Charlotte E Hart
FEELING WHITE

FEELING WHITE

An erotic novel
The second part of The White Trilogy
Copyright ©2015 by Charlotte E Hart
Cover Design by MAD
Formatting by MAD

License Notes

Table of Contents

To Feel

English definition of "Feel".
-To be aware of (a person or object) through touching or being touched.
(No object) Be capable of sensation.
(No object with complement) Give a sensation of a particular quality when touched.
Experience (an emotion or sensation).

To Experience

English definition of "Experience".
-practical contact with and observation of facts or events.
-an event or occurrence which leaves an impression on someone.

Sensation

English definition of "Sensation".
-   A physical feeling or perception resulting from something that happens or comes into contact with the body.

Belligerent

English definition of Belligerent
Line breaks: bel/li/ger/ent

Adjective:
1, Hostile and aggressive
2, Engaged in War or Conflict

Origin
Late 16th century: from Latin *belligerent*-"waging war", from the verb *belligerare*, from *bellum* "war".

FEELING WHITE

By
Charlotte E Hart

2015

"A belligerent state permits itself every such misdeed, every such act of violence, as would disgrace the individual."

Sigmund Freud

Charlotte E Hart
FEELING WHITE

Chapter 1

Conner/Alexander

"Dick."

Looking down the steps towards the tarmac beneath him, he shuddered at the ominous wave sweeping through his skin. The electric river of foreboding would have been exciting for him a while ago, but not now and certainly not this time. Thankfully it had been a few years since he'd needed to be concerned about his friends' dubious behaviour, or had needed to consider carefully how to turn him back in the right direction again. The last time anything close to this magnitude had happened, it had been that irritating green-eyed goblin that pulled him back from the edge. He'd never forgiven himself for not being enough that time round but the guy had thoroughly fucking lost it and his own arsenal simply hadn't been enough. Pascal Van Der wanker Braack had apparently got something up his sleeve that he simply couldn't give, and while that sucked big time, it had at least worked. More than likely this was going to be another fucking nightmare, possibly worse. And at the moment, even after the entire flight to mull it over, he couldn't begin to imagine how he was going to drag back the rage still coursing through his own veins, let alone deal with the lunatic in full-on arsehole mode.

The immediate two phone calls to the prick had gone straight through to voicemail as the car stormed towards the private airport. He'd probably been off his face already; his normal damned reset switch usually contained alcohol of some sort so he'd eventually called Angie at the central hub to confirm that the flight to New York had actually taken place. Thank God she was a decent sort because she really didn't have to tell him anything. In fact, she was risking her job by doing anything to help him at all, and after the way he treated her last year, he was surprised by her pleasantness to say the least. Of course she did get the words 'dickhead' and 'arrogant twat' into their brief conversation. She was right and he deserved every word of it, not that he gave a shit about her reaction to him but he at least acknowledged it.

The Limo now waiting at the bottom of the steps seemed fucking hilarious for the type of activity he was likely going to be a part of for the next few days or maybe it would be weeks. Who in the hell knew what he would need this time to bring him back to reality? The one thing he did know was that the idiot would need someone beside him to rein him in. He was bound to get himself in all sorts of trouble. The bastard thrived on it, breathed it in and swallowed it whole while smiling through the pain, and nine times out of ten, the guy just found it to hurt people anyway. It's just what he was by nature - violent. Whether the fucking goblin and his tricks had managed to tame it or not was really irrelevant because it was always there, hiding and waiting for the next opportunity.

The world saw a man in control, a man who moulded himself into whatever he needed to be to gain money and status, but that's not what he was in reality, not underneath. He was a sadistic bastard with plenty of blood on his hands and a fucked up head to boot. And this new torment was going to be just enough to reverse the sanity, enough to start the shit all over again, because the loss of Elizabeth Scott would mean the loss of balance, of moral input, and that meant undiluted fury would reign again. Clearly the idiot was more than capable of looking after himself but it was the others that became involved that Conner worried about. The man's 'calm down' switch sometimes needed one insane amount of adjustment and more often than not, that was his job. To pull him back from the brink and find his friend again, his brother of sorts, the only family he damn well had left.

He walked heavily down the steps and pulled his coat around his chin. November in New York was sodding cold and as the wind whipped past his face, he thought of Belle - damned frosty. Would she ever be less so? God he hoped so. If he didn't make this right, he had a feeling the love of his life would be gone because there was no way she'd put her sister through the anguish of ever having to see either of them again, and unfortunately for him, she'd be right to do just that. Her sense of unwavering loyalty for Beth would rapidly diminish any feelings she had for him, if she had any at all that was. He still wasn't sure about that.

He'd warned the arsehole, told him how important this was, not to piss around with Beth and not to screw her over, but the bastard hadn't listened for whatever fucking reason. So now he was standing in New York in an attempt to not only save his friend's existence but also his own future, because without Belle, he would disintegrate. His own carefully constructed barriers had disappeared long ago where she was concerned and she was very much a part of him now, deep inside of him. He wouldn't make it through losing another chance of happiness because she was it for him - the first one since Katie and Jonah - his only chance of a family again, of a new future. If she left him now, he knew he would blame the prick forever and that just wasn't fucking acceptable, not at all.

Sliding into the back seat, the random driver closed the door on him and wandered off so he pulled out his phone and reached for the bar. Whiskey, nice fucking choice. Tipping back a large one, he refilled it and thumbed through the numbers till he found the right number. His finger hesitated for a second as he gazed out the window, following a helicopter chopping around the night air, and smiled to himself at the thought of happier times with his friend. It wasn't that long ago really that they were partying their lives away, but that was before the Scott women fell upon them and gave them a reason for living, really living. God, the man pissed him off.

How many times was he going to do this? Would it always be the same with him? He knew the guy's childhood had been pretty bad and that some serious shit had gone down at some point in his past, but what the hell sent him into uncontrollable rages was still completely unknown. He didn't even seem to care about what he did to people, violently or otherwise. Maybe it was that dick, Aiden Phillips, and his dealings that had done this to him. Or maybe not. Who the fuck knew? But why couldn't the man just level himself out and be something close to normal?

The thought made him chuckle. He couldn't even face the thought of the word *normal* being in the same sentence as the rather legendary Alexander White. It was just bloody ridiculous; the two just didn't fit together at all, and it was a damned good job he considered him his only family because it was the only reason he currently had for not killing the bastard. How the guy pulled off being a respectable businessman when his inner core was clearly filled with something

9

other than sense was unfathomable, but he just did somehow. The fact that he was possibly the finest looking male specimen on the damn planet helped but that wasn't why people admired him. They admired the philanthropist, the money-maker and the shark, all traits Conner admired, too, but underlying that was loyalty. He'd never had a friend he could call on regardless of anything and Alex White was just that, loyal.

The cityscape loomed up at him as he crossed the bridge into Manhattan and again he felt the aggravating prickling sensation reach his neck. He looked down at his phone with a sigh and pressed call.

"Conner," Andrews said sharply.

"Where is he?" he asked quietly.

"The Parlour," Andrews replied with his usual bored tone. He tapped on the privacy glass and told the driver where to head. The dull nod indicated that he'd heard him so he closed the screen and returned his attention to the call.

"How is he?" Another stupid question but there might be some hope that he wasn't currently killing something, or at the very least trying to destroy it.

"I think you know how he is," Andrews replied with a small chuckle. He rubbed his forehead then pinched the bridge of his nose to try and dull the constant throb as he imagined the image of the dick in full-on mode. It was nothing to fucking laugh about.

"Well, can you keep him there until I get there? I'm just coming over the bridge. I should be with you in about twenty minutes," he said as he poured another drink and knocked it back, hoping to clear his head somehow for the oncoming battle.

"He currently has four women in the room with him. I doubt even Alexander White can manage that in less than twenty minutes." Conner's eyebrows shot up at Andrews' witty retort. He couldn't ever remember humour being a part of the driver's repertoire. And the fact that the dick was with women at least meant he wasn't hurting anything... Well, to some degree anyway.

"I'm pretty sure he'll have a damned good try, and frankly I wouldn't be surprised if he managed it. We both know what a fucking maniac he is when the right mood sets in." He chuckled at the thought. If it wasn't for the fact that he'd come here to make the idiot see sense or kill him he'd be pretty impressed with the guy.

10

"To be honest, I doubt he'll be going anywhere for a while. He can barely walk, let alone fuck anymore. The likelihood is he'll pass out within the hour. He's already been at it for most of the day. This is the second group."

Conner sighed with something close to relief. At least he'd found him and that meant he could get him back to the apartment and lock him in until he sobered up.

"Is it just booze?" he asked, hoping to Christ that coke hadn't been introduced to the mix yet.

"So far, yes."

"Are the girls okay?" he questioned as he cringed at the possibility of a really pissed off Alex.

"Yes, they seem to be quite enjoying their sessions. There was one in the first group who looked a little ruffled, but Roxanne said she would be okay once she'd been paid off."

"Good, okay, that's good." He blew out a long breath and refilled his drink.

"Do you know what happened?" Andrews asked.

"As far as I know he left a note for Beth telling her it was over. Other than that, I have no idea. Everything seemed to be going so well. I don't understand any of it," he replied, still trying to wrack his mind for some other miraculous piece of information.

"He saw her with Henry DeVille. They were apparently too close for his liking. He thinks he saw something happening between them."

Conner's head instantly cleared of confusion. He saw everything in seconds and completely understood Alex's reaction to what he thought he'd seen or actually had seen. His ability to read his friend's mind had become almost second nature over the years so it was plainly obvious how this was going to pan out, and given that he was probably in love with Beth, the result would more than likely be ten times worse.

"Oh fuck, that's not good at all," he replied.

"Quite. He thinks she's been working with Henry behind his back. He believes everything has been a lie up until now. What do you think?"

"I don't believe it for a minute. There's not a bad bone in her body. Besides, you know how suspicious and paranoid he is. He's probably conjured up all sorts of images in his fucking head. What a

11

prick. Why didn't he just talk to her?" The moment the question had left his mouth he shook his head in irritation. Alex was completely unable to show any form of vulnerability or emotion up until lately. He had hoped the prat had gotten past that but obviously not. "I'm getting too old for this shit, Michael," he said with a huff.

"Can you ask Belle to clarify anything? Maybe if we get this sorted quickly enough, he won't go off the rails completely this time. And stop fucking whining. I've got ten years on you and two wars. I don't need your moaning," Andrews replied with a touch of anger threatening. Conner tensed a little but reined it straight back in. Michael Andrews was not someone to mess with and he'd been there with Conner every time Alex had gone ballistic. For years he'd been the only one Conner could rely on to help with the idiot in twat mode. Until the green-eyed thing turned up anyway.

"Yes, but you get paid for it, and stop pretending you don't enjoy it. I can already see you going all covert, you arsehole. Have you got your earpiece in yet?" he replied, laughing at his own sarcasm.

"Grow up. Where are you now?" Conner looked out the window and saw the Chrysler building.

"Not far, just coming up Lexington. Should be ten minutes."

"I'm in the upper bar," Andrews replied as the phone went dead.

He frowned at the phone for a few moments, not quite sure what to do next. He needed to call Belle and find out what the hell Beth was doing with Henry. How did she even know him? Surely it wasn't possible that Alex was right. He tapped his fingers on his knee, trying to engage his Alex brain for a few minutes. He'd learnt this trick a long time ago. The only way to try and understand Alex White was to become him for a while, to try and feel whatever he was feeling. He'd become so good at thinking the way that Alex did that he could almost envisage everything through his eyes. His paranoia was beyond abnormal and his destructive tendencies were quite immeasurable, but Conner's grasp of his emotions had solidified into something he could hold on to - something to help him guide the man back towards everyday life, or at least his version of everyday life, which was pretty strange to say the least.

Finding Belle's number, he hit call and hoped she'd have the right answer and not something that would make his 'Alex brain' suspicious.

"Have you located the bastard yet?" she asked angrily. No 'hi babe,' she didn't even say his name. He bit back a smile; he loved her smart mouth, what she did with it and what came out of it.

"Fuck, I love you," he replied as that smile emerged. He couldn't stop it. The woman was everything he'd ever wanted.

"Yep, I know. Has he got some sort of excuse for his wankerish behaviour? Actually, have you killed him? That's probably more acceptable to be honest." She was clearly still very pissed off. He sighed again at the thought.

"I don't know. I haven't gotten to him yet, but I need to ask you a question and I need you to be really honest with me. I have to know the truth before I get there," he said, trying to let her know how serious he was for once.

"Am I ever anything but?" she replied, sarcasm dripping from her beautiful tongue.

"Okay, how does Beth know Henry DeVille and why would she have been all over him at the Addison's charity ball?" The phone went silent for a moment and he heard her shuffling about and closing some doors. "Belle, are you still there?"

"Yes, I'm here. Beth just came in so I've gone into the bedroom. Why do you want to know about Henry?" she asked. He instantly sensed that she also knew Henry, which didn't make him happy at all.

"How is she?" he asked, trying to flip the image of Belle and Henry together away in his head. It was not a pretty picture.

"A bloody mess - slobbing about and refusing to eat. I wouldn't be surprised if she starts on the vodka soon and she hates the stuff." Conner felt his stomach drop at the thought. She was far too lovely for any of this shit. "Now, why Henry?"

"Just need to know."

"Okay, well if I must. I went to school with Sarah. They fell in love, got married and all that shit. Henry used to look after Beth at all the parties we went to. While Sarah and I were getting pissed and arsing around, he would get all protective and big brotherly over Beth. He was very sweet to her actually. I can't see why she would be all over him though. She never fancied him or anything, and he certainly didn't see her that way," she replied quietly.

"Right, well that's good news. Has she seen him recently that you know of?" he asked cautiously.

"No, we haven't seen Henry or Sarah for a long time. I keep meaning to pop to Barrington's but I just never get the chance. What's all this about, Conner? Because frankly, I'm getting bored and I've got a distraught sister pacing about outside."

"I'm not sure yet, but I think there might have been a huge misunderstanding. Can you not say anything to Beth about this and definitely nothing to Henry or Sarah? I just need to get to Alex and get him to listen to me."

"If you think for one minute that he can fix this then you're very much mistaken, Conner. I'm not letting him back here again. Misunderstanding or not, he is not fucking welcome, do you understand? I told you to go because you wanted to see that he was okay. That doesn't mean that I give a shit if he's alive or dead," she seethed at him. He felt the venom pouring off her even from thousands of miles away and knew that she meant every word.

"Belle, please don't let a mistake ruin this for them. He just-"

She cut him off. "He just makes a lot of bloody mistakes, doesn't he? Huh? Tell me, Conner, what would you do? If this was the other way around, wouldn't you want to kill him? He's a fucking dickhead and I hate him," she said, far too quietly for his liking, and he sensed her retreating from him.

He felt his own inner turmoil building at her words. She was so right and he couldn't find the fight in him to try and persuade her otherwise. Mr. White had royally fucked up this time and to make matters worse, he'd involved the best thing Conner had ever found.

"Belle, I-"

She cut him off again. "You what, Conner? You want me to accept that he's only human, that he's entitled to fuck up? Is that what you want from me? Because he's your little fucking brother or something you want me to say it's okay? Well it's fucking not. Who the fuck does he think he is? He deserves to die for this shit and you should want to kill him for messing with her, and us."

"Jesus, Belle, I do want to kill him. I'm so fucking angry that I want to rip him to pieces. He's potentially destroying the most

14

amazing thing in my life and if I have to let him go to prove how much I love you then I will, but, baby, please don't ask me to give up on him too quickly. He loves her. I know he does. I've never seen him so captivated, and she loves him, too. You know that. I can't let you stand in the way of seeing them happy if I can make it right between them."

Utter silence greeted him from the other end of the call. Great, now he'd pissed her off even more. Minutes went by with him listening to her breathing. She hadn't hung up. That was a good thing, right?

"Conner," she eventually said, almost nervously, which was unheard of for her. He felt his insides beginning to tremble with an odd sensation.

"Yes, babe?" Fearing what was about to leave her mouth, he hung his head and reached for the bottle in front of him. If she said it now, he *would* fucking kill the man.

"I can't..." Silence again. It was fucking disturbing. He clenched his fist around the tumbler in his hand and waited for speech of some sort. Nothing happened so he swallowed and hesitantly tried to tease the words from her.

"You can't what, babe? Talk to me. I know this is awkward as fuck but I won't let him ruin us. I promised you the world and I fucking meant it. You've got every inch of me, babe. It's all for you but I have to fix this. Please, Belle, don't make me turn my back on him."

More silence. The fucking dick better be worth this shit.

"Just don't let me down. I can't be in love with someone who lets me down again. If you think you know what you're doing then do it. I won't stop you," she eventually said. His heart leapt out of his chest so fast he dropped his drink into his lap. Did she just tell him she loved him?

"Did you just say you love me?" he asked, desperate to clarify the point for himself. The shock of the words was just too much for him. She hesitated again. "Belle, say those words again."

"I'm trusting you, so please don't fuck this up," she replied as the phone went dead. Of course she wouldn't say it again, would she?

He blew out a breath at the thought and ran his fingers through his hair as the car slowed. She loved him. She fucking said it, maybe not twice, but the words did actually leave her lips. He felt a ridiculous smile break across his face instantly and laughed at himself as a warm fuzzy feeling crept around his insides, drowning the horribly ominous one that had previously been lingering. He rubbed at his chest and imagined her fingers there, actually everywhere. Smiling at his soaking wet dick area, he grabbed at some napkins to mop up the stain and chuckled. First woman to make him spill a drink, too... Jesus, that woman was a lot of firsts.

The car pulled to a stop outside the infamous black building and he stared at the door, trying to pull every inch of his nasty demeanour to the forefront again. It was fucking harder than he thought. That warm, fuzzy feeling just kept circulating and making him smile again. This was not a place for warm fuzziness at all. This was not even a nice place - expensive, yes, full of the glamour that Manhattan necessitated definitely, but absolutely not somewhere for nice. This was hard kink. People were very ready for whatever they came in here for and revelled in it to the max. Nobody knew where the owner had come from but the fact was that she was into some pretty hard shit, pushed it and offered it with a class no other woman had ever managed. Roxanne was extraordinary in her own way, scary as fuck to boot, but absolutely in a class of her own. She probably knew the fucking goblin because he was just as bad.

The driver coughed in front of him and brought his wandering mind back to the task at hand. Yes, he needed to rid himself of the warm fuzziness. He shook his head at himself. That shit really wasn't going to help for what he was about to walk in on.

~

Alex stirred slowly. Something was irritating him and dragging him from his sleep. Whatever it was, it was uncomfortable and actually quite bloody painful. Rolling over onto his side, he reached out a hand to find her, then the obvious reality hit him square in the face again. She wasn't there, never would be again. He screwed up the sheet into his hand in frustration and immediately realised where the discomfort was coming from. His hand was screaming at him. He tightened it more and let the pain intensify. Anger coursed through his veins again and he let the comfortable numbing solitude sweep over him. The energy it took to control the rage was just too much for him to be bothered with, and considering he no longer needed to be a reasonable human being, he might as well start the day as he meant to go on. A drink, that's what he needed.

Opening his eyes a little, he pulled himself up and threw his legs to the floor heavily. The dull thud of wood made him widen his eyes. Where the fuck was he? He looked up at the wall of blue tinged-glass in front of him and sighed. Conner.

The beautiful New York skyline was staring back in at him in all its glory and he felt another sigh leave him. He loved it here. He'd wanted to bring her here and show her everything. She would have adored it, all the tourist traps and the cafe culture. He could just see her now running around in her jeans, not the least bit bothered by the amount of make-up she put on her breath-taking face as she dragged him out through the door in search of excitement. Fuck, he missed her.

Now he had to deal with Conner. He couldn't actually remember him turning up yesterday but the fact that he was currently sitting in his spare room was a good indication that Conner was indeed in New York. He had no recollection of the day before, which meant he'd been either completely arseholed or off his face on coke. He scrunched up his nose and realised that he'd obviously just been alcohol-fuelled for this particular outing.

Rubbing his hands through his hair, he was reminded of the pain in his right hand and dropped it in front of his face. All his knuckles were split open and the substantial bruising alerted him to the fact that he'd quite plainly hit something or someone. If it was someone, he'd hit them a lot. He shrugged to himself. He couldn't fucking remember anything so they'd more than likely deserved whatever they got. Even if they didn't, he couldn't give a shit anyway.

He walked over to the window and palmed the glass. The image of her naked in front of him was instant. He groaned at the thought and shook his head to try and rid himself of it immediately. She was just another whore, yet another let down regarding his damned emotions. Muttering and turning for the bathroom, he pondered why the bloody hell he was naked. Christ, he hated this not remembering thing. His complete lack of control disgusted him, but it did nothing to stop the fact that he wanted another drink. He also knew without a shadow of a doubt that Conner wasn't going to allow it. Well fuck him, he'd just go back to his own apartment and find some there instead.

Looking at himself in the mirror as he brushed his teeth, he tried for the thousandth time to find some sort of explanation for her behaviour. There still wasn't anything to condone her betrayal. She was just a bitch who'd connived her way in and destroyed all hope of the something more he was beginning to think of as a possibility. As if it ever would have been. He deserved fuck all of worth, not that she was even that anymore. He noticed varying shades of lipstick prints on his ribs and sneered in revulsion. Had he fucked someone last night? He couldn't even remember that. If he had then it clearly wasn't a memorable event, and besides, he had no reason to feel guilty about it if he did, so why the bloody hell he suddenly did was unreasonable to say the least. He brushed at the smudges of bright red in revulsion and pictured her lips glistening with lighter tones, her mouth parting to say his name. Whore.

Scrubbing his hands across his face, the vague memory of Roxanne came to mind. Oh, Christ, he'd been to The Parlour. He chuckled to himself. Pascal would kill him if he found out, and of course he was bound to find out. The man had far too many connections for his own good. Fraternizing with Pascal's enemies was always a stupid move but he'd find a way to douse the flames eventually. If he could find out what his fucking problem was with the woman it might help, but the bastard refused to speak about it. Whatever, it wasn't his problem anyway.

The shower, at least, was soothing to some degree and as he left the bathroom to find his clothes, he realised that he hadn't noticed them anywhere. Well, he certainly hadn't come back naked so they must be somewhere. He threw the sheets back, hoping that they would reveal his suit but it still didn't materialise. The sudden memory of Conner doing this to him before leapt into his mind. Apparently it was one of the dick's ingenious ways of keeping him housebound when nothing else worked.

Fucking great.

Aggravation at the thought of being holed up in this apartment with Conner poured across him, and at the same time, his own self-loathing reminded him of his own pathetic issues. Conner had an uncanny knack of reminding him of his inadequacies. He was the last person he needed to be around right now. He just wanted to go out and get shitfaced again. He had every right to be angry and he intended to vent it in any way he chose. At the moment, two thoughts were crossing his mind - women and drink. Conner could go screw himself because his big brotherly lecture was not going to work today. He hadn't even got a clue what was going on. Well, he didn't think he did. The fact that he couldn't remember anything meant that he didn't know if they'd spoken about it or not.

Swiping at a towel, he tied it around his waist and turned for Conner's room. He'd just take his fucking clothes instead because he wasn't about to be kept here like a bloody prisoner. He twisted the door handle and found it locked. Wanker.

Storming back up the corridor to the lounge area, he found the over-the-top space empty.

"Conner, where the fuck are my clothes?" he shouted angrily as he approached the kitchen area. The sun glinting of the stainless steel surface made him blink and he raised a hand to shield his eyes. On dropping it away from his face, he noticed the arsehole's back in front of the coffee machine.

"There's no booze here so I suggest you get your arse back to bed and sleep it off a bit longer," Conner said quietly, still making his drink.

"Fuck off. I don't want to go back to sleep it off. I want my bloody clothes. I need to go out. I've got meetings planned." He tried for the work thing, which actually made him think about work for a second and that led to Henry and his treachery. What the hell was he going to do about that? Why hadn't Mark got back to him yet? Was it Monday yet? Jesus, what a bloody mess.

"No, you don't. I called Louisa. She rescheduled your meetings. You have a week off. Go back to bed, Alex," the arsehole replied, still not turning around as he studiously pressed buttons on the machine. The rage began to boil again and he let it rise happily because for once, he refused to push it back down. Frankly, it felt too fucking good to try and switch it off. If Conner wanted a fight, he could damn well have one.

"Conner, give me my fucking clothes. I have to go. I'm getting beyond pissed off and I don't want to do anything I'll regret," he responded, hoping to God that his friend would take the hint. Slowly, the dick started to turn. He noticed the wince that left the arsehole's mouth and frowned. He was moving too slowly for his liking so he continued to watch the movement that was happening in slow motion with a strange sense of dread looming.

Conner eventually turned fully to face him. The sight almost made him sick. The entire left hand side of his face was a mess of black and purple, his nose had two strips of tape across it and his lip was cut open. He shuffled two steps forward, winced again and grabbed at his ribs in obvious agony while damn near collapsing to the floor. Lunging forward to grab him, he reached for his friend's arm but Conner's warning eyes bored into him.

"Back the fuck off, man," he seethed as he continued to glare viciously. Something was very bloody wrong here so he quickly stepped away and watched as Conner hauled himself back up to lean on the counter top. Minutes seemed to pass as he witnessed the clearly agonising movements of his friend trying to manoeuvre to a comfortable position until eventually he stood still and braced himself against the cupboard. "You know, I'm really fucking hoping you've already done something that you regret, Alex, because this shit really hurts, and if I let you do it for nothing then I'll just get on my plane and go back home."

His brow furrowed as he began to understand the meaning of Conner's words. He'd done this? Guilt consumed him in seconds as he staggered backwards to the chair and fell into it. Hanging his head, he grabbed at the back of his neck and tried to remember, anything to help him understand why the hell he would have done this to his only true friend. Fuck, why? Nothing.

"I'm sorry," he mumbled. What else was he supposed to say? He couldn't even begin to fathom what the fuck had happened, but one thing was for sure: he'd apparently beaten the hell out of the only important person in his world and that was incomprehensible.

"Are you?" Conner asked as he shuffled laboriously across to the other chair and slowly lowered himself into it. Alex's head shot up.

"Yes, of course I am. You know I wouldn't do this on purpose. I just... I can't remember anything about it."

"Actually, I don't know, because I can't remember much remorse when you did this to me," Conner replied as he drank some of his coffee and sighed. More of those fucking uncomfortable minutes ticked by while Alex tried to recall information and looked at the floor, totally disgusted with himself. The thought of lifting his head to look at the damage he'd caused again was disturbing enough, let alone having to actually explain why the hell it had happened.

"The keycard is in that draw. Go and get some of my clothes. I can't have this conversation with you while your sodding cock's looking at me. It's fucking creepy."

His head shot up again and he stared at Conner for a moment in utter amazement. Even after a battering from him, the man was still trying to be funny? He certainly didn't deserve any joking in this moment and he simply didn't understand this apparent loyalty the man had for him.

Conner watched him over the rim of his cup. There was no smile on his lips and it struck him how odd it was to see the man in a reflective mood. He was too quiet and too calm. It was making the heavy air of tension seem impossibly uncomfortable and he found himself wondering if this was Conner's breaking point. He'd put his friend through a lot over the years. Maybe this was the end of the line. If it was, he deserved it. Never had he been so revolted by his own actions, and the thought of what could have happened scared the shit out of him.

Eventually he broke his gaze from Conner, who hadn't even blinked during their little staring competition, and walked to the drawer. On opening it, he found the card and a very familiar diamond bracelet. He instantly sucked in a breath and ran his fingers across it. Her fucking perfume assaulted his nose and as he closed his eyes, he saw her face staring right back at him, those big brown eyes of hers tearing him in half just a little bit more. He felt the outer world disappear as she consumed his brain again, her fingers on his skin, her hair fanned out across his chest and those three fucking words falling from her mouth, the same ones he longed to hear again.

"She hasn't done anything, you know? You really have screwed it up this time," Conner drawled with distaste. Alex swung round to meet his eyes. "Go and put some fucking clothes on and then make yourself some coffee. It's time you heard some home truths, Alex."

He continued to look at Conner with his mouth gaping open like a bloody idiot. Did he just say that Elizabeth hadn't done anything wrong? What the fuck was wrong with the man? She quite obviously had, and that Conner was even daring to bring her up in conversation was just unbelievable. Rage welled again. Was he trying for another fight? Images suddenly flew to his brain with remarkable clarity - Conner pulling him by the shoulders from a woman who was cowering on the floor beneath him; his hand around her neck, her brown eyes a mixture of terror and dread, her fake red hair falling around her shoulders barely covering the reddened marks that were already on her skin. He could almost hear her screams of desperation as she scampered backwards while he was being dragged away from her. There were others in the room, too - a blonde tied to the wall and another one kneeling in the corner with her head covered, both crying and pleading for their release. He shook his head to clear the visions and instantly realised that he'd completely lost control, and that had Conner not been there yesterday, this morning would have been an entirely different scenario for him.

He shuddered and closed his mouth as more self-loathing consumed him. The culpability of his actions hit him so hard that he found it difficult to put one foot in front of the other as he tried to move towards Conner's room. Hanging his head in shame, he eventually opened the door and pulled some jeans and a t-shirt from the drawers, his brain trying desperately to shut the images off that were now rapidly coming back to him. Fighting, lots of fighting.

Buttoning up the jeans and pulling the black t-shirt over his head, he was suddenly reminded of his friend's loyalty again. He squeezed his eyes shut as the anguish slowly started to rise and he tried to dispel what he'd just thought about.

"If you want to hit someone then use me. I won't let you hurt anyone else," Conner had said as he'd thrown him against the wall, *violently.* And then the whole scene erupted in his mind. He cringed and slumped backwards onto the bed as he relived the moment when he'd done exactly that and Conner, his friend, had taken the entire thing without even trying to stop him.

Oh Christ, what had he done? Visions of Andrews eventually pushing him into a car ended the painful memories and then there was nothing again.

Sighing, he looked down at his hand and opened and closed his fist. He really was a worthless piece of shit. What sort of maniac would do that? He continued to sit there staring at the nothingness, trying to process how it had all gone so wrong. He couldn't blame her for this. Yes, she might have been the catalyst, but these actions were all his own and at the moment, he was damned close to walking himself right off the Brooklyn Bridge. He didn't have any right to be happy, never had, and regardless of what she'd done, she was still the most perfect creature that had ever been created. It sickened him to think that he ever thought love a possibility from her. Why the fuck would the version of her that he thought he'd known ever want someone as corrupted as him?

He noticed a movement in the doorway and realised that Conner was watching him.

"I'm sorry," he said again without moving his gaze from the window. "I remember now."

Conner stared for a few more minutes then slowly made his way across to the bed and sat down next to him with a loud exhale of breath.

"Good, maybe you can think a little more rationally now then, you dick." Alex couldn't help the rise of the corner of his mouth. There were few who could speak to him like that and get away with it. He supposed the man had more right than ever at the moment.

"Are you okay? I mean..." He gestured towards his face and body vaguely. The fact that the bruising matched Conner's hair would have been funny if anybody else had caused it. The blues and pinks seemed to roll together effortlessly.

"No, I'm not. It fucking hurts like a bitch. I'm still trying to work out whether I'll return the favour once I can move again," he replied as he crossed his ankles and stared back to the window with a Conner grin starting to form. Alex frowned and stood up. Shoving his hands into his pockets, he wandered back over to the view.

"She hurt me. That's never happened before and I couldn't think clearly. I shouldn't have started drinking. It was fucking stupid of me," he said as he thought of her with Henry, his hands holding her as they danced.

"No she didn't, you idiot. You hurt you," Conner replied sarcastically. His head swung round to Conner instantly. What the fuck did he know? He wasn't there.

"No, Conner, I saw them together. He was touching her and she was enjoying every bloody minute of it," he said as the image of Henry's hands on her legs ripped through him again like a knife. "And you can fuck off if you think I'm listening to any of your sanctimonious bullshit about this. She's a whore, maybe a perfect one, but a whore nonetheless."

"Do you really believe that of her? Is that what you honestly think she is?"

Alex sneered and turned back to the window. Whatever he may have believed of her wasn't relevant, was it? The bitch had destroyed any remnant of hope he was clawing onto. She was now just another pawn in a game.

"Yes," he replied, although the moment he'd said it that strange doubt shit flickered across him as her eyes bored through him again. He sighed and leant his head on the glass.

"Then you were right, you don't deserve her. I don't know why I'm bothering," Conner mumbled from behind him.

Didn't deserve her? Jesus, he'd tried hadn't he? He'd done everything a decent man should do and look what it had gotten him. He rubbed his head against the cool glass and snorted in disgust. Damned emotions weren't worth shit and now Conner wanted more from him?

"What do you want from me, Conner? She's fucking that bastard and helping him destroy me. I don't know how you expect me to handle that but you shouting her fucking praises is not helping."

"I expect you to fucking trust someone, Alex. Just give someone a bloody chance. Why the hell didn't you just ask her about it?" His head swung around to face the dick.

"What?"

"Why didn't you just walk up to her like a normal fucking human being and ask her how she knew Henry?" What, and play happy families or something? What the hell was he going on about?

"They were all over each other. You expect me to go give them a fucking hug? Join in?"

"Jesus Christ, you saw nothing, Alex. Your absurd brain made up something that wasn't fucking there. And it clearly still is. You're bordering on insane. You know that, right?"

"Fuck off. I know what I saw."

"No, you really don't," the dick cut in with his arms outstretched and a snarl forming. Alex raised a brow and sneered in return. This was getting irritating. Much as he hated looking at the man's bruising, if he'd tried this shit last night, he wasn't surprised he'd beaten the shit out of him.

"Conner, this is getting fucking dull. I'm not a damned idiot. They were-"

"OH, FOR CHRIST'S SAKE, GET A GRIP, ALEX!" The dick shouted at him. "This is Beth we're talking about. Beth. You're a complete fucking idiot. In fact, I should kill you for your idiocy. Did you even think about what you saw?"

"What the fuck is your problem? Look, I'm sorry about the face but I'm going. I've had enough of this, and I want a damned drink," he said as he headed across the room towards the door. This was getting old and being angry around an already beat up Conner was not wise.

"Of course you do. Standard fucking response." His eyebrows shot up as he stopped and turned back again. "Coke, too? Or are you just going to find a different kind of whore to vent yourself on again?"

What the hell?

He stared for a few seconds, trying to stop the rage, his fist suddenly clenching as he tried his damndest to not allow Conner his taunts. The man was the only one who did this to him, the only one who had ever found a way to tap into his emotions and use them against him. Well, apart from Pascal and that was entirely different. He pulled in a long breath and flexed out his hands as he looked at the pink and blues on his friend's face. His friend. Christ, the woman was even destroying his relationship with him now, the only decent one he'd ever been a part of.

"Why are you trying to wind me up? Whatever the fuck this was, Conner, it's finished, done. I'm not going to do this with you. I'm not going to stand here and listen to you."

"Jesus, Alex," the dick shouted again. He narrowed his eyes in return and took a step back as he forced his hands into his pockets.

"Conner, don't do this," he warned as his hackles got the better of him. Bruising or not, the man should know better. Conner sighed in response and stared back until his head dropped into his hands.

"Is it really that hard for you to just believe in something? Belle went to school with Sarah, you twat. They were best friends. They've all known each other for years. He's like a brother to Beth. It's your own bloody paranoia that caused all of this."

What?

He blinked in response as his chest constricted at the thought. What were the odds that this had all been a mistake? Okay, a catastrophic mistake but maybe it was possible that he'd gotten it wrong. Something never did feel quite comfortable about the whole situation, but he'd put that down to the fact that he'd never been in love before. In love. Elizabeth. Her eyes assaulted him again as he stared blankly into Conner's. He could almost feel her in his arms again, sense her moulding herself all over him, taste her skin, her mouth. He felt his fingers lightly tapping against his leg and opened his mouth to reply.

"I..." Instantly realising he hadn't got a fucking clue what to say, he just closed his mouth again and looked at Conner for more clarification on the matter.

"Well fuck me. Speechless? That's almost worth the pain," Conner said as he raised himself from the bed slowly and shuffled his way around the corner towards him. "Come on. We need some coffee and I need some more pain killers," he said as he grabbed onto the doorframe awkwardly. Quickly moving to his side, he grasped at his arm to support him. Conner tensed but looked at him with a smile. "Do not even think about going all knight in shining armour on me, you arsehole, and if you pick me up, I *will* find the strength to kill you."

"I..."

"Still nothing? Fucking amazing," he said with a huge Conner grin. It wasn't that fucking funny. In fact, nothing about any of this was amusing in the slightest. His mind wrapped around visions of her eyes in tears and then Conner's bruised face. What the fuck had he done?

"I don't deserve your humour, Conner. Please don't try to make light of this," he replied sharply as they continued down the hall. As much as Conner's wit was legendary, this just wasn't the time for it.

"No, you don't, so you better start planning what the fuck you're going to do to fix this."

He sighed as he lowered Conner to the sofa in the lounge. He had no fucking idea, and he still didn't even know if he believed he'd made such a stupid error in judgement. It just wasn't like him to get something so wrong.

"I'm going to make coffee. I need to get this drink out of my system and then I need to think."

When he returned with the drinks, Conner was stretched out across the sofa, fast asleep with one leg dangling over the edge. He gently lifted it up and pulled the blanket across him. Moving back to the chair, he sat down and started to sip at his drink. The taste was bloody disgusting but after he'd drunk it, he picked up the other one and swallowed that down as well.

Glancing around the room, he tried to find something to focus on while he thought about how to find a way back in. Eventually his gaze landed on the bracelet lying on the drawers. He walked over to it and brought it back to the chair with him, squeezing it tightly. She wouldn't make it easy for him and she had every right to make it as difficult as she could. In fact, the sudden realisation hit him that she might not want him back at all. Oh, that wasn't good. And Christ, Belle... He hadn't even thought about her. She would be peppering every conversation with how much of an overwhelming basket case he was. There's no way she would even allow her sister to consider the possibility of reconciliation. She would more than likely be pushing her sister to get straight back out there and drop him like a tonne of bricks. He had to give it to her, she was a formidable woman and he smiled at her loyalty. Elizabeth would never be alone with Belle beside her.

Two hours later and several more coffees, he was still sitting there trying to formulate some sort of plan when he heard Conner groan and attempt to sit up. He reached over for the concoction of pills and water and handed them to him. Conner threw the little tablets of happiness down his throat with complete ease and swallowed the water back. The man was far too comfortable with pills for his liking, but he supposed the guy had been swallowing various concoctions for most of his life. Tipping his head back on the sofa, he turned it sideways to look across at him.

"Have you worked it out yet?" he asked as he pushed his feet up onto the coffee table.

"No, not yet. I can't find a way past Belle," he replied with a snort of laughter. He knew Conner would appreciate the irony.

"Ah yes, my beloved. Don't worry about her. She might not be as inflexible as you think," Conner replied with a chuckle, which caused another groan of pain. "I'd be more worried about Beth. She's a mess, man. You've done some real damage."

"She is? I don't suppose I even deserve another chance with her," he said as he hung his head back down and stretched out his aching hand. "Or with you."

Conner smiled. "You might be the biggest dick on the planet, Alex, but you're my only family. How many other people do you think I'd do this for?" he said as he waved his hand at the bruising. "You know how much I love my face."

"Why the fuck didn't Michael stop me?"

Conner laughed and stood up slowly. "He was a little busy holding off the three guys who wanted to kill you. Apparently you'd already pissed off most of the Doms in the room by taking all their pretty little things. Poor little girls had been falling over themselves to go in with you." Alex sighed and thought of his apparent father figure.

"Oh, right. Is he okay?"

"Of course he is, '*Mr. I've been through two wars.*' The man should have been a cage fighter or something," he said with a grin. Alex nodded and got up to go and make more coffee.

Conner reached into his pocket and pulled out Alex's keys, dumping them onto the table in front of him as he walked towards the kitchen. "Now go home and sort yourself out. I trust I can leave you to your own devices without having to worry about you now," he said as he turned back and raised an eyebrow. Alex picked up the keys.

"Yes, thank you. I'll be fine now." He sighed and stood up. "You're not coming back with me?"

"No, I think I'd better stay here for a while and let this face heal. I doubt Belle would be very enamoured with me if she knew what happened. I'm guessing she probably wanted the violence to happen the other way around." Alex frowned. He hadn't thought of their relationship and what any of this could do to them. A surge of loyalty instantly reminded him that he should be here with Conner, that he should look after the mess he'd created.

"Then I'll stay, too. I don't think a few days will make any difference anyway and frankly I need the time to get my head together." Conner smirked as Alex dropped his keys back on the hall table and followed him through to the kitchen. "You want something to eat?" he asked as he opened the fridge.

"You're going to cook for me?" Conner chuckled as he took a seat at the breakfast bar.

"I think it's the least I can do, don't you?" he replied as he looked across at him. Conner raised a brow and pulled the paper across to read, flicking instantly to the business section. For a man that looked like a strung-out rock god, the genius across from him had one hell of a business brain.

"You're up two points on the stock exchange. Rumours of this deal are flying, man. You seriously need to get your shit back together," Conner exclaimed as he scanned the prices. Alex sighed at the thought of his company and the impending storm that was brewing. Henry De Ville was trying to destroy everything, and funnily enough, he'd just let him win the first move. All the dick had done was dance with her and his own fucking paranoia and jealousy had caused all this shit to happen. Clearly the bastard knew him far too well. He should have trusted her but instead he'd fallen for Henry's little game and left her alone, probably heartbroken.

"I told her I didn't love her," he said as he dumped bagels on the top and remembered her mouth moving around those words of love and happiness.

"I know," Conner replied, not lifting his head and picking up a pen.

"I think I lied," he continued quietly as he found a knife and began to look for bacon and eggs. The man never had anything to eat in his kitchens.

"I know." Conner sighed, almost with boredom as he continued scribbling. This was news. How the fuck would he know that?

"You do?"

"Of course I do, you dick. I've probably known longer than you have. You've been all smiley and shit." Alex pondered the ridiculous smiling shit. Conner was right. He'd never been a smiley and shit person. There had never been anyone to be smiley for.

But there was now, and he'd be happy to continue with that if she'd give him a chance to prove it. How he was going to take her forward into his life and explain all the crap in his past was unfathomable, but if she'd have him he'd try. That's what he'd promised her on that podium, wasn't it? That he'd try, that he'd give her everything and try to be a better man. She needed that because Elizabeth Scott was the kindest, loveliest creature on the planet, his angel, his reason for waking up and believing in something more.

"Do you think she'll have me back?"

"I don't know. Let's hope she thinks you're worth it," Conner replied as he lifted his gaze, shrugged his shoulders and started to draw rings around the numbers in front of him like a mad man.

Alex watched for a minute, trying to calculate his own worthiness. He wasn't worth shit and the man sitting before him was prime proof of that. How was he even going to try and say sorry for this?

He turned back to the bagels and sneered at his own pathetic behaviour. His fucking bastard of a father would be loving this. His eye caught Conner throwing the pen down in agitation so he looked back at him for whatever was coming next.

"Alex, if I think I'm going to lose Belle because of this, you're gonna be on your own. I'll be done, you understand me? I can't let this shit screw up what I have with her."

Fuck.

"Yeah, I know."

He did. If he didn't deserve another chance with his angel then so be it. He wouldn't let Conner's world fall apart, too.

Chapter 2

Elizabeth

"Beth, can you come in here a minute?" Belle calls from the office.

Quite frankly, no. The only two places that I am presently even vaguely comfortable with are my kitchen and my bed. The thought of talking business or discussing anything other than the temperature that I need to cook my beef at is of no interest to me whatsoever, so I hurry around the cooker, trying to turn the meat and sort the vegetables at the same time. If I ignore her, perhaps she'll sort it out by herself.

Nearly one whole week has passed since the most distressing and heart-breaking moment of my life, and still I can't think of anything else other than that sodding note and his intense blue eyes. They haunt everything. I can't sleep, eating is becoming a serious issue for me and just managing to get myself up in the morning is a feat in itself. If I wasn't so important to my own business, I would continue to lie in that bed constantly. It's warm in there, cozy, sometimes even a little tranquil. I've always wondered why people curl up into the foetal position when they felt threatened or unhappy. Now I know, because it's the only position that gives me any sense of peace or comfort. Every night since that day, I've crawled into my bed and scrunched up the pillow into my chest, refusing to acknowledge his bow tie that I threw in the bin the day before as I cried, and yet every morning I wake up with the damn thing grasped in my hand again.

The last place I want to be is here, and to be honest, as good as Belle and Teresa are being about the whole thing, I just don't want either of them near me. I can't cope with their constant looks of sadness at my misfortune. Belle is becoming bloody absurd. Never in her life has she been so sweet to me and it really is starting to make me feel like some sort of pariah.

This can't go on any longer. I have to find a way out of the fog. He is a shit. It's as simple as that and I can't let him ruin the rest of my life. I'm not stupid, not one of those silly girls that thinks their life is over. I know I'll get over this eventually, but in the meantime, I just need to find a distraction, something to take my mind off the constant craving for his stupidly gorgeous face and those consuming eyes. I've tried everything... Actually, I haven't tried anything other than sitting on my arse and wallowing in my own self-pity, but I just miss him so much. I could never have imagined that I could miss someone to the point of it physically hurting me, because that's how it feels, like someone is repeatedly hammering a stake into my heart, and then when they've finished they just rip the whole thing out and leave the hole gaping open, bleeding. He is so completely inside me that I feel like my right arm has been ripped off and now I can't function properly, his body seemingly still wrapping itself around me even though he's no longer here. I can still hear his thoughts and I swear the hairs on the back of my neck can still sense him, regardless of the distance between us.

I was a mess. I am still a bloody mess, but now I'm starting to get angry at my own mess. How could he do this to me? And how the hell could I let him?

"Beth, really, I need you in here," Belle shouts again at me. I huff out a breath and walk across to the office.

"What do you need?" I ask as I round the corner. I can feel the irritation in my own voice and try for a smile, not achieving it in the slightest. I don't know why I bothered.

"I wanted to know what you were going to do for the Orangry dinner party. I'm just writing up the menus," she says as she gives me that false, sugary smile that has started to become a permanent fixture on her face. It's bloody ridiculous and doesn't suit her in the least.

I instantly turn, walk back to the kitchen, grab my folder and return to the office. Thumbing through the pages, I find the appropriate section and remove the menu sheet I prepared a while ago. I actually did it the day of the fire and it leads me straight back to images of the evening that followed. So obviously I quickly screw my eyes shut and try desperately to dismiss the visions of the two of them laughing at the dining table and then playing chess. *Alex*. God, he was beautiful that night, the way his face softened to that slightly calmed level and the feeling of his hair in my fingers as he told me to give him everything I had. His darkened blue depths had prised the last of my defences away in that moment. *Bastard. Stop it, Beth!*

"Can I have that then?" Belle's voice pulls me back from my daydream, or nightmare. I'm not sure what I'm supposed to call it anymore.

"Yes, sorry, yes. Here it is," I reply as I hand it to her awkwardly.

"Were you thinking about him again?" she asks quietly.

"Yes, no, actually I was thinking about both of them. You know the evening after the fire. That's the day I wrote the menu."

"Oh, right, yes, I never did get the pleasure of Pascal. Frankly, I wish I had. He sounded completely intriguing," she says with a very dirty laugh. It's the first time I've seen her laugh in the last week and it makes me smile. She's been so busy trying to be pleasant and sweet that she's stopped being the big sister I'm used to, the sister I need.

"I need you to stop, Belle. I can't take your niceness anymore. I have to get back to normal and I need you to help me do it," I say without thinking about it at all. She stares at me for a while as if trying to make up her mind how she's going to respond. Eventually, she opens her desk draw and pulls out a bottle of vodka and two glasses. Pouring two really quite large shots, she hands one over to me and downs hers, indicating that I should do the same. I do. It still tastes revolting. Why on earth she likes the stuff is beyond me.

"Good, right well, if the slobbing around and feeling sorry for yourself shit is finished with, I suggest you get your act together and start to think about getting out there again, because seriously, he is such a tosser and really not worth your time at all. Do you still have Pascal's card?" she asks. My eyes shoot to hers in surprise. Where the hell did that come from?

"What? You have to be kidding me. You think seeing him will make me feel better somehow?" I pretty much shout at her. The thought of seeing any man is disturbing enough, let alone one that's as troublesome as Pascal.

"Yes, I do. I think that someone making you feel beautiful and wanted again is exactly what you need. And you did say he was ridiculously cute," she replies as that wicked grin returns.

"I don't think I said he was cute, Belle. Cute is most definitely not a word I would use to describe Pascal Van Der Braak," I reply as I remember his hands on my waist and his groin against me in the kitchen as we danced.

"Ooh neither would I. The man's completely gorgeous. I only got to meet him once but it was a flash of heaven before me. I've never been into dangerous types myself but there was definitely a part of me that was drawn to him, something about the way he just mesmerised me." We both swing our heads at Teresa as she hovers in the doorway. "Drinking, are we? Where's mine?"

"You know him?" I question, unable to understand why she would have ever met him, albeit completely understanding her statement.

"Well, no, but I was at his club once a few years ago with a friend of the same persuasion, and you know how I'll try anything once," she says as she reaches for the vodka and takes a shot out of the bottle.

"What are you talking about?" Belle asks in obvious confusion. I cringe at the thought of what she will think of my new-found lifestyle choice. I've never gone into great detail about what Alex introduced me to and how much I enjoyed it.

"You know, BDSM and kink and stuff. Some of it was actually very entertaining. I kept the handcuffs. I wasn't enthralled with the spanking part of it, though. Never really was one for pain," Teresa replies. Belle's eyebrows rise as she looks over at me with a new expression. I think it's utter shock.

"Have you turned into a kinky bitch? And why the bloody hell didn't you tell me about this?" she says as she pours another shot for us. I hang my head a little, although why I feel embarrassed is a mystery to me. I suddenly remember Alex... *Head up unless I tell you not to.* I pull it back up and smile privately at the memory. Dickhead. I hate him.

"I didn't know what to say about any of it. Frankly, I was just starting to get my head around it when it was over. It didn't seem worth mentioning by then," I reply as I down another shot. It tastes better this time. It's clearly a grower.

"Right, well, you have to call him then. He sounds absurdly naughty and exactly what you need to get over the arsehole."

"Oh my god, did he give you his card? He doesn't do that like ever. He's renowned for it - very particular in his choices so I hear." Teresa giggles at the side of me. "You have to call him. It will do you no end of good."

"Really?" I look at them in complete astonishment. Is this really the smartest move? It certainly doesn't feel like it to me if I'm honest.

"Absolutely," they both chime in together. Shit.

"Honey, we just can't watch you like this anymore, and if a night of Pascal will make you smile again then you should get straight on with it," Belle says from the other side of her desk, her feet now propped up on the top. Smile... Yes, Pascal could probably make me smile, more than likely nervously, but even the thought of him brings my lips up into a curve.

"Right, okay," I reply slowly as I think of Alex. He'll find out about it, won't he? And it will more than likely send him completely of the rails. Not because he gives a shit about me but just because he doesn't like to share. Or maybe he won't care less? Well, sod him. He gave away that right when he told me he didn't love me, by way of a fucking note. I should go out with Pascal. The girls are right. I need out of this fucking nightmare that I'm currently swimming around in and Pascal will definitely be a distraction. Whether it will be a good distraction or not is yet to be decided.

"Good girl. Now, where's the card?" Belle asks. "You might as well get on with it before you change your mind."

"I'm not doing it now. I need to finish this food for James. I'll do it when I get home later." Belle narrows her eyes at me. "I will, I promise. Just not now."

"Right good. What time is it?" she asks no one in particular as she walks out the room, hotly pursued by Teresa into the shop. I follow with yet another sigh of indifference. That's happening a lot lately, too.

"Twenty past five," Teresa replies. I wander across to the door to turn the sign. There isn't any pastries or bread left anyway and James will arrive through the back door in twenty minutes or so.

I gaze out the window at the busy London streets and watch all the cars backing up. Why people don't use the tube is still beyond me. A grey sports car turns the corner and I smile at the thought of his

Aston Martin. It was so like him, refined and elegant, not overtly flashy or some other such on trend brand, just pure and sleek.

"When will James be here?" Belle asks, snapping her fingers and pulling me from my gaze.

"About half an hour. Everything's ready," I reply as I make my way back to the kitchen, suddenly feeling incredibly deflated again.

"You could always give him a try again," she says as she follows me and grabs a carrot. I frown at the thought as I move some pans around.

"I don't think so. Something tells me he might not be enough anymore," I reply as I begin loading the part-cooked dishes into the catering trays. She raises her brows and continues with her nibbling. "I'm just... I'm just different now. I want different things. He gave me new insight, taught me stuff and now I need... Oh I don't know what I need, but I do know that it isn't James anymore."

"Will you be okay with Pascal, you know, with all the kinky stuff?" she asks as she waggles her hips at me in what can only be described as a pathetic attempt at provocative. I giggle at her. She looks ridiculous and it feels good so I smile warmly at her.

"I think so. He's pretty intense but I think he'll be a gentleman and I don't intend to sleep with him so hopefully he'll behave himself," is my response. God knows why because a *behaving himself* Pascal is highly unlikely.

"Well, you just keep me informed of where you are. I don't know the man for toffee and I don't want you in trouble," she says as she helps me carry the trays out to the van.

"I promise I'll let you know. I'll even give you his number if you want it." She moves around the counter and looks around uncomfortably.

"What's it like then, you know, the whips and stuff?" I look at her. She actually seems to be blushing a bit and I can't help but laugh at her.

"You don't know? I would have thought that you might already have had some playtime," I say, thinking of my conversation with Alex about Conner.

"Why would I? I've never... What are you saying? Do you know something I don't?" she asks, the blush disappearing as she clearly cottons on to what I'm suggesting. "Does Conner...?" I raise my

36

eyebrows at her and smile. "Oh, well, yes, he is quite... I suppose he... Right." She turns and walks into her office, obviously frustrated at her lack of information. I follow her.

"Belle, I don't know anything for sure. I only know snippets of what Alex would tell me. He was very private about things. He just indicated that Conner helped him with stuff. He never said that Conner was still into it so if you haven't seen any chains hanging around then maybe it was just a phase for him."

"Right," she says again as she throws some vodka down her neck. "You want one?"

"No, I'm going to finish up and go home. I want a long bath and a glass of wine. It's time for me to get myself back together. One week rule remember." She smiles and comes around the table for a hug.

"One week rule, yes that was a good one," she replies as she considers the rule we made up regarding getting over a man. I'd only been seventeen, but we'd used it ever since, giving each other one week to slob out and cry about it before the other one of us kicked backsides and started life back up again. Well, my week is nearly up.

"When's Conner back?" I cringe inwardly at the thought of him being with Alex. I know they've been together in New York. Belle has tried to be discreet about it but I have to accept the fact that my sister has found a good one in Conner and that I'll be seeing him again soon. The thought makes me sodding uncomfortable - not because I don't like him. I do. But just because he's so closely connected to Alex. I still love him; there's no getting around it, and regardless of how I tackle it, I'm going to have to stand in front of Conner and tell him I'm fine, that I've gotten over it and that it's okay. But it's not okay because no matter how hard I'm trying to fight it, he is still revolving constantly like a snake in my head, as if he won't let me go, wrapping himself around my spinal cord to control every nerve and feeling, still breaking my heart again, hourly.

"He said Thursday or Friday," she says quietly with a shrug. "He's been in LA. Apparently he had something to sort out." She looks guilty and I know why, but she really shouldn't.

"It's okay, Belle. You know that, don't you? He's good for you. Just because Alex and I aren't together, you shouldn't feel..." I can't help the tears that suddenly spring up and flow down my cheeks. She wraps me up in her arms and squeezes tightly. Several painful minutes later, I push away from her a little as the feeling of irritation at my own pathetic behaviour raises its ugly head again.

"I love you, honey. I'll drop his sorry backside if it will help. You know I will," she says as she rubs my back and tries to soothe away the tears. I sniff them back and shake myself.

"You will do no such thing. He adores you and you should enjoy it. You deserve a man like him." She smiles and wipes at my tears, gazing at me for a minute.

"Right, so anyway, tell me more about this BDSM debacle. I think I might need a step-by-step run through of what he might expect from me," she says. I snort a bemused laugh out because I know all about it, don't I?

"It's not something I can just explain like that, Belle, and I'm not sure how much I know anyway. He was the expert, not me, and I'm not entirely sure I saw even half of what's possible." She looks confused.

"Do you mean we need more alcohol?" I smirk and make my way back through to the kitchen.

"James will be here in a second. Why don't we wait till we get home?" I call back to her as I continue to sniff away my tears and wipe my cheeks. If I can get away with not having to discuss it at all then I'll try. The very idea of having to go through that sort of information is not entirely appealing, given that the only man that has ever touched me in that way is the one man I'm trying desperately to forget.

Unfortunately, something tells me deep down that there isn't a cat's chance in hell of forgetting Alex White, but just maybe I can pretend that he isn't the only man in my mind. Maybe I can at least try to convince myself that I can find more elsewhere. I have to because more with him just isn't a possibility anymore and that means it's time to let him go. He doesn't love me and there's nothing I can do about it.

~

Three hours, the tube ride from hell and a bottle of wine later, I find myself lying in the bath, trying to stop myself from thinking about him, again. Being naked and surrounded by soothing warm heat is not helping me in the slightest. Every time the water swirls around me it reminds me of his hands and the way he moulded them over me or his weight as he dragged his body over mine with that effortless dominance that left me utterly lost and completely his. Every bubble seems to highlight the showers we shared together as he pushed me against a wall and showed me a new version of sex that I couldn't have imagined previously, and each drip of the tap keeps pulling me back to that bloody clock, its heavy tick tock reminding me of his home.

"Sod off," I scream at no one, trying to tell Alex exactly how I feel about him and that he should get out of my head. I haven't even had the chance to vent at him. The man just upped and left in the middle of the night, leaving me with a note, okay a very explanatory note but a note nonetheless. I never saw him as a note kind of man. Why didn't he tell me to my face? He seems to have no problem telling everyone else what he thinks. Fucking coward.

Shaking myself irritably, I get out and head to my room, feeling remarkably happy about the fact that I feel so angry. It's giving me the confidence I need to make the call to Pascal. It's a strange feeling for me. Normally I do the whole suffer in silence thing, hoping to not cause too much of a fuss about my feelings, but for some reason I feel stronger somehow, as if I have a right to feel extremely pissed off about the whole situation and that I should do something about it. Well, that's exactly what I'm going to do. Belle is right; this moping around thing is done with and I'm going to call Pascal.

I move toward the dresser and pull out some shorts and a t-shirt. Yanking them on, I grab a brush and head to the kitchen. Coffee? No. Wine? Standing there for several seconds, I try to make up my mind what I want to drink. Never have decisions been so difficult. When the hell has that happened? *It's a bloody drink, Beth.* I grab the wine and head to the sofa, collapsing on it with a serious bang.

Oh, Jesus, I'm going to call Pascal. Who on earth thought this was a good idea? Oh yeah, me and both of my girls. Really? This is not a good idea.

Swiping his card from the table, I palm it in my hand for a few minutes. It's nothing like the man at all. Alex's card made me feel him, the elegant scrolled writing and the thick heavy embossing of the card itself shouted style quietly and had a businesslike quality that made you feel that you were dealing with superiority and power. I feel myself running to the bedroom to get it before I even realise what I'm doing. Pascal's card just feels wrong somehow. I sit back down and lay them both on the table in front of me.

Pascal's card is black. The weight is just as thick but the writing is a simple block font in white and there's no embossed detail to it. It feels clinical, cold even, and that's not an image I've ever imagined of the man. He's fantasy and almost ethereal in a devilish sort of way. He's bloody dangerous, that's what he is. It amuses me that his card gives away so little of who he is and I chuckle a little. The irony of the two cards is quite perplexing. Alex, the man who gives so little emotion away but seems to let himself flow through his business card, and then Pascal who shows you exactly what he is with no remorse or apology and yet his card delivers nothing to you.

Do I really want to see him?

As much fun as I will probably have with him, Alex will find out about it. It's not exactly getting myself away from Mr. White, is it? I should be looking elsewhere, socialising in a different part of town and trying to find new people to be around. The fact is that being near or around Pascal will lead to seeing Alex again. Mind you, being around Conner will mean exactly the same thing and there isn't a bloody thing I can do about that either. I have to admit that the introduction to his preferences has opened my mind to a new world, and much as the thought of doing anything with anybody other than Alex scares me to death, it's obvious to me that I won't be happy with anything else now. He consumed me, showed me a different route, and my body yielded with such enthusiasm that I can't go backwards now even if I try. But for that, I need the right type of man and there is only a few ways of finding them. Unfortunately, Pascal is a damn good starting point. The fact that it's Alex I want to learn from, give my heart to and feel above me is... Well it just isn't possible anymore.

Sucking in a long breath, I gulp down a large glass of wine and look back at the cards. One last thought of Alex and I reach for Pascal's card and dial the number.

"Yes?" His voice is clipped, almost annoyed. My inner slut recoils instantly. I have no idea what the hell I'm doing or frankly how to do it.

"Hello, Pascal, it's..."

"Ah, my English rose. I could never forget how enticing that voice of yours is. It reminds me of your mouth and all that I want from it," he says in his very familiar smooth voice. I smile.

"Well thank you, Pascal. It's lovely to hear yours, too," I reply, scrabbling around to regain my nerve. *Cool, Beth. Cool and in control.*

"Mmm..." I can hear the cogs in his brain clicking over with measured timing. "So, my dear, what do you need from me? Entertainment or protection? I believe those were our last words when I left you with Alexander?" he asks, his voice dripping with the usual Pascal naughtiness.

"I don't think you offered me protection, Pascal. You actually said you'd fight for me," I reply as sexily as I can manage as I try to knock him off balance a bit. The only real way of dealing with the man is to play him at his own game a bit. If I let him take over, I will be utterly lost, or maybe that's the point? Oh, fuck it!

"I would willingly kill for you, my rose, but I believe you have your own protector closer to home than I, do you not?" Oh, I haven't thought about this at all. What do I say now? Do I tell him I've been dumped? There isn't much point in lying. He's going to find out anyway. Actually, it surprises me that he doesn't already know. Perhaps there's a way around it.

"You told me he would be worth my love, Pascal. He was not," I answer sharply with as little emotion as I can.

"Ah... So very English, my dear. Even in your anger you are pleasant with your insinuations. Did he fuck someone else or was he too cowardly to give his soul to you?" he says as I hear the pop of a cork on the line and laughter in the background. Clearly he's having a good time.

"Probably both, Pascal, but he isn't my concern anymore and I'm not interested in discussing him with you, so I was wondering if the other offer of your entertainment might still be available?" I ask, trying to get the image of Alex with someone else out of my bloody head. Not nice at all.

"Of course it is, my dear. I told you to come to me when he bored you. I was, however, positive I would never get hold of you again." He chuckles. "Such a fool... Now, what are you doing next Friday evening?" he asks. I feel nerves race up my spine at the thought of this really happening. "I'm afraid I have to go to Berlin tomorrow morning for the week and unfortunately it cannot be avoided or I would cancel it for you."

"Next Friday is fine, Pascal. It will be perfect actually," I reply softly. At least I'll have an entire week to get my head around the idea. There isn't an event booked in on the Saturday so I can do what I want, whatever that might be.

"Oh, my dear, you sound thoroughly dull and extinguished. Do not worry, my rose, we shall soon resolve that issue. I shall have you squealing with delight the instant I get my hands on you. Remember how sinful you are, and do wear something that leaves little to my imagination." I can see the devilish smile creeping up his mouth. It's actually very appealing.

"Okay, Pascal." I giggle stupidly. It's ridiculous but at least something feels nice for once. "I'll try to find something suitable for you."

"Good. I'll send a car for you at eight thirty. Bring an overnight bag with you and please give your sister my number. I would hate for her to worry." *What?*

"Pascal, I..." I don't know what to say. I don't want him thinking I'm a sure thing for his taking. No matter how mischievous he is, I'm unfortunately still in love with Alex. Or maybe I should let him have me. Perhaps he can dispel the man from my brain. If anyone can, it's more than likely him.

"Elizabeth, you want entertaining and in my world, that means all night. I will not accept anything less from you. It could only be compared to crushing a pupa before it has achieved its metamorphosis and that would be supremely disappointing to say the least."

Oh...

"Right, well I'll pack a bag then. Where will we be going?" I ask, suddenly feeling a little concerned about what the man is up to.

"To my club of course," he replies with a snort as if the very idea of going elsewhere is beyond him. "I have a feeling the sight of you in my dungeon may be my undoing." He chuckles and I instantly feel a little sick with nerves. *Dungeons, really?*

"Umm... right. I think I should probably go now before this gets a little too much for me." I have to get off the line before I change my mind. Regardless of how much his green eyes are lingering in my mind, Alex's blues are disappointingly merging fast.

"Of course, my dear. Just one more question if I may?" he asks, far too politely for my liking. It immediately reminds me of Alex again and I can sense what type of question is coming from his far too kissable lips.

"Yes, Pascal?" I try for relaxed and casual.

"Steel or rope?" I freeze, my insides hardening instantly at the thought of rope. Alex is so good with rope. It's his thing. The thought of anyone else using rope is just wrong and completely uncomfortable. Why am I even considering this question? I'm not doing anything with Pascal anyway, am I? Probably not. Although my little inner slut is certainly warming up to the idea as I feel my groin alight to the idea.

"Steel," I reply without thinking too much more about it. Have I just given Pascal permission to use handcuffs on me? Oh god, what am I doing?

"Mmm... yes, he is rather good with rope, isn't he? Quite the master of it in fact." He remains quiet for a moment and I know he's giving me time to think more about if I want to go through with this. "I won't allow him between us, my dear. I assume you realise this?" I frown, as I understand what he's trying to say. "If you come to me, I expect you to be ready for me alone. I will not compete with him." Am I? The ability to remove Alex from my thoughts while I'm with Pascal is certainly not going to be easy. I don't even know if I really want to yet. How am I supposed to not compare the two of them?

"Pascal, if I come, I'll be ready," I reply smoothly. At this moment it's the only honest answer I can give and I've given up on the playing games thing. I'll know by next week if I can really do what he asks, and if I can't, I'll cancel it. Simple. Silence follows my statement for a few moments.

"Excellent. I'll look forward to the pleasure of your company next week then, my rose," he eventually says.

"Yes, me too," I reply as I nervously chew my thumbnail and flip his card over in my fingers, unfortunately realising that I'm trying to get used to the feel of it under my fingers.

"Goodnight, Elizabeth," he clips, suddenly seeming a little cold again.

"Goodnight," is my reply as I end the call and stare into the room.

Ten minutes later and I'm still staring around the room, not really looking at anything, just continuing with flicking his card around in my palm. No matter how hard I try, though, it just doesn't feel comfortable to me. The words *unfamiliar* and *unproven* cross my mind. I have a feeling Pascal is probably very *proven* though, just not to me, not like Alex was anyway.

Who is Pascal? I have no idea whatsoever really. The man is immeasurable. I just know that his behaviour around me made me feel appreciated. No, that's the wrong word. Maybe desired is a better explanation of how he made me feel. I'm sure he makes every woman feel like that. It's part of his job, after all. I watched the woman flock to him in Rome as if he were their saviour. Clearly the man is distractingly handsome, but it's more than that. He has that same tortured soul thing happening that Alex pulls off with such precision and beauty. It's some sort of aura they have around them that just makes you want to run to them and let them devour you in a bid to rid them of their sins. What sins does Pascal hide? He said Alex and I reminded of a different time in his life. What was that life like for him? I try to envisage a kinder Pascal, a man who shows a loving nature. He showed me snippets of him in Alex's kitchen when he told me how much Alex felt for me. That man seemed nice. Well, apart from the fact that he was outrageously groping me at the same time. The thought makes me chuckle to myself as it reminds me that I probably won't be meeting the nice version next week and I highly doubt Pascal has any intention of anything *nice* being lined up for me on our date.

Blowing out another breath at my confusion, I head back into the kitchen, shaking my head, to get a cup of tea. For some reason the wine tastes sour as if there's nothing pleasurable about it anymore. Skimming the counter top with my fingertips, I remember Alex pushing me down on top of it and shudder. Closing my eyes, I press my palms face down on it and let the vision flow around me - his mouth on me, his hands holding me down, those damned icy eyes demanding more from me. "Chess," I mumble softly to myself to snap my own head out of the moment. It doesn't work. I wonder actually if I'm trying to shout it to him somehow, to make him stop with his relentless twirling around inside me. Unfortunately, he isn't doing this to me, I am. This is all me because he's made his feelings clear.

I hear the keys in the door as I remove the teabag and turn to see a soaking wet Belle looking furious as she throws her bag onto the table and storms into her bedroom. I fill another cup and wander into the lounge. Plonking myself down onto the chair, I grab the two cards and tuck them into my pocket.

"You okay honey?" I call.

"No, I'm fucking not. Look at that," she says as she walks across to me half dressed, chucks a magazine at me and then huffs back off into her room, presumably to continue changing her clothes. I look down at the image in front of me. *Oh dear!*

Conner is sitting in a very modern looking bar, surrounded by what can only be described as playboy bunnies. To be fair, he isn't touching any of them but they're certainly touching him. The man with him is very American looking with teeth so white they almost knock me out. He's probably mid forties and, regardless of the casual attire, seems to have businessman pouring out of him. I scan down the page to find out who he is. Tyler Rathbone, apparently. I have absolutely no idea but the man looks expensive and very cutthroat, as he seemingly drags the women to him, not that they appear to need much persuasion. Looking back at Conner, I try to study his reaction to what's happening around him. He seems relaxed. It's then that I notice the dulled bruising around his face, which shows he's been fighting. Nothing all that new as we've seen it before, but the fact that he's been with Alex sends shivers across me. Is he okay? What do I bloody care? Bastard deserves it!

"One week he's been gone and he's all over them. Look at the fucking git," Belle seethes as she flings herself on the sofa and grabs her tea. "And he's been fighting again. What is so bad about the man's damn life that he needs to fight?"

"Honey, I honestly don't think he's all over them. He's not even touching them and you know what the paps like to make of situations that look bad," I reply, trying to calm her down. Conner wouldn't do anything wrong, would he? Even I'm questioning it as I think it. What the hell do I know about men anymore?

"Well, yes, even I have to admit he doesn't look all that into it but what's the sodding face about?" she says a little more rationally.

"I don't know. It might have something to do with Alex, I suppose. He did seem awfully mad when he left here," I muse as I continue to look at the picture.

"Well fuck him. I doubt he's even thought of the fact that this could come back to bite us on the arse. This is not good for our business," she says as she snatches the magazine from my hands and launches it across the room. I stare in disbelief.

"That's what you're worried about? That this will affect us?" Does the woman have no sentiment at all?

"I can't be seen to have a relationship with *that,* Beth. We're high end caterers. We can't be dragged into that kind of crap. We'll lose business left, right and centre if this becomes the norm." Oh, I hadn't thought of that.

"Oh, right, aren't you worried though?" I ask tentatively. She is supposed to care about him, after all.

"About what? Him? He's a big boy and he's clearly survived yet another brawl. No, I couldn't give a shit about his face. I just need to find a way to do some damage limitation. Unfortunately for us, we do not have enough wealth to be able to ignore the papers, unlike idiot boy here," she says as she begins to tap her fingers against her chin. "Perhaps I should go out with someone else? You know, be seen out with another man for a few nights."

"Belle, I don't think that's such a good idea. I don't think Conner will be very happy about it when he finds out, and you know he will," I reply quietly, hoping to put her off the idea, knowing it's bloody pointless but at least trying. Her face flies to mine with anger spilling out of it.

"When will you get it, Beth? Stop thinking about them all the time. This is about us. They're all fucking arseholes. I will not risk our business for any man, regardless of how I feel. You need to wise up and quick. I love you but you cannot let them rule your emotions anymore. It's pathetic," she spits at me. "Oh, fuck it, now I'm really sodding mad."

"Belle, calm down, honey. I didn't mean you shouldn't be irritated. I just don't want you to lose him," I say as I reach over and rub her arm.

"Well, the dick shouldn't have behaved like a bloody Neanderthal, should he? What a prat."

There is quiet for a while as I watch her formulate a plan in her own mind. "Okay, so I need my little black book. Who's good for a date?"

"Belle, can't you find another way around this?" I ask hesitantly.

"No, and frankly I don't want another option. I told him not to screw this up and that's exactly what he's doing. It'll do him good to worry a bit," she says as she yanks her bag from the floor and starts digging around in it. "Did you call Pascal?"

"Yes, next Friday," I reply as I sip my tea, watching her thumbing through her infamous book.

"Good for you," she says as she smiles wickedly. "Now there's a name I haven't seen for a while. He'll do nicely. Blythe MacDowell, what do you think?" I roll my eyes at her and laugh. He's a match made in heaven, I'll give her that.

"I haven't seen Blythe for a year or so. Is he still here or is he laird of his Scottish castle now?"

"I don't know, but he'll come back for me. We had a lot of fun together."

My brain rapidly displays images of the burly Scotsman and his effervescent charm. He's probably the funniest man I've ever met and his charisma is something to behold. You can't help but have fun with him. Of course it helps that his six foot rugged good looks keep you constantly guessing what's under his kilt, whether he's wearing it or not.

"Well, I think he'll get right up Conner's nose and the rest of the social network will be alerted in minutes of his return. I'll call him now. Perfect."

"Belle, just for once will you think less unemotionally about this? Conner loves you. Please don't ruin things." Her eyes narrow as she closes the book and chucks her phone on the table.

"Okay, I'll wait till the morning. I'm still calling though."

Oh god, could something just be easy and simple for a change? Before these men came into our lives, everything was calm. Will it ever be that uncomplicated again? Something makes me doubt it.

Chapter 3

Alexander

The boardroom was full of waiting employees, yet he simply couldn't drag up enough energy to bother with the meeting that he'd called at short notice. He'd forced every head of department to drop everything to get to this meeting so that he could get control of his business again, but that had been a few days ago and now he just felt like going home to the solitude of his study and reading a book or something. He was like that a lot lately - all over the fucking place.

After flying in from LA on Sunday, he'd given himself some time to process the last week and then called Louisa and told her that he was back on board and needed a whole lot of things put into place.

The phone call from Mark Jacobs on Monday had reminded him that he did indeed have a hell of a lot to lose and that he needed to get on with saving it. Regardless of his own stupidity regarding Elizabeth, she was not his only concern at the moment and until he felt secure within himself and his accumulated wealth, he was of no bloody use to her anyway. She more than likely wasn't going to accept him back anyway. Why the hell would she? He'd just proven how little he deserved her.

He'd spent the last week manoeuvring his way around varying company profiles, trying to get all his cards in place for the oncoming storm. Tyler Rathbone was, for now, his friend and new business associate, and that meant he could stop relying on Henry's funding and find a way to get this deal completed behind closed doors. If he could just keep his shit together and force the Chinese to comply, he'd be home and dry.

The meeting with Rathbone had been brought forward a few days because of Jacobs' unusually boring lack of fucking information regarding Henry's misgivings, which had incensed him to the point of sorting his own bloody way out of the issue. The only useful piece of information he'd managed to find was a snippet about a younger cousin that had apparently gone off the rails years before. The family had hushed up the whole thing, but it seemed drugs and a bad temper had been the delinquent's downfall. Mark had promised to look into the matter further and get back to him as soon as he knew anything else. His results on Evelyn Peters hadn't been much more interesting either. For a damned good investigator, Mark Jacobs had done a thorough but completely unproductive job, but at least he was continuing his search for more about the woman, which was reassuring. Why he was trying to prove she was related to him was beyond him. He knew she was family of some description because he could feel it every time he looked at her picture. The thought was distracting, though, and until he had some firm evidence, he just couldn't bring himself to think it possible or even begin to deal with the shit that was swirling around his own head about it. Thankfully, Conner had given him the emergency home address details of her mother. When he had the balls or time to deal with it, he probably would but until then, he'd let Jacobs keep digging around.

After he'd argued with Conner about going to LA and meeting Rathbone, Alex had eventually called his plane and gone to the airport anyway. It seemed it was the worst place in the world for Conner to be seen with the bruising on his face because of the parasitic tabloids. He had felt pretty guilty about that given the circumstances, but it couldn't be helped at the time, and regardless of his feelings for his saviour, his territory was in danger. He was going to sort it out.

He smiled at the thought of his friend grumbling his way up the jet's steps at the last minute and muttering about the fact that he was a complete dickhead and that he didn't deserve his loyalty in the slightest. Given the beating he'd handed to Conner, he was lucky the guy was even talking to him so he had to agree. At the time it had prompted him to consider visiting a shrink of some sort. Given the situation with Elizabeth and his now obvious paranoia around her, he knew he needed to do something. The blackout with Conner had worried him to the point that he believed it was possible that he might hurt her at some point if he lost it again. He couldn't keep on pretending that he could deal with all this emotion without talking to someone about it, so yesterday he'd done just that.

Strangely, he'd found it quite a cathartic experience. Dr. Keith Schroder had been an interesting man and far cleverer than Alex believed possible of a psychiatrist. He could only remember vague images of other shrinks he'd had to deal with when he was younger. They weren't very positive memories. He'd found them to be quite naïve in their analysis of his apparent condition at the time. He didn't have a condition; even he knew that. He was just fucking mad and a bit of lunatic when it came to taming his temper. Schroder had been intelligent, resourceful and quite inventive. He had also been the most unemotional man that he'd ever met. Not once had his face changed its shape or positioning. He'd been calm and somewhat pragmatic the entire time. No matter how much Alex had tried to divert attention with his normal ambiguous manner, Schroder had keep his inquisition gentle but forceful. Damn, the man would make a hell of a poker player. He liked him immensely, and Elizabeth would, too, if she'd ever agree to go with him.

What he was going to do about her was still a quandary. He'd picked up the phone so many times that he'd lost count, and every time, he'd put it down again with a disappointing thud against whatever surface it landed on. He just couldn't find the right words to tell her he was sorry and that he wanted her back. She'd be a fool to take him back anyway. He didn't deserve her, and how he was supposed to convince her when he couldn't even convince himself was becoming a problem he was unable to solve.

"Love." He mumbled the word out loud to himself as he tapped his foot on the floor and stared at his screen. What he was looking at he couldn't even remember. She was continuing to consume most of his thoughts. She had done since the moment the wheels had touched down in London. He'd somehow found the ability to push her aside for a while when he was in New York and LA so he could concentrate on other matters, but the moment he knew he could touch her again, he'd become almost desperate for her. The need to feel her against his skin again and disappear into that calm place he'd adored so much was almost unbearable in its relentless attack. He'd never had that before, and he was damned if he'd lose it now.

He looked up at the window and felt his whole body relax into the vision of her, her red hair falling over her shoulders and those big, beautiful brown eyes pulling him towards her. "Perfect," he sighed out as he felt the soft smile spread across his face.

The phone suddenly ringing on his desk broke the moment abruptly and he sneered at it as he pressed the button sharply.

"Louisa," he snapped, trying to remain calm with the woman.

"Sir, do you want me to cancel this meeting or are you coming in?" she asked, professional as ever and completely on his side as usual. He sighed and picked up his phone from the table.

"No, I'm coming in. Just give me a minute," he replied.

"Yes of course, Sir," she said as he put the phone down.

Shrugging into his suit jacket, he walked over to the door and pocketed his phone. Just as he reached for the handle, he rubbed at his eyes and shook his head. Very little sleep over the last week was beginning to take its toll, and the constant pain of missing her was muddling his brain to a fucking disturbing point of distraction.

"Go away, Elizabeth. I can't do this with you in there," he muttered to himself. She softened him and chiselled off his edges, and right now he needed those corners sharp, rough and angry. He drew in a long breath and headed out of the door. This wasn't going to be pleasant for any of them but he had a feeling he'd feel a lot better when he left this meeting. After all, barking orders around and making people feel like shit was one of the more effective versions of himself, so that's what he was about to do.

As he approached the boardroom, he smiled to himself, remembering her standing there in that little business suit, all gorgeous and perky with her hair neatly pinned. God, how he longed to pull that hair again, to sink himself inside her and forget everything else. What day was it? Friday. Fuck it, tonight he was going round there. If she said no then he'd have to find another way in, but he had to give it a go. This bloody ridiculous being nervous about it shit was just not sitting comfortably with him at all. After this, he'd be more ready to face her and hopefully more ready to hold his head up and take whatever she threw at him.

Muttering and grumbling greeted him as he rounded the corner and took up position at the top of the table. The entire team turned toward him and plastered on their best happy faces. Well, they weren't going to be fucking happy in a minute. Picking up a pile of filled document folders that had been placed in front of him, he threw them down the table and sat down heavily as he unbuttoned his jacket. He watched with his fingers steepled under his chin for a few minutes as the usual grabbing and polite shuffling took place, carefully scanning the faces and trying to glean important clues about demeanour and posture. At the moment he didn't trust anyone apart from Conner. Everyone in this room was a potential threat.

"Sam, Nicola, don't bother picking one of those up. You're both fired. I'd like you out of my building within half an hour. Louisa will accompany you immediately," he said instantly as he noticed them glance at each other far too suspiciously for his liking. Louisa raised herself from her seat beside him with a completely impassive face and went to stand at the doorway waiting for them. She had no idea what was happening but she did her job immaculately and loyally. Nicola did the correct thing and made for the door. Sam, however, decided to have a temper tantrum. His head of negotiating apparently thought it appropriate to negotiate. Idiot.

"Mr. White, you can't do that. I have a contract and I haven't done anything incorrect or detrimental to the business. It's in my contract." He looked around the table wildly and found Westfield. "Tate, tell him. He can't just bloody fire me," he continued as he flailed his arms around amusingly. Westfield quite rightly just stared at him with that lawyer's face that Alex had always admired.

"Sam, would you like me to list your failings in front of this table? I am more than happy to." Alex grinned as he leant back into his chair, crossed his legs and let the atmosphere do the rest of the talking for him. He could feel the bastard rising back up in himself and revelled in it - that feeling of cold, disciplined defiance coursing through his veins like a slow burning fire that had no intention of being dampened. The man started shifting uncomfortably and looking nervous. Alex chuckled. "Good, now go. Please do try and sue me if you'd like. We all know how Tate enjoys a good fight."

His head of negotiating obviously thought better of his own argument and lowered his head as he made his way to the door to join the others. Tate smirked at Alex from the other side of the table. The gesture was too intimate and left him still questioning Tate's loyalty. Was he friend or foe? He still didn't know and that made him damned uncomfortable in this room. There was too much information available in here or anywhere in this building, frankly.

"Right, now that's over can anyone tell me why I lost profit in two departments this month? I am a little fucking irritated and getting ready to think about a few more of you." Silence greeted him as they all looked over at him with either shock or fear imprinted across their faces. "No? Okay, we'll go one by one then, shall we? Karen, open up to page fourteen and tell me why the hell three hundred grand has been wasted on fucking policy that you should have be able to do in your sleep." She scampered around to the page and then looked back at him with a nervous expression.

Christ, this was going to be a long meeting.

~

What time was it? Jesus! Eight-thirty? Was it too late to go to hers now? It would be at least nine before he got there, probably later given Friday night traffic. He pulled his black wool coat on and pressed the button for the lift. The afternoon had dragged but there was no denying its effect on him. He felt invigorated, alive. It was interesting that scaring the shit out of people always put him a good mood. Perhaps he should talk to Keith about that.

"One," he said quietly as the doors closed and he blew out a long breath steadily.

The doors opened again and he strode across the lobby, nodding at his receptionist as he reached the doors. He didn't even know her name. When the hell had she arrived in the business?

Andrews waited patiently for him at the car with his normal bored expression.

"Sir," he said as he closed the door and went around to start the engine. "Where to?"

"Elizabeth's please," he said as he reached for the Cognac, trying to stop the tapping foot thing that seemed to have become a permanent fixture over the last few weeks. Neck rubbing was enough of a tell so this foot thing was damned infuriating.

"Yes, Sir," Andrews replied quietly.

He took a steadying sip and watched the London nightlife drift by the window. Dropping his head back against the seat, he closed his eyes and began to run through his carefully prepared speech - the one he hoped would be enough for her. He would tell her what a fool he'd been and how much he loved her, that he would give anything for her to give him another chance, to prove he was actually worthy of her love. It suddenly occurred to him that she might tell him that it wasn't enough and that he would have to prove it, or that she simply wasn't interested in his idea of love, and the nervous ball that he'd been trying to dispel came raging back. Damn, a few lines of coke would help sort all this shit out. He bit back the need and wrinkled his nose up at himself in disgust.

"What the fuck am I doing?" he mumbled to himself as he reached for another drink.

"I think you're going after what you want, as you've done hundreds of times before," Andrews said from the front. Smiling to himself, he realised he hadn't reinstated the privacy glass and chuckled as he opened his eyes.

"Thank you for your insight, Andrews, but I'm not sure it helps," he replied as he watched Andrews' brows rise in the mirror.

"It should do. Have you ever been turned down before?" he said with a snort of humour. Alex smirked and downed his drink.

"I think this is a little different, don't you?" he said sarcastically as he looked back out of the window.

"Perhaps, but it definitely will be if you turn yourself into someone else for her. I doubt she'll thank you for it," he said calmly as he raised the screen back up and effectively gave Alex his own space again.

He considered that statement carefully. He hadn't thought about it like that. For whatever reason, she had fallen in love with him for exactly who he was. He hadn't hidden or softened for her particularly. Well, maybe he had a little but only because he'd wanted to. Yes, she'd probably pulled the fun in him out to play again but she'd loved each part of him with equal measure, it seemed, accepted his flaws and differences. She'd in no way seen his darkened depths in their entirety, but there hadn't been enough time for that and he wasn't entirely convinced that he would ever need that of her anyway. Andrews was right, though. He'd spent all this time telling himself to beg for her and actually, she'd fallen for a man who would never do anything of the sort. Would she prefer that man to come to her door and demanded her attention again?

Pinching his brow and laughing at himself, he realised he'd been going about this in completely the wrong way. Was this what love did to people? Sent them into another level of thinking that made them change into someone else? She'd found her balance with him the way he was and he'd taught her to believe in herself. She wouldn't want a begging fool. She'd want the Alex White she knew and hopefully still loved.

Pulling her bracelet out of his pocket, he rubbed his thumb backwards and forwards on it and watched the road weaving its way towards her apartment with a new sense of hope. Perhaps if he simply told her the truth and then swept her off her beautiful feet again, he'd have her home within a few hours.

"Shall I wait, Sir?" Andrews asked as he opened the door.

"I think that's probably wise," he replied with a chuckle. "God knows what's going to greet me in there."

"Yes, Sir, but I'm sure you'll be fine," Andrews said with a wink. Alex looked back at him and smiled. The man was a rock. He didn't deserve him, either. He couldn't even make up his mind if he was comfortable with the *"Sir"* thing anymore, given what had passed between them regarding fatherly intent. Something had shifted a little somehow. He shook his head and kept walking. He'd think about that shit another time because his focus was only on her at the moment.

He made his way across the foyer of the building, pressed the button on the lift and watched the numbers as they counted backwards. He felt his foot tapping again and instantly stopped it. *Fucking ridiculous, White. Stop it!*

The ride up in the lift went by in seconds, giving him no more time to think about it and he stood before the door, trying to calm himself for whatever he was about to receive. Lifting his hand, he knocked with purpose and waited. He did not get the response he was hoping for.

"Mmm... The great Alexander fucking arsehole White, how very depressing," Belle drawled as she blocked the doorway from him. Shit, he hadn't thought of this scenario. He'd been sure she'd be out on a Friday night.

"Belle, can I see Elizabeth?" he replied curtly. There was little point in pleasantries with her. She wasn't impressed. He got it. Neither was he.

"I assume you're joking because last I heard, you were the complete bastard who didn't deserve one second of her time," was her response as she took a step forward and made him move backwards a little. He frowned and put his hands in his pockets.

"I'm not leaving, Belle. I need to see her. I was wrong," he said slowly, trying to keep his temper in check and show the woman some respect. She was, after all, completely correct in her description, no matter how much he hated being spoken to in such a way.

"Yes you were, you fucking pig. How dare you? To her, of all people. She's nothing but kind and loving and for some unknown fucking reason, she was completely devoted to you," she seethed as she held his eyes fiercely. He immediately understood Conner's infatuation with her and smirked at the thought.

"Belle, if you would just let me in, I-"

She cut him off. He smiled and relaxed his stance. He'd let her have her minute or two for the time being. She probably deserved it.

"I'm not finished yet, you dick. You will listen to what a complete fuck up you are. I can't believe you have the balls to stand there and smile at me. Are you trying to charm your way past me? It won't fucking work, arsehole. I am immune to your bullshit. It's actually quite revolting, but please do enlighten me with why the hell I should even begin to let you at her again," she said with venom as she narrowed her eyes and crossed her arms at him. It actually made him flinch a little and made him consider whether Elizabeth's temper was as strong as her sister's.

"Because I love her," he said aloud for the first time. It made him smile, regardless of the situation, so he said it again. "I love her, Belle, and you're right. I've been a complete dick, but you have to give me the chance to talk to her. You know I'll get around you if I want to anyway," he replied. Her eyes widened just a little. Clearly the love comment had stirred some emotion in her so he continued with his smile. Immune or not, he could see her caving in.

"You're a fucking arsehole, White, and I hate you," she responded as she glared but thankfully took a small step backwards.

"I appreciate that and understand why, but can I see her?" he asked as he moved forward.

"Fuck off," she sneered again. Clearly she wasn't caving very quickly.

"Belle, I just need to see her for a minute. If she doesn't want me here then I'll leave."

She stared, quite maliciously for a woman. He was impressed, still fucking irritated, but impressed nonetheless.

"You can't, not tonight," she eventually said, her eyebrow quirking with something that amused her.

"Why?" he asked, suddenly feeling very suspicious of her changed demeanour and attitude.

"She's out this evening," she replied smugly as she folded her arms and snickered.

"Where? Who with?" he asked as realisation started to dawn that she was possibly out with another man. His hackles instantly raised their very ugly heads with a vengeance.

"I don't think that's any of your business." She smirked, and that was fucking annoying. His anger bubbled to the surface instantly as he felt his mouth tighten. Sister or not, she was becoming tiresome.

"Belle, you will not stand in my way any longer. She deserves to know. I have allowed you your moment, now tell me where she damn well is." He sneered as he stepped forward and used his increasing size to force her back into the hallway. To her credit, she hardly stepped backward at all, just stared at him with her face full of contempt again.

"How long will you manage this time before you fuck it up... again?" she asked as she turned back into the apartment. He could feel the loathing pouring off her and tried to calm down a little.

"I won't, not this time," he said quietly as he followed her. She picked up her wine glass and looked over the rim at him. It made him chuckle. Conner did the same thing when he was irritated. "You know you're a lot like him? It's easy to see how you two work so well together."

She snorted and rolled her eyes. "Were you with him in LA when he got papped with women dripping all over him and bruising on his face? Do you think he considered the implications to me or my business while he was having a good old time fucking his way around the states?" she replied with distaste. Alex frowned. He hadn't thought of the effect on Scott's. Conner clearly had when he tried to argue the point.

"He's a good man, Belle, and he loves you. Now please, where is she?" She stared again. Her fucking eyes were almost as bad as her

57

sister's at ripping him in half, but they simply didn't have the same grace. They were harder somehow, broken maybe, a view he knew very well. Eventually, she sighed and lowered her glass.

"She's with Pascal, at his club," she replied with irritated resignation.

"WHAT?" he yelled at her. "Fucking hell... No!" he shouted again as he turned and stormed from the apartment. He hit the button on the lift so hard it shook. Grabbing at his pockets, he found his phone and fumbled through the numbers for hers and pressed call. "Pick up, pick up..." Voicemail greeted him. He smacked at the lift again angrily.

"Alex, what's the matter?" Belle asked behind him nervously. She'd obviously picked up on his instant worried tension and thankfully not assumed it was just a jealous rage.

"Call her, Belle. Now! Tell her to leave," he shouted at her as he scanned back through his numbers to find Pascal's. He'd fucking kill him if he laid one finger on her. He watched as Belle looked shocked and then bolted inside to get her phone. She arrived back, shaking her head and signalling voicemail. The lift doors opened. "Keep trying her. Leave messages, anything to get her away from him. He's not whom she thinks he is," he said as he got in the lift. She pressed her hand against the door as it began to close.

"What are you telling me, Alex? Do I need to be really worried here?" she asked, her voice panicky and shaky, those eyes softening a little. He realised what she meant and tried to quiet himself a little to ease her mind.

"No, I'll be there before then," was all he could find in his brain to help her. He wasn't sure if he would be but there was no point worrying her with no reason. "Call me if you get hold of her," he continued as he brushed her hand off the door and watched it close.

He found himself pacing furiously before the doors opened again, and he ran to the car like a man possessed. He couldn't let Pascal even think he had time to play with her. Christ knew what the man would come up with.

"Eden," he shouted at Andrews as he got to the car. Recognizing the apprehension in his voice, Andrews leapt into action and floored the car out into the traffic. He swiftly grabbed at the bottle of scotch and drank some. The instant the alcohol hit his throat, he threw the bottle as hard as he could straight across the car at the window. Fury welled up inside him at the thought of Pascal's hands anywhere near her as he gazed at the liquid pouring across the carpet with disgust. Not only did she belong to him - and the bastard should have known better than to try without asking permission - but she wasn't anywhere near ready for the sort of debauchery that man would be considering for his amusement. Regardless of the current situation, Pascal shouldn't have even thought about touching her, and as he grabbed at the other bottle, he balled up his fist in frustration and slammed it against the console. This was his own fucking fault. If he hadn't been such a complete arse, none of this would be happening.

Abruptly, he looked up. What time was it? Pascal never started his real entertainment until eleven at the earliest and he would be making this evening pull out as long as he could. He would want her all night. He would savour everything about her carefully, methodically and let his mind wander as he watched her move and calculated her reactions to the things around her. Looking at his watch, he let out a breath. It was a little after ten so she would probably only be drinking at the moment. He knew Pascal so well that he could almost plan the evening out in his mind. He relaxed back a bit and tried to cool himself off. She'd be okay for now. He looked out of the window to see where they were and it was still too far away for his liking. Traffic was slowing them considerably and he cursed the Friday night frivolities that were happening all around him.

Grabbing at his phone, he hovered his finger over the call icon. What was she doing with Pascal? It was the first time the thought had popped into his head and he frowned. After two weeks she'd decided to go out with another man? Yes, he'd treated her appallingly but what had made her get straight back out there, and with Pascal of all people?

He knew she would have reacted badly to his behaviour, but he'd expected her to crumble into a mess and sink into a hole of depression, not pull herself together and catapult into the hands of the devil, or at least a version of the devil. Perhaps she wasn't as breakable as he thought she was. Had she found an inner strength that he was unaware of or had she always been tougher than he'd assumed? He realised that he didn't know her nearly as well as he thought he did and that made him more nervous than he was earlier. Did she want Pascal to show her more of their world or had she gone there thinking it would simply be a good distraction? Surely she knew what she was doing. She must want what he could offer her or she wouldn't have gone to him, would she? Although she most definitely didn't know what Pascal was capable of doing to her if the mood took him, and it probably would. She was everything he liked to destroy.

Suddenly unsure of what to say to Pascal other than *'I'll fucking kill you if,'* he put the phone back into his pocket and decided to wait and see the reaction on her face for himself. Christ, she might even tell him to leave and carry on her night with the shit. That definitely wasn't going to happen. Regardless of how she felt, he wasn't going to allow Pascal one touch of her beautiful body. She was his and until they had talked, she wasn't going anywhere without him.

Twenty long minutes later, the car pulled up to the nondescript black door, the symbol of Pascal's dragon firmly imprinted into the gold disc beside the name. He licked his lips and wondered how this was going to pan out as he waited for Andrews to open the door. One thing was for sure; his temper was still bubbling away inside and he couldn't decide whether to send it away or use it in full force. He'd wait and see how he felt when he saw them together. He needed to gauge her reaction to him so he could decide how to proceed.

"Wait here," he said to Andrews as he walked to the door, unclenching his fists and trying to regain his impassive appearance. The door was opened for him by the nameless bouncer who must have known who he was, so he walked down the elegant green staircase to the security suite. Three short knocks later the door was opened by Hayley, Pascal's PA. He walked straight past her and sat at one of the monitors.

"Hayley, where is Pascal?" he asked sharply without looking at her as he tapped away at the keyboard, switching screens so he could search for him. He couldn't see him anywhere.

"Mr. White, I can't let you-"

He cut her off. "You'll let me do anything I damn well please or I'll inform Pascal of the skimming you've been doing for the past three years. I'll also tell him about your affair with his brother and the information you gave him regarding his balance sheet," he said as he tried to gain the access codes for Pascal's private suites, although why Pascal would be in his own apartment with her was completely unknown. "What's the code for Pascal's apartment?" She looked at him in shock.

"Please, Sir, I can't give you that. And I didn't give anything to Fabrice."

He lifted himself so quickly she didn't have a chance to step away and stumbled backwards into the wall at his scowl.

"You're a fucking liar and I don't have time for your shit. Tell me the code now and you might have a hope at saving your job," he sneered as he inched closer and grabbed her arm. She cowered and began to shake at his force.

"Haven216," she responded quietly as she looked at the floor. He sat again and watched as the screen came to life.

"Lock the door and sit in that chair," he said as he studied the two of them sitting at the dining table drinking wine. "And put your phone on the table. I wouldn't want you getting any fucking stupid ideas."

Oh Christ, she looked amazing. Although the image of her in Pascal's dining room was completely unacceptable, he couldn't help but watch her as she crossed her long legs in another indecently short dress. The flash of thigh sent his pulse racing instantly as he let his eyes drift across the rest of her and blew out a long breath. The deep red dress clung to every curve on her and accentuated her pale skin tone magnificently. Her slender arms were bare apart from gold wrist cuffs that matched the gold heavy chains around her neck. He'd never seen her look so bloody appealing and found himself moving to adjust his rapidly agreeing cock. Her luscious red locks tumbled down her back effortlessly as wave after wave gently encased her cheekbones and hid some of her face from him but as he watched her incredible mouth move he fell deeply in love all over again. She was perfect and he was damned if he'd let her go, especially not to Pascal.

He, of course, was being his normal arrogant self as he sat there in what appeared to be a black Gucci suit. Unfortunately, looking as impeccable as ever in his more modern guise, for a near forty year-old man, he looked bloody good. He was casually studying her. Actually he was fucking leering, but to the outsider he would have appeared completely ambivalent about the woman in front of him. He most definitely wasn't. Behind his facade were a multitude of sins presently being concocted. He could see the glint of arousal from the way the man tapped his cheekbone thoughtfully and widened those penetrating green eyes as she moved her hair. Too many years had been spent learning from the man for Alex to not be able to read his every single movement. Each small inclination of hand or mouth was a signal of his next focus or his impending explosion of aggression.

She abruptly stopped talking and looked at the door. Alex noticed her barely-there movements and watched the way her face frowned briefly as if she was aware of something. She rubbed her arms and licked her lips quietly, almost as if she could sense him close and it confused her. He smiled at the image of her doing the same thing every time she knew he was near her but couldn't see him. He'd often gazed at her minutes before he pounced and the thought made him chuckle as he realised thankfully that she still loved him, or at least she could feel him.

Pascal's gaze didn't waver as he smiled across at her movements and picked up his phone. He said something to her and glanced up at the camera, his eyebrow raised mischievously. She resumed her conversation but kept her arms around her tightly as if she were suddenly uncomfortable with the air around her. Pascal chuckled and typed something into his phone. Alex's own phone vibrated seconds later and he couldn't help the smirk that shot across his face. He plucked it out of his pocket and swiped.

- **How much longer do I have to play before you come in and get her, dear boy?**

He quickly replied. How the hell Pascal knew he was here was still utterly perplexing, even after all these years. The man always seemed to know somehow, but the fact that he did know meant that nothing more would happen between them.

- **Not long, and if you keep looking at her like that, I'll kill you.**

He continued to watch as Pascal received the message and erupted into fits of laughter. The man seemed far too jovial for his liking, and the thought crossed his mind that maybe Pascal was actually being loyal in his own delusional way. He clearly hadn't touched her. Regardless of how fascinating he found her, he hadn't done anything inappropriate up to this point and frankly that was unusual in its own right. The very fact that they were having dinner in his apartment was out of the ordinary. He couldn't remember a time that Pascal had ever taken a woman into his home. Had he been so ready to condemn Pascal that he hadn't thought about him being decent in the slightest?

Christ, he really needed to get a grip on this paranoia thing and calm down. He still didn't trust that Pascal didn't want her, but for now at least, it appeared that his friend was being gentlemanly. He doubted his mind was in agreement, however Pascal was controlling his body for once and that in itself was a sight to behold. Pascal controlling his desires was not something Alex could ever remember witnessing before. That was the entre point of Pascal - to not control himself.

He looked on as Pascal stood and offered his hand to her and then wrapped her into a dance hold, his long fingers travelling her skin smoothly as he obviously tried to entice an explosive reaction or a sexual one out of him. He turned her so that he could look into the camera as he kissed her neck lightly. Alex immediately felt his whole body stiffen at the seductive vision. It wasn't the reaction he expected from himself and as much as he didn't like it, he couldn't deny it was there. His gaze dropped down to her legs as Pascal dipped his knee provocatively in between them and pulled her tighter against him. She glided effortlessly as she moulded to him and let the music take her. Pascal's gaze held firm with his as he dropped his hand downwards and fingered the bottom of her dress, just below her arse line, and as that look of sexual carnage embedded itself across his face, Alex began to feel his pulse quicken again while he watched him kiss her shoulder languidly.

He groaned at the sight and sucked in a breath. Too many times had he been a part of this torment with Pascal, and he normally liked nothing better than to watch and be goaded into frustration and dominance while Pascal would get them ready for him. But this was different, rubbing somehow closer to the bone than it ever had before. Unfortunately, it didn't seem to make a damn bit of difference to the way his body was reacting to the sight before him. The man just knew him too fucking well.

He shouldn't be feeling like this. He should be angry, furious even, but the erotic energy around the pair of them was simply too much, so shaking his head irritably, he stood up and switched off the monitor. Pascal could have his few minutes with her because within an hour, he expected to have her back in his house, and then in his bed, exactly where she belonged.

Suddenly remembering Hayley, he looked at her. She was still sitting there nervously pulling at her skirt and fiddling with her thumbs. He sneered at the very thought that she might be thinking he wanted her.

"You don't need to worry about your job. Pascal knows it all already. For some reason he quite likes you," he said as he unlocked the door and walked out. Plucking out his phone again, he thumbed down to Belle's number and sent a text.

- She's fine. I've got her now.

The response was almost instant.

- That is yet to be decided, arsehole.

He rolled his eyes and kept walking.

Chapter 4

Elizabeth

O h good god, what am I doing in here with him? I can't breathe. I'm so nervous, not necessarily because Pascal is being difficult. He isn't. He's being charming and wonderful and so positively normal it is actually a little unsettling. I've never seen him so... well... normal. His exaggerated over the top-ness seems to have been quietened somehow and he appears to be something like he probably was before the Pascal of today. Mind you, I don't actually know the Pascal of today all that well so I'm not entirely sure if he is different or whether this is the way he behaves in a normal date-type situation. Does he even do normal date-type situations?
Probably not, Beth.

I have to say, I expected him to be all over me like a rash. I expected him to come on so strong that I would have no choice but to surrender, but he hasn't been like that at all. Clearly he's been flirtatious and downright dirty at some points, with those intoxicating green eyes zapping at me like a moth to a sodding flame, but I just get the feeling he's trying to temper himself down a bit. It's almost as if he wants to take it slow. Maybe he's been giving me the opportunity to leave if I want to? I have no idea, and frankly I am still so confused about my feelings for Alex I can't quite comprehend how I should be viewing my circumstances at all.

I'm waltzing - well, not waltzing because that would suggest politeness and there is nothing remotely polite about this dance - around his dining room with a ridiculously short dress on that Belle forced me to wear. The mood in his apartment is as low and seductive as I imagined and the space around us screams eighteenth century boudoir. Long, purple curtains frame the Georgian architecture beautifully and low-hanging crystal chandeliers funnel light around the room gently, highlighting heavy dark woodwork and doorways. Artwork covers the walls in abundance, reminding me of a stately home, and I wonder yet again who Pascal is. It wouldn't surprise me if he was some sort of royalty with his aristocratic European accent, and that reminds me that actually I still don't even know where he's from.

I also still have no idea how I'm supposed to understand the fact that I am becoming slowly aroused by the man, regardless of the fact that I'm still hopelessly pining for Alex, and to top it all, I keep getting the feeling that he's here somewhere. I can feel him. I don't know how but it's as if the hairs on my neck are pulling me in another direction, away from Pascal. I've never believed in that mumbo jumbo rubbish about being connected to someone, but at this moment, I am questioning that somehow. I can remember the same feeling in Rome when I felt him before he spoke while my eyes were closed in the afternoon heat on the Pantheon plaza.

I close my eyes tightly and try to bring myself back into the moment with Pascal, and a very nice moment it is. The soft tones of Norah Jones are floating around in the background and Pascal's hands are being really quite well behaved in their wandering. His knee, however, is not, but at the moment I really couldn't care less. I am empowered by his suggestive movements, and given Alex's betrayal, I force myself to relax again and enjoy every single minute of his flirtation. Well I'm trying, and I would if I could just get the sodding feeling of Alex being here out of my head. It's like he's watching me or something equally ridiculous.

He couldn't be here, could he? I suppose he could be here. There's nothing to stop him being at Eden. It would be a bit coincidental if he decided to come here on the same night as my arranged date with Pascal. Does he know about that? Has Pascal told him? *Don't be stupid, Beth. Get on with the leg grinding.*

His shoulder kissing is becoming slightly more intense as I feel the scrape of teeth against my jugular, and I smile at the thought of him being an actual vampire. It still suits him so well. He looks just the part this evening in his black expensive suit, his hair tied at the nape of his neck and his shoes polished so highly that I can see my reflection in them. His long, elegant frame glides in a way that leaves me with no doubt that he's completely in control of himself and possibly me if I'm honest. Unfortunately, none of this is doing anything to distract me from his face. His hypnotising green eyes are almost draining me of any resolve I had of saying no tonight, and his wicked mouth continues to tease me with visions of torment and lust.

"Can you feel him, my dear?" He whispers quietly against my neck as he twirls me stylishly.

I absolutely can, but I am so shocked by his question that I instantly start to move away. How does he know how I'm feeling? And why has he suddenly mentioned Alex? He tugs me back to him aggressively by the arm and growls. His hold is so brutal that I instantly get a clear indication of the dominant man in him and rapidly begin to feel a little edgy of his behaviour. "I know you can. I can, too. He crawls around inside you, doesn't he, my rose? His fingers on your skin almost burn with the passion they create," he says more fiercely as he grazes my backside with his fingers. I have no idea what he's suggesting because Alex told me he had no interest in men. Maybe he does?

"Yes, I feel him," I reply as I try to relax into him again, to calm his hold a little. His mouth moves to my neck again and then draws up towards my face and I realise that he's going to kiss me. I freeze in his arms. All thoughts of rationality start to disappear as I hold his eyes with mine and try to decipher in split seconds if I want to do this. "Pascal, I-"

Before I get a chance to speak, he pushes me violently back towards the wall and forces his weight onto me, and oh god it feels good. I gasp in response but instantly let him smother me as his fingers grasp my arm and pin me to the wall.

"Maybe I should just have you now, my rose. Maybe I should just hold you down and take what I want from you before he has the chance to stop me. Hmm?"

I'm suddenly a quivering wreck. I have no idea how to respond to that, and the fact that his other hand has moved to my throat really isn't helping.

"Pascal, I don't think-" His hand squeezes viciously. There's nothing soft about it at all and as I begin to struggle for air, he smiles at his hold on me. I actually can't decide if I'm turned on or scared to death at the way his eyes dance with amusement at my response.

"I can feel your pulse, Elizabeth. I know what you think. You like it like this, don't you? Is this hard enough for you or would you like more. Should I have you against the wall, or over the dining table?

Perhaps I should just force you to obey and not allow you to think at all. Would you like that, my rose? Hmm, tell me. Give me a reason to fight him for you," he says unnervingly calmly as he grips my throat tighter and slowly pulls my arm up behind my back.

My eyes widen at the thought as my core unfortunately tells my brain to sod right off for even thinking of refusing him. He watches my face with interest as if surveying a new plaything. He's more than likely completely right because I would probably be very happy as his new toy. I open my mouth to say something but there's nothing forthcoming at all so I close it again and wait with bated breath for whatever's about to happen.

He keeps up his relentless stare as I shake in his hold, until he runs his tongue over his teeth and lets out a small sigh. A brow rises in possible frustration, or irritation. I'm really not sure which, but given my ridiculous panting and the fact that I'm very close to saying yes to him, I suck in a breath to attempt some form of control. His grip eventually softens a little and I exhale a breath as he takes a step away from me and gently loosens his hold until he lets go. His damned intoxicating emerald eyes don't waver in the slightest with their intensity as I flex my fingers and watch him back away from me slowly. My body seems to reel from the loss, and bizarrely, he's somehow managing to make me feel vulnerable without him close, so much so that my arm reaches out to him before I can stop it. His amused smirk returns at my actions as his eyes travel to my hands.

"Mmm... While my fingers itch for you, my rose, I'm afraid he's near now so kiss me and let me taste you. Just one taste of a different life and then I'll let you go. Unfortunately, I know it's him that you want, and as expected, he has come for you."

He has?

Why Alex has come for me is suddenly and rather confusingly of no concern to me at all, because I absolutely want to kiss him. I want to feel his mouth on mine and I want to feel his hand at my throat again. I can't stop myself as I nervously move towards him. My mouth seems drawn to him and for some reason, I need to do this. I need to feel like I've made a decision one way or another about him - that I'm making a choice, because he's giving me that now, the choice. He's not forcing me to yield to him, simply asking for a taste of me. His lips quirk just slightly as if he knows exactly how I'm feeling and is revelling in his strange power over me, but he doesn't move closer. He just waits for me to get to him before twining those fingers into my hair and pulling me into his hold.

And oh god, his kiss is so soft, so warm, and so consuming that all thoughts of Alex drift away for a moment. His lips move with grace across mine, and as his hands move to the back of my neck, I melt further into him. His tongue moves purposely against mine as he groans in the back of his throat and pulls me tighter, deepening an already passionate embrace and evoking feelings I never thought possible from him. I am almost lost in him, revelling in this intriguing and overwhelmingly beautiful softness as I whimper helplessly in his arms, when he all too quickly slows down and pulls his teeth delicately back over my lip. My body screams at the thought and leans into him again to keep up the momentum but I know it's ending as his mouth tenses a little on mine and he groans again.

He pushes me away a little as if annoyed with himself at something and leans his forehead onto mine, rubbing his thumb over my throat. I can't stop my rapid breathing as I grip onto his suit jacket and lick my lips at the image of him just taking what he wants, now, instantly, wishing in some way that he would just show me what I want from him and make me stop thinking.

He eventually chuckles a little and moves his head away from mine to smile at me, a soft, warm Pascal smile that I swear will haunt my dreams forever. Not the normal naughty one I've come to love in some way but a new version that I'm sure is only reserved for a few rare and privileged people who get a glimpse of the real man he is, or was.

"For another life, I think, my dear. I knew he would never let me have you," he says as his finger meanders along my jaw and I instinctively bend into his hand and nuzzle. "I will always be here should you need me to entertain you, and I am, of course, still happy to fight for you should you wish it."

I smile at him fondly and with something close to love or maybe lust. I can't decide which as he watches my reactions to him carefully. Is he asking me if I want him to fight for me right now? Possibly, but I know I don't. As beautiful as Pascal is and however uncomfortable my ache may be, he's not Alex, and now that I know he's here somewhere, I know who I want. Is that a mistake?

I continue to gaze at him and can't help wondering what life would be like with Pascal. Would he be more trustworthy? I somehow doubt it, but something about this moment makes me question the thought immediately. His green eyes look full of honesty for once and not devilment. Whatever he is, I know he's a good man deep down, that he could be something more than he currently shows. But as visions of ice blue eyes hit me again, I sigh out at the possibility of someone else. There isn't anyone who's ever going to make those damned eyes go away, is there? Fuck.

"Thank you for being a good man, Pascal. I wish I could do this but you know my heart is with him, much as it irritates me. You've known all along, haven't you?" I reply quietly as I gaze into his eyes, actually quite annoyed with myself as to why I don't want him as much as I want Alex. He sighs.

"There was a good man once, my rose, and I shall endeavour to find him for you again should you call, but for now I'm afraid I must condemn him to hell again," he says softly as he turns, picks up the wine and hands me mine. "Unfortunately, he is a fool for true love, and no good for my image at all."

"Pascal, why do you hide yourself away? I can see you now and you're wonderful. You deserve to be happy with someone. Please, be who I know you are," I reply as I watch his demeanour change and another man take his place. Mr. Untouchable has returned.

I shake my head at him and reach out to his lips, lightly touching them with my finger. He looks a little confused, and then before I know it, I'm closing the space between us again and kissing him. I feel his hand brushing my hair back as he returns the kiss, but can sense the distance he's creating in his mouth. All intimacy seems to have disappeared and I feel oddly bereft without it, as if he's not allowing me in anymore, our moment apparently gone as he pulls away from me.

"He's here, my dear. Do not let him win you easily," he says with his trademark devilish smirk promptly back in place. I laugh softly and turn to sit at the table again. It appears we won't be doing any of this little thing we've just had again.

"Okay, Pascal, if that's how you want it." He resumes his position opposite me and raises his brow roguishly.

"How I wanted it, my rose, has nothing to do with what just transpired. It would be limiting to consider anything other than what currently is, don't you agree?"

What the hell does that mean? Sodding riddles have reappeared, it seems. I have no idea how to respond to that so I gaze back at him and try to fathom some sort of reply as my mind repeats the sentence.

"Will you make it awfully hard for him, my dear?"

Oh that's better, safer to some degree. My brain scrabbles around for the topic of Alex again as I watch him lick his lips and I shake my head at my own confusion regarding the man.

"I don't know yet. He hurt me. If I'm honest, I don't even know why he's here and I'm not entirely sure how I feel about it anyway," I reply as I look at my wine and try to process what I'm feeling.

Do I want him back? Yes, of course I do, but under what terms? And how the hell am I going to trust him this time? Pascal would probably be much easier, I'm sure. I look back up at the disturbingly evil grin... Maybe not. "Why do you think he's here?"

"He loves you. He does not yet understand what to do with that feeling," he says nonchalantly as he fills a brandy glass and offers me one. "Love, for him, will be perplexing, a conundrum of sorts."

"Why did he leave me then?" I ask on a snort of laughter.

"I really don't know, Elizabeth. Perhaps you should ask him. He does so hate a direct question that he can't manoeuvre his rather delicious body around. Pressure appears to unnerve him remarkably well in the correct circumstance."

My mind wanders for a moment to a vision of the two of them together. What have they got up to in the past? And why does Pascal refer to him in such a sexual manner? Those small, almost unnoticed, movements between them spring into my mind and I realise that they've been together in some way. At some point something has happened. I know Pascal's bisexual. Not only have I been told but he makes it obvious in his lust for Alex and the way he speaks about him.

"Are you in love with him, Pascal?" His brows rise immediately and a stupidly sexy chuckle erupts from his mouth as that real smile graces his mouth once again.

"So forward, Elizabeth... You are quite astonishing in your assumptions."

"Well, I'd like to know. It's obvious you two have history of some sort and I'd like to know how you feel," I reply firmly as my self-belief with him grows. He remains still as he leans on his hand and furrows his brows, possibly in agitation or discomfort, his finger brushing against his lips as he thinks over his response.

"What I feel for Alexander appears to go much deeper than love, my dear, so I try not to analyse it to any significant degree. I'm afraid it confuses even me," he says as he continues to watch me. What the hell do I say to that?

"Right, well, that's interesting," is all I can come up with. I'm not sure how to feel about his acknowledgement. "Do I have to worry about the two of you? Because, like you, I won't compete, Pascal." Unbelievably, I am on a roll of confidence and if I'm potentially going forward with Alex, I want to be aware of my competition all of a sudden. My own feelings for Pascal are confusing enough. The thought that Alex might have some as well is beyond irrational in my brain at the moment.

"No matter how much I like you, Elizabeth, I can't honestly tell you that I wouldn't fall at his feet should he ask it of me. I have been there before, and as you know, it is an exquisite place to be. I would never dishonour myself by refusing him," he says as he smirks wickedly at me.

I stare at him with slightly narrowed eyes. At least he's admitted something but the man is confounding and I'm really not sure how I should feel about what he's just told me. I'm not even sure how I feel about kissing him this evening and what could have happened had it not been stopped. His ability to never answer a question directly is bloody infuriating and I'm left feeling uneasy with his answer as I continue sipping my brandy.

His finger still taps softly against his lips as he smiles at me thoughtfully and I can't help smiling back at him. He is naughtiness personified. It's in his nature and for all the world, I wouldn't change a thing about him. No matter how exasperating he is, he has become someone I now consider a friend of sorts. Whether I'll live to regret that decision or not is entirely unknown to me, but regardless of his feelings for Alex, I could never imagine him not being part of his life.

"Have you ever slept with him?" The question is out before I can stop it. I'm not even sure if I want to know the answer. His eyebrow rises as he licks his lips.

"Slept? No," is his short response. *Helpful, thanks.* Perhaps I wasn't direct enough.

I open my mouth to ask again but we both stiffen at the same moment and I know he's felt it, too, that zap of something cold tingling across our skin. I instinctively rub my arms and watch as Pascal relaxes comfortably back into his chair as if he's had years of practice at dealing with this Alex effect. *Of course he has, Beth.*

"He has your key?" I ask, slightly perturbed at his almost peaceful posture. Why can't I do that? *Pathetic. Sort your shit out, Beth!*

"He has my soul, my dear. Why would he not have my key?" he replies, licking his lips as his eyes spark to life playfully. Arsehole. I roll mine back at him and wait for Alex to materialize while I try desperately to achieve casual and unflustered. I want Alex to feel intimidated and uncomfortable. I want him to be awkward and unprepared but unfortunately I know he won't be and secretly, and rather bizarrely, I'm glad of it. If he came in here meekly, I would probably laugh at him.

Looking across at Pascal, I realise again how sodding confused I am and wonder if now would be a good time to leave. I could just go and avoid the strange scenario I'm about to enter. *No, Beth, stand your ground. He's an arsehole.*

I cross my legs and elongate them as best as I can, trying to achieve my best nonchalant and sexy pose as the door opens. Pascal smirks at me but doesn't move his eyes from mine as he swallows his brandy with a heavy noise. I try to turn my head but for some unknown reason, it feels stuck in place as if I dare not remove my eyes from Pascal's. It's probably because I know that the moment I do, he'll have me in tatters again and I'll do anything he wants. I'll use Pascal for the moment. His amusement should be able to keep me together if I can just hold onto it.

"Alex," I say quietly as I continue to gaze at Pascal. "What can we do for you?"

I'm really trying but the nearness of him is so enticing, I feel like throwing myself at him. The need to just feel his mouth against mine again is so consuming that I want to give up the fact that he hurt me so badly and drop to my knees. All thoughts of his disloyalty vanish, as I smell that familiar scent linger under my nose. Unfortunately, that promptly sends an extremely carnal message straight to my groin and I feel that crazy leg tremble thing that Pascal hasn't quite gotten close enough to this evening.

"Elizabeth." Oh god, I'd forgotten how good it sounds coming from his lips. "I need to talk with you and I would prefer to do that at home," his velvety voice says confidently as if he knows it's a foregone conclusion that I'll go with him. I realise that it probably is, but Pascal's rising brow tickles me and I can't stop the infectious humour creeping across the table to me.

"Really? You want to talk? Well I'm afraid I'm having dinner at the moment. Perhaps you could leave a sodding note and be on your way," I say sharply, trying to twist the knife. I hear his low growl and sense him stepping closer to me. My skin flushes immediately and I curse myself for my passionate response to him. *Stay in control, you idiot. Stop biting your thumb, Beth.*

"That is a fair point and I deserve it, but it won't deter me from the fact that you *are* leaving with me in the next ten minutes."

I close my eyes at his forceful tone and blow out a breath. How on earth do I want to do this? Slowly opening them again, I turn to look across my shoulder at him and my insides melt to a liquefied state. My mind instantly muddles again as I look up into his hardened blue eyes and hold his gaze as firmly as I can. I don't know what I want from him or from myself but I do know that he is still the most captivating man I have ever seen and I itch for him to hold me and remove the damage he's done. I just don't know if he can.

And good lord, he looks magnificent standing there. He's all bad man casual in his black jeans, jacket and boots and I realise that I'd almost forgotten how broad he is. Compared to Pascal, he seems huge in his demeanour and physicality and I feel myself squeezing my thighs as that ridiculous panty combusting thing begins to stir again. His shirt matches his icy eyes tonight and the colour somehow seems to intensify his hold of my face as his impassive gaze refuses to let me go. His mouth twitches briefly as I swallow and I know he knows what I'm thinking about. *Bastard.*

He moves a step closer and offers me his hand. I frown as I look down his corded forearm to that hand. I know the damage it's capable of and I'm not entirely sure if I trust myself in it. I look back up at him and notice the light blue has gone and the darkened, sea-deep version is seeping through. He's getting irritated by my hesitance and unfortunately becoming even more infuriatingly attractive as he does so. His black hair has that unbelievable just fucked look that I love so much, as if he's been running his wicked fingers through it repeatedly, and his neck muscles are starting to show his impatience. It's the most tantalizing display of erotica I've ever seen from him and I know I'm about to give in. I can't help it. I want to go with him.

"Take my hand, Elizabeth. Now." He growls at me. I flinch a little at his now extremely stern voice and realise I have to take some control of my traitorous thoughts. He has been a complete dick and regardless of how much I want him, I have to show him how I feel about his behaviour. I try for apathetic, hoping that will be emotive enough to get my point across.

"No, Alex," I say as I stand and move to Pascal. His gentlemanly instinct had him rising the moment I did. "I might take it when you've explained yourself to me." Pascal's smirk turns into a wide grin of mammoth proportions as he places an arm around my waist and chuckles.

"My rose, it has been an absolute pleasure," he says as he kisses my hand and walks me to the door. "Please come back whenever you like." We both turn to Alex as he mumbles something behind us about a hundred years. Pascal barks out a laugh and helps me into my coat as Alex sneers at him and continues to watch us carefully.

"Thank you for your entertainment and candour, Pascal. It has been thought provoking to say the least." Pascal chuckles and steps away from me. I move into the doorway and look back at Alex, who is now staring furiously at Pascal.

"Alexander, do not look at me like that. From what I gather, this has been entirely your own fault, dear boy, and if she comes back to me, I will happily oblige her anything. Your temper, exquisite as it is, may not be enough to stop me next time," he says as he points at the doorway. "Now go, the pair of you, before I change my mind about my options."

Alex continues to stare at him as he walks towards me. Something unknown passes between them as Pascal frowns at him and then he drops his gaze to the floor slightly. Whatever just happened was intimate and I watch in fascination as Alex nods his head. Apparently he's now happy with his little internal conversation with Pascal. He turns to me, inclines his hand forward and gestures for me to walk along the corridor towards the exit. I stand for a moment, looking into his eyes, feeling unsure as to what the hell I'm doing. Pascal's lounge suddenly feels slightly more appealing and I wonder whether I should go back in. I don't know if I can do this again with Alex. He hurt me and yet I miss him. I could finish it here, right now, and move on with Pascal. His damned eyebrow raises as if he's challenging me into a discussion and I feel my resolve kick in again as I narrow my eyes at him looking all sodding gorgeous. He smirks. *Arsehole.* Okay, I want him, but he's going to hear my wrath. I turn, hold my head up high and stride like the best of them towards the probably waiting car.

Keep it together, Beth. For god's sake keep it together!

~

"Lovely to see you again, Andrews. Thank you for the safe journey," I say as I take his hand getting out of the car. I've done it purposely as I know it winds Alex up and I need to feel some sort of power over him. Clearly it's not working because my stomach is doing bloody cartwheels.

"Miss Scott, you're welcome," he replies quietly. I look up at those ominous red doors and feel the shiver run down my spine as I let go of his hand and he walks towards them.

Alex walks around to me and for the first time, touches me on the small of my back. Instant heat rushes around every inch of my body and I look up into his eyes sharply, almost gasping for air. He smiles softly and replaces his hand again. Not a word has been uttered between us as we made our way here and yet I can feel his emotion swirling around his head. He watched me all the way but didn't make a move to touch me or move closer. He just sat there looking thoroughly beautiful and absolutely fuckable in his dark, thoughtful mood.

"God, I've missed you," he says tenderly as he brings his other hand to my face and runs his thumb against my cheek. I thankfully manage to still myself before I roll hopelessly into him.

Taking a step away, I look down and try to find some piece of anger that I have inside me to be vengeful, but if I'm honest, it's just not there. His very presence is enough to make me feel at peace again and the thought of tumbling into bed with him is making me feel far too comfortable around him. *Why did he leave me? Why did he mess this up?*

His hand suddenly tips my chin back up and I look back into his slightly anxious blue eyes.

"Head up, Elizabeth. I can assure you that you have no reason to be looking down - quite the opposite, actually," he says as he lets go of my chin and gestures toward the house.

I take my first few steps and then feel my breath quickening. Sudden thoughts of how much I love him flood my senses and I realise instantly that I seriously don't know what I'm doing, that I can't beat him at this game and that I'm probably going to get hurt again. I feel the panic rising, and try as I might, I can't push it away. I freeze in place and stare at the open door. I can hear the tick tock of the grandfather clock and it sends images of my last moments here flooding back to me. That bloody note etches itself back in my brain and I suck in a breath of air, trying to remove the sick feeling that is welling its way up my body.

His arms wrap around me from behind and I feel his breath against my neck. It's warm and comforting somehow, his hard body moulding to me as well as it always does. His fingers manoeuvre their way somehow up to my throat, stroking firmly, and I moan at the welcome desire that makes me tip my head back into him instantly and forget.

"I know you're nervous, Elizabeth, but please hear me out. I need to tell you how I feel." His voice is so soft I can hardly believe it's him, so full of course emotion that I melt willingly into his hold. We stand there silently for a while, me looking at his door, him breathing me into him and squeezing me tightly as if trying to stop me from running. Eventually I pull away from him and walk forward into the house with my legs trembling and my arms crossed over my chest. Perhaps they'll shield my heart... Who knows?

We walk into the lounge and I gaze around at the familiar surroundings and try to process how I'm feeling. My eyes land on the chessboard and I realise that the pieces are still in the same place as the last time I was here.

"The board hasn't changed," I randomly blurt out. I'm not sure why but I haven't said a word to him since we were at Pascal's and I need to say something. He chuckles. It's wonderful to hear that sound again and I smile privately.

"Nothing's changed. I haven't been back here since the last time I saw you and..." He stops and I turn to look at him with my brows up. He looks a little lost as he brushes at some imaginary fluff on his shirt and I almost laugh because it's so unlike him, but I stop at a small smile. I know what he's saying and for the moment he seems a little on the back foot, which makes me feel a bit more in control. "Would you like a drink?"

"Yes, please," I say as I shrug out of my long coat, throw it on a sofa and sit down. He raises an eyebrow and smirks a little at my sudden change of behaviour. "Anything red?" His head quirks to the side and he takes his chance to glance up and down my body as I kick off my shoes dramatically.

"Right, we're doing this in that way, are we?" he replies sarcastically as he grumbles to himself and saunters off into the hallway, leaving me to watch his glorious backside.

Stop it, Beth!

He casually walks back in, having removed his jacket, with a changed expression and pours out two glasses. Handing one to me, he brushes his fingers over mine apparently casually but knowing exactly what he's doing and moves to sit next to me. My eyes narrow. I will not make this easy for you, Mr. White.

"No. Over there," I say as I point to the chair. He rolls his eyes and smirks but does as I ask while gracefully putting himself in the other seat. I then realise that it might have been a bad move because now I can't get away from his sodding eyes, so I tuck my legs up beneath me and hide behind my glass. *Oh for god's sake. Head up, Beth.*

"How have you been?" he eventually asks.

"What a ridiculous question," I reply sharply. It seems I have reverted to confident mode, or perhaps it's *I don't give a shit* mode. I really don't know, but his look of surprise makes me smile so I decide to keep going with it.

"I suppose it was. However, given your *date* this evening, I wasn't too sure," he replies as he swirls his drink, sneering a little at his own thought. Is he suggesting that I shouldn't have been out with someone else? *What the hell?*

"Mmm, yes, I was having a nice night. Pascal is quite the entertainer, isn't he?" I say suggestively, hoping I've hit a nerve. He stares at me for a time, that cold almost pissed off face forming regardless of how much he's trying to mask it. As I continue to look at him, his eyes drift downward and I notice something else. Hurt? Or pain, perhaps?

"Did you want him tonight, Elizabeth?" he asks as he frowns and takes a drink. Oh bloody hell, so not ready for that question. Shit... Yes, I did, but not as much as I want you, unfortunately.

"Why am I here, Alex?" I say impulsively, not prepared to discuss Pascal at all and suddenly just wanting to get to the point. He glances at his hands and then sighs.

"Have you missed me?" he asks as he watches my face for any reaction. I gaze back as best I can without emotion.

"Why should it matter? You left me with a note telling me that you didn't care." I take a sip of my wine haughtily and try not to frown at the taste because Christ, I hate the stuff, regardless of the price tag.

"That was a mistake," he says as he abruptly stands and walks out of the room again. Where the hell is he going? A few moments later he returns with a bottle of white and smirks at me. "You should have asked for white, Elizabeth," he says as he removes the red from my hand and passes me a glass. *Bastard!* I can't believe he noticed that.

"The word has become difficult to say easily," is my response as I take the glass. He sits down next to me and rests his elbow against the back of the sofa with a thoughtful gaze as I rapidly scoot away from him.

"Elizabeth, you got caught up in my own mess of a brain. Something is happening in my business that caused me to react badly to seeing you with someone. I was wrong in what I did and how I left. Actually, I should never have left at all, and now I'm trying to make that right. I miss you and I want you back." I look up at him and try to process the words. *He misses me?* If he misses me, why did he go?

"Why did you then? Go, I mean?" I reply softly. All confidence has disappeared as I feel like I'm exposing myself to him. Trying to stop the tears that are threatening, I shift back into the sofa a bit more and move further from him. He smiles and reaches out for my hand. I look down at it warily and scowl a bit.

"Don't run from me, Elizabeth. I know I screwed up and you're hurt but I hate myself for it and I just want to prove how much you mean to me," he says as he watches me. "I told you once on this sofa that I didn't do relationships, well now I want one, very much, with you if you'll have me."

His mouth is mesmerizing as I watch it form around the words I've longed to hear from him. The small smile that's breaking across those long and very kissable lips makes my mouth water as I feel the words swelling inside me. He wants me. He wants me to give him another chance and try again. Can I? Do I trust him?

I look up into those icy blue eyes and see the warmth coming from them that no one else sees. He means what he's saying. I know that. I can feel it, but for how long?

"Touch me, Elizabeth, and tell me you don't feel the same," he continues as he holds his hand out. "I won't touch you again unless you ask me for it. I don't deserve you and I know that."

God, I want to touch him so much I'm aching. The thought that I could be in his arms again in seconds is so consuming that I don't think I've got the will power to say no. Every inch of me is begging my mind to let go and give him my all again. I can feel the moment my brain gives in and it's like a lightning bolt of reaction rushing through me. My fingers tingle to move towards his hands and as I slowly extend my hand to him, I know I can't be without him, that I can't take the chance of not trying again.

Those first few seconds of touch are like a summer meadow and a steam train colliding at the same time, and as I watch his fingers entwine with mine, I feel like I'm home. The warmth is soothing and electrifying at the same time and I'm instantly lost in him again. He pulls me towards him with such force that I whimper at the memory of his hold on me. His strong hands grab at my body in familiar places that feel so natural and he pulls me onto his lap with ease. His fingers glide their way up my ribs and into my hair as he tilts my head to the side roughly and kisses my neck with a passion I've not felt before from him. I feel my hands wrapping into his hair as I tug at it and push his mouth deeper into my neck. I'm suddenly desperate for him and also bloody angry at my own weakness over the current situation. Grabbing hold of any inch of resolve I have, I let go of his hair and pull away from him before I can't. I know I have to find a way to the truth before I can trust him with myself again and I know he's going to try his hardest not to tell me. But this is not the time for secrets and if he wants more then he's going to have to be honest.

I stand up and try to stop the panting that's emanating from my mouth pathetically. Shuffling backwards and bumping into the coffee table, I desperately search for my sanity and composure as he watches me with an amused expression. Is he bloody laughing at me?

"What are you doing, Elizabeth?" he asks confidently with that sodding eyebrow raised, as if he knows he only has to grab me again and I'll go straight upstairs with him. I probably would.

"Moving away from you," I reply, not really knowing where I'm going but knowing I have to get there and find some space away from his hands. Kitchen. Yes, the kitchen's good. No romance in a kitchen.

I quickly escape the lounge and head down the hall, only to notice the peninsular unit as I walk in, which automatically gives me visions of hungry sex - then the kitchen table, which sends the note flying back to my brain with a punch to the ribcage. Why the hell am I here? He doesn't love me. I should leave - get out of here before it all goes wrong, again.

I hear him coming into the room behind me and move across to the coffee machine, basically to escape him, but the thought of it tempts me into having one and I start the process almost robotically. He chuckles behind me and I turn to glare at him. I am so not happy that he's amused by me. He holds his hands up in a look of surrender, smirks and then leans against the units, crossing his unfairly exquisite legs and looking thoroughly smug with himself. I feel my eyes narrow and turn back to the machine.

"You find the situation amusing, Alex?" I ask, irritated by his stance and apparent feeling of superiority around my discomfort.

"No, you just reminded me how much I like you in my house. It always suited you and it's comforting to see you here again," he replies as he kicks his leg about and lowers his head. Oh... That's actually quite sweet. I'm still not bloody happy about the smirking thing though.

"Well, I'm not feeling very comfortable. I don't even know why I'm here," I say as I glance across at him and gesture to the coffee glasses. He grabs them and walks them to me so I step back abruptly and let him place them on the machine. *Don't let him touch you, Beth.*

"Still thinking about leaving?" he says quietly as he presses buttons and the scent of coffee fills the air around us.

"Yes," I breathe out gently as I wrap my arms around myself, still in the hope of shielding my heart somehow.

"What do I have to do to keep you here?" he asks as he carries the two glasses to the table.

I watch him carefully as he holds out a chair and gazes back at me with the same adoring eyes that I saw once before. I walk over, take a seat and realise that I don't know what I want him to do.

"I don't know, but I do know that I can't just fall back into this with you. You have no idea how much that note hurt me," I reply as I look down at the table and draw a circle with my finger around the very spot that he left it in.

"I am sorry, Elizabeth. I revert to type when threatened and I'm fucking hideous at that point," he says with a sigh. His fingers run through his hair and land on the back of his neck. "There is something I need to tell you to help you understand. I'd hoped I could avoid it this evening, that maybe we could discuss it in the morning."

What? Did he just assume I'd stay? Fury wells up in me with such force that I can't even begin to control what's about to come out of my mouth.

"Threatened? I never threatened you. I loved you. How dare you assume that I would stay with you after what you did? God, you're an arrogant bastard, Alex." Oh wow, this feels good. "You throw my heart on the floor and shrug it away without so much as a backward glance and you expect me to just give in instantly and what? Beg for you or something? You're a fucking arsehole. How many women did you sleep with while you were away? At what point did you think that you might have made a mistake? Who the fuck do you think you are?"

I'm seething and as I watch him sit back and take what I'm giving him, I decide to have another go before he gets the chance to

82

respond. He starts to open his mouth as my shaky finger points at him. "You can't just do that to someone and then decide you've changed your bloody mind. I loved you and I thought you felt somewhere near the same. I gave you everything and you destroyed it, with a fucking note. And what the hell was that about? Didn't you have enough guts to tell me to my face? Was I so unworthy that a note was all you felt I deserved? You're a fucking coward."

I can't take the tension in my grip on the table anymore and stand up so I can pace or something, anything to get rid of the pain that's starting to come flooding back again. Tears start and I know I'm crumbling. He gets up and moves toward me with a hand out. "No. Stay away from me. I won't let you manipulate your way back in with that ridiculously gorgeous body. It doesn't work like that and I won't let you do this to me again, Alex. I can't go through it again. You ruined it and I... I... You can't do this to me."

My throat catches through my tears before I can finish as he continues towards me. I back up into a cupboard door and realise there's nowhere left to run as he approaches. My hands curl around my face and I sink to the floor in the hope that it will somehow swallow me up. Where are those fucking fairies when I need them?

Strong arms wrap around me and before I know it, I'm being lifted from the floor and walked along the hall. His soft mouth is kissing my forehead gently and I realise he's heading for the stairs.

Shit. No. Do I want that? No, I don't. Oh god, yes, I do. No!

"Alex, no. I can't-"

He cuts me off. "Shh, baby, trust me for a minute." I have no idea why but I do. Either that or I'm too exhausted to care so I hold onto him and let him take me up to his room. He glides across the dark room to the bed and it's all I can do to stop myself from lifting my head and touching my lips to his. His mouth is so close its driving me insane as he puts me down in front of it and reaches for the hem of my dress, never removing his eyes from mine. I know I could lose myself again in those blue eyes so easily and gasp at the thought of being naked around him, but I find some tenacity and put my hand down to stop him. His face softens as he grasps my hand firmly and moves it out of the way. "Nothing will happen tonight, baby. Not unless you want it to, anyway. It's late and you're tired," he says as he reaches for the dress again and hesitates as if asking for permission. I nod and he slowly lifts it up my body, dragging his fingers along the way. Unfortunately, I can't help the moan of pleasure that escapes my lips at his touch. His wicked slow smile shows me exactly what he's thinking about as he lingers his hand on my spine, reminding me of his pressured weight against me, and then sliding it around my waist and dragging his fingers on the way, he drops the dress to the floor. Reaching around me, he pulls the covers back and lowers me backwards, pulling the duvet up to my bare chest. I've never felt so warm and comfortable as the familiar feeling of his bed envelops me and I watch him walk to the other side.

Slowly, he removes each piece of his clothing as I gaze at him. He still looks gloriously edible and my resolve almost shatters again as I imagine his mouth on me, his teeth. *Oh God, Beth, stop it!* Eventually, having tortured me with his stripping, he gets in beside me. I can't begin to fathom why I'm in his bed or why I feel the need to curl up to him so I just go with it and enjoy the warmth as his hard body wraps around me. He tucks my head under his chin and strokes my hair as he kisses my temple. It's so soothing that I almost find myself forgetting what's happened as I listen to his heart beating steadily in his chest.

"Sleep, baby. We'll talk tomorrow," he says quietly.

I feel myself drifting as his fingers continue with their rhythmic caress and I try to let the night's emotions disappear. Unfortunately, regardless of how confused and angry I am, he feels as perfect as he always did and I know that in the morning, I'll give in again. Whatever I feel at this moment is too much for me to deal with so I let myself fall towards the relaxing cadence of his body as he breathes in and out.

Tomorrow we'll talk. Yes, tomorrow.

Chapter 5

Elizabeth

It's morning. I know it is because I can see the light spilling from under the bottom of the curtains but I am refusing to acknowledge it. If I do then we'll have to start talking again and at the moment everything is too perfect to ruin. He's curled up behind me with his hand gently stroking my stomach and hip and god, it feels so right, so wonderfully consuming and peaceful that I just want to pretend that everything's okay for a while longer.

I wonder what it is that he's been thinking about for the last hour while we've been lying here, me lying stock still trying to pretend that I'm still asleep and him breathing quietly. I know what I've been thinking about and it has everything to do with his hands and what they're doing to me. He's not really doing anything but the mere fact that I can feel him nudging against my back is so distracting that I'm desperately trying to stop my body backing into him shamelessly. Those ridges and bumps are somehow melding into my own again and forging that state of closeness that we once had. The weight of his body pressed against me is so evocative that I'm slowly giving in to my own temptation. Would it hurt to just have a quickie? *Yes, Beth. Get your priorities straight. You are still pissed off.*

Right, quite.

"What are you thinking about?" comes drifting over my shoulder huskily, breaking my quiet contemplation and reminding me how bloody lovely he is.

"I'm not. I'm sleeping," I reply stupidly as I pull the covers up to my chest, still refusing to admit that we need to talk. I can feel his smile into my neck as he kisses it leisurely, dragging those damned lips over very appealing pressure points that I'm positive he's fully aware of.

"You haven't been asleep for an hour or so, baby. You were happily backing into me until you woke up." *Oh bollocks. Shitting bollocksy balls!* I so hate my body right now.

"Right, well, as we've now confirmed that I'm awake, I suppose I'll get up. I shouldn't be here anyway," I say as I try to move away from him. He clearly doesn't think that's acceptable as he tightens his hold and pulls me back. It's useless, I know it is, but I struggle as best I can.

"Don't," he mutters quietly as he uses his other hand to wrap around my chest.

"Don't what?"

"Leave, run, fight me... I need you to stay," he says softly as I still in his arms and savour the words. Beautiful as they are, he doesn't really mean them. If he did, he wouldn't have left me in the first place, would he?

"You don't need me Alex. You just don't like the thought of not having something that you think you deserve," I reply as I try to banish the comforted feeling that's starting to flow. I don't trust it and I won't be held to ransom by his body, regardless of how good it feels against my skin.

"I do need you, Elizabeth. If I'd wanted to just have your body, I would have taken it last night and you would have let me. You know you would so don't pretend otherwise, and I absolutely don't deserve you," he says sharply as he brings his hand to my throat and squeezes slowly. My body instantly arches into him as if I'm bloody powerless and I start to let the feeling take over. He groans and presses himself into me harder. "Do you want a reminder of how we feel together, Elizabeth?" He growls as his hand drops down to my groin and pulls me into him again. No... Yes... Christ, I don't know!

His fingers find their way between my legs and I open them for him. I can't stop my traitorous body from reacting to his hand as he starts to circle my sweet spot with his firm unyielding touch. It's so familiar that I know what's coming next and I can't help but widen them more as my hand moves to the back of his neck and grasps on. He's going to make me come quickly. I can sense it in him. He's telling me that I'm his and that he can do what he wants with me, to me, and unfortunately at the moment, he's absolutely right. My body reacts in exactly the same way as it usually does around him and the passion and desire begin to sweep through me as the temperature rises around us. His hands grab on as he spreads me wider, hooks my leg over his hip smoothly, then runs those fingers back upwards towards the ache he's already created inside me.

As he's grinding into me, he's becoming more forceful with his movements and I realise quickly that this isn't enough for me. I know without a shadow of doubt that I want him inside me and no matter how hard I try to talk myself out of it, my body rolls toward him helplessly. It's the only movement he needs to understand what I want from him, because he's so swift at pulling me towards his waiting mouth that I gasp at the power of his hold as he kisses me so passionately that I struggle to breathe. Our tongues entwine so forcefully that I can't stop myself from nipping at his lips lustfully, eliciting a growl of pleasure from him while he rolls me onto my back and I moan at the exquisite, heavy feeling of him above me. I instantly open my legs and wrap them around his torso, pulling him down onto me, which causes another groan of satisfaction as his hands move to my face and he pulls back to look at me as he catches his breath. I try to resist touching him but it's futile and I lay my hands on his chest and feel the electricity spiking off him. His blue eyes are dark and piercing as he watches me move my hands over him. His muscles constrict and ripple under my fingers as I wander around his stomach, feeling the hardened ridges. I'm trying not to think, to just feel and relish in the feeling of him on me, but his mood seems so thoughtful and almost dreamy as he moves his head down and kisses my chest quietly that I begin to wonder what he's thinking again. His mouth moves further down and I moan loudly as I realise where he's going. I arch my hips up into him as he drags my panties down my legs, kissing the length of them as he goes and then licking his way very seductively back up.

"Tell me what you want, Elizabeth. I'll give you anything," he whispers as he blows a breath across my sensitive nub and moves his hand leisurely across my stomach. His searing eyes look up at me and I instantly melt as his warm tongue flicks out across me. It's like a magical current of pleasure and seduction is somehow weaving its way back into my mind and I tip my head back, relishing in its power over me. His mouth closes over me again and I buck at him, trying to free myself from the intensity. His hand automatically holds me down with the force I recognise and I sigh in the delight of his strength and remember his fingers around my throat.

"I want you inside me, Alex," I say softly as I reach for his hand and pull him toward me. As he crawls over me, I feel his body pushing down on me and grasp the back of his head, moving him down to me for another kiss. His mouth is so delicious that for a few seconds I forget the need to have him buried in me, but as he nudges my knee sideways, I groan at the thought and greedily wrap around him again. His fingers grab at my face as I close my eyes and wait for the blissful feeling of him entering me. I open them back up to look at him and find him gazing at me with an unfamiliar look that leaves me utterly breathless.

"Don't close your eyes, not once. See me," he says as he begins to slowly push himself inside me. His mouth opens as he sucks in a breath and then pushes more. His size continues to stretch me and the euphoric feeling that hits me is heady and intoxicating as he consumes me again. I gasp at the weight of him deep inside so he pushes again as if proving a point to me. "How do want this, Elizabeth?" he says as he stills inside me. "Do you want me to fuck you or make love to you?"

His voice is so husky and coarse with lust that I just look up at his handsome face, panting and flicking my gaze between his eyes and his mouth. How the hell should I know? He wants me to speak? It's not possible so I follow my gut instinct.

I pull on his hand and move it to my throat. It's safe there. I can handle it that way and then walk away from him. That wicked smile of his arrives as he licks his lips and grips onto my neck gently. He pulls his hips back deliciously slowly and starts to move. The friction is immediate and so intense that I feel myself beginning to clench around him straight away as the build of my orgasm takes hold. Increasing his rhythm, he pushes against my throat a bit more with that expert pressure of his and grabs me into him.

"Yes," I hiss at him as his force increases with every punishing stroke and his answering groan into my neck tells me he's nearly there as well. His fingers bury into my hip as he uses his body to push me into the bed, with each brutal thrust almost trying to get so close that I have no way of escaping him. I couldn't if I wanted to because the feeling of stars is nearly there as his hand tightens around my throat again and I tip my head back at his growl. The instant I do, my nub rubs against him more powerfully and I begin to explode.

"Alex, God, yes..." I hear myself shouting as those lights start flashing behind my eyelids and that serene place beckons me. The feeling of him still moving increases the intensity and has me moaning with lust for him. His fingers grab at my face and force me to look back at him as he releases my throat and pounds into me slowly. I can feel his darkened blue eyes reaching back into my soul and tugging me back to him with every stroke as his other hand wraps under my neck and pulls me closer.

"More, Elizabeth. Give me more." He growls as he crushes me into him and bites at my lips. I moan in response and let every inch of myself revel in the feeling of him on me again, his muscles twisting, his scent reminding me, and his damned voice owning me again with each word uttered from his mouth. Skin slides across me beautifully as he closes the gap between us further and tempts me back towards everything I need from him. His strength, his very presence is enough to tell me there's no going back. I love him. Every captivating thing about him seems to fit so well within me, so fluidly.

There's no room between us now and I feel almost part of him as our bodies move together seamlessly and he continues with his rhythm, his eyes still continuing their intense assault as I moan deliriously with each circle of his hips and feel my body tighten around him again. My hands grasp at his back in an attempt to pull him nearer, and as I feel him swelling inside me, my mouth moves to his. I'm overwhelmed and completely lost beneath him as he responds breathlessly with beautifully soft lips rolling his tongue smoothly over mine and gripping my thigh tightly.

"I missed you," falls from my lips before I can stop it. He hesitates slightly then continues his relentless driving as I rise to meet each thrust and give him every inch of my body that I can to increase the pressure between us as it builds. Pulling his mouth from mine, he curls his face into my neck and lets his body begin to spasm in a peaceful pulse of movement. The euphoria that hits me is mind numbing, earth shattering, just him and me in a never ending wave of joy, just this one last time.

FEELING WHITE

"I love you," he breathes out into my neck as his jaw tightens with his release and groans out deliciously with the pleasure of it. My eyes fly open instantly. "I love you, Elizabeth."

Did he just say that?

No, he couldn't have, but he did. He said it twice, actually. No, don't be stupid, Beth. He doesn't love you. What did he say then if he didn't say that? He did, didn't he?

I can't move at all because if I do, I might have to touch him again or something and the very fact that he's still breathing rapidly into my neck means that I'd have to touch him to get him off me. My hands have stilled so completely at the shock of his words that I don't know what to do, and much as I'd like to believe what I heard, I just can't, because why the fuck would you leave someone that you love?

I'm confused yet again, but I think I'm more angry than confused because I just can't understand why he would put me through any of what's happened if he feels like that. I was happy to just have sex and feel him on me. I made a decision to enjoy the nearness of him and just have one more time. Okay, I probably felt love on the way through. In fact, I felt every intense emotion I've ever felt around him but I wasn't about to tell him that. I know that *missing you* bit slipped out but I was just caught up in the moment.

But this is not what I expected and now I have no idea how I feel. Oh, sod this.

I heave as hard as I can and quickly roll away from him when I've found an inch of space, grabbing the sheet as I go, and promptly stand on the floor, staring at him with narrowed eyes. The sheet is so tightly wrapped around me that I almost laugh at my own absurdity, given the fact that we've just had sex, but for some reason, I pull it tighter and try to process my thoughts. Perhaps I shouldn't. Perhaps I should say the first thing that pops into my head and pressure him.

He's moved to the side of the bed and is sitting there looking back at me with equally narrowed eyes and a frown, but his face has an underlying tone of amusement, which causes my blood to boil a bit more because if he's bloody laughing at me, I'll kill him. I try desperately to look for deceit in his eyes because I know that's what he does when he wants something, not in a vindictive manner but the man has made millions, possibly billions, out of being a manipulative sod and he's damn good at it. But all I can see is a forthright Alex, the

Alex who knows he's in the right and is ready for a fight about it. He wouldn't say those words if he didn't mean them, would he?

His face returns to cool and controlled while he studies me carefully, almost weighing up his newest opponent in a game of minds, and I can feel my nose twitching as I watch him and try to work out what I want to say. His brow slowly arches at me as he rests his elbows on his knees and supports his chin with his hands.

"Whenever you're ready, Elizabeth," he says expectantly. He clearly doesn't know what he's dealing with so he just sits there waiting.

"What did you say?" comes out of my mouth before I can stop it. I so wish I could put my hands on my hips right now.

"I'm not sure I should say it again if this is the reaction I get," he replies quietly as he runs his hands through his hair.

"You can't say that sort of thing. We... We had sex, Alex. That's it. That's all. You can't take those words and-"

I am abruptly cut off as he stands up in all his magnificent glory and takes a step toward me. I back up rapidly, not daring to allow him to touch me again.

"We did not just have sex, baby, as you well know," he says as he keeps moving and I keep retreating.

"You don't mean it. If you did, you wouldn't have left," I blurt out as I hold my hand up to him, trying to halt his progress. It doesn't work.

"I do mean it. Do you believe I would ever say those words if I didn't mean them?" His sodding eyebrow arches again as he stops and stares at me with astonishment in his eyes. Well no, but that's not the point. Why would he say it then?

"You manipulate people. You admit it yourself. It's what you do," I reply as I clutch at straws for some reason for him telling me he loves me.

"Why would I try to influence you?" is his response as he opens his palms and sighs at me. My eyes become slits. He's hiding something; I can see it in him.

"Because you..." I don't know. "Because you want me back, to trust you again." He moves forward again. Predatory Alex is returning and I realise I have to keep him away until this is finished.

"Do you trust me?" No... Yes... But you're not telling me the whole truth and you have to.

"No," I reply sharply as I hit the wall. Why am I always banging into things around him? *Pathetic.*

"Liar." *Bastard.*

"No, you broke this, us," I say bitterly as I wildly motion backwards and forwards between the two of us with my hand.

"Yes, I did, but I want to fix it," he says with frown as he drops his head a little. I know I'm hitting some nerves so I decide to go in for the kill.

"Why?"

"I've just told you why. I love you," he replies with a confused face.

"No, not that, that's ridiculous. I mean why did you leave me?" Did I just say that being in love with me was ridiculous? *Get a grip, Beth.*

"You think me loving you is ridiculous?" His expression is one of amazement and frankly he's got a point, but I can't let him get away from the truth now. I'm on a roll, and while he hasn't got any time to think, I keep pressing.

"Yes. No... I don't know. That's not the point. Why did you go?" You will answer me, Mr. White.

"I thought you were lying." His game face has returned and I inwardly groan in frustration at his mask coming back.

"What about?" I ask immediately, not giving him a chance.

"Loving me." What? Who does he think I am?

"Why would I lie about that?" I reply as I throw both of my hands in the air and then realise I've dropped the sheet. It skims to my feet. Shit. Oh, balls to it. I seriously don't care at the moment.

"To manipulate me, to throw me off guard," he says as he skims my body with his eyes and smirks a little at my now hands on hips stance.

"That's stupid. Who the hell would lie about being in love with someone?" I shout at him in utter shock.

"Plenty of people when they want to destroy you," he mumbles to the floor as he grabs the back of his neck and moves his head from side to side.

"What are you talking about? I don't understand," I reply quietly as I notice his agitation building. He's clearly getting frustrated and I know he'll clam up if I don't tread carefully.

"No, you wouldn't, because you are absolutely guiltless and I misjudged a situation catastrophically because I am most definitely not." He sighs as he moves away from me and grabs his jeans. Pulling them on, he turns to the dresser and pulls out a green t-shirt.

"Alex, please tell me what the hell you are talking about because I'm completely lost here," I say as I stare at him and try to figure out where he's going with this.

"I'm not having the rest of this conversation naked, and I refuse to have that fucking bastard in our bedroom." What? Who on earth is he talking about now? And *ours*? Really?

"This is not our bedroom, it's yours, and unless you fill me in on what sounds like some pretty relevant information, I'll never be setting foot in here again," I reply sharply. I feel like stamping my foot at his reluctance to just tell me what it is. He walks into the bathroom and brushes his teeth.

"Elizabeth, please, just get dressed and come downstairs. I'll make some coffee and we can continue with this." I watch him as he walks by me with a frown. "Your clothes are still in the wardrobe if you'd like them," he says as he leaves and heads down the landing.

"Why the hell are my clothes still here?" I say to myself while I stare at his retreating body pulling the t-shirt over his head. Beautiful as it is, something looks strange about his back so I tilt my head and study him moving. Something seems off balance somehow. Then it hits me - a new run of numbers on his tattoo. What the hell?

I frown at the door and wonder what to do now as I glance down at my body, realising that I can hardly walk into his kitchen with nothing on. Sneering at myself, I stomp across to the walk-in wardrobe and pull open the doors. He's right. All of the clothes that he bought for me are still hanging in exactly the same place. I wander over to the drawers and pull out a brown shirt and pair of skinny black jeans and yank them on furiously. Much as I'd like to debate the stupidity of these clothes still being here, I want the conversation more and if that means I have to wear them, so be it. I can hardly wear the scrap of material that was last night's dress. *Hairband? I wonder...* Wandering back across to the bedside table on my side, I open the drawer and find a black hair tie that I left here still staring at me. He really hasn't removed a thing of mine. He did say he hadn't been back here since he left for New York. Where has he been then? I stride to the bathroom and open the cabinet. All my creams and make up are still in there and so, thankfully, is my toothbrush. I grab at it and viciously scrub at my teeth while I try and fathom the reason he would do any of this and who he thinks I've been working with to destroy him.

Looking up into the mirror, I remind myself that I am stronger now, that he made me stronger, and that I should keep looking him straight in the eye. I have nothing to hide and I've done nothing wrong. Slamming the cabinets closed, I give myself a quick once over and head out towards the stairs. Unfortunately, I'm met with the sound of *Adele's* album drifting up to me and I hesitate as I listen to the words.

"Should I give up or should I just keep chasing pavements?"

God, he's good. Belle would be laughing at his audacity and flying in for the kill.

I, however, desperately want to believe every word that leaves his mouth, and as I listen to the rest of the song, I know he's trying to tell me something. Regardless of the heartless bastard that left that note for me, I've seen the other version of him, the one who's learning what it feels like to be open to his feelings again and trust a bit more. Has this really all been just a misunderstanding? It's possible, and if he did feel used or lied to for some reason, he would have done exactly what he did and reverted to the callous arsehole inside, giving no thought to me whatsoever. I'm actually surprised he didn't throw me out by the scruff of my neck and humiliate me even more, given what he apparently thought happened. Well, either way, the only way I'm going to get to the bottom of this is to go and find him.

My chest rises and falls heavily as I descend the sweeping burgundy carpet to the hall. I have no idea what I'm about to hear and for the time being I'm still not entirely sure what to do with the happy feeling that's starting to flood me as I ponder whether we can get past whatever this is. However, as I reach the kitchen and see him sitting there at the table staring out into the garden blankly, my heart thuds energetically in my chest. I love him, desperately. I know because the heat of emotion that rises as he senses me and turns his head is overwhelming and I long to run over to him and tell him. His features

94

soften into a smile as he watches me in the doorway and then stands and walks to me. His hand reaches for my face and for the first time, I nuzzle into him and close my eyes.

"Come and sit. We have a lot to talk about," he says as he guides me across to the table and passes me some coffee. He sits and stares at me for a moment with a smirk. "Ask away," he continues.

Where do I start?

"Where have you been?" I ask as I pick up my drink and sit back in my seat, savouring the taste.

"New York, then LA, then the apartment," he clips.

"Why the apartment?"

"Because I've never *had* you there and I needed to think clearly. I struggle to do that around you. Thinking of you is distracting enough." Well I suppose that's a complement of sorts...

"What do you think you saw?"

"I saw you with Henry DeVille at the Addison's ball." *Henry?*

"Right, and what does Henry have to do with anything?" I ask in complete confusion.

"I didn't know you knew him. He's trying to ruin me so I assumed something that I now know was not the case," he replies on a sigh with a small shrug of his shoulders.

"What do you mean? Henry's not like that, and why didn't you just ask me about it?" He stands abruptly and I watch him walk over to the coffee machine and press more buttons as he reaches over to the cupboard for more glasses.

"Elizabeth, you have to try to understand the world that I live in. It's all lies and manipulation. That's the way it works. If I was correct and I had asked you about it, you would have told Henry and then he would have stepped up his game. If I let you believe that I just didn't feel the same as you, Henry would have assumed that you'd failed in your quest to seduce me and would have been none the wiser. It wouldn't be that surprising to him that you couldn't control me. Nobody else ever has."

I sort of get that I suppose.

"I still don't understand. I've known Henry since I was a child. He's a good man. Besides, he said he was a good friend of yours," I say as I cross my arms and feel myself becoming even more confused by the situation. The thought of Henry being anything other than fantastic is just plain weird.

"I thought so, too, but now I know differently," he replies as he sits back down with two fresh drinks, good timing given that I've just drained mine.

"Didn't you think you knew me better than that? How could you think that I'd be capable of conspiring with someone in something so disgusting?" He sighs and looks out across the garden.

"You know, you're right. It is quite beautiful out there," he says, pointing his finger to the garden. I roll my eyes at the obvious deflection and keep going.

"Alex, do not try to change the subject." He smirks at the window and drops his gaze as he returns his eyes to mine and his face breaks into a wide smile.

"You're really very good at this when you get going," he says, tapping the table with his wicked fingers. I try not to look at them because I know he's still trying to manoeuvre to a more comfortable place by teasing me.

"I'm glad you approve but you're still deflecting." I fold my arms and raise my brows at him. He sighs, pinches his brow and crosses his legs. The look of a tired man seeps into him and I almost feel like backing off and letting him just relax.

"You were so different, Elizabeth. You began to strip me down and find a way through the layers. You encouraged me to take time off and to relax, you asked me to question everything I had become, you said you didn't want my money and you never asked for anything but my time. Don't you see how I could see that as manipulation? That's so new to me. Every time I was with you, I took my eye off my business and in doing that, I could have been giving power to Henry."

Oh... Stupid Beth, how did you not see that?

"Oh, I see what you mean now." I slump in my chair, finally understanding exactly what has been going on in his brain. No matter how stupid, I can see precisely why he reacted the way he did.

"Yes, quite," he replies over his coffee.

"Well, I still don't see how you could trust that stupid instinct over me. I told you I loved you. I meant it," I say almost sulkily as I swing my legs. I feel like a child the moment I've said it and stop myself from going further.

"I have done very well out of trusting my instincts and I still will. I only hope that my lapse in judgement hasn't ruined what you felt for me," he replies as he searches my eyes for warmth. There still isn't much, regardless of how I'm feeling inside. I need to know more.

"When did you realise you were wrong?" He shifts in his seat a little and I struggle to hold back the smile that's forming at his discomfort. I'm in control here and I can't help but feel a bit proud of myself.

"Conner talked some sense into me a couple of days later. He found out from Belle about Henry and made me listen to him," he replies with another small shrug.

"What? That was two weeks ago. Why have you waited so long?" I am suddenly exasperated at him. He notices my raised voice and leans back away from me.

"I had something to deal with, and I honestly didn't know what to do to make it right again. Then when I finally decide to sort it out between us, I find that you're out with Pascal." His brow furrows as he glares at me. "What the fuck did you think you were doing with him?"

"Having a nice time. I think I deserved it given what you did to me for no reason whatsoever," I reply with a casual stare, daring him to continue with this heated line of questioning and his irritated tone.

"Do you want him?" he asks abruptly with a frown of anger looming. Jealous? Good.

After pulling the moment out as long as I can and watching every emotion cross his face, I smile at my own amusement at his behaviour. Given that I left with him last night, does he honestly believe that I would choose Pascal over him?

"Apparently not as much as I want you for some unknown reason." He breathes in deeply and softens the glare that has developed.

"Good, that's good." The words are soft. "I didn't know. Pascal can be... persuasive."

"Mmm... Yes, he can." It's all I'm willing to give him at the moment. It really won't do him any harm to keep being a little nervous about it, and I can mentally feel Belle slapping my shoulder with a triumphant clap. *You go, girl!* His eyes and lip curl instantly, telling me he's not happy with my response, so I change the subject quickly.

"What are you going to do about Henry? And do you know why he's doing this or what it is that he's doing?"

"Annihilate him, and I'm working on that," he sneers with a bark of disgust at the mention of his name. He's clearly really pissed him off somehow and I make a mental note to try and find out why.

"Why? He's not achieved anything yet and I'm sure that you're now preventing him going forward with whatever plan he has."

"He threatened me, and nearly ruined everything I've worked for. Why the fuck would I let him get away with that?" He looks so confused at my question that he opens his mouth to continue and then shuts it again with a perplexed face.

"I don't know. It's just that he's a dear friend and I don't like the thought of him being left with nothing. Sarah is like family to me, and-"

He cuts me off quickly as if sensing my compassion over the issue and trying to dismiss it.

"Sarah's the one who told me and she'll be fine. She's a very clever woman."

I bite back the immediate feeling of jealously that randomly pops into my head at his acknowledgement of another woman. I frown at myself and take my cup over to the sink, trying to dispel the image of Alex and Sarah together. Perhaps that's why she looked at me oddly at the ball. Have they slept together?

"Look, can we talk about something else or go somewhere for the day? I assume you don't have to work today as you're still here, and I would very much like to spend some time with you," he says as I suddenly feel him standing behind me. I turn to look at him and wonder what to do next. Do I want to spend the day with him or do I want to go home and think about all this?

"Alex, I need some time. I don't know how I feel about any of this." He reaches his hand around me and gently pulls my ponytail forward across my shoulder. His small, almost sad smile has me melting. This wasn't his fault. Well, it sort of was, but we just got caught in a crappy situation. Regardless, I'm still hurting and I feel like I have to process that feeling first.

"You're still the most perfect thing I've ever seen, Elizabeth. I'm sorry I hurt you but can you please just trust me when I tell you that I do love you. You have no idea how much you mean to me and I want to show you... Just let me show you," he says as he brushes his fingers along my jaw and tilts my chin up to him. Suddenly my knees are doing that trembling thing again, and as I look into his soft eyes, I know I'm giving in. My heart is leaping so rapidly at the thought of happily ever afters that I can't stop my arms from reaching up to his neck and running my fingers through his hair. I love him and he's saying he wants me. What idiot would turn their back on such a feeling? Not me, that's for sure, and if I just try to forget, I know we'll get through this.

"Okay," I say quietly as I look up at him and smile. "Where shall we go?" The one thing I do know is that I need to avoid the bedroom or any other available surface. I need to be with him as a person before I can truly allow myself to believe anything else. I want to feel his emotions and go from there. Maybe a day together in a relaxed atmosphere is just what we need to try and rediscover ourselves.

"Where would you like to go?" he asks with a raised brow. "We can do whatever you want to."

"I don't know. I need to call Belle, though, and let her know what's going on."

"She knows. I saw her last night." *He did?*

"Oh, well I bet that was fun for you."

"Fun is probably not the first word that springs to mind," he replies on a smirk as he continues to rub my cheek with his thumb. "Now, can I suggest a shower and then lunch somewhere?"

"A shower sounds great."

"Good, go on up. I just need to do something first and I'll come and join you," he says as he releases me from his grasp and wanders off.

As I leave the kitchen, I swipe my phone from my bag and send a text to tell Belle I will be staying here for the day. Her response is instant and makes me laugh out loud.

- **I hope you're making the bastard suffer! How was Pascal?**
- **Pascal was different, and I'm not being easy if that's what you're referring to.**
- **Be careful, honey. Call me if you need me. Love you.**
- **Okay, love you, too.**

Having giggled my way past the study and noticing Alex on the phone, I climb the stairs with a lighter feeling than I've had in weeks and head to the shower.

Twenty minutes later, I'm sitting wrapped in a towel having finished my hair and make-up, in the wardrobe looking at the clothes and trying to decide what to wear. Where are we going? And do I want to wear any of these clothes anyway?

The shower in the background stops and he wanders into the room, drying his hair with a towel, completely naked. My eyes run over his astounding physique as I scan the length of his frame and practically drool at him with lust. *Close your mouth, Beth. He's doing this to wind you up.*

He meanders his fingers across his clothes, twisting and turning as he does so while I stare at the tattoo undulating across his shoulders, remembering it's meaning - to wage war. Am I about to witness him going to war with Henry? Probably. Then I notice those numbers again and gasp. It's the date I served at the White Buildings for the business luncheon. He put me on his back? Wow. Shit, that's... I have no idea what that is. He marked himself with my dates, our first meeting.

"You put me on your back?" I question incredulously.

"I did," he says nonchalantly as he pulls out a dark brown suit and white shirt, seemingly dismissing the fact that he marked his skin for me, or maybe it's for him.

"You're not going to explain further?"

"Some other time maybe, when you're ready to hear it."

Oh, right... I'm pretty sure I'm ready to hear it now if I'm honest. Having said that, knowing Alex it might be a little too deep for the light and breezy atmosphere I'm hoping to achieve this afternoon.

"Where are we going?"

"Out for lunch."

"You need a suit for lunch?"

"Yes." Okay, where the hell is he taking me? I thought we were doing chilled out.

"What do I need to wear for whatever you've planned?"

He wanders across to my side of the wardrobe and grazes his fingers across a blue dress, shakes his head and moves on. I watch on in amusement at him choosing my clothes for me. He finally stops his hands at a deep purple, wraparound, knee length dress and takes it out. His eyes move to the set of shelves and he reaches for a pair of matching shoes and a Chloe bag that I love. He turns around and deposits them on the floor next to me. I can't help but giggle at him as he kisses me lightly on the lips and turns back to his own side of the wardrobe.

"I trust you can manage your own underwear?" he says as he reaches for his own shoes.

"I think I'll find a way somehow," I reply sarcastically.

"I'd be more than happy to help." His eyes meet mine over his shoulder with a devilish glint and I smirk back at him.

"I'm sure you would, Mr. White," I reply as I drop my towel in the wash basket and move past him to the drawers in the bedroom to find suitable underwear. The dress is tight and needs something smooth to go underneath it. Mind you, I've lost a few pounds since he bought it so perhaps I could get away with some lace, and since I know how much he likes me in lace, it won't do any harm to tease him with it. Leafing through, I find the lavender set I am after and quickly slip into them. They feel amazing. Annoying as it is, expensive things always seem to sit better against my skin and I muse the thought as I return back for my clothes and hear the low growl come at me as I sashay past him.

"If you're doing it on purpose, it's working," he says as he buttons up his shirt and shrugs into his jacket. God, he looks amazing. He's got that *don't mess with me* glare going on that always disables any defence I've got, and his eyes seem to have deepened in colour a bit. Trying my hardest for casual, I continue with getting dressed.

"I'm sure I don't know what you're talking about, Mr. White," I reply as I slip my feet into the very high shoes and reach for the dress. He is on me in an instant and he means it. It is the first time he's been so forceful in his touch of me and I sense every nerve ending standing to attention at his aggression as he holds me flush against the wall. I was beginning to wonder if he would ever return to normal. While his softness is beautiful in its own right, it isn't the Alex I know. Apparently I am now being reminded of the man I do remember.

"I think you know exactly what you're doing, Miss Scott. It won't take much for me to scrap my plans for romance and give you a different version of myself for the day," he says as he pushes his knee between my legs and grabs at my wrists. "We both know how much you want it."

My body is a quivering wreck as he kisses my neck roughly and drags his tongue along my collarbone. I can't believe I'm actually entertaining the idea of him doing this again, but for some reason I don't want to stop him in the slightest. *No, Beth... Trust. Romance!*

"Alex I... I want you to stop," I find a way to stutter out as he bites at my jaw playfully and I tip my head back and moan.

"No you don't," he growls instantly. He's right but I have to get myself out of here. I know we can do this. Sex isn't the problem, and dropping straight back into it isn't going to help me at all.

"Alex, stop," I mumble half-heartedly as I fight his grasp on my wrist. He must sense something is different because he lifts his head and gazes at me while softening his grip a little. After looking at me for a moment, he lets go of me and takes a step backwards as he blows out a breath.

"You're not ready." My eyes drop to the floor and I pull in a long breath as I try to stop the torrent of desire swirling around inside.

"You know I am. I just... I just need something more than this at the moment," I reply quietly as I look back up at him slowly. I don't think either of us knows what I need but he nods and reaches for my face.

"Okay, we'll do it your way for now," he says as he ghosts a kiss across my mouth and holds my chin. "But, Elizabeth, do not push me if you don't want the reaction you're for asking for. I might not stop next time."

Oh Mr. White is definitely returning to true form and I smile softly at the image of him as he lets me go, picks up my dress and helps me into it. His hands pull the material around my waist and fix the three black metal buckles into place at my side, smiling wickedly at himself as he more than likely thinks about cuffs and restraints. I giggle. He raises a brow and growls at me.

"Stop it, Elizabeth."

"Sorry," I reply as I try to contain my giggling fit.

"Why the hell did I pick this dress?" he says as he huffs and extends his hand to me.

"Because you like buckles, Mr. White," I respond, continuing to giggle as he drags me from the room.

"Because I like seeing you in them, Miss Scott," he replies as he pulls the last one very tightly against my skin and cinches in my waist. "And really, if you knew what was going through my mind at the moment, you would not be feeling very giggly about it at all."

Oh!

Chapter 6

Alexander

She said she needed funding. He could remember the moment clearly in his mind as she'd gazed out of the window and rambled on about banks and bigger kitchens. He was pretty sure she hadn't really even realised what she was saying at the time, but he'd heard it and moved it into a box in the corner of his mind for future use. The trouble was, now he didn't know what to do about it. He was entirely sure that her sister would probably be on board with his plan to invest. Well, she should be, given her business head. Mind you, he clearly wasn't her favourite person at the moment so maybe she wouldn't be enthused. But more importantly, the likelihood was that Elizabeth absolutely wouldn't be, regardless. The thought in itself would probably send her into a hissy fit, let alone him actually doing something with that thought.

He supposed he could do it silently behind her back, but that would mean her sister lying to her, which definitely wasn't going to happen. He could equally set up a company of some sort and procure a dull manager to do the job for him. The thought suddenly struck him that maybe he should just buy premises for them and let them do the rest. What did he own in that area already? He didn't know. It had been so long since he took any interest in that side of the business that he couldn't in all honestly remember. And did they even want to stay in that area?

Unfortunately, he realised that he knew very little about her business and cursed himself at his own lack of previous interest. Did he even ask her about it on a daily basis? Probably not. He was normally so self-obsessed with his own dramatics that he wouldn't think of asking her about hers. Presumably she was doing well with it? They owned a good apartment on the right side of town and the business premises they were currently renting would be extortionate. He knew because he owned a similar one about two streets off. He smiled at the memory of one of his first London investments. He could remember that building well because the bloody wreck had almost had him running to a loan shark.

Fuck, he really needed to get a handle on this relationship stuff. He wanted to know about her, all about her. He flicked at a pen on his desk and watched it roll to the floor. He smirked at it and then laughed at his own childish behaviour. She'd done that to him.

The moment at lunch when she'd flicked his lettuce at him had been one of the most endearing moments of his life. He'd tried for a moment of disgustingly erotic whispering and she'd just reached over and flicked his lettuce at him. He'd been so shocked by the movement that he'd burst out laughing at her audacity in the middle of The Ivy. That she cared so little about everyone's opinion was testament to how far she'd come, and he'd loved her more in that moment than he could remember feeling before. She'd been so free and happy as she giggled her way through the five courses and he'd relaxed happily for the first time in two weeks and just listened to her. Her voice was the most glorious sound he could wish for and he'd spent the entire time inwardly thanking everything and anything that she'd agreed to let him back in. It was on her terms and he sort of understood that, but at least she was willing to listen and give him a chance to redeem himself. The rest would come later, when she trusted him again. If she ever fucking did.

He stood from his desk and walked out of the door without even closing his laptop.

"Louisa, who runs my London property?" he asked casually as he wandered to the elevator.

"Tom Brindley, Sir. Anything I can help with?"

"No, thank you. He's on four, isn't he?"

"Yes, Sir." With that, he said the word *four* aloud and put his hands in his pockets.

When he walked out of the elevator, he looked around at the offices and open plan space and tried to remember the environment. He didn't even know when the last time he was on this floor was. The girl at the reception desk jumped up from her seat and threw him a nervous smile as she quietly placed something back in the drawer. The faint odour of nail polish wafted across his nose and he smirked at her. She couldn't have been any older than nineteen, and if he

105

remembered correctly, he wasn't exactly enamoured with work of any sort at her age either.

"Mr, White Sir, Is there something you need?" she asked as a blush rose across her chest and face. He wandered across to the desk and opened the drawer.

"Crimson," he said as he read the bottle. "Quite appropriate, given your face at the moment. Could I suggest you do some work, or do you not have enough to do?" She recoiled and fumbled with her fingers. "What's your name?"

"Justine Ellis, Sir," she said quietly as she looked at the floor. He had to give her credit when she looked up at him through her lashes and batted them together. She was quite a pretty little thing really - virginal and of no fucking interest whatsoever, but pretty nonetheless. He had never been enamoured with virgins, far too inhibited.

"Justine, go up to my office and tell Louisa that I sent you to help her. She will keep you busy enough," he said as he turned and walked off towards the office doors. He hoped Tom's name would be on a door somewhere because he honestly didn't know what the man looked like.

Opening the door, he found the apparent Tom shouting into the phone at someone with his back to him. He walked in and sat on a chair quietly to watch the man. He looked pretty average in height and build, decent suit and he still had his hair - always useful, but until he turned around, he couldn't quite make out his age. Christ, he was in full swing about some interest rate that was clearly unacceptable to him. Alex raised his brow, actually quite impressed with the man. He couldn't remember employing him but whomever it was that did had done a good job.

"Right, fine, you shit, we'll be pulling Hamilton road, the three buildings in Mayfair and the Mandarin holdings. Unless you come back with a number under two, you can fuck right off." Tom slammed the phone down with a groan and pulled at his collar before turning around.

"Shit! Mr. White? Shit... Sorry, I didn't know you were there." Alex continued with his smirk and waved him off as he registered that he was younger than his hardened attitude suggested. Tom reminded him of himself a few years ago.

"Sit down, Tom. What do I have in London that could be used as a commercial catering premises?"

"Umm... Let me think. There's Osterbruck Place or maybe Defoe Point? That's got a small car park and easy access to all major networks. I could probably work out some others but I'd need more information regarding size and capacity," he said as he looked Alex straight in the eye. He didn't even blink. At fucking last.

"Send me the details of them and anything else you think might be good. I'll need to know about current lease details and I only want spaces that I can make available within the next month or so."

"Mr. White, I'm pretty sure Tate can make anything vacant within a week, let alone a month." Alex chuckled and stood up. He was right.

"What were they offering on the phone?" he asked as he reached the door.

"Two point two above base. It's a good deal. I just want a bit more. With the nine purchases we've got lined up over the next month and the investment in the east end, every half point helps," he replied with a shrug. Alex smirked at him and wandered off with a wave of his hand. The man needed a raise. He plucked out his phone and called Louisa.

"How much is Brindley on?"

"One hundred and twenty, I think. His bonus will be twenty five percent." How the hell the woman remembered every detail of his business was quite inexplicable.

"Give him another thirty and raise him to forty percent. How long has he worked for me?"

"Around three years," she replied as she tapped away at her keyboard.

"Any Far East experience? Married? Children?"

"Not as far as I'm aware, no, and no. He does speak four languages though," she replied succinctly.

"Right, well find out, will you? I need someone for the Shanghai deal and I think he'll be perfect. It will mean constant travel and of course another contract. Could you get Tate to sort one? No. Wait. Louisa, do you think you could organise a new contract for him without Tate being involved?"

"I expect so, Sir. Anything I should be aware of?"

"No, not at the moment. Can you turn off my laptop? I'm going home."

"Of course, Sir, and thank you for Justine. She's being very useful."

"Good, you can keep her for a week or so. I know how you like a new pet." She chuckled in response.

"Have a good evening, Sir." He switched off the phone and headed to the elevator again.

On leaving the building, he stood outside and breathed in a deep lungful of air.

Where was she? It was Wednesday and he hadn't seen her since Sunday morning when she'd left him, regardless of how much he'd tried to lure her back into bed. She'd definitely found a new strength since he'd been an utter dick and left her. She was less compliant now and it turned him on like hell fired up. She was bad enough before; now it was almost impossible to resist her. She goaded him now, teased him and yet held herself back from giving him everything. He'd never found the chase a more enthralling task and was still relishing in the feeling of it as he picked up his phone and texted her again. He'd found their daily banter via text amusing and quite the distraction from the daily grind. He started to walk toward the park.

- **Where are you?**
- **At the wholesalers, talking to a very charming young man about cream. X**
- **What about cream?**
- **Whether it's better whipped or beaten. x**
- **I want you.**
- **Whipped or beaten? X**
- **Both, preferably with the cream.**
- **Mr. White I am quite appalled. X**
- **No you're not, Miss Scott. When do you finish?**
- **It'll be about six. X**
- **I'll pick you up. Be ready.**

He smirked to himself and sat down on a bench in the park as he watched the nannies and their charges running around and chasing birds. He loved this park, in fact he loved being outside and it

108

reminded him that he promised himself some time away. He wondered if she'd go with him and pondered her skiing ability. She'd never mentioned it, but she'd never mentioned chess or the piano and she could do both of them remarkably well. The thought of going away also brought the Lake District flying into his mind. He needed to get to see Evelyn Peters' family and although it was obviously a delicate matter, the only way he would know the truth was to stare into her mother's eyes and ask a few questions. Thinking of that and Elizabeth in the same moment made him realise that he wanted her to go with him, but he hadn't told her anything about the possibility of a sister. Was now the right time? She said she wanted to know him and he'd already done one of the hard bits by taking her to the bastard's house.

He frowned deeply as he thought of her that evening cowered on the floor in fear of him and screwed his fist up at his own stupidity. This was his second chance to make everything right with her, and if she wanted it all then she could have it all. Schroeder had said he should be honest with her and that he should take her with him to the next meeting if he felt it appropriate. Should he? She said she wouldn't hold anything against him, that she didn't care about the shocking bits, only that he was open enough to admit to them. Well maybe he was ready to tell them to someone, to her.

- **Do you ski?**
- **Yes. Why? x**
- **Want to go?**
- **Probably. When? x**
- **Not sure. Just wondered.**
- **Okay x**
- **Do you have plans for the weekend?**
- **No, free all weekend x**
- **I love you.**

Glancing down at his watch, he frowned and rubbed his neck. It had been ten minutes since his last text and she hadn't responded. Why wouldn't she say those words again? God, he wanted to hear them. Did she even still feel the same? He assumed she did otherwise she wouldn't have taken him back. Was it the same as the reason why she wasn't allowing any of his preferences to enter into the relationship? She'd stopped him the first time and then not pushed him into that guise anymore. Why was she holding back from it? He knew she wanted it. He could sense it on her and he was becoming desperate for it. He was trying to be gentle but it just wasn't in his nature and he wanted the other Elizabeth back. Fuck, it was actually unbearable. He wanted her to give in and let him take her back to the places she'd been before. He needed to feel it again with her, to see her flexing underneath his hands and bending to his will, but she had the control now and she was using it to her full advantage. Was she doing it on purpose?

Shaking his head to himself, he got up and headed back to the offices. He needed to get his car and then drive across town. His phone vibrated and he grabbed at it with a smile. Tom Brindley's email was not what he wanted but it did divert his attention. Defoe Point, interesting. It was exactly what she needed and in an excellent location - fifteen minutes up the road from the shop and big enough for them to expand at their leisure. Now how the hell did he make her see his reasoning for it?

He wanted to give her the world but he knew she wouldn't take it easily. She would just see it as him trying to buy his way out of trouble. Perhaps he should make her pay him for it. He'd had no intention of doing so, but at least she would see it as a business arrangement and not an overly priced gift. He smiled at her term for his extravagances on her and slipped his hands in his pockets. Lifting his head to look at the front of his building, he smiled and thought of the last few years.

He'd done this - from nothing to this.

A familiar face walking towards him in the crowd suddenly diverted his attention and he tried to stop the immediate angry frown that crossed his face. He couldn't get away now she'd seen him. He straightened his face and walked toward her as she put one long leg in front of the other. Models, whores the lot of them.

"Alexander," she said demurely as she air kissed him and he made the mistake of inhaling her perfume. He hadn't smelt it for a few years and it reminded him of another time in his life, one he wasn't proud of in the slightest. Had he been anywhere other than outside his own building, he would have shoved her into oncoming traffic. He hated her for making him despise himself more than he already did.

"Caroline, what are you doing here?" he said tersely as a sense of shame swept across him. He didn't want her here. She reminded him of what an arsehole he really was and furthered his own appreciation of how much he didn't deserve Elizabeth.

"Well that's a fine way to say hello. Actually, I was just passing and I wondered if you'd have Conner's number? He seems to have changed it since..." she said as she pawed at his chest with her orange fingertips and batted her fucking eyelashes. He stepped back instantly and sneered at her.

"Conner's with someone, Caroline and I doubt he'd be happy if I gave you his number. Why do you want it anyway?"

"Well, darling, life's expensive and I thought that maybe I could tell him a story or two," she said through her sickly smile. *Why had he ever found that attractive?* He grabbed her by the arm and dragged her across the road. "Stop it. You're hurting me."

"Shut up, Caroline. Fuck, will this ever stop?" he seethed as he almost threw her at the wall and then realised where he was and let go of her instead. He glared at her and reached for his wallet. "How much this time?"

"Darling, I think you can do a little better than that, don't you? I mean, really, is that all your friendship's worth?" she said as she swished her short blonde hair around. "Oh, and I heard about your new girlfriend. Is she very lovely, Alexander? Does she know who you really are?" He growled and shot her a lethal look as he glanced at a truck on its way toward them. *Just one fucking push.*

"I have one cheque in here, Caroline and I swear it will be the last one you ever get from me," he said as he scribbled the same amount as last time she did this. "You have tested my patience for the last time and don't fucking think of going near her. I will not be responsible for my actions if you get her involved." He pushed it at her hand and stepped back before his anger got the better of him.

Five years Miss Anderson had held this against him and he couldn't think of a way out of it apart from killing her or maybe giving her to Pascal. He knew she had the video somewhere but he didn't know where or with whom. The fact that she was Conner's girlfriend and apparent true love at the time was the only reason he was continuing to feed her money. If his friend ever found out about the affair, their brotherly relationship would be over. Conner was not a man to be crossed at any cost because he simply didn't forget or forgive. Three times he'd fucked her, three times! So far it had cost him three million. Christ, one million per fuck, and it really wasn't that good at all. Unfortunately, the bitch had the foresight to film the last time when he'd had another two in the room at the same time as her, and frankly she'd be playing that card for far too long now. He needed to find a way out of it. Yes, he'd been a fool but he'd been struggling with addiction and still hadn't completely found his way through his fog of fury and pain. It was still no excuse but he wondered briefly if he could tell Conner about it now. He was happy with Belle and maybe he would forgive him his sins - probably not, though.

"Just remember I still have it, darling. I'll do whatever I want and you will still do as I ask when I ask it of you," she said as she took a step toward him and went to kiss his lips. He recoiled and stared at her, astounded by her actions. "Was it really that bad for you? I have fond memories of you, darling," she continued as she smiled and then pouted at him.

"Just go, Caroline," he said as he turned away and tried to push the fury down. "I don't want you anywhere near me." He had no one to blame but himself really, and as much as he hated her, she was only doing what she could, given the circumstances. He'd been stupid enough to get into the situation and so he would have to pay the consequences of his actions. That was his world and the only saving grace was that he hadn't gotten her pregnant.

"Til next time, darling," she shouted at him as he looked over his shoulder to see her very thin frame gliding down the pavement in full model swing. Hopefully she'd trip and stumble into the road at some point. He frowned and walked back across the road to his offices, sucking in a breath and trying to find his calm again. Fuck, he hated being blackmailed. If the woman ever had the stupidity to turn up again, he'd finish it for her.

~

An hour later, he was sitting in his car a little way up the road from her shop and still wondering what to do about the building he wanted to give to her. He'd just wasted all that money on a woman he couldn't give a fuck about and the one who consumed him would hardly accept a penny from him. She told him to enjoy his wealth. Why shouldn't he, she'd said? Quite bloody right.

Getting out of the car, he slammed the door and walked towards Scott's. He liked the name. Not only was it hers but it was straightforward and to the point. The faintest flicker of the name Elizabeth White drifted through his mind and he stopped abruptly and tried to grab hold of it before it disappeared. What the hell was that thought about? Marriage? There was no way he was processing that image at the moment. She'd only just agreed to give him another chance. The likelihood of her considering that as an option was zero on a scale of one to ten. Chuckling to himself, he carried on walking and gazed at the red painted building. Their sign work was excellent and the style of font was spot on - modern but with a traditional twist. While Belle was the company front, he could feel Elizabeth in the fibre of the details emanating from the outside. She'd designed that artwork; he was sure of it.

He opened the door and wandered in. Teresa swung round, smiled at him and shouted for Elizabeth. He nodded in thanks and picked up a baguette for some reason, wanting to hold something that she'd created with her lovely hands.

"That will be three pound seventy five please." His head shot to Teresa as she took it from him and put it in a paper bag.

"That's extortionate." He almost choked at the price. She smirked at him.

"That's London, and when, pray tell, was the last time you bought a baguette?" she asked with a glittering smile. "Actually do you even carry money or are you like the queen?" He pulled out his wallet and found a twenty.

"Lovely, thank you," she said as she took it and went to the till. Elizabeth rounded the corner and looked at the bag in his hand then at Teresa.

"What are you doing, you idiot? Give him his money back," she said as she snatched it from her and handed it back to him with a shy smile. He couldn't have given a damn about the money as he smiled at her and felt his heart peel apart that little bit more. She was stunning, standing there with her hair scraped back and a smear of chocolate on her cheek. He moved toward her, grabbed her chin and licked it off her before he could stop himself. Her soulful brown eyes widened at the gesture and her full lips parted with a small moan. He stared into those eyes. She was so ready, it was killing her to stop it, and thankfully he could see it now because she was relaxing again. *Not long.*

"Well, he was amusing me. It's been a dull day. Honestly, you should have seen the look on his face... Priceless. Easy target. I thought he was some hot-shot or something." She laughed again as she walked past them to the front of the shop.

"Hi," Elizabeth said as she glared at the woman and then looked up at him through her long lashes.

"Hi," he replied as he kissed her gently and released her face. "Are you ready?"

"Yes, just give me a minute to get my bag." She walked into the back again. Unfortunately for him, it wasn't her who returned a minute later.

"Still being a fucking arsehole," Belle said as she collected the drawer from the till. Clearly it wasn't a question, more of a statement.

"Belle," he replied in acknowledgement of her existence. There was little else he could say until he proved himself. She was right to be protective. Actually, he admired her for it.

"Dickhead," she muttered under her breath as she looked directly at him and then returned to the back room. He bit back his frustration and waited for the only woman in the room who actually liked him to come back. A hand touched his back and he swung round to see Teresa smiling at him.

"I know you love her and Belle will come round given time. Don't worry, she's just a natural born bitch," she said. He looked down at the very small woman and felt a burst of thanks for Elizabeth's friend. For some odd reason, her opinion of him was more worthwhile than he could have imagined.

"Thank you," he replied quietly.

"Thank you for what?" Elizabeth's lovely voice said as she drifted back into the room looking like an angel.

"Nothing, it's private and you need to keep your nose out, missy." Teresa giggled as she waved and said her goodbyes. He turned back to Elizabeth and held out his hand. She smiled and took it as he pulled her out the door.

"You're driving?" she asked as he unlocked the car.

"Yes," he replied as he looked at her with a puzzled expression. What was wrong with him driving?

"It's just weird. You're normally being driven and you've never actually driven me anywhere." He thought about it for a moment and had to agree. This morning he'd just decided to drive himself. It was strange. He couldn't remember the last time he'd driven to the office and thinking on it, he'd really enjoyed it.

"Perhaps I'm starting to remember the simpler things in life," he said as he pulled out into traffic and smiled broadly at her.

"In that case I know the perfect place for dinner," she said with her mischievous smile as she told him to head for Barking. He felt his eyebrow rise but was so amused by her sudden mysterious behaviour that he indicated and manoeuvred them into the right lane.

Nearly an hour and a lot of heavy traffic later, they were sat in the car outside a small country pub. He looked across at her and watched her smile radiantly as she got out of the car and wandered towards the door. Her long legs encased in black jeans seemed to go on forever and her dark red hair tumbling around her cream shirt emphasized her soft pink lips effortlessly. She stopped and beckoned him to get out of the car. He wasn't entirely sure if he was horny or humbled by the way she just owned the space around her. Her face illuminated the ground around her as she held her hand out and pointed to the black and white thatched building. Hand holding, yet another wonderful thing about Elizabeth Scott. He chuckled to himself and got out to grab her.

"You're beautiful," he said as he picked her up and kissed the living hell out of her.

"So are you," she replied as she pulled her finger down his nose and kissed it. It was the sweetest gesture he could ever remember receiving and he laughed at it heartily as he dropped her to the ground.

"Where are we?" he said as he looked up at the sign. "The Spotty Pig?"

"My cousins lived around here when we were younger. We would meet here once every couple of months for lunch or dinner. It's wonderful. A nice family run it and it's all homemade," she said excitedly as she opened the door.

He looked around the interior and felt like he'd been transported to some sort of sixteenth century inn. The walls were all black and white and threaded with old crossbeams. Hundreds of old horse brasses hung from every available surface. The random pictures of some non-descript landscape that dotted the walls were truly fucking horrific but regardless, the place was packed full of people eating dinner and laughing. He swept his gaze across to the bar and noticed a large rumbling fire in the other side. It reminded him of cold winter nights and blankets across knees. The place had a warm, homely feeling about it and he instantly understood why she liked it. There wasn't a pretentious thing in the space that would distract from its comfort or appeal and he smiled back at her as the visions of a home with her swept through his mind.

"Can I order for you?" she asked as they approached the bar. He smirked at her.

"If you like," he replied as he watched her peruse the blackboard on the wall. Apparently there was only six meals to choose from.

"Okay, why don't you go and grab the chairs by the fire and I'll get us some drinks," she muttered as she continued her gaze distractedly, nibbling her thumb with her hand on her hip.

"What makes you think you know what I want?" he asked as she backed her arse into him and jumped at the unexpected contact. He grabbed her hips and pulled her back harder.

"I'll... I'll wing it and hope. I do that quite a lot lately." She giggled as he grazed her neck with his teeth and let her go. Wandering toward the swinging doorway, he gazed back to find her deep in conversation with the old man behind the bar. She looked perfect just as she always did and he felt his heart explode again. Unfortunately, he just didn't see the door in time before it smacked him in the face with full force.

"Alex! God, Alex, are you okay?" he heard as he lifted himself from the floor and moved his hand to his nose. Christ, it hurt. He registered her laughing quietly and turned to glare at her. His eyes were watering with the pain but try as he might, he couldn't form any thoughts of anger as she lifted her hand to her stunning mouth and tried to stifle her fucking laughter. The young girl beside him was shifting nervously and apologizing profusely so he assumed it was her who had banged the door forward. He glared at her instead, and she ran away.

"Are you bloody laughing at me, Miss Scott?" he said sharply. That was obviously her limit because she erupted into fits of hysterics and almost fell over as she bumped into a table. He quickly grabbed at her waist and pulled her to him with a growl.

"I'm sorry. Shit, that was funny. I mean... Sorry, it wasn't. It's just... Oh my god, I can't speak," she continued through her tears as she swiped at them and looked at him, then burst out laughing again. He couldn't help but grin at her laughter. It was infectious, and before long, the whole bar was joining in. It was the first time he could remember being the butt of a joke and being reasonably happy about it. Eventually, the old man came over, slapped him on the back and apologised for his waitress's blunder. He introduced himself as Mike and opened the door for them to go through, safely this time, with a wink at her. She giggled and nodded at him.

Alex pulled her through to the table and sat after she had. Thankfully she had managed to contain her laughter to the occasional snort and he shook his head at the whole ridiculous situation. What the boardroom would make of such a disaster was anyone's guess.

"Is your nose okay?" she said once she'd calmed herself a bit more.

"I'm sure I'll survive," he said after a pause. "I'm glad I amused you though," he continued as he took off his suit jacket and rolled up his sleeves.

"Better," she said as she gazed at him. He looked across at her questioningly.

"Excuse me? You don't like my suit?"

"I love your suit, and you in it, but I prefer you out of it." A small shrug glanced her shoulders. "You look more relaxed now and I like to see your skin," she replied as she bit her thumb nervously. He smirked at her and picked up his drink. It was a good reply and more importantly, an honest one.

"So what am I having for dinner?" he asked casually as he watched her pupils dilating at his tapping fingers. Fuck, he loved how responsive she was so he decided to keep the honesty thing going.

"Lamb," she replied as she licked her lips and shifted in her seat.

"What are you thinking about?" he asked as quickly as he could, staring into her eyes and looking for her signs as he continued his tapping. He knew them so well; he'd only have to see or hear a flicker of them and he'd know what to do next.

"Your hands." His gaze dropped to her lips as she parted them. He had an instant need to grab her and bend her over the table but refrained. Perhaps she needed more teasing to get back to herself. It seemed to be working in this moment.

"Where?" He kept his gaze as impassive as he could manage given the growing issue between his legs and slowed the tap to a steadier pace, watching as her eyes returned to his fingers.

"Throat," she replied as she grazed her fingers delicately across her own and swallowed slowly. It was mesmerising and he struggled to stop himself from throwing her over his shoulder. God, he wished they were in a private room. They bloody well would have been if they'd ended up where he'd been taking her this evening.

"How firm is the grasp?" He hoped the answer would be an honest one and not one she held back from this time. He needed her back and he wanted her happy about it, ready to be with him again and not the tampered down version she was currently asking for. He couldn't keep it up for much longer.

"Very," she said as she brought her eyes up to meet his. The sparkle in them indicated that she was ready for more again and he felt his whole body exhale with relief.

"Well, I'll see what I can come up with for you then," he said as he abruptly stopped his tapping fingers and looked toward the approaching waitress. She placed their food, giving him a very shy smile and apologised again for the earlier incident.

He picked up his cutlery and waited for Elizabeth to do the same as he looked at the food in front of him. It was mountainous and he smiled at the thought of home cooked meals. After a beat, he realised that she hadn't picked up her cutlery and looked across at her. She looked suddenly nervous. Gone was the passion he saw a few moments ago and he tried to think of a way to get her back. He sliced into the meat and licked his lips as it fell from the bone.

"Would it help if I told you I was nervous, too?" he said as he lifted it to his mouth. His taste buds exploded with rosemary and deep rich gravy and he only just stopped the moan of happiness.

"I don't know. Are you?" she replied as she narrowed her eyes at him. Was he? He didn't know. Probably not in that capacity but definitely in how she perceived him.

"Do you want me to be nervous, Elizabeth, or do you want be to be what I am without opinion?"

It was the best honest answer he could give her, and Christ he cherished not thinking about controlling himself, just switching off and being what he was underneath. She raised her eyebrow at him as if registering his candid response and thanking him for it. She knew what she was dealing with. He wasn't going to hide from her anymore.

"I want nothing less than what you are, Alex. I'm pretty sure you're the one who needs to find the balance between those two, not me," she said with a soft smile as she picked up her knife and fork and dived into what appeared to be pork and apples.

A balance? He'd never thought about it like that before and spent the rest of the meal thinking about exactly that. Was that was she was trying to find in him? A comfortable balance of all the versions of himself that he played with daily? Didn't everyone do that to some degree, though? Play different people to different consumers? Wasn't that the point of what he did and how he'd made so much money doing it? Sometimes he longed to just be the angry young man he used to be, to just let all the aggression flow freely and be exactly what he wanted to be regardless of the situation. He was pretty sure that wasn't what she was after, but it did spark the idea that perhaps it was time to find himself again and find the balance she spoke of.

Having finished the meal, he leaned back in his chair and watched her pick at her food. She was clearly full but couldn't resist another bite. He didn't blame her. The food was delicious and he couldn't remember enjoying a meal more. He lifted his glass of red and drank the last of it with a real sense of pleasure, something he realised had been sadly lacking until he'd met her. How she'd done it was still a mystery, but she'd definitely awoken a new man and he was finding himself liking him more and more by the day.

She looked at her watch and frowned.

"Are you ready to go?" she said with a sigh as she looked across at him and smiled. He flicked his eyes to the clock on the wall - ten thirty. Where the hell had the evening gone?

"Yes, come on," he replied as he got up and extended a hand. She took it and followed, muttering about watching out for the door. He tightened his grip and she giggled. God, he loved that sound. He was so busy thinking about it that he was almost out the door before he realised he hadn't paid and stopped abruptly. She banged into him and giggled again as she stumbled backwards.

"I haven't paid," he said as he pulled her back towards the bar. She sniggered at him and stopped him for a kiss on the way.

"We don't have to," she whispered in his ear. "I doubt a couple of meals will break me." He looked at her in shock as her words registered in his brain, the very words he'd used with her in Rome to his own amusement.

"You own it?" he said as he looked down at her with pride and smiled at her deceit. He liked her little game very much. She grinned back at him with a shrug.

"Well, not just me. Scott's does. We couldn't let it die and it was so cheap at the time," she replied as she pulled him back toward the door, shouting her goodbyes to Mike as they left.

"I'm impressed," he said. It was honestly the only thing he could think of as she held her hand out at him. He frowned. What was she asking for?

"Keys. You've had three glasses of wine, Mr. White," she said as she stared him down. He rolled his eyes and threw them at her. She unlocked the car and got in with a beautiful slide. She looked good sat there and he felt the pride swell again.

"Are you as bad as your sister?" He suddenly remembered the epic journey where he'd almost lost his life, twice.

"Worse." She chuckled as she fiddled with knobs and buttons on the seat. "How the hell do you move it forward? Sodding expensive things have too many buttons on them." He reached over and kissed her as she slid forward a foot at his command of the correct button.

"And how many sports cars have you driven, Miss Scott?" he asked with a smirk as she floored it backward and lifted her brow at him.

"Worried, Mr. White?" she said as she spun the wheel in her hand so efficiently that he got the feeling he was being teased again as he gazed at her. Her cheeky little smile got his pulse racing instantly.

"You are a woman of surprises, Elizabeth," he replied as he closed his eyes and rested his head back against the seat. "Anymore this evening?"

"I think two is plenty of exercise for that old heart of yours. I wouldn't want you keeling over on me," she said with a giggle as she hit the accelerator and raced toward the road, screaming her delight as she went. He chuckled at her entertainment and looked across at her again. She couldn't be any more perfect if she tried.

Chapter 7

Elizabeth

I'm ready. I know I am. He's never looked at me before like he has been doing in this last week, and I honestly can't keep his hands out of my mind any more. The constant thoughts of what they'll do to me when I give him the chance to use them fully is beyond absorbing. I know he hasn't shown me everything yet, regardless of his actions in Rome. I don't think he's even begun to handle me the way he wants to. I can see it in his eyes. It's as if he's protecting me from something. Maybe he's protecting me from him? I saw something darker in Pascal's eyes and I know I've seen flashes of the same thing in Alex's.

We've had a week of loveliness and it's felt warm, kind and sincere. He's told me he loves me repeatedly, and now I believe him, but I can't tell him the same until this feels right again. I feel like I've been seeing a changed man - a man I don't know, and one that, if I'm honest, I'm just a little bit uncomfortable with. He's still in there and I know I told him I needed something different, but it just all feels contrived and unnatural, as if I'm pushing him to be someone he doesn't want to be, and I know I don't want him that way at all. I need him back and I need to trust him to let him be that man again. Why did he have to screw it up?

I'm lying in the bath, having had the busiest day of the year so far, trying to think of a reason not to trust him when he says he loves me. I've been up since five this morning, preparing everything for the weekend's bookings. The winter wedding of the Williamsons had me chopping and dicing for most of the morning, and the Bloomsburg Hotel's festive office party had me making nibbles and delectable treats for most of the afternoon and evening. James is thankfully running the event this evening as we both knew there wasn't a cat's chance in hell I'd be able to do it, and Theresa and Belle are doing the wedding tomorrow with the family chef putting all the dishes together for them. I'm so glad that it's turned out like that, because I simply haven't got the strength to say no anymore.

I narrow my eyes at my own toes as they poke out of the bubbles at me, as if they can somehow answer my questions for me. *Ridiculous, Beth. Just get on with it. You know you want it.*

I can feel my own body betraying my mind as it aches at the thought of him, and I brush my fingers over my stomach and down towards my thighs. I'm cursing myself under my breath, but funnily enough, I'm not stopping my hand as it weaves its way downward further and touches my nub with just the right amount of pressure. Without thinking, I feel my other hand wander toward my neck and smile at the thought of those dastardly hands as a moan escapes my mouth. The water swirls about around me and makes me remember his tongue as he snakes his way around my body, teasing me to within an inch of my life before he lets me get anywhere near the point of explosion, and then, when I'm about there, just stopping and holding me back again. I slip my fingers inside and think of him pushing my barriers, enticing me with that pleasure pain thing he does so well, biding my hands and hanging me up for him to view and...

"Right, I'm off." I'm instantly brought back to this world when Belle shouts through the door and I splosh the water over the side of the bath in an attempt to sit up. I don't know why. She can't see me but I feel caught out somehow and look at the door wildly.

"Shit," I mumble to myself as I throw the towel onto the floor to stop the escaped water from swallowing the bathroom up.

Everything okay in there?" she calls through the door.

"Yes, I was just... I was..." I stutter. I don't know what to say... *About to come?*

"Were you really? Naughty girl," she replies with a hysterical laugh. I throw mental daggers at the door and scowl at it.

"Stop talking to me through the door, you idiot," I say as I pick up the sponge and start washing. She opens the door and strides in, looking incredible in an electric blue dress, and plonks herself on the toilet seat.

"So what are you doing this weekend?" she asks as she picks up some blue nail polish and starts to apply it.

"Nice colour. Wearing it for any particular reason?" I reply with a cackle. "I'm sure he'll appreciate it. Are you even wearing underwear?"

"Yes, I know, and no. So the weekend?" She grins as she screws her nose up at the smell. I giggle. She always has hated the smell of nail varnish. I lean back again and sigh.

"I don't know. He hasn't told me anything, only that I need to be ready at seven and that he'll have me back here by Sunday night. I don't know how I feel about it all if I'm honest." She looks across at me suspiciously and puts the nail varnish down.

"What do you mean by that? You do still feel the same, don't you?"

"Yes, of course I do but I haven't let him touch me-"

She cuts me off abruptly with a look of disbelief. "You haven't had sex again yet?" she shouts incredulously. I roll my eyes and throw the sponge across at her. It hits the sink. I always was a terrible shot.

"No, silly, I mean I haven't let him get kinky yet and I think I probably will this weekend. In fact, I know I will if I'm honest. I just... I still don't seem to trust him and I don't know why."

"Probably because he's a fucking dick who acted like a pig," she replies. That's her best response as she shrugs and blows on her nails.

"Thanks for that, Belle, really helpful," I say as I slide under the water and remember the pain of him leaving again.

When I surface again, she stares at me with what can only be described as a weird look. I don't think I've ever seen it before and I tilt my head at her as I wipe the suds away.

"I think I love him, you know?" she says as she continues her gaze.

"Oh, right," I reply quietly. "Are you okay about it?" I know full well how she feels about being in love. It wrecked her last time after the bastard, Marcus Renfield, and she promised she'd never do it again. She swore she'd find a rich man who was fun and that would be that.

"He does love you, honey. Conner wouldn't have fought me so hard on it if he didn't think it was the right thing to do. I trust him. Perhaps you should, too?" she says softly in response as she stands up and starts to brush herself down in the mirror. *Conner fought her?*

"How can you say that? You haven't got a good word to say about him normally, and Conner would stand up for him, wouldn't he?" I say, trying to figure out where on earth she's going with this.

"Conner battled his corner quite effectively, and I say bad things about him because I think he's an arse. That doesn't mean that I don't think he's good for you. If anything, I think him being a dick probably helped you. You're stronger now, wiser around him. Use it to your advantage and don't let him make the same mistake again. If you're going to do this with someone like him, honey, you've got to give it everything. There's no point holding back because you'll only hurt yourself in the end and blame yourself when it doesn't work," she replies, her words slow, almost as if she's devouring each thought and processing them herself.

What the hell was that? Did she just do a complete one eighty on love?

"What was that? I'm sorry but I'm pretty sure you just spoke of love with some sort of fondness attached," I reply as I watch her fiddling with her jewellery. She looks nervous all of a sudden and I get out of the bath and wrap myself in my robe. Does she need me? What's going on in her head? "Belle, are you okay? What's the matter?" She turns around to look at me with tears brimming her eyes and I throw my arms around her and cuddle her as tight as I can. Tears? I don't remember seeing tears for years. I can feel her sniff them back before they fall from her eyes and she backs up and wipes at her eyes, shrugging away from me.

"I'm... I'm nervous, scared. What if he...? Do you think he'll...? Oh, fuck it, I don't know what I am and frankly I'm getting bloody bored with feeling like this," she says as she storms out of the room. I follow her and watch her throw herself on the bed, overly dramatically to be honest. Yep, definitely in love. I smile and sit down next to her.

"You'll wrinkle your dress," I say with a giggle as she sits up and looks at me.

"What does it matter? He'll have me out of it within twenty minutes anyway and I'll love every minute of it. He's got me, Beth, hook, line and sinker. I wasn't ready for him. I'm still not sure I am."

"Well, given your little pep talk to me a minute ago, perhaps you should just listen to your own words. He's not like Marcus, Belle. You know that." I think about Conner for a moment. "To be fair, he's not like anyone, is he? The man's a genius or something, and regardless of his blue hair, he is pretty gorgeous." She giggles at me and bumps my shoulder with hers.

"What a pair, hey? Could we not have found ourselves normal, dull, rich men? You know the ones who are a bit of fun and okay in the sack?" I look at her with a smirk and a sigh.

"I didn't even want a rich one. It still scares the shit out of me if I'm honest. Normal would have been just fine on its own. Alexander White is definitely not normal." She giggles again and snorts back a bark of laughter.

"Bloody stunning, though. I mean, are his legs as good as they look in trousers?" My head swings round so quick it almost falls off.

"Oh my god, are you having pervy thoughts about my boyfriend?" She tries to straighten her face and fails miserably as she bursts out laughing.

"No! Yes... But you've thought the same of Conner and don't deny it." I have to laugh because I have, early on, before I realised he was interested in her. He was one of the only wealthy people who'd never intimidated me for some reason. Now I just see him as a friend, but he's still a very cute friend.

"Actually, it was his shoulders. He's got very good shoulders, has Conner, cheeky too." I swear I hear her hiss at me and look at her with my mouth hanging open. "Did you just hiss at me?" She shrugs and gets up.

"I can't help it. He gets me all fired up. Fucking jealously, ridiculous I know. I really need to do something about that. It's far too obvious." She checks herself in the mirror and reapplies her lipstick. "Listen, I have to go or I'm going to be late."

"Where are you going?" I say as I wander out into the hall and make my way to the kettle.

"I don't know. Some basement somewhere, then I think he's sweeping me off to a friend's yacht. Even I can't keep up with him if I'm honest. Oh by the way, remember the shop's closed on Monday for new lights in the front and we're going to Mum's for lunch." How had I forgotten that?

"Yep, no need to remind me, and frankly I'm glad of it. I feel exhausted."

"I think we all do. We need to sort that holiday and soon."

"Yes, Alex mentioned skiing the other day randomly. Don't know what that was about but it did get me thinking," I reply as I shove her down the corridor. "Go. He's waiting."

"And so he should be," she says with a grin as she gives me a hug. "Have a good weekend, honey and let me know where you are when you find out."

"I will. You, too."

"Love you," she says as she closes the door and leaves me on my own.

I make a cup of coffee and head through to the lounge. It's only eight-thirty and the thought of curling up on the sofa and watching a DVD or some rubbish is very enticing. I flick the through the channels and try to let my mind relax into chill mode. Clearly it's not happening because the moment I try to focus on nothing, he comes flying back into my head with superb clarity and I find myself closing my eyes and letting him take over again before I know it.

Stop it, Beth. One night.

I lift my eyes open and shake my head as I chastise my head for letting him control it again. I don't even know why I'm bothering to fight it any more. It doesn't matter whether I trust him or not. I know I want him to be more again because the way he's currently behaving just doesn't feel quite right. Part of me wishes it did, but deep down, I feel like I'm stifling him, holding him back and at the same time restricting myself from enjoying every inch of him. I doubt there's a future for us if we don't get back to where we were anyway. He wants it... I want it... What the hell am I playing at? What am I trying to achieve here? *Shit, I'm still thinking about him. Stop it!*

I flop backwards on the sofa and stretch out. I am determined to relax and not think about him. The credits roll on the news that I have been aimlessly staring at and I flick the channels again. *Bridget Jones* flashes in front of me and I smile. Perfect. I crack my neck and bed in for the film. I love this film and it will definitely distract me from wandering fingers, hopefully.

I wake to find myself in darkness and the television doing that slight flicker thing it does when there's nothing on. What time is it? I squint over at the clock to see five in the morning staring back at me. Shit, I must have fallen asleep during the film. The last thing I remember is her walking through the market to Gabrielle's song. God,

127

I really was tired. I try to move, knowing that I should go to bed, but when I suddenly remember that he's going to be here in two hours, I think better of it and snuggle back down again. I'll have another half an hour or so before I think about hauling myself into the shower. I can't believe I spent the night on the sofa. Given what's probably going to happen tomorrow night and the lack of sleep I'll be getting, I should have got to my own bed and rested. *Idiot!*

What the hell does he want from me at seven anyway? Doesn't the man do lying in? And where is he taking me? Probably somewhere expensive, I know that much anyway. It'll be a day of opulence, or something ridiculous like lunch at the Ivy. Who goes to lunch at the Ivy for God's sake? He does, apparently. I smile at the thought of flicking his lettuce at him, which reminds me of his interesting whispering. There was a time I'd have been shocked, even appalled, but now I can't help but wonder what it would feel like to be suspended and blindfolded. I at least know why he likes ropes now. I can feel my groin completely agreeing with my mind and giggle at myself as I make my decision. Mr. White, you've got permission.

Regardless of my sleepiness, I can't help but reach for my phone and type in the word Shibari. The instant I do, several images spring onto the page. My eyes open with a start as I look down at the images of women wrapped intricately in rope and knots. One is lying flat downward as she hangs from four ropes. Her body has somehow been laced together with twisted bonds that seem to end at her neck. The man standing next to her has his fingers hooked downwards in her mouth and he seems to be pulling her toward him. With the other hand, he's holding the rope that's attached to her neck and gazing at her with a completely impassive face. She, however, seems to be in a trance-like state. Her eyes are glazed like she's been transported to another place somehow, but there's no denying that they're lust filled. I bet her mouth's watering around his fingers and I can guarantee she's itching to bite down. The energy it must be taking to take that pressure in her mouth must be consuming her. Her body looks taught and lean as if she's stretching every fibre of herself out for him with a strained pleasure that she can't deny herself. Is that where I go when I find myself in that peaceful place? Is that what he sees when he looks at me? What is that place? If she goes there, too, it must have a name. I need to ask Alex about that.

Scanning another image, I notice the time and jump up immediately. How I've done it I don't know, but I've been learning about bondage for nearly an hour and now it's six. Well at least I'm informed now.

By a quarter to seven I'm sitting outside my apartment on a bench, staring at the road. The last time he picked me up, he startled me by standing outside my door, which is not happening again. I am prepared, I am ready, and as I sit here in my long brown boots and jeans waiting for him, I smirk at the thought of making him force me again. That's what I want from him and that's what he wants me to give him. I won't have to do much. He'll read it in me. His eyes will read mine like an open book and I'll revel in it. Whatever it was that I've been scared about has deserted me and for the first time in a week, I feel somehow more relaxed.

Having done some research, I now know that it's a Bentley that's driving along the street toward me so I check my watch. Yep, he was going to surprise me again. *Not this time, White.*

I pull Belle's beige coat around myself, tuck my cream scarf in neatly and walk toward the car with a determination I haven't felt before. I am in control, I am strong, and I know what I want. He'll give me just what I want if I let him and I refuse to be a wreck about it anymore.

His foot hits the pavement and for whatever reason, all thoughts of my own powerful existence run away in fear and hide as he lifts his beautiful frame out of the car. His blue eyes hit mine and in a second, he's suddenly wearing that look - a darker blue - the look that tells me he's had enough of pussy footing around and he's going to take his control back. It happens in a split second. He was soft, now he's not and as I watch his body move aggressively toward me, I inwardly groan at my thoughts. God, I want him. He could have me this very second, right here on the concrete and I would probably beg for more.

His boots click loudly as he eats up the ground in long strides and gets closer. The wind blows his shirt flush against his skin and I just hold back a moan at the figure of him as it moulds across his chest. I can't breathe as I glance at his hands. Has he seen it in my eyes already? The slight sneer of desire that sweeps across his mouth tells me that he probably has and I feel myself moving quicker toward him.

He halts abruptly four feet away from me and holds his hand up to stop me. I'm so shocked that I still instantly, drop my bag and gaze across at him. He watches me intently for what seems like hours as we stand there in the wind, his hands in his pockets and my hands gripping my coat at the neck as if it will somehow save me from something. His head tilts just slightly.

"Are you ready, Elizabeth?" Am I...? Yes, I am.

"I think so." God, I hope so. Please don't break my heart again.

"This isn't the story of love conquering an addiction. You do know that, don't you? We've only just begun and this will be enduring." Wow, did I think that? I don't know. Jesus, it's a little early for this.

"I think so," I reply as a grip tighter to my coat.

"This is who I want to be. I revel in it and I'll take you further if you trust me," he states with no reservation whatsoever as his eyes give me one last chance to leave if I want to. I know that's what he's trying to tell me and I gulp down an unwelcome gasp of nerves. How far is he talking about?

"I... I don't want you to." I never wanted that. I just needed time.

"Are you sure?" he says as his eyes narrow slightly. "I can't be the man you've had for the last week forever, Elizabeth. Not even for you." I smile and take a breath as I look down at the floor. For the first time he's being himself again and I can't wait to have him back.

"I don't think I liked him much anyway. I think he was holding back," I reply with a smirk and a small chuckle.

His eyebrow arches at my comment as he processes it and then he smiles. It's one of the most glorious things I've ever seen and I can't stop my feet from moving again as he opens his arms and squeezes me into him. His mouth glances under my ear and he breathes me into him. For the first time in a while I feel like the real Alex is holding me again. His hand moves around my neck and squeezes hard as he tilts my head up to him.

"I've got something for you," he says as he pushes me away and reaches into his pocket. His hand opens to reveal my bracelet. "It never left me, not once." He lifts my left hand and places the diamonds carefully around my wrist. "Please don't take it off." I look down at it twinkling in the streetlights and smile as he raises it to his mouth and kisses it.

"Mr. White, are you getting sentimental on me?" I reply as I giggle at him.

"No, I just don't want you to give it back to me again. It's yours and it tells me that you're mine," he says with a wink and a smirk so I grin at him with that *I so love you* look. "Now, are you ready to go?" he asks as he picks up my bag and extends his hand toward the waiting car.

"Yes, where are we going anyway?" I ask as he pulls me to the car. He doesn't respond as he puts me in the car. "Hello, Andrews," I say as I slide in.

"Good morning, ma'am, nice to see you again," he replies in his monotone fashion as he pulls out into the road and starts our journey.

"God, Andrews, I do wish you'd call me Elizabeth or Beth or something. You make me sound like bloody royalty," I snap a little harsher than I intended. His eyebrows raise in the mirror and Alex looks at me with shock. "Well it's stupid, all this ma'am and Sir stuff. Honestly, I think everybody should just loosen up a bit." Where my sudden exasperation has come from, I'm really not sure, but I'm giving it everything and that means being me, too.

"Ma'am, I-"

I cut him off. "No, that's it. It's Elizabeth or nothing at all, I'm afraid." His eyes shoot to Alex's and I watch him look at me with narrowed eyes. "And don't you do that either. You can have me, Alex, anyway you want me, but there are some things that will be on my terms," I say with fire as I stare at him and give him my best *don't piss me off* look. Eventually, he opens his beautiful mouth.

"Feisty," he says with a smirk as he hands me a vanilla latte and picks up what I assume is a double espresso. "Michael, call her whatever she likes."

"Good, nice to meet you, Michael," I reply as I sip and look over at him.

"You too, Elizabeth." I turn back to Alex with a smile. He chuckles at me and shakes his head. First battle won.

"So where to?" I ask as I look at his gorgeous face and sigh dreamily.

"I need to go to the Lake District to see someone and I thought we could stay for the weekend. It's nice up there," he replies as he laces our fingers together and rests his head back to look across at me.

"Who do you need to see?"

"I don't know who she is yet. Her name's Mrs Molly Peters and I'm not sure what she means to me at the moment. That's why we're going." Interesting.

"Are you going to explain that any further because it didn't make a whole lot of sense?" I say as I bring my knees up and snuggle into the seat. God, I'm tired. He reaches into his bag and pulls out a file. "What's that?" He passes it over to me and I open the first page absentmindedly.

"Oh my God, who's that?" I ask as I shift in my seat and stare at him in bewilderment. He hasn't got any family. He told me that, but the woman in this picture looks so much like him it's actually slightly scary. If Alex had a sister, this is what she would look like. She's got the same eyes, the same questioning gaze and I can't quite get over what I'm looking at as I look back at him.

"Quite," he replies with a smile. "That's what we're going to find out."

"When did you...? How did you...? Why haven't you said anything?" I ask in complete confusion. How could he keep something so important from me?

"I didn't know what to think, and I haven't said anything because *you* have been a more pressing requirement to me lately," he says as he pulls me across the seat and onto his lap. I immediately straddle him and gaze at him again.

"Are you okay about it?" I ask as I hold up the picture and look at it next to his face. It really is quite freaky. They could be twins.

"I don't know yet, and with you sitting on my cock, I don't think I really care," he replies as he grabs the picture, throws it to the floor, puts his hands around my backside and yanks me towards him forcefully. "You're talking too much. There are far more appropriate things to do with that mouth of yours so kiss me, Elizabeth, and for fuck's sake mean it this time. You've made me wait long enough." So I do, with everything I've got, knowing that I've given him permission to do whatever he wants again and relishing the thought of it.

By eleven o'clock we're driving down the motorway in a blacked out Audi, heading towards Keswick. Apparently that is where Mrs Molly Peters lives. I find myself gazing out of the window, watching the beautiful scenery whizz past and thinking. The atmosphere on the flight was calm and collected as we talked about varying topics, but I could feel the underlying tension in him. He was nervous and I understood why. What would it be like to find out you potentially had a sister that you didn't know about? Especially when you thought you had no one in your life apart from an arsehole father. I tried to keep the conversation light and breezy. I talked about work and asked him about skiing. He asked me to go to Austria with him on holiday, and I said yes I'd love to, but unfortunately that was the extent of the depth of talking. Does he want me to root deeper? What exactly is he struggling with?

As we pull into a small town and make our way around roundabouts, I realise he's hiding himself away again. He's doing what he does best. To the outside world he'd look like a man in complete control, but to me he looks like a man in pain. Given our conversation this morning about me being ready for him, I have to help him out of this. It's more for me than it is for him. I know he'll be okay if he does this his way, but I won't be. He has to talk to me about this and let me be part of this for him.

"How do you feel?" I blurt out, hoping to surprise him into reacting as I watch his fingers tighten on the wheel.

"Fine," he clips as he continues to manoeuvre his way through the small town streets. I sigh and put my hand on his thigh.

"Alex, you are definitely not fine. Please talk to me. You brought me with you for this so let me help you." His eyebrow quirks up the tiniest bit as he turns onto another duel carriageway smoothly and looks for all the world like he's happy as Larry. But I felt his thigh tighten beneath my fingers. He's absolutely not fine.

"I'm fine," he says again. I'm not having this at all.

"Pull the car over," I say quietly. He keeps on driving. "Alex, I asked you to pull the car over." He still keeps driving. I undo my seat belt and reach for the handle.

"WHAT THE FUCK ARE YOU DOING?" he shouts as he lunges across me and grabs my hand before I get to the handle. I glare at him and shake his hand off.

"So stop the fucking car!" I scream back at him. He quite literally throws the car to the side of the road and slams on the brakes. His hands shake on the steering wheel as he sits there silently, breathing hard, and I suddenly realise that he's fuming with rage. I look across at his face, hoping that he'll turn to me but he doesn't so I get out of the car and take a few calming breaths. *Don't back down, Beth. Just hold on.* Christ, its cold. Where's my coat? Oh, sod it.

I hear the car door open after a few minutes and feel myself stiffen. I have no idea what I'm about to get but I've got to be ready for it. I will not let him shut me out of his feelings. He cannot tell me he loves me and then close himself down on me the moment it gets tough for him.

"What the hell were you going to do? Launch yourself out of the fucking car?" he shouts at me as he rounds the corner and kicks the car, denting it. Shit, he's still angry.

"If that's what it took to get you to talk to me, yes," I reply quietly, refusing to let him wind me up. He kicks the car again and I look at the second dent in amazement.

"Fuck," he says as he stomps off with his hands on his head. I watch him as he finds somewhere to stop and looks into the distance blankly. Where is his head at? What does he need from me?

He's kicking at the ground a little and looking up to the sky now. His hands have returned to his pockets and his stance looks a little more relaxed so I tentatively make my way over to him, hoping he'll open up. He pulls in a long breath as he hears me approaching and looks down at the floor.

"Have you calmed down now?" I ask softly as I gaze at him from a couple of feet away with my hands tightly wrapped around myself.

"Not really," he huffs, but I can hear he has and I smile to myself. God, I love him, every single bit of him.

"I love you," I say tenderly. "Let me in. Tell me how you feel." His head turns to me slowly and the smile that spreads across his mouth is simply breath-taking. He walks toward me, chuckling to himself, and pulls me toward him.

"Say that again," he says as he looks into my eyes with that beautiful smile still firmly in place. Is that all he needed? *God, what an idiot, Beth.*

"I love you, Alex White, and I need you to let me in. I want to know all of you. I want to feel everything with you and if you want me, you're going to have to give that to me because I won't do this any other way," I say as I grip his arms and hope that he understands. He apparently does because that damned eyebrow raises and he sucks in a breath. Before I realise it, his hand is around my neck and he's kissing me with such force that I'm losing all thoughts of sanity. My brain instantly transports me to a bedroom and I'm seriously considering letting him take me right here. He drops my neck and travels his hands down to my backside to hoist me up against him. He's so warm and I feel myself melting into him as my nipples peak against him, losing all thoughts of where we are as his tongue reminds me what it's capable of and his soft lips mould themselves around me. My arse hits the bonnet of the car and he pulls away and travels those lips down my neck as his hands find their way under my jumper and tease my skin with his grip on me. Suddenly I realise what he's doing. He's using sex as a way of getting around this. Little shit. Pushing him away a bit before I completely lose my body to him, I put my mouth to his ear.

"I love you, and you can distract me from this now if you want, but I will ask you again." His body tenses as his kisses on my neck still but he relaxes again with a sigh and looks back into my eyes.

"Spoilsport," is his response as he moves backwards and helps me into the car. "But can we please go somewhere warmer. Your nose is blue and I'll have to remove the disgusting thoughts I was having before I can find the more confusing ones you're asking for again," he continues with a smirk as he walks around the car and gets in. He's got a point because the moment my arse hits the heated seats, I sigh in response and relax back into the comfort of the drive.

"What were they? Your thoughts? The ones you need to remove," I ask as I turn my head towards him. Perhaps some naughtiness will help him open up.

"You have no idea what you make me think of, do you?" he replies as his mouth twitches and he continues staring forward.

"Tell me then."

"When you're ready, I'll show you, Miss Scott."

Oh, okay.

As we approach what can only be described as a stately home of a hotel, I gasp at the stature of the place. It's vast. The ivy that covers

135

the entirety of the outside gently drapes across every window of which there are many and the gardens are manicured to within an inch of their lives. I instantly imagine a lord of the realm and his mistress running through the pathways to their secret liaison in the summerhouse that I've noticed. My eyes follow the line past the small pretty building to find a forest of dense trees spreading as far as I can see. It's as if the hotel is hidden from the rest of the world, just for the special few to enjoy. He pulls the car up to the front and gets out as a man in full red livery walks towards the boot of the car elegantly. He's not rushing. He's probably dealt with hundreds of the Alexander Whites of the world his whole life and he is beyond composed as he smiles quietly and welcomes Alex as Mr. White and then offers me his hand. Clearly before I can take it, Alex moves in front of him with a low rumble of a growl emanating from his chest. I raise an eyebrow at him and slide my hand into his.

"You really don't have to. I'm all yours," I whisper as we walk to the door.

"I absolutely do, Elizabeth, and I will continue to do so," he replies loudly as he follows Mr. Red Livery to the desk.

The dark-haired beauty that sits behind the desk visibly falters as she looks up and sees him and then seems to manage to compose herself as she watches Alex approach. I can't help the snarl that crosses my mouth when I eventually catch her gaze. *Back off, bitch.* Her face pales a bit and I know I've hit my mark successfully, but ever the professional, she slaps her smile back on and turns back to Alex.

"Good afternoon, Mr. White, Miss Scott. Welcome to Battersby Hall. We hope you'll have a pleasant stay," she says as she looks down at her screen and fumbles with the keyboard. Alex chuckles to himself and looks across at me.

"You really don't have to, Elizabeth," he says quietly as he continues his chuckle and rubs his thumb on the back of my hand. The irony is not lost on me and I can't stop the smile that creeps across my face.

"I absolutely do, Mr. White," I reply as he leans across and kisses me. I'm so glad he did that.

"Why don't you go on up? I've got a phone call to make and I'll get all this sorted out," he says as he slides the door card across to Mr. Red Livery and nods his head toward the lift. The man nods in return and carries our bags while extending his hand forward. I smile back at Alex as his gaze lingers on my retreating backside and watch his shaking head as he chuckles again. He's obviously amused himself with his thoughts and I blush at them, knowing exactly where his head's at.

A few minutes later, I'm stood in the most exquisite room I have ever seen. Little man has gone and I'm alone, hesitantly waiting by the doorway because I can't even think about touching something. I'll break it if I do. My clumsiness knows no bounds around places like this and I know instinctively that the best thing to do is stand still and wait. *Bloody ridiculous, Beth. Move your feet, you idiot.*

As I walk around and gently touch everything that glimmers and shimmers in the opulent cream environment, I wander across to the window and sigh at the view that stretches for miles. It really couldn't be lovelier and I hug myself at the warm feeling that swirls around inside me. Could I ask for more? He loves me, I love him and he's whisked me off to an exclusive hotel in the middle of the Lakes for a night of remembering what we're all about. The image of the suspension ropes flashes across my mind and I look towards the ceiling. No hooks up there. *Well that will have to wait then*.

The handle on the door clicks and I smile again. Just knowing that he's behind me seems to bring a comfort back that I hadn't realised I'd lost as I feel my body relax.

His arms curl around my waist as he leans his head on my shoulder and looks out at the view with me. I can't stop my fingers from reaching up to the back of his neck and fiddling with his hair as his lips meet the side of my neck tenderly.

"You're stunning," he says quietly as he nibbles his way up to my ear and slowly turns me round to face him. I sigh with adoration and wrap my arms around him.

"Nice room," I say as I lay my head on his chest and watch the light glinting off one of the four chandeliers. The intricate patterns dancing on the wall behind it remind me of hundreds of diamonds sparkling and I look down at my bracelet, his bracelet. It reminds me of the sign in Pascal's office.

If you don't want to share it, cuff it, on the left with diamonds.

Oh, so he's cuffed me. No wonder Pascal was so interested in my bracelet. I hadn't thought about it that much at the time but now I know, I'm not sure how I feel about it. It's not real though, is it? I mean, not in the real world. Actually, I feel strangely honoured by the accolade. It's a bit like an engagement ring but not. No wonder he thinks of me as his, and to be honest, given his fingers and hands and what they're capable of, I doubt I'll ever be leaving him anyway.

"Alex, where do I go when... You know, when we... I don't know what happens to me when you do that to me?" I ask quietly. I don't even know where that came from but I want it answered so it's as good a time as any. He stands me up and looks at me.

"You want this conversation now?" he asks as his eyebrows shoot up.

"Well yes, I need to understand. If, you know, you said you'd take me further," I reply and move away from him and towards the sofa. He watches me move like a hawk and then sits down opposite me with his hand resting on his chin. His fingers meander across his lips as if he's trying to find the right words to describe what I feel in those moments.

"I don't do it to you. You do it to yourself. It's called subspace, Elizabeth. Some call it drifting," he says as he tilts his head and frowns. "And believe me, you look fucking irresistible in it."

Oh, right, well it has got a name then.

Chapter 8

Alexander

He sat and looked at her with a new hope swelling through his heart. She'd said she was ready and now she was asking questions of him regarding the whole situation. He was so taken aback by the question and the circumstances she was asking it in that he couldn't quite believe what she'd said as he stared at her. Did she really just ask that? He'd been pretty certain he was about get twenty questions about how he was feeling about meeting the apparent family Conner had found for him, but it seemed the tables were turning in his favour for the time being, so he watched her as the information sunk in and wondered where she'd go off to next. He inwardly smiled to himself. He still couldn't gauge her reactions or read what she was thinking at all. In the bedroom, she was so easy to read as she gave him every sign he could imagine, but in the normal world, where they were a couple, she was still a complete enigma to him. He propped his head up with his chin again and waited for her brow to unfurrow. They had a couple of hours to kill before they had to meet Mrs Peters and this was the best way he could think of to pass the time. If she wanted to know then he'd tell her and then show her, happily.

"Right, well, helpful as that is, I still don't know what it means," she said as her big brown eyes looked over at him with a confused expression. They softly flickered as he opened his mouth to speak so he closed them again and licked his lips. She blushed quietly and batted those lashes like a soft, cuddly bunny rabbit, dropping her gaze slightly as she shivered. He smiled and started again.

"When you're put in a position that your body and mind find hard to process, either through pain or the threat of aggression, two chemicals enter your system. Adrenalin will speed up your heart rate and deliver various feelings - anger, slight dizziness or tunnel visions are all common side effects. Your body will use them to help you run and flee the danger. Endorphins act differently. They will flood your body and relax your muscles, mostly to increase your threshold for pain. But they also calm you down so you can think clearly, which will in turn will also help you to run and flee the danger," he said as he watched her pull her knees up and unzip her boots. She threw them over the side of the sofa casually and he couldn't stop the chuckle that rose up through him. She was so perfect.

"Well aren't you the fount of all knowledge? And I suppose that danger is supposed to be you and your hands?" she said sarcastically as she thought up her next question and gazed at him with an adorable pout. "Is that why you tie me up? So I can't flee the danger?"

"You asked, Miss Scott, and no, I restrain you to ensure you relish the feeling and learn to embrace it," he returned as he rose to get something to drink. "I also enjoy watching your sexy as sin body fighting it and writhing in turmoil. That's the bastard in me just playing for fun."

On finding the fridge, he brought back a bottle of wine and two glasses and poured. She had her eyebrow raised as if she hadn't considered his sadistic thoughts when he watched her. She clearly hadn't got a damn clue what she made him think of.

"Why do I feel all drifty in it, like I'm almost watching myself from the outside?"

Christ, he hadn't had one of those for a while. He hadn't any idea that's how far she was going in. The very fact that he hadn't even given her any help in the matter only increased his admiration for her. She was a complete miracle for him and exactly what he needed her to be.

"Different people have different reactions to the chemicals. Some people fight them, some people actually feel quite ill and others just let their body take them wherever they need to be." He shrugged as he handed her the glass and she brought it to her fuckable mouth. Talking about this really wasn't helping him at all as he felt his dick agreeing with him.

"So, will I always go there?"

"Yes, when the reaction's right and if that's what I want to achieve from you." Which he very definitely did at the moment. *Stop it, White. Not enough time.* His face must have betrayed him at some point in that last sentence because her expression changed to one of curiosity as she rose from her seat with that mysterious smile and padded softly across to him.

"What do you want from me?" she asked as she knelt down in front of him and placed her hands on his thighs gently. God, he wanted inside her mouth. Just the sight of her on her knees between his legs was almost enough to make him come. Did she know? She licked her lips and glanced down at his crotch and he smiled when he realised that on some unconscious level she must. She was so in tune with his feelings that he sometimes hated to admit it.

"What do you think I want from you?" he said as he gazed down at her. She slowly stood and started to remove her clothes. He exhaled a breath as her top came off and he drifted his eyes down her body. Fuck, she was a goddess. Every curve was in exactly the right place, her waist dipping in delectably before reaching the divine curve of her hips and as she peeled her jeans down her long legs, he had visions of them wrapped around his neck and growled at her. Her hands reached for his belt and she tugged forcefully, which made his breath change into one of lust as he watched her nimble fingers trying to release his now painful cock from hiding. Once the fly opened, she grabbed at the sides of his jeans and dragged them down his thighs until they were on the floor. Then she slid his footwear off and discarded them over her shoulder with a sexy little smile that made his cock ache even more. Kissing her way slowly back up his legs, she started to undo the buttons on his shirt with her teeth. With each one she bit him gently on the stomach and chest until finally she was inches from his face. She looked into his eyes with an expression that he swore he'd never forget. It was an announcement of a returning woman, the one he'd missed so much.

"Is this what you want, Alex? Is it what you need?" Her mouth hummed around his as she teased him more with her tongue, never quite touching him. He bit at her jaw playfully as she began to make her way back downwards. He tipped his head backward and savoured the feeling as her delicious tongue licked and sucked its way down to his waiting hard on again.

A groan of exquisite pleasure slipped from his mouth as hers closed gently around the sensitive head of him and he moved his hand to the back of her neck to encourage her to take him deeper. She did, beautifully, and as she cupped his balls at the same time, another groan shot from his mouth. Fuck, her mouth was so soft and warm. He really wasn't going to last long at all at this rate. Her hand wrapped itself around him and started to glance softly up and down the length of him with that feather light touch as she mirrored the movement that her mouth was making. His head rush started as she delved deeper with her lips and he felt the back of her throat hitting the top of him over and over again. He couldn't stop the shuddering that hitched his breath at the feel of her. Her hand raked over his stomach as she swirled her tongue around his head and delved back down again.

"Elizabeth, stop," he said raggedly as he gazed down at her with his cock in her mouth. He closed his eyes, trying desperately to stave off the inevitable, but she was too good at it and she knew him too well. She grabbed hold of him harder but removed her mouth and he opened his eyes again to find her watching him intently as her hand moved up and down on him hard. It was eroticism gone mad and he moaned her name as she rolled her thumb across the top of him slowly and then lowered her head again, smiling sinfully as she ran her tongue up his length and swirled around him again. He couldn't do it much longer. It was just too much for him to watch her, and as she dragged her teeth back upwards and then plunged back down again, he reminded himself to never allow her this control this again.

Her mouth and lips tightened around him as she sucked down hard and dragged her teeth back up. He gasped a desperate breath in. Feeling the pit of his stomach buckle under the pressure, he grasped onto her hair and forced her head upwards so he could see her eyes. Fuck, he loved her eyes.

"Watch me," he growled at her as he began to feel his explosion beginning and moved his hand more aggressively, forcing her movement faster and deeper. "Watch what you're doing to me."

Her eyes widened as he panted heavily and felt his throat constricting around her gaze. The intensity of her actions increased as he tightened his grip on her hair and gasped again for air. He raked her head back again and pushed himself into her mouth, just to control the angle if nothing else, but as his legs began to shake, she gripped onto his thigh and dug her nails into him. That stab of pain was enough to force the last bit of control he had away from him and he gave into the eruption that was filling him with torture and sweet release. Only in the last seconds of his coming did he tip his head again and close his eyes as he pumped himself into her throat in violent spurts.

"Fuck, yes..." The sensation was euphoric as he felt her swallowing each mouthful, earth shattering even, and as he opened his eyes to look at her lapping and licking her lips around his spent cock, he found that he simply couldn't move. He was so transfixed on her form as she slowly wandered her lips up his body and eventually kissed him softly that he just sat there and let her do what she pleased. The taste of himself on her mouth made him feel a primal need that he couldn't remember feeling before, so he grabbed her suddenly and flipped her onto the floor, intending to show her exactly what that feeling was, even if he couldn't explain it himself. She squealed in shock but relaxed around him immediately as he continued to kiss her passionately. He felt so desperate to hold her close and feel her wrapped around him that he couldn't think of anything else.

She slowed the kiss quietly and gently pushed at him but he wasn't ready to stop. In fact he'd only just begun. He wanted more and he was damn well going to take it. She pushed harder.

"Alex, we have to get ready," she said into his neck as he bit harshly onto her shoulder and she moaned out in pleasure. "God, Alex, no, this is important," she said as she tried to get up. He smiled into her and moved down to her breasts, licking luxuriously as he went and savouring each mouthful.

"So is this," he replied as he held her wrist down to stop her getting enough purchase to move. She kept squirming, which was just fucking stupid because it just heightened the game for him, so he growled at her as he pushed more of his weight onto her and continued his path over her skin.

"If I have to safeword you, I'm going to be pissed. I refuse to use it unless absolutely necessary," she threatened. He laughed at her response and lifted his hand from her wrist as he clambered reluctantly back up her body to her face. "Thank you," she said as he kissed her softly.

"I just wanted to have some more fun with you," he said as he ran his tongue across her salt-laden lips and groaned at the memory of them around his cock, which was rapidly growing uncomfortable again.

"*You* just wanted to avoid going out, Mr. White, and as wonderful as it would be to have you inside me, I did what I did for you. You can have your own way later," she said with that gorgeous smirk.

"Don't you want to come, Elizabeth? You know it won't take me long. Don't you want to feel my fingers inside you, my tongue? Fuck, I want to bite every inch of you and..." he said as he raised his head to move downward again. She used the split second to roll from underneath him and bolted for the bathroom. He lunged for her and missed, which pissed him off immensely. She slammed the door in his face as he got to the door, and locked it. "Witch," he groaned at the door as he banged his head on it and regrettably resigned himself to the fact that they were indeed going out. Out to deal with feelings that he wasn't in the least bit ready to think about. Having said that, he was less tense than a while ago. Had she done that to him, just for him? Did she understand him that well? Probably. She seemed to feel things even before he did some of the time. He scowled at his own thoughts. How could she understand any of the shit that was in his head? Even he didn't comprehend it most of the time.

"Too slow, Alex. Getting a bit stiff in your old age, I think." She giggled through the door as he heard the shower start.

"You're going to regret this, Elizabeth," he shouted at her as he left for the other bathroom, chastising his own temper tantrum as he went. Christ, he loved her.

"I should hope so," she called back in a relaxed fashion. His eyebrow quirked as he looked back at the door sharply with hunger looming again. He could break it down, he supposed... That could work. Maybe not.

"Down boy," he said softly to himself. "Later."

~

The car was idling across the road from a small, white, detached cottage on a country lane in the middle of nowhere and he looked at her with his head tilted back on the headrest. She watched him carefully all the way here, but hadn't probed him on his feelings again, just let him stew in his own thoughts and find some clarity. He'd

144

realised that the tremendous dick sucking had definitely been a way to calm him and make him feel close to her, to give him that safety net that she seemed to offer, and it had worked because he'd spent the entire journey trying to work out what he wanted to tell her. She didn't know nearly enough about any of this to be comfortable with what could be about to happen, and he cursed himself for not being more open with her. She was so good at helping him. Did she even know how much peace she gave him? The word made him smile. It was a word he thought he'd never use with regard to himself. He gazed over at her and waited for her to turn to him.

"I feel confused, angry and nervous," he said as reached out and brushed his fingers across her cheek. When she eventually turned, she surprised the hell out of him by launching herself onto his lap and straddling him, but he smiled at her as she kissed his nose.

"Can I do anything to help?" she asked with another soft kiss.

"You already are helping," he replied as he tucked her hair behind her ear. "You're here."

She beamed back at him and then looked across at the cottage with a frown.

"Are you ready to go in?" He followed her stare. Was he? Hell if he knew, but there was no going back now.

"I think so," he replied. She kissed him again and giggled as she slid off his lap, grabbing her coat as she opened the door. He got out and met her at the back of the car.

"That was quite cool," she said, still giggling. He quirked his head. What was she talking about? There was fuck all cool about standing out here.

"What?"

"You... thinking so hard. I mean, it's normally me thinking. You're always very definite about things, all like, *Are you ready Elizabeth?* While I'm all, *I think so.* Guess I must be in control at the moment."

He chuckled and felt the pit of his stomach drop. In a way, she absolutely was. Strong, completely commanding her feelings and using every piece of that strength to help him stay focused, and he'd told her nothing about what she might find out in a minute, not given her a single piece of fucking information to let her know how much she meant to him.

145

He had to tell her something, anything.

"Elizabeth, I don't know what I'm going to get in here. This could be anyone. Please tell me that no matter what you hear, you'll wait for me to explain anything you don't understand," he said as they began to walk towards the house. She looked at him with a perplexed expression, that beautiful smile replaced with bewilderment, or perhaps doubt. He sighed. She hadn't got a clue what he was talking about.

"What's that supposed to mean?" He felt his feet shifting and his body tensed. He hadn't told her about his name. He hadn't told her all the details of his father or about his mother's apparent suicide. Shit, what had he done, bringing her here with no information? She took a step closer to him. "Regardless of what happens in there, Alex, I love you. I will always love you." He doubted it immediately but just tried to believe that she'd understand. She had to because he sure has hell wasn't going to lose her again.

"I love you too, more than you could ever know," he said as he got to the door and knocked twice, somehow trying to knock his shaking hand away.

They waited for several minutes before the door hesitantly opened and a small woman answered and stared at him. Her hands suddenly shot to her mouth and she burst into almost hysterical sobbing tears. Alex immediately reared back and looked down at the woman with apprehension as he let go of Elizabeth's hand, thinking that he might have to catch the woman or something. She thankfully sniffed back the tears after a few minutes and looked back up at him.

"Nicholas... My god it's you," she said as she threw her small arms around his waist and hugged him tightly. He didn't know what to do in the slightest and just stood there with his arms out by his side, trying to decide whether he should return the hug or not. Touching had never been his greatest emotional response so eventually he settled for a slight pat on the back. She was obviously distressed and the last thing he needed was her having a heart attack. The fact that she knew his name was a reasonably good start, he supposed. She seemed to compose herself as she took a step back and peeked around his side. He felt his heart clench in fear at the thought of Elizabeth and what the hell she would be thinking as he turned to look at her.

146

"Mrs Peters, this is Elizabeth Scott, my girlfriend," he said as he searched her eyes, hoping to god that it was still the case. She stared back for a moment with a shocked expression and then turned to the small lady.

"Nice to meet you, Mrs Peters," she replied politely with the warmest smile she could find, given her clear confusion. He continued his gaze across at her and silently begged for forgiveness. She didn't deserve to hear this information in this situation. He should have told her before now, and unfortunately her returning gaze wasn't as consoling as he'd hoped for so he sighed and turned back to Mrs Peters.

"Come in, please, come in. Where are my manners?" the woman said as she ushered them with her hands and then wiped her tears again. He ducked to get through the door and followed her through to a small kitchen that looked like it was still stuck firmly in the 1980's. It was immaculate, nonetheless, and she pointed them to chairs. She stared at him again for a moment before moving across to the kettle. "Tea or coffee?" she asked pleasantly as she fiddled about with cupboards.

"Tea, please," they both said in unison. Clearly Elizabeth also hated instant coffee and he smiled at yet another similarity.

They all sat in very uncomfortable silence until the woman placed their tea in front of them and brought over some sugar and milk. Alex glanced around the small space and wondered what he was about to find out. Who was this woman? He pondered reaching for Elizabeth's hand and then decided against it. He seriously didn't know how pissed she was at the moment. Unbelievably, as he dismissed the thought, her hand found his under the table and he looked across at her with a small curve of his mouth. She didn't return it with as much enthusiasm as he would have liked but then she had a right to be slightly irritated with him so he just turned back to the woman again.

"I've been searching for you for so long, I'd almost given up hope," the woman said quietly as she sipped her tea. Alex narrowed his eyes.

"Who do you think I am? And what am I to you?" She looked at him for a minute with a frown and fussed with her wedding ring before she answered.

"I think you're Nicholas Adlin, and if you are then that would make me your aunt, your mother's sister and a horrible, terrible person." His eyebrows shot up at her admission and he grabbed onto Elizabeth's hand tighter as she scooted closer to him. He couldn't speak. His mother didn't have a sister and why the hell was she a terrible person?

"I don't understand. I am Nicholas Adlin but my mother didn't have a sister. I would have found her if she did." He'd searched for years for more family, but eventually he'd just given up. Even Jacobs couldn't find anything remotely plausible.

"I can assure you she did. I dare say your bastard of a father neglected to tell you about my existence. I know he deleted every record of my life and truthfully, I was glad of it. It meant he couldn't find me," his apparent new family member replied with venom lacing her every word. He instantly knew she was telling the truth but struggled to process the information regardless.

"No, he did not, and I'm sure he could have removed your information if he'd wanted to," he seethed quietly, yet another thing to hate the bastard for.

"How did you find me then?" the woman asked quietly.

"It was accidental to a degree. Your daughter works for a friend of mine," he replied as he watched her reaction carefully. Did Evelyn know anything? The woman's hands shot to her face and she jumped up and started pacing the small space. Probably not, then.

"Oh my god, she hasn't met you, has she?" She paced a bit more. "God no, please tell me you haven't told her anything. Oh my, she'd know the instant she saw you. Please tell me you haven't," she begged as her hands came together in prayer stance. He chuckled to himself in derision as he presumed God had nothing to do with any of this. God clearly didn't fucking exist. If he did, he might have stopped the bastard that beat the shit out of him every night for years.

"No, I haven't. I've only seen a picture. I thought I might find out some actual facts before I introduced myself," he said with a lift of his eyebrow and a healthy dose of sarcasm as he crossed his legs.

"Good, oh that's good. Oh my, what on earth am I going to tell her?" the woman replied as she returned to her seat and seemed to calm herself again.

"Well, how about you tell me first and then we'll work it out together. Who is she to me?" he said as he took a drink of the tea. He instantly put the cup down. He hated tea. It tasted like piss and reminded him of the hot scaldings he'd received on a regular basis. The bastard had liked that form of pain.

"She's... She's your sister - well, half-sister," the woman replied as she looked down at her tea.

"You had an affair with my father?" he asked calmly. Her head shot up instantly and she appeared almost furious.

"No, I... Are you still in contact with him? What was your childhood like?" she asked with narrowed eyes that looked familiar for some reason. He shook his head as he realised she wanted to know if the bastard had been a good father. She clearly didn't want to hurt him with information that might not go down well. Sweet as that might have been, it was much too little, far too late.

"Absolutely not, and I have no loyalty to him at all." She tapped the table with her fingers steadily and he smiled at the gesture as he looked at his own hand. Did his mother do that as well? "And my childhood was unpleasant to say the least." She looked immediately upset as she frowned again and put her head down.

"He... He... Evie was... *is* a good thing. I love her very much and I don't want her to know. She thinks Tony is her father."

Elizabeth's hand tensed underneath his and he looked across at her beautiful, tear-filled eyes impassively while he thought of his father. She smiled quietly so he returned to the small woman.

"I doubt we can avoid that, Mrs Peters," he said as he stared at her with a heavy heart and understood. His father was violent. It wasn't a shock that he was also a rapist, but it was saddening nonetheless and his chest constricted at the thought as he looked at the small woman. She returned his gaze for a moment and then seemed to steel herself for another sentence.

"He killed your mother, you know? I couldn't prove it but I know he did," she said angrily as she stood and started pacing again. He watched her hands run through her short blonde hair and glanced over her frame. She wasn't any taller than five two, very petite figure and her clothes were dowdy as if she'd worked manually every day of her life. Would his mother have been the same? He hadn't even seen a picture of her. He knew nothing about her at all. At least he knew where his blue eyes had come from now.

"I assumed that he might have." Elizabeth's hand stiffened again so he rubbed his thumb across it in an effort to comfort himself as much as her. "Why didn't you help her?" he asked casually, taking in a breath quietly. The battle to stay controlled was becoming harder but none of this was the small woman's fault and exploding in front of her wasn't going to help anyone. Quiet and composed White was needed at the moment. He'd deal with the after effects later. If Elizabeth still loved him by the end of this, she'd be there to help him.

"I tried, so he beat me and your mother ruthlessly then raped me repeatedly in front of her. I was seventeen and scared to death. She asked me to take you, to run away but he wouldn't let me go, and then when I eventually got my chance, I just ran. By the time I plucked up the courage to come back, she was dead. I... I didn't even go to the funeral because I was too scared of him. When I found out I was pregnant, I was determined to make the best of it and then I met Tony. He made my life... easier. When Evie was three, I tried to find you again but you'd gone. No one would talk to me for fear of him and so I gave up. The system wasn't the same back then. You couldn't get information easily and with them changing your name, I had very little hope of ever finding you."

He nodded his head as he thought about all the information. He wasn't sure what to think. He tried to process it but knew he couldn't so simply stared back at her with what he was sure was a glazed expression.

"I see," was the only thing he could find to say.

The small woman fidgeted back into her seat and sighed as she looked across at him. He tried for a comforting smile but his heart was chasing itself so rapidly that his mind couldn't catch up so he just continued with his vague stare.

"What's your name now? I assume it's not Mr. Walters from our insurance company," she asked with a raise of her brow. He heard Elizabeth gasp at the look; eyes were clearly his mother's family trait and he instantly thought of Evelyn.

"That's quite scary and a little bit weird," she whispered from his side. He chuckled a little and squeezed her hand lovingly. She wasn't mad. That was a good thing and the thought calmed him a bit as his heart returned to a more careful beat.

"No, it's Alexander White," he said, frowning as he realised the name felt a little strange around his mouth. Nicholas Adlin hadn't been his name for a very long time, but for some reason, in the presence of a family member, it felt a little wrong somehow. He didn't like it in the slightest.

"What do you do, Alex?" the woman asked inquisitively as she removed their cups and boiled the kettle again.

"I run a business - investments and property, that sort of thing." She smiled and nodded in that vacant 'haven't got a clue what you're talking about' way that he so despised about people.

"And you, Miss Scott?" He turned to her to watch her reaction. He'd missed looking at her so gazed at her beauty in the hope of distracting himself from the level of unease that was still coursing through him.

"A catering business. Can I use your loo?" she replied without looking at him. The small woman motioned her toward the hall and told her to go on through. She did and he instantly felt lost without her near him and felt his heartbeat increase again. He scowled at his own weakness.

"Have you been together long?" the woman said as she placed more of the revolting tea on the table. He pulled his gaze from the door regretfully and returned it to her.

"A while, although I'm not sure she'll forgive me when we leave here," he said as he loaded sugar absentmindedly into her cup. She liked sugar; she had lots of sugar in her coffee. He couldn't believe it actually ended up tasting of coffee at all but she loved it so he put another spoon in and stirred, hoping that she liked it in tea.

"She didn't know?"

"No. I should have told her. She does know about my father and the care home but she... she didn't know my name or anything about my mother," he replied as he stared at the table and then glanced toward the door again, Where was she? He could feel his breath tightening at her not being close enough and realised he couldn't do this without her at all. That was clearly why he'd brought her here.

"She loves you then. I wouldn't worry too much. She wouldn't have held your hand through this if she didn't think she'd still be with you tomorrow," the woman said as she smiled and reached for his hand. He watched as it descended in slow motion. Did he move his hand or leave it there? He looked up at the woman as he felt it land on his and stuttered out a breath, struggling to bring another one in. His eyes shot to the door again as he felt what appeared to be panic welling up inside him. He needed her. Where was she? He pulled his hand away from the woman's warm fingers and stood up quickly, barely registering the teacup falling to the floor and liquid spilling across the floor as he barged the table out of his way.

"I need... I need to go outside for a moment," he said as he moved across the kitchen and hurried toward the front door, knocking pictures on the wall as he went. He grabbed for it and lunged outside, slamming it behind him. The first big lungful of air did nothing. The second did little better and he felt himself dropping to his knees, trying desperately to get some air. His hands hit the floor as he tried to stabilise himself before he toppled forward. What was happening?

His vision started to swim in front of him and he sat back on his haunches and grabbed at his chest while sucking in the air he needed. Why couldn't he breathe? Nothing was stopping the sharp pain that was stopping his ribs from expanding so he reached for his throat and clawed at it in the hope that it would help.

He heard the door open behind him and keeled over forward again onto his hands.

"Alex?" she shouted as she dropped down by his side and grasped at his face to turn him toward her. "Alex, what's wrong? Please, Alex," she said as he panted hard and scrabbled with his hands for something, anything. She pushed him upwards somehow and got in front of him, holding his face in her hands. "Baby, I love you. You have to breathe. Calm down and breathe," she said peacefully as she forced his eyes to hers. "Look at me. Look into my eyes and breathe with me."

He felt his hands grab hold of her shoulders as he steadied himself on her and looked at her lips as they opened and closed around her inhale. God, they were beautiful, so soft, so warm and precious. His body started to relax as he looked back into deep brown eyes that blinked gently at him and drew in another lungful as she moved closer. "I love you. You're okay. I've got you. Breathe."

His fingers eased their grip on her as he felt her fingers running through his hair and saw her mouth widening into a smile. Fuck, she was still the most incredible thing he'd ever seen. He moved into her hand and closed his eyes as he pulled in another breath and then looked back at her. She was still smiling and the moon seemed to create a halo around her. He frowned and reached up to her hair, drifting his fingers through the light that bounced around her face as he watched the light illuminate her features with an ethereal glow and sighed. He didn't deserve her, not in the fucking slightest. What he'd put her through tonight was bad enough. If she ever found out the rest, she'd be running for her life.

"Angel," he whispered to himself as his breathing slowed a little more.

"Alex?" she said with a puzzled expression. He watched his fingers find her face and moved them across to her lips. She wetted them before he got there and he drew her forward to him.

"I love you," he said as he pulled her toward his mouth. "I love you. I couldn't breathe without you." She shuddered out a breath and then met his lips. He wrapped her up in his arms and tried to show her everything she meant to him in a single intimate moment as he thought with his tongue. Love, passion, obsession and respect ebbed through him in waves. "Don't leave me again," he said as he pushed her back and gazed at her. Her breaths were now rapid as she flushed, her pupils dilated and her lips trembling with something... Was that love or fear? "I don't want you to leave me again."

She nodded and curled her frame into his shoulder as he held her tight and stroked her hair rhythmically. *Peace...* The thought lingered in his brain as he looked up at the stars and tried to imagine his life without her in it. She'd bought him peace when he'd least expected it or wanted it and now he couldn't even think of her not close to him, with him. *Family...* His mind whirled back to the woman inside and what he should be doing and then he looked back down at her in his arms. *Family...* She was his family. The other woman didn't matter in the slightest because as long as he had her, that was enough.

"Alex?" Her voice drifted up beneath him and he pulled her closer.

"Yes, baby?" he replied as he kissed her hair and wandered his fingers across her shoulder gently.

"My knees hurt." What?

He chuckled as he realised they were kneeling on the gravel and pulled her up with him as he stood. His vision instantly tilted again and he grabbed onto her. "Steady," she said as she righted him and took a step away with a frown. "Are you okay now? What do you want to do?"

Something wasn't right in her face. He could see it. She was almost cold in her gaze, calculated.

What did he want to do? He didn't know. At the moment, he couldn't feel further from *in control* if he tried, and the thought of going back inside was filling him with a dread that he didn't even want to entertain. What the hell had happened a moment ago was beyond unfathomable and he certainly wasn't in any rush to go back in and have it happen again. She was still here. She hadn't run a mile and screamed at him so at least he hadn't completely fucked that bit up, but she was pissed and that was the most important thing to deal with.

"I need to ask her if she has something I want and then we'll go," he said quietly as he looked at the door and brushed the dirt off his trousers. "Are you okay?" She stared at him pensively for a moment and then cuddled her arms around herself.

"Well, given that I've just found out that I know nothing about the man I'm currently dating, and that I was considering giving whoever that man is permission to suspend me from a sodding ceiling or something, I think I'm doing... not too bad actually," she said with a raise of her brow as she nibbled her thumb. He reached for her but she stepped away again. "No, Alex. Not yet," she said sternly. He frowned but nodded his head and walked to the door.

The woman was still sitting in the kitchen where he'd left her, but now she was crying again so he sat down opposite her and passed her his handkerchief.

"I'm so sorry. I didn't know what to do. I'm just so sorry," she said over and over again. He sat for a few more minutes and allowed her to cry it out. There was no way he was bloody touching her again. His angel came in and sat down next to him quietly. He didn't look at her. She was annoyed. He understood the gravity of his fuck up.

"Do you have a picture of my mother?" he asked when the woman eventually stopped weeping. She stood and walked over to the welsh dresser. Pulling out a photo album, she shuffled through some pages, removed a few pictures and then placed them on the table in front of him. He continued to watch the woman as she fiddled nervously again. He didn't want to look at the pictures, not here. He would wait and do that in private.

"She was wonderful," the woman said as she stared at him. "You have her eyes and probably her humour if that sarcasm is anything to go by."

He pocketed the photos and stood up at the thought. He supposed she would know but he wasn't prepared to think any deeper into that.

"Thank you, Mrs Peters," he said as he made his way to the door. She rushed after him and grabbed onto his arm. He stiffened instantly and looked over his shoulder at her. She looked humble and defeated, and he smiled a little and uncurled her fingers from his arm softly.

"Please stay. I've got so much to tell you, to show you. What about Evie?" the woman said fretfully. Elizabeth brushed past him and squeezed his upper arm as she leaned into his ear.

"Be nice, Alex," she whispered as she let go and opened the door. He watched her gorgeous arse go and shook his head. "Goodbye, Mrs Peters. It was lovely meeting you," she called as she stepped into the darkness away from him, again.

"We have to go. I'll call you in a few days when I've decided what to do. Thank you for your help," he said as he pinched the bridge of his nose and started toward the door again.

"Alex, wait," she called. "Please, just a second," she said as she rushed up the stairs. He stared after her and then walked out of the door. He'd wait outside. He could fucking breathe out there.

She hurried back down the stairs and gave him a small wooden box. "It's all I have, but I suppose it's more yours than it is mine," she said quietly as she touched the box and smiled at him.

"Thank you," he replied as he turned for the car. Suddenly something like guilt bit at him and he realised the woman probably felt dreadful regarding her inability to help for all those years. He stopped to look back at her. "It wasn't your fault, Mrs Peters. I don't blame you. I hope you know that. I just... I need time to think about this." She faltered slightly and then smiled again.

"Thank you. That's kind of you to say. And I understand. Just call me when you're ready," she replied. "Goodbye and drive safe." He nodded at her and turned for Elizabeth.

She was leaning on the bonnet, watching him carefully. He wasn't ready to see the steadfastness in her eyes and he hesitated for a second before continuing. She was either leaving him or about to kill him, and at the moment he really hadn't got a fucking clue which. She held out her beautiful hand and he reached into his pocket and threw the keys at her. She nodded and unlocked the car as he gazed at her.

This was going to be a bloody long car ride. Whether they would still be together by the end of it was questionable to say the least.

Chapter 9

Elizabeth

"I'm going for a shower."

That is the first thing that I've uttered since we left. I hurl the keys at the mahogany barley twist sodding expensive table and quite frankly couldn't give a shit if they scratch the hell out of the top of it. He's got enough money; he can pay for it, whoever he is. Bastard!

How dare he take me into that with no warning? Nicholas Adlin? Who the hell is Nicholas Adlin?

Alex is apparently. You'd think that was a pretty important piece of information to tell the woman you say you love, wouldn't you? But it seems in his world I am not relevant enough for him to trust me with his secrets.

I slam the door behind me and lock it firmly then I check it again. It would be just like him to sneak in and disable my anger with sex and it simply isn't going to happen any time soon. Twisting the lever on the shower up, I don't give myself time to think about going back out there to talk to him and immediately rip off my clothes. Heat - that's what I need and lots of it. Cold irritated and disgruntled - that's exactly how I'm feeling and dare I say, indignant.

Stepping into the water, I tip my head back and let the water wash over every piece of me. I scrub at my face with the sponge just to make sure that every one of the tears I nearly shed a thousand times on the journey home are firmly removed from my eyes. My fingers yank at my hair as I try to massage the headache away from my scalp with the lemon shampoo. It doesn't work, but as I continue to let the water fall, some sense of logic starts to wash over me again, even if I am still irked at his behaviour.

What the hell must that have been like for him?

His mother was killed by his father, his aunt was raped by his father, he has a sister and an aunt that he never knew existed and his father has hidden it all from him simply because he must be an arsehole of the greatest proportion. He's probably standing out there in complete turmoil while I'm in here licking my own wounds like a child because he didn't prepare me for any of it. Well, he did a few minutes before we went in, but that wasn't nearly enough and he knew it. I saw it in his eyes the minute she said his real name. I wanted to run at that moment, but when his hand gripped onto me, I couldn't do it, and regardless of how much I disliked him at the time, I simply couldn't leave him to do it on his own. He'd taken me because he needed me and so I gripped back and smiled at him through it all.

When Mrs Peters raised her brow at him, I was completely overcome with emotions for him. He was with his family again and he must have been so overwhelmed by the prospect. The way her face changed around sentences was so much like him, I couldn't take my eyes off of her and every expression had me thinking about his mother and what she must have looked like. Eventually, though, having smiled my way through most of it, I couldn't take the tension in my hands anymore and excused myself to the loo, just for a bit of space to process everything. He'd sat there the entire time with hardly a flicker of emotion or sentiment. It was as if he were treating it as a business meeting. How on earth he wasn't in tears throughout the whole thing was beyond me because I struggled to contain them and it wasn't even my family. I watched him from the corner of my eye throughout their conversation, trying to gauge his reactions and make sure he was okay but his complete lack of enthusiasm or reaction to her emotions was unnerving to say the least. I couldn't make up my mind whether he was hiding his anxiety or if he truly was being completely heartless with the woman.

She was so sweet; I could see it in her every move. She was probably the perfect mother who'd given everything to her child and loved every minute of it. He had made her nervous and uncomfortable and hadn't done a thing to help her feel at ease with the situation, but I suppose he didn't have to. She hadn't lived his life and his early years did not sound pretty in the slightest.

The panic attack had thrown me though, completely. I would never have imagined a man like Alex could even begin to think about how to have one of those let alone crumble to the ground himself. I'd watched my mum have several over the years and had learned how to deal with them, but nothing could have prepared me for seeing him in the middle of one. He'd looked terrified, as if he didn't know what the hell was happening to him and it had taken everything in me to say strong and bring him back to me without falling to pieces myself. Is that what the thought of family does to him? Is the thought that others might love him or need him so incomprehensible, given his bastard of a father, that it reduces him to panic?

I huff at myself as I step out of the shower, shaking my head, and look at myself in the mirror. What the hell do I do now? Regardless of my tantrum, I still love him and he probably has his reasons for not telling me any of it, although what they are, I have no idea. Has he been trying to protect me from something again? Why couldn't he just have talked to me about this so I would have had a clue what I was walking into with him?

I look down at my make-up and start the process of making myself look something like me again. If I am going out there, which I am because I can't stay locked in the bathroom all night, I'm going out there with full war paint on.

He hadn't spoken on the ride back, and at the time, I'd been so angry that I hadn't cared, but now I know he was probably just struggling with his new information and trying to find his way through it. As I pick up my mascara and swipe across my eyelashes a few times, I remember him clutching me and telling me that he couldn't breathe without me. Then I remember him asking me to never leave him again. I lean on the counter and try to work out how I feel. He loves me; this beautiful, complicated man has needed me to be his strength for the afternoon and as I gaze back up at the mirror, I realise he is more than likely still going to need that for the evening, too. This isn't going to simply evaporate for him. Whatever feelings he's having, he'll need to think about them, understand them and finally find a way through them. I gaze across at the door and cross my arms. How would I be feeling if I were him? A bloody mess, probably and very much alone, given his girlfriend's silence.

Rifling through my bag to find a lipstick, I smear it on and gaze at myself again as I drag the brush through my hair. It catches a knot and somehow ignites my brain into gear as I think about his hands on me. The slight pain causes me to remember his need for control. He must feel so out of control at the moment. His world has just been turned inside out and I'm in here feeling sorry for myself and trying to find an explanation for his inability to talk to me. Suddenly I remember the photos of his mother and gasp at the thought of him sitting out there all alone looking into his mother's face. *Stupid Beth. Selfish is so not you.*

I quickly drag the brush through my hair a few more times and then shake my head about in the hope that it might look somewhere close to sexy. Clearly it doesn't but that can't be helped as the hairdryer's in the bedroom and rushing out the door to dry it before I talk to him is just stupid. Pulling in a long breath, I shrug into the cream silk robe and reach for the handle. He needs me so he's going to get me. I have to help him find a way through this new problem he has to deal with. How? I have no idea, but I'll wing it and hope. Whatever happens, I love him and I think he loves me too, so I'll put aside my grievances and hope we can talk about them when he's found his way back to me again.

As I open the door, I find his eyes looking straight at me from the chair by the window. I could almost weep as I see the cold look in them as they stare blankly at me. If I'd ever seen dead eyes, I'd say they'd look like this and I don't like it in the slightest. Where's he gone?

The darkness of the room does nothing to help my sense of foreboding as I take a step forward nervously, although why I'm nervous I don't know because I've done nothing wrong. He's slumped in the chair with a large glass of something dark dangling from his fingers, watching me as if he couldn't care less what move I might make. I glance down to see the pictures of his mother are on the table in front of him at haphazard angles as if he's thrown them there, and the small wooden box is placed on top of them. His hand raises and he tips the whole lot down his throat then reaches down beside him to the bottle that I hadn't seen and refills the glass. His face is more detached than I've ever seen it and I'm suddenly anxious that he might not even want me here. I hadn't thought of that. Maybe he doesn't want my help at all. His demeanour is certainly saying he doesn't care. Or is it? Jesus, if I could just get a slight handle on his emotions, maybe I would have a hope of reading him.

What does he need from me? Does he want to talk? *Probably not, Beth.*

"Good shower?" His voice sarcastically rumbles across at me like crumpled velvet. Okay, he's pissy. That I can deal with.

"Cleansing," I reply with as much sarcasm as I can manage.

"Are you going to leave me now?" he says with no emotion at all. Okay, where the hell did that come from?

"You asked me not to so I won't. You also told me to give you a chance to explain so I will," I reply as I quietly move over to the chair opposite him and hope that talking a little will relax him. I definitely don't need explosive Alex anywhere close to surfacing. He tips the next glass down his throat again and pours two more. I gently pick mine up and sip at it while I watch him brooding in his own anger or frustration. I'm not sure which it is but regardless, it's sexy as hell and my core tightens. Maybe that's the best way to proceed... What the hell am I thinking?

"There's not much left to explain, is there? I think most of it's been said today already." He chuckles to himself and raises his glass again. Before I know what I'm doing, I grab the glass from his hand and put it quietly on the table. He scowls at me instantly but doesn't reach for it again. I am so not doing this with a pissed and drunk Alex.

"How do you feel?" I ask tentatively as I look into his eyes and hope they warm up. He sneers as his head turns sideways and he looks to the floor. What that means I have no idea. It could be one of a hundred emotions. "Do you feel upset or angry?"

"Both," he replies sharply as if that's a stupidly obvious question to ask. Okay, talking is definitely a no. I instantly feel irritated at his tone but realise as his eyes darken that this has to stay on course because it's pretty obvious what he needs by his manner. He wants his control back and it will have nothing to do with love for him at the moment. That's what I came back for, isn't it? I told him I was ready. Perhaps it's time I prove it to him.

"Do you want to feel better again?" I say as I pull the silk from my crossed legs and expose my thigh to him. His eyes don't move from mine but the small twitch of his mouth tells me he's noticed my move.

"I'm not in the mood for pleasant, Elizabeth," he replies with those storm-laden eyes drilling into mine as his fingers tighten on the armrest. My heart increases ten-fold as I begin to understand what I might be letting myself in for. I've seen flashes of those eyes before.

161

There will be nothing nice about what's going to happen next. Hot, more than likely. Nice, definitely not.

"I had assumed that, Alex." Did he honestly think I thought a nice make out session was going to make this alright for him? "Do whatever you feel you need to."

His head tilts to the side as if he's considering his next move. If I didn't know better, I'd think he was questioning himself, but he never does in this role and I know he wants it. Even if he doesn't, I apparently do because my heart rate is in overdrive and I can already feel the tingling between my thighs at the thought of what he might do.

Slowly I reach down and untie the belt on my robe, letting it drape open across my body for him as I watch his eyes, which still haven't moved from mine. I reach over into the glass and take an ice cube from it. If I'm going to do this, I'm going all in and as I glance the cold across my throat, I see his mouth part slightly and I at least know he's interested. I pull the ice down onto my chest and let the cold seep across my breasts. My nipples tighten instantly and I feel the moan leave my mouth breathily as I close my eyes. Letting my head fall back, I think of his hands and what he's about to do with them. Will it be too much for me? I've never seen him so devoid of feeling, never felt his touch when he's been so distant. I hear his breathing change and know he's thinking. It won't be long now. This isn't submissive. He's not in control of this and he won't be able to let me do this for long before he shows me exactly what he wants. I roll the cube down further to my stomach and gasp a little as it hits the top of my thighs. My legs uncross without me thinking about it, as if my core has a mind of its own, and I let go of every nervous feeling I've ever had around him and slide it across my nub. My other hand instinctively reaches for my throat but before it lands, his hand is there. I groan out at the feel of it and open my eyes to see him above me. His eyes are almost black and his neck muscles are taut. His fingers clamp hard around my neck as he pulls me upright and knocks my hand away from between my legs.

"It's not your orgasm to have, Elizabeth, it's mine," he growls as he pushes me backwards and slams me into a wall. I gasp out at his ferocity as he releases my throat and drags the robe off my shoulders with violent tugs. "Undress me," he says as he glares down at me. I stare in shock for a moment before sucking in a breath and reminding myself that he needs me, and that I offered this to him, told him he could have this his way. My hands reach out to him steadily and I can't believe how calm I feel as I gently unbutton his shirt. I can feel him watching my every move as I push it off his shoulders and run my fingers across his chest. He's so stunning that I can't help but put lingering kisses all over his body to try and soothe him as I reach for his belt and feel his heart beating through my lips. Slowly I make my way downwards to push his trousers and pants down to the floor and gasp at the manhood that springs into my face. God, he's perfect, the absolute epitome of masculinity. I gaze up at every rippling muscle and wonder what on earth I've done to deserve such perfection as I kiss my way back up his body.

He reaches to the floor and pulls the belt from his trousers. "Turn around," he says. I do instantly and I feel him wrapping it around my wrists tightly. My instincts make me tug at them but they don't move and my core ignites beneath me as realise how much I want this, how much I want him to do exactly what he wants to do.

He tugs at my wrists and drags me through the hall towards the bedroom. It's uncomfortable to walk sideways and his speed does nothing to alleviate the strain on my shoulders as he pulls me along, seemingly not caring about my comfort in the least.

"None of this will be for you, Elizabeth. It will be for me. You've offered it and I'm going to take it," he says in a monotone voice as he quite literally throws me across the bed. I scramble up as best I can with bound wrists and look at him with wide eyes. There's no anger or love in his movements as he draws in a breath and moves to the doorway without looking at me. "Stay there," he says as he walks away and leaves me kneeling on the bed.

Shit. I have not thought this through properly. I should be excited, and I am to some degree, but for some reason his sudden cool composure has me edgy. There is nothing flirty or fun about this. He doesn't even appear angry anymore, which is disconcerting. I could have dealt with that. I've had angry Alex before. This version is foreign to me, worryingly so.

He wanders back in with the tie from my robe wrapped around his knuckles and a bottle of wine. There's no glasses; clearly we're not drinking then. He moves across to the bed and I flinch a little. I have no idea why but I assume it's because I just don't know what's coming. He grabs hold of my hair sharply and tugs me toward him as he ties it up into a high ponytail. I can't hold the angle and all my weight is on my hair so I move my knees toward him to hold myself upright, but as I think I've got balance again, he pushes me sideways so that I fall. My eyes glance over at his. They're dead. There's nothing in them to read at all.

"Your comfort isn't relevant. You'll deal with any position I choose to put you in," he snarls, his lip curling menacingly as he stares down at me. Oh, that's not good at all. His head tilts at the obvious shock on my face but other than that there is still no expression to define as I gaze into his unblinking eyes. Where has his beautiful smile gone? His lips are hard and flat as he continues to watch me. A vision of a hunter pointing a gun at a deer flashes through my mind and I gasp at the thought and let my eyes drift downward again, away from him.

"Better," he says quietly as he sits on the bed next to my legs and wanders his fingers across my ankles. I pull them away sharply and scurry my knees up to my chest, suddenly feeling the need to hide from him. His hands grab at me with such force that it actually hurts as he drags them back down and starts to turn me. I struggle against him as the beginnings of panic start to surge through me. I know it's stupid because I do trust him but I can't help it at the moment; he just seems so far away. I know my safe word. I know he'll listen if I use it. I *hope* he'll listen if I use it. Within seconds, his knee is forcing downwards into the middle of my back painfully and his hand is on the back of my head. It doesn't matter that I'm struggling because I haven't got a hope and he knows it. As my face hits the bed, I realise that this is what he wants. He's being overly aggressive in his touch; his demeanour is distant and cold. It's as if he wants to forget his feelings about me and just be what he is.

"Are you finished?" he says into my ear as removes his knee and increases the pressure of his hand. I can feel him wrapping my ponytail around his wrist as if ready to yank me towards him so I relax my whole body and drop onto the mattress, deadweight. His grunt of approval tells me he's happy with my response and I instantly get the feeling communication will be kept at a minimum.

Still holding my hair, I feel his other hand land on my calf and travel its way up my leg as his knee pushes between my thighs to open me up. His mouth starts to lick and bite at my shoulder and I can't stop the moan that escapes from my mouth at his touch. I close my eyes and turn my face to the side to get some air. *Just feel, Beth.* His touch is softer now. It's still aggressive but more relaxed somehow and I begin to feel my core tightening again. His hand finds its way between my legs and he thrusts what feels like three fingers straight in with ease. I'm panting within seconds and I sense wetness dripping from me as his fingers twist and turn, opening me roughly while not giving me chance to move away from him. He releases my hair and pushes his hand underneath my stomach toward my aching nub. His fingers find it and start to circle. He increases the pressure to the point of lifting me away from the mattress and my hips rise away so that my arse is in the air.

I feel exposed and vulnerable instantly but as he rams his fingers into me repeatedly, I know I'm going to explode soon. The feeling is torture and bliss rolled into one and my legs start to tremble beneath me. His fingers leave me the second he senses them trembling and he grabs my chin and hauls me up to him.

"I'm not ready for that yet," he growls at me as he drops his hand to my throat and kisses my neck, dragging his teeth and digging his fingers sharply into my hipbone. I watch as he tosses the robe tie in front of me and he continues with his biting, sliding his fingers back inside me. I instantly start the trembling again.

"Do. Not. Come," he warns. His voice is laced with hostility and it's enough for me to back off from the feeling that's bubbling away between my legs. He reaches forward and ties the sash around my neck tightly and with a sharp tug, pulls the dangling end of the tie across to my leg. He wraps it twice around my knee and then draws hard on it. My head and neck are instantly forced toward my knee and down into the mattress again as it drags on my neck and causes me to moan in pleasure. I honestly can't believe the feeling of restraint in this manner is so erotic but my aching core tells me otherwise as it begins to pulse at me again and heat travels across my skin.

"Do you want to be fucked now?" he says as his tongue swipes the full length of my quivering lips. *Oh god, yes.* "You taste like you do," he mumbles and then his hand hits me hard across my arse. I yelp

165

out and turn my head a little to see him. His eyebrow raises but that's all, and then he delivers another one. The pain is intense. There is nothing soft or sensuous about it so I close my eyes again and wait for the next, but as I do, I feel the quiet place calling me and let it wash over me. The next smack lands on my thigh and doesn't hurt as much, but the tingle is exquisite and seems to highlight my groin again. I suddenly feel like I can't breathe and try to move my head, but he pulls on the sash again and wrenches my head around and down further. The pressure on my throat is pure ecstasy and I moan into the mattress as pain and pleasure combine into a mixture of sheer unadulterated bliss.

"Alex, please..." I'm begging. I'm so desperate to have him inside me now that I can feel my inner muscles contracting of their own free will as if they're trying to entice him in. His hand comes down again on me and I feel the buzz in my core. I'm going to come. "I... Please..." I can't think anymore. All I know is that I'm about to come from nothing more than being bound and slapped and the ache is so bad that its persistent throb is agony.

"Don't you fucking dare." He growls as he delivers another one and yanks the sash again viciously. That's all it takes for me to start.

"I... I can't... I..." The feeling of delirium is coming at me so fast I haven't got a chance to hold it back anymore, and I let it go with full force as I tense every piece of myself and embrace the stars alighting. Teeth suddenly sink into my ribs and I gasp in a breath at the sharp pain, so quickly that the stars retreat and the haze of my impending orgasm clears. His soothing tongue licks away at the pain and before I know it, there is no pain at all and I'm drifty and peaceful again. The sash from my knee is unexpectedly released and he pushes me forward. I smile into the pillow as I hit it off balance and realise that this is his control. This is what he wants from me and he can have it all because I have never felt nearer to paradise in my life.

"You will fucking wait until I'm ready," he says angrily from above me as I fidget with my bound wrists. I can hardly feel my fingers and the pressure on my shoulders is becoming unbearable but his forceful hand between my shoulder blades soon redirects my focus as he pushes me downwards. He'll do it now. He's ready, I can sense it in his voice. His composure is slipping and his breathing is ragged. It's the sexiest thing I've ever heard and I try to clamp my thighs together to stop the oncoming bliss that's travelling through me in anticipation again.

His cock rubs across me once and I lift my hips eagerly to meet him while groaning at the thought of him stretching me. He withdraws instantly so I smile again and adjust my balance a little in readiness. Relaxing my hips away from him, I pull in a breath and wait as his hand draws down my back until he rests it on my hip bone and grabs at my throat with the other one. *Yes, more...*

"I want you inside me," I pant with rapid breaths. "Please, fuck me. Please."

"I don't care what you want," he says as he tightens his fingers and pulls me upwards to bite my neck. I moan out a breath and turn my head to him, licking my lips and searching for his mouth. God, I want to taste him.

"Yes, you do," I reply as I swipe out my tongue to his lips. He bites at it and then sucks it into his mouth with delicious swirls of his own tongue then releases it and sneers at me.

"No, I really fucking don't," he says as he shoves me back down and then spread my legs wider. I grunt out as he pushes me around until he's happy with my position and then rubs himself leisurely around me again. "But I am going to fuck you," he says as he thrusts himself in so hard that it takes my breath away and forces me towards the headboard. He pulls out and does it again, even deeper. "And it's going to hurt you. I want it to hurt you."

I cry out as I hear him growl behind me and groan again at the depth of his thrust in me. He feels agonisingly big, and as he rams back in again, I feel his hand reaching toward my throat again. That's all I'm going to need. I can feel it building with every stroke, and when his fingers connect, I know what will happen. I'm counting on it with every beat of my heart.

"Yes..." I hiss out at him as I grind back and he continues to pound slowly into me. He stills and leans over me.

"If I have to, I'll use your mouth instead. Don't move again until you're told," he snarls as he pulls out again and then slams back into me.

His pace is suddenly fierce and I haven't got a hope of holding back as he starts to voice his pleasure and shows me how close he is. His movements are so flawless that I start trembling before I can stop it. Every thrust that hits me sends jolts of pleasure up my spine and straight to my core, igniting the bliss that's coming, and every drag back fuels the stars that are beckoning.

"Oh god, yes," I cry out as he continues and grabs my throat. I lift my head and let him have it. I want his hand there. I need it so badly I'm screaming for it.

"More, give me more," he shouts as he squeezes his hand and slams in over and over again. The bright lights take hold of me and I begin to spiral. "Down, Elizabeth," he pants. I bury my head into the pillow and raise my hips up for him as he pushes his hand into the back of my neck and holds me there. He continues with power and a fevered pace, punishing me with every luscious stroke that hits me so deep. My orgasm takes me so hard that I shudder everywhere and groan as my core tightens around him and moan at the feel of him swelling inside me. My skin alights with quivering and my legs go lax, but his relentless grip on my hip keeps me aloft as he groans and starts his release.

"Fuck, yes." He growls as I feel him coming violently inside me. He pulses and floods me with warmth as he pours himself into me. "Christ, fuck." He grunts as he slows his movements and drops his weight down on top of me.

My shaking subsides slightly as I float in a sea of rolling waves of pleasure. I feel him wrenching at my wrists and realise he's undoing the belt that I'd forgotten was there. He throws it to the floor, chuckling to himself and I smile into the pillow, knowing that I've got him back again. That small chuckle is enough for me to sense his return and I sigh beneath him. Warm fingers travel the length of my side while he shifts his weight to settle between my legs again, kissing my lower back relaxingly and rubbing some much needed life back into my wrists. Whether it's for me or him I'm not sure, but as I calm myself and hold on to the delicious feeling crawling across my skin, I begin to understand the nature of him a little more clearly and tell myself to give it more thought at another time. Whoever and whatever he is, or whatever that was, it's mine now and I'll work him out someday.

"I'm hungry," he says out of the blue with his normal voice. I crane my head around to look at him. He's wearing his usual post-coital half cocky grin as he bites my back playfully and wanders his fingers along my skin gracefully. Malicious Alex has clearly left the building.

"I'm not doing that again. You'll have to wait," I reply with a raise of my brow. I couldn't find the energy if I tried. His returning smirk is almost enough to make me cry with love and I gaze at him quietly. That's the man I love. He shifts abruptly and rolls me onto my back with frightening ease as he crawls up me and rests an elbow by my head, his other hand instantly returning to between my legs and gently dipping inside me. My back arches straight into his hand without any help from me, clearly ready for round two whenever he requests it.

"I meant for food actually. You've satisfied my other appetite quite effectively for now. Having said that," he says as he draws his fingers up my body towards my mouth, "I'll be happy to watch you eat this first."

My lips part as he places his fingers into my mouth, dripping velvety liquid into it as he does so and swirling them around my tongue. The taste is divine, salty, sweet, musky. Him and me, together, beautiful yet almost dirty, or perhaps filthy is a better explanation. Whatever it is, I definitely want more because my lips reach forward again as he pulls them away and puts them in his own mouth. "That's the taste of sin, Elizabeth. You'll find pain always tastes better," he says as he pops them out nonchalantly and reaches across to the bottle of wine. "Drink?"

I open my mouth and he gently pours the crisp cold liquid in. Guzzling it down greedily, I watch him as his eyes crinkle softly and he smiles. The light blue has seeped back in now and as he takes a long drink himself, I gaze at his throat swallowing. It goes straight to my groin and I moan to myself. Perhaps I have got another one in me.

"More?" he asks as he inclines the bottle with a devilish grin. He's so not talking about the wine and my eyes narrow as memories of his secrets eventually come back into my brain through the mist of the sex.

"I'm still pissed with you. You do know that, don't you?" His returning smirk does nothing to help with my irritation as he leans in to kiss me again. As much as I feel like turning away, I don't because his lips are far too tempting.

His weight is suddenly off me as he gets off the bed and stretches his neck from side to side. I groan at the vision of his arse and tattooed back walking away from me and roll over. It reminds me to ask him about the damn number again. Perhaps now is not the best time, though, given that I've only just gotten the reasonable version of him back. He throws his shirt at me and slaps my backside, so I yelp out. I have no idea why considering the ferocity of the slaps that happened mid whatever that session was.

"Get up. I'll order some food," he says as he saunters out of the room, pulling his jeans up as he goes. I roll back over and pull his shirt around me. It smells divine and I inhale deeply as I cross to the en-suite, thinking about the conversation that's coming. Do I even want to have it? How much do I really care? I know the information now. Is there any reason to rehash it with him and stir up bad feeling when he's clearly found his way out of his fog? Perhaps I'm more intrigued with what else there is lurking in his depths. What I do know is that I don't want to feel exposed with no readiness for some other situation that he might put me in.

I walk into the lounge and sit on the sofa beside him, trying hard not to let his chest distract me from my thoughts. Frankly, I could forget the whole thing and drag him back to that bed again. His head turns toward me and he runs a finger along my jaw as he smiles and leans his head back.

"What else are you hiding from me?" I ask quietly as I search for some answers from him.

"I'm not purposely hiding anything from you. If you ask me a question directly, I'll never lie to you," he replies with a mischievous grin. Ah, there's Mr. White again, great deflection.

"Alex, that isn't a fair response and you know it. How do I get answers from you when I don't know the questions yet?" His grin continues as he quite effectively infers my point precisely.

"Yes, I suppose that's quite a problem for you." I turn away from him in exasperation. What the hell am I supposed to do with that?

"Still not fair," I reply with a pout. He sighs and pulls my chin back around to face him again.

"Elizabeth, I've done some atrocious things in my life, most of which I have no regret about in the slightest. I know I am absolutely undeserving of your affection, let alone your love, and if you think I'm going to offer up my history on a platter for you to dissect then you're sorely mistaken. But if you ask me then I will answer honestly." His eyes tell me he means it and for the time being I feel mollified but that doesn't mean I feel happy about it at all.

"I didn't even know your name," I say in a small voice as I gaze at him.

"Yes, you did. Nicholas Adlin was weak and pathetic. You wouldn't have liked him at all and neither did I. I haven't been him for a very long time." His voice is suddenly clipped and short and I sense the agitation building again.

"Alex, if you put me in a situation where I'm not forewarned again, I can promise you I won't be so compliant next time."

He sighs and shakes his head as he turns back to me. "I should have told you. I left it too late and then I didn't know how to phrase it or deal with it. I am sorry for that. It was wrong of me but you have to understand that this is as new for me as it is for you in some ways."

Right, well, at least he's apologized. A sharp knock on the door breaks me from my thoughts as he gets up and wanders toward it. I can't stop my face from following his frame moving along elegantly. The swing of his gait is purposeful and yet oh so casual. How does he pull that off? My eyes first hit the young serving girl who's pushing the trolley in. Her face immediately beams at him in a seductive manner and I roll my eyes and giggle to myself. Frankly, it's getting boring watching them fall at his feet. Knowing I do it myself is ridiculous enough. I watch him extend his hand to the room and notice him staring at me.

"What?" he asks without removing his eyes from me. The girl faffs around and puts the silver covered platters on the table while blatantly trying to catch his eye again. Thankfully he's not looking so I smile at him.

"It appears I'm not the only one who's interested, Mr. White." She instantly looks at the floor and hurries toward the door. "Perhaps she'd like to join us. You never know what kink she's into. Do we have any whips with us this evening? I think I have some buttplugs dotted about." Her face shoots to mine as it turns the colour of beetroot. His raised eyebrow and questioning gaze have me amused but I don't change my serious face in the slightest.

"No, not for this weekend, Elizabeth," he says with a chuckle as he passes the girl a bundle of notes, dismisses her with a wave of his hand and heads towards me with a smirk on his handsome face.

"And what do you know about buttplugs, Miss Scott?" he asks as the door closes.

"Absolutely nothing at all," is my giggling response because I may have heard of them but never would I entertain the idea. His licking of lips has me assuming he knows exactly what they're used for and probably has plenty of experience in the matter.

"Then that was naughty," he says as he holds out his hand. I take it and he pulls me over to him.

"Good tutor." I smirk in return.

"Good student," he replies with a wicked grin. I so love that smile. "Who needs some lessons in anal manipulation by the sounds of it." My eyes widen at the thought as he squeezes my backside softly and draws leisurely circles around the cheek. "I could always invite her back in and let you try it on someone else first."

If my eyes were wide before, they're now damn near jumping out of my head. Did he just say that? And the seriousness of his face is quite disconcerting to be honest. Oh my god, I don't even know how to reply to that. My mouth opens and then closes again in disbelief. Is that what he really wants? My eyes flick to the door and then back to him. He suddenly widens his mouth into one of those glorious panty-dropping smiles in amusement. He's fucking laughing again. Arsehole.

"Bastard. It's bloody ridiculous. All this salivating over you is quite disturbing," I say as he pinches my backside. "Ouch, and talking of salivating, what's for dinner?" He crosses to the table, towing me behind him and abruptly turns back.

"Did I hurt you?" His face is suddenly deadly serious again and I move back a step.

"Don't be stupid. You've pinched my arse a hundred times, I always say ouch. It's just the shock." What a bizarre question.

"I didn't mean just now. I meant earlier," he replies with a frown as he glances at the bedroom. Oh, right.

"No," I reply instantly as I reach for his mouth with mine. It was painful but it was bliss. How can that be described as hurt? He turns back to the table with a sad smile. "Hey, why the sad face?" I say as I catch it in my hands and spin him toward me again.

"I don't know. It's just... Being with someone I care about and being like that, I..." He's stuttering? Oh my god, he can't find the words, which of course starts me off with a shit eating grin at his confusion.

"Well, I'm glad you're confused about it. I'm constantly baffled about all of it. And of course you yourself are a complete enigma, Mr. White, so imagine how I feel. At least you know what you're doing," I reply as I step up to the table. "Now what's for dinner? I'm starving." After shaking his head and chuckling, he lifts the lids on the trays and I look down and then across at him in utter amazement.

"Dinner madam?" He smiles.

"That looks a lot like posh fish and chips," I exclaim with my hands clasped to my lips.

"That it does. I'm afraid I couldn't get fat soaked wrappers and plastic forks, though, so it's only half naughty. We'll make up for the other half later." Oh god, that is so sweet.

"You remembered?" I say as I think of Rome. His eyebrow lifts as he picks up a chip and puts it in my apparently open mouth.

"I remember everything about you, baby. I've never taken a woman to a high-end restaurant and had them tell me they'd have preferred fish and chips before. The moment is etched quite firmly in my mind. In fact, I've had some quite explicit images of your body and greasy fingers ever since," he says as he takes one for himself.

"Wow, that's... impressive, and actually a little bit tormenting," I reply with the biggest grin I have. This is what love is - remembering the little things. Good lord, he's good.

"Mmm," he mouths as he picks up the plates expertly. He even looks good holding plates, for God's sake. "Now, table or knees?" he asks as he juggles the plates to one arm, waiter style, and picks up the napkins and cutlery.

"Carpet, and we must have a crappy movie - something funny, and when on earth were you a waiter?" He chuckles and moves across to the lounge area. I follow him quickly.

"I had to earn my keep to stay with Giuseppe's family. Sixty hour weeks were the norm. I can also make a mean cocktail. Get the blanket." I do and lay it out on the floor in front of the hyper modern flat screen with a smile. "Want to know something else?" he continues as he places the food down.

"Always." Information is always good.

"A month after trying to steal that apple from their kitchen, his mother made me stand by her side in the kitchen and make an apple pie. She glared at me the entire time and spoke so fast in Italian that I didn't understand a word, but each time she smacked my hands with her spatula, I learned a very valuable lesson,"

"Which was?"

"Watch extremely carefully and learn, and under no circumstances put your fingers in a hot pie." He chuckles at the memory and then his eyes light up. "She also taught me to throw knives," he says as he picks up a steak-knife sharp end first and points it at a canvas picture on the wall of a woman. "Necklace." He launches it at the wall and it amazingly lands in the middle of the red heart pendant on a chain around her neck.

"Wow, that's extraordinary," I say as my gaze lingers on the heart around her neck. Could he have aimed it anywhere else? Please. "I hope it's not a metaphor." His gaze drops from the picture to mine instantly and he crawls across to me and kisses my nose.

"If it is, it was my thought and therefore my heart. You're right in the middle of it, Elizabeth, and I wouldn't want you anywhere else." Okay, that's all kinds of lovely and so not what I expected.

"Sweet," I reply sarcastically as I reach around him for another chip.

"Yes, even I'm amused by my own statements lately," he says as he moves back to his own food thoughtfully. "Did it get me off the hook for being such an arse?" His sexy chuckle is almost infectious, almost.

"Absolutely not. You'll have to give me more for my forgiveness."

"More of what?" he says devilishly with a twinkle of lust forming.

"Information," I reply as I bite into my fish. "Sex will not get you out of this."

"What do you want to know?" he says casually as if it's the most normal thing in the world for him to tell me everything about himself.

"Where did you go earlier?" I ask without skipping a beat. Quick fire is definitely the way forward with him. He instantly stills his chip to mouth movement and hovers for a second.

"That's difficult to explain." His brow furrows as he dips it in his red sauce and pops it into his delicious mouth, so trying to deflect. I can't help watching his mouth though.

"Try." *Stop looking at his mouth, Beth.* I do and gaze at his eyes instead. They're still as captivating as ever and I smile at own absurd reaction to him as I watch his brain ticking over. Thirty minutes ago I was bound and slapped, and now we're having a normal conversation over fish and chips in what is probably a thousand pound a night suite on a blanket on the floor. Well, not a normal conversation, obviously. He abruptly wipes his hands on his napkin and sits up straighter.

"I have managed my life to a degree without feelings being involved. Emotions are debilitating for me so I try to stay focused on anything but them. If I am emotional and I become that way inclined, I disregard them immediately. It's the only way I can stay in control of the world around me. Dominance, for me, is about being decisive and resolute. Unfortunately, if my feelings become involved, I can't think clearly enough and therefore I am no longer dominant in my nature, which is most definitely not the point." His brow furrows again for a second as if he's searching for something. "I suppose the act of domination in itself tends to direct my focus elsewhere, which in turn enables me to organise my mind effectively again, and subsequently controls my emotions."

Oh bloody hell, could that have been any more complicated?

"Well that's psychology at its best," I reply with a frown as I nibble on a chip. I'm really not sure I understand any of it, so what I'm supposed to say is anyone's guess. I think I've memorised the statement so I'll have a think about it later.

"Is that all you want?" he replies as he returns to his chips as if he's just told me about *Little Bo Peep* or something equally mundane. I still can't stop watching his hands as he sucks at his fingers.

"Well, you don't always act like that, so what made tonight different? I've never been with you when you've been so..." What was he? Foreign? Cold? Scary?

"Removed? Distant? Disconnected?" he cuts in as he shuffles forward and pulls my hand directly to his heart. Within seconds he's shifted me onto his lap and wrapped an arm around me. I don't know how to describe him. I lost him to a place that is apparently okay for

175

him, but for me it was unknown, intimidating even. Yes, still hot, but nervously so.

"Unfamiliar… You were unnerving and cold, like you didn't want to acknowledge me, like I couldn't give you enough or something," I reply quietly. He nudges my head into his neck with his chin and traces patterns on my arm soothingly. He's also not answering, which can only lead me to believe that was the intention in the first place. Why would he want to remove himself from me?

"I'd like you to help me with something, if you could," he says eventually in a soft voice. I have no idea what on earth I could help him with.

"Okay," I reply with bated breath. It's unlikely I can assist him with anything, but if I can then I obviously will. Who wouldn't do anything for the man?

"I have a meeting next Thursday that I'd like you to attend with me, if you can."

"Okay…" I still have no idea what he's talking about but I'll go. Shit! I have a busy day on Thursday. "Oh, wait, what time?"

"Six thirty," he says as he moves his hand to my head and twirls my hair. Oh, that's nice.

"Oh, that's fine then, great. Would you like to volunteer more information about the meeting?" I'm now intrigued.

"Not particularly," he whispers as he moves back and tips my chin up to him then frowns. Shit, have I got red sauce on my face? "Do you know I've hardly had to tell you to keep your head up at all? Are you finally believing in yourself?"

"Good teacher," I say as I gaze at him and smile. He really is. For all his versions and fuck ups, he gave me this strength, whether he meant to or not, and through joy or pain, I am stronger because of him.

"No, Elizabeth, I simply showed you the way. You've found the destination all by yourself," he replies with his mouth mere inches from mine, soft lips reaching for mine quietly as he nips and then sucks in my bottom lip. "You are more than I could ever be. You are truly astounding and you have already surpassed any expectation I ever had of you," he continues as he lowers me toward the floor. Oh right, we're going there again then? Yes, please. I fold my hands around his neck and bring him down to me, his eyes light blue with a hint of darkening that makes his intentions clear as he picks at the top button of my shirt.

"Stay with me this time," I say as I lean my head back and sigh at the feel of his weight on me again. Please stay with me. Make love to me. Hold me close.

"Try as I might, I never left you last time, regardless of what you might have felt at the time," is his response as he makes his way down my body and nudges my legs apart. "If I say your name, baby, you'll know I'm still there with you."

I breathe out a sigh of relief as he splays his hands under my back and lifts my chest up to him. My back arches and with one swipe of his tongue over my already hard nipple, I'm begging... again.

Chapter 10

Elizabeth

After my mum's usual three course, Sunday-on-a-Monday lunch with all the trimmings and a good few glasses of wine, Belle and I are making our way back to London in the peeing down rain in her car, trying not to talk about the fact that mum looks ill. She wouldn't talk about it and she refused to even hear of us helping her out in the kitchen, but we could both see it. I especially noticed the way Dad was fussing around after her and then he did the washing up. That did it for me. The last time he did anything remotely domesticated was when she had her mastectomy.

Shit.

I've been trying very hard to think about my wonderful weekend to take my mind off it. Obviously it had its complications but it was still fantastic. I've never felt closer to him. Saturday night and Sunday morning were spent making love, giggling and running around naked. After the first round of confusing Alex, he turned into a genuinely open and expressive version of himself, still brutal but happily so and he even surprised me by telling me some more about his childhood. Vile as most of it was, I still appreciated him opening up to me about it. If I ever meet his father, I will not be able to contain my rage and will more than likely explode at him.

We both looked at the pictures of his mother. I gasped in shock at the similarity while he quietly studied her face with no obvious expression. It was clear to see where he'd gotten his eyes and mouth. The young woman was beautiful, and her long blonde hair and blue eyes dazzled me even from the photo. Her smile was captivating. It had a serene quality that made you feel at peace with yourself somehow and it struck me at the time that I hadn't seen that smile from Alex. Hints of it maybe, the slight tilt that encourages true happiness, and yet his mouth was so similar to hers that I knew he should be capable of the full-blown version.

Does he have any peace in him at all? His height, build and dark hair clearly come from his father and there's also a hint of something around his eyes that doesn't belong to his mother. I only ever see it when he's angry or frustrated but it's definitely there, lurking, waiting for the storm to brew up. Is that where he gets his anger from? If it is then his father probably put it there with his abuse. Bastard.

"So what do you think?" Belle's voice lifts me from my memories. "Do you think it's back?" I turn to look at her as she grips the steering wheel as if she's going to rip it off at any second. She probably is, knowing her.

"Oh God, I hope not. I'm not sure she can go through it again. She was such a mess last time and Dad definitely can't deal with it. Did you see him washing up?"

"Yep, it's not good, is it?" She's making a statement and I don't answer her as I turn back to watch the road with sadness rolling across me again. Mum will never make it again. She barely made it the last time.

Cars whizz past us at a rate of knots as if they're all desperate to beat the London rush hour. I don't know why they bother. London is always in rush hour. It never stops, aside from early Sunday mornings when at least a few people try for a lie in. A small white car sidles up beside us and I notice the little boy in the back. He turns towards me and gazes across. I can't help but think of Alex as his blue eyes twinkle at me and his little tongue pokes out. I poke mine out and giggle at him but inside I'm crying. Did he ever smile as a boy? Did he even know what a genuine smile was or how it felt to be happy? Does he even know now, as a grown man? It's suddenly my mission to make sure he does.

"Are we going home or to a bar? It's only five but I think I could do with a drink, preferably four," Belle asks as we hit the outskirts.

"Where's Conner today?" I ask quickly. She looks across at me in confusion.

"And that's of any significance because...?"

"Well, Alex is around and I thought it might be nice to all have a drink together, and as you never went with the *wind up Conner by seeing someone else* method, I assume everything's okay again. Maybe we should just call them and see if they're about. I'd really like if you and Alex could get on again." She looks at me with narrowed eyes and then shakes her head at herself. She doesn't like him. I get it. But honestly, she's the one who pushed me back, well maybe a little, actually not at all, but she did say he was good for me, sort of.

"Oh right, yes, he's at the office today so he'll probably be up for it. Text him for me," she says as she throws me her phone. I do. The responding beep within a minute tells me it's from him. "Open it up, see what he said." I do and instantly gasp.

"I'm not even thinking about reading that out loud, Belle. It's revolting. Needless to say, he'll meet us at INK if we want at seven thirty." She laughs at me.

"I assume you didn't tell him it was you then? He likes phone sex. It's his thing. Go on read it to me." I'm sure my face is beetroot red as I glance down at the words again.

"He says he wants to... Well, it's to do with dildos and his big..." I can't finish it as I watch her dissolving into fits of hysterics beside me.

"You, young lady, cannot seriously be embarrassed about that with all the shit you're currently up to with Mr. White, and text him anyway, I need to know where to go. I don't even think INK is open at this time of day," she says through her giggles. I'm also now chuckling to myself at the thought of my mortification. It is a bit ridiculous.

I pick up my phone and text.

- **Hey, do you fancy a drink with Conner and Belle at seven ish? x**
The response is pretty quick.
- **Where?**
- **We're coming into London now. Is INK open yet? x**
- **It is for you. Gate access for parking 11324453. Press 9113427745 on the back door key pad. Once you're in, release the alarm with Meritato27.**
- **Wow, that's a lot of numbers x**
- **I'll get there as soon as I can. Help yourselves. Music's behind the bar, fourth button on the top panel.**
- **Thank you, Mr. White. x**
- **You're very welcome, Miss Scott.**

"We're going to INK apparently. He's given me a shit load of access codes to get in," I say to Belle as she turns into Kensington. I look up to see where we are and smile.

"Free admission to the bar? Well fucking fantastic. Ooh isn't this where Alex lives?" she says as she scans the houses with the eyes of a hawk.

"Yep." I can't help the smile. She really does have a thing for big houses. "Where does Conner live anyway? I never have asked you."

"Apartment on the river, penthouse of course. Actually, I think it's two knocked into each other," she says with a wry smile. "Ostentatious, very modern and very computerized as you can imagine. I have to enter my handprint just to get in the door. The fucking coffee machine makes your coffee by recognizing your voice." She's chuckling again.

"Next you'll tell me he has robots cleaning for him," I reply with a laugh.

"He does, two of the little freaky things, weird if you ask me but there you go." I open-mouth gape at her. *Really?* "So which is his?" she says, still scanning the road so I point at the oncoming gates. She immediately slams on the brakes and whips the car over to them. "Holy fuck!" she exclaims as she looks up the drive. I giggle. It is pretty bloody impressive and I remember feeling exactly the same the first time I arrived here. In fact I still do most of the time.

"Quite," I reply as I gaze at those now more friendly red doors and think of who lives inside. The manicured front lawn has been cut to within an inch of its life and the ivy creeping along the front looks glorious as it dips gracefully along the edge of the windows.

"Has he asked you to move in?" she asks out of the blue as her brow furrows and she sighs. "Because that would make such a nice family home."

Where the hell did that come from? Family? From Belle? Really? And move in with him...? Oh my god, no, well... No.

"What? No, we've only just got back together," I reply sharply as I give her my best *what the hell are you on* look. "Has Conner?"

"Yes," she replies with a small twitch of her mouth. What? She's so thinking about doing it.

"Really? Wow, that's... Bloody hell, what did you say?" I can't believe he asked her. I'm shocked to say the least. Mr. Avery permanently off the market will probably send every magazine into overdrive or something.

"No," she replies as she indicates and pulls out into the traffic again. "It's his apartment. If I do it, we'll get somewhere together. I want joint custody of my own home, thank you very much."

"I can't believe you're thinking of this. I mean, it's wonderful and I'm so happy for you, but I just never thought you'd go all in and really try this again." All thanks to Marcus Shitfield, of course.

"I love him, mindboggling as that is, and he's damned persistent," she says with a shrug as if there's nothing left to question. I suppose there isn't with Belle. Once she's made a decision, she's normally full-on with it.

"Well you should go for it then," I exclaim as I grin across at her. She looks slightly baffled by her own admission suddenly. "If you want to, that is. I mean, you don't have to obviously. You could just keep dating and think about it later." She still looks perplexed.

"Would you? If he asked you, I mean?" she asks as she pulls up to some traffic lights. "How would you know if it's the right thing to do or not?" Would I? I doubt it, but maybe.

"I don't know. I haven't thought about it. Conner is more open with his feelings, Belle. Alex is... Well, he's complicated to say the least," I reply as I imagine being with him full time. Whether I could keep up with his mood swings or not is incomprehensible but the thought of waking up in those arms every day is truly enviable.

"Right, well, I think that deserves a conversation and a few drinks, and what are we going to do about Mum?"

"I'll call Dad tomorrow. He never could lie to me. If I have to, I'll travel back and play for the truth. I might even beat him, and I've gotten better lately," I reply as I laugh at my own obsession with beating Mr. White at his own game.

"Yes, I've noticed you playing at home. Mr. White likes chess then?"

"Mr. White likes all sorts of games, Belle. He's also very good at every one of them. That's his *thing* as you call it."

Thirty minutes later and we've managed to crack the gate code and park the car. The back door access was equally easy but the now loud, high-pitched screaming coming at two second intervals from the alarm panel is setting my nerves on edge to the point that my brain can't apparently spell any more. What the hell is Meritato anyway, for Christ's sake? I try one last time and thankfully the screaming turns to a dull four-tone beep and then miraculously the entire place lights up as a computerized female voice welcomes me as Mr. White. Mrs White, thank you. What? Fuck, why did I think that? *Shit, ridiculous... Stop it, Beth. Idiot.*

Belle smiles as she encourages me forward. I hesitate as I look along the length of the corridor in front of me. I can't believe he gave me all the codes to get in here. I know he says he loves me but this is real trust in me, faith. The thought warms me and I smile as I sweep my way along the corridor as gracefully as I can, completely in control as if this is my home, hopefully towards a bar because frankly, I have no idea where we'll end up.

Thankfully, after two more doors, that's exactly where we end up, straight into the bar. Belle claps her hands together like a child, removes her jacket and throws it on the bar with happy abandon.

"Righty ho then... What shall we start with?" she says gleefully as she wanders her hands across all the bottles. I shake my head and settle in front of the white bar on a stool to watch her attempt at bartending. She launches at varying bottles and then dips to a fridge. "Oh, fucking hell, I'm in heaven. Look at all this alcohol. Where's the music?"

"Fourth button on the top panel apparently," I reply as I scan the area. There is no panel. We both look again for it.

"Found it," Belle says as she leaps up onto the back bar, frankly very impressively in those heels, and presses the fourth button. Thumping, hard-core beats hit my ears so suddenly I jump up and giggle at my own stupidity as I nearly fall off the stool.

"Can we change it?" I scream at her over the deafening noise. It's fabulous for a night out at eleven ish, but five thirty in the afternoon, not so much.

"Absolutely fucking not!" she screams back as she returns to her drink mixing, dancing to the beat and grinning like a fool. Oh, she's so on one!

She looks good behind a bar and as I look down at my skinny jeans and heels, I suddenly realise that maybe I might too, so I dance my way back to her with a shrug of indifference and help her with her cocktail making. This is more than likely going to get very messy because it's quite obvious why we're drinking - Mum.

Quite a few very strong drinks later and we're both well on our way to merry-go-land. The music is still thumping out around us and Belle has even decided to turn it up. I have taken the opportunity to take my drink to one of the podiums and have a go at being a diva, something I've never even entertained the idea of doing before, but it seems that Belle's idea of Cosmos and Singapore Slings has given me that edge of idiocy that you watch every other girl having at somewhere around midnight. I realise it's only about six thirty but I couldn't give a rat's ass at the moment because I'm just happy to take my mind off my mum. The euphoric melody of *Delirium's Silence* is slowly pulling every wanton sexual move out of my body as I glide my hands over myself and up into the air with every intention of belting out the song. I'm so hot that I've tucked my t-shirt up into my bra so that I can give my stomach some air, and the feeling of being exposed is somehow increasing my need to grind on the pole that's stuck in the centre of my podium. Christ knows how she's done it but Belle's even managed to find the light system so the pink, yellow and blue hues that swirl around us seem to open up a green light for us to let rip to the thundering beats. I glance around to see that she's decided to take the other podium now and we grin wildly at each other as the bass drops in and our bodies give in completely to the rhythm. Bloody hell, she's good. She could easily have been a stripper, and I watch in awe as she spins herself around the pole and then randomly licks at it seductively. Who she's doing it for I have no idea. I burst out laughing but then decide that it was, in fact, stupidly erotic so I have a go and find myself instantly wanting to have sex with my pole. *Alex. My pole is Alex?* Yes, it seems my pole has become Alex, and suddenly I want to give it everything as I throw my leg around it and lean backwards. I've seen that move somewhere, some model or something. I can do that. Fortunately for me, I can do it and am in fact quite good at it as I find my balance and try a few other moves. My hands move to the grip I use when my wrists are bound and before I know it, I'm spinning, hopefully gracefully, around it and letting the music take me far away as it starts to come to an end. I can hear the song finishing in my mind but my body doesn't want to comply, doesn't want to finish its grinding and twirling, and as I run my back across the pole to stop myself, I open my eyes to search for Belle. She's standing stock still, watching me with a gaping mouth.

"Fuck me, where the hell did you learn to do that?" she shouts across at me as a less thunderous beat kicks in. "That was... I'm not even sure what that was."

"Quite," a very familiar voice says from the darkness. Both our heads immediately spin towards Conner and I instantly scan for Alex. Fuck. "It's a good job he's not here, Beth, because that would not have been acceptable for me to watch at all. I have a feeling I might have gotten my very attractive head ripped right off," he says as he saunters out of the gloom into the light. My half pissed state is obviously in full effect now or my sexual tension is because I can't help but notice how good he looks in a suit.

A suit? Really? Yes, a black suit. He looks all kinds of right and wrong in it. I shake my head at myself and watch Belle leap gleefully off her podium into his waiting arms. He devours her instantly as if he's never touched her before and I smile at them as I step back to give them a little privacy. What they're about to get up to is probably not for me to watch and I giggle to myself as I make for the steps quite unsteadily.

The darkness envelops me again as I round the corner behind the DJ booth and hands suddenly grab at me and slam me against the wall. My heart leaps into my throat instantly and then his body meets mine. His hips thrust into mine as he kicks my legs apart and before I know it, the zip on my jeans is yanked down and he's roughly pushing them down my legs. His aftershave assaults me as hot, panting breaths travel up my neck towards my face, and when his mouth meets mine, it's like an explosion of desire within me bursts forward. He crushes me against the wall and growls that unmistakable sound low in his throat as his hand finds its way into my soaked panties and his fingers slide into me deliciously. I tip my head back instantly and try to stop the moan that is desperate to escape my lips, but when his mouth bites down on my nipple, I can't stop the groan that erupts. He pushes my jeans down one of my legs with his foot and I slip out of my heeled shoe so that he can do it easier, pulling my leg up as he tugs the bottom of it off completely.

I open my mouth to say something but he instantly brings his finger up to my mouth to silence me and I gaze into his playfully darkened blue eyes as he removes it again and grabs at my leg to hook it around his waist with a wicked smile.

"Be quiet," he says as he unzips his suit trousers and pulls my hand towards his cock. "Do you feel that, how fucking hard I am for you?" Oh god, I do, and as my fingers wrap around his length tightly, he grunts and swipes at my hand to move it away. "Not enough, baby. I want inside you."

I can't believe I'm about to do this. Belle and Conner are here somewhere and the thought makes me squirm a bit, but the first touch of him against my quivering core and I'm lost in him again, eternally. One very hard drive later and he's so far inside me that I can't stop the exquisite groan of pleasure that springs out of me again. His hand immediately covers my mouth as he slides back out and then slams back in again repeatedly. His dark eyes stay locked with mine as the corners of his mouth quirk teasingly and I tremble around him. I'm so close, for some unknown reason I can't even begin to hold it back so I don't. He hasn't told me to so I let go with everything I've got around him and delight in the feel of his ridges rubbing the very inside of me.

Something about him holding me against the wall and covering my mouth only heightens every passionate response so I yield completely and let him guide me. His grunt of approval at my acceptance lets me know how much he needs this, how much he wants me to allow his roughness, and as his hand clenches more around my mouth, I grab onto the back of his neck for support. My nails sink in as I feel the next wave of pleasure rolling towards me and embrace it with open abandon. He does this, frees me to give in to him and let go of something I never knew I had. Every hard thrust bruises my back against the wall as I wildly try to suck enough air in through my nose to keep up with his pace, but then he widens his hand and almost closes off my air completely. My mind reels at the thought of no air so I tense instantly and begin to panic a little, only to feel him push more of his weight into me and lift me from the floor.

"Stay with me," he whispers hoarsely as my safeword flashes through my head and I realise that I can't say it even if I want to. But before I know it, the thought has disappeared into a feeling. It's only his penetrating blue eyes that I see, only his overwhelming body that I feel against me, pushing me once again towards a new experience.

And oh god, his hips are forcing harder now, punishingly so, and I can feel him thickening deliciously inside me so I tense my leg around him and let my orgasm take hold of me. I feel every brutal stoke as his breathing shallows and he lifts his head, revealing straining neck muscles and a suddenly taught aggressive jaw. I watch his shoulders stiffen as he begins his release and starts to buck his hips erratically at me, stretching me wide and tensing his hold on my waist.

"Fuck, you feel good," he growls out as I whimper into his hand and try to gasp for some air. He tightens it again and grins as if he's enjoying the sensation of me struggling under him. "Can't you breathe, Elizabeth?"

My eyes widen at his dark amusement, yet at the same moment all sorts of pure bliss roll over me, seemingly dulling and yet somehow heightening each conscious touch as he slams into me again and again and squeezes that hand tighter. I can't breathe, and I'm not even trying anymore because whatever he's doing is so consuming that I don't care. My legs grip onto his relentlessly pounding hips as I stare into those eyes and watch as he groans and removes his hand to allow me one quick breath before he replaces it with his mouth. The world seems to blur as every part of me becomes focused on sensation, completely overriding the need for air as I feel him shudder inside me and we ride out our heavenly pleasure together.

Slowly he brings his mouth away from mine and I immediately pant for the air he withheld from me until he replaces it again then nips at me. "Still perfect," he whispers as his eyes dance with that amused devilment.

"Mmm," is all I've got as he lazily grinds into me and I try to smile at him adoringly, still gasping in much needed oxygen. His white shirt wrinkles around his neckline and his eyes sparkle ice blue again as he draws his fingers over my lips and smiles.

"How did you like not breathing?" I don't even have words for that so I just stare back and wonder what else he's got in his box of sexual tricks. Who knew not breathing was one of them? "Quite debilitating, isn't it? Somewhat euphoric, though, in the right moment." I'm still panting for air, and again, I have no fucking words at all, only some strange quivering that continues to ride itself all over my skin as I try to bring some semblance of order back to my frazzled brain.

"I think I'll have a pole installed in the bedroom." Oh Christ, he was watching me... My eyes widen. "Quite the performance," he says as he slowly pulls out of me and reaches to straighten my jeans. I shuffle them back up and do my belt up as he sorts himself out.

Why I'm suddenly embarrassed by my dancing is beyond me so I drop my head a little and watch him running his hands through his, literally, just fucked dark hair with a permanent smile on his handsome face. He slants his eyes toward me. "Are you looking at the floor, Miss Scott?" he says with that rising brow of his. "Because we both know how I feel about that." My head shoots up again.

"Yes, I just... I didn't know you were watching," I reply as I sink back to the wall for balance and chew my thumbnail. Mortified is not the word, but at least he's not angry or some other ferocious emotional response.

"How could I not?" he says as he moves towards me. "You were hot as hell and completely immoral. I don't think I've ever seen something so lust-worthy." Okay, well, I can feel better about myself then. Clearly I'm not bad at that pole thing, and Christ, he looks good. I so want him... Again. My core clenches fiercely as I look at his shoulders moving off then glance at his hands. All I want is for him to bend me over and do his worst, show me everything he's got. I can't even process my thoughts as to why but I know I want it, any way he chooses.

"I think I need fucking again," I blurt out without thinking as he extends his hand to mine. Even I can't believe I've said it and as I watch his eyes swing back to me sharply, I groan at the snarl that meets me. He's immediate in his glare of darkness. Everything disappears apart from his eyes and the sudden proximity of his hand at my throat.

"Is it the tequila, Elizabeth, or have you finally found your voice?" he says as he forces me backwards and goes to that eerily still place of his. My back hits the wall and I moan again at the thought of the Alex in the Lake District. I relax completely, ready for anything he's about to deliver and smiling at it, wanting it more than life itself for some odd reason.

"Anything you want, Alex. Do anything you want," is my slightly hazy answer. I can't even remember the question. Was there one? God, I hope he's rough. Shit, I'm horny. I clutch his hand and squeeze it tighter around my neck, hoping to spur him on or something. Unfortunately, he flexes his hand and slowly let's go of me. It's not the response I was after so I frown at him. He chuckles. It's really not funny.

"Now's not the time baby, but the attitude is fucking perfect," he says with a raised brow as he moves in to kiss me softly. It's not enough, but he's probably right and it'll do as I wrap myself around him. "Come on, I'll see what I can do for you later." He winks at me and grabs my hand again, so I take it and follow him through to the bar to see Belle and Conner sitting there drinking. Belle looks just as dishevelled as I feel. She's probably just had the same *hello* as I've received and I smile our secret smile at her as she glances at me and smirks.

Conner turns around to see Alex and instantly holds his hands up in surrender with a surprisingly wary look on his face. Even in my drunken state I notice the flash of uncertainty in his eyes.

"I swear, man, I was only watching Belle," he says quietly. Alex chuckles and slaps him on the back as he rounds the bar and pours them both a large Scotch. Conner visibly relaxes again. I have no idea what the hell that was about. Surely Conner wasn't really expecting his head literally being ripped off?

"To be honest, I wouldn't blame you if you weren't," he replies dryly. Belle's eyes widen and she slaps his arm over the counter. Conner's eyes instantly hit mine with a devilish grin, so I slap him as well and then we all burst out laughing.

Several minutes later, I realise that there's no one else in the bar apart from us. Why the hell I hadn't noticed before is anyone's guess.

"Where is everyone?" I ask.

"We don't open till nine and I made the staff wait in the back. Tom was fucking leering at you," Alex sneers as he walks out the back. I watch him with a frown, wondering where exactly happy Alex has disappeared to because he's apparently gone all emotional about something.

"He won't like sharing you, Beth. I'm actually really surprised he didn't twat me one," Conner says softly behind me. Belle arches her eyebrow and bursts out laughing again.

"God, we were only dancing. That's just ridiculous," I reply as I knock back the rest of my Belle creation. I have no idea what I'm drinking anymore but I do feel very pissed now. In fact, is Conner actually moving or sitting still?

"That's just him, Beth. Don't rile him. It's not fucking pretty at all," he says as I watch him sway in front of me. Was that him or me? Oh, he really is quite pretty.

"Well what a dick. If you ever get like that with me, I'll twat you one," Belle responds as she staggers off her stool. Conner grabs at her before she hits the deck. Christ, we really are pissed.

"Possession is nine tenths of the law, precious," he says as he lifts her back up with a glorious grin. He's so in love - cute, blue-haired genius, very pretty indeed. Where's mine gone?

"Fuck you. Nobody's bloody possession," she slurs to him as she looks at me. "You, toilet, now, hair... Fucking mess." Oh, right. Shit hair, not good. I get up, stumble a bit and grab onto his shoulder, which is big. Yes, big. Good shoulders. Good arse, too, nice lips. Where the hell is Alex?

"You look damn fine in that suit, Conner. Very cute... Yes, cute, blue hair, oh wow, pink tips..." I'm giggling now. I can't think at all. Why is the floor moving?

"Get your arse over here," Belle shouts at me as she grabs my arm and we both wobble towards the corridor. "You're so pissed." She laughs.

"You are so much more pisseder, pissdisder, wankered." I giggle as I clutch her arm and navigate the floor. We're obviously ten again.

"Would you ladies like a lift to the bathroom?" Conner chuckles behind us. We both try to glare at him but hit each other's heads together instead as we turn around. *Subtle, Beth, really sodding elegant.*

"Shit," is the only word I can find as we right ourselves and I head for the toilets with Belle swaying beside me. I can see the corridor; it's over there. Why won't it just stay still for a minute?

"Christ, Beth, what did you put in those drinks?" she says as we reach the bathroom door.

"Me? You made them. I just put the orange juice in. I think... Didn't I?" I can't remember a sodding thing. She pushes on the door. I follow and fall straight over her as she tumbles to the ground in what can only be described as a whirlwind of over-acting and dramatics.

"Christ, Belle, get the hell up. What the fuck is going on? It's normally me," I say as I crawl my way up the wall and try to find the sink units. She doesn't bother to get up, just belly crawls commando style across the floor. I can't stop the fit of hysterics that bursts from my lungs as I watch Action Woman trying to make her way to the toilet.

"Oh, shitting hell that's funny. You look like Barbie gone all CIA or something." I giggle as I lean my weight on the counter top and try to look at myself in the mirror, which keeps moving, or maybe it's dirty for some reason?

"At least I haven't got an eighties hair do," she laughs as she strips her jeans off and sits on the loo. "You look like a cheap fucking Vegas hooker." Oh, holy fuck, I do!

My eyes are a bag of black mascara and my hair, well my hair has done its frizzy I don't give a shit thing. Honestly, I couldn't make it look less like crap if I tried. Clip? Have I got a clip? Rifling through my bag, which happens to be Belle's because I've picked up the wrong one, I find a brown crocodile clip and set about doing something with my hair while I wipe at my eyes and try to regain some impression of order. Belle finds her way over to me, on her feet this time - well, nearly on her feet - and starts the process of damage limitation on her own face. Giggling our way through various mascaras and lipsticks, we're eventually reasonably happy with our appearance again.

"I think I'm going to take Conner home. I'm in need of round two," Belle says to me quite abruptly with a serious face. I burst out laughing and fall back towards the toilet. Then, remembering that I actually do need to pee, I start to take my jeans down. "Are you coming?"

"Was earlier," I giggle at her. She bursts out laughing and zig zags for the door.

"I'll see you out there in a few," she calls as the door closes. I stare at the wall and try to focus my fuddled brain back into gear. Water, that's what I need. As I'm pulling up my jeans, I hear the door opening again and giggle at the thought of Belle crawling back across it again.

"Jesus, what have you forgotten now, you stupid cow?" I shout as I try to organise my belt and look up. It's not Belle, and I step backward into the toilet again as a man I don't know looks me up and down with a lecherous smile. He's big, and I'm suddenly very aware of my vision swimming and my inability to focus on anything. I shake my head about in the hope it will bring some order to my sight. Thankfully it does a little as my heart rate speeds up at the potential danger. Why is he looking at me like that?

"This is the ladies. You should be next door," I say quietly as my non-pissed brain races back to me. He looks a little too confident for my liking and I realise he knows exactly where he is. He grins; it makes me shiver. "I'm not sure what you think you're doing but Alex is out there and he's not going to be happy if-" No more words get out as he lunges forward, knocks me backwards into the toilet and closes the door behind him. I open my mouth to scream but his hand is instantly over it.

"Shut the fuck up, bitch. I watched you earlier. You like it like this, don't you?" he sneers as he grabs at my breast with his hand and pushes his erection into me. I have no idea what to do but instinct suddenly kicks in and I start kicking and pushing at him furiously. He's too strong and I can't get a decent shot in whichever way I try. He roughly turns me round and holds me up against the toilet door. "All his whores are like this, begging for it. You're all fucking sluts," he mumbles as he undoes my belt and flicks the button on my jeans. *Christ, Beth, get it together. The door opens inwards, toilet's behind you, mouth covered, bite! For fucks sake bite!*

I wrestle my head around to loosen his grip on me, which only gets me a maniacal laugh and a tug of my jeans but it does dislodge his hold a little. My teeth find his finger as I clench down as hard as I can and then throw my head backwards, hoping to find his face or nose or anything. The resounding crunch lets me know I've hit something and I scream as loud as I can as his hands fly away from my mouth. I turn and shove at him with all my might as he topples backwards clutching at his nose and lands on the toilet head first. Scrabbling for the door, I unlock it and bolt as fast as my feet will take me, but just as I get to the door, his hand grabs onto my arm and yanks me back to him. I scream as hard as my lungs can manage and send my arms flailing around at him, slapping and kicking for all I'm worth, nails clawing and lunging for eyes, anything to stop him and give me a chance to get to the door again. I keep screaming in the hope that someone will hear but as he gets a hold of me again and swings his hand at my face, I know I haven't got a chance. The crack that sends me flying across the room towards the sinks instantly causes the room to spin around me and I grab onto the sink to steady myself. A hand grabs at my jeans again as the other one wrenches my arm behind me and bends me over. Oh, fuck no!

My head is throbbing and the pain from the strike on my cheek is pounding so badly that I'm struggling to see straight, let alone fight back. I try to move away from him but he yanks at my arm again and I cry out in agony as I feel my shoulder pop a little. He smacks the back of my head forward and I bash it on the sink unit and slump forward with a groan. I know I should fight but I can't move away from him as he shoves me forward again, pinning me and snarling at me.

"Now shut the fuck up and stay still, you whore. I'm gonna fuck you and you're gonna take it," he grunts as he licks my neck disgustingly and his rancid breath hits my airways. I heave in repulsion but my head hurts so much that I just try to find my peaceful place. It's safe there, quiet. "We all know how he treats his women, darlin'. I bet you like it rough, dontcha?" he whispers disturbingly as he tugs my jeans again and I hear his zipper. That's enough for me to find my voice again and I scream. No fucking way am I making it easy for him. I might like it rough but not from him. I will not be raped easily.

Picking my foot up, I slam it down on his toes and am rewarded with an injured shout of pain but his hold increases and he gets his hand in the front of my jeans. *Oh no, oh no, oh no...* I squirm again and clamp my thighs together, hoping like hell that this isn't going to happen. Clearly no one can hear my screams in here. The music's too loud and there isn't any women here apart from Belle, but I keep trying anyway in hope. In one last-ditch attempt to get noticed, I scream Alex's name at the top of my lungs as I feel my jeans moving down across my arse and my arm being yanked up my back again. Nothing happens and I realise that it's going to happen. I'm going to be raped, and no matter how much I struggle, I can't get him off me. My body stills and my eyes swim again with tears as my mouth starts begging in hope.

"Please don't do this. I don't want this, plea-"

Suddenly all the weight on me is gone and I heave out a breath as I warily lift my aching head to see why. The vision that hits me is both comforting and scary as hell and I jolt myself upright and grab onto the counter behind me. Alex has him pinned to the wall by his neck and is repeatedly smashing his fist into his face with such force that the resulting blood splatter lands on my t-shirt. I slowly look down at it and heave again as the room starts to spin. I look back up to watch him let go of the man and let him slump to the floor then shove him to the ground with his foot as he starts kicking him viciously in the head and stomach. I struggle to process what's happening in front of me as my vision sways a little, and I gaze on in slow motion, listening to the grunts of aggression and bloody spluttering. The man has given up fighting back or even trying to protect himself and is now floundering around limply. He's going to bloody kill him!

No, he can't kill him; that would be bad. I shake my head at myself as I see Alex crouch down over him and pick up the man's neck so that he can throw some more punches at his face. His eyes are wild with violence and brutality, his body tensed to hell as if he has no intention of stopping any time soon and I realise I've got to stop him. I take a wobbly step forward.

"Alex, stop," I say quietly. I can hardly hear my own voice as I reach my fingers toward him. He hauls the man back up and throws him against the wall and continues with his beating. "Alex, please, you're going to kill him," I shout out, trying to get his attention. He's so engrossed in the demolition of the man's face that he can't even hear me. I move forward a bit more and try to grab his arm before it connects again. His eyes swing to mine for a second before he pushes me away forcefully and returns to his pounding. "Fuck, Alex, stop!" Nothing. "Please... Alex? Shit... Please!" I realise I have to get someone and make for the door as best I can, holding onto the wall and screaming for Conner, for anyone.

I make it to the corridor before I fall to my knees and start to heave again at the thought of all the blood and scream again for help. Conner is by my feet in seconds with a confused expression and I point wildly at the toilet, grabbing onto his shin.

"Stop him, Conner. He's going to kill him." He bolts for the room and Belle quickly gathers me up into her arms and tries to lead me away, but I have to go back. I have to know that Alex is alright, that Conner's stopped him before it's too late.

"No, Belle, I have to go back." She's dragging at me to go the other way so I shove at her and push her to the floor as I grab the wall and run back to the bathroom. "Get the fuck off me!" She clutches my arm back to her.

"What the hell happened?" she shrieks at me. I can't answer. I just have to open the door. "Beth, what happened?" My hand grabs the handle and I slump back to the ground as I gaze at the scene before me and lean against the door.

Conner has both of his arms wrapped around Alex's elbows and is trying his damndest to restrain him from going back to the man on the floor while quietly talking into his ear. He's jerking wildly in Conner's grasp and bellowing violently as he tries to free himself and then slams his head back towards Conner's face. He dodges effectively and continues with his murmuring. I can't hear what he's saying but it seems to be working as I watch Alex slow his movements slightly. My eyes glance at the man on the floor. He's breathing, just. The coughing up of blood and the heavy rasping noise coming from his throat let me know as much so at least I know he's not dead. There's not much of his face left, though, and the strange angle of his thigh looks revolting as it jars out sideways.

"Oh holy fuck, what happened, Beth?" Belle whispers over my shoulder as she sits down next to me and wraps her arm around my shoulder, pulling me to her protectively. I just stare at Alex as Conner eventually lets him go gently and he begins pacing with his hands on the back of his neck. He seems a little calmer now, still sneering with fury but thankfully not doing any more about it. My eyes glance at the man on the floor again and watch as he continues to bubble blood from his mouth and nose. Alex moves across to him and shoves his injured leg sadistically, causing the man to gurgle a scream in agony. I can't even begin to process where *my* Alex is because this isn't him, so who the hell am I looking at here? All that behaviour was sheer animal, no thought or sense, just callous, brutal violence.

"Belligare," I mutter quietly as his tattoo flits through my mind. Who the hell am I in love with?

That wasn't a businessman. That was a man who'd fought before, and who was happy doing it, who was so involved in a merciless killing spree that he couldn't even process his girlfriend behind him screaming for help. That was a fucking nightmare waiting to happen and as I watch him simmering away in the corner of the room, looking down at the man he's nearly killed with no emotion other than a sneer, I realise I know absolutely nothing about him, nothing at all.

Who the hell is Alexander White? Or Nicholas Adlin, for that matter?

I can't even begin to comprehend how much else is in his closet, regardless of how much I think I love him, so I do the only thing I can think of as his head turns toward me slowly and he takes a step forward. Thankfully Conner holds up his hand to stop him.

"Drink," I say as I haul myself up and pull my eyes away from him to head for the bar. Belle grabs me and helps me toward it. I walk straight behind it and pour the scotch that they were drinking earlier with a shaky hand, tipping it straight down my neck. I refill it and tip another one down.

"Honey, slow down," Belle says quietly as she reaches for my hand. I shrug her off and pour another one. "Well at least pour me one then," she continues as I glare at her. Why I'm so angry is anyone's guess? I was very nearly raped. I should be a cowering heap of nerves but for some reason, I'm just furious, with myself? Possibly. Or with him? I don't know. He was protecting me. I should be proud and thankful but the ferocity that was in that room was not part of the man I love, or was it?

I have no idea, absolutely no sodding idea.

Is this the rage he controls? Is this why he needs his preferences? Is this what his father was? Is he nearer to his father than I thought? Shit, what the hell was that?

"Are you okay?" she asks quietly. Completely and utterly, not.

"I was attacked in the toilet. Alex pulled him off." My voice comes out methodical and calculated as if I'm telling someone else's story. She gasps and moves to hug me. I back off instantly. I don't want anyone touching me, not even her. "I want to go home," I say as I pick up my bag and head for the front entrance. She follows behind me quietly.

"Honey, you need to report this. We need the police here." I swing round so fast I almost knock her over and glare at her. Is she fucking kidding?

"Did you just see that in there, Belle? He's nearly dead, for fuck's sake! Alex will be arrested and go to jail because of me. No fucking police, okay?" I shout at her venomously. I can't stop my rage from exploding all over her. She backs up and stares at me with a shocked expression so I continue my scowl, daring her to continue.

"Belle, can you give us a minute?" Alex's calm voice comes out of the darkness behind her. I freeze and glare over at him as he wanders casually over. Not a hint of anger is left on his beautiful face now as I boil away inside and picture him fifteen minutes ago, pounding the shit out of a man's face. You wouldn't even know what had just happened if you didn't notice the blood oozing from his knuckles and the spray of crimson splattering his suit and shirt.

"Okay," she says quietly as she reaches out to me. I take her hand and give it a squeeze then let go and return my gaze to Alex. He looks down at his hands and then shoves them in his pockets with a frown as she walks past him back to the bar.

"Are you okay? Did he... Did he touch you?" he says shakily as he looks straight at me.

"Do you mean did he fuck me, Alex, like all your other whores?" I spit at him.

"What?" He looks instantly confused and takes a step toward me. I step back. I have no idea who the hell the man is and at the moment, I seriously don't like him, hero or not.

"He said he watched us, and that I liked it rough, just like all your other whores." I glower at him and he stops. All his other whores, just like me, ready for anything, willing to give him anything he wants. I'm suddenly disgusted with myself.

"No, it's not like that, Elizabeth... I love you," he replies as he reaches a hand forward to my face. I step back again and look to the floor.

"He said they all knew how you liked it, how your whores loved it, how they begged for it." I can't look at him anymore. I don't even know how I feel about anything, including him. I don't know him and I was nearly raped. My shaking starts again as I try to make my brain process information logically.

"Baby, no. I love you. Please," he says as he curls his fingers around my shoulder gently and pulls me to him. God, that feels good... and bad.

"Is that what I am, Alex? Just another one to fuck? According to him, I am?" I mumble into his chest as the tears start to finally surface. His chin rests on my head as he sighs out and rubs my arm soothingly.

"No, baby, you're everything to me. I can't breathe without you," he replies quietly as I listen to his heart thundering rapidly. As his arms squeeze around me, I let my tears flow and finally sob my heart out into his body. "Shh, baby, it's okay. I've got you." His words only worsen my tears as I wonder who it is that's got me and my legs give way beneath me. Warm arms wrap around me before I hit the floor and I let myself be carried to wherever he's taking me as I stare across his shoulder at the corridor and wonder where the man is and if he's still alive.

"Is he alive?"

"For now," is his response. I have no idea what that means, and frankly, I really couldn't care less. He's not dead. Alex isn't going to jail for murder. That, for me, is okay at the moment.

Before I know it, we're outside and he's lowering me into the car gently with a small smile. I don't return it. I can't. I just stare at him because I can hardly move, let alone manage an emotional response. He walks around the front of the car and I watch him pull off his jacket and shirt then grab another shirt from the back, having wiped his face on the bloodied one. It's a comfortable movement, like he's done it a thousand times before. His tattoo flashes at me under the streetlight and I suddenly realise he's got something hiding in that brain of his that's vicious, deadly even, certainly something more than I ever thought possible. As he gets in, I notice his knuckles again and briefly think about how much they probably hurt before the vision of the man's face hits me again and I look across, hoping to clear the image. He stares back at me with no regret whatsoever.

"Is that who you're hiding from me?" I ask. It's more of a statement because I know the answer and clearly so does he because he just frowns a little and then starts the car. I have no energy left to fuel more conversation on the subject so I try to relax and gaze at the dashboard as he drives us out onto the road. His hand finds my fingers so I limply hold it and stare out of the window into the darkness as he makes two phone calls. One to Conner to let him know we've left and another one to an unknown voice. I switch off and close my eyes as I begin to drift into an alcohol-fuelled, numb sleep.

Chapter 11

Elizabeth

I vaguely remember getting back here last night, just like I vaguely remember being put under a shower and then in this bed, but apart from that, I remember nothing. I think he watched me from the chair at some point because I remember waking up in the early hours and thinking he was sitting there gazing, but now I have no idea whether it was real or just a dream.

I roll over and see a glass of water and some painkillers. I feel the smile pulling at my face as I reach over quietly and grab the water. My head is already letting me know how much I drank last night and the idea of ridding myself of the ache before I get up is, frankly, awesome. I glance at the clock on the table - seven. Okay, I've got some time before I have to get myself to the shop. There's only the party tonight to prepare for so I swallow the pills and sit up a bit. Clearly Alex isn't here and I heave out a sigh as I begin to let myself think about last night. Having thought about the fact that I was very nearly raped for a few minutes, I decide that it isn't worth thinking about because that is exactly the point - *nearly* raped, not raped, thank god. My own emotionless response to the thought shocks me, but regardless, I am apparently more consumed with who the man downstairs actually is. It's not that I'm not having a reaction to being assaulted; it's just that watching Alex in full-on kill mode is more disturbing than the other thing that happened, or didn't happen.

I lift my hand to my cheek and frown as I am reminded of the smack across the cheek that sent me barrelling across the room. Pushing against it gently, I am amazed to feel that it doesn't hurt too much at all. Christ, I really did get away lightly with the whole situation. The thought makes me shudder. If Alex hadn't have got there in time... Well he did, so I don't need to think about it anymore. Where is he anyway?

Swinging my legs out, I head for the bathroom and try to work out how I feel about his behaviour in the cold light of day. My anger and confusion last night were clearly to do with the amount of alcohol consumed and the situation, because this morning, I can't quite find the abhorrence that rolled across me last night. The feeling is now more like surprise or sheer astonishment. I mean, I knew he could fight. I remember him hitting that Draven guy in Rome but last night was lethal, absolute deadly brute force being aimed at another human being. He could have just hit him a few times and left it at that, but he seemed intent on killing him, which goes way past the normally allowed explosion of violence when put under pressure. It wasn't defence of any kind. It was an unadulterated act of violent aggression, no holds barred, and more worryingly, it was as if he enjoyed every minute of it. The way his frame moved around his vicious punches and kicks showed balance and precision in his ferocious delivery. It suddenly seemed even worse to me. It wasn't a gung ho throw yourself at the maniac moment. No, he knew exactly what he was doing and he gave it everything. And then there was that changing clothes thing at the car. His face was completely relaxed as he wiped another man's blood off it and put on another shirt. It seemed like he'd just left the gym or something equally mundane. Other people wouldn't do that, would they? They'd be revolted by having someone's blood on them, maybe even be sick or something.

What was that? Where the hell did he learn that level of ferocity, and more importantly, why?

~

A cleansing shower later, I throw on some slim-line black trousers and a grey shirt, apply some foundation to cover the reddened marks on my cheek and forehead, then the rest of my make-up and make my way down the stairs to find him. I still don't know how I feel about the whole *beating the shit out of someone* thing but decide that I'll know the moment I look at him. I'm not afraid of him; I know that. I'm just confused about him, yet again. I duck my head around the study door to see if he's there. He isn't so I keep on walking to the kitchen and as the smell of freshly cooked bacon hits me, my stomach rumbles greedily. When did I eat last? Oh yeah, lunch at Mum's, because that was so much fun.

"Morning, Miss Scott," a woman's voice says from around the corner. I look up, instantly startled. She stands there smiling at me with a frying pan in her hand. "One egg or two?"

"Umm... One please," I reply as I look her over - probably early fifties, slightly greying hair. Quite a large lady but well dressed and very smiley. She seems honest or kind or maybe both.

"I'm sorry, I haven't introduced myself," she says as she wipes her hand and offers it to me. "I'm Mary Jenkins. Please call me Mary." Oh, Alex's housekeeper! I clamp onto her hand and smile in return. Clearly she knows who I am.

"Nice to meet you, Mary. Is Alex around or has he gone to work already?" She hesitates for a moment and then swings her eyes to the garden with a frown.

"He's out there, Miss Scott, been out there for about an hour," she replies as she returns to the cooker. I gaze out and eventually see him at the very bottom of the garden, sitting on a bench staring at the park beyond.

"Why is he out there?" I mumble absentmindedly to myself as I cross my arms and wonder what to do.

"He was pacing, Miss Scott. He goes outside when he paces," she says softly. My eyes shoot to her back. This is news to me. She seems completely unfazed, as if she's seen the act a thousand times. I return my eyes to the garden and then go down to the hall cupboard to retrieve my coat. Shoes? No shoes... "My wellingtons are in there if you want to borrow them," she shouts to me. Is this woman a mind reader or something? I pull on the smallest green boots I can find and march my way back to the kitchen.

"Thanks for the wellies, Mary. Could you hold the breakfast for a few minutes?" I ask with a smile as I pull on the French doors.

"Already turned off, Miss Scott," she replies with a wink and a hearty laugh.

"Please, Mary, call me Elizabeth or Beth. I've already had this conversation with Michael," I say with pleading eyes. Her returning gaze is a little wary but she eventually smiles.

"Alright, Elizabeth," she says as she plonks her tea towel down on the work surface in a determined fashion. Something makes me think Alex has already told her not to.

"Thank you," I say warmly as I click the door open and walk into the cold December frost. Nice woman... I wonder how long she's worked for him.

The gravel crunches beneath my feet as I make my way along the path towards him and take in my surroundings. I've never been out here before and I am truly awed by the beauty of it. The huge patio that I stepped out onto screamed modernity with its vast cream table and chairs but the rest of the garden is elegant and graceful, as if it has been tended with loving affection for hundreds of years. How the gardeners manage to get flowers blooming at this time of year is beyond me and the red and yellow flower beds and the short box hedging in strict rows shows award winning design detail. The massive lawn at the end of the first terrace of beds is large enough to play cricket on and framed with a low brick wall. There's a summerhouse off to the left, which is obviously Victorian with its intricate detail and glass shimmering side panels. It actually might not be a summerhouse at all. It's so big it could be considered a small house. Neatly trimmed tall hedges line both sides of the garden and at the end of the lawn, there is a selection of seating areas overlooking the park, and there he sits in a brown wool coat with a thick scarf wrapped around his neck. My heart lurches with love as I watch him tug at it and throw it on the bench beside him. For some bizarre reason, it reminds me that I never really see him with anything around his neck, no ties or scarves, only black tie events and he doesn't keep them on very often for those.

I crunch on a bit further and he eventually turns to look at me. His warm smile is breath-taking so I return it gleefully and run to him as he extends a hand to me. I'm so in love with him, regardless of his animalistic tendencies.

"I see you've met Mary," he says as he gazes down at my wellies. I giggle and snuggle into him as he wraps his arm around my shoulder.

"What are you doing out here? Beautiful as it is, it's eight in the morning and you never come out here," I ask as I gaze into the park beyond. It really is beautiful.

"I was thinking of you. The garden reminds me of you." Oh well, that's lovely, I think, unless he's talking about weeds, not that there are any in this garden.

"Why?" Lovely as it is, I don't have clue why a garden would remind him of me.

"The peace that's on your face when you gaze out here is truly extraordinary. I thought I might come out and try to find some of the same emotion," he replies as he tips my head back and gently kisses me. I melt. "Are you okay this morning?" I snuggle closer into him. Am I? I think so. He picks up his scarf and wraps it twice around my neck as he gazes at me. I nod at him and return to my snuggling. He's so warm and his distinct spicy aftershave invades my senses as he kisses the top of my head.

"How's that going for you? You know, the peace finding?" I giggle. He doesn't respond, just sighs and rests his chin on my head as he strokes my hair. Minutes pass as we both look out and watch the horses going about their daily exercise with their riders on board.

"You wanted to protect me," he eventually says quietly. What the hell is he talking about?

"What?"

"After all you'd been through and all you'd witnessed, you told Belle not to call the police," he replies as he tightens his hold of me. "That was, actually it still is perplexing to me."

"Of course I did. You would have been arrested." My eyes lift to his in amazement; did he really think I would be so selfish?

"I probably deserved to be." Well possibly, yes.

"Maybe you did, but I wouldn't have been the one who allowed it. You were protecting me." He sighs again and tucks me back under his arm.

"You are so strong, Elizabeth. You should be wrecked but yet here you are, with me and the fucked up offering I have for you. You have no idea what your trust in me means but I don't deserve your compassion or loyalty. You could do so much better for yourself than me."

Right, that's enough of that Mr White.

I sit myself upright and turn to face him. He suddenly looks a little uncertain so I smile at him and run my fingers over his lips. How can this be the same man as the one I saw last night?

"I love you. My compassion and loyalty are part of that love. You have them whether you think you deserve them or not," I say as I watch his eyes stare into mine. They're smiling with something as I catch them crinkling at the corners, then his frown returns. Is he ever without one?

"I was so incensed, so furiously angry at what could have happened that I couldn't think of anything but killing him," he says as he runs his hand through his hair and then brings it down to rest gently on my cheek. He rubs his thumb over my bruise and stiffens. "And I would have had you not stopped me."

"I didn't stop you. Conner did," I say as I gaze at him with a puzzled expression. "You wouldn't stop when I asked you." *Begged you, frankly.* His face softens and that warm smile creeps back across it as if something's funny. It really isn't. We're discussing killing a man at eight in the morning, for God's sake. His cool demeanour at removing the blood from his face flashes across my eyes again and I can't believe it's the same man in front of me. He's done it before; I know he has and now I can't deny how intrigued I am about it.

"What Conner *said* to me stopped me, baby. He's not physically capable of stopping me and he knows it, but he is the only one who can talk me down," he replies with a small shrug. What the hell does talk him down mean?

"What do you mean?" I ask hesitantly. I really don't like where this is going. It's as if he's admitting he loses all normal levels of sanity on a regular basis, which I apparently can't stop him from doing.

"He told me that I would lose you if I carried on, that I would destroy a future with the only woman I have ever loved because of my inability to control my anger. It was enough to clear the haze. *You* were enough to clear my haze," he says reverently as he grazes my lips with his finger and leans forward.

"Oh, right... Well that's..."

"You don't deserve this in your life and I've tried to keep it under control, to be better, but when I saw you in there with his hands on you... I just couldn't stop it. I didn't want to. Do you know what that would have done to me? You're my world. Everything is you."

Any thought I previously had about how much I love him has just tripled. I seriously don't care if he's a serial murderer at the moment because he's just told me the most beautiful thing I've ever heard, even if it was in a random bizarre sort of way. I stare into his crystal clear blue eyes and watch the wind ruffle his hair about. He truly is the most gorgeous man I've ever met and he's mine, absolutely mine. I lean forward to kiss him and then decide that it would be far more comfortable to just get on top of him so throw my leg over his lap and dangle my feet behind the bench. He looks instantly shocked but quickly puts his arms back around me and shuffles me forward onto him with a smile.

"Okay, well given that I've now seen it, where does it come from? And more importantly, why are you so... well, accomplished at it? And frankly, a little too comfortable with it if I'm honest. Is it to do with your father?" I ask as the vision of him slamming his fist into the man's face floats through my mind. I shiver as the same hand gently traces patterns on my back and wonder at the dexterity of that hand. "What else are those hands responsible for, Mr. White?"

He draws in a long breath and hugs me towards him so I wrap my arms around him and snuggle into his warmth. Unfortunately, I can feel his hesitance, his avoidance, and know without a shadow of a doubt that this conversation is finished for now. At least he isn't trying sexual manipulation so we're a step closer to normal.

"Always pushing for more," he says into my neck.

"Always," I reply as I kiss the side of his neck and feel him tilt his head back to allow more of it. My core clenches at my own thoughts surrounding this spot on him as his hand finds the back of my head and firmly holds me in place. Just as I'm actually feeling completely lost in the moment and ready for more, he abruptly stands up with me still wrapped around him and starts walking towards the house.

"Now's not the time. It's a long conversation and I have to go to the office for a meeting... As long as you're okay, that is?" he says with a sudden worried expression. I grin at him and kiss him again.

"I'm fine. You got there in time, and I think he came off worse than me in the long run."

"He should be dead," he growls as he hitches me up on him and looks across at the summerhouse with a quirk of his mouth, then shakes his head and keeps going forward. He was so thinking about sex. I smile and grind myself down onto him. "Stop it, Elizabeth."

"What? I didn't do anything," I reply as he drops me on the floor with a snort of laughter and opens the door to the house. Bacon

205

assaults my nose again and my stomach grumbles at me as he walks towards Mary and she smiles at him with a warm face. His body language softens around her and I watch on in fascination as he interacts with her. It's nothing like his demeanour with Mrs Peters. It's like the behaviour a son would have with his mother. She never touches him nor he her, but they fluidly move around the room together as though they've always known each other.

"Have a seat, Elizabeth," she says as she puts the eggs in. His eyebrows shoot up at her familiarity as his gaze lands on mine. I narrow mine and stick my tongue out at him. He laughs and shakes his head, probably in amazement.

"Thank you, Mary," I reply as I take my seat. He brings two cups of coffee over and sits opposite me with a paper so I instantly smirk at him and his *Times* broadsheet. That damned brow rises as if he senses my amusement and dares me to challenge him on the matter.

"With all the forms of technology around, you still choose to read an actual paper?" I laugh out as Mary places two delicious looking pates of breakfast in front of us.

"Paper feels better in my hands. It's tactile, flexible," he replies as he swipes his glasses from his pocket and puts them on. Wow, utter sexpot has arrived. He's pretty damn good without them, but holy fuck... The black thin frames sit right on the bridge of his elegant nose and accentuate his bright blue eyes to perfection. He reminds me of all those teacher fantasies that girls talk about at school and I giggle to myself as the thought of canes crosses my mind. I dare say Mr. White is probably quite handy with one. "Something funny, Elizabeth?"

"Thinking of classrooms," I say as I bite into some of my bacon. His mouth twitches in amusement as he turns a page and peers over his frames at me, which causes immediate leg clamping to occur. Oh my god, the man's an utter fiend, and I really have to go to work so I lower my eyes again in the hope of dispelling the very inappropriate visions that have arrived. "Are you tired? You said you only ever wear them when you're tired."

"A little," he replies as he begins demolishing his plate of food. "Are you still okay for Thursday night? And by the way, I assume you're coming to Conner's party with me on Saturday? "

"Oh shit, I'd forgotten about that. Yes of course, and yes Thursday's fine. I'm intrigued," I reply as I stand and take my plate over to the dishwasher while I mentally scan my wardrobe for something appropriate. I haven't got anything but Belle more than likely has. Actually, I have all the stuff upstairs. I wander back to him and grab my bag off the back of the chair as he sips his coffee. "Do you mind if Michael takes me in? I need to get going."

"I'll take you. Andrews is on holiday," he says, dropping his paper. "Just give me two minutes." He strides out of the kitchen and runs up the stairs. On holiday? I fiddle with my bracelet while I wait for him and smile at its glittering diamonds. I haven't taken it off since he gave it to me again, not once. I shower with it and sleep in it. Where I go, it goes. I can't help but grin at the meaning of it, and the fact that I'm that important to someone, to him. Of all the people on the planet, I never expected someone like Alexander White to see me as special in any way, and as I watch the diamonds glinting back at me. I wonder what it is that he sees in me.

Two minutes later and he sweeps in, picks up some keys from the key rack and takes my hand as he leads me through the back of the kitchen. This is new. I have no idea where were going. Two corridors and several doors later, he's pressing numbers into a keypad by the side of a steel door. It opens sideways with a swoosh of air and I damn near fall over as I look at the interior of what is, I assume, the garage. I look over the badges and know nothing about any of them. Yes, I can drive a fast car because of Henry's incessant mania, but some of these look super fast. *Ferrari, Lamborghini, McLaren, Range Rover*, three bikes that I have no idea about. The *Aston Martin* is at the front and the *Bentley* sits in the corner, looking decidedly sober in comparison to the flashes of blue, red and white on the other cars.

"Well that's a lot of cars, Mr. White," I say as I run my fingers across the smooth lines of what is apparently a *McLaren*.

"They're fast, and I do like my toys," he says with a chuckle. "Which one do you want?"

"I have no idea," I reply, gazing on in astonishment while he fiddles with a lock box by the keypad. "What else do you have hiding in this house?" He chuckles again and throws some keys at me.

"Lots of things. We'll take the *Aston*. You can drive," he says as he stands by the side of it with his hands in his pockets, looking thoroughly beautiful in his three-piece grey pinstripe suit. "I quite like you in charge of me." I smirk at him and run over to it like a schoolgirl, not that we'll be going anywhere fast at this time of day in London traffic, but maybe I can hurtle up the drive in style.

~

Wednesday morning is what it promised to be: quiet, thank god. We've got no parties or dinners planned and so I get the day to potter around my kitchen and prepare for tomorrow afternoon's Christmas 'drinkie-poos' at the Carrington house. That's what Mrs Carrington calls the shindig that she holds every year. It will only be nibble type things so all I need to do is organise myself. All the ingredients are in the back ready and James is coming in tomorrow morning to help me before we need to be serving at lunchtime. I should be able to make it back to meet Alex at six-thirty as the party finishes at four and as long as traffic doesn't hinder us, which it possibly will, we'll be fine. However, with Christmas shopping starting in earnest, the streets are so hectic and the roads even more so that I'm potentially winging it as usual in the hope that all will be well. It reminds me that I haven't bought a sodding thing yet, and what I'm going to get for Alex God only knows. What the bloody hell do you buy someone like him?

The day rumbles along quietly and can't help thinking about what happened on Monday. I felt fine on Tuesday morning, but talking with Belle about it last night seems to have brought the whole thing back to me with a vengeance. I was very nearly raped, in a toilet, drunk. If Alex hadn't got there in time, I would be in a very different situation now - possibly in hospital, maybe even... No, I'm not thinking about that. I shudder at the thought and turn back to my vegetable preparation, slamming the knife down onto the chopping board with a loud clank. I need some self-defence lessons. I will not be in that situation again. Yes, I'd had a bit of throw your hands about defence when I was at school, but I couldn't get away from that man. No matter how hard I tried, he completely overpowered me. I briefly wonder whether I should ask Alex to teach me and then quickly flick my thoughts to someone more professional. Not that Alex couldn't teach me to kick butt very enthusiastically. He obviously has more venom than anyone I've ever seen but he's too close to me. I need someone I'm happy to hit without feeling guilty about it. Actually, thinking about it, there's been a few times I've desperately wanted to kick his butt. Perhaps he is the right choice after all.

"Belle, who do we know that can teach self-defence?" I ask as I round the corner into the office.

"I don't know anyone but I think Teresa took some lessons a few years ago," she replies as she straightens her skirt and slips on her heels. "Right I'm off then. Is she still coming over tonight?"

"Yes, she bloody well is. We haven't had a good girly giggle for ages. You pair and your boyfriends have been decidedly neglectful," Teresa shouts from the front. I don't know how she hears everything but she always does.

"Okay, I'll see you both at about eight. I've just got to get this meeting with the Bauers out of the way then I'll definitely be ready for a drink," she says as she walks out the back door with a wave. I walk the other way to find Teresa. She's closing down the shop and fiddling about with the flowers that arrived yesterday, from Conner this time, astonishingly. The combined smell of his lilies and Alex's Roses that arrived today are, while wonderful, starting to overpower the shop somewhat. The idea of a deli come bakery is that you smell the food, not flowers.

"Let's take them home," I suggest as I pick up the two vases and carry them into the back. I wrap them up in some greaseproof paper and hand a bunch to Teresa.

"God, you two are bloody lucky - two incredibly hot, incredibly rich bachelors chasing your arses all over the place," she says with her typical giggle.

"I'm not sure that lucky is the right word, honey. Alex, for one, is hard bloody work, albeit totally worth it," I reply with a wink as we walk out the front door and pull down the shutters.

"How the hell are we supposed to carry these on the tube without killing them?" she says as she fumbles to find a comfortable holding position for the huge bunch of lilies and gardenias. I'm messing around with my pink and lemon roses while trying to lock up the padlocks.

"I have no idea. Carefully?" I reply with a snigger as I start to walk up the street with her.

The noise of London envelops us as we march our way ungracefully toward the tube station and try to avoid every oncoming person in case we attack them with our bouquets. We don't talk that much. One never does at this time of day. It's far more important to just look where you're going, and the fact is that while I love London, the people are aggressive as hell at rush hour. They're all so desperate to get home that they'll happily knock you flying if they can get one step further in front of you. Give it an hour or so and they'll change into beaming lights of joy and happiness but at the moment... well, just watch your step.

Just as we're about to descend the steps, I hear my name being called and look around for the very familiar voice with a smile of delight plastered across my face. The door opens on a black limousine at the side of the road as that black cane knocks at the floor twice to get my attention. I turn to see Teresa open-mouthed gaping at the car and nudge her to follow me over. I poke my head inside to see him lounging with a glass of champagne and that disarmingly naughty grin of his.

"Would you two lovely morsels like a carriage to somewhere?" he says as he lifts his flute to me. "There is more than enough room in here for a ménage a trois, my rose." I smirk wildly at him and watch his green eyes rove over me.

"Well thank you, kind sir," I reply as I tug a blushing Teresa's hand and step inside. He winks at me and then turns his intense stare to her as she seats herself in the corner as far away from him as she can and gazes out the window. Even I am a little puzzled at her sudden bizarre behaviour as she fiddles with Belle's flowers. Never in my life have I known her to be anything but open, honest and relaxed.

"Am I to presume she is afraid of me, Elizabeth?" he asks as the car pulls back into traffic. Her eyes instantly shoot to his and I watch her steel herself again. If there's one thing she isn't it's scared. She grew up with four brothers, and while she's nervous for some reason, she's definitely not afraid. I watch her demeanour change to one of conflict and lift my eyebrows at her because I have no clue as to what she's doing. I know she thinks he's hot so why isn't she doing the normal Teresa flirty thing? Even I can't disagree with that because, frankly, he looks bloody good sat there in his probably *Armani* suit and light pink shirt, effortlessly looking like every woman's fantasy. He's not Alex. There's something more ethereal about him, and he hasn't got that raw, maybe damaged appeal that Alex holds so well but he absolutely has something I can't get out of my system.

"No, *she's* damn well not afraid of you," she suddenly spurts out quite assertively, bringing me back from my unfortunate lusting. I really need to get rid of that. His mouth immediately turns to a huge grin of mischief and I can't stop the laugh that comes from my mouth.

"Oh, my dear, you do keep exceptional company. What is her name?" I begin to open my mouth but she cuts me off before I get a chance.

"If you want it, you'll have to ask me directly, and nicely." Okay, where the hell has this little spitfire come from? And what is she trying to achieve? I'm really not convinced this is the best way to deal with Mr. Van Der Braak at all. I continue watching the little floor show with amusement and a certain amount of trepidation. He's never been anything but gentlemanly with me, well apart from the clear dominance thing, but I've seen his attitude towards others. I wouldn't want to be on the wrong end of that cane any time soon.

He stills for a moment as if trying to solve a conundrum. I've never seen him look hesitant before and it intrigues me. He reaches for my bouquet and snaps off a rose head before I think quickly enough to stop him and leans toward her.

"May I?" he asks quietly as he hovers his hand by her face. She continues her glare without the slightest movement. He extends his arm and tucks the rose behind her ear. "I am not sure I need your name, little one. Your bite appears to be quite enough," he says as he leans back again and gazes at her. She still hasn't removed her eyes from him but her face has softened a little. She's such a sucker for romance.

"So, my rose, how are you? Is Alexander behaving himself?" he says as he continues his gaze at her. She eventually looks out of the window and effectively dismisses his attention. Is she trying to wind him up?

"Good, Pascal, thank you and yes, although I would never ask him to behave himself too much," I reply with a smile as he turns his elegant body to me. "How are you? What have you been up to?"

"Bored, that is what I am. Life is deathly dull and underwhelming without the pair of you available for my entertainment," he says with an exasperated sigh as he reaches for my hand and brings it to his lips. I smile with warmth at him and think back to last time we were together.

"Well, perhaps it's time for you to find that more meaningful thing we talked about, Pascal," I reply as he strokes his hand over my bracelet and chuckles to himself.

"Mmm, I am afraid I find that unacceptable, my dear. I am sure temptation will present itself soon enough but I must admit, my patience is wearing a little thin," he says as the car pulls to a stop. "And now even you are taken from me again," he says as he points his cane at our apartment. How on earth did we get here that quickly? Maybe the floorshow took longer than I thought. My eyes shoot back to his. How did he know where I lived?

"How did you...?"

"If something interests me, there is nothing I do not know, my dear."

Oh, right. I'm still not sure what I should think of his interest in me or my own in him, frankly, so I smirk at him and gather up my flowers in the hope of escaping those green eyes.

"You should come over for dinner sometime. I'm sure Alex would enjoy it and I certainly would," I say as a female driver opens the door. She's gorgeous, not unexpectedly.

"Thank you for the lift," Teresa says abruptly as she steps out without even looking at him. He doesn't acknowledge her in the slightest.

"I'm afraid I have been banished from talking with you for the time being, my dear. He will need time to calm himself," he replies with a sad smile. I hate it instantly and can't stop my finger reaching forward and grazing over his lips. He stills completely and looks almost lost for a moment before grabbing my hand from his lips. I can't believe Alex would do such a thing, would he? Maybe he would in this twilight world they appear to live in.

"Well that didn't stop you offering me a lift, did it? I'm sure you know your own mind, Pascal. This is the real world after all. And I'll work on Alex. It appears he's behaving like a child," I say, leaning in to kiss his cheek. God, he smells good. He moves his head at the last second so my lips land on his and the warmth of them instantly reminds me of his apartment. I pull back quickly and his eyebrow quirks up, those emerald eyes twinkling again and his naughty smile returning. It's much better, however, his licking of lips has me thinking very inappropriate thoughts again.

"Go now, Elizabeth, before I forget my manners and drag you back in here. You know how I despise decency," he says as he releases my hand with a final brush of his fingers. I grin at him and step out of the car. "And do give your little friend my number when she's ready. She may be an interesting diversion for a while, until you're ready for me, that is," he continues with a chuckle as he slides back into the depths of the limousine.

"Goodbye, Pascal," I say quietly as the driver closes the door on him and snarls at me. I can't contain my laughter at her as she wiggles her hips back to the driver's door. Yes, he's probably had her, but if she thinks he belongs to her she's got another thing coming. I doubt the man will ever belong to anybody.

I turn for the apartment and see Teresa standing at the entrance of the building wearing a smug, self-satisfied grin on her face.

"Oh my God, what the hell came over you? Are you out of your mind?" I ask her in amazement, walking over to elevator. She grins stupidly at me and presses the button. "No seriously, Teresa, that's Pascal you're messing with."

"I know. Sensational, isn't he? Always thought he was gorgeous," she replies with a giggle as I unlock the door and we throw our bags to the floor. "Wine?" I nod at her and grab the glasses.

"I don't understand. If you like him, why did you act like a complete arse?" I have no idea what her plan is but it's not one I would have considered. She wanders over to the sofa and deposits herself on it. Having put the flowers in two vases of water, I go to my usual chair and slump down.

"Well, Beth, I wasn't entirely honest about the last time I saw him. I actually spent the entire night salivating over him as I watched him use and dismiss at least fifteen women. They were all throwing themselves at him, as I'm sure you can imagine. It was quite humiliating for them really. I remember thinking then that if I ever got a chance to be within ten foot of him, I wouldn't be like that in the slightest. A man like that needs something unattainable. I dare say that's why you're of such interest to him. He's a very bad man and I absolutely want every mean inch of him, just for one night you understand," she replies casually as she pours the wine and relaxes back. "I really do like this olive green colour you've got on the walls. Where did you get it from?"

I gape at her in surprise. She said she didn't like the bondage and pain thing. Well, she'll be getting it from him. I can't believe she's even thinking about it if I'm honest and what's more disturbing is the little nagging twinge of jealousy that's winging its way over my skin. What the hell is that? And wall coverings? Really?

"Jensons, it's around the corner, and you do realise he's kind of kinky? In fact, he's all kinds of perverted apparently. I thought you said you weren't into it?" I reply as my phone beeps in my pocket. I pull it out to scan the text.

- Go to the front desk. I've left a present for you.

Alex... Oh, a present. God, I hope it's not one of his overly priced gifts. I wish he would just understand that and accept it. I'd be in a shack with him, well maybe not a shack, but certainly a normal kind of lifestyle. Normal, I giggle to myself as I make my way to the door because that word just doesn't sit well with him at all.

"Just got to get something, honey, back in a moment," I say to Teresa as I shoot out the door and press the call button. What's he left for me? I practically run across to the desk. The security guy looks at me with a smile.

"You've got a package for Elizabeth Scott?" I say excitedly. He ducks his head down and passes me a small white envelope. I thank him and shoot back to the lift as I open it. A key falls out and I stare at it in puzzlement and then slide out the card as the lift doors open.

So you'll always have somewhere safe to run to.
What's mine is yours. Your alarm code is CHESS.
Ax

Oh Christ, is this his house key? Wow! Well that's unexpected. I don't even know what to think about that. It's not an overly priced gift; that's a good thing. His reference to safety is definitely about last Monday night and that's really very sweet. What's mine is yours? That's... I don't know what that means at all. I'm confused. I suppose when you're in love with someone that's what you do, give them your key, but the thought hadn't even crossed my mind. In fact, Alex hasn't even been to my apartment for more than a few minutes. I open the door and go immediately to the safety of my chair.

"Oh good you're back. So did Pascal ask me to call him?" Teresa asks as she tops up her wine.

"Yes," I reply quietly while I study the card in front of me. Am I ready for this with him? I love him and he says he loves me. That's good. Why am I thinking about this? It's just a key, but it's not for him, is it? This is probably the first time he's ever been so open with anyone, the first time he's really let someone in and tried to give them everything he has. I'm instantly overwhelmed as I begin to realise the importance of his love for me, of his commitment to me and of my understanding of him. He would have killed that man, not because he couldn't control himself but because it was me. It suddenly strikes me that if it had been another woman, he might well have ignored it. Every piece of him he reveals is like another layer of skin being peeled back to uncover another uncomfortable truth that he hates to admit to me. He's slowly lowering every barrier he ever put in place and now he's removing the one barrier that could keep me away from him: his home. He's giving me the key to his solace. A tear hits the card and I realise I'm crying happily, with love for a man I thought would never open up everything for me.

"Well, where the fuck is the fucking wine? What a bunch of knobs. Jesus, a party for four hundred in two days? What sodding planet do some people live on?" My head shoots up as I wipe at my tears and I see an irritated Belle launch herself at her wine already poured by Teresa. "And what the hell is wrong with you, Snotbag? Mr. Good Legs fucked up again?"

"To be honest, I was about to ask the same thing," Teresa says from my side as she snatches the card from my hand and scans it with a smile. "Well, well, well, moving in, are we?" she says as she passes it to Belle.

"I'm not sure that's the point of the key," I reply with a chuckle as I lay it on the table in front of me and pick up my drink. "So what about the Bauers? A no-go then?"

"No, definitely not. I told them we could do it in February at a push, but in our kitchen, four hundred people in two days, with no prep time? Not a hope. We need a bigger kitchen. It's as simple as that. And with Mum, well, you know... God, I hate saying no to good money."

We would normally use Mum and Dad for this sort of thing but after my phone call with him on Tuesday afternoon, it isn't even a consideration. She'd begun testing again, not that either of us needed clarification on the matter because it was pretty obvious. He sounded devastated and to be honest, so were we. We'd all been through this before and while she'd made it out the other side of breast cancer safely, it had damn near killed her the first time. Second time, who knew? He'd sounded so upset that I very nearly got in the car and belted down the motorway, but he'd told me to stay away, that he wasn't going to tell Mum that we knew because she'd worry too much and that wouldn't help with her stress levels. Regardless, I was going on Friday. Belle couldn't but as James had been a complete star and promised to do the whole of prep and serving for Soresbury Halls Christmas buffet, I had the time so I was going to use it.

"Well, have you sorted figures for the loan yet? Let's get our backsides to the bank. The Spotty Pig's doing well and we could always stick that in for collateral if we have to. The base rates are very good at the moment. We need this as soon as possible. What do the accounts look like?" Belle gawps at me and even Teresa flaps her mouth about. "What?"

"Bloody hell, girl, where has Miss Business-brain come from? You normally just sign the paperwork and leave the rest to me," Belle says as she begins taking off her clothes and walks into the bedroom. She comes back out in a pair of leggings and t-shirt.

"I think someone else's business brain is rubbing off on her," Teresa says with a giggle. "You better watch your figures, Belle. You're the one that called him - what was it? - oh yes, *a pure business brain on a killing spree with hands made for butchery.*" I watch her wander over to the kitchen and rifle through the take-away drawer. "I'm calling for pizza. Normal for everyone?" We both nod.

I think about that for a moment. Is that the man I'm in love with? He seems to have changed so much since those first few visions of him. I'll have to ask him. He'll be highly amused at that description of himself. His control of Pascal flits through my mind. How does he do that to a man like Pascal? And why? Control, hands made for butchery, who is he deep down? And how am I managing to release a bit of him?

216

I still have no idea. It makes me wonder whether he's softened in his work environment, too. Funnily enough, I hope not. While it was nice to watch the people at the ball see his more emotive side, he's clearly done very well for himself being a total shit. It suits him, and as long as I get the other, more honest version of him, I really don't mind.

But Belle has definitely struck a chord. I've been thinking more and more about the fundamentals of business since I've met him. Regardless of him being a callous bastard, which was never going to be my style, he does induce a more focused side of my mind to commit itself to numbers. I'm good at what I do, but I've always left all the business matters to Belle. She's very good at them. I've never felt guilty but for some reason over the last few months, I've just been more interested.

I look at the key on the table and smile. He's changing me, just as I'm apparently changing him. First my confidence with wealthy people, then my sexual appetite and now I'm becoming a numbers lady... Well bloody hell, I like every one of those changes with a passion. I stretch across for my phone and giggle to myself as I text him back.

- Thank you, I love you too. X

Chapter 12

Alexander

The drive had given him time to think. He didn't need it because he knew exactly what he was going to do and it didn't take a fucking genius to work out why. That the fool had the stupidity to even think about touching her was incomprehensible, but people did strange things and god knows she was stunning. No, stunning was too plain somehow. Maybe arresting was more acceptable.

Guy Chambers had been a trusted employee for almost three years. Alex never really cared that much for the man but he had always been on time for his shifts, he'd served his time as a bouncer in an exemplary manner and had on several occasions sorted out some difficult scuffles, but he never thought of the man as a rapist. It just confirmed his inherent distrust of people and reminded him to start looking behind the persona again. Most humans were simply out for themselves and it seemed this particular person had seen fit to try his luck with Elizabeth.

The dick had called her one of his whores, and that they all knew what Alex liked. Did they fuck. No one in his club had ever seen a fragment of what he liked. If they had have done, they would never consider touching what was his, but it made him wonder how many times it had happened before. Not that he gave a shit if the man had fucked every other girl he'd had before her, only that he'd been disrespected by not being asked for permission first. Well, it wouldn't be happening again anytime soon regardless. Guy had tried that move on the wrong woman this time - his woman, his air to breathe.

He sneered at the thought as he pulled onto the dirt road and crossed the old wooden bridge into the quarry. Rolling his phone contacts for Mark's number, he called as he brushed some dirt off the dash of the Range Rover. He really should have Andrews take it for a valet. He didn't use it much but the dust was disgraceful and he didn't appreciate having to sit in filth, regardless of the situation.

Waiting for Mark to answer, he scanned the area and pulled to a stop under the old garage area.

"Yep," Mark answered breathlessly after a while.

"What the hell took so long?" he asked tersely. Christ, he hated waiting.

"Oh, I was having a bit of fun, sorry, mate." He shook his head and started to climb out of the car.

"I assume he is at least still alive?"

"Oh yeah, I wouldn't have finished him," Mr. Jacobs replied with a chuckle as he removed his shirt and jacket and folded them up on the back seat along with his phone. The jeans didn't matter. He had to be in a suit in an hour or so anyway. Rolling his neck around, he locked the door, pulled the garage door down and headed for the old iron gates that led into the pit. The cold air instantly hit his chest, causing a refreshing shiver as he descended the steps and focused his eyes on the dimly lit area. Two underground lamps lit the old mine shaft weakly as he made his way along the familiar roughened ground and remembered the last time he was here. Reggie Hanson had been a wealthy but idiotic small time crook, looking to gain access to the big boys by blackmailing London's notoriously neurotic Drugs Lord, Aiden Phillips, Alex's employer at the time and friend now. Well, friend was a little past the mark, but respected ally was probably an acceptable compromise. But needless to say, Mr. Hanson had never had the opportunity to blackmail anyone after he'd been dealt with in the pit.

He watched his boots get dustier as he continued his descent and mentally chastised himself for not bringing shoe polish with him. Christ, he'd bet his life on the fact that Jacobs would have some. Shit, business had made him forget all those little details that had kept him from being found out before. He'd perfected the art years ago but now he was a fucking softy in comparison to the way he was when this was his life. His every waking moment had been based on who needed what from him, and how much he had to inflict to get the information required, or shut someone up completely.

He shook his head and chuckled to himself as he entered the vast space deep beneath the ground and heard Mark's laughter coming from the end of it. If there was one thing Mr. Jacobs enjoyed, it was nearly killing a man and then giving the poor bastard a chance to recover - a technique Alex had learnt to admire, albeit not necessarily use himself. His own choice of amusement had been firmly rooted in someone's sense of fear, of what could happen before it inevitably did. It still was really. He'd spent plenty of time taunting, torturing and goading to get whatever he needed from them before he did what he was paid to do.

Flexing out his fists and stretching his hands as he wandered across to the pair of them, he noticed that Mark had even gone to the lengths of untying the prick completely and letting him think he had a chance of getting away. *Fucking idiot.*

Guy Chambers was on all fours, spitting up blood again and scrabbling about in the dust, presumably to try and find something to hit his attacker with. Alex inclined his head to the side and crouched down in front of the man as he pushed his own hands into the dirt and then rolled the chalky grit into his palms. The man was a mess of blood and bruises, just the way he fucking should be. He was only still breathing because Alex had been more concerned about getting Elizabeth to safety and away from what she'd watched him unleash. Her look of disgust had been firmly implanted at the time she'd thrown it at him and he could still feel it now, burrowing under his skin, making him feel something other than the nothing he normally felt in these situations.

Just as he went to rise, the dick lifted his head and spat at him. He watched the blood roll down his chest and frowned. While the blood was significant, it wasn't even nearly enough for what was about to happen. He stood up, grabbed a metal chair that had been discarded and began the process of wrapping his hands. He hadn't intended on it but the rapist scum could be carrying any fucking disease. He noticed that Mark had not had such foresight. He probably didn't care either. Actually, on further examination it seemed Mark hadn't used his fists at all. A long length of lead piping had been his weapon of choice, apparently.

"No hands this time?" he asked of Mr. Jacobs.

"Nah, AP likes us to look a bit cleaner these days, says we need a weapon. I've never had much time for guns - too quick," he replied with a shrug. Alex rolled his eyes at Mark's weapon and got a returning grin of utter pleasure. God, he'd almost forgotten what a maniac the man was.

"Guy, why did you think it appropriate to rape my girlfriend?" Alex asked as he tied the last of the bandage off and walked over to him. There was no response other than a spluttered cough so he kicked him in the head and watched him fall to his side with a cry of pain. A few moments later, he hauled himself up to a kneeling position, so he kicked him back over again. The fucking arsehole didn't deserve to be anywhere other than on the floor. "Shall I ask you again? You see, I just can't fathom why you would sentence yourself to death."

"Fuck you!" Guy yelled as he spat out some more blood and had the audacity to look him in the eyes. He would have laughed if the little shit hadn't have actually tried it with Elizabeth. Of all the whores the man could have chosen, possibly did, she was not one of them and never would be.

"Well, eloquent as that is, it still isn't an answer. I just want to know if you thought I was going soft? You know who I am. You were Aiden's before you came to me."

The dick made some gurgling noise that sounded something like a word but he couldn't hear so he aimed a punch at his nose. The cartilage crunched gloriously beneath his fist so he hit him twice more for good measure and then circled him while looking for signs of retaliation. There wasn't any. Unfortunately for Alex, this wasn't what he was after at all. The man was so exhausted and beaten up that he didn't have a hope of fighting back or talking very well apparently. "Any answers yet?"

"Why not?" the man mumbled almost incoherently. "Just another fucking whore." Alex was so shocked at the admission that he took a step back.

"Did he just say why not?" he said to Mark in utter amazement. Mark shrugged and swung his pipe about again. "Did you just suggest that you tried to rape her because you hadn't got anything better to do?" he asked as he stamped on the man's knee, relishing in the crack that resonated in the space around them. The awkward angle of the joint and the cries of pain made it obvious that it was broken so he crouched and tore at the joint more until it felt completely loose in his hands. More screams of pain and hand scrabbling later, his own irritation began to set in. He couldn't get the old feeling back. He wasn't enjoying the torture as he once had, and he felt slightly

221

disgusted by his behaviour for some fucking irrational reason so he stood up.

Looking at Mark, he wondered if he should make this go on longer than it needed to just to ensure that Mr. Jacobs knew he was still capable of it. He narrowed his eyes at the man rolling around in the dirt. He probably should but the fact was he didn't have the enthusiasm for the fun of it anymore. He loved her and just wanted the man to pay for his idiotic behaviour. He didn't care if the idiot learnt a lesson or not because he wouldn't be around to change the way he acted, and therefore his opinion didn't matter in the slightest.

He watched Guy give up on the floor beneath him and pondered his next move. The man didn't deserve to live, not because he was a rapist but because he choose the wrong woman and the wrong man to cross for that matter. Would she ask about this? And if she did, what would he tell her?

He presumed she wouldn't be too happy to find out that the man she loved had killed someone, even if it was Guy Chambers. He hadn't even begun to process what she might think of all the others but then he wasn't going to tell her so that didn't matter. He sighed as he looked down at the man and held his hand out to Mark for the lead pipe. He heard the laughter burst from Mark's mouth as he passed him the lead and walked off towards the entrance.

"I'll see you in ten, mate," he called as his footsteps echoed out of the doorway.

Alex stared for six of those minutes as he listened to the man start the begging process and clamber up to his knees again, as best he could with the damage there. They all did that, begged for their lives as if it would make a difference to him somehow. It never did, so he just gazed at the stuttering fool. The image of her asleep in his bed after the event drifted through his mind as he remembered watching her all night so he could ensure she was safe and promised himself to never leave her alone again, to keep her protected. She'd looked so small in that foetal position and he'd stroked her beautiful head until she'd stretched her lean body back out again and finally relaxed enough to sleep peacefully. That she'd trusted him enough to fall asleep at all, given her attack, was so mesmerizing that he'd just stayed there and watched her breathing, kept his fingers attached to hers to remind himself of her touch, even though she hadn't wanted to give it to him. He wasn't surprised at the time. He must have disgusted her with his actions.

Eventually the thought that he had other matters to attend to today stirred him back into action so he raised the length of lead, looked into the man's eyes, smiled at them widening in fear and then smashed it repeatedly into the side of his head. Sadly, the dull thud of cracking bone did nothing to appease the angry visions of the fucker's hands on her, but it did release a little of the tension that it had created for him. However, if the experience was supposed to be cathartic in some way, it fell short of total exoneration so he snarled at his own infuriation with the man and gripped the pipe tighter. As he delivered another heavy blow, it was suddenly apparent in his mind that this was probably what loving someone did to the prospect of revenge. It appeared that it wasn't enough to see the recipient dead for his actions or even to be the one to inflict the sentence. Given that he'd never cared about someone before, he'd presumed that this would solve the problem. It didn't it seemed. He wondered if he should have made the man suffer more or if he should have made Elizabeth watch the event. Or maybe she should have done this herself. Would that have been more therapeutic somehow? Who fucking knew? So he just kept slicing the pipe through the air in his normal methodical manner, as if it were nothing more than a tool for work of some sort. It wasn't normal to be this dispassionate about killing, he was sure, but as all the old numbness crept over him, he watched the blood splatter the dirt and smiled. Exonerated or not, this fucker wasn't ever going to touch her again. He wouldn't ever be touching anything again.

There wouldn't be anything left of the fucking body.

When he thought he'd done a thorough enough job of ending the man's existence, he watched the jerky movements of the body impassively as the residual movement of damaged nerves finally gave up their fight for life as well. He pushed his own boot onto the corpse's chest hard and heard the whoosh of air leave the fucker's lips for the last time with a sneer as those dead eyes stared back lifelessly. He tilted his head at the figure and tried to find a sense of shame in himself, or maybe remorse of some sort, but there was nothing again, just silence and the echo of his own breathing in the cold space around them. Disgusted with the lifeless form, he drew in a long breath and cracked his neck back into place while circling his shoulder about. He really was getting too old for this shit. He'd said he'd never do that again. But then he'd never loved before, never loved *her* before, and whether she liked it or not, he'd kill for her. He just had and he'd do it again in a heartbeat.

Hearing the sudden unison clicking steps of the Tomkins brothers arriving behind him, he turned around to hand the pipe to one of them. He never did know which one was which. The twins were Mark's clean-up crew so their job was to dispose of everything clinically without a trace of anything ever having happened. He nodded at them as they saluted with their customary smirks and went about their business professionally. The smell of chemicals penetrated his nose before he'd walked five paces, and he smiled at the thought of Guy Chambers burning in acid as he listened to the pair of them chuckling, bantering even about him still being a brutal bastard to have onside. They were right, or they were where Elizabeth was concerned anyway. Christ knew how he'd ever gotten away with this respectable image he apparently pulled off.

Well wasn't that a fucking happy half-hour? He unwrapped his hands and used the bandages to wipe off some of the blood that was smeared all over him while trying to work out how best to clean up his boots. Tan and blood were not a good combination, yet another forgotten thing.

When he reached the car, he doused himself with a bottle of water, changed out of his jeans and started to put his suit on. Mark leant on the car in front of him with that self-satisfied, smug expression of his. Alex snorted at him in amusement and bucked his belt.

"Just like old times, hey, mate? Thought you might have come in a suit this time though," Mark said jovially as he pulled up the garage door. Was it? It didn't really feel like old times for some reason.

"Can't get the blood out of Saville Row," he replied quietly as he grabbed his phone and scrolled through for Henry's number. Mark chuckled in response.

"Yeah, AP says that, too. Okie dokie, so I'll see ya soon," Mark said as he jumped into his red *Porsche*. How he'd gotten over the rocky ground was beyond comprehension. "Oh, and by the way, I found out something about that cousin of DeVille's. I'll send you the paperwork. I think he might have been one of yours." Alex raised a brow. At last a piece of useful information.

"What was his name?" Frankly there had been so many he doubted he'd remember.

"Grant Monroe the third. Don't think you knew that then, though."

No he didn't, but he did remember Monroe, whining little prick as he'd been at the time.

"Thanks," Alex replied as he got in and started the engine. Mark Jacobs didn't need to know anymore. "Right, round two," he muttered to himself as he brought the phone up to his ear and called Henry with a more animated smile. It was becoming a good day.

~

The phone call to Mrs Peters had been difficult but unfortunately, it wasn't his fault that the woman had lied to Evelyn all her life. Regardless of whether she wanted to tell her daughter or not, he was going to meet his half-sister on Saturday night anyway so he didn't really have much choice. He'd made it as comfortable as possible by offering to have Mr. and Mrs Peters flown down and put up in a nice hotel, but frankly, what else could he do? She apparently wanted to see Evelyn before the event at INK to tell her about the whole sordid situation, so they were travelling down to London tomorrow. What the hell she was going to tell the poor woman was anyone's guess? He hadn't given the old lady much time to prepare for the fact that she was about to tell her daughter she was a product of rape, but then he didn't have much time to play with and frankly, he wasn't sure he gave a shit anyway. His memory drifted to Elizabeth and her words of comfort as they gazed at pictures of his mother - his dead mother. Was his mother dead because of her own sister's weakness? He'd told her he didn't blame her but he wasn't entirely sure if that was true. Yes, his father was a vicious bastard but surely they could have gotten away from him if they'd tried harder. He shook his head at his own thoughts as he remembered his own pathetic attempt to get away from the bastard. It wasn't until he'd stolen the neighbour's car that any of it had been discovered and then the care system had swooped in and apparently saved him, which was a fucking

225

joke. He'd learnt how to be a tyrant in that place, not how to become a civilised human being.

He draped his napkin over his thigh and glanced around the restaurant as he waited for Henry. The phone call had taken every inch of his self -control, and given this morning's earlier entertainment, he was still suitably in the mood to kill. That, however, was not the plan. His game was to get closer. He knew it would take some doing but he needed to find a chink in Henry's armour and find out what he was planning. He knew that the funding from Tyler Rathbone would see the deal through so he didn't need to worry too much about that, and now, at least, he knew it was more than likely related to Grant Monroe, which could cause an extremely irritating problem for him. He needed some leverage of his own because it seemed this would become a war of who had the worst dirt. It worried him that DeVille might have proof regarding his past that would bite him irrevocably on the arse, but at the moment, what the hell could he do about it? He couldn't pay him off and he couldn't bribe him because he didn't have any concrete dirt on the man. Christ, he couldn't even hurt him because the lord of the manor would be missed too much. Fuck it, Mr. Jacobs needed to dig a lot deeper, albeit Henry wasn't a killer and what was worse than that?

The brown haired waitress smiled at him seductively as she delivered his brandy and then swished her skinny arse out of the way. He found himself staring and envisioning Elizabeth's long, lean legs walking away gracefully with a far more appealing sway to her hips. Unconsciously, he noticed his finger tapping on his knee as he remembered the hotel in the Lakes and her yielding behaviour for him. She'd let him have that time with her purely for his own benefit and god he loved her for it. He briefly toyed with the idea of taking her to Pascal's club this evening. She had proved she was ready, but would she want to go given that she was manhandled on Monday? Mind you, twenty minutes before that she'd shown him everything he wanted from her with her *do anything you want, Alex,* comment. Christ, that had been good to hear. And then of course there was still the issue of Pascal himself. Unfortunately she wanted him; he could see it on her face and in her body. That was fucking complicating to say the least. Much as he'd shared all his other women with the Dutch rogue, he couldn't quite bring himself to share her, regardless of the stirring of uncomfortable desire he'd felt when he'd watched Pascal hold her. If he could just get to the point where he honestly believed the love she had for him then maybe he'd be able to give her what she wanted. She probably didn't understand her want for two different men, as it was unlikely she'd ever ventured into those types of situations before him, but if she wanted it, he was sexually aware enough to not try and withhold it from her. Inevitably it would probably happen anyway. His dilemma was also too self-involved for his liking. As he'd never loved before, he had no idea if he'd be able to watch impartially as he so often had done prior to her. And did she really want him anyway or was it just the normal hypnotising way that Pascal seemed to have with all women? The fact that his friend had actually seemed genuinely interested in her was also a conundrum of disturbing proportions. He had even thought to challenge him in the matter, which took some serious amount of backbone, not only because they were friends, but because Pascal had never even shown a hint of attraction for anything real. If he allowed any of it to happen, would he challenge him again? For now at least he had relented and told Alex that he would stay away until he saw fit to put them back in the same room together. Perhaps he should just get on with it and see how the situation developed. Who fucking knew?

He swilled his brandy around a few times and then downed it, signalling the waitress for another. Henry appeared in his line of vision and tapped the waitress for a drink, probably a gin. Alex plastered on his executive smile and gestured at the chair as the blonde Lord of the manor arrived.

"Alex, good to see you," Henry said with his overly enthusiastic grin. Alex very nearly rolled his eyes at the very idea of them sitting here and being polite while both plotting dastardly deeds. Fucking ridiculous.

"Henry, sorry to have called a short-notice meeting but I just want to finalise the Shanghai funding, so we can move on and think about our discussions regarding Russia," he replied, trying to engage his once friend in more deals.

"Jesus, straight down to it, huh? Well, I brought the files you wanted and the varying associated documentation, so all I need is your final signature and the money's yours, and mine, of course," Henry replied with his once enigmatic smile and a chuckle. Alex knew that smile better now. It was his *you haven't got a fucking clue* smile. It struck him that hadn't been the way when he'd smiled at Elizabeth, which was obviously his genuine one. She'd clearly been telling the truth and he inwardly cursed his own distrust of her. "Have you anything in mind for Russia? I know Matthew Stuce-Triapold is looking into his grandfather's land out there and is undecided as to whether to sell or not."

"That's interesting. How's he doing? Financially, I mean?" he asked as the waitress returned with their drinks. Gin - so predictable. Henry grinned conspiratorially and took a long drink.

"Not that well, there's definitely acreage up for grabs at a very good price I should say," he replied with a wink. Alex stored the information as it was probably reasonably useful even if he knew he would never be dealing with Henry again. Money was money. He'd take it anywhere he could find it, and Matthew was a half-decent human. He nodded his head, effectively ending the business discussion as he took the files Henry passed him.

"So how's Sarah?" Henry's body tightened quietly and Alex knew he'd hit a sore spot but chose to ignore the reaction. He couldn't help but think of the poor woman being in love with him and not the man opposite.

"She's well. Carrington's is booming and she's thinking of opening a new shop in Paris. I suppose it will be good for her," he replied as he perused the menu. "Anyway, tell me about your involvement with the Scott girl."

Ah, he'd been waiting for this one and was still unsure how to handle it. Did he tell him how important she was or did he let the bastard believe she was another mere conquest? Given that Henry actually liked her, she wouldn't be used against him, would she? Maybe she would. Just as he was considering his response, his phone buzzed. He looked down to see the text and furrowed his brow instantly.

- **She still smells divine, dear boy. I envy you too much for my own liking.**

Pascal, what the fuck did that mean? Where was she? And why the fucking hell was Pascal close enough to smell her?

228

"Problems?" Henry asked as he sniggered dryly across his menu at him.

"Yes, a small one," he said as indifferently as he could, racking his brain as to where she was. She said she'd got a big party to cater for today so it was unlikely Pascal was near her.

"If you need to go, it's of no consequence to me. We can do this another time," Henry said while he flagged down the girl and placed his order. Steak - another predicable thing about him. Why he ever bothered to look at a menu was anybody's guess. Alex stared at the man's Nordic features and wondered why he hadn't seen all the predictabilities before.

"No, it's fine. I'll deal with it later," he said as he glanced at the menu and pretended to be looking. Regardless of his outward appearance, jealousy was surging through his veins and he was desperate to get to her. He looked up at the waitress and smiled. "I'll have the cod please and bring a bottle of the Sancerre will you? We've got a lot to talk about." His gaze landed back on Henry as the bastard chuckled and slapped his hand on the table.

"That's what I like, a man that does what he wants." He shooed the waitress away and leaned across the table. "So tell me, what's she like? Does she ride as well as I might think?"

The thought made him cringe but he raised a brow and resigned himself to the fact that this was going to be a long lunch of lies and deceit. Perhaps he'd at least have more information by the end of it, though, because sitting here close to the man he'd once considered a friend was one of the hardest games he'd had to play in a very long time. Thankfully, after this morning's events, he felt a little more invigorated by the thought of playing again. He picked up his phone and texted Pascal his response. That fucker could have some of his real thoughts instead. Mind you, the bastard enjoyed pain far too much.

- **Don't make me warn you again. You won't like it this time.**

Two and a half hours later, he stepped onto the pavement outside the restaurant and passed the valet his ticket. Within two minutes, his *Aston Martin* screeched around the corner a little too enthusiastically for his liking and he glared at the young chap as he got out.

"I'm so sorry, Mr. White. It's just... Well, I haven't driven a *Vanquish* before and I got a bit... well, you know?" the boy said with a decidedly naughty grin. Alex couldn't stop the chuckle that fell from his mouth. At least he was honest. He tucked a fifty in his hand and slid into his seat. Just as he was about to pull away, he called the boy back. He wasn't even sure why.

"What's your name?"

"Joe, Sir." The boy looked sheepish. He obviously thought he was about to get a berating.

"Do you intend to do this for the rest of your life?" he asked as he gestured to the restaurant.

"Preferably not, Sir, but I need the work," the boy replied, looking truly confused by the line of questioning.

"Well, Joe," he said as he wrote a number on a piece of paper. "If you call this number and ask for Trudy, she'll show you how to drive one properly. She might even have a job that's more appealing." The boy looked at the paper and then back at him with an excited laugh. Alex smiled as a feeling of genuine happiness engulfed him. It was a good feeling and he wondered what on earth had made him offer the boy a chance without knowing if he deserved one or not. "Tell her it was me. She's a complete bitch but she can drive a car."

"I don't know what to say, Sir. Thank you," the boy replied as he pocketed the paper.

"That's all you need to say, Joe," Alex said as he closed the window and headed for the office.

That's what being good felt like then. Given that he'd killed a man this morning, he supposed it might balance out the nature of the day somehow.

Staring at various spreadsheets and documents, he was surprised to suddenly realise that Louisa stood in front of him with a confused look on her face. He took off his glasses and pinched the bridge of his nose to try and ease the headache that had formed over the last... What time was it anyway? He checked his watch; it said it was six-fifteen. Fuck! There wasn't a cat's chance in hell he was going to make it to her in fifteen minutes. He jumped up and started throwing things about. Louisa chuckled at him, and his eyes shot to hers.

"I have been trying to buzz you for the last half an hour, Sir," she said as she continued her giggling. He'd never heard her giggle so he stopped and looked at her for a moment. "Just go, Sir. I'll sort all this out and have your driver pick it up." He could have kissed her as he launched around the desk with a smile and grabbed his suit jacket.

"Thank you, Louisa," he said as he opened the door and almost ran for the lift. Just as he was getting in, she called him back.

"Sir, hold on," she said as she darted to the desk. She picked up a package and gave it to him. "I sent the red dress for Miss Scott. You'll want this." He opened the package and glanced inside with a smile.

"As always, Louisa, you have been very useful." He smirked as he backed into the lift. "How much do I pay you again?"

"Not nearly enough," she replied as she crossed her arms and returned his smirk. He said the word one aloud and let the doors close. The woman should have been a lawyer or something. She was far too good to be doing his shit. He'd give her another raise in pay and a holiday. If only he could make all her problems go away.

The drive over was laborious to say the least. He'd actually spent most of it sitting in traffic jams. When he eventually pulled up, he slid the details of Defoe Point into the side pocket of the car, grabbed the package Louisa had given him and made for the front of Scott's. On opening the door, he was rewarded with a vision he didn't think he'd ever forget.

She was sitting with her leg elegantly draped across the other one on top of the shop counter and her arms splayed out either side of her. The black heels flashed a red sole at him, which matched the dress to perfection, and as his gaze travelled the length of those incredible legs, he noticed the black laced, corseted waist section that pushed her breasts up deliciously as she leant towards him. His eyes eventually met her enthralling face and he swore his heart stopped at her gaze at him. Her soul-melting chocolate eyes seared into him and the slow curve of her lips stirred his dick straight into action. He realised instantly he wanted nothing more than to take her somewhere and show her exactly what his hands wanted to do to her. In fact, he wanted to show her here and now.

"Hi," she said. "You're very late, Mr. White." He couldn't stop himself as he strode toward her and wrapped his hand around the back of her neck.

"You are perfection, Miss Scott," he said as he pulled her mouth to his and revelled in the feeling of her soft lips against his. Her tongue slipped onto his with the sweetest hint of strawberries and he devoured it as he thought of every way he was going to have her tonight. She eventually released his mouth gently and smiled again. He swirled his fingers in one lock of tumbling red hair and returned her gaze. Fuck, he could look at her forever.

"That's quite a hello you've got there," she said as she leaned forward and kissed him delicately again. His dick throbbed again and he shook his head at his own enthusiasm for the woman in front of him.

"That's a very appealing look to say hello to," he replied as he helped her down and watched her run her hands down the dress. Stunning - there wasn't an inch of room left in it but she somehow managed to make it look refined. Others would have made the outfit appear slutty, but her grace held a more polished appearance. He grabbed onto the lacing at her back and cinched it in tighter. She gasped and then moaned as his other hand travelled to her throat. "Shall we do this now, Elizabeth? Have you ever fucked in here before?" Her body instantly said it was willing and he smiled into her shoulder as he kissed it.

"Alex," she rasped out breathlessly. Christ, he loved hearing her say his name. He released the lacing and let her go. He'd got other things to show her at the moment. They'd have to wait until later.

"I wanted to show you something," he said as he held out his hand and led her toward the door.

"I thought we were going to a meeting? I was slightly confused by your choice of outfit, I have to admit," she said as confusion marred her beautiful brow. He scanned her again. She couldn't look more exquisite if she tried.

"It is a meeting," he replied with a wink.

"Oh, right, well, I'll be interested as to why I needed to wear something so... tight then." He laughed at her as he watched her pulling the shutters and locking up.

"I like you in restricted situations, Miss Scott." He smirked as they got into the car.

"Yes, I realize that," she said quietly as she crossed her legs in the car and let the dress ride up her thigh. He pulled out into easy traffic and reached across for her leg. Her skin sent a bolt of electricity straight to his groin and he chuckled to himself at the effect she still had on him.

They drove in relative silence as he tried to think of how he was going to handle the next half an hour. He still didn't know how she was going to react to what he'd prepared so he was *'winging it,'* to use her term. He didn't often enter into negotiations of any sort without knowing every possible outcome, but this one was unusual for him. He'd never given a building to anyone before so he had no idea how it was going to pan out. The next turning set his pulse racing, and smiling to himself, he realised he was nervous. He tapped his fingers on her thigh and she turned her head to him and giggled.

"I'm struggling with whether that's nerves or excitement," she said as she grabbed his finger to stop him and brought it to her mouth. He inwardly groaned at the vision, made another turn and parked the car in front of the building.

The Victorian warehouse had been used as a printing factory for the last five years. It was a two storey building, which had been renovated to a high standard about two years ago. The main body of the building was largely open plan and the second floor held office suites and a large conference room. Alex had scouted it after Tom Brindly had sent the details through. It was perfect for them to expand into. It would need kitchens fitted and probably dividing walls built in, but he'd already applied for preliminary planning permissions and with his contacts, everything would be fast tracked anyway so she could be in here by early next year. He drew in a long breath and got out of the car. Walking around to her door, he felt those nerves pinch at him again and shook his head at his own insecurity regarding her. He hoped this was the right thing to do and that she wouldn't take it the wrong way but in all honesty, he knew she wasn't going to be ecstatic about it.

"Where are we?" she said in obvious bewilderment as he helped her out. She fiddled with her dress and looked over at the building. Christ, she looked incredible. He was desperate to kiss her again or have her against a wall. He couldn't make up his mind, which made him smile. He'd never been all that bothered with kissing before her.

"I love you," he said. "You do know that, don't you?" She stared at him, still confused, and then her whole face softened at his words. He adored that those words did that to her face. He only hoped that his next ones wouldn't remove that look.

"I know. Well, I think I do anyway... And I love you, too, but I still don't understand why we're standing outside a dark building. Is it a club or something? Because seriously, I think they need a bouncer to announce themselves or at least a bloody sign." She giggled and wrapped her arms around herself.

"No, it's not a club, Elizabeth," he replied as he gazed at her mouth. "It's yours."

She gaped at him as if not understanding what the hell he was talking about, and then after a minute of staring, her eyes narrowed a little as realisation started to set in. Her body tensed as if ready to blow and his eyebrow rose with amusement at her anger. He knew she wouldn't be happy about this but he was fucked if he was entering into conversations about her paying rent or buying the property from him. She was having the building and that was the end of the matter as far as he was concerned. His lawyers had drawn up the paperwork already and all he had to do was get her to agree to sign it. She simply didn't understand how little this meant to him financially and because of that, she thought it was an inappropriate thing to offer. He sauntered over to the building and unlocked the door. "Are you coming?" he called as she stood there scowling at him.

"No, I am most definitely not. You can take your building and-"

He cut her off. "Elizabeth, get your absurdly glorious backside over here now before I make you," he said, dropping his voice to that octave she responded so well to. She flinched but stood her ground defiantly and raised her brow at him in challenge. Christ, how he liked her little challenges. He was sure if she could have, she'd have stamped her foot at him. He chuckled and took one step back towards her. She retreated and held her blood red nails up at him. He couldn't stop himself from licking his lips as he imagined her hands on him and pictured her up against the darkened brick wall behind her.

"Alex, this is not acceptable. I know you think it's okay but really it's not. I can't do this. Please, Alex, try and see it from my point of

234

view. You may have more money than sense but that's not what I want from you. I just want you." She was almost begging him. He sighed and held out his hand. Why could she just not take something from him? He wanted her to have it all.

"Just come and have a look, please, Elizabeth," he said as his hand hung in the air. He had no idea if she'd take it or not. "Baby, I bought two buildings bigger than this yesterday, in cash. In the next month, I'll apparently be buying nine more in this country. I have more land in the states than I know what to do with and my portfolio in China is about to triple. Add into that that I'm thinking about Russia and a ski resort in Austria and perhaps you can begin to imagine how much I'm worth. This," he said as he waved his hand at the building behind him, "is not a big deal to me in the slightest. I want you to have it. I want you to expand your dreams and be excited about your future. If I can help you achieve that then I will and that's not up for discussion."

Her beautiful eyes continued with their assault of his as they stood there. He'd never felt so emotionally challenged in his life as every part of her honest and decent personality held firm. It wasn't in her nature to be happy about this sort of thing. He knew that and it was one of the reasons he wanted her to have it. He'd never given a thing to anybody, simply because nobody had ever deserved anything from him. She made him want to give her everything. She gave him peace and therefore she deserved it all. Eventually, her mouth moved to say something, then she closed it again and he smirked at her because he'd always found the move ridiculously adorable. When the hell the term adorable had entered his life he had no idea. He inclined his head as he waited for her to find her voice again.

"Don't stand there smirking at me. I am not happy. You don't understand, do you? This isn't what we're about, Alex. You can buy or give things to everybody else if you want, but all I want from you is your emotions and your loyalty. To know that you trust me with your feelings is all that's relevant to me. Your wealth is of no importance to me unless it's to do with your own self-worth. Please, don't ask me to be okay with this. I can do this on my own," she said as she waved her hand at the building. He loved her more with every precious word that left her lips. "You don't have to prove anything to me because I don't want you to. You are everything that's important to me and all I need from you is your love."

He had to hand it to her; she couldn't have tried to decline an offer better than that. He smiled at her as she dropped her lovely face to the floor. She knew he wasn't going to give up and as she sighed with frustration at him, he moved towards her again with a growl. She looked up at him through her lovely lashes and brought her thumb to her lips.

"Elizabeth, I'm afraid you're going to have to prove all of what you've just said to me," he replied as he picked up her chin. "If you expect me to believe the depth of your emotions then you'll have to prove them to me."

"I... I don't understand," she replied as she gazed at him. *Fucking perfect.*

"Take the building." He wrapped his arm around her waist and pulled her to him.

"But I've just told you that–" He cut her off with his mouth as he devoured hers and revelled in the taste of her again. Never had her mouth tasted sweeter to him as he began to really believe that his money meant nothing to her. Her moan of desire let him know exactly how she felt as her body moulded into him delectably and she ran her fingers up to the back of his neck.

"Take the building because I love you, and because I've never wanted to give anything to anyone before," he whispered into her neck as he made his way downwards to her breasts. "Take the building because it's what my emotions tell me to do for you, and take the building because it's what my loyalty demands me to do for you. You have no idea of the loyalty I have for you." He heard the narrowing of her eyes rather than saw it as he felt her body stiffen against him.

"That's quite obviously blackmail, Mr. White," she said in an irritated tone from above his head, which was now forgetting the reason they were even having this conversation. His dick was once again doing the thinking as he eased a nipple from her corset and gently bit down on it. "And doing that isn't helping your cause any." He pushed her backwards to the car and forced his weight onto her as he lazily rubbed himself against her thigh.

"I think it might be helping quite a lot actually. You're far more pliable and you're smiling, which is a damn good start," he said as he lifted his head and looked into her beaming face. "Take the fucking building, Elizabeth, and prove that you love me."

"That is not playing fair," she replied quietly as she rolled her eyes at him and sighed. He chuckled and moved back to her chest.

"Fair's overrated and boring, as you well know by now." She groaned in frustration, or desire - he couldn't tell which and frankly didn't give a shit. Either was fine by him. He could do something interesting with either.

"What was in the box?" she said abruptly as she tugged at his hair. His sudden confusion jolted his head up to look at her.

"What box? What the hell are you talking about?" He had no idea, and the fact that he wasn't consuming her with his nipple biting was intriguing.

"The box Mrs Peters gave you." Oh, that was fucking clever - naughty girl, always after the elusive information.

"Ah, are we going to play for it? Tit for tat, so to speak?" She grinned as she broke away from him and headed for the open door. He watched her arse walk away and wondered if he could bend her over something quickly to navigate her away from the emotions she was after.

Not a fucking hope, White.

"We haven't played for a while, have we?" she called as she entered the dark building.

He couldn't help the smile that crept across his mouth as she disappeared. She was far too smart for her own good and too sexy. Frankly, he hadn't got a fucking clue how he was supposed to keep up with her. He still didn't know how she'd managed to break down his defences but he was beginning to realise that he was damn glad she had, because feeling her swirling around inside his head was probably the best sensation he'd ever felt. He only hoped that she wouldn't hate what she found in there when she delved a bit further.

Chapter 13

Elizabeth

Oh shit, oh shit, oh shit, oh buggery balls and shit! I cannot believe he's doing this. No matter how nonchalantly I've walked into this huge sodding building in the guise of playing some sort of game, I can't begin to imagine how I'm going to turn down this offer without pissing him off, or worse, hurting his feelings. Why the hell can't he understand that I just don't want this from him? Yes, okay, even I'll admit it's an amazing opportunity, but how could I take it and not be left feeling beholden to him? Regardless of how much he wants me to prove my love, I can't take it. I mean, how would that look to the rest of the world?

Oh yes, hi. My name's Beth Scott and my boyfriend gave me this vast building so that I could realise my dreams. How sweet. Yes, Alexander White. Yes, the one with stupid amounts of money. Yes, the one that every woman wants to bed, and no, of course I'm not with him for his money or his incredibly stunning body. I really just want him for his beautiful but damaged soul.

Even to my own ears it sounds ridiculous. If this was someone else, I would be laughing my backside off at the pathetic attempt to convince someone that the money wasn't important. The truth is it is important but only with respect to the fact that I don't want it from him. It's his, not mine. I have my own and no amount of him pressing this on me is going to prove any different.

At what point doesn't he get that I just want him? I don't even know if it's possible to separate the man from his wealth. I see snippets of a man who just wants to be himself, but then he's gone and in his place stands a man that simply commands the respect of others because of his power. I mean, how many people have that many cars in their garage? And what sort of man gives a building to their girlfriend? And frankly, why would he? It's not like he needs to. We'll probably get our funding from the bank at some point because we're a pretty safe bet in this economy. His words linger uncomfortably in my mind. *Take the building because I love you, and because I've never wanted to give anything to anybody before.* Is this so unusual to him, to give something freely and with some sort of sentiment involved? Is this what he thinks love is?

Oh, and bloody hell it's big. I flick on the lights beside me and gaze around the space in front of me. Cavernous would seem a more appropriate word. Regrettably, I can't stop my mind from imagining it becoming a modern catering unit. There's so much room that it would be so easy to install a bakery kitchen and a functions section. The steel stairs that climb up the side of the building obviously lead to office suites on the second level where I can easily see Belle lording herself around and shouting orders over the balcony to her *staff* below. I giggle to myself at the thought of it and walk towards the middle of the empty floor. My ridiculously high heels click loudly on the industrial floor as I wander and spin slowly, gazing at the sights. The inside is completely white. The irony is not lost on me in the slightest and I find myself looking back toward the door to see him standing there watching me. His solid body leaning on the doorframe casually and his icy eyes pierce me even from this distance. His slight smirk and arrogant gaze let me know that he can see what's travelling around my head and god, he looks good in that three piece black suit - infuriatingly so. The man could quite easily be posing for GQ in this moment and would certainly be making the magazine a fortune as the women of the country flocked to buy it and hoped that one day they'd meet him. Only they won't, not if I can help it anyway. Well, they might, but they still can't have him.

As I run my eyes over him, I stupidly let my mind wander to his hands, which instantly sends visions of darker lighting and the click of my heels as I struggle for balance reminds me of steel and then restraints. My legs start their trembling as my groin tightens at the thought and I clench my thighs in the hope of staving off the inevitable. His eyebrow rises at me from across the room and his smile grows wider. How the hell does he see that? Shit, I wish I had something to hang on to because I could seriously faint at the panty dropping vision in front of me at the moment. *Oh god, stop it, Beth! Get a sodding grip of yourself.*

"What was in the box, Mr. White?" I ask as I land my hands on my hips. The act in itself gives me at least a little more confidence around him. Oh god, he's leaving the doorway and heading my way. Why does he have to be so bloody gorgeous? He is so going to try and seduce me into having this building from him. Not going to happen.

"Why do you want to know, Elizabeth?" he replies as walks behind me and starts to circle around my body. It's like he's perusing his prey and I can't help but feel instantly intimidated again. Will I ever be able to feel in control of myself near him? My skin electrifies under his intense scrutiny and I drop my gaze a little then whip my head back up quickly. Looking submissive in any way is not going to achieve my goal in the slightest.

"I don't, if I'm honest, unless you want to tell me that is. I just want to know how you feel about what was in the box." He stops his circling in front of me and reaches into his inside pocket. A long, rectangular box is withdrawn from within and my eyes narrow immediately. The red bow indicates that this is yet another present of some sort and I suck in a breath to calm the impending storm that's beginning to brew inside my mind.

"Do you mean this box or the other box? And have you got any idea how much I want to fuck you right now?" His amusement at my irritation is not only fuelling my feelings but it's seriously beginning to make me question how this is ever going to work between us. But yes, he's making his feral glaze pretty clear to me and unfortunately, try as I might, I can't stop that trembling thing again.

"The other box, because you can't possibly be thinking about giving me another gift, Alex. I might not be able to contain my anger much longer. You know how I feel about this." His mouth softens a little as he presumably thinks about my response.

"Hurt, amusement, regret, sadness and then resolve," he says with no expression at all as he closes the space between us and tucks the box into the front of my dress casually. How he's found any room I have no idea. This dress was made for the smallest Beth possible. And what the hell did all those words mean anyway?

"Excuse me?"

"You wanted my feelings about the box of my mother's belongings. Now you have them. When you accept the building, I'll tell you why. This is a negotiation, is it not?" No, this isn't a bloody negotiation. This is me finding a way to not accept this building, something I'm sadly not finding a way to do at the moment.

"I can't..."

"Elizabeth, don't tell me you can't out of some moral commitment to yourself. You are everything I wished I might find for myself and never truly believed that I was entitled to. If I have amassed a fortune for any reason other than to share it with you then please tell me what it is?"

"Alex, that's not the point here and you know it." His sigh of frustration ends my sentence as he backs away and pinches his brow.

"That's exactly the point," he says with a huff of displeasure as he paces. "I have not been a good man, Elizabeth. I am still not a good man and if I had the slightest bit of decency, I would have let you go before I even got my hands on you, but just watching you move was enough to make me hope for something more. This money is part of me. It will not go away and you will have to find a way to believe that you are deserving of my affection in any way I see fit to deliver it. If you could give me something I needed, would you withhold it?" I throw my hands up in annoyance. The man is exasperating. What a ridiculous statement.

"Well of course I wouldn't, but what could I possibly give you that you don't already have?" He spins so quickly that I stumble backward. Thankfully, he catches me by the arm and steadies me.

"Take the building and I'll tell you what you give me. If you want all those emotions from me then you're going to have to give me what I want in return."

"No." I will not barter money for feelings. His eyes bore into mine as he tightens his hold on me and frowns. He clearly isn't used to getting a firm *no* in his world. Well tough, this is the world of love. It's a little different than business and he will learn that I only want him.

"You are so stubborn, Elizabeth. If I told you I would end this if you didn't take the building would you accept it then?" Oh god, please don't do that! My eyes falter as I feel the power of his voice and my throat almost strangles me with its response to the possibility that he would. His stare is relentless, as if he can't comprehend my point of view at all so I raise my head and return his glare.

"No." I won't be scared into it. I will stamp my foot at him in a minute, though, because beautiful as his words have been, I still refuse to take this from him. "I don't want this from you. You can't bully or cajole me into taking something from you that is just too much, Alex. If you love me it's because of who I am. If I let you shower me with your wealth then I will become someone that I'm not. How will you think of me then? I will just be another money grabbing bitch and you will resent it. It will change us and I won't allow that. I just want your love, Alex," I reply, throwing my hands up in the air. I seriously don't know what else to say to make him realise what this means to me. Why can't he see what this sort of act does to me?

I feel his hand loosen on my arm and then watch as he walks away from me and puts his hand on the back of his neck. "Open the box, Elizabeth," he says as he wanders around. What box? Oh right, the box that's tucked in my cleavage. *Stupid Beth.*

"Alex, I..."

"For Christ's sake, open the damn box. I swear I'm going to fucking explode if you don't just do one thing that I ask." Okay, so pissed off Alex is arriving, someone I was hoping to avoid but apparently I haven't managed that. I gingerly remove the ribbon and open the box to probably reveal some expensive jewellery or something, but instead I am presented with a dark red tie. What the hell?

As I take it out of the box and run my fingers across the expensive silk, I look back up at him in confusion. I haven't got a clue what this is about.

"It's for me," he says quietly as he stares at it in my fingers and chews the side of his lip. It's something I've never seen him do before and I suddenly realise he's very nervous of something. I still have no idea what he's trying to tell me but I'm guessing it's reasonably important so I take a step toward him as he reaches up to his top button and closes it up around his throat. Are his hands trembling? "Come and put it on for me."

I move across to him and drape it around his collar. He instantly pulls me forward and kisses me tenderly but I feel the stiffness in his demeanour and his eyes hold something I've never witnessed before. I can only liken them to the time in his father's house, apprehensive maybe, or fearful even. He nods imperceptibly as I gaze into those blue eyes and wonder what on earth is going on behind them and why he's bizarrely asked me to put a tie on him in the middle of our argument.

242

His mouth tightens as I tuck the material behind his collar and do up the first knot.

"My father would put his tie around my neck when he dragged me up those stairs." I drop the silk instantly and try to take a step backwards. His hand clamps around my waist as he pulls me back harshly. "No, Elizabeth, I want you to understand exactly what it is that you give me. Keep going," he says as he pulls in a breath and focuses his eyes on my mouth. I nod as I reach up again and pick up the material softly and start the second stage of a Windsor knot. "I haven't ever worn a tie because I can't breathe in them. You were the first one to make me forget the pain." My fingers freeze at his confession and I gaze up at him. "You still do."

"Alex, I don't know what-"

He cuts me off. "I haven't finished. Keep going," he says softly while he grips onto me tighter and furrows his brows at the feeling of my fingers moving again. "He would make sure it was on my skin and then he would tie it so tightly that it would almost strangle me. His favourite entertainment was to tie the other end to the banister and make me stand three steps down so I was almost hanging, then he would kick my feet from underneath me. Sometimes he would taunt me with his hand and then pull it away when I was close enough to reach it. Other times he would simply keep kicking me until he got bored."

His face is expressionless again as he recalls the events and I cringe at the thought and swallow my disgust. He watches me lick my lips nervously and the side of his glorious mouth curls upwards so I do it again and he broadens his smile. "You see, just watching your mouth makes it go away. You have no idea how liberating that is for me. I have spent my entire life waiting for something to take the pain away, Elizabeth." His eyes return to mine and I pull the long end up to thread it through, but the thought of pulling it tighter scares the shit out of me. I pull my eyes from his, look down at the red tie and wonder what to do next. What the hell must that have been like for him? What sort of arsehole does that to a child? I can't do this to him now. No matter how much he trusts me, the thought of him recalling something so painful because of me is revolting and I feel my tears welling up at his discomfort. His thumb brushes across my jaw.

"Tighter, Elizabeth. Yours are the only hands I want to feel at my throat. Yours are the only hands I will ever allow there because this is what you give me." My eyes lock with his again as I tentatively pull on the silk until it's finished. He releases a breath and swallows against the restriction. "You give me the peace I crave, baby. You remove the memories, and you give me the freedom of a future I never thought possible."

We stare at each other for what seems like an eternity until my mouth opens, trying to formulate a response. I fail miserably and close it again as I take in the man in front of me in a tie. I don't know how I'm supposed to feel about the fact that he's wearing it or what to say to him at all. Is he wearing it for me or for him? I'm not even sure if I like the fact that he's wearing it at all. If the thought of it causes this sort of feeling for me then what the hell is it doing for him? The emotional response to a situation like this is to be overwhelmed with love and happiness, I'm sure, but I can't get the image of a father and his little boy standing on the stairs out of my head. This is so huge for him that I begin to understand what it means to him to have that strip of red around his neck. That he's only be able to do it with me at his side is humbling to say the least and that this man could need me in such a way suddenly breaks any amount of control I was containing, so I let the tears run freely down my cheeks.

He grabs at my hand and lays it across the tie near his chest, and as I scan my fingernails against the red silk, I realise that he had this planned. He wanted to tell me this as he gave me something. He was going to give me his feelings and memories as a way to extinguish the flames that he would create by trying to give me the gift of a building. All I've ever asked him for is his feelings and love and this was obviously his way of balancing the scales in his favour. He tips my head up with his other hand and smiles softly.

"You didn't have to tell me about this," I say as I stare through my tears at him and he brushes them away. My fingers can't stop themselves from trying to remove the frown lines from his forehead as I gaze into his eyes and try to send messages of adoration and love. I have no idea what to say to convey how much I feel for him and how proud I am of him.

"Well, I knew some sort of negotiation would probably have to be endured." He chuckles quietly as he pulls my face to his and claims my lips hungrily. I melt into him with a new-found sense of love and wrap my arms around his neck. Eventually he breaks away and leans his chin on the top of my head and we stand there for a moment, wrapped around each other.

"Please take the building. I need to give you this to help you understand how I feel about you and I don't know any other way of explaining how much I love you." I can't begin to fathom how to say no to him given what has just transpired so I do the only thing I can think of.

"Okay." It's nowhere near enough of a response but as I gaze at his throat, I honestly can't think how to say thank you to something like this. Regardless of how much he seems to be in control of himself, I'm still a disgraceful mess of tears and emotions. "On one condition," I say as I move my fingers back up to his neck and start to undo the tie. His brow mars in confusion at my actions.

"And that condition is what, Miss Scott?" I pull violently at the bloody thing and throw it to the floor beside us then undo his top button - *much better.*

"That you never wear one of those things again," I reply as he stares at it with a raised brow. Clearly this move was a surprise for him and I grin at the instantly more relaxed Alex. "If you want me around your throat, it will be against your skin only."

I'm actually really inspired by my own surprising statement and reach my lips up to drag kisses all over it, as if trying to wash away the years of agony that must linger there. He groans into my neck and picks me up. Before I know it, I hear the clanging of metal beneath his feet and realise that he's taking us up the stairs. I still don't remove my lips from his neck as my core ignites with lust. I know exactly where this is leading and his grunt at the banging of a door only increases my want for him.

My backside hits a table and I push the jacket from his shoulders frantically as he looks down at me. My fingers move to undo his waistcoat swiftly and as he shrugs out of it, I move onto the shirt and eventually reveal his perfect skin. His hands yank at the lacing on my dress until it loosens and I travel my hands madly over his belt until it finally releases. He pushes at my dress roughly until it skims my hips and lands on the floor beneath us. His breathing spikes as his gaze rakes over me in my lace hold ups and thong with more animal lust than I can ever remember seeing before.

"Fuck, you're incredible," he says as he reaches forward and skims a finger over my sensitive nipple. I know exactly what I want and I'm happy to give it to him as I back up onto the table and lie back down against it, spreading my legs for him as I go.

"Show me how you feel, Alex," I say as I push myself further along the table. Clearly this must be the boardroom. His reaction is instant as he climbs over me and licks his way up to my mouth. Hot shivers course across my skin as his mouth connects with my body and I feel my ache beginning to build. I'm desperate for him and as I grab hold of those muscular shoulders and draw his face down towards mine, his hand finds its way between my thighs. Pushing them wider and forcing a hand down to hold me in place, he suddenly thrusts into me with no warning whatsoever. An exquisite groan of pleasure echoes in the room and I revel in the feeling of him filling me so completely. His fingers wrap around the back of my knee as he wraps it around his waist roughly and he pushes in again deeper.

"Always so fucking good," he growls as he lifts his head and grabs hold of my hair. "Tell me you love me." My body responds before my brain engages and arches up to him with a moan of desire as my core clenches around him and he increases his pace.

"Oh God, yes, I love you," I groan as he kneels up and drags me down towards him, impaling me again. My eyes fly open to see him tipping his head back and moving his undulating body in perfect synchronicity with mine, one hand on my stomach and the other under my back to increase my arched frame. He flicks his thumb across my nub at precisely the time I need it and I shout out his name as I let my orgasm take hold of me and scrabble my hands around for something to grab on to. His eyes come back to mine at his name being called and I watch his expression turn to one of love in a split second as his own release starts to build.

"Say it again," he growls, as his breathing turns rapid. He suddenly pulls me up to him and continues his rhythm without missing a beat as I grind down onto him and kiss his neck frantically.

"I love you." His arms tighten around me as his movements become less aggressive and his mouth skims over mine tenderly. He's close to the edge, so close that I can feel him shaking as he tries to cool himself down. My body reacts immediately by clamping around him and milking him for everything he has. Suddenly desperate to feel him flooding in me and have that connection that binds us together, I wrap myself around him and lick and suck at his throat, my throat, the throat that belongs to me.

"Again…" His groan is delicious.

"I love you." I can't get close enough and his arms are forcing me so tight to him that I'm struggling for breath. My thighs push me upwards and downwards on him as I try to get closer still and he grunts out his pleasure. "I love you, Alex."

"Christ, I love you. Come with me." It's all I need as my body shakes into oblivion and I feel him thickening inside me. "Fuck yes," he groans as I feel his warmth spilling inside of me and I let the stars alight behind my eyelids with every panting breath, forcing another delicious aching pulse of our combined bodies.

"I love you," I murmur into his mouth as he meanders his lips along mine while our breathing settles. This is my time to tell him all that I feel and what he gives me.

"I love you so much it hurts. You deserve everything from me and I want you to take everything I have. I'm all yours, Alex. You're worth every second of my thoughts and my love, you always have been." He pulls his face back to gaze at me as he brushes my hair from my face reverently and pulls me closer to his body. His searching eyes seem like they're trying to tell me something but he doesn't open his mouth; he just keeps looking at me and running his fingers across my back. Eventually he blinks his eyes, frowns a little and moves us to the side of the table so we can dress.

"Nice underwear," he says quietly as he watches me slide my dress back on while he does up the buttons on his shirt and tucks it in his trousers.

"I'm glad you like it." I giggle as I turn my back on him so he can do the lacing up. He does and I can't stop more giggling as he cinches me in tighter. "I'm not sure I'll be able to breathe if you keep that up." He doesn't speak, just keeps tying the lace tighter until his hands still on my hips.

"When did you see Pascal last?" he says over my shoulder in that voice that makes me tremble a little. Where the hell has this version come from and why are we talking about Pascal? Shit, he shouldn't have given me a lift yesterday. Do I tell Alex or not? Is he going to be pissed? Well, he can't be at me; I haven't done anything wrong. *Don't tell him, Beth, best not to.* "And do not lie to me, Elizabeth." Oh, Fuck!

"Actually, he gave Teresa and I a lift home the other day, funnily enough," I reply as nonchalantly as possible so as to diffuse any potential anger that might be threatening. "He just happened to be passing," I continue as I turn around in his arms and take a look at him to see who I'm dealing with. Definitely darkening blues so I smile sweetly and rise up on my toes to kiss him. He accepts this kiss but pushes me away a little.

Oh for Christ's sake, I seriously can't keep up. Two minutes ago he was giving me buildings, telling me intimate details of his childhood and making love to me on my own boardroom table, and now he's mad at me? It was just a lift.

"Do you want him?" What? Oh my god, he's jealous? After everything we've just been through?

"That is the most ridiculous question I've ever heard." I can't even begin to look at him as I stride through the door and try to dampen the fact that in a small way, yes, I do. Why is completely unknown but it doesn't mean I'd ever do anything about it. His hand grabs my arm before I make it to the top of the stairs.

"That's not an answer, Elizabeth."

I turn abruptly to face him and shrug out of his hold. Infuriating man, gorgeous, yes, irreplaceable definitely, but this is not acceptable regardless of how correct he might be in his assumption. My eyes narrow and my hands suddenly become living accessories of my mouth as they wave in his face to get his attention.

"Alex, did you not hear a word I said in there? I love you. *You.* No one else. Whatever you may be thinking about Pascal, stop it. He's not relevant here. I could have had him but I chose you. I still choose you. And while we're at it, keeping Pascal away from me is ridiculous. He is your friend and he's done nothing to dishonour that friendship. In fact, he was the one who told me to go with you and that he knew it was you that I wanted." I can't even believe I'm poking him in the chest as he backs away from me a little and looks almost shocked at my venom. I suddenly realise I am enjoying my rant and decide to keep going as he stares at me and begins to open his mouth. "And shut that mouth before I completely lose it. Do you have any idea how much I have to put up with when women are around you? They drool over you as if you're the last available man on the planet. Clearly you are the most incredible thing most of them have ever seen, but honestly, it is hard bloody work trying to convince myself that I'm the only one you're interested in, and frankly, I don't believe it myself most of the time. So you having jealous hissy fits over your friend is just... well it's just fucking stupid."

There, rant over. His fingers close around mine, which are still attached to his chest, and he drags me towards him with a slight smirk on his face. He's fucking laughing at me? My mouth opens again.

"Actually, I was just going to tell you that you could have him if you wanted him, that I would allow it if it would please you," he says as he pulls my hand behind my back and holds it there tightly in his grasp, his damned brow rising at me as he waits for an answer.

Wow, shit, didn't see that coming. What on earth do I say to that? Apparently he's not jealous. I have no idea what to say, and the fact that I can still feel him seeping down the inside of my thigh is a tad distracting. Who has these types of conversations? Cleary anything but a quick no is going to give the game away. Does he want me to sleep with Pascal? He is sodding kinky after all? His grasp on my wrist tightens and it instantly reminds me of Pascal's pressured grip, which is not fucking useful in the slightest. In milliseconds my brain searches rapidly for the correct answer to this question as his unwavering eyes hold mine. There absolutely isn't one, in any variety of worlds.

"Would it please you?" he asks again, licking his lips.

"No, I told you, I choose you," I reply as quickly as I can. Much as the thought may appeal in some small way, I am not going down that road. The man in front of me has everything I need and my love for him only increases as a smile creeps across his beautiful face.

"I know what you told me, Elizabeth, and I believe you. However, I told you I would want to take you further and there is nothing I would deny you. Sex holds no room for pretence. Your deceit will only fuel a desire that can't be realised, and that, I'm afraid, is not my idea of love," he replies smoothly. He might as well be talking about a shopping list for all the emotion he has in his voice, and I stare up at him with something like amazement in my eyes. I haven't got a bloody clue what I'm supposed to say to any of that. Does he want me to have sex with his friend? We've just had an intimate connection of love and now he's discussing threesomes? How can someone with such a jealous streak and explosive temper even begin to process this as normal? It's not normal, but then nothing about the man is normal, is it? Christ, I wish Belle was here, or even Teresa. Maybe they'd have a sodding answer. Even Conner might give me a hint as to what the hell the man is trying to achieve. Maybe it would help if I understood what the hell was going on between him and Pascal. Oh, fuck it!

I shrug my wrist out of his grasp and sigh with exhaustion. This has probably been the most challenging two weeks of my life and frankly, I can't find the energy to deal with this anymore. No matter how much I need him and love him, at the moment I just feel like I need space to try and find a way through every emotion that's flying through me.

I turn and walk away from him with nothing more than the clicking of my heels. I haven't even got the enthusiasm to hold my head up anymore so I hang my head and walk down the stairs while glancing at the floor space below, which is now mine. It doesn't hold as much interest as it did before as I walk over it and out of the door.

I stand by the car waiting for him to lock the door and watch his body as it moves fluidly around. Every inch of him is dominant in some way and I wonder what that actually means to me anymore. I feel like I know him intimately one minute and then in the next second, he floors me with some piece of information or demonstration of a man I still sadly know nothing about and don't understand on any level. He wanders across casually and opens my door for me with a tilt of his head, as if there is nothing left to discuss, as if he's right and he knows he is. Sadly, he probably is and I curse my traitorous body for thinking about Pascal in any way whatsoever. Damn those intoxicating green eyes.

"Would you like to go for dinner or shall I take you home?" he says as he slides into his seat and reverses out of the parking area.

"I'm pretty tired, can you just take me home, to mine please," I reply as I gaze out of the window. I can't look at him. If I do I'll change my mind and I just need to be alone to think.

"Okay," is his quiet response. It shocks me. I was pretty sure an argument would ensue and I watch him from the corner of my eye as he heads out into the traffic and turns for my apartment.

The drive remains silent as I ponder what it is that I need time to think about and before I know it, he's parked underneath our building. As we walk to my apartment, I can't make up my mind if I want him to come in with me or not. Belle's at Conner's for the night and I relish the thought of the house to myself. I unlock the door and turn to look at him. His devilish smile has returned and I can't help the softening of my heart as my gaze lingers on his mouth.

"Coffee?" I ask as I reach down and throw my shoes in the doorway.

"Oh thank Christ, she speaks. I was wondering if I'd scared you to the point of running," he replies as he swats me on the backside and makes his way into my kitchen. Unbelievably, he appears to know exactly where everything in my kitchen is as he busily gets cups out of cupboards and flicks on the kettle. "Don't you have a machine?" he asks as he sneers at a canister of instant.

"No, we drink tea here, never got around to buying one," I reply as I wander off to the bedroom to get changed. I need something comfortable on and a quick freshen up down below.

Ten minutes later and I'm greeted with a very relaxed Alex lounging on my sofa, having removed his jacket, drinking his tea from one of my mugs. I stare at him for a moment. It seems so odd to see him in my space. Our whole relationship has been based at his house and I find it strangely uncomfortable to see him sitting casually in my home. That expensive black suit seems too easy on him for this sofa and that black hair too perfectly dishevelled. It's as if he's too big for the space around him somehow.

"Better?" he says as he points to my cut offs and *Jack Jones* green t-shirt.

"Different, not necessarily better," I reply as I pick up my tea and sit beside him.

"So what's on your mind apart from me giving you a lot to think about?" he says as he turns toward me and pulls my hair back out of the grip I've just put it in. I raise my brow at him. "I like your hair down. Sue me. My legal department will eat you alive." He smirks at me as he runs his fingers through it. "If I don't first, that is." I can't stop the giggle that bursts through my mouth. His eyes immediately flood with warmth and I lean my head onto the sofa and gaze at him.

"You always give me a lot to think about. Half the time I don't have a clue what to do with what you make me think about."

"Well that sounds confusing," he replies as he grins wickedly and sips at his tea. My gaze lands on his hands and I feel the blush rise across my cheeks at my less than wanted thoughts.

Oh get a grip, Beth!

"It is." *Very, always.*

"Mmm... What else? Something else is troubling you." Oh, so now he's a bloody mind reader as well. I only wish I had that ability. Perhaps I'd have a hope of gleaming what it is that goes through his mind then.

"I think my mum's got cancer again." I might as well get straight down to it. His face tenses as he grabs my hand and pulls it to his mouth.

"Why on earth didn't you tell me?" he says as he frowns at me. "I wouldn't have been so cavalier with you if I'd known what you were going through."

"I don't know. I only found out on Monday when we went for lunch. It was pretty obvious she wasn't well so I called Dad on Tuesday. I'm going to see her tomorrow. Dad told me about testing but he doesn't want her worrying about us worrying, so I'm going to wing it and see what happens."

"Is that why you got so drunk? You should have called me straight away. I could have helped. Christ, Elizabeth, you're the one pushing me for emotions all the time and the minute you've got something to deal with, you hide it from me?" he says as he runs his hand through his hair in frustration. He begins to open his mouth again when the door buzzer goes. Who the hell could that be? "Stay there," he says as he gets up and goes to answer the door. Several clipped words later and he walks into the kitchen area with a large box and begins opening it. I wander over to him to see what's going on and gasp as he pulls out the large machine.

"Is that a fucking coffee machine?" I seriously can't believe he's bought a bloody coffee machine at this time of night just because I haven't gotten around to getting one. And where the hell did he get it from? This is getting beyond ridiculous.

"Yes. Either you have one here or you'll have to move in with me. I cannot abide bad coffee and I fucking hate tea," he says as he pushes things along the counter top with his back toward me to make room for the thing that looks just like his. My mouths instantly gapes as my brain processes his words.

"Did you hear what you just said?" I reply in utter shock. He pauses for a second and then carries on with his fiddling.

"I'm perfectly aware of what I said," he says as he plugs the machine in and fills the water section. "Open this," he continues nonchalantly as he hands me some scissors and coffee beans and flicks on the switches.

He wants me to move in with him? Well, actually, he can't do or he wouldn't have bought the coffee machine, would he? Clearly he doesn't want me to move in with him. I can't stop the wave of disappointment that rolls across me at the thought as I gaze at his back and his perfectly toned backside. *Oh stop being stupid, Beth.* Well he can damn well have the money for the marvellous thing. I wander over to my bag and grab my personal chequebook.

"How much was it?" I ask as I sign the cheque and fill out his name on the header line.

"Why is that relevant?" he asks over his shoulder as he turns and looks at me. His body instantly tenses but a smirk begins to adorn his beautiful face. "Oh, I see... Three thousand."

Oh my god, for a bloody coffee machine? Well, I can't back out now so I scribble the amount down and push the cheque across to him with a smile. He promptly picks it up and gazes at it before ripping it in half and dumping it in the bin. The bastard!

"If that's staying here then I'm buying it," I practically shout at him as I point at the machine. He chuckles and lifts the glass cups out of the box without a word in response. "Alex, I'm serious. This is not okay." He turns with a sigh and spreads his hands on the counter in front of me. My groin tightens at his height over me as I sit on the other side and look up at him. Damn him.

"If you think I'm accepting a penny from you, you're sorely mistaken, and besides, it's as much for me as it is for you," he says with a pleading expression. "Do not do this again, Elizabeth. We've talked about this. Just let me be in love with you and stop pursuing an argument that doesn't need to happen."

Is that what I'm doing? I thought I was just standing up for myself. His hand grazes my cheek as he turns back to the machine, which is now dripping the wonderful smelling coffee into the glasses. Actually, I have a right to stand up for myself even if he does make it hard. I try to fathom a way of getting three thousand pounds into his bank account and suddenly realise we actually do his catering. It's pretty simple really. I'll just pay the money into our account and not charge him for part of the next lunch. Brilliant. God, I'm good, sneaky too, apparently.

"So tell me how can I help with your mother?" he says as he sits down opposite me and places the coffees down then reaches behind him for the sugar canister and starts loading my drink. "And how the hell do you stay so toned with this amount of sugar?"

"If you met my mother, you'd understand. It's in the genes. Belle's not so lucky. She has to work like stink for her figure, and there's nothing you can do unfortunately. I can only hope she has the strength to fight it again," I reply sadly. There really isn't anything anybody can do, but the thought that he cares gives me some comfort, and as his hand finds mine, I gaze up into his face with the hope that he'll help me through it. "I'd like you to meet her, you know, before she gets too ill. She'd hate to meet you at her worst." His face looks suddenly confused.

"You... You want me to meet her?" His tone is incredulous as if it's the strangest thing he's ever heard and I realise he's nervous as I watch him chew the side of his lip.

"Of course I do. Why wouldn't I want her to meet the man I'm in love with? If you want to, that is. You don't have to. I just thought... Well... Oh, I don't know," I reply, questioning if he even wants that amount of closeness with a family unit. He clearly has no idea what a decent family means and I don't want to push him in any way.

I stir my coffee uncomfortably as I wait for a response. I have no idea what's going through his mind. Two hours ago we were arguing about buildings, thinking about his abusive bastard of a father, making love and then discussing Pascal. Now we're sitting here talking about him meeting my potentially very ill mum and I haven't got a clue how I'm holding in the tears that are threatening to spill again.

"Have you told your parents about us?" he eventually asks quietly as he gazes at me across his coffee.

"Of course I have. Not in intimate detail, obviously, but they do know who you are. I'm pretty sure my father might kill you if he knew any more." My wry smile is clearly not lost on him as he blinks his eyes a little and looks down at the table, furrowing his brow.

"I'm positive he would. I daresay nobody will ever be good enough for his little girl. I'm certainly not." His sad smile almost breaks my heart and I grab his chin and tilt his head up without thinking about what he needs to hear. I want him with me and I want my family to meet him. His strength is what I need right now to help me through the time to come, not his insecurities.

"Can you come with me tomorrow?" His eyes search mine for a few minutes as if he's trying to make up his mind if I'm serious or not. Does he honestly still believe he's not worthy for some bizarre reason? "I really want you to come with me. I want to show you off. It will do my mum the world of good to look at you. Dad's well past his prime," I say with a giggle, trying to lighten the mood. The curl of his lip lets me know I've managed it.

"Okay, what time do we leave? I have some things I need to do in the morning," he asks as he leans back and flicks the machine again, all the way up, damn Pascal.

I gaze at him and wonder what on earth tomorrow will bring. Alexander White in my family home will be a sight to behold and probably a very emotional state of affairs.

"Around ten. Can we take the bike? Dad will absolutely love it."

Chapter 14

Elizabeth

The ache in my knees is unbelievable. We are not on the same bike as the last one as apparently this one is faster. Well it might be, but it definitely isn't more comfortable, and why he needs a faster bike is beyond me. When I suggested going to Mum's on the bike, it was mainly for my dad's benefit. He loves anything with two wheels, although I do have to admit I still love the feeling of being wrapped around him and the vision of him at nine in the morning, head to toe in bike leathers was well worth the effort of waking up as he pressed the buzzer repeatedly.

Why haven't I given him a key yet?

Where he'd been and what time he'd left this morning was unknown, but his glorious smile on seeing me had completely smashed any concerns I had about him meeting my parents.

Gripping around him tighter as I think of his playful banter this morning, I shift about, trying to get comfy again. He seems to be in an extraordinarily good mood and I sigh contentedly as he reaches back and squeezes my thigh, then indicates into a service station looming on the horizon. Oh, thank god!

Seconds after he's found somewhere to pull up, I leap off the bloody thing and stretch every limb in an effort to bring some blood back to varying extremities. Thankfully, given it's the middle of December, it's actually a very sunny day so I unzip my jacket and remove my helmet to get some fresh air around me as he climbs off.

"You okay?" he asks, clasping my hand and leading us into the building.

"Just a bit tense, I guess. Seriously, that is not a comfortable bike in the slightest," I reply as I point back at the dark grey whatever it is. "What is it anyway?"

"Triumph, and I don't remember saying that being with me would be comfortable in any way, shape or form. Perhaps I should teach you to ride one, and then you could choose your own comfort. Until then, you'll have to deal with what you're given, Miss Scott. You appear to handle other painful situations effectively enough," he replies with a wink as he saunters through the sliding doors, swats me hard on the arse and heads for *Starbucks,* looking ridiculously sexy with that stupid helmet hair. How he manages to make it look all sexy bad boy is a complete mystery. I so want him right now. It makes me wonder if there's a convenient room available at that hotel next door, then I notice the time. Balls, it'll have to wait till later. My groin screams at me in protest and pouts at seeing my parents instead of ravishing the man beside me, but tough.

"Actually, there might be something you could teach me," I ask casually. He orders some coffees and waves the change away when the guy offers it to him as he gestures over to a table by the window.

"Really? I like the sound of that. Anything to have you doing my bidding has to be of the utmost importance." I giggle as I slap at his arm playfully and gaze across at him.

"Well it doesn't have to be you, but I really want someone to teach me some stronger self-defence moves. When that happened on Monday, it just reminded me how useless I am in a struggle. He completely overpowered me and anything could have..." I shudder at the thought of what could have been and look down at the table. His growl makes me lift my head back up instantly.

"He won't hurt you anymore. But I think self-defence is an excellent idea. However, if I taught you, would you use those moves to repel me as well?" he says with an amused grin. I love him all the more for trying to dismiss the subject and keep the atmosphere light, but it does beg the question of what actually happened to the man. The last I saw, he was barely breathing. What happened after we left that night? I didn't want to know before, perhaps because I didn't care or perhaps because I just didn't want to think about it, but now, now I feel like I need to know for my own peace of mind. The bastard should obviously have been castrated, but I wouldn't like to think of him being dead. Someone must have taken him to hospital or something and I remind myself to ask Alex about it at another time. Today is not the day for it and I bring my thoughts back to the present and the lovely man in front of me, who may also be the most confusing individual I have ever met. What were we talking about? Oh yes, defence moves.

"And when would I need to use them on you, Mr. White?"

"Well, with my aggressive preferences, who knows? To be honest, I'm not sure I like the thought of being on the receiving end of my own handiwork very much. I quite like being able to overpower you," he says as kisses me chastely and then looks across at a group of men that have gathered around his bike with a curl of his lip. "But I can teach you viciousness if that's what you want. You will just have to promise me not to use it against me when I'm being a bastard."

Oh right, well that really fills me with confidence. I'd never thought of him being that aggressive with me. The thought has me strangely aroused and I lick my lips as I watch his agitated face. Clearly his precious bike is rather important to him and I'm slowly becoming amused by the thought of him going all primal on the poor guys around it. I may have been shocked and somewhat appalled the last time I saw it, but for some reason I'm now eagerly awaiting its next arrival. Is that strange? Probably is... I think I might need to see someone about this because surely that can't be normal. To want him aggressive with me is bad enough; to want to watch him aggressive with someone else is possibly psychotic or something. So screwed.

"Go show me some belligerence, Mr. White. It's really quite erotic," I say smugly. His head swings back to me and the laughter that erupts has me beaming with delight at him.

"Still full of surprises, Miss Scott. I thought you didn't care that much for my temper?" he says as he jumps down from his stool, and I notice that one of the unfortunate idiots has decided to get on his bike. Oh dear. "Wait here and be good."

"As if I'm ever anything else," I say in mock shock, picking up my drink and watching him leave.

As soon as he steps foot outside the door, one of the lads looks up and they all burst into fits of hysterics at the poor guy sat on the bike. Sadly, this only fuels the guy into becoming even more of an idiot by remaining on the bike. I shake my head as the others back away slightly on Alex's approach. God, he's beautiful. Even the way he moves has me panting with lust or something and I can't quite believe I'm getting horny at the thought of him becoming angry. His frown is now firmly planted across his forehead and the scowl that's gracing his mouth is really quite disturbing. The guy has obviously decided to continue with his stupid behaviour, regardless of the owner's proximity, and is apparently even having an argument with Alex now. Well, it's a one-sided argument, with small guy talking and Alex becoming more and more furious. I can see it now as his face becomes less expressive and his demeanour changes to one of impatience, body completely still, muscles tense. Primed would be the word. It makes me realise that although I may not understand his mind completely, if at all, I do understand his body with more clarity than I'd given myself credit for. Perhaps I should try and read him like that more often.

One of the lads in the group takes a step toward Alex aggressively and I almost jump off my chair to get help as I start to realise what's unfolding in front of me, then decide to sit tight and see what happens next. I'm rewarded by watching Alex turn on the young lad with frightening speed, not giving him a chance to move any further. He stumbles backward from the unexpected move and lands on his backside, which causes the rest of the group to jeer and shout at the guy on the floor. Guy on the bike has begun to look a little less sure of himself as Alex turns back to him and says something. I clearly can't hear it but I watch the colour drain out of the guy's face as he gingerly gets off and backs away with his hands in the air. Obviously whatever it was that Alex said has had the desired effect because the entire group then seems to apologize to him and move away. I swear one of them even bows in apparent shame and trips over his own feet. Mr gorgeous man turns and walks back towards me with a smile and a wink so of course my thighs clamp together again at this weird attraction I have to his more feral side.

Sitting down opposite me, he finishes his coffee as if nothing has happened and I shake my head at him with a giggle. "So commanding, Mr. White. I think one of the little ones actually wet his pants." He chuckles and looks at his watch.

"We should go. I don't want to get you there late." I smirk at him and raise my brow.

"You'll take on ten guys but you're worried about my parents?" I reply with amusement. "Mr. White, are you a little nervous about meeting my dad?"

"This is probably one of the most important meetings of my life, Elizabeth. So to answer your question, yes, I am a little." His face shows me how serious he is, and as he lifts his hand to the back of his neck, I realise just how much he's worried about it. My heart melts for him and I lean across and kiss him on the nose.

"Don't be silly, Alex. They're just people and they'll love you just like I do. Do you think I'd take you if I didn't think you were worth it? Just be yourself and everything will be fine," I reply as I jump down and reach for my jacket. He frowns and carries our helmets out behind me.

"Why did you make me bring you on a bike? Nothing could be worse than seeing your daughter arrive on the back of one of these," he mumbles as we get on.

"Actually, Dad has a real thing for speed. He's the one who taught me to drive. He loves bikes so I thought it might make you feel a little bit more comfortable. Now grow a pair, Mr. White and get your playful side back again. I need all the amusement you can manage for today," I say as I reach forward and knock his visor down. He shakes his head at me and pulls away.

"You will definitely pay for that comment later, Miss Scott," comes growling through my helmet and I giggle and grab on as he picks up speed, approaching the motorway. I know I will and frankly I can't wait, but at the moment, I need to concentrate on Mum and making sure that she knows how much I love her. Alex can just get on with being what he is. He'll be fine. He pulls my hands tighter around him and leans forward. I shift my feet to find a better position and then squeeze tighter.

Oh shit, here we go.

~

Nearly an hour later, we're pulling up outside my family home and I jump off before he's even stopped the bike. The door opens as the engine shuts off and dad walks out, smiling quietly with open arms. I launch myself into them and hug him as tight as I can. I can't even begin to contain my tears. I thought I'd be in control but one look at his face and I'm in bits. *Really strong, Beth. Well done!*

Eventually, after much head stroking and sniffing, he releases me and stands me back to look at me as he always does.

"Always knew you had some of your old man's need for speed in you, Bethy." His gaze lands on Alex as he removes his helmet and walks across to us. "So this is him then, the chess player?" he says as he gives Alex an extended once over with an expressionless face and straightens his shoulders. Apparently he's going to play killer dad for a laugh. My dad couldn't be less of a killer if he tried. I somehow have my doubts about the man he's approaching though.

"Yes, Dad. Alex White, meet my dad, Alan Scott," I say as I watch Alex extend his hand. He might be nervous but he's not showing it if he is. He's in full-on charm mode. His body is soft and relaxed with a hint of *don't piss me off*. It reminds me of the first time I saw him work his boardroom - in control but not needing to assert it.

"Nice to meet you, Sir." My dad's eyes narrow as he shakes his hand and holds on a bit too long. Sir is not a word I ever expected to hear coming from Alex and I smile at the vision of it. It doesn't sit comfortably on his tongue at all but I love him for trying.

"Are you competent on that thing, son?" Dad asks as he nods at the bike. "Daytona 675, isn't it?" Alex immediately looks impressed and smirks a little.

"Yes, very competent, Sir and you're correct. It's one of my favourites." Dad starts making his way over and Alex gives me a small smile as he follows him. My eyes follow his backside as I lick my lips. So not the right place or time to be thinking about sex.

"Right, I'm making tea. Is Mum in yet or is she still at the bakery?" I call over to them.

"She'll be here in about twenty minutes, love," Dad shouts back as he holds his hand out to Alex for the keys and waves me off. Well that's Dad and Alex sorted.

I wander into the house and down the hall to the kitchen, hanging my jacket and helmet up on the way. Still sniffing back my tears a little, I put the kettle on the aga and look around the kitchen with fond memories, remembering Belle and I doing our homework on the vast pine table and eating bacon sandwiches. The kettle boils until it screams at me and I fill two cups with tea and pour water into the cafetiere. It's not a machine but it is real coffee at least and it's the best I can do for him at the moment. I take my tea and walk straight out of the back door to go to my favourite place in the world - the summerhouse. When I reach it, I notice that the swinging seat is out and almost burst into tears again. Mum loves that seat. It's probably why Dad's dragged the old thing out again. She spent the entire summer sitting out here when her hair started falling out last time. I swallow some tea and sit gently onto it to try to sort my head out. I cannot go bursting into tears when she gets here. I don't know what I'm going to do but I just need her to know that I love her and that I'm here if she needs me.

"There you are," Alex says as he strides up the garden path, looking a little perturbed with a mug of coffee. "I think your dad's taking my bike out in a minute." I burst out laughing and stare at him.

"You are joking? He hasn't been on one for years." The sound of the engine roars to life in the background and I smile at the thought of my dad revving the engine. Regardless of my fear of the machines prior to Alex, Dad has always been an advocate of speed. I think that's how he wooed Mum all those years ago.

"He really is taking it, isn't he?"

"Looks like it. He'll be fine and your precious bike is in safe hands. He used to race," I reply as I pat the seat at the side of me. He looks at it warily and I can't contain my amusement. "Scared, Mr. White?"

"Very, Miss Scott. Is it safe?" I giggle at him as he sits gingerly at the side of me and wraps his arm around my shoulder. We sit in silence for a while and swing backward and forward, listening to the birds while I think about Mum and what's to come. She suddenly appears at the backdoor and I catch her looking out at us with a smile. I squeeze his hand and nod toward the door. An instant Alexander White award-winning smile is plastered across his face as he pulls me up and marches me toward her. I watch as she melts at the vision of him and practically throws herself out of the door to greet him. Well, that's Alex and Mum sorted as well. The blush that stains her cheeks as she pulls him into a hug is overwhelmingly sweet and I roll my eyes at Alex in full on panty combusting mode. Honestly, the man could make the sodding angels weep. He's even pretending he's actually enjoying the hug. I seriously doubt that he is. He certainly didn't like it from his own aunt, so it's unlikely he's happy about my mother being so touchy feely with him. Which is a point... Did he ever talk to Mrs Peters about his sister and when they were going to meet? Yet another thing I need to ask him about. I assume that Evelyn will be at

Conner's party, given that she works for him, and that's tomorrow night. He must be thinking about it. Is he okay about it? I'm a shit girlfriend. Why have I not thought about this before now? *Rubbish, Beth, just bloody crap!*

When my dear mum eventually unwraps her slightly too clingy hands from him, she stands back and gives him the once over with a remarkably disarming grin.

"Well, you're certainly a big boy, aren't you? First rate, darling. I would say he's quite the catch. If I was twenty years younger, I'd-"

I cut her off rapidly, knowing exactly what's about to leave her mouth as his expression turns to one of intrigue. "Mum, please!" Alex chuckles beside me as she turns to me and air kisses me on both sides.

"Bethy, please don't go all frigid on me. The man's an Adonis. Is Belle's as attractive? I knew you'd both find good ones in the end. You see, Alex, it's in the genes. We positively drive back unsuitability. One can't make great babies without the correct gene pool," she says as she links arms with him and heads them down the hall. His brow rises at her as she beams up at him. She may be ill but it obviously isn't stopping her going straight in for the kill. I was so hoping this wouldn't happen, "How many children would you like?"

Oh. My. God!

"Mum, you are absolutely not getting an answer to that question," I cut in as I hurry to catch up with them before she forces him to speak. However, it does get me thinking. Does he even want children? I suppose he might not, given his childhood. It reminds me that this whole scenario must be really quite strange for him so I gaze across at him. Thankfully, he's got a warm face on as if he's enjoying my mortification. Bastard.

"Bethy, I just want to know the truth. We all know I may not have that long and I want to know that he's the right one. I will not beat about the bush with my questions any longer, young lady. Time is of the essence," she says as she looks directly at him.

Well holy shit, I so didn't see that coming.

It makes my heart break and my breath halt at the same time as I stare at her dumbfounded as to what I'm supposed to say in return. My eyes flick to Alex, who is refusing to look away from my mum but has somehow managed to hold his enigmatic mask without flinching.

263

"Well, Alex, are you the one who will make my daughter happy?" Astonishingly, he doesn't miss a beat as his smile widens at her.

"If you think it acceptable, Mrs Scott, I would be honoured to make your daughter very happy for the rest of her life," he replies confidently as he turns toward me. "Should she want that from me, of course. I think I have made my intentions reasonably clear to her."

I have no idea what I'm supposed to say in this situation. I just gape at him. Did he just tell my mother that he wants to get married at some point and have babies with me? Yesterday he was telling me I could have sex with another man if I wanted to - the king of the kink world at that - and now we're talking happy families... What the hell? I seriously have no clue whatsoever. I'm completely lost. He lives in another world.

"Well, given that you got her on that death machine that I've just seen Alan on, I would say she'll probably say yes, if and when you ask more directly. And I hope you do so rather quickly. Life is far too short for silly games."

I'm still staring at him with my mouth open as he turns back to her and nods quietly with a frown forming around his beautiful eyes. I possibly didn't handle that announcement from him all that well. Maybe I was supposed to beam with delight or jump into his lap or something equally as dreamlike, but frankly, I'm just so shocked I can't even begin to process the statement. I shake my head from its fog and turn to my mum as she gets up. After all, she's the one I'm here for.

"Mum, I wanted to ask about-"

She cuts me off with one of her death stares as we all hear the rumble of Alex's bike returning.

"No, I won't hear of it. I am ill... again. That is the end of it. If I have any other information for you, I'll let you know. Now stop making this poor man uncomfortable and tell him how much you love him while I go and check on your father. I'm surprised he's made it back in one piece to be honest," she says as she scurries out of the kitchen with her bob swinging and leaves us alone. I look across at him and try to form some words. Nothing comes to mind, unfortunately, and I fiddle with my fingers as I look at the table.

"I'm sorry she put you under that pressure. You really didn't have to say anything, and I..." He reaches across and tilts my chin up. Why is he always doing that?

264

"If you're going to tell me that you don't want the same, Elizabeth, you will damn well look me in the eyes when you say it," he says tersely as he drills me with his. My heart rate is now through the bloody roof. "I meant every word I said, and unless you're about to refuse me, I would suggest you don't say anything else until you're ready to do so."

Okay, that I can manage. Saying nothing is exactly what I want to do because I still can't form sentences in my head, let alone through my mouth. The fact that Alexander White is sitting in my family kitchen is strange enough; the thought that he may have just proposed in a roundabout manner is frankly bizarre. I sit quietly and gaze across at him with a small smile. His lips quirk up into a smirk at my refusal to speak. It's apparently all he needs to be happy again because I watch the wrinkles unfold in his forehead as he gazes out of the window.

"I like your mother's honesty, albeit a little heads up would have been nice," he continues with a chuckle. I smile back at him as I feel the tension leave my body at his more relaxed demeanour. Love rolls across me and almost floors me as I watch him lift his head and broaden his extraordinary smile at me. His eyes suddenly twinkle mischievously and it makes me wonder what else is going on in his mind. Probably sex - it's normally his default setting.

"I love you," comes out of my mouth without apology or regret. I do, unequivocally, and I want him to understand that. I want him to know that regardless of anything, I will always love him. He nods at me as my parents walk back in and reaches for my hand.

"Son, I think I've broken your bike," my dad says as he holds up a piece of something dark grey and a handful of bolts with a perplexed expression. "I'm not sure what happened but now it won't shift out of gear." Alex furrows his brow again a little then bursts out laughing as he stands up and rolls up his sleeves.

"Have you got tools? Let's see if we can fix her." He chuckles as he winks at me and follows Dad out of the door. Clearly he's a mechanic as well. Is there anything the man can't do?

"That's a mighty fine piece of ass," my mum says as she watches them walk away. I assume she's not talking about Dad. Oh, help me!

"Mum, really? I came here to talk about you. I think you've embarrassed me, and him, enough for a millennium."

"Bethy, you must marry that man. It's imperative. Anyway, tell me about this Conner that your sister's dating. She won't tell me a thing. You know how she is. Is it serious? And does he really have blue hair? And which company does he work for? And what possessed you to get on that bike? Actually, scrap that, even I might get on again for that man. You must drool permanently." She looks at me expectantly as she puts the kettle on again. I roll my eyes but she's right about the drooling; even I'll admit that.

"Mum, please, I just want to know about the tests and about what happens next. Can you at least tell me that?" She sighs and turns back to me.

"Darling, I'm not going to think about it too much again until the time comes. I will fight it again if I have to, and I will have the love of my family around me to help. Just let me be happy for now and enjoy seeing you and Belle finally finding someone important in your lives," she says as she brushes a tear from my eye. That's my mum, a hopeless romantic and always thinking of us. I decide it's best to fill her in on Belle's gossip and give her what she wants rather than continue with the other horrible topic. I grab my phone and search the internet for the best picture of Conner I can find - preferably not one of him brawling. It's not easy, but I eventually I find one of him outside his office looking dapper in a blue pinstripe suit and give the phone over to her.

"Oh my, that really is blue hair," she exclaims as her eyes widen. "That's definitely a *Prada* suit, though, so he at least has some style, and he's a rather a big boy, too."

"Actually, he's got pink tips on it at the moment as well. Belle dared him, and he hardly ever wears a suit. He is absolutely besotted with her, though, and he's a good man. You'll like him. She even mentioned moving in with him."

"Really? Well that's astonishing," she says as she continues looking at him. "He really is quite handsome the more you look at him. Do you think he'll always have blue hair?" she says as she tips the phone sideways.

Alex walks in through the door and completely steals my attention as he walks behind her to the sink to wash his hands. His eyes flick to the phone screen and he shakes his head with a smile.

266

"Sorry to interrupt, ladies, were you ogling men?" My mum's face turns beet red as she slaps his thigh. "And yes, Conner will always have blue hair. However, I think your other daughter is beginning to make him pull it out so he may not always have hair at all."

"That's my girl. I do hope you realise what you're letting yourself in for, Alex?" she says with a giggle. It's so much like my own that I can't help but join in.

"I'm extremely happy to let myself in for anything that Elizabeth wants," he says as he looks across at me with his panty dropping smile. I restrain my giggling fit and try for calm as his gaze holds mine, licking his lips over my mum's shoulders and raising that bloody brow at me. I squeeze my thighs together and shake my head at him just as my dad walks in behind me. I can't stop exploding with laughter again at the rate at which Alex's face changes to one of seriousness. Mum looks confused. Well at least it's not me this time.

I finally finish my little bout of hysterics and wander over to Alex, who quietly puts his arm around my waist.

"The bike's going to have to be fixed. It needs new parts so a car will be here in about an hour if that's okay with you. I've got something I'd like to share with you since we're in the area," he says. I have no clue what he'd like to share with me but nod my head and look at Dad, who's hovering in the corner with a grin on his face as he watches us. Alex, it seems, has won over my entire family. Well, nearly... I'm pretty sure Belle's still not that happy about him but she is trying, which for her is a positive step towards happy.

"I think it's time for cake then," Mum says as she jumps up and puts the kettle back on the aga. "Walnut, chocolate or raspberry ripple?" My stomach rumbles.

~

Leaving Mum's house was the hardest thing I've had to do for a while. It was probably the nicest time I've had with her in ages. As usual, she'd fallen into giggling fits as Alex had regaled her with slightly naughty stories of varying situations he had been in during his life and I'd watched in awe as he'd delivered an admirable performance simply to make her smile. She'd blushed and gasped her way through the whole thing. It seems he can work any woman into a frenzy. Dad also

267

smirked his way through the conversation while gazing at mum in adoration, and when the time eventually came to leave, he pulled Alex into a hug and thanked him for making his wife smile. The moment brought tears to my eyes, but for all his performance with my mum, he went instantly rigid in Dad's arms, as if he simply didn't know what to do with the moment. Dad coughed slightly and backed away, trying to pull the intimacy away again but it was too late. I could only watch as Alex waved him off awkwardly and walked out the door towards the car as he smiled back at Mum. All I was able to do was hug them both and say sorry to Dad. How was I supposed to explain to him why Alex had reacted in that way? It wasn't my story to tell, and to be honest, I didn't entirely understand it myself. And now, while we're being driven to lord knows where, I am still trying to work that out as I lean onto his chest and listen to the thud of his heart beneath my ear. Perhaps I should just ask him? He's been pretty quiet since we left, not off with me or anything, just thoughtful and slightly distant.

"Thank you for all of that," I say into his shirt. His arm tightens around me as he kisses my head and rubs my arm absentmindedly.

"I think it should be me thanking you. Your parents are wonderful. I've never felt so welcomed by unknown people," he replies quietly. "I'm only sorry I left your dad feeling uncomfortable."

"It's okay. He'll understand; don't worry. Well, he won't, but you know what I mean. How could he? He doesn't know anything about your past so he'll probably just assume you're a little rigid or something. Anyway, forget about it. It doesn't matter. Actually, it does matter, not to him but to me. Why did you react like that?" *Tactful, Beth!* I have no idea how I managed to make that sound like such a disaster, but I've asked now so at least I'll get an answer.

"I've never had a man older than me hug me in such a way. It felt... strange," he replies instantly as if he's been thinking about the answer for a while. Well, at least my assumption was right.

"You reacted the same way when Mrs Peters hugged you. Was it the same feeling then?"

"No, that was distrust. Unfortunately, I still have that feeling regarding her," he says with an unapologetic tone as pulls me across his lap to straddle him, his face suddenly changing. "Take your top off. I want to watch you come."

Okay, definitely emotion avoidance, and actually, I couldn't give a damn. I've wanted him all day and he's known it all day. I pull my jumper off and throw it behind me to the floor. He immediately slips the cups of my bra to the side and bites at my nipples roughly. There will be nothing relaxing about this and my groin pushes toward him as I tilt away from him to increase the friction against it. His right hand flicks the button on my jeans as his left supports my weight and he shoves them down a little to make room for his deft fingers. I moan at the feeling as he pulls his head up to look at me and inches his fingers inside me.

"Oh god," I groan softly as I rub into his hand and feel the ache subside that has been desperate for his touch. His other hand finds its way into the back of my jeans and he reaches down further than I expected and rubs at my other entrance. My eyes fly open at the movement and I still in his arms.

"You've never been fucked here, have you?" he says as he drags the finger forward to get some of the moisture he's creating and then increases the pressure until he pushes a finger in slowly, inch by inch. My eyes widen at him as I absorb the feeling. No, I haven't, and I can't even begin to describe the feeling of it being filled. Dirty, raw and penetrating are the only words that come close to what I'm sensing as both his hands work gently at me. His thumb flicks across me with a growl of possession and I feel the beginning of my orgasm taking hold. Intense pleasure starts at my neck and seems to radiate downwards to every nerve in my body. "I'm going to fuck you there, baby. I'm going to drive myself in there so hard you'll beg me to keep doing it," he continues as his fingers work in unison, faster and with more force. I moan against him as my body begins to shake at his words and thoughts of him behind me. "And when I've done it enough times, you're going to let another man do it so I can watch from beneath you." Shit, I can't form thoughts. *Oh God, Pascal.*

His intense eyes and the thought of what he's just said send a bolt of lightning straight to my core and it ignites as I pant with lust at his words and tip my head back to absorb every moment of the bliss he's creating. "Oh god, Alex, yes," I call out as my body moves of its accord to enhance the rhythm he's creating within me naturally, as if I've done this a thousand times. Each slide backwards and forwards causes friction in another direction as I feel his fingers rubbing together inside me. Sudden shivering takes hold of me as I erupt with the most explosive and mind blowing sensation I've ever had. Every colour of the rainbow flicks across my vision and I stop breathing completely as my head comes back into line with his and his feral gaze lets me know he was deadly serious. I can't stop intoxicating green eyes flashing through my mind as I look back into his darkened blues. I know that's who he's thinking about, and as hard as I try to dismiss them, I can't, so I let them wash through me as I move on his fingers and look into the eyes of the man I love.

"Breathe, baby," he says softly as he removes his finger leisurely while continuing to grind his original hand in me, his thumb massaging me back down slowly with a rhythmic cadence that seems to lull me back to a peaceful place of compliance. I watch his eyes as he stares into the very heart of me to ensure I'm listening to what he's told me. He wants me to be ready for this. He told me he'd take me further and that he'd want everything from me. It appears he's now beginning to let me hear his thoughts more vividly and I have absolutely no idea how I feel about it. I can't even fathom a thought regarding how his words make me feel - only that he's probably right because I know that when he tells me to do something, I will, more than likely without hesitation.

Eventually, he gently removes his hand and buttons my jeans up again as I gaze into his face with unsure eyes. His hand strokes across my jaw and moves its way around the back of my neck.

"You are exquisite, Elizabeth, and I will give you every piece of the damaged soul you ask for in return for your acceptance of it. That's all I ask of you, that you do not condemn me because of it," he says steadily with a slightly pained expression. Condemn him? Never, but I do want to know why.

From somewhere deep within, I find the courage to just ask the question.

"Why Pascal?" I could have expanded but, frankly, there's no point. He might as well continue with the honesty. He's hesitant for a moment, slightly shocked even, as he glances at my lips and then chuckles.

"I've never had to answer that before. I'm not quite sure what to say," he replies as he picks up a piece of my hair and twirls it around his finger. "Pascal is a known quantity, I suppose, and you want him.

He's the only one I'd allow this with," he says with a shrug. No, I don't. Yes, I do. No... Or do I? No fucking clue anymore. Should I say I don't want him again? Clearly Alex wants the experience anyway, but I thought he didn't like to share...

"Do you?" Oh, shit! That definitely came out without any thought at all. Well sod him, I've always wanted to know.

The silence stretches as he presumably thinks about his response and continues with his twirling of my hair. Well he hasn't said no and that's what I expected so what does that mean? It's one thing knowing that Pascal is in love with him, or *something that goes much deeper,* but to think that maybe Alex has feelings for him in return is slightly perturbing. I can't compete with that. I don't even know if I want to be part of that. I will admit that I'd probably do it, but suddenly the thought of three people's feelings being involved in a game is terrifying. Not that Pascal would care. He's clearly been dealing with his feelings for a while. I drop my face away from him because I can't hold those eyes anymore. He might know what he's doing here but I absolutely do not.

"Head up, Elizabeth. Let me look at those eyes while I think about this. They ground me enough to be honest," he says firmly. Oh god, he does want him.

Time seems to roll on as his face stays unchanged and he tries to find his way through his thoughts. I just sit and stare at him expectantly in the hope that whatever leaves his mouth next is comforting to some degree. What am I doing even discussing this? My inner slut maybe stripping her clothes off but my mind is not in agreement at all. This is quite plainly ridiculous.

"My history with Pascal is clouded with mixed thoughts, Elizabeth. He has been a tutor, a tormentor and a confidant. He allows me to be exactly what I am with no judgement or sense of consequence. In fact, he encourages it to the point of stupidity sometimes. Do I want him? No, Elizabeth. I am not bisexual, nor gay, much as he might want me to be. But I do need him for certain elements of my preferences. He knows me well, is extremely skilled and he knows the rules that I require of him," he eventually says. I have done nothing but watch his mouth move and try to process the words that have left it. He doesn't want Pascal. I can breathe again because there would have been no competing with that amount of testosterone. Clearly there is a strong bond between them with regard to sex, but if he's being honest with me, it's nothing more than that. What it means they've done together before, I'm still not sure of, but I'm now pretty sure it's been hedonistic to say the least. However, it does beg the question of how he hasn't seen Pascal's feelings for him before. Maybe he has?

"Do you know that he loves you?" I ask as I climb off him and sit on the cool leather again. His brows shoot up as if he has no idea what I'm suggesting. I eye the *Cognac* in the centre console. I might need some. Actually, I do need some so I reach over and pour some into the cut crystal glass. Immediately chastising myself for mid-afternoon drinking, I tip it back and savour the flavour. This ridiculous conversation is setting my nerves on edge but the sharp burn that hits my throat is wonderful so I have some more.

"Why the hell would you think that? I doubt it very much, Elizabeth. He knows better, and besides, the man is incapable of it," he replies as he pours himself a drink and looks out of the window. "You know you do make things complicated sometimes. It's only about pleasure and sometimes amusement."

What an unbelievable statement. If he thinks this is only about that, he needs his head examining. He probably does anyway. I gape at him. Has he never had one single feeling about anyone before me? Has he never even considered that Pascal might have feelings for him? And what the hell has he given any other poor woman that he might have considered an *amusement* previous to me? The face of the cutthroat bastard blossoms across his features from somewhere and I ponder what emotion has just shut him down. I watch him over my drink and try to suppress my need to jump him. I so wish he'd stop looking so bloody gorgeous all the time, especially when he's all ferocious. That strong jaw and unyielding mouth are simply too distracting sometimes.

"I didn't think you liked to share," I mutter, almost to myself really because it appears talkative Alex has left the car. His body tenses as he turns back towards me with a look of distaste. It's almost enough to make me jump out of the window. He could kill with that look, that slight sneer of disgust or perhaps the beginnings of rage.

"I don't, Elizabeth, so I suggest you think about that before I put you in a room with both of us. I can assure you I will be thinking an awful lot about it," he replies as he continues to stare at me.

Well that makes the whole thing so much easier for me to understand. Not.

Incomprehensible.

Chapter 15

Alexander

No matter how he thought about it or which vision he created for himself, the thought was just wrong and unfortunately completely enthralling. To see her in Pascal's arms would simply be too fucking much and Alex knew it. Regardless of how fucking erotic the sight might be, he didn't, in all honesty, know if he'd be able to stop himself from killing the bastard. Why the hell couldn't he just get the vision out of his head and keep his damned mouth shut? He loved her. Every single bit of her beautiful body and mind belonged to him, his to do with as his chose, and here he was wanting to see her with Pascal. He had assumed, obviously wrongly, that he wouldn't want this. He certainly didn't like the man even looking at her, but he couldn't get that smirking bastard's sex-fuelled gaze out of his mind.

He'd never seen the man so enraptured before, and whether he liked it or not, he wanted to see more of it. Perhaps he just wanted to see it again so he could rip it away from the bastard. He could be a vindictive little shit when the mood took him and he knew it. But Pascal had done nothing to deserve his wrath, so something else must be driving his need to see them together and to be part of it. He didn't fucking understand it in the slightest, so when she had muttered the word *share* beneath her breath as she'd sat there looking absurdly decadent given her jeans and white jumper, he'd instantly been irritated to the point of disgust with himself.

He didn't know. How could he answer if he didn't know? He only knew he wanted it and so did she. She was probably bloody confused and given his temper regarding her, she was more than likely a little scared. Well so was he. For the first time in a very long existence of being completely in control of a sexual scene, so was he. Just the thought of her being more attracted to or possibly more interested in

Pascal was almost not worth the interaction, but clearly not enough to make it stop him wanting it.

When Parker, the driver that Andrews handed over to when he left for his holiday, looked at her when she got out of the car, Alex had to hold himself back from ripping his head off, literally ripping it off. The rage that surged through him as the man smiled far too seductively was consuming to the point of explosion. She nodded politely and then gazed back towards him with nothing but adoration while she reached for his hand. It softened the moment enough for him to remember where he was but not enough to stop him texting Andrews and telling him to order the jet and get his arse back tomorrow. He'd had a week, which was enough of a holiday for him. He was about the only one who Alex trusted around her. Well, him and Conner anyway. So why he thought he could do this with Pascal was utterly bemusing, and why had she talked about Pascal being in love with him? That was the most absurd thing he had ever heard. Yes, she might be in touch with her feelings but if she thought she could read Pascal's, she was sorely mistaken. He wasn't even sure if the man had anything that could remotely be considered a feeling of love, unless it was with regard to business. However, it did cross his mind that maybe the connection between them was a little more than simply fucking women and game playing. He did like the man after all. Maybe the master was a little more emotional than he'd considered before. That didn't mean he was in love though, did it? Fucked if he knew. Emotions were still a lost cause as far as he was concerned. Yes, he'd give her what she wanted, but whether he'd ever be comfortable with them was another thing entirely.

Now they were standing in the sleek, white foyer of the complex he'd had built four years ago. He shook his head and tried to bring himself back to the moment at hand and gazed across at her as she chatted amicably with the centre manager, Pauline Turbury. The woman was stick thin and haggard as hell, but given her start in life, he didn't understand how she was even alive today, let alone running a place as big as Addison's. He'd chosen her because of her empathy, because she'd been through more than anyone he'd ever met and because he was so humbled by her that sometimes he didn't even know what to say. It was still in her eyes. Even thirty years after the abuse, she still carried it around with her every day and when she

275

looked at him, she knew he did as well. No one else knew apart from Elizabeth but Pauline seemed to, and she did nothing but put her hand on his shoulder and smile. She never questioned him or tried to delve deeper but she somehow conveyed that she was there if he needed her. He would never need her but the thought that she was there was comforting to some degree. He had Elizabeth now. That was all he needed to get through each memory. She would give him everything he needed and probably more because he had no intention of ever letting her go. She was his and that was the fucking end of the topic. Pascal could go jump off a fucking bridge. He wasn't having her. He shook his head again in hatred of his own indecisiveness as a sound drifted through his head, an angel's voice beckoning him for more.

"Alex, are you coming?" she said as she flicked her luscious red locks over her shoulder. His eyes dropped to her mouth. Unfortunately, no, he wasn't coming and Christ, he wanted to, preferably with her lips wrapped around him. He chuckled at her enthusiasm and his thoughts. She was excited to see this side of him. Of course she would be, wouldn't she? It showed his emotions for what they were worth.

"Yes, of course. Is Sophie around, Pauline? I told her I'd like her to meet Elizabeth and she never did call me." Pauline's face fell a little as she walked them towards the stairs.

"Alex, Sophie has been having some problems. She has had some setbacks that have made her continuing progress a little more difficult. She's probably in the gardens. I'll go and find her. Why don't you two have a wander around and we'll meet you in the cafeteria in a little while," she said as she waved and clicked her way along the long corridor.

"What would you like to see first?" he asked her as he took her hand and led them up the stairs to the function rooms. He wasn't even sure what she'd make of the place. The people here were damaged. Hopeful yes, that was a requirement of them being allowed to stay, but they were all shells of people on their way to a more stable future if possible. The odds were that three out of ten actually made it through their pain, and while it wasn't enough, it was at least a start.

"I don't know. What is there to see? I don't want to interrupt anything important. I mean these people are all in therapy of some sort, aren't they? I suppose I just want to understand how they get to a better place, how you help them," she replied in a soft whisper as she hesitantly looked around. He chuckled.

"You don't need to whisper, baby. Addison's is quite open about everything that happens. The route to forward progression here is based on facing the issue, whatever it might be, and engaging in various different discussions or therapies that suit the individual best. Some work, some don't. I'm afraid it depends on the depth of the abuse," he said as he opened the door to the games room. Several familiar faces looked up and smiled at him. One particular young lady almost threw herself at him.

"Alex," she shouted as she ran to him and wrapped her hands around his waist. He stiffened instantly but tried to remain fluid to some degree. Tamsin was twelve when she was brought to the centre. She was now fifteen and on her way to being more balanced, but two abusive brothers had fucked her life up immeasurably. She raised he head slightly and glared at Elizabeth from his chest. He felt her hands tighten around his waist so he gently removed them. She was also known to be possessive and explosive. The irony wasn't lost on him at all, but she was becoming too attached to the wrong person - namely him. She curled her lip at him and took a step back as she continued her glare at her newest threat.

"Tamsin, how are you? This is my girlfriend, Elizabeth. I thought it might be nice if you could show her around the games room while I have a chat to Frank," he said, keeping a careful distance. His girlfriend, thank God, kept a warm smile plastered across her face as she extended her hand to the young girl. It wasn't a game to her. She wasn't showing her guts or guile; she simply seemed to be happy and unaffected by Tamsin's demeanour. He watched in awe, as his bewitching woman seemed to disarm the girl and began chatting with her about her hairstyle. Tamsin flushed and giggled like a child. Well, she was one - at least she could be here. He smiled at her and let them wander off to the pool table. Frank, the shrink, appeared at his side. He was a good one apparently.

"Quite a woman you've got there," he said as he pulled up a chair for them both. Alex growled at him; he couldn't help it. It was becoming the norm and she appeared amused by it most of the time, if slightly uneasy. The dick laughed.

"Yes," was the best answer he could find as he recalled his irritation and gazed at her sublime figure.

"Are you finally releasing yourself to someone, Alexander?" He chuckled at that. Frank had been trying his psychoanalysis shit with him for years so he turned toward the man and smiled.

"Tell me what's been going on around here, Frank. Pauline says Sophie's not doing great and Ben isn't looking too hot either," he asked as he looked over at the blonde haired boy. The nine year-old looked completely lost in his own world of window gazing as he swayed from side to side.

"Still using the avoidance technique then?"

"Apparently so," was his short response as he raised a brow. Frank smiled and looked across at the boy again.

"It's always like this, Alexander. You know that. Nothing comes quickly. Your impatience is heart-warming but we both know half these kids won't make it. We can only try, and unfortunately, Sophie's mother died, which she's finding hard to cope with," Frank said with a sigh. "But on the positive side, we have had eight others move onto Bernard housing. They're all going to college now and looking forward to life again."

It still wasn't enough. He felt like pounding the shit out of something as he relived a few moments at his father's hands, his face buried in the carpet as he'd been held down. Bile rose in his throat and he looked across at her. She giggled at him and waved her elegant hand. The vision of his father dissipated to a distant blur and he rubbed at his throat as he remembered her fingers there. Only ever hers.

"Come and meet Elizabeth, Frank. I think she'll like you. She's quite fond of talking about feelings," he said as he stood and wandered over to the angel who was currently sinking pool balls expertly, another thing he didn't know about her. He also couldn't stop watching her backside leaning across the table. God, he wished they were alone. He had a feeling she'd enjoy his current thoughts regarding the pool cue. He certainly would. Christ, her ability to distract him from his thoughts was miraculous to say the least. Tamsin stared at him as he moved forward but she didn't try to move and she even smiled a little as he approached his angel. Fuck, the woman had

278

done it again. She didn't even try and people loved her. It wasn't surprising as much as it was awe-inspiring.

"Elizabeth, this is Frank Stelling. He's the resident guiding enlightenment for the kids here," he said with a smirk as Frank tutted behind him and shook her hand.

"Hello, Elizabeth, lovely to meet you. Tell me, what have you done to our patron? He seems, dare I say it, happy." She beamed at Frank. It was almost enough to bring Alex to his knees and he swallowed his giddiness before anyone else saw it. God, he worshipped the ground she walked on.

"Well, it appears, Frank all you have to do is play a few games with him. He likes them you see and I love playing with him," she said as she licked her lips. His dick twitched. *Temptress*. He wanted her, immediately. Why he hadn't taken her in the car was a mystery. For some reason, he'd just wanted to please her and watch. That behaviour was still fucking odd.

Frank stood watching her in amusement. The man was too clever for his own good and as he looked across at Alex, he felt his defences around the man crumble a bit. He had been the one to give him Schroeder's number so he knew the counselling had begun. What he thought of Elizabeth was anyone's guess, but he was probably far more intrigued with how she had found a way in. He couldn't blame the man; he hadn't got a clue himself.

"Interesting. Games... I never thought of that," he said as he raised a brow and shifted his head to watch a small boy who was having some sort of aggressive blow out with the drinks machine. "It seems I am needed. Elizabeth, it was a pleasure. Alexander, give my best to Schroeder the next time you see him, and can I suggest that you take her with you next time?" he said as he walked off toward the boy with a wave. *Bastard*.

"Who's Schroeder?" she asked without hesitation. Tamsin looked at him quizzically.

"Not here, Elizabeth. Let's walk and we'll discuss it. Sophie and Pauline will be waiting for us," he said as he grabbed her hand, smiled at the young girl and led her out of the door.

"Bye, Tamsin, lovely meeting you," she called over her shoulder. His heart warmed at her care of a girl she'd never met before. "She's a remarkable young lady," she said as she continued looking back at her. "Why is she here?"

"It's not my story to tell. I'm sorry but I can't. You could come back and ask her yourself, though. She seems to have taken a shine to you. You can be as involved with this as you'd like to be. They're always looking for volunteers," he replied as they headed out the doors and through the garden to the cafeteria.

"Oh wow, look at this," she said as she gazed around at the gardens. He smiled at her love of the outdoors. "Someone really went to town on the grounds."

"It's important to be around beauty for rehabilitation," he replied, gazing at the most enchanting thing in the place. She stole the show with every fibre of her being. "I had the designers create small, intimate spaces for contemplation and large, open spaces for communal gatherings. It's critical for them to feel together but not overly crowded." She gaped at him.

"You did this? I knew you were involved but did you do all of this? Is this whole place because of you?" He'd forgotten she didn't know the extent of his involvement and frowned a little at the thought. Should he tell her the reasons why? Perhaps not now.

"Addison's was formed six years ago. I had this place built four years ago because the original location was unsuitable for more children. Come on, I think it's going to rain," he said as he tugged her hand and led them into the café. He didn't want any more conversation on the matter.

"You do know your distractions don't work anymore, don't you? You can't deflect me, and I still want to know who Schroeder is. But, Mr. White, I happen to love you immensely so I'll let you keep your secrets for now," she said as she wrapped her hands gently around his neck and kissed him on the cheek. He smiled into her face at her abilities and enjoyed the feeling of her skin on his.

"I love you, too," he replied, returning the kiss and moving away from her. He saw Pauline from the corner of his eye, smiling warmly at them and walked over to her. Where was Sophie?

"She's not up to seeing anyone. I'm sorry," Pauline said as they reached her. Alex smiled a little to himself as he thought of all the times in his life that he *hadn't been up to seeing anyone*. Frankly, it had been most of his life. Fucking parasitic do-gooders, pretending they had a clue what any of it felt like. If only Sophie knew how much he understood about how she felt.

"It's okay. I'll see her next time or tell her to give me a call whenever she feels like it," he replied as he looked at his watch. "We should get going anyway."

"Oh, that's a shame. It's been good to see you though. It always does the children a world of good to see you here. They look up to you more than you know," Pauline replied as she grinned at him. He smiled back but couldn't stop the irritation rising internally at her continuing approval of him. She knew nothing of how little he deserved their admiration.

"We'll see ourselves out, Pauline. Thank you for your time."

"Yes, thank you. It's such a positive environment and such a deserving charity. I feel honoured to have been here," Elizabeth said to her as they walked outside again.

"You're quite lovely, Elizabeth. Please be good to him. We all love him very much, regardless of how little he thinks he deserves it," Pauline said as she shook her hand and looked at him. He flinched at her words but regained himself quickly. "We'll see you again soon." She nodded at them both and with a wave of her hand, disappeared into the gardens.

"It appears everyone's in love with you, Mr. White. I shall have to keep my guard up," her lovely mouth said as she linked her arm through his. He frowned and walked them away to the safety of the car. There was no one there to fuck with his mind, only her, and she was allowed. Well, on his terms anyway. Who was he fucking kidding? She was so far in his mind that he hadn't got a hope of deflecting her. He didn't even think he wanted to anymore.

~

She was upstairs in the shower and he couldn't make up his mind whether to go and get her or if he should do the work that he should have done all day. He'd dismissed phone calls all day just to be with her, just to give her the support she needed. Her family were undoubtedly some of the best people on the planet, and that her mother would be struck again with cancer was just abhorrent. He reached for his phone and sent a quick email to his doctor. The woman would get the best. It was as much as he could do for her. That and be there for Elizabeth. He sighed and looked at his desk, then at the bookcase. That's where it had all started. He relived the moment with alarming clarity when she had ground onto his leg and made herself come as he'd held her against the shelves. He walked across to see if divine intervention had put her in that spot or if it had just been him. The first book he found with his hand was a collection of John Keats' poetic works. He chuckled and pulled it from the shelf to lay it on his desk. The melancholic poet was an overly dramatic, love-sick puppy, but his choice of wording was exemplary most of the time. Perhaps he would read it in a different light this time round and actually feel some of the sentiment involved.

He clicked on his laptop and was instantly bombarded with several hundred emails that should have been answered or at least looked at. He shook his head and closed the bloody thing. He couldn't concentrate on anything, let alone deal with it. He would be meeting his half-sister tomorrow and he still didn't know how he felt about it. He assumed she would either know by now who he was or she would currently be having a conversation with her mother about her rapist father, *his* rapist father.

Soft tinkling lifted his head from his thoughts and he realised she was in the music room. He smiled and walked into the lounge to get some brandy. The tones of Clair de Lune echoed along the corridor and he frowned in confusion. Why would she play that? He hadn't heard her play since he behaved like a dick. She must have the same feelings regarding the piece as he had now. It haunted him with bad feelings and he only remembered watching her as he'd cursed her for being a whore.

Clearly she wasn't and could never be, but the memory of that night was implanted nonetheless and he knew she would be thinking about it while she played. He wandered along the corridor with two full glasses of amber nutrition and was completely thrown as he turned the corner into the doorway. There she sat, in his shirt again, the dull glow of the lamp behind her again. It was as if he had been transported back to that night again. Everything was the same apart for his feelings this time. She looked across at him and smiled as her fingers traversed the keys.

"Come sit with me," she said as she stopped abruptly. "I want you to take away the memories."

He hesitated for a second. He had no idea why, but the vision of her sitting there was so captivating that for some reason he felt like moving toward her would be intruding or something equally rude. She held out her hand and beckoned him. His feet moved without him asking them to and before he knew, it he was sitting behind her, burying his face in her hair. She shifted forward a bit to make room and began to play again from the beginning. Time stood still as he listened to her and felt her body moving beneath his hold, kissing her lightly and moving her hair out of the way so he could watch her fingers. She was everything to him. He knew he had to find something to take this away from them and as she began to sniff with emotion, he felt his own throat constrict.

"I love you," he said as he moved his hands to her thighs and let his fingers trace patterns in her skin. "I never loved until you, and I will never love anyone but you." She missed a key and fumbled to get the flow of the music back. "I was a fool and will spend the rest of my life showing you everything that you deserve from me. I'll give you all that I am and hope that you can give me half as much in return, because you are my air, baby. You have my heart, my soul and my body. It's all for you if you want it. You can take it and do with it as you wish." She stumbled again at the mention of her own words and stopped, her fingers trembling as she inhaled sharply.

"I..."

"Keep playing, baby, or play something else. Help me find another way to tell you this."

She placed her hands over the keys and he felt his breath shudder at the thought of what piece would conjure up the right emotion for her. If she could only feel his own sense of hope and peacefulness around her, maybe she would be able to understand the depth of his commitment. "I love you. Make this go away for both of us."

She tinkled over the keys a few times and then shook her head and got up. He raised an eyebrow at her and watched as she walked around behind him.

"Turn around," she said softly in that beautiful voice of hers as she sniffed again and picked up her drink. He moved his legs around to face her and looked at her mouth as she drank half the glass. Surprising the hell out of him, she clambered astride him and fidgeted him backwards until she could reach the piano again. His fingers wrapped around her hipbones as he looked into her eyes. They still ripped him to shreds and he struggled to hold her gaze. She pushed herself as close to him as possible and ground down onto him as she stretched around him and began to play again. He smiled into her shoulder as the familiar notes of the same piece filtered into the air around them. For good or bad, Clair de Lune was going to be their music. It was his job to make it beautiful again. Perhaps it was only right that the piece had taken them through bad and good times.

He moved her hair again and kissed her throat as she found her way around his body, her groin moving across him and pressing onto his dick with fevered intensity. He unbuttoned his shirt and hers so he could feel her skin on him, which instantly electrified the air around them and had her moaning into him. Fuck, he loved that sound. He wanted inside of her immediately. He moved her around until he could pull himself free of his jeans and moved his hand to the side of her panties. She moaned again as he ripped the sides apart and discarded them, her fingers flinching at the keys as he lifted her up and pushed her down on top of his waiting cock.

Discordant notes rang into the air as they both tried to find their positions and adjust to the intensity of being together. He swallowed at the warmth of her sweetness wrapped around him and buried his head into her neck.

"Fuck, you feel good," he growled as he pulled her closer. She moaned and pushed down on him.

"Make love to me, Alex. Show me how you feel."

Christ, he loved hearing her say that. He slowly exhaled as she found her rhythm again and he started to move her gently backwards and forwards on top of him. Every stroke nearly had him exploding like a fucking teenager. The sound of the music and her heavy breathing only increased his desire to grab her and throw her on the ground, but in this moment, he was holding on so tightly that he never wanted to let go. His fingers dug into her back and pulled her closer to him as she squirmed to reach around him and find the notes she wanted.

"More," she moaned as he increased the friction and she rubbed herself on him. He moved to get a better angle and drove in hard. "Yes. Oh god, I love you," she hissed at him as her breathing started becoming erratic. He kissed his way up her neck and continued with his more forceful thrusts as the piece escalated. She matched his passion and drew her face back to look at him, stilling the keys.

"Don't stop playing, baby," he panted in roughened breaths as he gazed into her eyes and tried to show her all she wanted. She kept pushing into him and moaned out his name again as she trembled above him and fumbled the notes.

"I can't reach the-"

"I don't give a fuck. Keep playing," he growled, watching her captivating face as she began her spiral. Her lips parted, and that iridescent blush rose across her chest and neck beautifully as she tried to keep playing behind him. "Come, baby. Let it go for me," he said as he felt his own release building, thickening within her. Her muscles clamped around him and he couldn't stop the need to kiss the living hell out of her so he grabbed her face and slammed his mouth over hers. Her fingers were pulled from the keys but frankly he couldn't give a damn. She moaned into his mouth as she came hard around him and pulsated on him. It was enough for him to lose control and he let go seconds after her as she wrapped her arms around him and they rode out their moment in ecstasy together. Always together. Christ, he'd die without her.

He palmed her backside in his hands and kept grinding her into him with steadier pulls as he explored her mouth with his tongue and affirmed his need to stay connected to her. He hadn't got a fucking clue where that need came from but he knew he couldn't be without it and revelled in the feeling of her sliding up and down on him as he pulsed inside her. She eventually broke the kiss and gazed at him with a smile. He exhaled slowly as he tried to find some air again. She always managed to make him lose his ability to breathe or find it again so he listened to her as she tried to do the same and grinned at her. It was more than likely a fucking sappy grin, but he didn't give a shit. She did this to him, and he actually quite liked it.

"Maybe we could practice that again," she said as she giggled and ran her fingers through his hair. He loved that as well, her hands in his hair. He'd never allowed a woman that before.

"Often, I would hope," he replied, still grinning like a fool.

"We might even make it to the end of the piece one day."

"I highly fucking doubt it, but I'm happy to keep trying. Would you like another go now?" He twitched his hardening dick in her and she laughed. That wasn't the correct response so he picked her up and growled. She laughed again and much as he wanted to slam her against the wall, he smiled and took them over to the sofa by way of the brandy glasses. She grabbed them.

They'd been sat there gazing at each other for about five minutes when the doorbell rang. He cocked an eyebrow at her and she quickly began to do up her shirt, or rather *his* shirt.

"If we have guests, baby, you'll be doing more than buttoning up my shirt. For a start, you'll need underwear," he said as he stood up. "Wait here. I'll see who it is."

He walked out and found Conner opening the door in front of him. He narrowed his eyes at the thought of him having a key. He'd never given a shit whether he'd walked in before because there had never been a woman here before but now. Well, they could have been up to anything, anywhere.

"Wait longer next time," he snarled as he approached him. Conner's eyes widened a bit as he halted his movements.

"Shit, man, I didn't think. I'm all over the fucking shop. Jesus, did I interrupt something?" he replied as he glanced at his open shirt. Alex chuckled and ducked his head back into the music room.

"Its Conner, baby. We'll go into the lounge. Go get dressed." Conner's smirk was clearly uncontainable and Alex pointed a finger in the direction of the lounge with another snarl. "Don't be a sick fucker, Avery." Conner ambled his way in front of him with a frown and turned into the room without looking back. Good fucking job, too, because Alex couldn't stop watching her backside ascending the stairs with a lack of underwear. She giggled all the way and he shook his head at his own possessiveness as he headed for his friend.

"I am sorry, man. I'll ring next time," Conner said quietly as he poured himself a drink and then threw a log on the fire. Alex tilted his head at him as he sat and wondered what was wrong while he watched him pace about. Conner wasn't a pacer. He sipped his brandy and waited.

"What do you think about marriage?" Conner suddenly asked out of the blue. He was so taken aback he didn't know what to say. He opened his mouth to try but Conner stopped him. "I mean, she won't move in with me and I don't know what else to do so I bought this and now I don't know if I should or not," he said as he held up a small, square, red box. "Would you? Do you think it's too soon? It's too soon, isn't it?" Alex smirked at him and watched him continue to pace around. The man was being hilarious. He opened his mouth once more, but Conner started again. "I think she needs this from me. I adore her. She's fucking insane and I don't know if I can keep her or not, but I just want her with me, like all the fucking time, and I'm seriously all over the place about this. I mean, it's marriage, Alex, like kids and shit, and I don't know if I can do that yet." He eventually flopped himself down into a chair and stared at the fire.

Alex watched him to see if there was anything else coming as Conner took the box out and opened it to gaze at the stunning ring, Alex couldn't stop the whistle that rang out of his mouth at the clearly very expensive piece of *Cartier*.

"Do you think she'll like it?"

"I have no idea. Perhaps you should ask her and find out," Alex replied as he sipped his brandy again. He hadn't got a clue what else to say. The fact was that if Conner was thinking he wanted to do this then he probably did, "What do you want me to help you with?"

"I don't know. I just want to be sure it's the right thing to do. I have blue fucking hair, man. Is that what married people look like? I haven't got the slightest bloody idea what a married man should look like. Most of them look as depressed as fuck from what I've seen. And what if she says no? Shit, I'll die if she says no."

"I doubt she'll say no, Conner. She loves you," came drifting from the back of the room. Alex smirked again as Conner's hands fumbled with the box and his eyes shot to hers almost in terror.

Perfect fucking timing.

"Beth, shit, you weren't supposed to see this. How could I have forgotten you were here? Oh, for Christ's sake, now I've royally screwed this up," he said with an exasperated sigh as he pocketed the box and stood up for another drink. She headed across to him and Alex gazed at her effortless grace as she filled her glass and then sneaked a hand into his pocket to retrieve the ring box without him noticing, Alex grinned across at her and tutted with a shake of his head.

"Naughty," he said quietly. She giggled as she ambled her way back across to him and sat on the floor, leaning her head back between his legs. He couldn't stop himself from wrapping his fingers in her hair and fanning it out over his thigh as she opened the box and gasped aloud at the sight of the rubies and diamonds.

"Oh my, that is quite a ring," she exclaimed. Conner's eyes shot across to her as he patted his pocket wildly.

"Jesus, Beth, how the hell did you get that?"

"Pesky fairies." Alex chuckled as he thought of pick-pocketing in his youth. She would have made a superb accomplice. He stroked her hair and watched her gazing at the ring in adoration. Regardless of her thoughts on overly priced gifts, she clearly liked the connotation of this one.

"Conner, do you love her?" she asked as she closed the box and placed it on the table with a small sigh.

"Of course I do. What the hell is that supposed to mean?"

"Nothing, I'm sorry. It's just that she's my sister and I need to know that this is serious and not just because she won't do as you want her to. Belle is the way she is for a good reason and no amount of manipulation will make her change. I need to know that you love her exactly the way she is. She's been through enough without you adding to it."

"I don't even know what to say to that. You think I'd do this if I wasn't happy with exactly who she is?" he replied as his hands flew around. Alex smiled at his agitation. He couldn't help it; it amused him to see Conner edgy and frustrated.

"She won't move in with you because she's scared, Conner. Has she told you anything about Marcus?" His mouth snarled at the mention of another man's name and Alex noticed his temper flare across his features. It wasn't quite so amusing anymore.

"No. Who the fuck is Marcus?" he said angrily as he stomped across and towered above them.

"Calm down, Conner. If Elizabeth is trying to help you then I suggest you listen and take notes. Are you both hungry? Chinese okay for everybody?" he said as he stood up and glared at Conner. Conner drew in a long breath and removed his jacket.

"Yes, thank you. Sorry, Beth, I'm a dick. Who's Marcus?"

He walked out of the room and into the kitchen to retrieve his phone as he heard her saying the name Marcus Renfield. Whatever she was about to tell Conner was more than likely not good so he

288

called in the take out and scrolled through his messages for a few minutes to give them some privacy. They were all fucking boring apart from some business that Louisa had asked for. He quickly sent some replies and then noticed one from Pascal. He didn't even know if he wanted to open it. His finger hovered as he pictured the two of them dancing and remembered her words of Pascal's love for him. He couldn't stop his thumb moving.

> **- Alexander, I am bored to death without you. Why do you punish me with your absence?**

He had only one feeling regarding that: confusion. He didn't know himself, and he only knew that he couldn't play their games to full capacity any more with Elizabeth now in the picture. He didn't want any of their earlier entertainment any more. She consumed his thoughts and he had all he needed or wanted with her. Well, he would once she learnt more about him and truly felt his preferences. He could only hope she would accept them. She seemed to be doing okay so far.

He replied as he heard the gate buzzer go off.

> **- I need to talk with you. I'll call you next week. Are you in London still?**

He looked at the gate viewer and saw a young man loaded up with bags. He pressed the release button and walked to the door to open it. Handing the boy a fifty, he shooed him away and closed the door behind him. Just as he reached the kitchen, he heard laughter coming from the lounge so he assumed she had calmed the rage in Conner and settled his nerves a bit. She did that well - calm the storm in people. His phone vibrated so he opened it and gazed at the screen.

> **- I am yours whenever you need me, dear boy, regardless of the location. You should know this.**

Just the response he'd expected, but for some reason, it was beginning to take on a new meaning. The previously salacious thoughts he would have had regarding this comeback were now mixing together with jealousy, anger, resentment and something else that he couldn't quite put his finger on. He searched his mind for the unfamiliar feeling as he took some plates to the table and began unpacking the Chinese. It still wasn't apparent to him what the hell he was thinking about so he discarded the rubbish and selected some *Muse* to listen to while they ate.

She wandered into the kitchen with her arm linked in Conner's and it hit him like a tonne of bricks. Family... This was his family, and before he could dismiss the thought, Pascal drifted into his mind. His mind saw visions of the man's hands on her as he watched from a distance. What was that fucking thought? Why the hell would he consider Pascal family in one breath and then want to see them together? He would never consider the same thoughts regarding Conner, but then he'd never been that way inclined around Conner. They were more like brothers. Pascal was... something else. What was he? He'd never asked the question of himself before now until she mentioned it earlier. He'd just experienced a lifestyle that Pascal had mentored him in and never contemplated what the man actually meant to him. He was simply a highly skilled, and quite frankly depraved, son of a bitch who pushed him to be honest with himself regarding pleasure.

He took a seat and watched the two of them. Conner was beaming at something funny she'd obviously said and as he reached across to get some food, they both turned their heads towards him expectantly. Had someone asked him a question?

"Well, what do you think?" she asked. He had no idea what they were talking about.

"Sorry, I wasn't listening. What did you say?" She frowned at him with that look of hers that said *what's going on in your head? Tell me... Show me if you want,* then glanced at Conner with a bright smile and opened her mouth again.

"We were wondering about going sailing sometime. Conner tells me you have a yacht that you've clearly forgotten to tell me about?"

Meritato. The thought of seeing her on his yacht was pure bliss. A week of nothing but her naked and warmer weather was exactly what he wanted to do. Conner and Belle were not top of his priority list but he guessed it wouldn't hurt to have them there for a few days.

"Sounds great. When were you thinking?"

"I don't know. I'd have to look at the event list but we should be quieter in the New Year sometime," she replied as she stabbed at a pork ball. Conner chuckled next to her as he watched her bite it in half.

"Fuck, those teeth look as dangerous as your sister's." Alex shot him a look of death, and the dick laughed at him and sucked in a noodle. He raised a brow as he watched her eat the rest and imagined her tongue swirling around him. It wasn't even possible to describe the next image that floated through his brain. Needless to say, it involved her being tied up and possibly gagged, maybe in something red or nothing at all, ether would be fine.

"What? They're good balls," she said as she giggled and snapped her teeth at him playfully. He could almost feel her nails digging into him at the thought of holding her down again and making her scream. He was taking her to Eden. Whether Pascal was there or not was of no consequence. He just wanted her back in his suite again. It was time to start showing her who she was asking to see again. Perhaps it would make these ridiculous thoughts of threesomes go away so he could concentrate on other matters. Or maybe it would escalate them to the point of no return. Either way, he'd at least make a fucking decision and get on with it.

"So should I ask her then? What's the consensus in the room?" Conner said, abruptly cutting off his thoughts.

"I think you should make a decision and get on with it," Alex replied with his own words rattling around his head. Conner looked at Elizabeth for her opinion.

"I think you should trust what your heart tells you to do," she said as she picked up her drink.

Conner looked between the two of them with no more sense of purpose than he had when he first came to the house. Alex burst out laughing at his confused face. It was fucking priceless.

Chapter 16

Elizabeth

"*Come back to bed,*" he'd said as he grabbed me by the hair and tugged me toward the dark wood frame. His perfect naked form blinded me with its godlike physique, muscles rippling and that fine backside striding along, waging war on me. If only I could have. Instead, I'd twisted sideways away from him and lunged at the door in the hopes of escape. Well, not really *hope* because the fact was that I was dying to get back in that bed with him and let him torture me with some other new form of orgasm that I hadn't been privy to yet. However, work called at six thirty in the bloody morning.

"Witch," he'd called out as I descended the stairs.

"Love you. I'll be back by two," I'd called back.

"Take the Aston and be careful."

So I did. Well, once I'd worked out where the keys were and how to open the garage and the main gates. Frankly, I would have been quicker calling a taxi.

So now here I stand in my small and faithful kitchen, thinking about the really very large kitchen that he is giving to me - yep, giving to me. I still can't work out why he's doing it but it's apparently very important to him that I take it. He says it will show him that I love him. Why me telling him isn't enough I'm not sure, and how it relates to his bastard of a father putting a tie around his neck is completely unknown. But with a very heavy heart of unease, I've accepted and to be honest, I'm still pissed about it. I am yet to tell the girls about this but I assume they will be very pleased. What normal person wouldn't be?

Twenty eight bake-offs later and I've eventually gotten the food for the elevenses coffee morning at the Tushingham Hotel sorted and loaded into the van. We don't need to do anything else but show the driver the way, and waiting on staff will arrive at the venue in the next half an hour to meet him at the other end. Why we need them to be there every eight weeks is completely unknown. They never have to do anything but stand around looking pretty, and I still can't fathom why the hotel don't just do the food themselves. They say it cuts into lunch service. I suppose I agree in a roundabout way.

My phone rings on the work surface somewhere and I rush around the sodding mess I've created to find it. Obviously my feet get tangled in the rubbish and I trip and fall, Miraculously, though, my phone crashes to the floor beside me at the same time. I quickly answer it as I rub my foot and kick the rubbish in disgust.

"Shit, hello?" I say, somewhat inelegantly.

"Nice answer, Beth, very professional. You okay?" Conner's voice comes sarcastically crashing into my eardrums. Trust him to be the reason for my clumsiness.

"Yes, fine thanks. Just sodding dandy. Just fell over my own mess. Umm... actually, why are you calling me?" I ask with narrowed eyes. I have no idea.

"Houston, I think we have a problem," is his response. I don't like it. It's far too vague.

"What are you talking about?"

"Evelyn Peters has just emailed me to tell me she isn't coming this evening."

Oh! Not good at all. He finds family and she rejects him? What a bitch. I hate her instantly.

"Right, well, I don't think I can do anything about that. Besides, Alex will probably be happy about it," I reply, knowing he absolutely *won't* be happy but I try to make the remark as casual as I can.

"We both know he'll go all internal and start doubting his own worth again, Beth, and I for one don't want to see that side of him again, do you? It's scary as fuck to be honest. This new version of him that you've found is much better and I quite enjoy seeing it so I have a plan." Wow, shit, Conner really does know him well. I smile into the phone at his loyalty. I could kiss him; he's such a star.

"Okay, dude, what's the plan?" I reply with a giggle.

"Did you just say dude? Stop it. Sounds fucking stupid on you. Anyway, I was thinking you could go and have lunch with her, try to persuade her otherwise."

What? I don't think so. Female version of Alex, no thank you very much.

"I don't think..."

"Good, don't. I've booked a table for the pair of you at Clastro's and told her I need to meet with her about some software we're launching. She'll be there at one. Is that okay with you?"

Christ, Conner's on a dominant roll this morning. It's quite sweet, adorable really.

"Conner, what on earth do you think I'll be able to say to her? If she doesn't want to see him, I'm not surprised. How would you feel?" His response is immediate.

"I'd feel betrayed, confused, lonely and very much in need of some love. This is exactly the reason why she needs to meet with him and see that she's not the only one. And you, young lady, are the one to convince her. If you can melt him, you can definitely melt her."

Shit, that was good. I have no comeback to that at all. Bastard. Where the hell did this clever bugger come from?

"Did you memorise that speech?"

"Yes, I knew you wouldn't be too enthusiastic about it," he says with a humorous snort.

"I'm not, but I'll do it."

Of course I will. The thought of watching Alex's face when he realises she's not there is revolting, no matter how well he'll hide it. Conner's spot on. It would cause a turmoil I have no intention of letting happen. Miss Peters will be attending and will be enthused to see her new found big brother by the time I'm finished with her. I still hate her.

"My work here is done. I assume you'll know her when you see her?"

"I'm damn sure I will." Her eyes are as disturbing as Alex's.

"Bye, Beth. Have fun. I'll see you tonight." Yep, fun, that's exactly what this is going to be.

"Bye, Conner. Thanks a bunch." I huff as I end the call and start clearing up the rubbish at my feet. I check the clock and realise I've only got an hour to get myself sorted, get across town and think about what the hell I'm going to say to the woman. I'll wing it. That seems to have been working quite well for me lately and with any luck, those fairies might come along for the ride to give me a hand.

I thrash around the kitchen, trying to clear the devastation that is my workspace and then walk into the office. Hopefully Belle will have a change of clothes here because these jeans and t-shirt are not going to cut it with Miss Peters.

"Have you got a change of clothes here?" I ask her as she pounds at the laptop. She points her finger at the cupboard and returns to her serious face. I open it up and find a cream linen trouser suit and a green blouse. Clearly the matching shoes are below it. "Mind if I borrow it?"

"No, honey, go for it," she replies with no hesitation whatsoever. I quickly strip off and pull the expensive ensemble on. It's a tad long but certainly better than the previous outfit and the towering shoes help a lot. I grab my bag and touch up my make-up as I drag my fingers through my hair and try to make it do something elegant.

"What time are you getting there tonight? And do you want a coffee?" she asks as she stretches behind me and stands up. *Ooh coffee machine - must pay Alex back!*

"About eight-thirty I think. Listen, when is the next invoice for White's going out?"

"Umm, should be the twenty second, I think, just before we break for Christmas. Why?" she says, narrowing her eyes.

"Well I need to pay him back for that damn machine he bought and he won't take any money, so I thought we could leave it off his invoice and then I'll pay the company back. Is that okay?"

"I was wondering where that had appeared from. I'll pay half. In fact, why don't we just leave it and charge it to the business," she says. Go Belle! "How much was it?" Shit.

"Three thousand." She spits out her coffee, narrowly missing her suit.

"For a fucking coffee machine?" Yes, I said that, too.

"Yep," I reply casually.

"Oh right, well I suppose I should be getting used to it by now. Conner just spent that much on a new sodding tech toy. No fucking idea what it's for. I'm not even sure he does," she says, rolling her eyes. "Where are you off to anyway?"

"Lunch at Clastro's." I can't tell her anything else. I don't know if she knows anything or not. Has Conner told her? Who knows? I

295

haven't got time anyway. "I've got to go or I'm going to be late," I say as I rush out the door. "See you later, honey."

I don't hear her reply as I open the Aston door and slide in. I have no idea where I'm going to park. Actually, Clastro's has valet parking. Well, at least I'll look in control of myself as I rock up in an expensive car and hand it over to a young boy at one of London's swankiest hotspots. Unfortunately, I feel completely the opposite as I reverse out and head into the traffic. How the fuck am I going to manage a female Alex? I've only barely got a handle on him, so the thought of dealing with her is unnerving to say the least. As the traffic comes to a halt at traffic lights, I glance in the mirror and try for that Alex impassive face that he does so well, the one that says intelligent, confident, in control, not intimidated. I can't hold it for more than a few seconds before bursting into giggles because it's so not me. I can do the eyebrow thing, though, so perhaps I'll just eyebrow her into submission or something like that. Then I remember her face. I'm pretty sure she's going to eat me alive. So screwed.

~

"Thank you," I say to the young man as he passes me a ticket and drops himself into the car. He nods and smiles as he drives off really rather quickly. I turn toward the infamous black and red building and bring my head up abruptly as I think of Alex's words. *Head up.* I can do this. I can sit in front of her and hold my own. I am strong. I am the girlfriend of Alexander White and I will not let her ruin this for him. A doorman glares down at me as ascend the steps and my inner bitch recoils a little as my feet slow. Shit, I am so in over my head. *Oh get a grip, Beth! Move your bloody feet.*

I stride in my best *I own this space* style and casually walk up the stairs as if I've done it a thousand times before. For some reason, I can't stop the terse expression that seems to have materialised on my face at the doorman's glower. Maybe Alex is rubbing off on me in more ways than one. So, on approaching the hostess, I smile and ask for Mr. Avery's table. She extends her hand and beams at me. Apparently I have passed the expensive enough test so I return my face to its new, semi-irritated look. It feels strangely empowering to be so dismissive and I wonder why as I carry myself across the floor in what I hope are long, elegant paces. Several men gaze at me - two winking and one positively leering. I roll my eyes in amusement and continue forward towards my target with my expression unchanged.

The atmosphere around me suddenly seems to take on a somehow more electric charge and I instantly realise why as the hostess stops and waves a hand at the chair in front of me with a grin. As much as my body wants to freeze and recoil again, I pull myself together and sit down to look at her across the table. Miss Peters' pokerfaced gaze is as good as Alex's and I recognise those eyes the instant they hit me - the arching brow, the enigmatic expression that shows indifference but doesn't hide the threatening glare beneath. Her hair frames her face around her forehead in exactly the same way as her brother's and only accentuates the family connection. It's freaky. Even her ears are set in the same place as his.

We sit in silence for a few moments as we assess each other and I try to keep up this relentless staring contest, or maybe she's just wondering who the bloody hell I am. Probably the latter - best introduce myself.

I flick my eyes away from hers as the wine waiter arrives, trying to process whether I should be bitchy or more like I am with Alex. Who would she prefer? If she's anything like him, which she more than likely is, she certainly won't be bending over backwards for a friendly chat with me.

"What would you like to drink, ladies?" the young man says as he hands over a menu. Her eyebrow cocks at me again. Given she was expecting Conner, I have to say she seems to be handling the presence of an unknown woman rather effectively.

"A bottle of white please - something rich and spicy," I reply with a smile. Nothing changes on her face apart from the slightest lift of her lip at the same side as Alex as she looks down at her menu. It's frankly sodding weird.

"I didn't think he would send a dog to fetch his stick for him, Elizabeth," she says as she leans back a little and crosses her beautifully long legs, her tan pencil dress inching higher with a grace I could only dream of as she does. Both my brows shoot up because that shocked the shit out of me. It seems we are going to do this nastily. Christ, bitch alert.

297

"I am nobody's dog, Evelyn, certainly not Alex's, and actually, he doesn't even know I'm here," I reply as the waiter returns with a bottle of something. I haven't got a clue what it is but I trust his judgement and nod for him to pour.

"I thought better of Conner than this. I'll have to add manipulation and deceit to his rather impressive qualities," she says as she picks up her wine and cleans the stem with her napkin, sneering at it as she does so. I honestly can't breathe in that moment. Her look of disgust is so frighteningly familiar that I don't even know what to do, let alone say. So I, of course, have a giggling fit. *Helpful, full of authority, Beth. Well done.*

I gaze across at her and realise my attempt to outdo her *Alexness* is simply not going to work. I'm not even sure Alex will be able to beat her at it. Oh, sod it, I'm going for me instead.

"I'm sorry. I can't do this at all. Evelyn, please, I'm here to help. Let's just get on with why you don't want to come tonight and hopefully I can fill you in on what you're missing out on," I say with the warmest smile I can find. It's the one I use on Alex. Hopefully she'll find it as mesmerising. Something in her face softens a little and I notice a twinkle of amusement hidden in the depths of those blue eyes.

"You are very beautiful. Mum said you were," she replies with a sigh as she leans forward a little and taps her fingers on the table rhythmically - still freaky. "Elizabeth, I'm simply not ready to meet him. Yesterday my life was structured and happy. Today it is not. Would you not want a little time to think it all through? If you are the heart that beats for him as Mum says then I'm sure you'll understand my hesitance."

Wow, she said that? God, is that what I'm seen as? The heart that beats for him? Is that what she thinks he is? Oh my god, she's so wrong. I instantly realise that even if I don't see a cold man anymore, I suppose everyone else still does, including her, obviously. Come to think of it, I think even he does. I need to change that. The waiter approaches again with his pen so I glare at him as politely as I can and he leaves. Good boy.

"Evelyn, please call me Beth. I can assure you he has a very decent heart of his own. He just needs a little peace to settle in it. I don't know how much you know about him, but he hasn't been as fortunate as you. His childhood wasn't as *structured* as you say, and he just wants to meet a family he never knew he had. Can you understand that?" I return as I gaze at her and hope to tap into her emotional side. She clearly has one. It's more evident than her brother's, but then I suppose it would be given her childhood.

"Beth, I know exactly what the man is. I've done enough research in the last twelve hours to last me a lifetime. He's callous, cold and manipulative, probably a complete arsehole and definitely a player. If you choose to be associated with someone like him that's up to you, but I will take my own damn time making up my mind if he's someone I want in my life. He will not dictate my future simply because he's the infamous Alexander White. His title or connections are of no consequence to me. I don't even know if I want a brother in my life at all," she spits elegantly. I've never seen someone spit venom as beautifully as her, and while she's clearly wrong, I can't help but admire her spirit and need to be separated from his wealth. I stare over at her with narrowed eyes because, regardless of her cruel words, I realise I like her. She's so much like him it's ridiculous. It's like she's got all of his acumen and poise without his insecurities or tortured soul issues. He's going to love her.

"You would see that side of him because you haven't had a chance to see the other side of him, and believe me, you're spot on with your analysis. Actually, he's probably worse in some respects but when you break through that and find the man beneath, there's a very different version waiting for you. I love Alex very much and I want to do everything I can to make him happy. So tell me, what do you need to know to make you change your mind and come to this party? Would you like to talk to Conner about him instead of me? They're best friends and it seems you like him so maybe his opinion would help you. Equally, if you want to just see Alex privately, I can arrange that, too. I think he just thinks being at a function will be less intense. Although to be honest, I think the two of you are so alike that *intense* will more than likely follow you wherever you go. You're so much like him, Evelyn, everything, your mannerisms, your features. Christ, even the way you're sitting there looking at me as if you could rip my head off for even daring to challenge your thoughts, he hates that, too, by the way."

Oh yes, and there's that eyebrow inching at me. I snort out a giggle and shake my head at their similarities. "Look please, Evelyn, just give this a chance and let me help you both find each other. We both know you're intrigued, otherwise you'd have left by now, wouldn't you?"

Well, I've given that my best shot. Her face hasn't wavered in the slightest apart from the slight brow lift, also just like Alex. The smile that spreads across my face at the thought again is instant so I grab the bottle and refill our almost empty glasses to try and give her a moment to think about her response. Her brow furrows, yes, just like Alex. I almost choke on my wine as I try to contain another burst of giggles. She raises it and I watch in happiness as her face softens to the most relaxed I've seen her so far.

"Not an arsehole then?" she says through a tight smile. She's weakening. Go me.

"Sometimes, most of the time he's wonderful, though," I reply. Much as I love him, he can be a complete prick every now and then.

"Manipulative?" Oh, that's a good one.

"Definitely. Watch your back with that one, and ruthless with it," I say as I arch my brow at her. "Took me a while to figure that one out. I'm still trying if I'm honest but I'm slowly winning the game." She smirks.

"Player?" God, I hope not.

"Was he or is he?" She quirks her mouth up more and giggles a little. It's the first time I've heard her laugh, and there's nothing cute or girly about it, not that I expected it. My phone beeps so I pull it out to check it.

- Where are you?

I check my watch. It's two-fifteen. Shit, oh well, I'm trying to save his family. He'll get over it.

"Beth, I don't know how I feel. I can't be expected to come running into his arms or something equally as pathetic. I didn't even know I had a brother yesterday, let alone that I was a product of a sexual transgression. I just don't think I'm in the mood for a party or for acting like I care about someone I don't even know," she says with a sigh as she pinches her brow. I reach across and snag her hand away gently.

300

"He does that, too, you know? Please, Evelyn, just give this a chance. He doesn't know how he feels either and you'll both just have to work it out as you go along. I'll play middleman if you like but honestly, I think you're going to get along very well indeed," I reply as I sit back and realise that my work here is done. I have nothing left to give her and she's at least giving it some thought now.

"Thank you for coming," she says as she abruptly stands. "And please tell Conner his point has been made." I rise with her and drop some cash onto the table for the wine as we wander over to the door. My phone beeps again. I'll check it in a minute.

"Can I give you a lift somewhere?" I ask as I give the ticket to the valet.

"Would you want to meet him if you were me?" she asks quietly.

"Evelyn, I'm not you. I'm me, and I wouldn't be without him. He's my life. I can't imagine what's going through your mind right now and I sympathise, but I'm afraid I can't answer that for you. Just remember he isn't a monster, and he's just as nervous as you are about all this, not that he'd want me to tell you that," I reply as I watch the Aston screech around the corner and take a step toward it. "Do you want a lift? I'm going to him now if you want to join me?" She looks at the car with a smile and shakes her head.

"No, thank you. Is that his?" she questions. I giggle and nod at her. "Funny, I was looking into getting one last weekend, same colour, too." I smile warmly at her and wonder whether I should give her a hug or something. She sticks out her hand, clearly not a hugger, so I shake her hand and slide into the car.

"Do you want my number?" I call out as she begins to turn away.

"No, I know how to get hold of you, Elizabeth Scott of Scott's catering, sister Anabelle, Apartment 14, Risler Building." I look at her in shock. What is it with these people and knowing everything about me? "I told you, Beth, I like research and I'm a whizz at hacking all sorts of things. Your bank balance is pretty great, too," she says as she smiles brightly and turns again.

"That's just like him, too, knowing everything," I shout out as she waves and quite sexily swings her hips down the road. I pull out my phone again as I watch her sweep away. At least she doesn't walk like him, which would be all kinds of wrong.

- Elizabeth, where the fuck are you?

Okay, so now he's pissed off? Great. I check my watch - two-forty-five, fabulous. What's his sodding problem anyway? It's only forty-five minutes. Here I am trying to save his family connections and he's getting all pissy because I'm a little late. The word arsehole springs to mind. I quickly reply that I'm running late and that I love him then toss the phone on the passenger seat as I pull into the traffic.

Twenty-five minutes later and I eventually pull onto the gravel driveway, feeling slightly freaked out by the fact that for the first time I'm driving in here by myself. I even have a key to open the front door if I want, which is even more bizarre - lovely, but strange nonetheless. I feel the grin spread across my face at the thought of the word *home*. Could it be possible that I will move in here and set up home with him? I giggle at myself and actually start to believe that all of this is real, that Alexander White is a possibility for life. I know he loves me and that giving me free access to his home is a precious thing for him, and I assume driving his car is also an honour not often bestowed. So perhaps this is it. Perhaps I have met my mate for life. Then I realise I don't have any clue how to open the garage door. Balls! Not quite as *at home* as I thought then.

I park the car at the door and dig out my keys, hoping that he's not still pissed off about whatever he was pissed off about because I do not want this evening ruined for him, and us fighting is not going to start the evening off with a great deal of happiness, is it?

Opening the door, I hear the dark, heavy beats of some unknown music drifting along the corridors. At first I think it's coming from the kitchen and then the dull bass pulls my head in the other direction, past the music room somewhere. I put my bag on the table and wander toward the thumping notes as they get louder. I've never been down this corridor before and wonder where I'm going to find him. The walls are slightly less well designed here and the walkway seems to be narrowing a little. I realise I must be heading towards the old servant's quarters. All these old manors would have probably had hundreds of below stairs maids and butlers years ago. I pause as I struggle to know which way to go at a junction, left, right or the doorway in front of me. The music is louder here and I can't get a sense of which direction it's coming from, so I decide to wing it and open the door in front of me. It's clearly the right choice because the music is suddenly pounding my eardrums as I enter a small atrium. The ceiling is as high as the house and the skylight above casts a dreary glow across the space around me, making me feel ominously small for some reason. I can almost feel the beat of the bass in the fibre of the area as I edge forward. It's almost satanic in its relentless rhythm and I wrap my arms around myself, trying to implant some guts back into myself. Something feels weird, off, and I don't like it at all. Where is he?

I swing my head around, trying to find the source of the music. I can't find it so I clip my way to the first door and gently push it open. It's empty apart from a couple of pieces of old furniture so I turn again and head for the next one.

"Alex?" I call out, hoping that he can hear me above the noise. There's no response, just the same repetitive darkened notes. "Alex, where are you?" I shout a little louder as I reach the next door. The room's the same as the last. I rub my arms as a shiver runs across my skin and wonder whether it's him or the atmosphere around me. Perhaps it's haunted down here?

I reach the door at the end of the atrium and struggle to push it open quietly as it's so heavy. It's pitch black but there's a scent, a familiar smell that somehow draws me in and I feel my legs walk me in before I get a chance to think it through. The door slams behind me.

Shit.

I turn back to it in the hope that I'll find it because there's no way I can see it. Putting my hands out in front of me, I inch forward until I reach the wall and then start to walk along it until I feel the wood of the door. I fumble around until I find the handle and try to turn it but it doesn't move. Just bloody great, locked in a room. Could it get any more fantastic? I bang my hand on the door and shout out for help. No one's ever going to hear me over this music so I keep banging in the vague hope that Alex is about somewhere. Unfortunately, after ten minutes my hand begins to hurt and I give up. What the hell am I going to do now? *Nice, Beth, just so bloody clever.*

I slide down to the ground and sit against the door, gazing into the blackness. The music keeps pounding its disturbing melody, and after a while, I can feel myself rocking to its hypnotic chanting. It somehow seems to be pulling me to my peaceful place but instead of peace, there's a strange fear rattling through me. The sensation is not pleasant in the slightest and I shiver again as I duck my chin down to my knees and run my fingers along my arms, trying to process the feeling. Then it hits me like a lightning bolt as recognition sets in. The sensation is the same as before, when he was different, when he was detached and brutal, and I suddenly realise he's in here.

I rapidly search the darkness for him. Nothing. I may not be able to see him but I can sense him now that I'm searching for him so I pull myself to my feet and gingerly step forward into the blackness. I have no idea what we're doing but I assume this is something he's introducing me to so I find a spot, blow out a breath and wait with my hands hanging loosely at my sides.

"Alex, I know you're in here," I shout over the music. "I can feel you."

Several minutes later, I wonder if it was a figment of my imagination because nothing has changed. I'm still stood here in the same spot. The music has increased in tempo, which has increased my breathing a little but nothing else is any different, still pitch black, still no movement. Then I hear something to the right of me and I flinch away from it. Nothing else happens. *Stupid Beth.*

I shake my head at myself and think about heading for the door, then I sense something to the left. I quickly turn toward whatever it is and begin to tremble a bit as my senses turn up to hyper alert mode. My hands instinctively come up in front of my body as I prepare to fight. Given that it's Alex in here, I don't know what it is that I think I'm going to do but as something touches my hair behind me, I swing around to face it, hoping to god that it is actually Alex. The faint scent of him drifts across my face and calms me a little but my nerves are now so on edge that I can't stop the adrenalin running through me, or is it endorphins? What was that he said about the rush of chemicals? I circle around my own body, trying to figure out where he's coming from next.

"Are you ready to fight me, Elizabeth?" comes growling at me from the depths of the room.

What?

A hand grabs my ankle and yanks me forward, causing me to lose my balance. I splay my hands as I tumble to the ground to break my fall and manage to right myself before I smash into the floor. *What the hell is he doing?* Realising what's going on, I kick my shoes off and stand back up. I'm either learning how to fight or this is a very twisted version of his preferences. Either way, I'm not going on my arse again. I rip off Belle's jacket and take a firm stance as I try to find him in the darkness again. I still can't see a thing.

"Better," he says from somewhere. "You still don't look like the whore you are but we both know different, don't we?"

What the hell? I turn around, waiting for another attack from somewhere and try to contain my anger as I throw my hands up in front of me.

"Alex, I don't know what you're trying to-"

"Shut the fuck up. You're a cock teasing whore."

I gasp as a hand clutches my throat and throws me sideways without releasing me. My feet tangle with each other and I grab onto his wrist for support. "Fight me," he whispers quietly as he lets go and disappears again. I regain my balance and rub at my throat. Okay, so he wants a fight, or rather he wants me to fight him. This is definitely my viciousness lesson. I take a stand again and suck in a breath. I can't see him so I close my eyes and try to hone my senses to the sound beneath the deafening music. Hands clamp my wrists from behind and I twist from him and spin away as I wrench myself from his hold. He's on me again, in seconds this time, kicking my leg from beneath me and forcing me to the floor. I shove and kick out with everything I've got but he's too heavy and I can't budge him. "Money grabbing whore, useless and fucking worthless," he growls into my ear as he reaches a hand between my legs. Fury rolls over me at his words and I twist and turn in his grip until I shove him sideways and roll away. His hand grabs at my thigh so I kick him hard with my free leg and stumble away to retreat into a corner. He grunts out a curse and suddenly he's quiet again. My rage is building to the point of explosion at those words and my body begins to tremble. How fucking dare he? Is this his idea of a bloody lesson?

My eyes narrow at the space around me as I try to find a way to see him. It's still pitch black, unsurprisingly. The only thing for it is to trust my senses and hope that I can feel him near me as well as I usually can. Being pinned in a corner is probably not the best thing to do so I walk out into the middle of the room again and slow my breathing so that I can at least hear him while I close my eyes. The music abruptly cuts off somehow and I hold my hands up in front of me in the deafening silence. *Bring it on, White.*

Not less than thirty bloody seconds later and he's on me again, dragging me by my hair to the wall with my arm twisted behind me, where he pins me face first up against it and holds me with his body weight. For all my forethought, I don't have a bloody chance. I don't feel anything until the moment he attacks. Shit. I'm obviously not beating him with strength or agility, so I continue with my useless struggling a little in an effort to think of another way of manipulating this situation. His fingers dig in tighter and I wince a little.

"Did he feel good bent over you, about to fuck you? You wanted it, didn't you? Were you begging for it?" he sneers as he grabs hold of the back of my trousers and begins to tug at them. Something in me literally explodes at his words, or actions. I haven't got a clue but all thoughts of manipulation evaporate as I swing my head backward to connect with his and kick out with my legs again. Rage I never knew I had flows through me at the thought of that man and what he nearly did to me. I don't feel the dull ache that has spread across the back of my head. I don't feel the pain that's consuming my wrist as I struggle against his hold. All I can feel is body weight that I don't want on me and the memory of a man trying to rape me.

"Get the fuck off me!" I scream out loudly as I throw my head back again, instantly feeling the crunch of bone and yank at my arm until I feel it loosening. His other hand comes to my throat and before he can reach it, I swing my head and clamp my teeth down against his fingers. He grunts in response and tries to still my feet by pushing his body weight harder against me. In a split second, his hold loosens enough for me to pull my arm away and slam my elbow back into his ribs. He wheezes out a breath as I release my teeth and he grabs at me but I've already spun around and thrown my nails towards his face. He ducks but it's enough to allow me to push him away hard with my other hand, and as he stumbles back a little, it's all I need to launch myself at him with full force. I have no idea what I'm doing anymore but I can't seem to stop myself from attacking him. I know it's Alex but all I can see is the unknown face of a man. "FUCK YOU!" I scream again as I keep shoving and hitting out at his skin. Memories of the toilet door and the sink and his words in my ear only intensify my rage as I feel my nails shred his skin again. "Don't fucking touch me."

I see glimpses of Alex's eyes and mouth as he retreats backwards and lets me keep hitting him, so I continue, letting all of my frustration and anger pound into him. Screaming at him as he ducks here and there, I focus every violent blow at him to the point of seeing nothing else but blind fury until he stops and I realise he's hit the wall behind him. My arm comes back for another lunge without any thought to him and I release it with the intent of causing damage, but he grabs it before it connects so I raise the other one. He grabs that one, too, and tries to hold me still but I keep struggling, apparently still not content with my fight as his grip tightens around my wrists.

"Stop now, Elizabeth," he says quietly as he brings my fists to his chest. The snarl that leaves my mouth at his command has never before left my lips and even surprises me as I continue with my twisting movements with little effect.

"Fuck you. Let go of me," I yell into his face.

One of his hands suddenly grasps both of my wrists while his other arm wraps around me to pull me closer and he rests his chin on my head. "Shh, baby, slow down. I've got you," comes whispering at me. I can feel his heart in his chest as he continues with more soothing words to calm me, and eventually I haven't got anything left so I let the cloud clear and relax into him as his grip softens around me.

Finally, he quietly lets me go and sits down on the floor in front of me without uttering another word. I have no idea what I'm supposed to say to any of that. What the hell was that? Even I don't know where any of that anger came from and I absolutely didn't know I was capable of it. In fact, I'm pretty sure I could have killed him if he hadn't stopped me. What on earth was he trying to achieve? No idea. I'm confused yet again. Trust him to make me feel all over the sodding place. I collapse on the floor in front of him and try to process the last... however long it's been.

"Lights," he eventually says and I blink as the room lights up around us, then gasp as I look at his face. Blood trickles from his nose, and as I lower my gaze, I realise how much damage I've done to his torso. His beautiful body is marred with deep scratch marks and reddened patches. My eyes shoot back up to his in shock. "Mmm, feisty little thing, aren't you? You'll do very well when you're trained properly," he says as he wipes his nose and gazes back at me. "I'm impressed."

"Alex, I.... shit. I don't know what happened. I don't even know where that came from," I reply awkwardly. I haven't got anything else to say and I'm certainly not saying sorry. He made me do it. Well, I think he did. I don't even know if that's true or not. Did he have to say some of those things? I suppose if he was after anger, he did find it in me. Smartarse.

"It's called rage, baby, and believe me, I know the feeling very well. I'm going to teach you how to harness it and manipulate it. By the time I'm finished, no one will ever touch you again without your permission." His brow furrows as he pulls himself up. "Not even me."

He extends his hand to me so I take it and tentatively wipe some blood from his nose. His smile lifts the mood as he gazes down at me with soft blues. "I'm sorry," he says quietly while he leads me to the door.

"What for? The words or the pain?" I reply with a small grin. His mouth curls up into a smirk as his eyes twinkle with amusement.

"Both, but mainly the words. I just needed a way to rile you," he replies as he scoops up my shoes and jacket, well, Belle's. "You needed to hate me for this to happen. You need to learn how to hate."

"It appears you know me well, Mr. White. Let's hope I know how to push the same buttons on you should I ever need them." I can't think I'll ever need to provoke his anger. I'm pretty sure it bubbles millimetres underneath his skin most of the time, but the thought that I could is enjoyable nonetheless.

"I think you press buttons very effectively already. In fact, you can press those ones there," he replies as he inclines his head to the side of the door. There's a keypad on the right of it so I raise my hand. "Ten sixty six." I roll my eyes and smirk at the Battle of Hastings date, yet another war. Punching in the code, the door releases instantly. No wonder I couldn't get out.

"What is this room?" I ask as I glance back into it and notice a few other doors leading off it.

"It's a safe room, somewhere to hide out in case of emergencies or intruders. There's a bathroom and fully stocked kitchen over there, automatic lock outs and an intelligent computer system so you can monitor the house and call for help if need be. Suffice to say, it's supposed to be a good place to flee the danger," he replies with an ironic chuckle as he walks out, grabs my hand again and leads us through the atrium. My eyes wander over his bare back with sheer lust pouring from me. I have no idea why I'm suddenly feeling this way when five minutes ago I wanted to kill him. Well, not him, but someone who happened to be him at the time.

"Well, that's good to know, but what on earth were you doing in there?"

I can't help watching the way his tattoo moves under the pressure of his movements as he turns and bends around the corners. The beautiful script of belligerence stretching across his broad muscular shoulders evokes a feeling of aggression and then the dates reminding me of a man who's thoughtful and almost repentant of his life. I wish I knew what all those dates meant to him. I'll ask him at some point.

"It's dark in there. I like the dark. It gives me the space I need to calm down," he replies as he ducks through the next door and heads for the kitchen. Oh right, I have no idea what that means. Why would anyone want to sit in the dark? And calm down from what exactly? The man is still a complete enigma sometimes and quite possibly insane, given the last hour or so. I'm sure most men would have just given their girlfriends a few rounds in the gym and shown them some self-defence moves. Clearly Alex isn't most men. I'm not that surprised now I think about it.

"And you were in need of calming down because?" I ask, walking straight over to the medical cupboard as we reach the kitchen to retrieve wipes and various creams. He shrugs but doesn't elaborate any further, so I point at a chair and raise an eyebrow assertively. He looks down at his chest with a frown and reluctantly sits as I put the stuff on the table and begin cleaning up my attacking frenzy.

Unfortunately, the effect of his battered body seems to be causing the same undesirable response from my groin, which is quickly making my hands tremble with more lust. It must be that hunter-gatherer thing because I'm sure I should be feeling sad that I did this or even caring about his pain or something, but I'm not. I just appear to want more rough and tumble, preferably of the sexual kind. Does that mean I've suddenly become the hunter? I still haven't got a clue. Why would I be enjoying watching him flinch every time I swipe the antiseptic over his cuts? This has to be some sort of power thing that I'm not aware of.

"Feeling dominant, Elizabeth?" he says as I wipe at a particularly nasty scrape on his ribs. Of course he would know exactly what I'm feeling better than I would, wouldn't he? Arse.

Is that what I'm feeling? Is this what it does to him? Does being aggressive simply breed more aggression? It certainly feels like it to me at the moment because before I realise what I'm doing, I'm grazing my finger over another cut at his collarbone and climbing across him, licking my lips. His smirk does nothing to deter me from my mission, which is apparently to take control of some sort. He clearly doesn't agree as he pushes me off him, cradles my head and has me on my back on the tile floor in seconds. "Appealing as it may have been at the time, it's my turn now so I suggest you behave yourself," he says as he grabs my wrist, pins it at my side and mumbles something about being perfect beneath his breath.

I can't even say I'm struggling because I'm really not doing anything to stay in control at all as I happily let him have his way and moan out his name while he buries his head between my legs.

I seriously doubt that dominance is my forte. Yes, I might be feeling that way inclined but there's no denying who's in control here and it's blatantly not me. I know this because I'm beginning to beg and I can feel the words leaving my mouth before I can even try to stop them. I also know this because as he tugs at my trousers and manoeuvres my legs around, I'm yearning for him to be rougher, harder, nastier even, and somehow he understands this. In some way he knows everything I need seconds before it even enters my brain, and while he grabs my hips to roll me onto my front, I can't help smiling back at him.

"I think I've been bad," I say teasingly as I pinch at my nail marks on his chest and then moan out as he takes hold of my throat and pulls my back to his front.

"Baby, you don't know the meaning of bad. Let me show you," he says in that low tone of his as he nudges me forward to the table. My hands begin to tremble as he pulls the cord off the curtains and ties my wrists to the circular support underneath then casually wanders off into the kitchen. He reappears a few minutes later, holding a teaspoon, a candle and a stack of paperwork, which he puts on the floor in front of my face. My eyebrows shoot up. I have no idea what's coming next but those were the last items I imagined on a list of very bad things.

"Time for negotiations, Elizabeth," he says as he lights the candle with a very wicked smile and darkening blues, his finger running up the inside of my leg.

"With a teaspoon?" I still have no idea.

"Mmm, with a teaspoon."

The word teaspoon has never sounded so erotically tempting in my life.

Chapter 17

Elizabeth

I've gone with a floaty, flirty creation. Given my afternoon of meeting with the new found sister, beating up my boyfriend and then being tied to the kitchen table, I'm thinking that maybe a bit of femininity is in order for the evening. It's a deep blue lace affair of frills with off-the-shoulder details and a very nipped-in waist. It's stunning, clearly one of the very expensive ones and absolutely beautiful. It's also a bit short but sod it. For once I feel overly girly but in an incredibly flirtatious sort of way, and as I swipe the last of my mascara on, I smile at the thought of the afternoon's entertainment. A bloody teaspoon - who would have thought it? I still haven't got any words for it. Ingenious is the only one that's anywhere near close. And negotiations my arse. Signing ownership papers for my new-found premises while being put under that sort of pressure wasn't negotiating; it was... well, it wasn't sodding negotiating.

Heading out the bedroom and downstairs to find him, I ponder how this evening is going to end. It's ridiculous, I know, given that it hasn't even started, but I can't help but worry if he's going to be okay or not. Obviously she seemed to be somewhat more relaxed by the time I left her, but she might not even turn up tonight. I did my best but what's he going to be like if she decides not to turn up? Is it going to send him into one of his overly dark places or will he have enough clarity to realise that this is just as big for her as it is for him? I so wish I had her phone number because I would be phoning her at this precise moment to find out what she's doing so I can prepare myself for the outcome. Actually, should I tell him I went to see her? Is it going to piss him off if he finds out from her later? He clearly doesn't like being lied to or manipulated. Will he see it that way? Conner will probably know these things because I seriously have no idea. He's in a good mood, which is a start and not something I want to screw up in the slightest so I send a text to Conner in the hope of calming my sudden panicked state.

> **- Should I tell him I saw Evelyn this afternoon? He might flip out or something.**

"You are not going out looking like that," comes growling at me from behind as I turn towards the lounge. I spin round to see him looking absurdly glorious in a midnight blue suit. I could say the same if I'm honest. He's looking dangerously good.

"You bought it. I actually protested if I remember rightly," I reply as I wander over to him and kiss him on the nose. His hands immediately find their way under the loose skirt to my arse as he pulls me closer. Its easy access for him and his sudden smile of naughtiness and wandering fingers suggest he's just realised that himself.

"You're stunning, but do not bend over at any point. Unless it's in front of me, that is." I giggle at him and turn my head as I hear the front door opening. Andrews walks in, coughs uncomfortably and then turns his back to us. I can't help grinning back at Alex as he raises his brow and then chuckles.

"Sir, the car's ready," Andrews says in his MI5 voice. I let go of Alex and walk to the cupboard to get my coat.

"You can turn around now, Michael. I'm completely decent now," I say as I watch him with his nose to the door. He doesn't. He just walks out the door, refusing to look at us again. Alex helps me into my coat and walks me to the door.

"Do you have everything you need?" he asks as he scans my body.

"You're everything I need," I reply instantly as I grab hold of his hand. "Are you ready?"

It's a loaded question. I know it and so does he. His eyes flicker across mine with emotions he's not going to give me so I squeeze his hand, hoping that he gets the meaning of it. He nods at me and then kisses me as he leads us to the car.

The journey gives me no time to delve any deeper into his emotional state, and given that he seems exceptionally happy, I decide it's simply not worth pushing the matter. I'll simply stay close and deal with the effects later. Conner hasn't bothered to respond so hopefully

313

everything will be hunky dory and Evelyn Peters will arrive, be fabulous and we'll all giggle the night away. It's doubtful but I can always hope and at least Belle will be there for support.

"I've been thinking about Christmas," he says as he sips his *Cognac* and gazes across at me while we're winging our way to the party.

"Oh god, I know. I haven't bought a thing and I seriously need to get out there and hit those shops. It's only a few weeks away and I'm useless when it comes to getting this stuff done," I ramble back at him.

"Do you normally go to your parents?" he asks as his fingers graze their way up my thigh.

"Yes, but I didn't know what you normally did and I haven't had that much time to think about it." I haven't had time to think about anything.

"I was wondering if you'd like to invite your family to ours. With your mum being ill, I just thought maybe she'd like to be treated for the weekend." Did he just say ours? Meaning his, I assume.

"Did you just say ours?" His eyebrow rises as if he's rethinking what he just said. He'll definitely change tack with that one.

"Yes."

I stare in shock. My mouth opens and then closes again, his amused smirk continuing as if this is funny. He's right because it is. It's ridiculous.

"Are you suggesting I move in... again?" I can't believe I said that out loud but given his previous comment when we did the coffee machine thing, and the whole *what's mine is yours* note thing, I'm seriously beginning to wonder. He leans his head back onto the seat and turns his head toward me.

"Do you want to?" *Oh!* I stare again. Do I? No... Yes... Wow, I have no idea. This is so not expected.

"Alex, I..." I can't speak. Why can I never speak? And why does he keep throwing new questions at me that I have no clue how to answer? It's too early for that. Yes, I love him and I'm pretty sure he loves me, but seriously? Living together? Well, he has just given me a building because of the things I apparently give him in return. I still don't really understand that if I'm honest. But shit...

"Elizabeth, you don't have to answer that. Just know that I love you and I'd be very happy if you wanted to. I like you in my home and

I'd very much like to see you in it every day," he says as he brushes some hair off my face then runs his fingers over my lips. I could melt. In fact, I think I am doing. That was far too beautiful a thing to say.

"Okay," is my reply. That's it. I'm still focused on his fingers and lovely thoughts of happily ever afters as he chuckles and hands me my champagne again, because at some point, I must have put it down in the midst of my amazement.

"So, Christmas?" Oh god, yes, I'd forgotten about that.

"Are you sure?" Because a family Christmas and all the emotions that go with it is the last thing I'd expect him to want. It's another shocking thing to say the least.

"Yes, Belle and Conner, too. I normally spend it snow-boarding with Conner anyway and I just thought, well you don't have to if you don't want to. I just wanted to spend it with you and I thought it would be nice."

I'm across his knee in seconds and completely messing my face up on his lips. His quite lovely emotional being this evening is entirely overwhelming to me.

"You're amazing. I can't believe you've thought about doing this. It's a brilliant idea and I love you so much for giving this to Mum." He chuckles at my over exuberance and slides his hands up my thighs.

"We'll have to do it ourselves. I always give Mary two weeks off at Christmas and Andrews goes as well," he says as he gets dangerously close to my panties.

"Okay, I'm sure with our combined culinary genius we'll manage a turkey dinner."

"Okay then." He frowns. I have no idea what about.

"What's the matter?"

"I don't have any decorations or a tree."

"What, none?" Who doesn't have decorations?

"Well no, I haven't ever done that sort of thing before." Of course he hasn't because he's on his own. That is changing from this moment on.

"So we'll get it all tomorrow and start decorating, just the sort of thing to do on a Sunday afternoon,"

"Okay," he says as the car pulls up at INK.

"Are you ready?" I ask again as he stares at the window.

"Yes, come on."

INK has apparently turned blue. I'm not all that surprised really but I'm not sure how he's managed it. There's suddenly blue carpet in the foyer, blue tiles through the tunnel and even blue lighting making all the white surfaces look blue. Hilariously, he's even gone to the trouble of putting pink highlights on the ceiling. God, he loves her. I can't help but wonder if he's going to pop the question tonight. I also can't help but wonder if I should give her some warning about it. I haven't mentioned a word about my conversation with him. I didn't tell him everything. It's not my place to, but I told him enough to let him know why she's the way she is. He adores her and I know that now, but I am a little worried that she might say no simply because she's scared so I quickly scan around for her. And there she is, in a very tight and gorgeous cream silk dress that only Belle would have the guts or ability to pull off. I'd get it completely filthy within ten minutes of wearing it. She sees me and waves as she lounges on the bar, talking to a woman in an orange creation of some sort. It's revolting and I can see Belle trying desperately to not burst into fits of laughter at it. The rest of the bar seems absolutely packed with people who I assume either work for or with Bluetec, all beginning to shout drunkenly or doing that pretend dancing thing that happens when men think they're actually reasonably good at it. I'm so glad we've arrived late on because it's so much easier to deal with half drunken people than to have to do all that getting to know people thing. I do another quick scan for Miss Peters. Unfortunately, she's nowhere to be seen and that sends my pulse racing for all the wrong reasons. I can't have Alex turning into a maniac when all he's been is utterly wonderful so far. She needs to meet him just like this, when he's on top form and in full-on Alex White mode.

Conner ambles his way over to us and winks at me as he gives Alex one of his man hug things and I giggle at his choice of a bright blue suit and pink shirt. I have no idea how he's managed it but amazingly, it looks quite good on him. I'm pretty sure Belle won't agree with me at all.

"Beth, you look delicious," he says as he gives me a hug.

"Thank you, Mr. Avery. You look... interesting," I reply. It's all I've got. His face is a picture of shock.

"You don't like? These Scott girls have no taste at all, dude. Perhaps we should ditch them." It's not funny in the slightest so my eyes instantly narrow at him and then at Alex. He just chuckles and squeezes my hand.

"No, Conner, I'm pretty sure you just fucked up your own sense of appropriate this evening. It looks ridiculous, even for you," he says with a smirk of the greatest proportions.

"Fuck off," Conner replies as he straightens his jacket and tries for wounded.

"Happy to," Alex chides as he moves towards the bar with me in tow.

"No, don't go. I need you. Please don't leave me. I love you, Mr. White," Conner squeals like a girl from behind us as we all burst out laughing. Belle wanders across to us and beams across at him as he practically gropes her in front of us. I so love watching them together because seeing her giggling in a girly fashion is heart-warming to say the least.

"Right, what are we all drinking?" Alex shouts across the music as a sudden heavy bass line kicks in. "He's paying so I've had the good stuff brought up," he says as he pulls up the divider to the bar area and points at Conner. A very attractive barmaid in a very expensive looking outfit wanders over to him, smiles and then randomly kisses him on the cheek. My hackles are instantly on high alert. It's disturbingly not okay at all but Alex simply smiles back and then wanders off into the back room.

"Who's the bitch?" Belle questions beside me as she nods her head at the woman.

"I have no idea. I've never seen her before, but I'm not happy about the kissing thing," I reply as I narrow my eyes at her. She scowls back at me and that clearly makes the whole situation much worse.

"Ooh, I think there's going to be a bitch fight." Conner chuckles as he wraps his arms around Belle and looks across her shoulder at the woman.

"Who is she?" I ask as I find some sort of new anger and launch it at her through my eyes. Unfortunately, she just smirks and rolls her eyes as if I'm not even worth bothering with.

"That's Serena Bradley, Tom's sister. She works here on occasion when the big guns come in and spend their millions. She's extremely good at what she does." Belle elbows him hard and he recoils and stares at her.

"What the hell was that for?"

"Your really are an arsehole. Do you think I can't smell your pheromones pouring across at her? You're like a fucking dog in heat," she bites back at him. I've never seen her so spitting mad. This is clearly the jealously she was talking about.

"Belle, don't be stupid. I-"

She cuts him off just as Alex reappears and starts talking to the bitch again. I don't know which way to look.

"You know what, have her. I couldn't give a shit." She grabs my arm to turn away so I stare at Conner, begging him to make this right. This is not how I planned this evening and I absolutely can't leave the bitch with Alex. Thankfully, Conner has other ideas as to how this is going to pan out because the look of aggression that suddenly sweeps across his face is ferocious to say the least.

"Turn your backside back around and look at me," he says, very authoritatively for him. It even makes me jump a little. Belle stills for half a second then starts moving again. "Belle, don't make me fucking angry." Oh, actually, that's exactly the same voice Alex uses. He's clearly on a dominant roll. Belle swings round and snarls at him so I let go and flick my eyes to Alex who has now noticed the commotion and is on his way over, thankfully.

"Angry? You bastard. You do not tell me what to do. Fuck every slut in the place for all I care," she seethes quietly. It's quite impressive to be fair.

"Shut up." Oh no.

"What? Don't tell me to-"

"Shut the fuck up. Now." He's suddenly in front of her and growing. What is it with these men and that growing thing? She stares up at him with a scowl on her face and I swear she might even slap him. Alex wraps his arm around me from behind.

"What's going on?" he whispers.

"Jealousy, from her," I reply, equally quietly. "And from me. How's Serena?" His eyes swing to mine with a look of surprise but I can't hold it or argue about it because I'm too in tune with the other conversation that's going on.

"Are you bloody growling at me for a reason? And don't ever speak to me like that again, you-"

He cuts her off with, frankly, the most erotic kiss I've ever witnessed as he pushes her towards a wall while she protests, weakly. Other people get thrown out of the way and stand in shock at the couple as Alex chuckles beside me as if this is perfectly normal. Well, it probably is for him but obviously not for Conner. Actually, maybe it is but Belle just didn't know it. I certainly didn't.

"Is this behaviour normal for him?" I ask Alex quietly as I watch my sister get completely ravaged with a smile plastered on my face, and a rather unfortunate twinge in my groin as his fingers tighten on my waist.

"No, not particularly. I've only seen it once before," he replies with another one of his stupidly sexy chuckles. I'm still mad about the bitch thing but I can't help fidgeting at the thought of what's happening in front of me. "It's quite stimulating, isn't it? Watching?" he says as he drags a finger up my leg. I can't even begin to process being horny about my sister and her boyfriend, but I am. There's no doubt about it and his wandering fingers are only emphasising that point. Conner eventually releases her and steps back to get control of himself. She stares at him as if she's going to launch into another tirade so I cringe a little and wait for it.

"Don't you ever-"

"I love you. Marry me."

My hands fly to my mouth so quickly I actually smack my teeth. She gawps at him, Alex sucks in a breath, presumably in astonishment, and then Conner drops down onto one knee.

Belle's eyes almost pop out of her head as her hands go up to her mouth and she looks down at him in amazement. Tears are brimming my eyes as I watch on and hope to god that she says yes. I think I can even see tears in hers as she glances over at me. I can't help smiling back at her and nodding my head in encouragement. Alex's arms wrap tighter around me and feel him rest his head on my shoulder as he watches, hopefully with the same amount of interest.

"Annabelle Scott, will you please be my wife?"

Oh my god. My tears erupt as he opens that little red box and shows it to her. She gawps again. A handkerchief comes over my shoulder so I take it and hold that to my mouth instead, trying to stop

319

the never-ending flow. Is she going to say something? I don't think I've ever seen her lost for words before. Please say yes, please say yes.

"What do you think?" Alex asks into my neck as he kisses it, somehow sensing my internal question. I narrow my eyes. He's far too good at that.

"I... I don't know. I hope so," is the only answer I've got as I continue to watch her look between the box and Conner's eyes. He takes the ring out and grabs her hand. It's a forceful move; I'll give him that, and I just hope it's what she needs at the moment to help her decide.

"Will you?" he asks again. "Let me put this on your finger. I only want you."

My tears erupt again. I don't think I can even watch anymore but clearly I do, and then she nods. It's so small I doubt anyone else saw it, but I did. She glances at me again so I smile and mouth *yes* at her in the hope that she gets the hint. She looks down at him again with the most radiant grin I've ever seen from her.

"Yes."

God, it's a simple word but it means so much in this moment. Conner beams up at her and slides the ring onto her finger, and of course I erupt again into fits of tears. My sister's getting married to a blue-haired genius, and a lovely genius he is, too.

The entire room bursts into raucous applause and cheering. I hadn't even realised they were all looking or that the music had been turned off. When did that happen? I spin into Alex and cry my tears of joy straight into his shirt as he chuckles above me and strokes my hair, kissing my head softly. I try to stop but it's clearly not happening very quickly so he just keeps stroking and softly whispering lovely words to me while I try desperately not to think of myself in the same situation as my sister. It's not going to happen anytime soon but given our earlier conversation, I can't help my brain rambling away in my head. Eventually, I pull in a long breath and decide it's probably time to actually congratulate the happy couple again.

"Are you okay now?" he says with another chuckle as I lift my head to look up at him.

"Yes, sorry about the shirt. I'm just a bit... overwhelmed." He smiles gloriously and leads me over to them so I let go and literally fly into Belle's waiting arms as we hug each other nearly to death.

"Oh my god, I can't believe he did that," she says with an amazing smile firmly plastered on, and gazes at the beautiful diamonds on her hand.

"I know. Shit, I thought you were going to say no for a minute," I reply as we watch the man hug thing that's happening between Alex and Conner. They're both beaming at each other and it strikes me what this probably means to both of them. Presumably they've both been players for an awfully long time, and that time has come to an end. Well hopefully, anyway. Alex looks over and smiles with that loving smile of his that makes me melt as he extends a hand at the same time as Conner. We both giggle and walk over like stupid schoolgirls. It's all completely lovely.

It's then that I notice her about two rows back. Frankly, there's no way I could miss those eyes because I'm so attuned to her brother's that I'm struggling to maintain eye contact with her. She simply quirks her brow up and sips her champagne in that absolutely superior way that Alex does, so I let my smile broaden in the hope that she'll return to the nicer version I met earlier on today. Unfortunately, I realise all too late that means I've probably just announced I've already met her. Maybe he won't notice, if I'm lucky.

"That smile's only meant for me, Elizabeth. Who are you giving it to?" he says as he turns his head to search for what I'm looking at. There's no point lying because he sees her instantly and then stiffens immeasurably. If it wasn't such an awkward situation, I'd be very horny, very quickly.

She watches him as he stares back at her. It's really very disconcerting because, honestly, there couldn't be two more intense faces in the world at the moment and they really could be twins. Her face tilts slightly as if she's weighing him up as she raises her glass again and takes another sip. Apparently even she can't hold his full frontal assault with a completely impassive face and god, that makes me feel a little bit better about myself. However, she does surprise me with her next move, which is to suddenly walk directly towards us with a smile that would charm the gods, and yes, it's just like Alex's. His body doesn't change in the least but I can't stop the flutter of my heart as his hold on my hand increases.

"My brother," she says a little sarcastically as she stops in front of us and continues staring at him, still with that smile. I have no idea what's going on his mind because he has become absolutely unreadable all of a sudden. That mask is very firmly in place, which makes me question all sorts of reactions.

"Mmm, it would seem so," he replies as he holds her eyes. I flick mine over to Belle and Conner, who are gaping like fools at the scene beginning to unfold. I have to break this staring thing and get them somewhere quieter than this because it really could go very wrong if I don't do something.

"Evelyn, it's lovely to see you again. Shall we go somewhere a little quieter?" Alex flinches at my words and then I hear what I've just said, *again*, shit. Well now I've definitely given it away. Clearly we'll be discussing that at some point, but for now I'm more bothered about making this nice between them. She's his family after all.

"Beth, you look very beautiful, and yes I'd love to," she says as she leans her head in to air kiss me. This is new. We only did hand shaking earlier. And then I comprehend that she's trying to make Alex uncomfortable, trying to get the upper hand because she knows he's out in the cold on this one. Oh, what a prize bitch, unbelievable, and what's worse is that I started it. *Idiot, Beth.*

"I think this is between us, Evelyn. Elizabeth has nothing to do with it," he says sharply as he lets go of my hand and gestures for her to move away with him without even glancing my way.

He's mad at me. Sodding great. Well I'm glad I went to the trouble of making sure she came tonight for him. She nods at me and then casually wanders off with him towards the booth area while I gaze at his back, hoping he'll give me some sign of love. He doesn't at all. He doesn't even look back, and suddenly life seems utterly bloody awful. All afternoon and evening has been joy, laughter and fun, then my sister gets engaged, which is obviously wonderful, and now this happens. Fuck.

"Don't worry about it, Beth. He's just anxious," Conner says as he pulls me in for a hug. Belle squeezes my hand at the same time. "He still loves you. He just hates not knowing shit."

"That's why I bloody asked you whether I should tell him or not, which you didn't bloody answer," I blurt out loudly as I narrow my eyes at him. He frowns back at me as if he has no clue what I'm saying. "The text, Conner, why didn't you respond?"

"He couldn't. I threw his phone in the toilet," Belle says quietly beside me. I glare at her instantly.

"What the...? Christ, Belle, why would you... Actually, who cares? It doesn't matter now anyway, does it?" I reply with a resigned huff. I don't even know why I'm bothering to have a go at Conner about it because I should have known how he'd react to not being aware of everything. I know what's coming and it probably won't be pretty, so I can only hope they get on well and Alex doesn't return in a dark mood. Actually, I'm not even sure I want to take that risk. I could just go back to the apartment now and forget this whole being happy thing because really, I'm just not in the mood at all. Belle strokes my arm and smiles at me. It's sweet but not helpful in the slightest, so I gaze back at her with a small smile, desperately trying to say sorry for my outburst while inwardly wondering if it would be rude to leave them to it. I'll just slip off later. No one will notice if I'm not here and Alex will be in there with his new found sister for most of the night anyway. Even if he's not, I'm not staying around to be shouted at or something for simply trying to help. I plaster on my best fake smile and turn back to them both.

"Go mingle, honey. I'll be fine and you need to show off that ring," I say as I pick up her hand and almost burst into tears again at the sight of it. "And you, Mr. Avery are wonderful and I'm very happy for you." He chuckles at me and then pulls me in for another hug.

A large woman eventually butts in and grabs Belle's hand from mine to ogle the diamonds and before I know it, people are milling in between us and chatting to them about the whole engagement thing, so I let myself disappear into the background so I can make a run for it. Walking as fast as I can toward the doorway, I scan the area for Andrews, hoping not to find him hovering about so I can make a quick escape in a taxi. Clearly that isn't going to happen because he spots me immediately and stands up.

"Elizabeth?" he says. My throat constricts at his worried face and I struggle to keep the tears from falling again at his emotional response to me.

"Michael, I... I want to go home. Will you take me home please?" I stutter pathetically.

"Of course. Let me get your coat," he says as he rushes off to the cloakroom. I walk straight outside to wait for him and as usual, he arrives very quickly and hurries me to the car.

"Are you okay?" he says as he pulls the car away from the curb and heads in the direction of Alex's.

"No, Michael, not Alex's. My apartment, please," I reply, seriously not wanting to get into a conversation with him about it. He nods his head and turns the car around then thankfully continues all the way home in silence. Unfortunately, the moment he opens the car door once we've arrived, my tears erupt again. I don't even know why I'm crying anymore but I can't control the sobs that keep coming. His arms wrap around me tentatively and that's all it takes for every ounce of my exhaustion, nerves, pain and insecurity to flow straight out of me into his chest. I can't help it. I realise I'm crying on the chauffeur, but he's more than that to me now. He's a friend, someone who, for some unknown reason, I trust implicitly.

"Shh, you're okay, Elizabeth. It's okay," he soothes as he stands and holds me, gently swaying me backwards and forwards like you would a child. It's so relaxing that I eventually manage to contain my tears and gaze up at him with a sniff and a small smile.

"Thank you. I think I needed that," I say as I lean into him and then back away as my brain catches up with what's going on. He chuckles and releases me. It's a lovely sound and one I've never heard from him before.

"You'd make a good father, Michael," I say as I nervously shift from foot to foot, suddenly feeling very uncomfortable about my little outburst. He frowns.

"I hope I already do," he replies. He has children?

"Oh, I'm sorry. I didn't mean..." That's embarrassing.

"It's alright. I've got two, a son and daughter, both in their twenties and both at university. I'm very proud of them," he says with the biggest smile I've ever seen as he puts his hands in his pockets and looks at the floor. I'm shocked. He only looks about thirty-five, but clearly he isn't.

"Oh right, they must be a credit to you," I reply as I turn toward the building. He walks beside me and chuckles. It makes me smile again.

"It's nothing to do with me. Their mother is a great woman, but I'm trying my best." I put my hand on his arm and grin across at him. He's suddenly rather lovely indeed and completely swoon-worthy in a dependable sort of way.

"Thank you for bringing me home. You should go back now before Mr. Explosive realises I'm gone," I say as I reach for the door.

"Probably. Are you okay now?"

"I think so. If he shouts at you, tell him to go jump off a cliff or something," I reply with a giggle. He frowns again and holds the door for me.

"Goodnight, Elizabeth."

"Goodnight, Michael," I reply as I duck under his arm and head for the elevator, taking off my shoes on the way. I haven't even got the energy to walk. I just want a bath and my bed.

As I throw my bag down on the counter, my phone beeps at me so I dig it out and hope it's something good.

> **- Assume you've gone. Are you okay? Do you want me to punch the bastard? X**
>
> -

Belle, bless her.

> **- Yes, sorry. Not in the mood. At home now and no, don't you dare. Just enjoy your night and be madly in love. So happy for you x**

> **- Okay, honey. Sleep tight x**

I can only imagine the scowl on her face the next time she sees Alex, but sod it. I've had enough. I actually can't even be bothered with a bath so I drag the dress over my shoulders and head for my bedroom to find something more comfortable.

One hour later and I'm staring at the television, trying to stop my irritated rambling to myself as I sip at some whiskey I've found in the back of the cupboard. I'm hurt, obviously, but I actually feel slightly more angry than hurt. Yes, I know he doesn't like not knowing things, but I did it for him. I did it to make him happy. And yes, I realise I probably should have told him about it but then he would have known

325

she wasn't going to turn up and that would have made it uncomfortable for everyone. I was trying to help, for fuck's sake. How dare he go all moody about it and dismiss me? Was he trying to make me feel bad about being a nice person? And what the hell did he think I was up to? Is this another one of his paranoid *she's out to destroy me* things?

Idiot.

I seem to be becoming more and more annoyed as the minutes progress. All thoughts of poor Alex have now disappeared, to the point of me beginning to consider picking up the phone and shouting at him. Why would he ruin a perfectly nice evening by having a temper tantrum without asking me about it first?

Arsehole.

And I'm not even there to smile with Belle about her happy news. Yes, I realise this is my fault because I left but I left because of him. Didn't he think that maybe he should have waited to have this discussion with me later on?

What a bastard.

And I had to deal with yet another slut that he's more than likely slept with. Well, not slept with obviously, but had sex with. Clearly I'm the only one who gets the honour of sleeping with the man, but I'm not feeling very honoured about it at the moment at all. How dare she look at me like I wasn't worthy or something? Who the hell does she think she is with her gorgeous blonde hair expertly teased to perfection and her three mile legs highlighting her probably Alex screwed groin? Bitch.

Yep, spitting mad, so mad that I'm now pacing and considering what to do about my very pissed off state. I should go back over there and confront him about it. This is not the Alex White show where everything always goes his sodding way and the rest of the world be damned. He needs to know how his actions affect people, the most important person being me, obviously.

I narrow my eyes at the door and mull over my options. Is he still even there? He's not here begging for my forgiveness for his outrageous behaviour so I can only assume he's either still there or has gone home. He might still be sitting there with his sister, not even realising I've left. No, Belle won't have let that happen. She will have made her point very effectively by now, I'm sure. Sudden thoughts hit me of him being with the bitch. Oh, that's great. She will have latched her fingers into him and will now be helping him through his inner turmoil, probably using her tongue as medicine to soothe his poor tortured bloody soul.

Oh god, he wouldn't, would he? He might. I have no idea. What does he do when he's that mad?

In fact, did he have sex with anyone when he was in New York? That's what he does to get rid of emotional pain, isn't it? Takes me, aggressively, in that dark place of his with all his brooding beauty forcing its way into my heart again and tearing another layer away from me. Surely he wouldn't do that to us, to me? He loves me, or at least I think he does.

This is absolutely not good at all. What the hell do I do now?

I stare into the amber liquid that's swirling around the glass I'm holding and watch as it ripples its waves at me before lifting it up and tipping it back.

Sod it, I'm going to bed.

I'm clearly too tired to think rationally about any of this, and the last thing I want to do is get involved in a argument with him when I can't make sense of things in my own head. He'll verbally rip me to shreds or use his sexual glory to manipulate the situation to suit himself, which I will definitely give in to because Christ, he looked good tonight. I'll also very quickly see his pain and when that happens, I'll throw myself at him to help him, give him anything he needs to find his way back to me, or himself, or us. I have no idea what that even is but it's too bloody wonderful for me to want to avoid at any point. And I definitely can't bring myself to even vaguely entertain the possibility that I might turn up and find him with the bitch because that would be far too much to deal with at the moment.

So putting my whiskey glass into the sink and switching off the light, I make my way to my bedroom in the hope that sleep might be forthcoming. It more than likely won't be, but maybe if I cuddle up to his bow tie, I can pretend that none of this happened.

Tomorrow I'll deal with whatever it is that I have to deal with. So much for buying Christmas decorations.

sodding Christmas.

Chapter 18

Alexander

"**S**he lied to me," he said, glaring at Conner as if it was his fault. It sort of was now that he knew all the information. Thankfully Serena had now stopped her constant *please fuck me again, Alex* conversation and disappeared. She wasn't that good the first time and the thought of having anyone else wrapped around him now was frankly repulsive.

"So what were you gonna do? Screw Serena to make yourself feel better about it? I thought you were better than this, Alex. Fuck, what the hell is wrong with you? She didn't lie. She did it because she loves you and wants you to be happy."

Of course she did, because she's an angel whose sole purpose on this godforsaken planet is to make people happy, to make him happy, and his fucking paranoid brain was making him think all sorts of crap that he really shouldn't have even been entertaining, but he couldn't stop it. That darkness rolling over him in waves was like a comforting blanket of normalcy. It was where he was safest, where he was in control of his feelings.

"I wasn't doing anything with Serena. She just got me another drink." Conner raised his brow in that irritating *I know better* fucking way that he always did so well. Alex sneered and turned back to the bar. "Look, just fuck off, will you? If you think I want any piece of that whore near me again, you're wrong. I don't want anyone else."

No, he didn't. He'd just gone through possibly the most emotionally challenging hour of his life and when he came out, she was gone. Why he'd even thought he could do that without her was unfathomable. He'd been a fucking wreck but he'd been so mad when he realised that the woman he loved had gone behind his back that he couldn't even look at her let alone have her within ten feet of him. But he'd damn well expected her there when he finished. He didn't know what the hell he was going to do with her or what depths he would need from her, but he did know that he couldn't breathe without her, again. One hour of staving off another pathetic panic attack, one hour of hurt and anger, one hour of remembering his father's face, his hands, his bloody tie. One hour of looking into the eyes of a sister who had received every child's dream of a mother and father who loved her with every beat of their hearts, and what did he have? Only her, and she'd left him when he needed her most.

He deserved every fucking footfall of her running from him. What sort of man did that to the woman who loved him? The woman who'd met his sister and said everything that needed to be said to get her to turn up tonight. The woman who'd gone out of her way to remind Evelyn that Alexander White was actually just a man who was just as nervous as she was. The woman who'd clearly shone so brightly that his new-found sibling had no choice but to ramble on about how wonderful she was. Well, not ramble because Miss Peters was certainly not a rambler. Conner was right; she was scolding with her words to say the least. But whatever it was that Elizabeth had said, it seemed she made the difference in his sister's decision to give them a chance of a relationship of some sort.

Elizabeth.

What the hell was he doing here?

"So, why are you still here then?" Conner asked.

Quite.

He stood abruptly, not entirely sure why he needed her but knowing that he absolutely did. Was it the dark place churning through him or was it her arms that he needed and those sweet words of love? Maybe it was both. She seemed to stay with him through those times, and he couldn't dismiss her like he did all the others. Maybe the two opposite emotions were rolling into each other and creating something different for him now, some mingling of anger and passion.

"I'm going. Congratulations," he said sharply as he turned and headed for wherever Andrews was.

"Thanks, really feeling that," Conner grumbled behind him. Alex stopped and turned, trying to suck in his current odd feelings and find the pleasant ones his friend probably needed to calm him.

"You've done well, Conner. She's stunning and you'll both be very happy, I'm sure," he said with a genuine smile. He really was happy for Conner. Belle was a formidable woman but she was spot on

329

for him. The eye roll he received in return presumably meant he hadn't delivered the sentence genuinely enough. Well fuck it, he'd got more important things to deal with.

"That was fucking awful, White, honestly, absolutely terrible. I've never heard such utter bullshit. Just go and tell her how much you love her before my future wife beats the living shit out of you."

It was a good point; he could feel the death stare Belle had been delivering most of the night still penetrating his spine.

"I'll see you soon."

The drive was quiet. Andrews was in one of his non-speaking moods again, which most likely meant that he was pissed off or something else was wrong. Given that he'd taken Elizabeth home earlier, he probably knew how she'd seemed at the time, which was more than likely upset or emotional. It wasn't a conversation he was prepared to have. What the man was thinking was of no importance whatsoever because all he could think about was her, and what he felt like doing to her, with her, in her.

He gazed out of the window, wondering whether she'd even answer the door and then wondered if he would in her position. He still didn't understand why she had such faith in him or even why she loved him but she did so he kept holding onto that thought as the car pulled to a stop.

"Go home, Andrews. I'll call you if I need you," he said as he got out and slammed the door. He had no intention of going home. He'd just use her key and let himself in.

Turning that damned key was actually a bit harder than he thought it would be. It felt somehow intrusive or unacceptable for some reason, but he did it anyway while preparing himself for her reaction to him. Would she be asleep? It was entirely possible that she might be sitting there stewing herself into her own little temper about his behaviour towards her. She was becoming more forceful with her anger and it made her more fascinating to him every time she uttered a word in venom, and Christ, that vicious little demon she'd turned into when he pushed her this afternoon was hot as hell.

"How was your night?" he heard as he closed the door and walked into the lounge area, her voice laced with sarcasm. He smirked to himself and pondered her ability to know he was there before she saw him.

"Interesting," he replied as he moved toward the chair in the near black room. The only thing he could see was her long legs stretched out on the coffee table with the light from the window reflecting on her skin, that beautiful, creamy skin that called his fingers to mark it in some way and claim it as his.

He stood there waiting for another sarcastic comeback and was surprised when nothing happened, only silence as she studied him. She was getting very good at that now, finding her way into his inner battles and determining the most appropriate way to behave.

Would she feel his need for her or was she still too pissed to allow him what he needed from her?

If he was honest, he wasn't entirely sure what he needed. Just being here in the same room with her again was soothing him to some degree and calming him down from his furious agitation, regardless of what she was about to deliver.

"At what point did you get yourself a key cut to my home?" He smiled - obviously a little pissed then.

"I didn't. You left them in your coat if you remember," he replied as he thought of the coat she'd left in his closet the night he left her.

"Right," was her answer. It wasn't enough to give him a fucking clue where she was going with this. He supposed he could just grab her and get on with what he wanted but the need for her to offer it was so overwhelming that he felt himself tremble a little in anticipation that she might. Whatever she was doing, she was in absolute control of this moment and for some completely unknown reason, he was happy to allow it. So he stood and waited again. She'd done it before on several occasions now, somehow sensed his feelings and let him take her where he wanted them to be. His fingers began to itch to touch that milky skin as he gazed down on that leg and followed its line up to the top of her thigh, the faintest image of lace curling seductively across her hipbone and inwards towards her pussy. Obviously his dick instantly reminded him of exactly what he needed as his thoughts began to wander to everything other than her feelings regarding his actions this evening. Fuck it, he'd deal with the aftermath later when she was more compliant, when she'd done precisely what her body and mind was created to do, just for him, when he could give her those emotions she would be after from him.

"How do you feel?" she asked in that quiet, low voice of hers. Well fuck, maybe his order of events wasn't going to happen because there was no begging in her tone. It was a question she expected an answer to. It was clearly her way of making him uncomfortable, of getting her point across and making him vocalise it because she knew how he felt. She was the only one who ever did.

"I think you know, Elizabeth," he replied as she stretched her other leg out and then bent and widened her knees to allow him a glimpse of his quarry. Christ, she was getting good at this negotiating shit.

"Yes, but I want you to tell me before you show me. I want you to reach inside and tear out every emotion you've got so I can forget how fucking angry I am with you," she said with a sneer in her voice. She leaned forward and let her captivating but snarling face come into view, that flaming red hair tumbling over her naked breasts and highlighting every piece of perfection that she possessed.

All sorts of conflicting emotions and images rolled through his mind as he tried to connect all the dots and find what she was asking him for - the fear, the hurt, the pain, the torture and then the lust he felt as he learnt to recreate it for other uses and channel it. Her touch, then that fucking guilt that had receded over the years to almost non-existent, more fear, blood, screaming and begging, a warm embrace, her lips, her skin... He couldn't even begin to understand how to put all the thoughts and feelings into some semblance of order so he pulled in a long breath and gazed at her delicious mouth in the hope that it would help him to find his way through the conflicting imagery.

She opened her mouth to say something and then closed it again, probably because she was going to help him decipher it all and then decided against it. She was becoming an expert at making him talk and tell her the truth. She seemed to have the ability to pull every string on his bow very well indeed, somehow allowing him to believe that every thought might be heard without judgement or fear of reprisal. He wished it was ordered enough for him to give it to her, but every breath was still laced with his father and how fucking awful each day had been for him while his sister had apparently revelled in love, playing happy families. That bite of a right hook was still firmly implanted in his five year-old brain and that feeling of panic still rose as the bastard had looked down on him with a smug look of self - satisfaction then dragged him toward the stairs. The bruising still littered his body, regardless of the fact that the marks left long ago, and he still had that overriding need to constantly look over his shoulder because he might still be there, ready to do it all again with a smile, just to remind him how fucking worthless he really was, *is*.

"You disgust me. Look at how small you are. Look at how pathetic you are. You can't even fight back, can you? You don't even try. You'll never be anything because you won't even try to win, such a weak little thing. Do you need help, Nicholas? Stretch for my hand, boy, maybe you can reach me. Let's see what I've got to encourage you to try harder..."

Try harder, fight harder, wage fucking war.

He ground his teeth across the inside of his cheek to stop the prick of emotion that was rapidly threatening to break across his face. It was fucking pathetic but surprising nonetheless. He frowned and tried to steady his shaky breath as she held his eyes and kept pushing his buttons with hers.

Eventually she raised her perfect, lean body with a sigh and walked across to him.

"What do you need from me?" she asked softly as she gazed up into his eyes and wrapped her hand around the back of his neck.

He didn't know, but those big brown eyes were so overwhelmingly soul destroying that he had to get them away from him before he fell apart in front of her, so he looked over her head toward the window. Was that what she wanted from him? Did she want him to let it all out and fall at her feet? He wasn't sure that he could, even for her, but the fact that his heart was currently pounding erratically probably meant that she was getting him close to it.

"I don't deserve you," he said quietly. She moved her hand to his jaw and pulled his eyes back to hers, not allowing him to remove himself from her. The impact of those eyes on his again made him realise with acute clarity that whatever it was that was about to happen, he wanted to stay with her, always with her.

"Yes, you do," she replied as she trailed her fingers along the front of his throat and started to push his jacket off, her eyes never once leaving his as she continued her assault and kept pleading with him to give her more. "I love you. You deserve everything from me."

Not a functioning thought entered his mind as he heard those words and began to crumble a little more inside, his throat constricting with the possibility of that lost emotion of another type, of a release of some kind other than anger and then control. His barriers to the years of torment were crushing him internally, constricting inward and pushing the bile of emotions upwards towards his mind again where they were not welcome. He didn't want it, couldn't deal with it, was using every available technique to try and squash it back into its box and banish it again, but her god damn eyes kept pulling it upwards to the surface, begging it to release itself and give her the more she was pushing for.

"What do you want from me, Elizabeth? I don't know how to..."

"Yes, you do," she replied, undoing his shirt buttons and tugging on his cufflinks. "Show me, Alex. Let me see and feel all of you."

Her fingers travelled their way along his now bare chest and downwards to his belt, then sliding it from his pants, she held it out to him and continued with her gaze. His whole frame stiffened a little at the thought.

Was this what he wanted? Was it what she wanted? He was beginning to think about dropping down on his knees and letting her simply hold him and now she was offering up the alternative while still searching his eyes for the other response of more. Was he supposed to fucking choose what was happening to him?

"Elizabeth, I..." He hadn't got a fucking clue what he wanted but the emotions that were beginning to rapidly assault his senses were now overpowering him to the point of shaking. He fought against visions of that staircase and that tie, and the bastard's face as he sneered in repulsion at a weak, pathetic child who was just hoping to be loved, or even wanted, for fuck's sake. His fists tightened at the thought as his eyes flicked to the belt and then back to her. She stood there quietly, looking like the divine angel that she was with a wistful face, simply waiting for his reaction, seemingly completely at ease with either outcome. Her fingers gently held onto the black belt and gave him the chance to embrace the more comfortable version of himself if he chose to, but she could see him breaking, feel him losing the control he was desperately craving while contemplating giving it up entirely.

"Let me in," she said as she took a step closer and put her other hand on his chest. Tears welled as he looked down at that small hand and swallowed, trying to somehow will them back inside of him and not allow them any further. They were fucking weak and debilitating. His eyes flicked to the belt again. It was the only way to contain this and he knew it, and she clearly did, too. The pull of normalcy was so strong that he moved his hand toward it until he felt the warm smooth leather beneath his fingers.

"I can't give you-"

"Yes, you can." Her hand reached for his face then ran down his neck as she drew him down to her while he choked on the sob that was consuming his throat like fire. His fingers wrapped around her hand on the belt as he tried one last time to contain his torment and drive the tears back downward. He only had to take that belt and all of this would go away. Every disgusting memory would be chased back to hell in a matter of minutes.

"I love you. Show me, please, let me help you," she whispered into his mouth as her lips grazed across his.

Her fist pushed against the inside of his hand as she tried to relax her hold of the belt, or rather his hold of it. Time stood still and his logic reeled in chaotic uncertainty as an eternity of her lips and her body and her breath began to engage enough thoughts of love and adoration to overwhelm the repulsive visions that were still haunting his mind.

"I love you, too," he said as he felt the first tear fall onto his cheek and wet his skin. His fingers released her hand and the loud deafening clunk of the belt echoed in the room as it landed on the floor beneath them.

"I know," she said as she wrapped her arms around his neck and pulled him closer.

His knees instantly gave way to the barrage of uncontrollable new feelings coursing through his body, crippling any last defence he had against the pain. She dropped to the floor with him and continued to hold him as another lone tear ran onto her stomach, followed by another and another as he let every thought erupt into sorrow for a childhood he was denied. Then years of unbridled anger assaulted his mind, only heightening every sensation of shame and guilt to the point of self-loathing and hatred. Eventually he felt his weight become lax as her body curled tighter around him and rocked him slowly, soothing him to a rhythm of their own, somehow created from her passion and years of his own turmoil and inner demons.

He had no idea how long they sat there on the floor but each minute felt more like falling into hell as each disintegrating barrier opened up yet another fucking hurtful memory or vision to continue his torment. Flashes of the coal shed in the back yard, the toilet where he was allowed to wash his hair, the single mattress on his bedroom floor that the bastard pissed on repeatedly to mark his territory. Her soothing fingers brushed across his forehead gently, reminding him that she was still here, holding him, but it didn't stop the next visual of the bastard pushing his head into the cooker to check that the toast wasn't burning. He could still feel the burn in his eyes from the grill and bile rose back up his throat at the still lingering smell of his singed hair as he'd been pulled back out and thrown into the fridge door.

His hands gripped onto her hip, hoping to hell that she could keep him together when this was finally out in the open because she said she wanted this from him. She said she could help him through anything he had to give her, wouldn't run from him, would understand, and god, he hoped she could because this was it and she had caused it all. There was only the truth left to offer her after this, the devastating and brutal truth of the real man that she'd fallen in love with, the child he'd been and then the man he'd become because of a father who should have moulded him into a better person.

Christ, he absolutely didn't deserve her compassion and highly doubted her absolution when the time came, because come it would. Regardless of how he tried to hide it from her and in spite of his new image, she would find out because he would eventually break completely for her. She would make him do it unfortunately; he knew that with every beat of his newly awakened heart.

Her fingers ran through his hair softly again as she murmured calming words and gently began to release her hold on him. He didn't want her to so grabbed tighter to try and dispel the still crippling images that were taunting him and reminding him of his own pathetic weakness.

"Alex, look at me," she said as she tugged on his hair and tried to make him sit up. He fought against it, not wanting to hear her words. He just wanted to crawl in closer and stay in this place forever as she somehow helped him find an order to this pain in a way he'd never known before.

"I don't want to. I just want to stay here. Just let me stay here," he replied quietly as he drew in a long breath and let her scent envelop him in a cocoon of love and warmth, the skin on her thigh caressing his cheek as his lips lightly brushed over it.

"Okay," she said as he felt her lips on his temple, which caused him to realise that his dramatic tears had finally subsided, thankfully. He wouldn't be doing that again in a hurry. Her fingers gently moved back and forth across his back in a figure of eight pattern, caressing the very numbers of his life, the numbers of anguish and shame, and that damned guilt that had been chasing him around for years like a constant knife in the back. But her gentle persuasion was still lulling him deeper into his warm place of hope and something like profound optimism as those haunting visions of the bastard were slowly replaced with roaring wood fires and summer evenings on his yacht, all with her wrapped around him or under him. Nights in Rome or perhaps New York, showing her off to the world and letting everyone know exactly what they were missing as he claimed her publically, possibly by marriage or some other strange notion of commitment to the woman he couldn't breathe without.

"So what colour should I paint my building?" she said chirpily out of fucking nowhere. He turned his body in her lap to look up at her. She giggled a little and gazed back down at him.

"Where the hell did that come from?" he said, trying to ignore her perfect tits that instantly reminded him of his original purpose and began to slowly entice him back to his old self.

"Well, it's white. It's not really mine if it stays white, is it? That would mean it's still yours and it's not, it's mine, because you gave it to me, didn't you? And now it's official because I signed the paperwork, which you forced on me I might add, quite pleasurably in fact, but really, you gave me no choice in the matter, did you? I should paint it green or maybe orange. What do you think?"

Well she'd got his attention, clever little thing, and Christ, he loved her rambling. It was probably her way of bringing him back to the present and not letting him dwell in his fucking horrible place. Actually, he was quite enjoying his post horrible place that had morphed into a frankly bloody wonderful place but he chuckled and sat up to look at her anyway.

"I think you should leave it white. White looks good on you," he replied quietly as he reached across and tucked a lock of hair behind her ear.

"I think white looks good on me, too," she said with a huge smile that beamed that ray of light straight through to his soul again.

"And this White is completely yours. You're my world, Elizabeth Scott and I want you to know that. I want you to understand everything about me and how I feel about you. Let me show you. I need you to feel it in every beat of your heart because I won't be without you again. I won't let you go. I can't," he said as he grabbed her face and pulled her forward to his mouth.

Lips had never tasted so sweet. That she had held him and comforted him in his darkest moment seemed to intensify every feeling of love he had for her. His mouth caressed every inch of her lips to try and show her the depth of his feelings. She had no idea what she just caused him to do and what that gave him in return. His hands moved slowly across her throat then outwards across her shoulders and down to her hands as he brought them up to his throat and placed them around it.

"Take this, baby. It's yours. It's all yours. When you need the other man, I'll find him but for now, just take whatever you want and love me. I want to feel how much you love me."

Her big eyes widened at the admission but quickly fell back to a soft gaze as her fingers lightly gripped his collarbone and twirled gentle movements over his skin like some sort of symphony of light. He closed his eyes and relaxed into her touch again, letting her guide where she wanted this to go. Soft, feather-light kisses started at his neck then began to rain down on his chest as he let her chase away the last of his demons. There was nothing hurried or forced about her manner. She just let the tender caress of those lips keep trailing their way over his skin until she removed her hand from his throat and brought those lips back to his mouth.

She pushed against his chest so he rolled backwards to the floor and groaned as her breasts met his chest for the first time. The temptation to grab hold and sink into her was instant but he clenched his fists and waited for her next move to unfold. This was her moment. She'd given him so much tonight, all he wanted was for her to take everything she needed from him and do what she wanted.

In a matter of minutes he was naked and lying underneath her as she straddled him and continued with her sweet mouth, finding its way slowly to wherever she was going. His dick jumped to the constant soft tickling of her breast against it and again he fought every instinct to just throw her on her back and do what he wanted. The sharp bites of pain elicited ever increasing lust as she nipped and sucked her way across his body toward the place he wanted her to end. This submission to her was becoming slowly unbearable as she took every minute he was giving her and used it leisurely to entice growl after growl of frustration from him. Was she trying to wind him up?

Fuck, he wanted to show her how he wanted this, to give her every aggressive and passionate tendency that was now once again coursing with desire across his body, like a tornado slowly building. He was becoming desperate to reclaim his strength, to show her that the weakened man she'd comforted was only a small part of him, to remind her that that little boy was still just a memory and wouldn't be participating in their lives more often than absolutely necessary.

Did she know that? Did she understand him well enough to see exactly what he wanted regardless of what he'd offered?

Her mouth eventually landed exactly where he wanted it so he waited for the bliss that was surely coming as her lips travelled along the length of his dick. It was like a whisper of touch across his skin as her warm breath teased every sensitivity from him. One touch of her tongue and then no more than breath again as she moved her face around and let her hair float across his now over sensitive head. His fingers dug into the carpet as she drew the full length of her tongue across his aching balls and then twirled the damn thing all the way up to his tip too softly. He groaned out loud as she giggled a little and let her tongue rest on the head of him. Fuck, he was so close to flipping her on her back, or against a wall; anything would do. It was taking every last shred of control he had just to stay still and let her have her time because all he wanted now was to be inside her, forcefully, and as his aching dick began to throb with need while she continued to nibble on him gently, he grunted in annoyance at his own impatience.

"Look at me," she said as she licked lightly against him. His eyes opened instantly so he could gaze down at her. "What do you want, Alex?"

Her tongue flicked again as that wicked little smile lit up her face. It was like a lightning bolt across him as his last grip of submission began to fall apart.

"Inside you," he panted out as she dropped her tantalising mouth one inch down around him then sucked back up.

"No, Alex, tell me what *you* want," she said again, causing every primal and dominant part of him to rise to the surface again, literally growling in anticipation of what she was suggesting.

"To fuck you, hard," he replied as she lowered her mouth again a bit more and moaned into him, her eyelids fluttering closed as he watched her sucking and then releasing him. She hovered over him on her hands and knees, not moving, just waiting and trembling with want as she kept her eyes fixed on his. "To mark you, to bite you, to make you so fucking sore you'll never forget who was in you."

The corners of her mouth twitched a little as she sat upright and dragged her hand across her throat, her head tilting a little to let her flaming hair cascade down her back as her other hand reached out for his.

"There's the man I love," she murmured as she pulled him up to her and wrapped his fingers around her throat. "Come and find yourself again."

It was all the permission he needed to unleash every instinct he had to take her, fuck her, grab every piece of her and sink himself so far inside of her that she'd never be able to get away again.

He dragged her up from the floor and pushed her towards the wall as she whimpered softly in his grasp but moved in perfect synchronicity with his movements, feeling her way around his every step with a sixth sense and allowing him every brutal touch to her skin. He found her neck with his teeth and grazed them along her collarbone and then back up to her delicious mouth to devourer her again with his tongue. Her breathing became deep and methodical as he stepped back to watch in awe as she closed her eyes and began to detach herself slightly, expecting his force to take her to subspace. Her fingers grasped quietly at non-existent handholds on the wall for the support she might need to endure what he would do to her, and much as he adored it, he didn't want her drifting off. He wanted to stay completely connected with her and have her feeling and seeing every piece of what he wanted to share with her.

"Elizabeth, open your eyes." She instantly opened them and stared across at him with unadulterated lust pouring off her. "You stay here, with me. You show me everything."

Her breathing shallowed out instantly as he stepped closer and slammed his body weight into her, every fibre of his body wanting to get closer and deeper as he pushed closer and she moaned out in pleasure. His name whispered across the air and into his ears as she wrapped her incredible leg around his hip and grabbed at his back with her nails. Vicious little bites of pain caused a growl of frustration to explode from his mouth as she sunk her teeth into his lip and ground her hips into his dick. He had to get inside her. No amount of waiting or teasing was acceptable at all so he reached down and tore at the scrap of lace covering her so he could have her bare. Her cry of discomfort into his mouth only heightened his need as his hands roughly pushed her thighs apart to find her warmth. He wanted his fingers deep inside her, to feel all that heat and wetness that was just for him. He pushed three fingers in so hard that she squealed at the intrusion and gasped back a breath as she looked at him with wide eyes, those fucking beautiful eyes that took his breath away every damn time. His fingers pulled back out and then rammed in again. She groaned and held onto his shoulders as he nearly lifted her from the floor with the force of his hand. Christ, he loved that look, so completely his, every inch of her glorious body perched on his fingers waiting for release or instruction. Her mouth quivered with words she couldn't form as he twisted his hand to increase the friction for her.

"Oh god," she moaned as he rubbed rhythmically with his fingers and let her feel how close she was. A few touches in the right place with the right amount of pressure and she was exactly where he wanted her, trembling with anticipation and ripe for the taking.

His dick was throbbing to be inside her, actually fucking painful with need to be buried to the hilt but his mind was too involved in watching her fall apart in front of him, to see her vulnerable for him, to watch her every movement as she flexed, pulsed and eventually

341

collapsed on him. Her nails tensed in his skin as those eyes began to flutter closed and her breathing escalated, showing her nearness so he pushed his hand into her throat to bring her back.

"No, open them, let me see every fucking second of this," he seethed as he flicked his thumb across her clit to stimulate her further. She locked her eyes with his and let her weight fall onto his hands with a groan as he began to circle his thumb.

"Oh yes, fuck, Alex. Yes... more," she hissed as she started to grip his fingers. Spasms began taking hold and clamping around him. He spread his fingers to feel every movement deep inside her as her muscles started their constricting and the flush of orgasm raced across her skin, blushing her cheeks and widening her pupils to the black holes of desire he wanted from her.

Her panting only increased his need to bury himself inside her so he withdrew his hand and offered it to her. Her mouth instantly sucked at his fingers as she groaned around them, which made his dick jump to attention again and remind him of his goal. But, yet again, he found himself so mesmerised with her mouth that he just watched as she licked herself off him and then pulled his mouth towards her. Never had he felt so attached so someone, so completely part of someone else's pleasure that he was forgetting to breathe again. Her fingers wrapped into his hair tightly as she scratched her other hand across his lower back viciously, inducing the tension he needed to move again. His sudden grunt at the pain made him lift her by the throat. He had no idea how she knew it was coming but she grabbed on and wrapped her luscious legs around to support herself for the oncoming attack.

"Fuck, I need inside you," he said as he shifted her weight to get the leverage on the wall he wanted. She gripped on and raised herself a little so he could manoeuvre her and position his cock. The head of it was poised and waiting as he pushed her throat back so he could look into her eyes again when he lowered her onto him. Her scream of desire was all he wanted as he pulled her down onto him and drove in as hard as he could, hitting her core and letting the sensation of her envelop him as he pulled back out and forced his way back in again. She gasped out again and grabbed on as his hand continued to hold her throat against the wall. She was the sexiest thing on the planet. God himself couldn't have created a more divine looking creature, and as her eyes widened, he gripped onto her arse and bent down to pull her tight nipple into his teeth. Biting down harshly, he was rewarded with her agonisingly sweet moan of pain and as her nails dug in further, he released the last of his control. The bite of those nails induced all kinds of thoughts and visions. His back clenched at the bliss that was beginning to build with every thrust, and her now biting teeth on his neck only furthered his primal tendencies.

He lifted her and moved towards the bedroom. He wanted the mirror, wanted her to watch what she looked like while he fucked her, to see the way she writhed in front of him and screamed when she came. Putting her down in front of it, he pulled out and turned her to face it then pulled her wrists behind her back and grasped them tightly in one hand.

"I want you to watch yourself, watch me fuck you, see yourself as I do," he rasped out as he wrapped his fingers around her throat and angled her forward a little. The torture that followed was beyond anything he'd ever felt as he rammed back into her and felt her falling forward into his hand, gasping as he yanked her hands to stabilise her. Her pussy tightened around him every time he increased the force on her, her hands, her throat. It seemed every movement of his brutal intent only heightened her arousal and took her one step closer to her explosion. His cock threatened release each time he looked into those eyes or watched her lips panting with each thrust, her perfect tits moving gracefully as he slammed in again and she lent further forward into his hold, pushing against it with need. Her eyes fluttered closed as she tried to hold on to her orgasm so he released her neck and bit into her shoulder to make her look up again. Her eyes flew open as she yelped in agony.

"You will fucking look at me. I don't care how you control it but you will let me see you when you come," he growled as he pushed her towards the wall again and placed her hands on it. Gripping her hips, he picked up his pace and watched as she began to crumble around him. Her fingers scratched at the wallpaper and her legs began to tremble as he pounded into her. She arched her back and pressed back with every inch of strength she had to increase the force for them both.

"Yes, Alex, fuck me, please. More..." She moaned as she reached for his hand and pulled it between her legs, grinding herself onto it and gasping as he changed the angle of her body. His fingers stretched downwards to feel himself moving in and out of her as he pressed his thumb hard against her clit and flicked upwards onto it. It was all she needed as she clamped hard around him and shouted out his name with her release, her body quivering as she struggled to hold herself up while he continued to slam in as hard as he could.

He couldn't get deep enough or close enough so he grabbed her and pulled her back towards the bed, literally throwing her onto it and pushing her legs apart as he crawled across her and drove back into her again. Her head tipped backwards as she called out his name again and reached her hands to the headboard for something to hold onto, her fingers whitening under the strain as he kept up the relentless momentum. All thoughts began to evaporate as he let the blinding pleasure of his own release take hold of him. Primal need began to ebb through his body as he gazed down on the woman he loved, writhing beneath him while he gave her every forceful touch he could. Her hips would be bruised, his teeth marks were already glowing on her skin beautifully, and her pussy would be raw and punished to perfection, and Christ, he loved her for taking it from him, for giving this to him. She gave him everything.

His tension built to uncontrollable levels and the ache that consumed his balls was ready to break so he leaned down to take her lips in his, rolling his tongue around hers as she moaned out incoherently and began shake beneath him. Fuck, he loved that shaking, too. Her muscles clamped and spurred him on to his oblivion as she moulded herself to him. Her hands found their way to his hair as she pushed his head away from her to look at him with those eyes that consumed every breath he had.

"I love you," she breathed out as she fell apart under him again, her body rising and arching into him gracefully. He wrapped his arm under her back and plunged into her one last time before he let his own release flow. Every thought disappeared apart from intense love as he gazed down at her eyes and watched her pleading for him to get closer, her fingers clawing at his jaw with need as she pulled him down to her mouth again.

What the hell she saw in him was inconsequential. Whether he deserved her or not was completely irrelevant because she absolutely didn't need to plead or beg. She had him, every fucking inch, and there was no way she was ever going to be without him whether she liked it or not.

"Mine," he said, shaking with his own release and closing his eyes in utter bliss as he leaned down into her neck. "Always mine."

Chapter 19

Elizabeth

Well obviously, why didn't I assume this?
Christmas decoration shopping with Alex actually means us sitting at his house while another one of the most beautiful woman I have ever seen directs men backwards and forwards from a truck with ridiculous amounts of trees, baubles, floral embellishments and all the other general bits and bobs you need for a festive season. I can't even say that I mind that much. It would probably help if she wasn't so sodding gorgeous and efficient in her perfectly cut business suit that, if I'm honest, is a little too short and low cut for professional, but she absolutely pulls it off. She's sauntering around the place as if she owns it, pointing at men to garnish every available surface with some other beautiful garland or arrangement of some kind, and while I'm not intimidated by her, she's absolutely not my favourite person because she keeps touching Alex a little too much for comfort. Those frequent hand brushes and that batting eyelash thing she keeps doing appear to have no effect on him but on me, definitely.

However, the red, white and green decorations are very nearly completed across the lower half of the house and I have to admit that the rooms look incredible. There's a twelve-foot tree in the lounge and dining room, a smaller one in the kitchen and elaborately tiered centre pieces on all the tables. Stunning really, there's no getting around it. The woman's bloody brilliant at what she does. Unfortunately, she also seems to want to *do* Alex, so clearly I hate her. Serena, thousand mile fucking legs, was enough for me last night. I seriously don't need more competition today.

I pull my jean covered legs under me and sip at my coffee as I think about Mr. Sodding Wonderful who is currently shouting at someone on the phone in the kitchen. Alpha male has definitely returned with a vengeance this morning and while I'm very happy he let his guard down so completely last night, I'm also very happy to see him back to his normal self - well, his version of normal anyway. Beautiful as he was in all his raw, brutal turmoil and emotional as I felt about it at the time, I can't honestly say I'm entirely comfortable with what the hell it is that I'm supposed to do with that information, or what it means for him, or us. I still don't understand what made him crack last night but it must have been something to do with Evelyn and the way she made him feel. It was clear to me that I had to help him get back to his usual self as soon as possible because that amount of breaking for anyone would be hard to cope with. So I let him find himself again, in the way he found himself best - and god did he - while he took me with him, gloriously and with a connection he'd never given me before. We haven't spoken about it because I don't want to see him crumble again and he's giving me the vibe that he absolutely doesn't want to go there again anytime soon. That's fine for the time being because, thankfully, the one thing I do know with absolute clarity is that he loves me. What that means to him I really don't know but it does appear to mean that I'm not going anywhere anytime soon. And I am extremely happy about that.

I suddenly realise I haven't even asked my mum and dad if they'll come at Christmas yet, so I pluck out my phone and call them in the hope that they'll say yes. If not, Alex has just gone to an awful lot of expense for no reason whatsoever.

"Hi, darling," Mum says after the first ring. I swear to god the phone is permanently attached to her hand. "How's that delicious man of yours?" Oh god, here we go.

"Fine, Mum, and I'm fine too, thanks for asking," I reply as I stand and walk to the kitchen for more coffee. Efficient woman smiles brightly at me and saunters off towards the front of the house again so I stick my tongue out at her back childishly.

"Of course you are, darling. Anyway what are you calling for? I've already had Belle on the phone this morning sounding very pleased with herself for some unknown reason. Any ideas?" Yes, but clearly I can't tell you if she hasn't. Why hasn't she? Odd.

"No, no clue at all." I hate lying to Mum. I'm also bloody awful at it.

"Right, well as long as you're both happy. So what did you want, darling?" Oh please let this be good news to her and not her *do you not think I'm capable* speech.

"Well, Alex wondered, actually we both wondered if you'd like to come here for Christmas? Everybody to come here, I mean. We'd very much like to do lunch here and for you all to stay for a few days." I'm literally screwing my face up as I wait for her reaction, which could easily go either way as I reach for the steamy knob on the coffee maker, trying not to think about Pascal and watch a now very angrily pacing Alex outside the French doors.

"Right, darling, well I'll ask your father," she replies quietly. It's not a good response.

"Mum, please, we've had dinner at yours every year since we were born and I just want to give you a lovely day where you don't have to do anything." She remains quiet for too long as I watch Alex storm into the lounge via the other glass doors. "Mum, are you still there?"

"I'm perfectly capable of doing a lunch, Beth." I roll my eyes. I so knew this was coming.

"I'm not saying you're not. I just thought it would be nice to do something different and it was all Alex's idea. He thinks you're both lovely, and obviously, Conner will be here too so you'll get to meet him because you know Belle won't be taking him home anytime soon..." I'm rambling, playing the wonderful boyfriend thing because that will weaken her. I just want her happy and well, for god's sake. "Please, Mum, Dad will definitely come. You know that. Just say yes, for me, please?" There's another pause long enough to eclipse the sun.

"Elizabeth Scott, manipulation is definitely your forte. Of course we'll come. I'm sure it will be fabulous and I'll be very pleased to look at the backside on that divine man of yours for a few days." Oh my god, the woman is disturbed. I'm positive eyeing up your daughter's boyfriend is unacceptable. What on earth she's going to do when Conner gets in the room too is quite worrying. Perhaps we should invite Pascal as well because that would definitely would make her Christmas. Actually, I'm not convinced even I could handle that amount of testosterone, which reminds me of the Alex/Pascal situation that we still haven't talked about since he gave me a building and then nonchalantly told me to have my way with his friend. I need to talk to him about that, soon. I can't even deny that I'm interested because I know I am. Who wouldn't be with those intoxicating green eyes? What the hell does that mean about me, or about my relationship with Alex? Clearly I have no bloody idea at all.

"Okay, Mum, that's brilliant news. I'll let Alex know and get back to you about details and stuff nearer the time."

My heart's not in the conversation anymore. Alex is slamming things around in the background and a pair of vivid green eyes have now distracted me to the point of no return.

"Lovely, darling, now I don't have to stick my hand up a turkey's-
"

"Bye, Mum, love you," I cut across her, seriously not wanting to talk about anything in arses when Pascal is still floating around in my brain with his devious fingers working alongside Alex's. My brain is obviously delivering far too many interesting visions for me to even begin to cope with so I hit the end call button and exhale a long breath.

Another loud crashing noise comes from the study so I suck in a breath and wander towards the noise. All the delivery drivers and the woman seem to have disappeared and apart from the swearing and slamming, the house seems to have gone eerily quiet. I grip onto the doorframe and lean my head around to take a peek at what I'm dealing with, and oh god there he is. He seriously should not be allowed to exist. Every time I see him, my breathing becomes redundant. He's standing behind his desk, one hand fingering the keys on his laptop, the other holding his phone to his ear, his mouth moving around every snarled word he's uttering. I have no idea what he's saying because I literally can't function enough to focus on words. He's simply too damn sexy for coherent thought and that angry frown is just causing all sorts of other salacious imagery to invade every corner of my mind. After last night's explosion of sex and emotion, I can only describe myself as a wanton hussy. He was everything a man should be, soft, gentle, open, honest and then aggressive beyond belief as he reminded himself and me exactly who and what he is. My inner slut and me clearly want more of the same again because I simply can't stop my very sore bits tightening for another opportunity.

He opens a file to the left of him and scowls at something written within it then turns for the window and stands there looking out at the garden, hand in pocket, pulling his trousers tight across his arse and highlighting those muscular legs very successfully. His broad shoulders are accentuated by a waistcoat leading to that very tight midsection and that six-pack that I love so much. Then of course, what's actually hiding in his trousers, thick, beautiful, hard and damned aggressive in its nature. Oh good lord, I could explode just looking at him and my core reminds me of that by clenching very dramatically again, causing my knees to buckle a little.

Most women would be afraid of this moment. They would retreat and let him calm down before they entertained the idea of letting him rid himself of his angst, but apparently not me. No, my fingers are itching for him, to give him his release and offer myself up for him, to take his aggression and turn it into something more powerful for us, something so mind blowing that I'll never forget him, never leave him, never even think about it because he has everything I need and he couldn't ever do anything bad enough for me to not want him. He's mine and I'm his, and there's no more to say on the matter.

Where the hell Pascal fits in is mystifying, but we'll work that out at some point, I'm sure.

I wander across to him and wrap my hands tentatively around his waist from behind, hoping for a good reaction. I couldn't care less if he's rough as long as he doesn't dismiss me. His anger doesn't scare me; it's his refusal to show emotion that does. His hand gently lands on mine as he continues his swearing and cursing into the phone. It's as if he's body is with me but his mind is with the person on the phone. Well, if that's the case, I suppose I could use his body wisely so I drop my hands down to see how interested he is in release. Apparently he's very interested as I curl my hands around the hard length of him and rub slowly. He doesn't move, just lets my fingers continue wandering while he covers my hand with his and forces my pressure on him a little more.

My feet seem to let my brain know that I want him in my mouth because I'm walking around the front of him and unbuttoning his fly before I'm even aware of it, dropping down onto my knees and grabbing hold of his glorious cock so that I can lick and suck my way around it greedily. His fingers are in my hair, tipping my head up towards him so that he can watch me with his darkened blue eyes while he still talks, or rather argues, into that damned phone. My tongue swirls around him and I feel the first reaction of dominance as he grips my head harder and pushes himself as far down my throat as he can. His breathing hitches a little as his brow furrows, probably at a question he's been asked. I smile around him and continue with my deep sucking, just the way he likes it. Lifting my hand to his balls, I caress them around each other and squeeze a little until I notice his thigh muscles tensing. His cock begins jumping in my mouth so I start dragging my teeth back along him and licking the pre-cum off his head. His low rumble and flexing fingers let me know exactly where he's heading. Add that to the fact that he's now beginning to tremble in my hands and I can't help but tease some more. I withdraw and run my tongue across him until I reach his balls and then flick and tongue my way around them. His sharp tug on my hair lifts me back towards his length as he pushes his way back into my mouth. Jesus, even without talking the man can force me to do what he wants. I take him as deep as I can get him and then swallow, hitting him with the back of my throat and that added pressure.

"Fuck it," comes growling down at me as I see him throwing the phone on the floor so he can lean on the wall in front of him. "Christ, I love watching you do that. Suck me harder, deeper." He grunts while steadily beginning to fuck my mouth. So I do, each delicious mouthful ending at my throat every time I push that bit more to accommodate him. His speed starts to increase as his balls rise in my hand and his movements become more erratic. I'm so hungry for him that I let my teeth engage a little as I increase the suction to taste that warm salty flavour. I'm suddenly desperate for him to come. I want to know that I've given him the release he needed, that I took his turmoil and turned it into something pleasurable for him.

"Fuck baby, take it, swallow," he growls as he stills and then erupts into my mouth. His salt laden cum coats the back of my throat and I keep sucking until the last of it pumps into me. His body recoils as I pull hard one last time to keep his ecstasy going. "Shit, stop. Oh Christ, that's..." he stutters on a shaky breath as he forces his thumb into my mouth to release my hold of him then caresses my jaw with his hand, trying to regain his breathing.

I watch him with a grin of ridiculous proportions and mentally slap myself on the back for a job very well done. His face is slackened and he's got that soft, warm smile going on that tells me he's extremely well sated. Go me!

"Better?" I ask with a giggle as I look into his eyes and see that beautiful smile light up his face.

"You are entirely too good at that," he says, still panting.

"Well I'm glad you liked it," I reply with a wink. "I thought you needed to calm down a little."

"That was a very important phone call. I should spank the living shit out of you for interrupting my discussions," he says as he grips my chin. *Okay.*

"Go on then," I reply as I get up and stretch my legs. This kneeling thing really is hard work. Lord knows how these real submissive women do it all the time.

"What?" He looks incredulous, as if I've shocked the hell out of him.

"Spank me, whatever you want," I say nonchalantly as I clench my thighs in anticipation of what I might get, but he's in a good mood so it'll be fine. I hope.

"Are you goading me, Miss Scott?" And now that damned eyebrow is up, his eyes sparkling mischievously so I narrow mine a little. I may have just given him a bit more permission than I was expecting he'd want.

"Anything to get your mind off work and on me. It is Sunday after all," I reply as I wander towards the door.

"My mind's always on you," he says as he buttons his trousers, saunters across to the desk and closes his laptop.

"Really? It wasn't fifteen minutes ago. I thought we were doing Christmassy things." Apparently I've gone into stupid mode, or at least willing for anything mode.

"I can't believe you're tempting me into this. What do you want, Miss Scott? Are you feeling neglected?" he says as he stares me down with those narrowing eyes. I can almost feel his brain working out some very dastardly plan. Hopefully it will have something to do with a teaspoon.

"Very." And why the hell I've just pushed him further is beyond me but I do like my little moment of empowerment around him so I smile sweetly and put my hands on my hips.

"I can rectify that. Where would you like to start? Are you aching for something?" he asks as he moves toward me, slowly. I suddenly have no idea what's coming.

"Well, now that you mention it, you appear to have gotten off okay." *Idiot, Beth*. This could get a little rough. I brace my feet to the floor and hope the playfulness in his eyes keeps coming, not that I'd mind it rough obviously, but I would like him to stay with me at the very least.

"You're being very demanding, Miss Scott. Perhaps you're ready for something a little more fulfilling. I think maybe it's time to take you back to Eden."

What? That was not expected - forced to the shelves maybe, some kinkiness with a whip or something similar definitely. I'm comfortable with that, obviously, more than comfortable, actually, but Eden? Really? Which of course means Pascal. Does he know I've been thinking about it or is he just pushing me like he said he would?

"Oh…" It's all I've got. It seems I can't even form words.

"Quite." And he's loving my discomfort, an arrogant smile plastered on his face, blue eyes staring straight into me and refusing to let me escape from thoughts of his equally devious friend. Bastard.

"Umm…" My own power seems to have abandoned me at the mere thought. Scared almost to death seems more appropriate at the moment.

"Is that what you want, Miss Scott? Are you ready to play a bit harder?" he says as he rolls his sleeves up and effectively highlights those strong forearms and those hands that are still made for butchery, mine presumably, and now he wants to add another pair to the party.

"Ummmm…" It's still the only pathetic word I have, just a bit longer this time.

"Not quite so forward now? Are you losing your nerve, Miss Scott? You told me you were ready for me." He's stalking closer now. I swear the man could make a jaguar look like an amateur at cat and mouse. I edge backwards a little towards the door, which causes his eyebrow to rise again in challenge. I don't know why I'm bothering because I know he's going to win; he always catches me.

"Yes, I am. It's just I'm not sure how this works and you know I've never done that sort of thing and I'm not entirely sure what you expect me to do with…" I can't even say his name, green eyed monster, assuming that's what he's talking about. Is it? Maybe he didn't mean that and now I've let him know I've been thinking about it and... Oh god, I'm so screwed.

"Expect you to do with what, Elizabeth? Or maybe you mean whom?" I swallow. What the hell do I say to that? "Do tell me what it is that you're assuming here?"

"I... Uh... Well, you said that... You know... And I'm not sure how I feel about any of that yet."

It's ridiculous, I know, but honestly how does one talk about threesomes casually? And frankly, there is nothing casual about either of them, or dare I say it the pair of them together.

"Have you been thinking about it enough? Have you wound yourself up to the thought of his hands on you again? Did it feel good to be at his mercy, Elizabeth?"

And how the sodding hell do I answer that one safely? He might explode at me, or be hurt, or be jealous, but he wouldn't be asking me these things if he didn't want the truth, would he? And this was all his idea, wasn't it? I look to the floor. He doesn't like to share. He told me to think hard about that before he put me in a room with Pascal. I still don't know what that means but I'm pretty sure he'll need to know that he's the most important person in the room. "Is there something interesting on the floor, Elizabeth?" Arsehole.

I'm utterly exasperated with what I'm supposed to say next so my brain eventually gives up and goes with honesty.

"I have no idea what you want me to say, Alex." Because I seriously don't. I have no way of understanding the dynamics of this sort of thing, or the after affects for that matter.

"What do you want to say?" he replies as he moves away from me with a smirk and sits in a chair. He gestures to the other chair so I cross the room and tuck my feet up under me as he continues to amuse himself with my reaction. "Tell me what you find so confusing." Okay, I'm continuing with honesty, I might as well, given the topic.

"I don't want to hurt you, or me, or us," I eventually reply, having gazed at his still amused expression. His head tilts at my response and a frown crosses his features.

"You think that me letting you fuck Pascal will hurt me?"

God, I wish he would be a little more pleasant about it. Mind you, maybe that's the point. To him, sex is simply that - sex. I really need to understand his disconnect with the act in itself, or hopefully his previous disconnect with it.

"Well, yes." Can't he see that? Or is this normal for him? Perhaps it is, given he's never been in love before. My eyes drift to the floor again in complete confusion. I could never allow him to sleep with another woman in front of me so why does he find it acceptable the other way round?

"Do you love him?" My eyes instantly widen as I suck in a breath. Really? Does he think that? Although I ... Do I? No, well maybe I , no.

"God, no." He chuckles and his smirk returns as he reaches out for the decanter of Cognac and pours two glasses.

"Well why do you think it would hurt me then?" he asks as he places one beside me and sips at his own nonchalantly as if this is a perfectly normal conversation. It's not - well, at least not for me. I need some answers.

"You said you didn't like to share. I've seen you jealous. I don't want that again. You're more than enough for me, but you seem to want me to have sex with him and I don't understand it at all because I definitely don't want to see you with another woman. This is not normal relationship behaviour, Alex. Most men wouldn't be okay with this sort of thing at all." His panty-dropping smile is almost enough for me to rip my clothes off and jump on him. His finger moves around the rim of his glass as he licks his lips and gazes across at me.

"I never said I was normal." Well, no. Clearly not, but we are trying for a relationship.

"I know, but this is... I don't know what this is, but I-" He cuts me off with an arrogant chuckle and a wave of his butchering hand.

"You're still thinking too much, Elizabeth. I want to see you pleasured in every way and I'm honest enough to admit to what I am. I want to watch you fall into yourself and experience every sensation available. If I can offer that to you then why would I refuse it you? And I don't want another woman. If I ever do, it will be for your benefit, not mine," he says, crossing his legs. My benefit? Really?

I think not. I'm absolutely not interested in that, but at least I sort of understand his reasoning for Pascal now. What I don't understand is how he can separate his jealousy.

"But he's another man..." Even I think that sounds ridiculous. Clearly he is. I can't even finish the sentence. *Stupid Beth.*

"Obviously, and quite depraved, but nevertheless I trust him. And besides, he won't be the dominant man in the room. He never is."

Right, so here's the crux of it. If I could begin to comprehend what the two of them are to each other then maybe I could find a way to do this comfortably. Are they lovers? He said not but there's definitely something going on. Pascal is in love with him so what does the man actually mean to Alex? Apart from being a mentor and friend, that is, which is just not enough information at all.

"Okay, and that's another thing... What have you two been up to before me and why are you comfortable with this around him but no one else?"

He gazes at me for a moment, his brow furrowing and releasing as if he's trying to work out what to tell me, or maybe how much to tell me. His mouth parts to begin and I swallow at what I might hear. What if I don't like it? Can I accept whatever it is he's about to say? Clearly he's far more experienced than me in the bedroom department, but how far does that go? He once told me he wasn't inclined to behave like a very decent dominant and that it had become restricting. Has Pascal had something to do with that? Made him behave inappropriately somehow? Not that I can ever see Alex doing something he wasn't entirely in control of, and to be honest, I have no idea what a dominant really is. I only know him and how we are together, so is this normal?

His fingers rub slowly across his lips, apparently still deliberating his response, so I pick up my drink again, hide behind it and wait, hoping for complete honesty and partially dreading it.

"Everything, Elizabeth. There isn't a sexual or plausibly decadent act we haven't been up to, as you so gracefully put it. Well, apart from fucking each other that is. We have been extremely corrupt in our adventures, and while I'd like to tell you it's all his fault and I haven't been the instigator, I can't, not in the slightest. I can be just as sadistic in my tendencies as he is, more so really," he replies as he downs his drink and starts tapping his fingers. His stare is relentless as he continues to think. I know I shouldn't talk yet because he's clearly got more to say on the topic, and as my heart continues to thunder along, I can't help but think I'm in way over my head. "I have already tried to tell you what I am because I want you to understand, but some things will not be pleasant to hear so don't ask too many questions unless you're ready for the answers. With regard to how I'll feel about seeing him touch you again, I really don't know. I've never loved a woman before now so feelings have been irrelevant to our games. Pascal has simply been an extension of my preferences and now I want him to be an extension of yours."

Well, fantastic, sadistic tendencies? I suppose I sort of knew that, but when he actually says the words out loud, it's a little more disconcerting. Has he been holding back entirely? And really, what the hell does he want me to do for him in the future? I really can't fathom what else is more sadistic than a whip but I have a feeling the man sitting casually across from me certainly does.

"Oh." And there's that stupid word again. What else can I say? But what if he doesn't like what he sees when Pascal's hands land on me? Will he explode and change his mind? Will it damage us? And do I really even want this, knowing how much they've done together? They're probably more in tune with each other than we are. It's not like I'm a sodding expert in these matters but I think egos could be bruised all round if this happens. The statement I made about them being formidable together suddenly seems overwhelmingly tantalising and completely terrifying. My mind whirls back to the two of them at the chess table when I said it. I should have seen it then when Pascal chuckled at my words. *Stupid Beth.*

"I won't let you tell me you don't want this. I've seen the way you react when he touches you. I've watched the way your body moulds against his, and while you may not love him, you certainly want to feel him on you, don't you?"

I have nothing to answer him with. When has he seen us together? Was he watching at the club that night? No, how could he be? We were in Pascal's apartment... Unless there was a camera. Was there? Is that why I could feel him? Every single piece of logical thought has now disappeared because this whole scenario is absolutely not sensible, or normal even. It has utter devastation written all over it. And what on earth will I be part of anyway? Will they... well, you know... touch each other as well? Because that could be interesting... Or maybe not. I have no idea.

"You told me once that you weren't inclined to behave like a very decent dominant, that it had become restricting for you. What exactly did you mean by that?" Because seriously, I need to understand more about this. Clearly I trust myself in his hands but with Pascal as well? Will it wind him up to new levels I'm not aware of, some merciless bastard that may throw me to the wolves for fun. Unfortunately, his frown and narrowing eyes are doing nothing to help my nerves at my own thoughts. I know that look. It's the one that says he doesn't want to tell me something.

"That was before I loved you," he says quietly, turning his face from me. He's hiding something. Every inch of his cocky appearance has left the building and he looks a little lost all of a sudden.

"Why does that make it any different? You still want the same from me, don't you? And I really need to know what you're asking of me here," I reply, wishing I could turn his eyes back to me. He sighs and fiddles with his glass as he stands and begins pacing. Oh shit, what the hell is he going to tell me now?

"A true dominant gives everything to his sub, cherishes her, looks after her every need, and does everything in his power to ensure she is fulfilled, happy and safe. It's not a chore for him or an obligation of necessity. He wants to do it, needs to even, regardless of the amount of time he has with her. It may be love for some or just a primal urge for others but fundamentally, a truly decent dom treats his lover like a goddess and worships the ground beneath her feet," he says as he shoves his hand in a pocket and looks out of the window with another sigh. "I have not been one of those men, Elizabeth. I've never been known for kindness or decency in any way, and while there are some who've enjoyed what I've offered, many have been left feeling used and humiliated, mostly because I wanted it that way. While it may sound horrifying to you, I told you that I wouldn't lie so I won't. You deserve to know who I've been."

Lovely, just what I wanted to hear from the man I love, the same man who wants to put me in a room with another man and continue to take me further into his self-indulgent lifestyle. I can't even say it surprises me that much. I've seen his temper so I know his not so pleasant side. It's not someone I'd like to be on my knees with. Maybe Pascal does though?

He turns around and offers me a small smile as I gaze across at him and wonder what any of that means to me. He's never been that way with me. He's only ever shown me how to trust him and allow myself to revel in his hold of me. He loves me, has shown me his heart, his tears, his childhood. He's probably given me more than he's ever dared to give anyone so I'm not surprised that I'm not that bothered by his past behaviour. I just need to know how *decent* he'll be with me.

"Are you saying that because we're different you'll treat the situation more compassionately? That it will mean something more than it has done before?" I ask, hoping that his response will ease my tension around the whole situation.

"It will mean everything to me, Elizabeth, because for the first time in my life, I want to worship someone - you. Don't you see that? I want to give you everything you need without thought to myself because I love you. And I'm sure we will find our way through how compassionate you want the situation to be when the time comes."

Oh, right... Well that's a little more relaxing I suppose. I can't stop the girly giggle that escapes me as I gaze at him moving back towards me with a wider smile. He crouches in front of me and runs a finger along my jaw. "Everything will be exactly as you want it, baby. Every single inch of you will be adored, and whatever I think you need will be given in earnest."

Okay, that wasn't quite so girly or lovely. In fact it's got me thinking all sorts of things as his blues bore into mine with something like lust pouring from them. His fingers leisurely travel circles around my thighs and I drop my eyes from his at the very inappropriate vision of Pascal's fingers on the other thigh. Actually, maybe it's not inappropriate any more?

"He said he'd been on his knees for you," I randomly blurt out. I've become so absorbed in thoughts of sex, passion and panic that I apparently no longer care what's coming out of my mouth. His mouth unfortunately twitches in amusement again. I'm so glad he's finding this all so funny. Really, it's positively wonderful to be discussing threesomes with the man I love while he hovers in front of me in all his superiority, looking completely unaffected. The word deviant springs to mind.

"He has, several times. Would you like to watch him there again?" *Sodding eyebrow.* Normal arrogant, self-assured and sexy as hell Alex has returned with a vengeance.

Oh shit, oh shit, oh shit...

I have absolutely no idea. Do I? Possibly. Maybe not, but what would I know? I've never been here before and it's yet another stark reminder of that fact. But the image of Pascal on his knees in front of Alex is now firmly imbedded in my mind. The two of them in all their masculine glory as they reach out to me, fingers stretching and muscles rippling, sweat trickling across their skin, hot breath steaming through a dark room... Oh god, I have to stop these visions if I'm to have any hope of keeping it together.

"Would you? Is it what you want or need?" I ask hesitantly as I try to search his eyes for some kind of emotion that involves Pascal, because that scares the crap out of me if I'm honest.

He stands up abruptly and takes hold of my hand, lifting me up to him, his other hand wrapping around my back and pulling me toward his body. All six foot four of him coaxes me into his hard frame as he tugs the back of my ponytail playfully to make me look up at him.

"I want and need you, Elizabeth. Nothing will change that. Pascal isn't a threat to you in any way. He is just someone that I can use to give you something more entertaining, and thankfully he knows exactly what he's doing," he says smoothly as he threads his hands in my hair and lightly kisses me on the lips. I'm sure I mumble something about him being more than entertaining enough on his own but I'm so lost in his lips that I can't even remember what I was thinking. "So anyway, what do you think of the decorations?" he says as he releases me and wanders off in the direction of the kitchen. His hands nonchalantly placed in his pockets leave me feeling even more confused than I was at the beginning of the conversation. Well that isn't strictly true, but I still have no idea how I feel about the whole idea. I suppose I'll just have to wing it when it happens. I can always use my safeword, can't I? Because that will stop them, won't it?

~

Monday afternoon has been utterly crazy. In fact the whole day has been bonkers if I'm honest. Having been dropped off at work, I proceeded to crank up the music and dance stupidly while I made the lunches for two different hotels, both prepped and ready to go for eleven. James arrived, flirted outrageously with me, actually asked me out on a date again, which was damned awkward and then left with a smile. I get the feeling he won't be giving up in a hurry. It seems his run-in with Alex has made him up his game. Interestingly, his more assertive manner is far more appealing than his former self. I have definitely become a slave to this dominant nature that some men seem to possess. It makes me wonder whether all men are capable of it if they just delve a little deeper and latch onto their base instincts. Bless him, he reminded me of a teenager in full-on horny mode, nowhere near as aggressive as Alex in his nature but he was definitely giving it a go.

Anyway, after he disappeared with his truck full of beef for the Daresbury Hotel, and I'd sent the other van full of chicken on its merry way to the Rochester Hotel, I thought I'd have a quieter afternoon, but no. Why would the world of pastry be nice to me in the slightest. The right honourable lady something of something called Belle at twelve-thirty to ask if there was any way we could provide catering for her afternoon tea party at four thirty because their usual company had let them down. Belle zipped in the kitchen, handed me a note and rolled her sleeves up, shouting, "Five fucking thousand pounds for some sandwiches and cupcakes. Can we do it? Yes we can." Thanks, Belle. We have had a giggle though.

Tonight we're going to have a bottle of wine and talk about weddings. Teresa's staying over and I've decided I should probably tell them about the building I've acquired from my loving man. Yes, the one who wants to watch me getting it on with another man, the same one who tried to lure me away from him. Well, we were on a break but that's not the point. I wonder if I should talk to Pascal about all of this. Alex probably wouldn't like that, would he? No, not. *Stupid Beth.*

Where is he today anyway? It's nearly five. He said he had meetings all day and then was going to a charity boxing match this evening. That's one I'm glad I'm not going to. Fighting for defence is one thing, but fighting for pleasure is entirely different. I just can't get my head around the thought of men actually enjoying beating each other for amusement. Why would someone want to hurt someone for fun or sport as they call it? What sort of sick mind enjoys pummelling a man until he's almost passed out? It reminds me a little of Alex beating up that arsehole that tried to rape me. Clearly that was defensive, but regardless, something about his demeanour after the event left me feeling cold, uncomfortable somehow, as if on some unconscious level he'd actually enjoyed his fury a little too much. Weird. Conner's going, too. Belle is not quite as disturbed by it as I am but she turned down the invitation to go with him, declaring getting pissed with her little sister as a far more appealing evening. She's right because honestly, there is so much shit swirling around in my head that I'm struggling to breathe sometimes. Alex, Mum, Pascal, buildings, Belle and Conner, Teresa and Pascal - oh, I'd forgotten about that one - Evelyn and new found family, which leads me back to Alex again because, yes, he's there quite often. That also reminds me to ask him about Henry because he hasn't said anything about what's going on with his business lately. Add into that the constant menu of meals and delicacies that I need to prepare, manage and pull together on a daily basis and I'm feeling utterly exhausted. I can't remember the last time I just sat still for a few days and relaxed without this constant need to analyse or over think everything.

A holiday - that's what I need and soon. I wander over to the doors and pull the sign across as the girls file towards the door, giggling and laughing like teenagers as Teresa gazes at Belle's ring finger whimsically. She's a hopeless romantic, bless her.

"So what's the first topic of conversation this evening?" she says as she pulls the shutters and I lock up.

"Well, clearly more about wedding proposals and lovely things like that," Teresa replies. I can't stop smiling as I watch Belle grin back at her.

"I've got a bit of news as well, if you're both interested." Their heads shoot to mine and then straight to my fingers. "Oh god no, not that. I think one wedding is quite enough," I say as we begin to walk towards the tube.

"Right, well what is it then? Oh fuck, you're not pregnant, are you?" Belle asks with a look of horror splashed across her face. I'm not sure if I should be offended or not so I just continue walking and fiddling with my bracelet.

"That is still the most beautiful piece of jewellery I have ever seen," Teresa says as she grabs my hand and gawps. "Other than the rock on Belle's finger, obviously. I seriously need to get myself a man of calibre."

"You'd love the choker then," I reply casually as I giggle at her shocked face.

"What fucking choker? You never said anything about a choker," Belle interjects. "Why have I not seen a diamond choker? That's absolutely unacceptable, Snotbag."

"Quite right, you tell her. Christ, the man's got too much money for his own good."

Well wait till they hear the next bit then.

"Anyway, do you want to hear my news or not?" I ask, still pondering how uncomfortable I'm about to feel. It definitely isn't sitting well with me yet, regardless of my proving my love to him, and his throat and that little boy standing on the stairs.

"Okay, hit us with it," Belle says as she links arms with me and looks at her finger again.

Right, here we go.

"Alex gave me a building, a big one. I signed the paperwork on Saturday. We're moving Scott's." It's more of a fast ramble than a proper sentence I'm so desperate to get it out of my mouth. It sounds even more bizarre out there in the open. Both girls stop and shoot their faces to mine.

"A building? He gave you a shitting building? What sort of present is a fucking building?" Belle screams in the middle of the high street.

"A damned expensive one, I'd say. Where is it?" Teresa asks with a wicked, dreamy grin plastering her face as she twiddles with her hair. I don't think I've ever seen it before so I can't quite categorise it.

"Defoe Point," is all I've got. I don't remember the address.

"Oh holy mother of God, do you know how much stuff is worth up there?" Belle shouts.

"No, and I absolutely don't want to," I reply as I glance around the street. "Can you please keep it down? I feel strange enough about this already without the rest of the world knowing."

"But, Beth, honey, you're probably a millionairess now. You do realise that, don't you? Possibly twice over. I mean, I haven't seen the place, but Juliana sold her one bedroom flat for four hundred thousand," Teresa whispers conspiratorially as she nudges Belle and ushers us to the underground.

"I said I didn't want to know, and anyway, it doesn't matter because I'm not selling it so we better get planning a move," I reply as I try for casual and walk blindly to the tube that's waiting.

"But why did he give you a fucking building?" Belle eventually says. Her look is absolutely priceless.

"To realize her dreams, silly. God, for a smart woman, you're so stupid sometimes. That's what a man in love does for the woman he needs," comes rushing out of Teresa's mouth - ever the romantic. I can't help but grin at the statement, though, because it's absolutely right even if I can't give them the reasons. Belle looks between the two of us as if she has no clue why this is happening. To be fair, I'm still not entirely sure, but he has his reasons and they're not reasons I can share with her.

"Right, okay... Well we need to get organised then," she eventually says with narrowed eyes. "When can we see it?" Business Belle has apparently reappeared. I smile at her and get on the train.

"As soon as you want. I've got the keys. But first I need a chat and a good girly catch up over a bottle of wine or three."

Preferably with no drama.

And no fights.

And no discussions of threesomes, or Pascal.

And nothing at all to do with death or illness.

Maybe I need a couple of days completely on my own.

Chapter 20

Elizabeth

I haven't got a clue how it's happened but it's suddenly Thursday. I've been almost killing myself trying to get everything together for various parties and special seasonal luncheons across London. Cleverly, Belle hasn't even entertained the idea of doing anything outside of the city centre for the entirety of the festive season so I've been ensconced in my kitchen from five am until eight most evenings, desperately trying to hold the whole thing together. The very first thing we're doing when we move to the new premises is hiring another chef. I've been toying with the idea of asking James to come on board full time with me, but I just can't quite work out whether it's a sensible move or not. I mean yes, the guy is an amazing chef, but with this thing hanging around us, I'm not convinced that it's the smartest thing to do and I'm positive Alex will not be in agreement at all.

I did at least manage to get my Christmas shopping done online last night. While I went to Alex's on Tuesday after work, I knew I would be starting early this morning so I stayed at home with Belle and tried to buy everyone's presents in one fell swoop. Clearly that wasn't possible because I still haven't managed to find anything that someone like Mr. Wonderful could need or want. What the hell do you buy someone like Alex White for God's sake? All the other presents are done and dusted, of course. I don't even know why I thought I would manage his online. It was never going to happen, was it? And to be honest, I want it to be more personal than that anyway.

It's now ten past five and I've got half an hour to get the rest of the kitchen sorted and then a further twenty minutes to do something with myself before Andrews picks me up. I don't know why he's picking me up because Alex wouldn't tell me. He just sent me a text last night to tell me to be ready by seven and to wear something short. I have assumed he meant sexy and not lie on a beach and suntan yourself short, which means we're going somewhere swanky. It'll probably be a club so it's a sodding good job we have a shower here so that I can wipe the afternoon's food prep off of me and revitalise to some degree. It's also a good job I have a day off booked.

"So I called Pascal." My head whips round to see Teresa narrowing her eyes at me. "Ha, I knew it. You don't like it, do you?" she says with a smug smile. My hand stops its maniacal wiping to try and fathom what the hell she's talking about, and then I realise that the pit of my stomach is telling me that she's right. For some utterly bizarre reason, she's absolutely right. I don't like it at all.

"What on earth are you talking about? Why would I not like you calling Pascal? I'm just a little concerned, that's all. It's your health risk, not mine," I reply, trying very hard to extinguish the jealous little bite of something that's going on down below because it's just stupid. She raises a brow and keeps staring. It's very her, far too bloody astute about emotions of every kind. I plaster on my *you go girl* face in the hope that she believes me.

"Well, that's good then because I'm meeting him on Sunday. Given that I have Mondays off, it seemed the best night all round. I daresay I'll need recovery time," she says with her naughty little smile as she wiggles her hips and smacks her own arse. I can't help but burst out laughing.

"I think you'll be getting more than a light smack on the backside, Teresa, but if you're game I'm sure he will be."

And I'm still trying to contain my irritation at the thought. Why the hell would this bother me? She's lovely and he needs someone just like her, doesn't he? But he won't, will he? Want her, that is. Okay yes, in the sexual sense, but not in the mate for life sense. He'll just use her and then dismiss her, and why I'm jealous of that is anyone's guess. Perhaps I'm not. Perhaps it's just concern.

"Listen, honey, just don't go falling for him, will you? I don't think he's the settling down type and I don't want to see you hurt or injured."

"Don't be bloody stupid. One night, Beth, that is what the man's made for and that's exactly what I'm going to get from him," she says as she wiggles off with a silly grin. I get back to my wiping with more venom than I had a few moments ago. Clearly I need to have a think about this at some point because I have no right to feel jealousy of any kind, especially about my friend having a good time with someone like Pascal. Maybe I should call him and tell him to back off or tell her he's changed his mind, or maybe not. What right do I have to tell Pascal what to do? None, and I'm sure he'll let me know that in his very aristocratic way. *Stupid Beth.*

Amazingly, I'm ready on time. Teresa's already left and I'm just about to make my way outside in my short, brown, suede dress and Belle's cream coat when I notice a thick brown envelope on the counter top so I swipe it up and put it in my bag. Belle must have left it there or something and I hate leaving anything hanging around that might be important. It's unlike her but she's been a bit dappy since her engagement. So now I'm waiting on the side of the road for Andrews to appear and surprisingly he's late. I'm not entirely sure I'm happy about that. He's normally so punctual. I hope nothing's happened to him. Ten minutes later and I'm still waiting and wondering whether I should call Alex because this is not usual at all. What if something has happened? I pull my phone out and notice I've missed a text at some point from an unknown number. Maybe its Andrews letting me know he'll be late.

> **- You need to look at the photos. He's not who you think he is.**

What the hell? What photos? And who isn't who I think he is?

This has to be a wrong number or something equally odd because I haven't got clue what any of it means. A screech of tyres makes me jump so I lift my head from the phone to see what the noise is then laugh. Andrews is almost flying along the road in the Bentley, clearly annoyed at himself for being late, so I stuff my phone back in my pocket and walk to the kerb. A very efficient Andrews jumps out with a scowl and opens the door for me.

"Michael, this door opening really isn't necessary," I giggle as he pushes me in a little forcefully. "Umm, any reason you're pushing me?"

"Sorry, just bear with me for a minute, will you?" he says tersely as he hits the accelerator and sends me reeling backwards in the car. "Seatbelt," he shouts as he floors it again.

"Okay," I reply as I strap myself in and try to work out why he's travelling so fast. "Are we late or something? Well clearly we are, but why are you going so fast? I'm sure Alex would rather me alive than-"

"Was everything okay in the shop?" he clips as he scans the road.

"Yes, why?" At the quick left-hand turn, I grab onto the handle and try to keep my dress from riding up to my crotch. Always elegant.

"Nothing unusual? Suspect?" MI5 agent has clearly arrived.

"No. Well, Belle left an envelope out but she's been a bit all over the place since Conner and..."

More acceleration ensues as he floors it again to the right. Shit, the sedate Bentley can move, it seems. I hang onto my dress a bit more. Suede on leather seats does not appear to mix in the slightest.

"What's it like? Size? Description?" Oh for God's sake, apparently we're on a covert operation of some sort.

"Umm, brown, A4 size, you know like, an envelope?" I'm rolling my eyes at him now while I'm trying to hang on. What other sort of envelope is there? Well, I suppose there are white ones, too, but what does that matter?

"Where is it?" The car comes to sudden halt and he turns and glares at me. It's quite scary. I haven't seen it in him for a while.

"In my bag. Why?" I reply, completely confused as to why he would want Belle's stuff.

"Give it to me. Have you looked inside it?" he demands as he continues his glare and beckons his hand at me.

"No, not yet. Look, Michael, what's going on? I'm not giving you Belle's stuff. It's nothing to do with-"

"Now, Elizabeth!" Oh shit, that was loud. I flinch instantly and dig into my bag for the offending item and pass it over to him. He nods, rips it open and does a quick scan in his lap so I can't see. Bastard. "Hold on again," he says a little more quietly as he accelerates back into the road again and appears to begin searching for something again so I just hang on and keep quiet because I seriously don't like angry Michael. He's very frightening. Why is everyone in Alex's world not normal?

I hear the phone link in as he dials someone.

368

"Andrews?" Oh, that lovely, velvety smooth voice comes drifting into the car and I feel at peace all of a sudden, and a little horny if I'm honest.

"Sir, we'll be late. I've got a situation that I'm following up on," Andrews clips.

"What situation?" Alex asks. His voice has suddenly become all businesslike and very demanding. I can almost feel his suspicious eyes coming at me so of course my core clenches, hard. It's completely ridiculous but I can't help it so I close my eyes and revel in it.

"Someone was in Miss Scott's shop and I'm trying to locate him. It seems he left a package." My eyes fly open.

What? That is... What the hell?

"What do you mean someone was in my shop?" I practically scream at him. While I was in it? In the bloody shower? But the door was locked, wasn't it? How could someone get in? Andrews ignores me and keeps scanning every incoming street.

"Get her here now. You can go back out." Alex is clearly pissed now. I can feel the fury bubbling off him as his voice lowers and turns gravelly, utterly hypnotising. I so shouldn't be thinking about sex again.

"Yes, Sir," Andrews replies in a quiet voice as he continues staring at the streets. I'm not entirely sure he's listening to anyone. He seems entirely focused on finding my burglar come thief come whatever the hell he was.

"Michael, how do you know someone was in my shop?" I ask with narrowed eyes as I once again grab onto the centre console as he throws the car around a corner towards the back streets.

"When I pulled up he was running out. I went in and saw you were safe in the shower so came back out to see if I could find him," he says, all matter of fact. He saw me in the bloody shower? Did the other guy? Alex's growl does nothing to hide his irritation at the image that is now floating through his mind. I have a feeling Michael will be getting an earful at some point.

"Just get her here, ten fucking minutes ago, Andrews," Alex seethes quietly. That's definitely not good. Quiet means thoughtful, or not thoughtful at all, both of which are bad.

"Yes, Sir. We're about fifteen minutes away," Andrews replies. The line goes dead. I'm not sure who ended the call but I'm assuming it wasn't the man in the front.

I sit and wonder why someone was in my shop, and more importantly, I wonder what it is that's in that envelope. It suddenly reminds me of the text message. Are there photos in that envelope? And if so, of who? I stare at the back of Andrews' head and ponder asking him to let me have it back. It seems he thinks it's none of my business but it is, isn't it, because it was left in my shop, for me to see.

"Michael, what's in the envelope?" I ask as sweetly as I can in the hope of influencing his calmer side.

"Nothing for you to be worried about," he replies brusquely as he begins to drive a little more calmly.

"Well, sweet as that is, it was left for me so I'd like to see what's inside," I say in a more authoritative tone, because his *bless her little cotton socks* attitude is irritating as hell. "And I'm now assuming it has something to do with a text I received, so tell me or show me please."

"What text?"

"It told me I needed to look at the photos and that he wasn't who I thought he was. Now, I have no idea what that means but I'm beginning to assume that there are some photos in that envelope of something I should be aware of for some reason." I am met with silence. It's not helpful.

"Michael, what's in the envelope?" Still nothing, and now I'm officially pissed off. In fact I'm acting just like Alex would. I can almost feel him rumbling around in me. "Stop being fucking awkward, Michael, and tell me," I snarl. It's actually quite impressive for me. The shit raises the privacy screen and effectively ends the conversation. Arsehole.

Ten minutes later and we're pulling up outside a tube station that I've never heard of - Chatsteel Avenue. I'm completely clueless. Why we'd be at an underground station is mystifying. I'm still irritated enough with Andrews to not want to talk to him so I wait for him to open the door and then glare as best I can. Unfortunately, his MI5 agent mask is firmly in place so I'm not convinced my hatred has had any effect at all. He gestures his hand to the steps and nods in the direction of the locked gate at the bottom of them. My curiosity is on high alert but I'm still refusing to say anything to him as I descend the stairs and come to a halt in front of the battered old gate.

"You have a key on your key ring," he says. I do? Really? Unlikely, but I dig them out anyway and fiddle with them until I find a key I've never seen before alongside Alex's. I unlock the gate and walk through, expecting him to follow me but he shuts it behind me and I hear the lock click back into place.

"What are you doing?" I ask a little nervously as I glance around the darkened area and wrap my coat around me.

"He'll meet you down there. Just keep walking and follow the music, Elizabeth," he says as he nods his head again in the direction of the dark tunnel in front of me. I'm not at all happy but if Alex is down there then I'm sure everything is reasonably normal. He doesn't retreat, just stands there waiting for me to move, presumably to make sure I'm safe or something. How the fuck he would know, given that I'm about to walk into the pitch black, is confusing to say the least. Still, I turn on my too tall heels and stride away from him in what I hope is a display of superiority because I will not back down from my irritation with the man. Who the hell does he think he is, not allowing me to see my own things? I'm having severe words with Alex about this, as soon as I find him, that is.

Oh shit, it's dark. I seriously can't see a thing as I clip my way along the tunnel and listen for anything that will give a glimmer of a clue as to where I'm going. There's nothing to indicate a direction or a source of light so I keep following my instincts in the blind hope that they'll lead me the right way while running my hands over the brick walls. Eventually, I hear the tell-tale echo of footsteps and then the dull thud of music coming from somewhere in front of me. My relief at hearing something is so overwhelming that I realise I'm smiling for the first time in the last hour, so I pick up my pace and continue forward.

Heat starts to seep into my bones as I pass a small row of candles on my right in the shape of an arrow, pointing me in another direction. I turn that way and shrug out of my coat. The thud of a bass line is getting progressively louder, which causes me to move in time to the beat of it. I find myself swinging my hips as I hopefully glide along, now looking completely in control of who I am and where I'm going. I'm not, obviously, but I can't help but feel increasingly more empowered by the seemingly corrupt nature of the passage that I'm allowed into. My irritation with Andrews is slowly disappearing as my thoughts drift to quite captivating images of strange dungeons and a certain tall and dominant man. I have to give it to him; he certainly knows how to evoke a sex driven atmosphere wherever he leads me.

Lanterns are now lined strategically along the sides of the wall, highlighting the way forward and thankfully indicating an end to this mystery at some point. Small doorways draped with dark green velvet are off to the sides and random gold name plaques are embedded in the floor beneath my feet as I walk over them. I'm not sure what they mean but a few of the surnames seem familiar somehow.

I fluff up my hair in the hope that I'll be seeing Alex soon and run some more lip-gloss over my lips as I catch the dim sound of laughter and glasses clinking in front of me. Clearly I'm nearly there and thank god, because if I swing my hips anymore, they might fall off or something. It's an undeniably sexy and soul grinding entrance to a venue. All I want to do is dance my backside off and fall into this hedonistic mood with abandon. Two men soon come into view, standing side by side in front of another gate. They're big - like wrestler style big. I suddenly feel very small but this hip swinging is not going away anytime soon so I glide towards them and put on my award winning, Belle style smile.

"Your key, ma'am?" big oaf one says in an American accent. Key? What key? Does he mean the gate key? I pull them out and pass them to him. He swipes them over a blue pad on the wall and the gate clicks open. Okay, so I'm officially a member of some underground club that the mere mortals of the world know nothing about, which could be a little scary if I thought about it too much.

"Name?" Big oaf two says, as he scans me up and down lecherously. I narrow my eyes at him because I am a *feisty little thing,* am I not? Who the hell does big oaf think he's looking at. I am Elizabeth Scott, girlfriend of Alexander White and owner of my own company. It seems a little of my anger is still firmly rooted because my own authority knows no bounds as I land my hand on my hip and curl my lip at him. I quite like my snarl. It's new for me but does appear to get results.

"Her name is mine and not for you to hear. Let her through, Wade." Alex's voice comes drifting around the corner as I see his dastardly hand reach through the gate for me. Both men instantly step aside so I walk towards the gate and clasp onto those fingers, which immediately twirl me in toward him so I hit his chest with an oomph. "Good evening," he says to me as he clasps the back of my neck.

"Hi," I reply, relishing in his hold of me as I gaze into his icy blues. I don't even know what he's wearing because his mouth is mesmerising me towards it as he licks his lips and broadens his ravishing smile.

"I could smell you coming, baby, hear your footsteps, your legs lengthening as you got closer to me, sense your beauty before I could even see you," he says as he dips his head to mine and licks along the seam of my lips smoothly. My mouth parts to give him access but he pulls away and gazes down at me. "Still so perfect."

"Well that's a lot of lovely things to say," I reply, even though I'm not entirely sure what I'm supposed to say to someone saying they can smell me. But the rest of it was truly lovely, and really I couldn't ask for a more stunning man to be saying it to me.

"Mmm, I'm sure I'll find more things to say later, which will probably not be quite so lovely," he says as he trails his fingers along my thigh and reaches in between us. My eyebrow shoots up, not at the thought of what he's doing but the fact is there are people everywhere. I try to move backwards, and he chuckles and tightens his hold. "Are you refusing me?"

"Well, yes. Much as the thought is appealing, we seem to have company," I reply as a gaze around at the small space. It's full of people - very expensive looking people - all sipping champagne and laughing with each other. Every woman is made up to the nines with designer clothes and each man is in a suit of some description. Brick walls line the room and a long bar is across the far side, also filled with people. There appears to be another gate at the right of the room, which has ornate gilding all around it. Smoke and low, slow bass rhythms swirl around the room, creating a strange sense of dirty luxury, which of course sends my mind reeling with undisclosed thoughts regarding where we are and what's going on.

"Where are we?" I ask as I bring my eyes back to his. His deviant smile is firmly set in place.

"It's a secret, a place for the privileged few who have the right to be here," he replies as he grabs my hand and leads us across to the bar.

"Okay, and how did you earn the right to be here? What's it called, and shit, is that the Chancellor of the Exchequer?" I ask as I halt, seeing exactly who I thought I'd seen with his hand leisurely groping the arse of another man. He's married, to a woman. It's all very odd.

"I'm not at liberty to say, and neither are you," he says sternly as he nudges me forward again. "You do understand the concept of secrets, I assume?"

"Of course, but... wow. Am I not allowed to ask any questions at all?" He chuckles again as the waiter passes him a Cognac and me a glass of champagne. I'm pretty sure I would have preferred a brandy, or three, because as I scan around, I notice more and more people of a very high profile, all nodding at me and raising their glasses as if they're happy to have me in their strange secret society. I smile back in the hope of appearing cool and collected, but Christ, I have never been in a room full of so many important people. I'm talking about the people who run our country, and the people who pump the money in behind them.

"You can ask all the questions you like, but I would suggest you make them the right ones," he replies, looking up at a clock and turning off his phone. He's turning off his phone?

"How do I know what are the right questions?" I ask as I realise everyone else is also turning off their phones and starting to whisper to each other. Something is definitely going on. He smiles lovingly at me and tucks my hair behind my ear. "Do I need to turn my phone off, too?"

"Good idea," he says as a small woman sashays by us with a smile and heads towards the opposite wall. I can't help but watch her as the room seems to part to allow her access to her destination, which is a large brass disk on the wall. She lifts her hand and the room falls silent as she picks up a stick and bangs it against the disk. A loud booming noise radiates around us and the room turns to face her.

"Ladies and gentlemen, Madam is happy to have your company this evening and hopes you will enjoy your time with us. Please follow all the rules of engagement and make your way through to the auditorium so we can begin," she says as she gestures her hand out to the gilded gate beside her.

Rules of engagement? Where on earth am I? Are we going to fight or something? Because I'm pretty sure this dress wasn't made for skirmishes of any sort - well, maybe the sexual sort. Oh shit, is that what she means? My eyes shoot to Alex's. That bloody brow rises as his smirk ignites.

"I hope you're not feeling shy, Elizabeth," he says as he puts his hand on my back and pushes me toward the gate. I plant my feet. I am not engaging in anything with anyone but him, and I'm not doing that in front of anyone else either. He links his fingers into mine and kisses the back of my hand. "It's alright. You really don't have to participate if you don't want to. We have the means to avoid it."

Oh, okay then... I think. He pulls me forward with our joined hands toward those now ominous looking golden gates and rubs his finger back and forth across mine, probably trying to lull me into calmness of some sort. I'm not calm. I can't even begin to imagine what I'm about to see through the other side of this gate.

As we reach it, Alex raises his hand and puts it on a white pedestal, which appears to scan his hand and then beeps quietly, showing the number one hundred and twenty seven on the wall in front of him. He indicates for me to do the same. I have no idea why because it definitely won't recognise my fingerprints but I gingerly place my hand down. Apparently it does know who I am because it beeps then shows the number fifteen so Alex tugs me forward again. Fifteen is my number, it seems.

"And it knew my handprint how?" I ask with narrowed eyes at the devil in front of me.

"Andrews is quite resourceful," is his reply. So now I have visions of the bastard dusting my prints around the house. MI5 shitbag.

"I'm not happy with that man. He disrespected me," I say, quietly seething at the reminder. He squeezes my hand and ducks his head under a low beam as we wander along a long thin tunnel and I gaze at his very appealing back view and hold on tight.

"The last thing Michael would do is disrespect you. He was simply doing his job, Elizabeth, which was to protect you," he replies.

"But you don't know-"

He cuts me off. "Yes, I do, and we'll talk about it later but for now, shut up, unless it's to say something nice about my backside." Okay, how he knew I was looking is beyond me.

"I'm quite happy to say something nice about yours, sweetcheeks," comes chortling from behind me. I swing my head around to see a very attractive blond man staring directly at my arse.

"Because that is a seriously nice piece of ass." I'm not sure if I should be offended or flattered, but Alex's immediate stiffening hand causes me to wince a bit in reply.

"I would suggest you keep your opinions inside your head, Toby. Life can be short for those who don't use their mouths wisely," he says as he keeps walking forward. I snigger at the comment and follow on to God knows where.

Eventually we come out of the tunnel into a large, dome shaped room. Half of it is sectioned off into private seating areas or rooms of sorts, which are stepped up the side of the space like opera boxes, and at the front there appears to be a stage of some sort. The woman who banged the gong is already standing in the middle of it with a microphone headset on and what looks like a gavel in her hand while people begin to find their seating areas. Alex tugs on my hand and leads us to the third row up and along a corridor, towards the centre of the dome. What on earth I'm about to see is still utterly perplexing, but I suppose I did tell him I was ready for whatever he had. It seems I'm about to find about a bit more about Mr. White's preferences.

He ushers me into a door and we find ourselves in a small, black, three-sided room with two large, red leather chairs facing the stage - very cosy. He takes my coat and gestures to a chair so I sit and cross my legs. The door opens behind us and a waiter delivers a bottle of Cognac and two glasses before whispering something in Alex's ear and then leaving. It's all very secretive and I'm inwardly becoming very excited about what's going to happen in this new little world of his, so I take a large gulp of alcohol.

"What did the waiter say?" I ask as casually as I can manage.

"He told me bidding starts at twenty this evening," he replies with a smirk.

"Bidding for what?"

"You'll see."

The room in front of us goes dark apart from a spotlight on the woman and then a panel comes up in between us with a handprint scanner and a keypad of numbers. Alex immediately puts his hand over it and keys in some numbers. I assume it's some sort of security thing or something else required of this secret society.

"Ladies and gentlemen, thirty-four is starting proceedings this evening so when you're ready, please begin," the woman says as she moves to the side of the stage and presses a button. I have a number - fifteen. What the hell does that mean and what is number thirty-four starting?

The stage floor opens up and the biggest circular bed I've ever seen in my life rises up from beneath it. It is becoming apparent that this definitely to do with sex.

"Did you like the look of anyone in the room?" Alex asks as he gazes over at me with a chuckle and slightly darkening blue eyes.

"Oh my god, are you serious? What is going on here exactly?"

"We pay to get someone on that stage. If they want to, they'll do it. If they don't, they'll try to outbid us for their freedom. They have two minutes to make their decision. It's all about how much money we've got and who else is on the stage to play with," he says with a wink. "I'm expecting to be quite a bit poorer by the end of this."

"Umm…" Yes, I know it's pathetic but really, what does one say to something like that? They're playing with money to watch sex or force someone into it? There's something not quite right about it at all. Has Alex been on that stage? And shit, what if someone bids for him? Or me?

"Elizabeth, we're all big boys and girls. Everybody who is here is well aware of what's going on," he says as he grabs my hand and sips his drink. Right, yes, of course they are. Apart from me, that is. Well I wasn't. I'm now acutely aware of the live sex show come auction that is about to begin.

A very tall and very beautiful naked, blonde haired woman walks into the middle of the stage and crawls onto the bed then proceeds to put her hands between her legs. I absolutely can't stop the gasp of shock or the undeniable core clench that hits me like a tonne of sodding bricks. Alex chuckles again, takes my hand firmly and rests it on the scanner.

"Give me a number," he says with a very mischievous little smile. "Any number will do. It's just to get you used to it."

"Forty-five," I reply with a small giggle because I have no clue what I'm doing or what number forty-five looks like. He punches the number in and the scanner lights up beneath my fingers. Almost immediately, a small shock passes back through my fingers and I try to move my hand away but he keeps it there.

"He just told you to fuck off and countered with another twenty. If you want to see him, you'll have to bid again and take your chance. The next shock will be a little stronger," he says with a chuckle. Meanwhile, two men have now walked onto the stage completely naked and are beginning to get very involved with the woman.

"I assume they agreed to their bids then," I say as I watch them in sheer fascination as they begin to move her around the bed and work their mouths all over her. She happily lets them move her around until one is at her mouth and the other is at her ankle.

"Clearly they were happy to engage," he replies as another woman walks onto the stage. "And so is she. Now what are you going to do about your man? Will you let him beat you or do you want to watch him fuck someone tonight?"

Holy shit, this is so not what I thought it was going to be. Watch a live sex show, bid someone to join in, get a shock if they refuse, and get horny at the same time while sitting here next to God's gift to the female species. I assume I'm bidding with Alex's money here so maybe he should make the decision. I don't even know what the man looks like. He might have three eyes for all I know.

Said sex show is now in full swing and I realise that I'm leaning forward in my seat to get a better view. Presently, one of the women is giving a blowjob and the other is spread on her back as the other man gyrates on top of her and sucks her breasts. It's the most stimulating thing I've ever seen and my panties are already starting their combusting thing.

"Elizabeth, you're running out of time," Alex says as he taps the panel to show me a countdown timer that is currently at thirty-eight seconds.

"What does he look like?" I reply without removing my stare from the bed and tilting my head a little. I should possibly be embarrassed by my interest but let's be honest, it's Alex sitting beside me, and he bought me here so clearly he wants me fascinated by it.

"You're being picky about how attractive he is?"

"Yep, isn't that the point?" I'm suddenly very into this, a game of sex, with high stakes and a very appealing view. I thought I wasn't a gambler but it seems I am because random statistics begin tumbling around my head like nobody's business as I continue to watch the show and wonder what's coming next.

"No, not always. Sometimes it's just about control. However, he's six foot ish, brown eyes and not in bad shape, I suppose." He sounds okay. Dull, but not disgusting at least.

"Hit it then." He punches in the number again and I tense to wait for the shock. Nothing happens, thank god, but suddenly a number fifteen appears on the panel.

"It appears you're in demand, Miss Scott. Are you going on stage?" *Shit, shitty shit.*

"Absolutely not," I reply instantly. "What do I do?" He chuckles at me and strokes my cheek.

"Hit slash fifteen. It'll send a shock." Good one, I can do that, so I do. Suddenly I'm shocked back. Apparently my man isn't playing ball. It really sodding hurt that time as well. Fifteen flashes again. Arsehole apparently isn't giving in either, so I hit slash fifteen again and look across at Alex for some sort of guidance. It is his money after all. He's sitting there looking all captivating and gorgeous in a relaxed fashion with a shit-eating grin on his face as if he knew I'd enjoy this. He's right. I do.

"How much am I worth to you?" I ask nervously, because I'll hit those buttons all night to avoid that stage if it's left up to me.

"You assume I don't want you down there," he says with that eyebrow. Is he suggesting that he does? I swallow the bubble of fear that suddenly grips me. Thankfully, after a few seconds of deadpan staring, he smirks. "Just play your game, baby," he says as he lifts his drink and gazes across at me. I immediately punch in forty-five again and wait.

The lure of the sex show pulls me back and I lean forward again to see at least ten people now, all in varying positions, men on men, women on men, women and other women on men. It's a whole lot of fucking and gang banging and I can't even deny that there isn't a small part of me that wants to be on that stage with them, losing myself in the hectic frenzy of love making and brazen acts going on in that bed. It's very tempting if I'm honest. I look back at Alex to see him still watching me intently, his increasingly darkening blue eyes staring back at me. The next shock that hits me has me jumping out of my seat. Alex laughs and gestures for me to sit on his lap, so I do and put my hand back down, actually pretty pissed off at the pain that has just been delivered. Fifteen flashes again and then again, and then again. Oh shit, does that mean three people are bidding for me now?

I punch in slash fifteen three times and then hit forty-five again. I will have my man on that stage. I will beat him, and I absolutely won't be going down there myself. My inner slut is telling me I'm a moron but I'm trying not to listen to her as Alex begins stroking my inner thigh.

"I want to fuck you very badly at the moment." And oh yes, that's exactly what my inner slut wants to hear, only I can't concentrate because the number fifteen keeps sodding flashing. Thankfully, I haven't received another shock at least. Does that mean my man's going out? I look down at the counter, which is on three seconds, two seconds, one second.

"Yes," I scream out in triumph at beating the bastard as Alex chortles away behind me and pushes my legs apart further.

"Do you think you can keep going under pressure, Elizabeth?" he asks as he manoeuvres me about on top of him. I hear the zip of his fly and turn my head to face him. "I want you to watch while I fuck you, and I want you to keep playing at the same time."

That probably isn't possible if I'm honest, but hey, I'll give it a go. At least I only have to keep hitting slash fifteen now. His fingers make their way up my thighs to my very eager core and begin to slide their way around me. My head instantly falls back on his shoulder as I let that feeling take hold of me and start the climax that is inevitable. He pushes it back up so I'm watching again.

"Concentrate, Elizabeth. I need you to learn how to deal with all this. Control yourself, watch them fucking each other, keep your mind on the game and command your own body," he rasps out into my neck as he circles his fingers and then pushes them inside me. Oh god, I've never been so turned on in my life. There are at least twenty couples now, doing just about anything to each other on that stage and much as I try to clear my mind of his fingers, the feeling is overwhelming.

I notice a man walking onto the stage from the corner of my eye so I focus on him. I think he's mine. He's about six foot and reasonably cute in a sensible sort of way. He looks up at our box and winks, which has me giggling instantly. Fifteen flashes again so I punch in my refusal and let my mind come back to whatever Alex is doing because it seems my concentration has let me control the effect of his hands to some degree. He's being quiet for him, not pushing me hard or fast, just leisurely playing with me and fondling. It's nice, peaceful somehow, but the visions going on in front of me are starting to become increasingly erotic. People are coming all over each other, cocks inside every hole available. Moaning and screaming are beginning to make their way to the crowd watching, slapping sounds as people smack each other and then more moaning.

I feel Alex begin to lift me upwards slightly as my eyes flick to the panel. Fifteen flashes a few more times so I send my refusal again and leave my hand on the scanner. His rock hard tip brushes against me and I moan out as he rubs it across me. I watch my man lining up a redhead who reminds me of myself and I groan at the thought. His cock juts out in front of him as he pushes his fingers into her arse and then drives himself into her. Her head tips back as she takes him deep inside her and pushes back against him.

"Counter," Alex says. "Concentrate." I swing my eyes over to the panel and enter my rejection just as Alex pulls me down on top of him slowly. I stop breathing completely and let the sensation consume me as he fills me bit by bit and then begins to rock me backward and forward on him.

"Oh god that's good," I rasp out as he hits every available surface inside me and puts his fingers back on me. My man on stage is going at it like a jackhammer now as the woman begs him to fuck her harder. That's exactly what I want, more, harder, faster. My number flashes again so I punch in and push back on Alex with force, causing the delicious friction I'm craving. He drives in deep and begins to fuck me with long, slow movements.

"You're good at this," he whispers. "Shall I try harder to distract you, baby? Do you think you can keep going if I make you come?" I have no idea but the woman is now licking her way around two cocks as my man keeps hammering into her. I'm doing okay at keeping it together but frankly I'm beginning to lose the will. Everyone is screaming their pleasure out, my core is tightening with each thrust from Alex and his circling fingers are threatening me beyond belief. Fifteen flashes again and I'm struggling to think coherently, let alone move my hand to focus on numbers. He pushes me forward a little and growls as I try to move my fingers to the numbers. It seems my ability to stay reasonably self-aware is irritating him so I smile, punch in and watch my man close his eyes and give in to his own release. My core ignites as if I have no will at all.

"Oh god, Alex..." I moan out as he grunts behind me and I feel him thickening inside me. I haven't got a hope. I'm going with this and I hope to hell he's going to deal with the keypad because I couldn't care less as he keeps driving in and pulling me back onto him.

"Fuck, you're amazing. Come for me, baby. Let it go." He groans as he removes my hand and punches something into the pad. I do and watch as my man collapses on top of the woman he's been screwing while I gazed at him doing it. I made it happen, and Christ, that feels unbelievable.

"Yes," I hiss out as everything starts to explode behind my eyelids. Alex growls as he continues with his deep rhythm, pulling me back down onto him with harsh fingers as he thrusts in a few more times before grasping me around the waist and pushing me down onto the floor. My hands connect with the carpet as he raises my hips up and begins slamming into me with reckless abandon. Long, hard, punishing strokes as he grabs the back of my hair and tilts my head up, forcing me to keep watching the show in front of us. My core constricts around him instantly as I see my man move towards a woman and grab hold of her legs so he can bury his head in between them. I'm panting. I haven't got a hope of containing anything because the feel of Alex thickening, the brazen sights in front of me, and the combined sounds emanating in this room have me instantly ready to come again. I can't stop it. I don't want to. I can hardly breathe at the feelings swirling and tightening and riding me over the wave of assaulting stimulation.

"Fuck me, please. More," comes stuttering from my mouth as I dig my nails into the carpet and watch the woman arching her back into my man's face. My core violently begins to explode as Alex rewards me with more aggressive pounding and his hand around my throat. More stars, more lights, more... Oh god, more everything as my legs shake into oblivion and he uses his strength to keep me aloft.

"Fuck, yes," he growls out as he grabs my thighs to hold me to him firmly and finds his own ecstasy. Widening my legs, he pushes into me further as I open my eyes to watch the rest of the show. I feel him filling me with his release and revel in our connection. His mouth kisses my shoulder languidly as I ride out my tingling and allow my breathing to calm down a little. My man eventually raises his head and is immediately accosted by a different woman who licks his face clean. Another stuttered gasp escapes me as he casually wanders off the stage with a salute towards our booth and winks again. Alex chuckles behind me. I have absolutely no fucking idea what's funny about any of this. It's the single most disturbingly erotic thing I have ever been a part of.

"Well I hope Felix had a good time because I damn well did," he says as he continues slowly, moving behind me. I seriously don't have any words for what I've just been engaged in. "Are you okay, baby?"

I rise up to rest myself on his lap and put my arm behind me to finger his hair as I watch people starting to disperse from the stage and wonder exactly that. Am I okay?

I've just been completely lust driven by a sodding orgy, which I not only enjoyed watching but helped to happen by buying a man to be part of it. That man performed for me while I was thoroughly fucked from behind by my devilish boyfriend and was more than likely surrounded by other people doing the exact same thing inside their little rooms. It's a mystery to me as to whether that's okay or not. And all the time we've been wagering against each other and spending money as if it's going out of fashion, which for once I'm actually quite happy about. But should I be? Alex is clearly okay with this. It's probably quite normal for him and his unusual hands. So do I feel okay about this? Surprisingly, my gut is telling me that I do, and funnily enough, it's telling me and my inner slut that I'd joyfully do it again.

It suddenly strikes me that my number is no longer flashing on the panel. Thank god because I handed him the trust to deal with it and hoped he would. And why didn't he get flashed, so to speak?

"How did you stop the game?" I ask quietly as I turn my head and let my lips wander across his. Shit, he tastes good. I mean, he always does but something about this whole thing has made him taste more... primal maybe.

"I punched in an amount to stop them asking for you, upped the ante so to speak," he replies as he grins wickedly and nips at my lips.

"And how much was I worth in the end, Mr. White?" I ask with a giggle as I move away from him and try to sort myself out. I can hear doors opening and closing all around us so I presume it's nearly time to leave. He gets up and downs the rest of his Cognac with a chuckle, looking absolutely gorgeous as his eyes sparkle playfully. I could easily drop down to my knees for him at any given moment.

"We'll find out in a minute when I sign it off at the bar, where I'm sure Felix will have something to say about being pushed so hard. He's not been challenged that vehemently for quite some time. Being an Earl tends to gain him a certain leverage in here so let's go and buy the man a drink, shall we?" he replies as he gestures toward the door.

Oh shit, an Earl? Of where? That could be little awkward. Actually, given the surroundings, it might be quite good fun because I daresay they're all very comfortable with their little game, which is now mine, it seems.

Sod it, I'm all in.

So I smile and walk out, feeling just that bit more empowered than I was before tonight. Mr. White is quite clearly turning me into a sex fiend.

I think I quite like it.

Chapter 21

Alexander

S taring at his desk, he tapped his fingers and continued to try and hold in the fucking explosion of fury that was about to come out. Deep breathing wasn't working. Pacing wasn't working. Even rational or logical thinking weren't working because he had come so close to losing her and he knew it. If Andrews had been ten minutes longer, or if she'd decided to look at them rather than think they were Belle's, she would have seen it all. She would have suddenly known everything he was desperate for her not to know. It was bad enough that he was going to have to discuss this with his apparent father figure, but the thought of having to somehow explain himself to her was just... Well, there wasn't a word strong enough for how he felt about that.

She was upstairs sleeping and he'd managed to avoid this conversation all day because he'd made himself too busy to be available for Andrews, but unfortunately he did need to know. If the man was going to do his job properly then he would need to know where the photos had come from and why Alex was in them, with a knife and a dead man at his feet.

At this point, he wasn't entirely sure whether Andrews would even stick around to help him at all. If there was one thing a Special Forces guy didn't like, it was being kept in the dark. And he had most definitely been kept in the dark.

It had happened a long time ago and he hadn't got a fucking clue who had taken the pictures. He'd been so caught up in the act of violence itself that he hadn't been as careful as he had later on, when it had become more of a business for him, something to be planned more accurately with a little more restraint. He did know that there had been two people in the room with him that night because he was looking at the corpse of Keith Drummond, a bent private detective looking into Aiden Phillips' drug involvement, which AP hadn't been happy with in the slightest. So he'd done his job efficiently, coaxed the information out and then ended the threat to his boss. Ben Levington and Mark Jacobs had been the other men with him, people he had assumed he could trust at the time. He'd assumed he could still trust Mark but now he was reconsidering that thought process. Maybe he couldn't? And Ben, well he didn't even know if Ben was still alive.

Christ, now he needed to talk to AP, the last person he wanted to be associated or seen with in his current life. He was the equivalent of a mafia boss, but needs must so he stared at his phone for a few minutes. At least if he got some fucking control over what the hell was going on, he might be able to keep this shit from surfacing any more. To do that he needed Andrews to be all over this like the professional he was - if he even would, that was. There was no point avoiding it anymore so he hoped Michael Andrews would forgive him his sins and help him sweep them the fuck away. He'd just found his reason for living and he was damned if it was going to be taken away from him.

He picked up his phone and dialled Aiden then pressed the button for Andrews. He might as well witness the call. It might give him a clue as to who the hell he'd been working for all these years.

"Alex." Aiden's brusque tone and shortness were clearly exactly the same as usual. He never was much of a talker unless it came to the principles of death. It had been fine by him at the time. Andrews walked in the room so he put the call on loudspeaker, nodded at him to sit and leaned back into his chair.

"Aiden, how are you? Good, I hope." Treading carefully round AP was a necessity of life. There was a certain mutual respect but it only went so far.

"I'm well. Life is as good as it can be. What can I do for you?" Alex chuckled a little. The man was still as straight to the point as he always was.

"How are Amira and the family?"

"Cut the shite, Alex." The man snorted in derision. Alex chuckled again. Okay, he'd cut the shit.

"Do you remember Keith Drummund?" he asked as he stared at Andrews, who sat there completely motionless, his face an impassive gaze of unknown emotion.

"No. Who is he?"

"*Was*, an attempt at a private detective," he replied as he looked at another photo on his desk and scanned for evidence of someone else in the room. There still wasn't any.

"No, a bit fucking irrelevant for me to be bothered with." Well, that was true.

"Is Ben Levington still around?" he asked as he shook his head at his tattoo. If it wasn't for that, you wouldn't know who was in the photos. There weren't as many lines but the distinct writing was there as plain as day. Apart from that, it was only his back view and a switchblade in his hand. He chuckled to himself as he moved across the room and opened the hidden cupboard in the shelves. Fourteen numbers later and the safe clicked open.

"No, Levington became overzealous with his mouth, drugs. I have no idea why these people take them although I'm obviously glad they do. How's that going for you?" *Dickhead.* It was AP who'd started him on the road in the first place. Not that he'd minded at the time, but the constant lure back was irritating to say the least.

"Fuck off," he seethed in reply. He could throttle the man for his influence if he was honest. As much as he'd found some kind of solace in his previous life, it was screwing up his present, which included the angel upstairs. Andrews still sat there, immobile. He was probably memorising the entire conversation, and given his raised brow, he had more than likely worked out who AP was.

"Now, now, check that temper of yours. You know I don't like it, and it's not useful to me anymore." He took a deep breath and tried to regain his control. The bastard always could get a rise out of him, but he definitely wasn't a man to piss off. Andrews narrowed his eyes as he watched him backing down. To be fair, it was a very rare occurrence and probably quite confusing for the guy. He pulled the offending blade from the safe and threw it onto the table. He'd need to get rid of it, which irritated the hell out of him because it truly felt like a piece of him, an extension of his arm somehow.

"Aiden, I received some photos that could only have been taken by one of two people. Ben is one and Mark is the other. Do you know anything about that?" he asked assertively, being careful not to cross that thin line of disrespect as he watched Andrews pick up his blade to examine it.

"I hope you're not accusing me of something? Because that shit's not going to end well for you, Mr. White. I don't give a fuck who you think you are," AP snapped in reply. He rolled his eyes. The man was as suspicious as he was. Maybe that's where he'd learnt it.

"No, no, not at all, Aiden. I just need to know what I'm dealing with and you're the link here. I thought Mark was okay but now I'm not sure, and I have no idea about Ben," he replied as he stared at Andrews who was beginning to look a little hostile. Alex poured a drink and pushed it towards him as he filled another for himself. There was silence for a minute as AP presumably worked out if his paranoia was in control or if he was.

"Let me dig around. I'll meet you on Tuesday for lunch. It should give the tabloids something to talk about, and as I'm trying to show a professional image these days, you'll do me the world of good."

It wouldn't be doing him any favours at all, but if the guy wanted to do this face to face and it might help him figure out who the hell was after him, apart from Henry, then he'd do it. In fact, was this all linked to Henry? He hadn't processed that thought yet. Was Henry trying to warn Elizabeth off before he struck in some other way? The fucker clearly liked her, no matter how disgusting he'd been about her at lunch to try and throw him off the scent. Could she be in some sort of danger? That wasn't acceptable at all.

"Right, thank you. Tuesday it is. Text me where and when," he replied quietly as he started to sift through the photos again and rubbed his eyes.

"Mark told me about your little outing the other day, says you're still a special motherfucker, but then you always were," the dick said as he chuckled. Andrews' eyebrows shot up. Fuck, now he'd have to tell him about that as well.

"It was necessary," he replied as he downed his drink. It was time for this conversation to end. He knew where it was going.

"Did it still feel the same? After all this time, did it still give you that buzz you always needed, cleanse the turmoil?" Aiden asked. Andrews sneered. He had no idea why because he'd probably killed hundreds of people in his time.

"No, but it didn't stop me. It still wouldn't. I suppose once you're good at something, it's just muscle memory," Alex replied as he looked over at his bodyguard come chauffeur and wondered what was going through his mind. He supposed the man just thought he was a loose cannon sometimes, a frustrating child to have to deal with while being paid. It was a shame he ever had to know the truth because he kind of liked the fact that Andrews thought of him as a son.

"Ha, fucking muscle memory. Jesus, I miss your disinterest, Alex. You always did make me laugh," Aiden replied with a hearty chuckle, as if they were talking about riding a bike. But they weren't, were they? They were talking about murdering someone, and something inside started biting him with that fucking irritating guilty feeling again. He looked up at the ceiling. She couldn't find out about this. She would leave him. She would hate him and probably rightly so. It wasn't going to happen. He looked at the floor and sighed at the thought. How the fuck was he ever going to explain this shit to her?

"Aiden, I have to go. I'll see you in the week, and thank you again," he clipped. He had another chat to get on with and then he wanted her arms, because they might make some of this annoying fucking crap go away or at least quieten it somehow.

"Okay, see you then. And, Alex? Make sure you're in a suit. I need you at your best," the dick replied as the phone clicked off. *Wanker*. The man had far too much information about his past for his liking. He had a damn video somewhere that he'd threatened him with on occasion and he'd never be able to get at it. Mind you, if he ever went down for any of it, he'd take the shit with him.

He sat quietly and refilled his drink as Andrews stared at him. There wasn't a flicker of emotion or anything to give away how he was about to react to the enlightening conversation. So he waited. He really wasn't sure what he was waiting for but it didn't seem appropriate to talk for a while so he just continued to sit and stare back. Andrews wouldn't run to the police; that much was clear. There was too much about the man for him to entertain the idea of being a snitch, but he might just walk out of here. Not because he was offended, more because he didn't know the facts and that would be irritating the fuck out of him. What does a man who believes he knows someone think when they hear that sort of information? What would Conner think if he ever found out?

Fuck, there was emotion involved in this and he didn't like it one little bit. His past had been about a lack of emotion. It had given him the ability to do what he did with ease and even a sense of pride. But now, Andrews' continued stare was beginning to make him feel uncomfortable, as if he should be ashamed of himself. It wasn't a pleasant feeling.

Looking down he noticed his fingers tapping on the table and then realised his leg was bouncing, sure signs of his own nerves, pathetic reactions really. Here he was, having had a friendly conversation with the notorious Aiden Phillips while looking down on a selection of photos that incriminated him beyond doubt in the death of a man, and all he was worried about was how his apparent father figure might react. Feelings... Why he'd allowed them again was completely unknown. He looked at the ceiling again and smiled. He'd allowed nothing; she'd made him do it without even trying because her angelic presence was simply beguiling in its effect on his conscience. Regardless of the consequences, he wouldn't change a damn thing about it.

The dull thud of his knife landing on the desk bought him back to the man in front of him. Apparently it was time to start talking.

"How many?" Andrews asked impassively as he picked up a photo and looked closely.

"Why is that relevant?" he replied as he knocked back his drink. To be honest, he didn't fucking know anyway. He'd done his job at the time. Counting wasn't a prerequisite for being paid.

"I want to know what I'm dealing with, what exactly it is we're discussing here," Andrews replied as he picked up a marker and started circling areas on the photo. "The fact that you're talking to Aiden Phillips doesn't fill me with confidence that this was a one-time occurrence. So how many?"

He narrowed his eyes at the man. Loyal as he might be, he wasn't sure he needed to know everything about those years or why it had started in the first place.

"More than that one." It was all he was prepared to give. He was still the employer in the room as far as he was aware, and much as he didn't want to lose Andrews, this wasn't going to be a bare all type situation. He just needed him to do his job.

"Professionally? Or because you were a stupid fucking idiot?" Andrews asked as he threw the photo back on the desk and leaned back with a calm gaze. Funnily enough, both were apt descriptions.

"If you'd asked me that a few months ago, the former would have been true. While it still is, the latter is beginning to encroach a little," he replied with a small chuckle. He still wasn't remorseful but the woman lying in his bed certainly made him question his actions to a degree. Andrews just stared again with his impenetrable face. He'd always admired that look, but now it was disconcerting to say the least. Eventually he sighed and smiled a little so Alex let out the breath he didn't realise he'd been holding.

"I'm sure it is. Love tends to do that to a man's conscience," Andrews said as he sipped his drink and walked over to the bookcase. "Well, at least I know why you're so quick with your damn hands now. I always was a bit curious if I'm honest. I often wondered if you were more than you seemed and it appears you're probably more lethal than I am. More fucked up with it, mind you."

Alex sighed and shook his head as he watched Andrews' brow furrow. Emotional as this was, it wasn't going to do anyone any favours. The man simply needed to know the truth and then help him get on with clearing up the threat.

"Michael, I need to know if you're on board with this. I won't discuss all the details with you and frankly, the less you know the better. I'm sure you're aware of who AP is and now what it was that I did for him, so while your interest is warranted, can I suggest you just give me a yes or no so that I can find a way through this shit and move on?" he said, hoping the reaction would be a positive one. He liked the man, he really did, but involving him in his own murderous past was confusing the hell out of him.

Andrews sighed and wandered back over to the desk.

"I know Mark Jacobs. I don't believe he would double cross you but I haven't dealt with the other chap so I think we should look into him a little more. How much did you do with him in the room? And what was his purpose?" He knew Mark? Interesting. Regardless, Andrews was right. He hadn't had a lot to do with Ben himself either, just a few jobs here and there. He smiled across at what he now knew was a friend. It seemed he was staying despite the situation, which was a good thing.

"I think I agree about Mark, and Ben was generally a lookout. I only did a few jobs with him so I have no real background on him. However, I'm now wondering whether this is linked to Henry, which is causing me to worry about Elizabeth. She obviously knows nothing of any of this so I want her kept safe whether she likes it or not. Whatever you think you need to do, if the time comes, you do it. You protect her at all costs, do you understand? " he said as he looked across at the man and felt his heart clench at his own thoughts. He'd die before she was harmed. "Whatever the consequences to me, Michael, you keep her safe." Andrews chuckled and finished his drink.

"You didn't need to say that. I would leave you for dead to protect her every time. She's worth a thousand of you Alex," he replied as he stared coldly. Well at least they were on the same page with that declaration. Alex nodded and stood up.

"Okay, let's do this tomorrow. I'm going to bed," he stated as he put the photos in the safe and closed it. Andrews picked up his blade and moved to the door.

"Before I go, what happened the other day, do I need to know about it?"

"No, it's dealt with. It was personal, and nothing to do with any of this. Well, apart from the fact that Mark was there, which may be something we need to look at."

Andrews raised a brow before turning for the door again with a shake of his head.

"I'll deal with this," he said as he wandered off, spinning it around on his hand like a new toy. "Shame, it's quite nice really."

Alex rubbed his fingers together and watched his blade leave the room. It was a shame. That damned thing had helped him out on many occasions and not only that. It had made him the man he was today, given him the strength to become something more than the scared child he'd been. Whether that was positive or not was undecided, but she seemed to quite like who he was now. He supposed the blood that lingered on it was at least being removed from his life, which meant hers as well.

He closed the door and headed up the stairs in the hope that she would give him some comfort to counter the never-ending crap of his past. If he could change it now, he probably would but he couldn't, could he? It's who he was, and it seemed it was finally catching up with him with alarming fucking timing. The people in his past were coming to get him, coming to destroy all he'd worked for, and all Conner had helped him achieve, more than likely with force. They weren't the manipulators and sycophants of business he'd been so worried about her handling when they were first together, the ones she'd actually handled with ease once she lifted her beautiful head and found herself. No, these types of men were out to cause pain, physical and unyielding trauma, and if they were good at their jobs, which it appeared they were, they'd put her right in the middle of his shit-storm to weaken him.

If this was Henry, though, he'd stepped so far from normal deceit and treachery that it made his blood boil with unadulterated fury. But then, if it was him and this was connected to the cousin, then why bring her into this at all? Maybe he really was just trying to get her out of harm's way.

Deciding he needed to talk to Andrews about it in the morning, he walked into the bedroom and gazed down at her while she slept peacefully, unaware of him above her. Anyone could be here now to attack her and she wouldn't have a clue. She could be taken and used as a pawn or simply finished while she slept by the men he used to call friends. They wouldn't think twice about their task and if they had some fun along the way then all the better for them.

The shudder of fear that skated across his skin burned a hole straight through to his newly formed soul as he brushed her hair from her face and she mumbled his name. If that happened, he'd kill everything that moved. Everything that breathed would be a target for his revenge and he wouldn't care because she was everything that existed for him. There wasn't a thing on the planet that meant more than her and her ability to cherish him, to love him, and show him that peace he craved. So it was a fucking good job he'd begun her concentration training. Although he'd done it with Pascal in mind at the time, she could use the same mind-set to help protect herself. Harnessing her rage and turning it into defensive aggression was an easy enough step to take. She just wouldn't know what it was for, and hopefully she'd never have to. But if she did, he was damned sure she'd know exactly what she needed to do to save herself.

~

Saturday

"But I'm sodding working, you arsehole. You can't possibly expect me to go out to a party in four hours with absolutely no notice when I've got to be up for five o'clock tomorrow morning. I damn well told you about this last week. It's Lady whatsherface's daughter's eighteenth birthday. Why the hell didn't you tell me earlier?" she seethed as she flung her hands around in the air and sent daggers across at him with those beautiful eyes of hers.

Okay, yes, he'd probably forgotten about it, and he'd also forgotten to tell her about the Oakley charity fundraiser for Cancer Research tonight, which given her mother's current predicament was probably fucking stupid. But to be honest, his mind had been on other things yesterday, like sorting out shit-storms and protecting her from his past. Maybe he should have told her last week. Actually, why he hadn't told her about it when Louisa sent him the reminder a fortnight ago was a bloody mystery. However, regardless of the fact that he was possibly in the wrong about any of this, watching those long legs stomping around the kitchen in a pair of tailored trousers and heels was beginning to make his dick throb. Every single stride was filled with hostility, every hand gesture fuelled with undiluted irritation, which probably should have made him concerned or maybe even humble. All it was doing, however, was winding up the machine that was waiting to corner her and rip the damn things from her legs, bury his face in between those creamy thighs and make her beg until she relented and told him she loved him. Fuck, she was incredible, and given this new scathing anger, absolutely captivating.

This was the first time they'd had an argument of any sort really, apart from the obvious one where he was a complete idiot and left her, which was a fair point well made. It was one of the most erotic things he'd ever witnessed. His blood was almost boiling to the point of rage but something was keeping it simmering away steadily before it erupted, thankfully. Maybe that was what love did to a disagreement, softened it slightly, made it more of a negotiation than an ordering system. But his mouth was itching to just tell her she had no choice, that she was his and that meant she had to be with him at the event in spite of her work commitments. He'd even tried to go with the *"you will"* tactic at the beginning. It didn't work, and he very nearly got a slap in return. That made him horny as hell, too, so he thought he'd try again.

"Elizabeth, I couldn't give a damn whether you've got to work or not. I told you about my world and I expect you at my side tonight. This is your job as my lover."

That, and the fact that he could keep her near him this way. He had to go and he wanted her safe with him. Her eyebrows rose to unbelievable heights as she stared across at him, possibly in amazement, her hand suspended in mid-air.

"What the fuck was that?" she eventually responded, indicating that she wasn't at all happy with his demand.

"What?"

"Did you just imply that my work isn't important, that my company's success isn't as significant as your fucking profile or something?" Oh, he saw what she meant.

"No, but that doesn't change the fact that you are coming tonight, even if I have to dress you myself. I will not accept no for an answer," he stated in reply. He wasn't having it. She would do as she was told so he could look after her. That was his job.

"Oh no, you never fucking do, do you? The great Alexander White. Who would dare to say no and live to tell the tale? Well, fuck you. I'll do what I sodding well please, and that includes not going to your stupid party full of mindless sluts who will be leering all over you... again."

Now she was really pissed off. This was clearly a family trait. His dick was damn near jumping across the room at her. Feisty wasn't nearly enough of a word. He moved a step closer as she sneered at him and put her hand on a coffee glass, possibly with the intention of launching it at him.

"If you continue to swear at me, I'm going to get into a tantrum, and you really don't want to see it, Elizabeth. You're beginning to piss me off." He couldn't stop the undertone of malice that laced his voice. It was natural, a part of him, and she was about to get its full force regardless of the depravity that was torturing him, and his dick.

"Really? Well, given that I've seen you hurl a fucking lamp, smash your fist into a wall, beat a man near to death and tie me down,

I'm not entirely sure what else you've got, Alex. I'm not fucking scared of you, so you can get those thoughts out of your dominant fucking head right fucking now." His eyes widened in surprise. Yes, she'd got a point, but the fact that she'd kept going regardless of his temper flaring up was simply astonishing. Never had he endured an argument that continued to threaten his patience without smashing a fist into something. Clearly he'd underestimated her resolve when it came to a fight, and that was a mistake he wouldn't make again.

"What the hell is your problem? It's a damn party, which you are going to, with me, whether you like it or not." Her glare of disgust told him he was losing this battle of wills. He watched her fingers tighten around the glass. "And don't you fucking dare throw that glass at me."

She did, with acute precision, and she threw it with absolute venom. If he hadn't dodged it, it would have smacked him right in the face. Instead, it ricocheted off the cupboard and bounced across the floor in front of him. He smirked. He couldn't help it. She was utterly wonderful, entirely unbalanced and in complete control of his heart.

"Well, insightful as that was, go upstairs and get a damn dress sorted out." He was still smirking. She wasn't amused because she moved her hand to another object and glared again. Unfortunately, it happened to be a paring knife. His eyebrow shot up at the same time as his respect. "Are you intending to kill me with that? Take your best shot, baby. Plenty of others have tried," he drawled out, imagining the prospect of her at his throat. It was strangely erotic. She dropped the knife in apparent disgust and walked straight past him without looking. He couldn't help staring at that stunning mass of red hair tumbling over her shoulders towards her curvy arse as she went.

"No. In fact I'm going home. Fuck off," she said quietly and kept walking straight to the front door, which she opened. He couldn't fucking believe it.

"Elizabeth!" he shouted irritably as his mouth caught up with his brain. She was not leaving him.

"Oh fuck you, Alex. You're not ordering me around like some damned employee. Who the hell do you think you are?" she yelled as she kept going.

"You will not walk out that-" She was already out of it and halfway up the drive before he could finish. Where the hell she was going was beyond him. He stormed out and caught her by the arm.

She instantly rounded on him like wildfire with bitch-like eyes and a snarl, so much so that he actually took a step back at her vicious glower.

"Do you honestly think this is the way to do this? Huh? You might do what you want when you fuck me, Alex, but you will not command me to do anything outside of that. You're damn well delusional if you think I'm having that sort of shit," she screamed at the top of her lungs in the middle of the bloody drive. Enough was enough.

"Get back in the house," he said quietly. Christ, he was horny.

"Piss off, you arrogant bastard!" And that just made it worse. The look of venom made his fists tighten. Her reddened cheeks, her tight nipples in the cold air, her defiant stance, damn, everything about her said force me.

"I'll say it one more time, then I'll make you. Either that or I'll fuck you right here." He was completely serious. He couldn't give a damn about anything other than being inside her as soon as possible. Her eyes narrowed as she considered the options. Surprisingly she wasn't moving, just standing there with her hands on her luscious hips. Did she think he wouldn't?

"Fuck me all you like. We both know you'll take what you want anyway. You'll be doing it on your own though," she replied poisonously as she continued to stare. It shocked the shit out of him. Not the fact that she was giving in, because she wasn't. What she was doing was withholding what he wanted, her love, their connection, the thing he wanted above all else. Oh, what a clever girl. She couldn't, though, could she? She couldn't let him have her and just turn it off?

Her sneer told him maybe she could.

"You couldn't turn it off if you tried. You damn well want it as much as I do. I can read it in your every move, see it in your eyes, Elizabeth. Do you want me to force you to admit it?" he seethed in response, watching her lips part slightly, that evocative blush rising across her chest. He could almost feel the wetness sliding down her thighs, taste her on his tongue.

"Try me, you piece of shit."

Fuck, it was the most delicious invitation he'd ever received. He took a step into her space. She backed up and continued with her fierce look of disgust so he lunged for her with every intention of dragging her to the floor and showing her exactly what she wanted. Unfortunately, an unknown car pulled into the top of the drive so he froze and glared at it.

"Fuck," he muttered as he watched it come to the front door and park. The next sight was not a pleasant one at all, and certainly one he didn't want Elizabeth around for. The long, slender leg and very blonde hair were followed by a flirtatious smile as she gazed across at them with the devil resting on her treacherous shoulders. Caroline Anderson. What the hell was she doing here? And how much fucking nerve had the woman got? At his home? Really? Christ. He turned back to the only woman he did care about. "This isn't finished. Go in the damn house," he said quietly. Caroline had already gotten a display of his anger. He wasn't going to give her any more ammunition to blackmail him with.

"Oh you'd like that, wouldn't you? Is this another dirty little secret, Alex? Have you fucked this one as well? Of course you have. Who haven't you fucked? Come on, Alex, introduce me to your little friend. Maybe she can enlighten me as to who the hell you men think you are," she replied a little too loudly. Caroline cackled behind him. He could have killed the bitch instantly. And why had she suddenly said *men,* as in plural? Fucked if he knew.

"I don't want you involved in this. Go inside," he said again, trying for calm. It wasn't working. However, his dick had at least deflated at the sight of Caroline.

"No," she replied as she marched away from him defiantly towards the enemy. "I'll introduce myself, shall I?" Where the hell this woman had appeared from was a complete enigma - sexy as fuck, yes, controllable, absolutely not. This was not going to end well. The thought of her finding out about this shit was enough for all rational thought to disappear. He caught her arm and drew her back to him with a very sharp tug.

"Get inside the house. Right. Fucking. Now. Don't make me do something I'll regret," he seethed quietly in her ear. She stilled instantly so he pulled back to look at her. All colour had drained from her face, which instantly made him feel sick, but he kept up his malicious stare in the hope that it shocked her enough to listen. He just wanted her gone.

"Alex?" she whispered as her beautiful lips parted and he watched the tears form in her eyes. Her breath shook with each inhalation as she struggled against his grip, eventually dislodging herself and staring at him with searching eyes. Her face was a picture of betrayal and hurt. She wasn't scared. No, she was disappointed, possibly disenchanted, and she was right to be because he'd just given her a hint of the bastard he was. She eventually dropped her eyes to the floor and headed for the door with a shattered expression. He knew he'd just crossed a line and it was a line he'd have to work damn hard to get back over but it was too bad. He needed to get this bitch off his property and out of his fucking life. Elizabeth didn't need to see or hear what was about to happen, so he waited until she'd closed the door and then turned on Caroline with no thought whatsoever. He was damned if he'd keep having this conversation with her any longer. There was enough shit going on without her adding to the mix.

"What the fuck do you want?" he shouted as he pushed her to the side of her car. Her sickly sweet smile vanished instantly as she squirmed against him.

"Well, I..." she stuttered. It was pathetic and quite unlike her. Perhaps fear was the best way forward.

"You've got ten seconds to come up with something useful to me, otherwise I might just break your fucking neck," he said, tilting his head as he took a step backwards and left her to think. She had a choice to make. She could keep pushing this or she could let it go. He was hoping she'd make the right decision. Her face contorted as she tried to work out how serious he was. She should have known better. She'd seen him in action. He meant every fucking word.

"Alexander, I still have it. You know what it could do to you," she said snidely as she made the wrong damn choice. Christ, he hated dense women. He didn't give her a second to think, gripping her by the wrist, he spun her away from the car and opened the door. Then shoving her in, he stormed round to the driver's side and got in.

"Buckle up, Caro. We're going for a little drive," he said quietly as he slammed the Mercedes into reverse and hit the accelerator.

"No... Where are you taking me? No, Alex..." she stammered as he floored it up the drive.

"Shut the fuck up. I told you I wouldn't do this again. I fucking meant it. You're a useless fucking whore. It's about time you got what's coming to you. Did you think we'd do this forever, Caro? Did you think you'd hold this over me for the rest of my life?" he said with utter contempt as he pondered her pet name. Conner's voice rung in his ears, reminding him of his own self-loathing, which led him back to what he'd just done to the woman he loved.

"Alexander, please, I didn't mean... I just need the money," she stuttered again. It pissed him off more. This was all her own fault. He'd given her so many opportunities to back off and leave him the fuck alone.

"I don't give a shit. You've played me for the last time. Christ, your pussy wasn't even that good," he replied quietly as he remembered the last time he'd fucked her. Slack was the best word he could find.

"Please don't do this. I'm sorry."

Yeah, whatever. Sorry meant not a damn thing in this world, especially not from someone who meant so little to him. She was an irritation he simply didn't need any more. The quicker she was disposed of the better.

"Too late, Caro. Too damn late," he seethed as he shook his head and headed towards Eden. Pascal could use a woman like her, or he'd at least send her to one of his many *friends* to play with. She wouldn't be seen or heard from for a very long time. It was exactly what was needed, and he sure as hell wasn't marking his own fingers with her.

"No. God no. I'll burn it, okay? Please...I'll destroy it. I promise. Please... Fuck, where are you taking me?" she screamed as she grabbed at the door handle. He pressed the internal lock system and kept driving, then considered unlocking it so she could throw herself out into oncoming traffic.

"You know exactly what's happening here, Caro. You know who you're fucking around with. You always have. Maybe you'll learn some manners in someone else's hands," he replied quietly as he thought of her being sent to Europe in a crate, or maybe being bought by one of Pascal's associates and sent across to Dubai for some prince to entertain himself with. Oddly, the vision didn't present the kind of satisfaction he'd normally feel. Instead, that sense of guilt or maybe even shame hit him in the gut. His mind wandered back to Elizabeth as he felt Caroline tugging at his arm and begging.

"Please, Alexander, please... Don't do this. I can't deal with it. You know what'll happen if you let him take me. Shit, you can't be this heartless. Please..." She screamed at him as she hit his arm and frantically threw herself at the door again.

She was wrong. He was this heartless, or he had been. He frowned and looked down at his hands on the steering wheel. There wasn't any strain in his knuckles and there wasn't any tension in his body. He'd obviously reverted to not caring mode, apparently happy with his decision to do something wrong, something he should be ashamed of in the real world. He shook his head as her eyes tortured him again. Elizabeth, those brown pools of liquid chocolate swirling through his mind and softening all the sharp edges.

She'd be ashamed of this. She'd be disgusted with him, wouldn't she? Because her sense of right and wrong was firmly in place as she navigated the world and settled for nothing less than just and true.

Is this what he still was - a worthless piece of shit? A man who could dismiss lives so easily? That's what she'd said, wasn't it? *"Try me, you piece of shit."*

Her face floated through his mind as he'd inadvertently threatened her. She'd looked almost broken, disappointed, tired. Christ, she'd looked so tired, like she'd given in. Two minutes previous to that and she'd been flying so high, flying in her anger, flying in the justification of her superiority and god, what an angel she'd been in that moment, full of life and vigour. What the hell had she been going through since they'd met, dealing with his world and the fucked up sense of acceptable that he had offered her? God, she was beautiful, holding him in his darkest moments, giving him the peace he craved, helping him to see a better life, a more fulfilled existence, a possibility for more...

What the fuck was he doing?

Caroline was still squirming and screaming in his ear for him to stop the car, to let her out, that she was sorry, begging him to let her go. He pulled the car over into a lay-by and switched off the engine.

He hadn't got a damn clue what to do next. The woman still had the video and he needed that to go away, but he didn't necessarily need to do what he'd first intended.

She sat there quietly, sniffing and cowering against the door, black mascara running down her face and masking her beauty. She was quite pretty under all that deceit, all the more attractive for her fear, but she wasn't of any interest to him. He had his angel waiting for him, waiting for him to do the right thing and prove he was a better man.

"Where's the film, Caro?" he asked with a sigh as he turned in his seat to gaze across at her. "I'm tired of this. I just want you to go away."

"It's... It's at home, in the safe. I promise I'll burn it. Please, just don't..." she stuttered through her tears.

"I'm going to send someone round to pick it up at seven this evening. If you're not there waiting for him with everything you've got, I'm coming back for you. I won't be turned twice, do you understand? I will finish this next time."

She nodded her head rapidly so he pulled the car out into the road and drove back towards the house. He had an apology to make and a woman to hold, if she'd have him. Having driven a while, he glanced across at her and wondered what had turned her into such a nasty little whore. Her life should be good - a famous model, still attractive, still in her prime.

"What made you like this, Caro? Why are you so angry with me? Why blackmail me?"

She stared at him and wiped her face with her fingers, a small chuckle falling from her lips.

"You have no idea, do you? I loved him, Alexander. I loved him and you seduced me into your arms. You ripped away the only thing I ever had of any importance and didn't give a damn. You destroyed my life," she replied quietly as she looked back at the road.

"Why did you then? Why let yourself be persuaded?" he asked, genuinely interested for some bizarre reason.

"Have you seen yourself in full-on mode? You were stunning. I couldn't stop myself. Pathetic really when I think about it - the love of a good man for a ride on another. Such a waste," she said with a small sigh.

"He didn't know. You could have stayed with him. I never would have said anything," he replied as he pulled up to the gates and parked the car. She laughed at him, full on laughed. She was pushing her fucking luck because he still wasn't in the best of moods with the bitch.

"Oh, he knew. I never told him it was you but he knew somehow. That's the worst part of it. Don't you see? He chose you over me. He forgave you and threw me out as if I was a waste of his time. I probably was because no decent person would do that to someone like Conner, would they?" she said as she raised a brow and ran some lipstick over her mouth. "Do you still play with people regardless of the consequence, Alexander? Still crave the game?"

Shit.

He opened the door and walked towards the gates, not bothering to take another look at the woman who'd played him like a queen for the last few years, blackmailed him repeatedly when Conner knew all along. Christ, he hated her, clever bitch. Well it was over now. He didn't even need the damn film for fuck's sake. What the hell he was going to do about Conner was perplexing to say the least. Why had he done that? Why would he choose him over Caroline?

He shook his head and crunched along the drive, trying to formulate a plan with regard to the woman who was inside. There wasn't one really, was there?

Just fucking apologise.

Damn well beg if he had to.

She deserved so much more.

Chapter 22

Elizabeth

Spitting mad. Actually, I can't even find a word for how mad I am. How dare he try to scare me?

Unfortunately he did, quite a lot in fact. It was in his eyes. They turned just like they did when he almost killed the shit that tried to rape me. Cold, distant, removed and yet so intent on damage that I honestly questioned if he'd hit me if I refused to do what he said. So I walked away and now I stand here in his bedroom, watching him walk back up the drive toward the house, toward me.

If I wasn't so furious, I'd be admiring his body as it glides across the ground with precision and eats up the ground beneath his feet as if its unworthy of his attention for a second longer than necessary. I'd also be salivating over his face and the way his piercing eyes are frowning at the door as if he's about to tear it off its hinges to get to me. I'd absolutely be fantasising about peeling off that black sweater and running my fingers over his muscles, tracing my way around his tattoo and imagining inscriptions of other dates - marriage, children, a future.

Thankfully I'm pissed off beyond belief. I was mad enough before, although he was managing to win that war with his talk of sex and forceful behaviour. I almost dribbled at that point, regardless of my irritation, but having watched him drive off with another woman and not include me in his little plan, whatever the hell it was, I'm now livid. I should have left. I thought about packing my stuff and hightailing it out of here before he got back but I haven't finished with him yet, not by a long shot. I just haven't quite worked out what it is that I'm going to say yet. I so wish he'd been ten minutes more because I almost got my brain around how I felt, and now I'm flustered again. Arsehole.

And what the hell does *"before I do something I'll regret"* actually mean anyway?

I can feel my foot tapping away as I continue to gaze down at him, wondering what it is that he's going to say when he finds me. Is he still mad? I'm not even sure he was really mad when we were arguing, but he sure as shit was when that overwhelmingly attractive woman turned up. I'm pretty sure I've seen her somewhere before. She was like a poster girl of gorgeousness, all mouth and sultry eyes, tall, effortlessly glorious in that actress or model type way. I obviously hated the look of her immediately, and as the bastard didn't deny it, I can only assume he has been there before. Why wouldn't he? The woman is stunning. So is he.

Why on earth am I still here? With him, I mean. He's the most incredible thing most women have ever seen and I still can't quite wrap my head around what he sees in me. Why would he give me, of all people, his love, his childhood, his fears?

Actually, I don't give a shit. I'm still pissed off. I refuse to question my own self-worth when he's just treated me like a... a... I don't know what he treated me like but it wasn't sodding nice.

What's so important about the damn party tonight? I don't even know why I have to go with him. At least I was giving as good as I got. Thankfully my own self-confidence at being ordered around kicked in with full effect and I wasn't backing down in any way, shape or form. Given his inability to tell me anything about that envelope full of something that I should be able to look at, I'm still feeling quite irritated. It's about to continue because I swear if he walks in here with his *"you will do as you're told"* head on, I might well rip his off. *Feisty Beth.*

I have to admit it's probably not all his fault because I've been in a mood all day. Unfortunately, the thought of Teresa going to Pascal tomorrow is disturbing me. I don't even know why. She deserves a nice time. I love her dearly and I want her to have all the best things that life can offer, but for some unknown and probably completely inappropriate reason, I'm feeling possessive. God knows why. Pascal isn't mine in the slightest - nowhere near it. I've got my man and he's beautiful and he loves me. He's currently an arsehole but that doesn't matter because I still adore him. So why do I think I have any rights over Mr. Van der Braack? It's very annoying and utterly ridiculous.

I also truly don't want to see her get hurt, emotionally that is, and he will more than likely do just that. Not because he tries to, just because he's the type of man she'd fall in love with regardless of how much she protests. Belle would have the answers to these questions. Alex probably would, too, if I dared to ask him, but given our current situation, it's probably not the best time to ask because that would be wonderful, wouldn't it?

"Alex, I realise we're having our first real argument but could you please tell me why I don't want my best friend to sleep with the man you want me to have sex with? Yes, the same man that I also want to have sex with regardless of the fact that I'm in love with you. And maybe him. Oh yes, the same man that you've been - what did you call it? - oh yes, sadistic with in the past, probably with hundreds of women and possibly men."

Definitely not. Mind you, perhaps that's exactly what I should say. He is the one that's created all of this turmoil around the man after all.

I should just send Pascal a text and tell him not to meet her. I could do that. He told me he would help if I asked him for it, didn't he? So maybe I should just call in that favour. He can only say no, which would more than likely let me know that I shouldn't travel along this road any further. If I can't trust the man, I certainly shouldn't be having sex with him, should I? Because he's nothing to me in the grand scheme of things, is he? He's just an extremely good-looking man who happens to be one of Alex's friends and is probably unfairly brilliant in bed. I'm not sure who I'm trying to fool. I like the man. It may be unreasonable but it's true nonetheless.

Picking up my phone, I gaze down at the man I love who appears to have stopped moving for some reason. He's staring at the door with his hands in his pockets, looking thoroughly beautiful and a little perplexed. I can't help the small giggle that escapes my mouth because it's so unlike him to look that way and I'm so glad he's feeling as messed up as I am. Mr. In Control seems to have lost a bit of it, thank God. Maybe he's questioning what he's about to walk in on as much as I am?

Good. Arsehole.

- Pascal, I don't want you to see Teresa tomorrow. She deserves more so I'm asking for your help. Please do the right thing. Your Rose

I shouldn't end it with a kiss, should I? I'm not even sure I should end it like that full stop. Your rose? Really? *Stupid Beth.*

Sod it, I will start saying what I mean to these damned domineering men that have suddenly become a part of my everyday life. What chance do I have if I don't say what I mean? And really, I am his rose I suppose. He calls me that, and for whatever reason, I do feel connected to him in some strange way, some unusual pull that I can't deny. Maybe he does that to all women? It's yet another thing I have absolutely no clarity on whatsoever.

I hit send and hope he's true to his word. I know I'll have to deal with Teresa at some point and also my guilt associated with it, but I'll find a way through that when I have to.

Now, Alex. I look out the window again and, oh god he's gone. That can only mean he's in the house so I swiftly swing my head around to the door and suck in a huge breath to prepare myself for whatever it is that I'm about to get involved in.

Nothing happens.

In fact, ten minutes later and I'm still standing here with nothing happening. This was not expected, so clearly I'm now biting my thumbnail, wondering what the hell to do because this silent thing can't continue and I have no idea whether I should be going in search of him or just waiting for him to come and find me. If I go to him, am I backing down? Is he playing some sort of dominance dance with me to see who will win this battle? My phone beeps, making me jump a bit and unfortunately highlighting just how nervous I really am. I thought I was in control and feeling fine about how to handle Alex. It appears I am not.

- The right thing for whom? You should be cautious with your feelings, my rose. You sound a little covetous with your demands.

Bastard.

Trust the man to know exactly what I mean without me actually saying it. I roll my eyes at the message and continue to hope that he'll get the point and do the right thing. Whether it's genuinely for Teresa or just me is questionable, but I'm still working through that one. It is, of course, highly possible that he'll ignore me and do whatever the hell he wants anyway, but I've tried and I'm not giving him anymore to play with than that. I certainly don't want to get my feelings for Pascal involved in any of this. I've got enough to deal with where Alex is concerned because try as I might, I can't stop myself from wanting to go and find him so we can make this better somehow. I'm still mad but as long as he shows some contrition, we'll be fine. Well, we will when he tells me who that woman was and why he drove off with her.

Making my way down the stairs, I search for signs of life then hear tinkling of piano keys. There's either someone else in the house or he's in the music room. I'm pretty sure he won't be wanting an argument in there so I try to relax myself a bit in the hope that we won't have to endure more screaming. It's our room, our lovely room, the room that holds our song and makes me remember all of the emotions surrounding how he makes me feel, all of the newly found love he has swirling around inside him that he gives to me because he's only ever loved me, and will only ever love me apparently.

My hand pushes the door open to see him standing over the keys with a glass of Cognac in one hand and his fingers hovering over the notes. His face seems pensive almost, lost in his thoughts, which are more than likely dark.

"Do you play?" It comes out a little shakily but something has to break the silence, and funnily enough, I've never asked him the question. He doesn't turn to me, just keeps staring at the piano and sighs.

"No, I could never create something as beautiful as music. That sort of thing is intended for fingers like yours," he replies quietly. He's in tortured soul mode. My heart very nearly combusts at the thought because we caused this. Together we verbally assaulted each other and made us both weaker. God, I hate that. Well, that and the fact that he's just driven off with another bloody woman.

"Oh, I don't know. I think your hands can do plenty of things very beautifully indeed. In fact I remember begging for them to work mercilessly." He frowns and taps the keys again.

"Only when touching you," he replies softly as he turns toward me with a gentle lilt of his mouth. It's so sad, so despairing that I immediately want to run into his arms so that I can wash all of this away and make us fit together again. I wrap my arms around my chest

408

for comfort as his eyes gaze across at me. His mouth opens as if he's about to tell me something and then he looks at the floor. I'm keeping my mouth shut. I did my bit and started this conversation, tried to keep it light and make him comfortable. Now it's his turn because he needs to make this better. Eventually, his head comes back up and he gazes again, warm blue eyes smoothing the path for whatever he's going to say, and those lips quietly opening and shutting with no actual sound until he's found his words.

"I told myself I would be better for you, that I would try to change my behaviour so that you wouldn't fall foul of it, and I haven't lived up to that. I'm sorry for making it sound as if your business wasn't important because it is. In fact, it's exceptional, given the current climate," he says as he begins to pace about. My eyebrows shoot up as I stay rooted to my spot and watch him, because self-made millionaire, Alexander White, just flattered my business. He also appears to be doing quite well in the apology section of this statement. "And I despise that I frightened you purposefully. It was wrong of me. Actually, it was fucking unforgivable. So now I'm extremely irritated with myself for being so unreasonable and am uncertain of how to make this better for you. I just wanted you close to me. Frankly, I've never done so much damned apologizing before in my life and I'm not entirely sure what to do next."

His frame comes to a halt three feet in front of me as he searches my eyes again for an emotion that he can hold onto. I can feel him trying to work out if he's done enough or if I'm expecting something more from him. Some regret was expected, but that was way past what I thought would come out of his mouth. I'm really struggling to hold back the grin that's tickling the corners of my mouth because that was just wonderful, utterly apologetic and completely dream worthy. I'd probably swoon if I wasn't still gripping my arms quite so tightly. I think I may have just won a battle, I think I may have proved my point effectively, and I think maybe I should apologise, too.

"It wasn't all your fault. I'm pretty sure I said some horrible things, too, so I'm sorry for that," I reply quietly as I gaze across at him in all his masculinity, sex oozing off his brooding face, then quickly remember that he did still drive off with a woman. "I am not sorry for standing up for myself, though, because you cannot order me around.

You do know that, don't you?" He rolls his eyes at me and reaches for my hand.

"Yes, Elizabeth, you were quite vocal with your retaliation," he replies as he fiddles with my bracelet and pulls my fingers to his mouth with a very deviant smile. "And I think I actually liked it, oddly enough."

He did? He didn't seem like it at the time. And is he damn well laughing at me? My snort of irritation doesn't go unnoticed as his face flattens a little and I snatch my hand away from him.

"I'm glad I amused you. I'm not sure I can say the same of you if I'm honest. Who was that woman? And why did you get all... threatening, which I'm not very happy about by the way?" Might as well get it all out there why we're still not perfect. If we're going to argue again, I'd rather do it before we make up. His eyes close as he lets go of my hand, shakes his head and wanders back towards his glass of brandy. It's not a good sign.

"Her name is Caroline Anderson and I didn't want you involved in what I had to say to her. It wasn't pleasant. She's an old acquaintance that is no longer of concern to me or you and I think it's best if we leave it at that."

Not a hope in hell, Mr. White, and shit, I knew I recognised her - *Vogue* model extraordinaire, albeit shorter than I thought.

"Do you honestly believe that's an acceptable explanation for threatening me? What is it that you didn't want me to hear?" My hands are beginning their waving about thing. Thankfully I'm wearing clothes this time so there's no need to hold a sheet up.

"I'm not discussing this," he says tersely with a sudden hardening of his eyes. Mr. Pissed Off is returning. My snarl of anger shifts back into gear as I feel my eyes narrow at him.

"Yes, you bloody are. If we go any further it's with no barriers. We can have another damn argument if you want to." He is not backing away from this and I will not feel threatened without a very good reason so he better have one. His fingers pinch his brow as he lets out a long breath.

"Just let this go," he says quietly as he walks past me and begins to leave the room.

"Alex, I want a reason for you behaving like a caveman. If you expect me to forgive you for treating me like a slave then you need to help me understand why." I'm hoping that might appeal to his intelligence. Frankly, I'm beginning to doubt my own around him at the moment. He stops and turns to face me with his hand pocketed and what appears to be a pained expression. His sigh doesn't give me much hope either. My brow goes up as my hands find their way to my hips. I'm so not backing down on this one.

"Fine, I fucked her three times. She was Conner's girlfriend at the time and he was in love with her. I didn't give a shit and pursued her so that I could have her. She's been blackmailing me with that for years and I'd finally had enough. Has that satisfied your curiosity, Elizabeth? Do you feel better now you know what sort of man you're with?" he replies with that underlying cold tone of indifference that he does so well. No self-disgust, no apologetic tone, just the facts - how very businessman of him.

I don't even think I have a response for that. I thought Conner was his best friend. I'm sure my face is saying all that needs to be said because I can feel it screwing up in confusion. Blackmail? Does that really go on? And why would he do that to his friend? Wow, he really is a bastard. I'm in love with a complete fucking arsehole, a traitor.

"Right."

It's all I've got. At least I know why he didn't want to tell me. I suppose he did tell me he wasn't a good man. It appears he really isn't. If I'm honest, I'm struggling to even look at him. What a crappy thing to do to your friend. Is he the least bit remorseful about it or is it just something he does with no care for the other person involved? I haven't got a clue what to do or say next so I just stare at the floor in the hopes of making this go away.

"You see, this is why I didn't want you involved. This is not who you are, and it isn't what you want to hear from me, is it? But this is what I have been, Elizabeth. In fact, I've been far worse in some cases, and while I am trying to be better, I can't reverse my past for you," he says from the doorway. I still can't look at him so I cross the room and plonk myself down on the sofa, staring blankly at the alcohol table and wondering whether I should have some.

"No, I don't suppose you can," I whisper in reply because he can't, can he? And what's worse is that I really don't know anything about what he's done to people in his past. He's always told me he didn't deserve me and I suppose this is the type of thing he meant.

Because to pursue and have sex with someone who belonged to your best friend is just abhorrent to me, just plain horrible. Why would he do that? Did having no one love him as a child make him unable to empathise with someone else's feelings in that sort of scenario? Or did he just do it with no regard to Conner's feelings at all because he could? Either way, it just makes him a man with no moral compass whatsoever, doesn't it? And a complete bastard in my books. What other shit does he have in that damned closet that he's going to hit me with at some point? Christ, the man is some sort of lethal killing machine, with no ability to empathise, who enjoys sadistic sexual pursuits.

My fingers find my temples in a bid to rid myself of the flash of images that pass before me, blood, Conner's happy, in love face, Alex with a blonde woman and then our argument, all the time laced with that threatening tone that lingers over his words and actions. It doesn't work as my mind continues to spin with vile visions and angry voices, visions that are beginning to show me who he really is, or at least was. It's not the man I know but it clearly is the man he could be without me.

"I don't understand why you would do that. Why would you want to do that to him?" I ask as he hovers behind me. I'm not even sure I want an answer. He sits down on the opposite sofa and looks at me with sad eyes.

"Because I could. I'm a bastard like that, Elizabeth. I wanted her and therefore I took her," he replies with a small shrug - a fucking shrug as if it's a completely acceptable answer. It really isn't. Where on earth my Alex is in all of this is a mystery because this man is not him.

"You didn't care that it would hurt Conner?"

"If I didn't care, I wouldn't have paid the whore off, would I? I just didn't care enough to stop me from doing it in the first place apparently," he replies as he leans back into his seat and rests his head on his hand. "I'm not proud of it if that's any help, and I've just found out that he knew anyway. She got three million out of me and he knew all along. He never said a word to me, never hit me, never turned me away, nothing. Why would he do that? Why would he continue to be my friend when I'd just ripped away something that he wanted desperately?" he asks. Actually, I'm not sure that he's asking me, more musing to himself as if he hasn't got a clue why someone would forgive him.

I eventually lift my head from my hands and stare at him with a sigh. What the hell does he need to understand how much people care about him, that he might deserve love in spite of his actions? Does he seriously not get that Conner could want him more than his misdeeds, might want to give him a chance to redeem himself or at least prove himself again? God, his father must have done a real number on him. Either that or his sense of appropriate is so misguided that he can't see right from wrong at all.

"Do I seriously need to answer that?" His faced looks confused. "Honestly, Alex, can you not see why he let this happen?"

"I don't understand his response, no. He should have beaten me to death, or at the very least let me see how much he loathed me for what I'd done to him," he replies with a frown. "It's what I would have done." Oh god, the man really doesn't have a clue.

"That's what decent human beings do for the people they love, Alex. They forgive and forget because they can't bear the thought of being without someone. They worry that their life would be somehow less fulfilled or perhaps meaningless without that love. Clearly you were more important than Caroline was to him and he decided you were worth his loyalty or maybe compassion. I'm not sure which, but regardless, Conner must love you very much. You should be honoured by his allegiance, Alex. You should also be very proud to call him a friend and a confidant."

He snorts in derision and shakes his head at me. I don't know why I expected anything less. The man knows nothing of love or real feelings.

"Well he's a bloody idiot then. He shouldn't have forgiven me. I clearly didn't merit his compassion as you put it, still don't." He's possibly right if I'm honest, but it doesn't stop me wanting to rub his tortured soul and make him love himself a little bit more.

"Why do you do that? Why do you believe you're not worthy?"

"Because I'm not. Isn't it obvious?" Oh bless him, arsehole father.

"Not to me it isn't. I believe you're worth every second of my time and effort, but if you truly believe you're not deserving then

413

maybe I should just move on and find someone else who is, someone better?"

Unfortunately I couldn't, even if he told me to, and as his narrowed, dark blue eyes fly to mine, I raise my brow at him in challenge because he needs to see this, needs to understand how good he can be. He needs to remember the man who treats me like a queen and gives his time to Addisons with so much care that it's almost humbling to witness.

"I don't want you to leave me," he snarls through clenched teeth. I'm not surprised by that either, and I can't stop the small smile that brightens my face as I shake my head at him. His face softens back down a bit as he leans his elbows on his knees and clasps his hands together, rubbing his thumbs across his lips. "And that was uncalled for."

"Was it? Really? I can't do this on my own, Alex. It won't work if you don't believe, too."

"Mmm," he replies with a small smile. It doesn't reach his eyes and I know he doesn't really trust what I'm trying to say. He's still too busy trying to burn me into my seat in the hope I won't run for the door. At least I'm starting to work him out. I shake off my thoughts and move on to something more positive.

"Are you going to apologise to him?"

"I'm not sure if I know how to. It was a long time ago," he says as he gazes at me.

"Why don't you just start with something like, 'I'm a complete fucking arsehole. I don't deserve your support or friendship and I'm very thankful that you forgave me?' I think that will probably work."

It would probably work for me. Mind you, the fact that he has very nice shoulders, an incredible backside and a beautiful smile work for me. I'm not sure Conner will have the same core clenching response as I do. His aptly timed beautiful smile appears smoothly and does exactly what it's intended to do, weakens me completely.

"Okay, I'm a complete fucking arsehole and I don't deserve your support at all, yet alone your love, and I'm seriously hoping that you'll forgive me. Is that working?"

Bastard. Yes, how could it not?

"You really are a shit. Your panty dropping smile won't work on Conner, you know?" I narrow my eyes. He works me far too well. I have to try and work on that at some point.

"I know," he replies as he stretches his fingers to my knees with a lick of his lips and chuckles. "It does appear to be working on you though."

"It's not funny," I snap. I don't know why I'm bothering with the façade of still being angry. I'm already imagining those fingers working higher. It makes me wonder how surprised I really was about the information in the first place because I should be utterly devastated and I'm really not. His apparent nasty side is yet another thing I'm in love with for some unknown reason, and the fact that he is clearly a deviant little shit and yet is trying to be better is frankly wonderful.

"Oh I know, not funny at all," he replies with a smirk, dropping down onto his knees in front of me and pushing my legs apart so he can get in between them. My weak attempt at keeping them together really is pathetic.

"Don't ever threaten me again." His hands wrap behind my back and yank me toward him so abruptly that I actually squeal at the force of his strength. But as my core hits his warm body, I instantly feel like I'm home and safe again.

"I will never try that again, I promise. You have full permission to attack me if I do, or leave without hesitation," he whispers into my neck, dragging his teeth along my collarbone. My head lulls back to give him access as all memories of arguments disappear and forgiveness kicks in with a vengeance. "Fuck, you smell good."

"And how are you going to make it up to me?" I'm ridiculous. I'll admit it because regardless of how much I'm trying to keep this going, I couldn't care less as I grind into his hard stomach muscles. All I can think about is having these trousers pulled off me and possibly being carried up the stairs. Actually, I couldn't care less. Right here on the floor would be great, too. In fact, as his hands begin to push me back further, I'm pretty sure we won't be moving anywhere at all. His sudden halting and relaxing grip makes me sit back up and look at him. He's frowning again. "Oh god, what are you going to tell me now?"

"This is not me being *better*," he says as he backs away from me and stands up. Oh, it's not? It felt a whole lot better to me if I'm honest. My core instantly stretches across the space to him as if it could pull him back all by itself somehow. Clearly it can't but that's how it feels nonetheless.

"It's not?"

"No, that was me avoiding being a prick, so we're going to scrap the damn party that you're so averse to, drop them in a very large cheque as an apology and then I'm going to take you somewhere special. After that, you can get a good night's sleep before your very important and very early job tomorrow."

Right, I'm not sure that was what my thighs were hoping for, but as I watch him walk off out of the room, I have to admit I'm impressed. He's certainly learning and that can only be a good thing. The fact that he's left me here spread open for him, watching his perfect arse and panting like a sodding idiot is possibly not.

~

An hour and a refreshing shower later, he grabs my hand and leads me into the garage.

"Take your pick," he says as he moves to the back of the space and punches some numbers into the keypad on the wall. A grey box emerges from the wall and reveals keys - lots of keys. I blankly look around at all the very sporty things and wonder which would be nice. To be honest, I quite fancy one of the bikes but given my dress and his probably Saville Row suit, it's probably not going to work. It would have been nice to wrap myself around him and hold him close for a while to bring us back together again, though. He hasn't touched me since he left me in the music room and I'm beginning to long for his hands on me again, to feel him on me normally so we can move on.

"You choose, I haven't got a clue," I reply, although the *McLaren* does twinkle at me rather vigorously. How the hell I'd get in it elegantly is quite another thing.

"*McLaren* it is then," he says as he beeps something and the garage door opens.

"How did you..."

"Magic. You might want to have a word with those pesky fairies that keep hanging around. They keep telling me what you want," he replies as he opens the door for me and I try as best I can to slide in gracefully. It doesn't work and he ends up getting an eyeful of my lace top hold ups, possibly my laced covered crotch, too, as I eventually sit. "You're not making it very easy for me to be a gentleman, you know?"

I look up at him with a smirk, pulling my black dress down again slowly.

"What on earth gave you the impression that I was after that, Mr. White?" His growl of self-restraint as he shuts the door and walks around the car at least lets me know he's thinking about it. Maybe I should just push him further and get us back in the house quickly. I scan the interior of the car. There isn't a chance in hell we'll be doing anything in this cramped space, which instantly reminds me of the fact that I've never actually had sex in a vehicle, or on one for that matter. My mouth quirks up as the idea takes hold. This fantasy of mine could be lived out by the end of the evening.

About forty minutes later we're pulling though a set of very ornate wrought iron gates that appear to lead to an extremely large house set back along a winding driveway. I'm not entirely sure how I've survived the drive without being killed. Alex may well be a good driver but it appears sports cars and wet London roads are not to be messed with. Unfortunately, that didn't stop him throwing it around every corner available. My inner slut shrivelled up and died about ten minutes into the journey as she held on for dear life and tried to breathe her way through the fear. Strangely, she also revived herself at some point in the last ten minutes in a completely different state of mind. All she seems to be able to think about is kneeling and begging.

"That was not the nicest journey I've ever been on," I state as he laces his fingers in mine and walks me to the entrance of the building, which screams eighteenth century elegance at me. Ten steps lead up to a black front door that is flanked by two men in royal blue livery, top hats and the works. He turns back to me and abruptly pulls me to his mouth.

"No, but that fear's got you ready for me, baby, hasn't it? Your eyes are dilated, your lips flushed and full. I bet your pussy's dripping with arousal and you'd do anything I ask as soon as I asked it. Shall we just do it here on the steps? Or maybe on top of the car? Perhaps the other diners would like to watch. What do you think?" he replies with an arrogantly raised brow and a smirk. Arsehole.

"Actually, I'm dry as a bone." I roll my eyes and keep walking. I will not allow him to be completely in control even if he undoubtedly is. "And that is the least gentlemanly thing I've ever heard."

He chuckles behind me and firmly swats my backside just as we reach the door, making me yelp in shock. The doorman coughs uncomfortably then smiles at me. Alex glares at him so I roll my eyes again and keep walking then stop immediately as I hit the foyer. I have no idea why he's brought me here but language like that and my little black dress have absolutely no right to be entering the space at all. It's a sodding palace.

I quickly swing my astounded eyes back to his. His soft smile greets me as he takes my hand again and leads us across the vast marble floor towards another set of opulent doors, each step of his dominantly possessing the ground as he somehow casually owns the space around him. I tug on my dress and glance around to see if anyone's noticed that I'm not in designer clothes, all the time chastising myself for not picking out one of the expensive ones Alex bought for me. Several couples are loitering around and staring at us with their eyebrows raised, probably questioning who the ugly one with Alexander White is.

"Stop fidgeting," he says as he turns back to me before his hand opens the door. My eyes fly to the ground. Shit, this is too much.

"Sorry," I mumble in response. "Alex, I... God, why didn't you say something? I would have worn someth-"

He cuts me off. "Head up," he says as he lifts my chin tenderly. "Elizabeth, you are stunning, and the only one who holds my love so remember how much you're worth and stand by my side. Those are your numbers on my back. They are there for a reason. There is nothing in here that you can't handle with ease."

"But, I..." I don't even know what to say. I also don't know why I'm suddenly so nervous. I've done this sort of thing before with him and I managed okay. He leans in close enough to my ear to send quivers of desire coursing through me again.

"Shall I take you in caveman style? Throw you over my shoulder and bite your arse to let them know whom you belong to before we eat off the table like civilised humans? Will that remind you who you are?" His arm wraps around my back and I know he means it. Not going to happen. I shrug away from him and raise my chin with an amused smile. "Good girl. Though I was quite enjoying the thought actually."

"Don't even think about it." My glare comes rushing back as I notice a unfairly gorgeous dark haired woman flashing her eyes at Alex and making her way over. His chuckle softens it straight away.

"Better. Now, are you ready?" he asks as he cocks his head at the door.

"I think so," I reply with a wry grin.

"Yes, I think you are, too," he says as he pushes the handle down and opens it.

The gorgeous woman follows behind us and stands a little too close for comfort as she sashays very beautifully alongside me and winks. I'm not entirely sure what I'm supposed to do with that so I smile back in the hope that it was the correct response. Given that it's Alex who's bought me here, I don't even know where I'm being led. This could be yet another sex thing.

"Cecily," Alex says in acknowledgement as she winks at him and lengthens her stride. I watch her black hair swinging along her spine seductively in her open backed dress and sigh. This world of his is very definitely filled with the most dazzling people. Really I'm no match at all, but I keep my head up and try for casually elegant.

"And she is?" I ask as she reaches another set of doors. He frowns a little. Oh God, he's had her too. There really isn't anyone he hasn't slept with, is there? My head droops again. I really haven't got a hope. Every time I pull myself back up, he hits me with another crappy thing or another stunning woman to deal with.

"Cecily Winchester, mistress of Aiden Phillips," he replies as he squeezes my hand tighter. Oh, I've heard of the man, some big time crook that's heavily into drugs - well, selling them anyway from what I know. I'm sure there was a thing about him in the news last year.

"How do you know her?" I ask, desperately hoping that he'll tell me some other reason why she's winking at him. Having said that, she winked at me and I haven't slept with her. He pulls my hand to his mouth and kisses it.

"Same circles I suppose, wealth mixes with wealth in London. And no, Elizabeth, contrary to your beliefs, I haven't fucked everything that moves," he replies with a small chuckle as we catch up. Her head swings back to him and I swear her smile lights up the room.

"Alexander, tell her the truth. You simply wouldn't dare, would you?"

"Stop it, Cecily. Remember who you're damn well talking to," he replies quietly with a snarl. It's oddly malicious given her flirtation.

"Oh, Alexander, your threats don't bother me in the slightest. You should know that by now. They never did," she says as she pats his chest and swirls her dress towards the door again. "Have you come to see him?"

Him? Who's him? Is she talking about Aiden Phillips? Why would he know that man?

His past comes rushing back into my head at full force. Oh holy cow, a very bad boy, that's what he said, wasn't it? But he couldn't mean that sort of shit, could he?

Balls, I've entered the sodding mafia zone, yet another little place that Alexander White socialises in it seems. *Get your game face on, Beth.*

"No, I didn't know he was here. And I assumed he would be with Amira on a Saturday, not with his little after-thought." My lips twitch at the comment. He's a snide bastard I'll give him that. Her face is a picture of irritation.

"What the hell are you looking at?" she says as she suddenly turns on me with a very unfriendly face. The winking moment has apparently gone. I can't help but follow Alex's lead because the woman's head is far too far up her own arse, regardless of her beauty.

"I'm really not at all sure," I reply scathingly as I let my eyes glance over her slowly. Unfortunately, there isn't an imperfection anywhere. Bitch.

"She's sweet. I'm loving the innocent look, Alexander. Does she know what you really are?"

Oh, and now she's pissed me off because no I don't. I only know what he allows me to know, but I damn well know him better than her. I know his pain and no one but me knows that. She can fuck off if she thinks she's taking that away from me.

"Honey, there's nothing innocent here, so please remove your fake arse tits from my face before I rip them off for you," I seethe as gracefully as I can while moving a step towards her and letting go of his hand. Evelyn and Belle would truly be in awe of my performance because she actually steps back a bit as her eyes widen. Clearly no one

420

normally pisses on Aiden Phillip's mistress. I'm not even sure I should have if I'm honest, but I continue my irritated glare anyway and hope for the best.

"I think this conversation is finished, Cecily," Alex cuts in as she regains her poker face and opens her mouth. "Elizabeth, shall we?" he continues as he extends a hand in front of him and I walk through the door with a smile, not bothering with a last glance at her. His smirk of amusement is enough for me to know I did okay as she huffs behind us and clips off back the way she came. I think I just won a battle again, or maybe annoyed a mob boss's plaything, which instantly has me questioning what the hell I've just done. Mind you, she deserved it.

"Feisty." He chuckles as he places a hand on my back and kisses my cheek. "I think I've created a monster. You've definitely found your voice, haven't you?"

"Well what a bitch. I can't believe you have to socialise with these people. How do you know Aiden Phillips anyway? It's like the bloody twilight zone this world of yours, sex clubs, secret societies and now London's equivalent of the sodding mafia. Honestly, Alex, you could scare a girl off. It's all quite unnerving. I could really do without this shit. I mean, what the hell are you going to throw at me next? Is there some diabolical secret in your past that might send us all to jail or something?" I reply as I stride onwards, firmly entrenched in my annoyance. I'm really quite disturbed by this strange existence that he resides in, which I'm now clearly part of, and while I'm not entirely sure what I thought I was signing up for when I fell for him, I'm pretty sure it wasn't this.

I suddenly realise I'm on my own when I reach another door. How many sodding doors are there anyway? And where on earth are we going? I turn round to find him standing about fifteen feet behind me, looking extremely brooding in all his masculinity, dark blue eyes staring at me and jaw twitching in... possibly nervousness? What the fuck now? Haven't got a clue.

"What?" I ask, because I really haven't got time for this shit. I am suddenly on a roll of irritation. This day just gets better and better. Arguments, ex-lovers, bastard boyfriends and now crooked acquaintances and mistresses - yep, what a lovely Saturday.

"You said it didn't matter," he mutters quietly. Oh god, he is nervous. My heart almost shatters at his lonesome look, that little boy in the rain, peeping through his outward appearance just for me to see. To every other person here he's still Alexander White, mogul, six foot four with hands made for butchery, but to me, in this tiny second, he's lost, worried and looking to me for absolution of some sort. I smile softly and wander back towards him with my hand reaching for his throat, my throat. Caressing it gently, I nuzzle my head on his chest and blow out a much needed breath. How I'm finding the strength for any of this is beyond me but one touch of his body and I relax a little again.

"It doesn't. None of it will ever matter. I'm sorry, it's just been a long day." His arm wraps around me and pulls me into him.

"No, I'm sorry. This was supposed to be a nice night for you and my *shit* just got in the way again. Look, shall we just go home instead and have a take out? I could even cook for you if you want, massage maybe? In fact, can you swim?" What?

"Random, but yes," I reply as I gaze up at his concerned face while he scans the area around us with narrowed eyes. It appears he's now looking for a threat of some sort.

"Good, let's go and get you wet then."

Chapter 23

Elizabeth

I can't move any muscle on any part of my body. It's eight in the evening and I've done nothing but run my backside round for the entire day. The fact that he exhausted me all night in his damn swimming pool - yes, swimming pool. It appears the Victorian summer house is actually a twenty five metre swimming pool and jacuzzi come sauna type of building - really hasn't helped. Two hours of varying positions and some very interesting inspiration from Alex later and I was very ready for bed. He carried me back to the house in a bathrobe and dropped me onto the bed to sleep before today. I woke up feeling more tired than I did the night before. No amount of pressure for me to go back to his this evening worked because I seriously need some sleep, in my own bed, without him and all his tempting ideas or his body.

And what a bloody day. A profitable one, yes, but oh my god I'm so tired I could sleep for a week. While the day has been flawless and the birthday celebrations for one of London's wealthiest bachelorettes went off to perfection, I seriously need some help. Given that James couldn't work today and I had to work with a small team of people I hardly knew, I barely survived the experience without major disaster. Belle was, of course, incredible and managed to scatter her brilliance over every potential nightmare, which thankfully meant no one was any the wiser. She was a very happy bunny by the end of the day with several new contacts for future events. I'm so glad we have a bigger kitchen coming.

So now I'm sitting, well actually almost lying, in my chair with my feet resting very inelegantly on the coffee table, thinking about trying to move my hand to get to the wine. Belle is equally flaked out on the sofa, staring at her ring absentmindedly while glugging on her own glass. We're apparently waiting for Teresa to bring more wine. I'm assuming this means that Pascal has done the right thing and that she hasn't seen him today. I'm still perplexed by how this made me smile stupidly but I'm not over thinking it. Frankly, I haven't got the energy.

"So, wedding plans?" I ask as I haul myself up and reach for my drink.

"Long engagement," she replies with a snort. "My idea, not his. I just want to keep it like this for a while and see what happens."

I narrow my eyes at her and her unenthusiastic face. I haven't had the chance to talk to her for ages and her lukewarm response is confusing to say the least.

"Are you going to move in with him?"

"I might," she says as she stretches her neck about and then refills her glass.

"Okay, what's the matter? Last week you were smiling giddily and flashing that ring around for the world to see and now you're acting like you couldn't give a damn about him." Her face is a mixture of confusion and soft wistfulness all of a sudden as she sighs at me and looks over.

"He told me some things about his past that I've not been able to process properly. I suppose I've only got myself to blame because I did push for answers, but it doesn't mean I'm entirely happy with his response. It's just made me realise I know nothing about him if I'm honest, and now it feels fucking strange to have this ring on my finger."

Oh, right, well I know that feeling, obviously not the ring but the utter confusion over who a man is. That's completely normal for me.

"So what do you want to do about that?"

"I don't know. How much do you know about Alex? Conner told me some things that I never thought he was capable of. I'm beginning to question who these pair really are," she says as the door flies open and a furious yet gorgeous looking Teresa stomps in and helps herself to the wine without even saying hello. We both look at her in shock as she downs one glass and then clearly decides the bottle is a better idea so lifts it and begins drinking it down.

"Whoa, girl, what's got up your arse?" Belle asks as she looks in the bag and pulls out five more bottles of wine. Teresa eventually stops drinking and discards the bottle.

"Irritating fucking Frenchman, or whatever he is, that's what. What a fucking nerve, cancelling on me at the last damn minute. Who the hell does he think he is? This is me, for fuck's sake. Nobody cancels on me. I mean, look at me. Would you cancel on this?" she fumes as she waves her hands at herself and her very expensive looking purple dress with matching purple heels that are obviously new. I have to admit she looks utterly beautiful and I cringe at the thought that I made her this angry. Well, Pascal did, but fundamentally it was me and my possessiveness. I can call it *doing the right thing* as much as I like but in reality, I just didn't want him with her because it felt wrong somehow.

"I absolutely wouldn't cancel on you, honey. You look completely fucking awesome. He's a dickhead, whoever he is. Who is it by the way?" Belle asks, clearly unaware of the plan.

"Pascal fucking Van Der fucking Braak, cock faced arsehole," she shouts to no one in particular. This was definitely not a casual thing for her like she suggested to me. I've never seen her so wound up by a man in my life.

"Dutch then," Belle replies nonchalantly as she meanders over to the kitchen and brings back a bag of crackers and some cheese.

"What?" Teresa says, staring at Belle, still fuming.

"Dutch. Van Der Braack is a Dutch surname. I didn't know that was his surname. Why didn't someone tell me this?" It is? Right, Dutch. Oh well at least I know where he's from now. "Actually, I think we did a thesis or something on the family in St. Peters - very blue blood, third removed from old royalty. Shit, is he part of that family do you think?" I knew it.

"What the fuck has that got to do with anything?" Teresa replies, stomping off to my bedroom, probably to help herself to some of my comfy clothes. Two minutes later she returns in a pair of my shorts and a hoodie, still looking furious as she picks up a glass and starts glugging again.

"Come on, honey, calm down. You knew what he was like. I did try to warn you."

Again I'm cringing but she needs to get over this. I definitely did the right thing, regardless of my own reasons because Teresa would have been even worse if he'd actually played with her. She barks out an irritated snort and falls on the sofa next to Belle.

"I'm more furious with myself than him if I'm honest. When did you last see me like this? It's ridiculous that a sodding man can do this to me regardless of his blue blood, probably vampiric I should think." My splutter of wine doesn't go unnoticed as she smirks a little mid-paragraph. "I just can't believe I let myself get that hopeful about it. I mean, the man's an arsehole to women, isn't he? God, I'm an idiot," she replies as she repeatedly slams her head against the back of the sofa. Belle smacks her across the face and glares at her.

"You are definitely not an idiot, but he absolutely is a fucking arsehole if he's turned you down, honey. Anyway, you said he'd cancelled. Maybe he just had other stuff he needed to do. Beth said he's got businesses all over the place. Perhaps he'll just rearrange or something," she says as she nods at me. It's not going to happen, because of me, but I think I'm supposed to agree and help her feel better about this or something. Should I just tell her the truth or make up some shit that will keep stringing her along? Christ, I just want at least one of us to find a reasonably normal one for once, and Pascal is emphatically not normal. He might be for the right woman. Unfortunately for her, that woman is not Teresa.

"Let it go, honey. The man's a dick, granted a very attractive one, but you knew this would just be a fling. You told me that yourself. Please don't get so wound up by this. He might call you again but in reality, it'll still end up the same way. He was never after more than one thing. That's why I was trying to warn you off," I respond to her as she pulls up her legs and looks into her wine glass as if that's not the answer she was looking for. I might be a bitch for doing all this but now I'm very glad I did because the sight of her so unhappy is very nearly killing me. My fingers are itching to call him and tell him what he's done. Unfortunately, he won't care and fundamentally it's all my fault anyway, isn't it? God, I feel like shit. She eventually shifts in her seat and looks up at me.

"You're right, Beth. I don't need a man like that, do I? Plenty more fish and all that. Just do me a favour and slap the shit out of him the next time you see him, will you? I'm deleting his number as we speak," she says as she pulls her phone out, swipes a few things then flings it on the table in apparent revulsion.

Slap Pascal? I could do that. He's more than likely never had a slap, though he's given plenty I'm sure. I'm disgusted with myself as I smile privately at the thought and hide my face behind my glass.

"Right, well now that's sorted, when are we going to see this building of yours, Miss Moneybags?" Belle asks as she loads enormous amounts of cheese onto a cracker and begins munching. Suddenly very happy with this change of subject, thank you Belle, I brighten my face and think about tomorrow.

"Well, we could go tomorrow if you like. The shop's closed and I'm not seeing Alex until the afternoon so what do you think?" I ask as I help myself to some of the very appealing looking cheese and down it with some more wine. They both nod their heads and relax back again.

"Did you think about more staff?" Teresa chimes in. "You'll definitely need another chef and we're likely to need someone to run the shop if I'm coming with you. Actually, are you going to need another pair of hands for prep as well? God, this is actually a lot to think about. What about the new catering benches and cookers and stuff?"

"We're going to need a new chef, two more catering hands and someone to run the shop daily. I've looked into a loan for all the stuff we need at Defoe Point, but I'm just not sure how much we'll need until I see the space," Belle replies as I stare at her in shock. Clearly she's been organising herself well, as usual. I haven't thought much about it at all, apart from the James bit.

"I was thinking we could ask James," I say. Their heads shoot back to me.

"Because I'm sure Mr. White is going to think that's a fabulous idea," Teresa says with a roll of her eyes as my phone beeps at me. I grab it and swipe as Belle starts in.

"Well fuck him. James is great and I think it's a perfect call, honey. Ask him and see what he says."

"Okay, what about the catering stuff?" I reply as I glance down at the screen.

-   **It appears your presence has engrained itself, my rose. I am not normally so easily persuaded. I**

trust my decent behaviour will be rewarded at some point when I call on it.

Oh god… What on earth does he think he's going to get in return? Belle and Teresa are mumbling along in the background as I try to understand what I've just done. I assumed, obviously wrongly, that he would just do this for me. Clearly I should have known better. He wants something from me, which he's going to get anyway if Alex has anything to do with it, but what if he means on his own? Before I get a chance to reply, my phone beeps again.

-   **I've missed you today. Hope work was okay. I'll pick you up at two tomorrow. Love you x**

Oh god, that makes me feel like even more of a shit. I should tell him about this before Pascal gets any stupid ideas in his head. Perhaps not by text, though. Tomorrow will be good. Alex will be able to deal with him and put him back in his place, I think. Why did I get mixed up in any of this? With speedy fingers, I reply to the man I love first.

-   **Love you too. My day was very long and very tiring. How was yours? See you tomorrow X**

Now Pascal.

-   **Thank you for your decency, Pascal. Your reward is my affection and gratitude to the man I know is still in there. Your rose.**

That should work. He likes me nipping at his soft side, I hope. Actually, he might be thinking extremely inappropriately about anything but his soft side. I glance over at Teresa and feel guilt biting at me, then rapidly squash it back down. Whatever he is to me, he wouldn't have been that to her. He would have used her and then unceremoniously dumped her without thought. I've done the right thing here. Beep again.

-     **My day was underwhelming without you to play with. Like I said, I missed you. x**

My smile broadens at the thought of him playing with me, just like he did in his pool, jacuzzi and sauna as the rain pelted down on the glass roof. I'm almost wishing I was there again, in his very deviant hands, being manhandled and loved, but I seriously need my bed tonight.

"Who are you smiling at?" Belle asks with a smirk.

"Who do you think? That was clearly a very naughty thought she was having," Teresa replies as my phone beeps again.

-     **Gratitude is displayed in varying ways, my rose. I would prefer yours bound and gagged. That voice of yours distracts me from my usual thoughts.**

Oh shit, my face must be flaming. The arsehole is definitely after something. Actually, it makes me realise that Alex has backed off on all that stuff a little. I'm missing it a bit if I'm honest. He's still aggressive but there haven't been any additions to our sex life for a while.

"I'm thinking that was explicit to say the least," Belle says as she pours me more wine.

"I'm really not happy about all this sex talk. I'm feeling very under used over here. Will one of you find me a damn man and quick," Teresa states with her first giggle of the evening. I smile at her and swear to myself that I might just do that. Alex must have other friends apart from the obscenely nonstandard ones I currently know. My fingers travel to my phone again.

-     **I missed you too. Think of something to do with me tomorrow, anything you want x**

His response comes back as I'm texting Pascal.

-     **Well you asked for it. Try to piss me off a bit before I get to you x**

So I dump his text and reply to the man I love instead because my brain has suddenly ratcheted up a notch into, *whatever you want, Alex* mode, which is completely enthralling and utterly riveting. I have no idea what the man will come up with next. His ability to turn inanimate objects into sex toys is astounding.

> - **Getting you pissed off seems to be something I can do easily enough. Until tomorrow. I love you x**

As I stare at the two girls chortling away between themselves and begin to imagine Alex's hands all over me, Teresa's face promptly reminds me of Mr. Van Der Braack. I narrow my eyes at the thought. I can't keep doing this texting thing behind Alex's back because he will flip if he finds out. I could use that to piss him off a bit, I suppose. But I'm not sure that's quite what he meant. I am assuming he meant it in a fun sort of way. Actually, I miss his darker side a little. Why is still mystifying. However, there's just something very appealing about it in a slightly scary sort of way. Why hasn't he taken me to Pascal by now anyway? Or the club at least. Is he waiting for me to ask? Or is he still keeping me away from him, or vice versa? Not that I'd want him pissed off for that scenario. That could be way too detrimental to my personal wellbeing. And thinking about it, we haven't tried any... well, *back door* activity again since the car. My fingers find my phone.

> - **I'm his to play with, Pascal, not yours. Please don't make this difficult, but I am grateful to you nonetheless. Your rose**

The response is almost instant. I have no idea how people text that fast.

> - **It will be your decision, my rose, not his. It may never be his choice again.**

What the hell does that mean? While my inner slut may be hitching up her skirt and leaping fences to get to the very corrupt aristocrat, is he suggesting that I'm somehow in control of all this? And actually, does Pascal know what's going to happen anyway? Surely not. Having said that, they have done this sort of thing before and he's more than likely ready to do Alex's bidding at the drop of a hat, isn't he? But what does he mean by this not being Alex's choice. It's all his choice, isn't it? Well, I've obviously got some say in the matter but fundamentally, he's the one who sees all this as normal, not me.

I'm still very much out of my comfort zone on this.

I drop my phone on the table and gaze back at my girls in the hope of distracting myself from very inappropriate visions. Thankfully, another glass of wine or two later and I'm well on my way to not thinking about any man at all. The only thing on my mind is giggling and acting like a complete idiot as Belle knocks up the music.

It seems we won't be having that early night after all.

~

In the very cold December light of day, getting completely inebriated last night was not the best way to alleviate feeling tired. I'm dressed in my long, black, flat boots, black jeans and a black jumper. I did try to brighten up the look with my red, three-quarter length, Mont Clare coat but to be honest, I'm still so hungover that I couldn't care less what I look like. Thankfully, I did at least get a very good lie in, which resulted in me not even getting out of my bed until eleven o'clock. Belle's attempt at the coffee machine seemed to work a bit so three double shots later, I think I vaguely resemble a human of some sort.

Monday's London traffic is its normal busy self. I still don't really understand where any of it's going, but then London never seems to stop. It just keeps zooming about and getting its job done, whatever it is. Now we're all walking along the road towards what will be our new building, my building, and I still can't believe he gave it to me as we approach the corner arm in arm. Belle's giggling like an excited schoolgirl. It's the wealth of it all. Frankly she's a whore for a bit of power. Teresa is unfortunately still looking a little forlorn, which keeps kicking me in the guts. I'm such a bitch. I really do hate myself for making her so sad, but it was never meant to be so I'll just have to make it up to her somehow. Who knows? Perhaps I should take her into one of Alex's many interesting twilight zones. Maybe she'll find someone there, probably another arsehole though.

We round the corner and are immediately greeted with various work and trade vehicles. My eyes shoot to Belle who instantly arches a brow at me.

"Doing a little decorating, are we?"

"Uh, no," is my response as I continue forward and watch a man unload what appears to be a stainless steel sink unit.

"Well someone is," Teresa says as she catches up with me, fluffs her hair and instantly launches herself at a really quite attractive blond man lifting a heavy looking bag with no shirt on. It's bloody December for God's sake.

"Can I help you, love?" one of the other men asks as he gives me a once over and stands in front of the door. At least this one's wearing clothes. Still, I don't like his smarmy tone in the slightest.

"Yes, could you move out of the way so I can get into my building," I reply snarkily as I take a step forward.

"As far as I'm aware, love, you're not Mr. White and therefore, no."

Arsehole. Another up himself git I've got to deal with and frankly my head hurts too much.

"As far as I'm aware, Mr. White's name is not on this building. Mine is. If you want to call him on a Sunday, please do. Actually, use my phone. I can't wait for his response given that none of you should actually be touching *my* building anyway," I reply as I stretch it out to him and glare my best *piss off* face at him.

"Umm..." Mr. Arse appears to not know what to do with himself all of a sudden. My feisty Beth kicks in at his show of weakness.

"Oh get out of my way, will you?" I state as I brush past him and walk into the building.

Oh. holy shit.

The entire space has been completely decked out with everything I could ever want, perfectly at that. Stud walls have gone up to partition areas and create separate kitchens. Storage and refrigeration units have been discretely positioned so as to not see them. Every piece of stainless steel is probably the highest quality that I've ever seen and I know because I've been longing for that cooker I can see twinkling away at me in the far corner. I take another tentative step forward with my mouth still gaping as I hear the rush of footsteps behind me.

"What the fuck?" Belle shouts as she reaches me.

"I know." It's all I've got. The place is immaculate and planned to precision. The workman wandering around give the three of us varying degrees of wolf whistle and leering stares as they carry yet more new units about. I'm sure if they knew who I am, or more importantly who I'm with, they wouldn't dare to look let alone give dirty glances.

"Alex," I whisper out in awe as Teresa touches me on the back and then wraps an arm around me. I can't believe he's done this for me. I can't believe he gave me the building in the first place let alone did all this as well. It must have cost a fortune.

"Oh, that man has it bad for you, honey," she says quietly with another squeeze.

"How much have you asked for on the loan, Belle?" I'm not even sure why I've asked but for some unknown reason, I need to know that we could have afforded this without him, that maybe I could pay him back somehow even if it is over the next hundred years.

"Fifty thousand, but it never would have filled this space. We would have needed hundreds of thousands to achieve this. The trade staff in themselves probably cost that much. I didn't realise it was so big," she replies as she looks around again and then upwards. "Oh Jesus, is that offices up there, too?"

"Yep, your own personal heaven, go have a look," I suggest, mainly because I need some time on my own to evaluate how the hell I feel. I pull away from Teresa who thankfully seems to get the point because she marches off after Belle who is now excitedly running up the steps with her heels clicking and echoing around the space. I can't help giggling at the thought of the boardroom table that she's about to find and wonder if it's been cleaned since the last time I was here.

I wander forward into what seems to be designated as a baking kitchen and open a huge set of double doors. Every utensil and type of cookware is carefully placed inside, right down to the varying shades of cutting boards for different foods. Double draining sink units, microwaves, prime cookers, chilling cabinets, vast baking ovens... God, there isn't a thing that has been missed. Alex knows nothing about what would be needed here so he must have had some chef come in and order everything for him somehow. In fact, with this amount of work it must have all been ordered and discussed prior to me even saying I'd accept the place. I hoist myself up onto the work surface and stare around me again at everything he's done for me. I have no idea how to say thank you for this and there's clearly no way I'm paying him back. How does someone say thank you for something like this? I struggled to say thank you for the building in the first place.

I can feel the tears welling up as I try to come to terms with everything he means to me, everything he's done for me. I just hope to hell that I can give him the same in return because he'll never be able to understand how much I love him, how much I crave him near me and what his love is to me. How on earth can I make him see how wonderful he is?

I swipe away my tears and just stare, still in disbelief. I have no idea what it is that I've done to deserve him but I'm so glad for it regardless. For all his oddities and different little realities, he's mine, and he continues to amaze me every day.

I'm not sure how long I've been sat here, swinging my heels against the units and trying to think of a suitable response to his gift to me, but it seems to me that there just isn't one. I can only love him and hope that's enough. I'll just try to show him everything that love should mean, be there for him, protect him, cherish him and give him the peace he says he finds in me. That's all I've got to give him anyway, isn't it? So I'll continue to do just that and allow him his mistakes and his past. Regardless of whatever's in it that I don't know about, that's where it should stay, because that's what he wants from me, to accept the man he is today and to forgive him his sins. I swipe a tear again and close my eyes while I listen to the screaming that's emanating from upstairs. It wouldn't surprise me if there's a full suite of new computer systems and office stuff up there, probably supplied by Conner as his gift to Belle. What a pair of diamonds in the rough we've found.

"I haven't bought anything to negotiate with this time," he says from behind me somewhere. I smile to myself and keep swinging my heels quietly. I'm not at all surprised he's here because it's just like him to pop up when I need him most, as if he could hear me thinking about him and knew I wanted to have him wrapped around me. In all reality, Mr. Arse from outside probably phoned to check out who the maniac woman was.

"I'm not sure you've got anything left to negotiate with, have you?" I reply as I look at his reflection in the stainless steel splash backs in front of me, his arms crossed as he leans against the door frame and smirks at my back.

"There's still plenty to use, baby. I'm just not willing to discuss this with you. Actually, it was supposed to be a surprise, which you have now ruined," he replies as I watch his image taking steps towards me. My body hums with that familiar feeling as his hand extends to my hair and twirls a lock in his fingers. My head instantly leans toward him and rests into his hand as I close my eyes again and let his warmth infuse me.

"Then thank you, it's a wonderful surprise," I say quietly as his other hand wraps around me and pulls me back towards him.

"That's it? No argument?"

"No, just thank you and I love you." His chuckle is beautiful, so beautiful that I want to see it so I quickly spin on the counter and push myself towards him. Perfect crotch-grinding level - clearly by his raised eyebrow and twinkling eyes he's aware of this fact, too. I've clamped my legs around him before I've even thought about it.

"Is it okay? Do you like it?" My response is to pull him even closer and lean my head into his chest, breathe him in and let him make me feel safe and warm. "Should I take that as a yes?"

"I want you inside me," I reply as I nuzzle my head again and dig my hands under his shirt so that I can feel his skin. It's all I want at the moment, and I refuse to not be completely honest about it, just skin on skin and preferably a bed. His amusement reverberates through his chest and straight through to my soul as he leans in and rests his chin on my head.

"Oh, sorry," Teresa says from behind us as she flies into the room. I lift my head and peer at her. She's doing the Macarena with her hips. I think she's trying to suggest I should thank my man properly. I damn well would if everyone would piss off.

"Teresa," Alex says in acknowledgement, as he turns round to look at her interesting moves with a smile. She flushes a little then smirks to herself.

"Well, he deserves it," she says as she nods her head at him and sashays out of the room just as Belle walks in and heads straight for him. I have no idea what the look in her face is trying to impart but the fact that she has wrapped her arms around him and kissed him on the cheek before I've taken another breath has me gawping instantly. He looks equally shocked and clearly has no idea what to do with his hands. She pulls away and pats him on the chest as she turns away.

"You did good, White. Not such a fucking arsehole after all," is her comment as she leaves. I'm still too shocked to look away from the door as she shuts it.

"I think you just made it into her 'genuinely liked' books." He chortles to himself and leans back into me. God, he feels good. My core ignites again as his lips meet mine gently.

"You still want me?" he asks as his fingers travel south toward a place I'm desperate for all of a sudden. "Do you want me all over you?"

"God, yes," is my breathy reply. I don't seem to give a shit about the workman milling around or the fact that my sister and best friend are circulating the grounds. No, I want him instantly inside me so that I can show him everything he is. He pushes me backwards onto the surface and crawls up on top of me until we're lying down and I moan at the weight of him on top of me, wishing we were naked. He lines himself up with my unfortunately jean-clad crotch and braces his elbows by my head, his hands resting on my face gently.

"Why did I do this for you?" he asks as those light blue eyes blink softly at me.

"Because you could," I reply quickly, trying to get my lips to his as he gently rubs his hard length against my clit, which is screaming at him for more pressure. His hands push my head down again softly.

"Why else?"

"Because you love me." This rewards me with the pressure I was craving. Apparently it was the right answer.

"Mmm... Fuck, I love watching you, why else did I do this?"

"To help me... realise... Oh god, that's good... my dreams." I'm struggling now if I'm honest. Words are becoming hard to formulate. His tongue gently dips into my mouth as he feathers me with the sweetest kisses he has and keeps rolling his hips slowly, each thrust bringing me closer to finishing the ache he's created.

"Why else, baby? I need to know you understand," he says, his breath coming harder now as he reaches in between us, quietly unzips himself and pushes my jumper up to expose my stomach. I'm sure I should care that he's about to do this with everyone around but I don't, not in the slightest. His rhythm starts again. It's not too quick. It doesn't need to be because he's somehow managing to find the exact spot I need to come.

"Because I give you peace." His lips come down on me with passion as his speed increases a little with heavier thrusts. And oh shit, it's all I need. My tongue entwines with his as my hands find his hair. His quiet groaning into my mouth as I pant for air finishes any last thoughts I had about whether or not to do this here because my back arches up into him as I lock my leg around his.

"Tell me," he says as my core starts to splinter and alight. I throw my head back and let him take me there.

"I love you." His hand tilts my head back to look at him, his eyes smiling while his beautiful lips pant out with restraint. He's waiting for me, so I let him have everything as my body writhes for its bliss and then begins to shatter beneath him.

"Again," he says, moving higher up me and groaning against my neck, now rubbing himself against my stomach as his fingers keep me spinning through my glory. He grabs hold of my hand and drags it down to wrap around his cock and starts to pump harder into it as he grunts out in pleasure.

"I love you," I mumble out as I try to think of words and mould my other hand over his backside to push him down into me. His weight increases as he slows his movement slightly and looks back into my eyes with a groan.

"It's all for you," he rasps out as he stills completely and I feel his wet warmth spilling across me with his release. Eventually his hand lazily wanders and begins to push his come around my stomach, across my ribs, and then pushing my bra cup away roughly, he palms it all over my breast, all the time watching what he's doing and smiling to himself. My eyebrows shoot up, This is new, obviously what he meant by *all over me.* His face lifts to mine with a very deviant glint to his eyes as he moves some more to the other breast, squeezes my nipple sharply then rubs his hand up to my throat. The scent of him assaults my senses as he raises his fingers to my mouth, silently commanding me to suck them, so I do and relish his taste on my tongue.

"Mine," he states with a tilt of his mouth and a raised brow while I'm still licking.

I don't think I've ever had come purposely used to... What? Mark me somehow, because that's exactly what he appears to be doing. It's kind of territorial and he really doesn't need to but I can't help my smile of amusement.

"Yep, all yours. Mr. White," I reply as a giggle escapes me and I run my fingers through his very sexy looking, just almost fucked hair.

"You're damn right," is his response as he travels his teeth across my lips and nibbles. It's far too polite and I'm so ready for more. I push my hips up into him again to indicate exactly that.

"This is not very sanitary for a baking kitchen."

"Couldn't give a fuck." Neither could I if I'm honest.

Unfortunately, having slowed down from my, *very lovely explosion, which didn't quite cut it but was enough for the time being*, I'm reminded of who's around us as a loud banging noise starts up in the background, followed by a drill.

"Well that's ruining the moment a little," I say as I try to move. His hands find mine and hold me down again.

"Nothing could ruin me covering you in my come. You're not showering for a fucking week. I like you smelling of me," he replies.

"How very primal of you, Mr. White." His growl of agreement has me imagining all sorts of things again as he pushes his now hardening cock into me again. "Again?"

"I'm debating putting it in your mouth this time," he says with a cheeky grin as his lips meet mine again and he lets go of my hands. He could. I really wouldn't mind. Frankly, the man can have anything he wants at the moment.

"Beth? Is it safe in there? Because we're going," Belle shouts through the door, breaking us from our gazing contest. Alex groans and rolls his eyes as he moves backwards and puts himself away. I pout at him but tuck my breasts back in and try to sort myself out while sliding from the table.

"Yep, all decent, honey," I call back and the door opens. Well, as decent as I can be with him smeared all over me. His smirk of amusement at me wiping my neck earns him a small glare in return.

"There's nothing decent about fucking on your own food prep area, but hell, I would have done the same," she says as she turns to Alex and smiles. It really is a genuine one and my heart lurches at the sight of them interacting nicely. "Listen, I just want to know if it was you or Conner that sorted the computers and shit?" He chuckles and grabs my hand as we all walk out.

"I hadn't gotten around to the *computers and shit* as you say, so I think it's safe to assume Conner's involved. Although how he knew or got in here is beyond me," he replies as I gape again at my vast workspace and squeeze his hand, so in love.

"Sneaky bastard, well that's really quite sweet of him," she says, almost to herself as she looks up the stairs again. I follow her gaze and notice a blue bow on the door. Definitely Mr. Avery. I check my watch and notice it's almost two,

"Why don't you call him and we'll go and have lunch somewhere? Where's Teresa?" I reply, scanning the area. I can't see her anyway.

"Possibly hooking up with a very nice looking joiner over there, last seen pulling her neckline down a little and going in for the kill," Belle states nonchalantly as if this is perfectly normal. It possibly is to be fair, and given the Pascal thing, I'm happy for her.

"Not on my fucking time she's not," Alex says as he stiffens a little.

"Oh, stop being such a dick. He's off the clock apparently," Belle replies as she swipes out her phone. He sneers at her as if he's still not happy with that response. I don't suppose I would be if I was paying their wages either. I tug on his hand so he swings his eyes down to mine.

"Let her have this. She was hurt yesterday so this might help a bit," I say quietly as I inwardly cringe at my own guilt and hope he doesn't ask any more questions. He instantly narrows his eyes at me. I have no idea whether it's the fact that she's been hurt or that he can see me hiding something.

"What are you not telling me?" Clearly the latter then. Fuck, why does he have to read me so well? I really have to work on this impassive thing that he manages all the bloody time. My thumbnail comes up to my mouth without me even realising it. It was a stupid move because his eyebrow is now arched and questioning. Oh, sod it. I knew I had to tell him anyway so I might as well get it out of the way. I look over to Belle to make sure she's out of earshot and glance around for Teresa again. No sign. Good.

"I... Umm..." His eyebrow manages to lift even higher. Fuck. "Look, Teresa was going to see Pascal for some entertainment and I didn't want it to happen. I couldn't persuade her otherwise so I texted

Pascal and asked him not to, so he called it off, which it seems really hurt her feelings so I'm really glad he did, otherwise it would have been even worse and that would have been really bad. Unfortunately, now he appears to think I owe him something in return for his *decent* behaviour, which I am obviously grateful for given his normal indecent behaviour but... Well... You know. Anyway, I told him no, and to not make it difficult, and that I was yours but he said that it wasn't your decision, that it was mine. I'm not sure what he means by that but I get the feeling that he wasn't accepting no for an answer. So now I'm a bit confused as to what I'm supposed to do about any of that."

There, it's definitely a rushed explanation but it's all out there now. I've done nothing wrong apart from try to save my friend. Well, that's not strictly true but it's near enough for this moment. His completely non-expressive response is giving me nothing to work with at all. Shit.

"Mmm." And that's not really helping either.

"I'm sorry if you feel deceived. I didn't mean to. It just sort of all happened and I didn't want to see her hurt by him, mentally that is, or physically either."

He's still standing there looking at me, not a flicker of anything crossing his features. Belle wanders back towards us and smiles.

"He's calling Clastro's and will meet us there in twenty minutes. I've let Teresa know and she's not coming. Well, not with us anyway," she says as she smirks wickedly then flicks her eyes between the two of us. A second or two more of impassivity at me and then his enigmatic smile is back in place as he turns to her and gestures to the door, letting go of my hand as he goes. FUCK!

I catch up with them and search for any sign that this is okay and it doesn't matter to him, but he's not giving me an inch of anything. I have no idea whether he's angry or hurt or some other emotion that he's masking with that business smile. Belle slides into the back of the Bentley as Andrews holds the door open for us.

"Alex, are you okay? I really am sorry," I ask hesitantly. He looks down at me for a moment and then dips his head and kisses me on the forehead.

"We'll deal with it later, baby." Well, I got a *baby* in response so it can't be too bad, can it?

I smile back at him and then scoot myself into the car, hoping that he'll just relax and not drift away into whatever distant place he goes off to when he feels... whatever it is that he's currently feeling. I still haven't got a clue. I look back up to him to see his now pursed lips twitch at something as he stares at me with a slight frown for a second longer and then closes the door on me.

Well this will be a nice lunch, won't it? And an even nicer conversation later.

Yep, can't wait for that.

Shit.

Chapter 24

Alexander

Two more fucking meetings later and he was almost ready for what was coming.

An hour's discussion via conference call with the Chinese was certainly enough to stir his blood up to boiling point but at least they seemed to be getting on well with Tom Brindley, which had taken the heat off the conversation a little. It appeared the man was completely competent in the art of steering a happy direction out of something that was beginning to turn nasty. If it wasn't for his irritating mentor, he might have been able to manage it himself but he couldn't get Pascal out of his head. He'd actually spent most of the conversation trying to come to terms with what he was about to do. In all honesty, he still wasn't sure if he was actually comfortable with it but it needed to be done. The man needed to know who was in control. It wasn't him, or her.

Unfortunately, he'd also had to deal with Aiden Phillips this afternoon, who, to his credit, looked every bit the businessman as he sauntered into the restaurant and smiled. It even felt genuine to a degree. That Saville Row suit didn't quite sit as comfortably on his shoulders as it would on a man who actually traded in legitimate dealings, but he done a fine job of trying to pull it off. It wasn't hard to see why he'd done so well for himself in such a nasty little underworld. Not only was he a handsome fucker with his rugged devil may care appearance, but he had brains as sharp as a knife. Always had. So sitting with him in the Ivy had both attracted undivided attention and forced the lesser people to scurry away and hide in fear. The conversation had been pleasant and quite agreeable in a random, threatening type of way, but it had delivered the information he was after and thankfully given him some much needed backing if the time came. He hoped to hell he wouldn't need it, but he was grateful for the support nonetheless given the potential war that was coming.

Ben Livingston was a traitor to his own kind. He'd been dismissed for drug addiction, ironic enough in itself, but then he'd done the stupidest thing possible and decided to join the opposing team. It seemed a bit of extra work on the side had led him to various avenues including odd jobs for some high profile clients in London, blackmail, extortion, the occasional hit. Although Aiden knew nothing definite, it wasn't beyond the realms of reasonable doubt that he could easily be working for Henry. Whether he originally took the picture wasn't provable but he trusted his instinct that it wasn't Jacobs so that only left Livingston.

He'd left the restaurant with a smile and bounce in his step. Things were coming together, albeit the favour he now owed AP was one that would loom over him for some time. When the man called in that favour, he'd have no choice but to honour it regardless of what it entailed. Aiden Phillips was a man of his word and when he said *"atrociously"* with regard to death, that's exactly what he meant. He had a feeling the man enjoyed trying to taunt him back into his old world. Funnily enough, it didn't hold the same appeal anymore. It was probably to do with the goddess that had recently enlightened him to the merits of right and wrong. He still didn't deserve her respect or trust in him to do the right thing though. He'd just spent an hour giving a known criminal and drugs baron all kinds of help with regard to cleaning up his appearance and acting like a truly decent human being, front as it was.

This was only emphasized by the fact that the damned parasitic paparazzi had been hovering all around them as they'd left. Two shots of handshaking had Aiden beaming with delight and grabbing his arm to prove what a changed man he was. He was a fucking liar; that's what he was, no matter how many quotes he gave about fundraising and charitable ventures. Alex had returned the smile and shook his head when questioned on his relationship with AP, offering a smile and a wave of secrecy. It would be enough for the tabloids to offer AP support but hopefully not enough to condemn White Industries into the gutter.

A meeting with Tate in which he'd lied his backside off to avoid giving away too many details, and then another forty minutes in his office discussing Andrews following Jacobs around for a while, just to see how honest the man was being, and he'd almost lost the will to live. Would his life always be this complicated? To be fair, it wasn't dull and mundane anymore but for Christ's sake, was there a chance he could just give this normal thing a chance?

Before her, he'd been so bored but at this point, he'd kill for a bit of the normalcy she was offering, a bit of that elusive contentment she was hinting at and pulling him toward.

And this thing with Pascal wasn't helping. He presumed that whatever he was feeling with regard to the man was yet again another abnormal thing to contend with. What normal man would be interested in pleasuring her with another man's hands. More importantly, why did he want it so much? Pascal was already proving how much of a game it was to him by interfering and teasing her. It was bad enough that he'd had to scoop her away from him in the first place but contacting her behind his back was just idiotic of the man.

And how fucking dare he?

Trying to manipulate his way in and get to Elizabeth by going for her friend... He'd known she'd never allow it and ask him not to go ahead with it, ask him to *"do the right thing."* The bastard didn't know the meaning of the statement. He had to admit it was clever of him - stupid, given that it was probably going to happen anyway but ingenious nonetheless. Well, he was going to get something now. It wouldn't be what he was after but he'd definitely be getting it.

When he'd eventually gotten home and found her asleep on the couch, he'd almost changed his mind. She'd looked so peaceful and beautiful lying there with her hair fanned out across the arm, in his home, her home. Christ, he wanted her there with him all the time. He missed her touch every minute it was away from him and rushed to get back to her. He'd never spent as much time in his house as he did now. How he was finding the time was beyond him. Before her, he was at the apartment all the time and in meetings or partying until the early hours. In fact, he should be getting back to New York and dealing with other matters that he'd left there but now it appeared that all he wanted was to be with her and continue thinking of all the things their future could hold. Perhaps he should take her with him. That would keep her safe and close to him, wouldn't it?

If he could just get this shit with Henry out of the way and this threatening crap to disappear, he'd make sure she knew how much he longed for that future. He'd make sure she knew exactly what he wanted for the rest of their lives and just how special she was.

But instead of letting her rest, he'd decided to get this thing with Pascal finished with, or at least started. He really wasn't sure which it was and wouldn't be any the wiser until he saw her reaction to the situation and more importantly felt his own.

So here he sat, watching the world go by in the dark and occasionally glancing over at her as Andrews drove them steadily towards Eden. Each corner in the road brought on another strange sense of discomfort or maybe it was just anticipation. He wasn't entirely sure how to categorise it because he'd never felt it before. Every time he gazed across at her, his fists tightened a little in possessiveness, then her radiant smile would disable any anger that was beginning to build and pull the breath right out of his lungs again. She loved him. For whatever incomprehensible reason, she loved and cherished only him. He could see it in her eyes, in the way she let him hold her, fuck her, make love to her. He didn't deserve it, not one little bit, but he wasn't going to lose it and he damn well wasn't going to let someone else ruin it.

Her long legs uncrossed and then crossed again in that loose skirted sage dress as she pressed her lovely lips around her glass of Cognac and chatted about Belle and Conner at lunch yesterday, who had seemed a little at odds regardless of her over enthusiasm about all the computers being provided for her. He'd narrowed his eyes at Conner at the time but he'd shaken his head and said he'd call him later. Were they having problems already? Fuck, that was the shortest happy engagement he'd ever heard of.

Her sudden bark of laughter pulled him back to the moment as her warm fingers patted his hand. "Alex?" She'd asked a question, obviously.

"Yes," he replied. It was a fifty-fifty shot at getting the answer right and he'd do anything for her anyway so it didn't really matter.

"Oh please, you can't possibly tell me you're one hundred percent happy about having all of them over for Christmas." *What? Who?*

"Well, I-"

She cut him off. She had a knack of doing that. It was fucking wonderful so he smirked at her and leaned his head back on the cool leather.

"You weren't even listening were you?" she asked as she reached her hand over and brushed his jaw with that feather-light touch of hers that had him instantly yearning for more. "You look tired. We don't have to go out for dinner. You should have said and we could have just stayed at home, had an omelette or something." Fuck, that was tempting, but so was the other thing he was about to do, not that she had a clue what was about to happen.

"I love you," he said as he turned his lips into her hand and kissed her palm. Her skin smelt of honey and wild flowers, just as it always did, so he let the familiar fragrance envelop him and tried to bring some order to his chaotic thoughts.

"I love you too," she replied as that captivating glow crept across her cheeks and the car glided to a stop. He watched her glance out of the window and notice the black door with its embedded disk. Given that she'd been here before, she clearly knew exactly where she was. Her face shot back to his with an uncertain expression, her lips trembling a bit as she brought her thumb to them. He just stared at her as he continued to kiss her palm and hoped she'd be alright. She knew it was coming at some point anyway.

"Umm, what are we doing here?" she asked as she composed herself, rested back into the seat and gazed into his eyes, almost accepting but just a little hesitant. She was right to be. He hadn't got a fucking clue what he was doing. He just knew Pascal needed putting straight and this was the best way to do it.

"I'm dealing with Pascal. I told you I would, and you pissed me off successfully," he replied, dropping her hand and opening his door as Andrews appeared at hers. She'd asked for this in a roundabout way with her texting the other night. She probably didn't expect this but the opportunity had presented itself so he'd use it to full effect.

"Oh right," she said as he rounded the car. Grabbing her hand, he walked towards the door and wrapped his arm around her waist to stop her before they reached it. He didn't know what he wanted to say or how he wanted to say it, but she needed to know it regardless.

"I need you to do exactly what you're told when we're with him. I need you to look into my eyes and do everything that I tell you with no other thought than what I want from you. Do you understand?"

"I... I think so," she replied shakily.

"I want you to trust me to look after you because this is about us, not him."

Well, it was a little but she didn't need to know that.

"Okay, I always trust you," she said as her face lit up with a relaxed smile, clearly suddenly understanding to some degree. He was glad at least one of them did.

"I need to tell him something and this is the best way to do it, but if you don't want his hands on you, this is the time to say so." Her eyebrow arched beautifully. Apparently they didn't need to discuss that bit. He supposed they had already had that conversation and at least she was admitting it now.

"As long as you're there... I want you to enjoy yourself, Alex. Whatever you want, remember?"

Fuck, his cock twitched. That wasn't entirely the point but that damned mysterious, sexy as hell smile of hers was beginning to make this game all the more fun. He'd never played Pascal like this before and she appeared to be completely on board, as if she knew exactly what was coming. Maybe she did. Her ability to read his mind was still perplexing.

Placing a gentle kiss on her lips, he laced their fingers together again and knocked on the door. Ten seconds later it was opened by Hayley, who ushered them in with her head lowered and gestured towards the stairs. Clearly she was still cowering. It suited her. She should keep damn well doing it.

"Where is he?" he called over his shoulder as they made their way along the corridor and into darkness.

"He was in his office. I'm not sure where he is now," she replied quietly as she walked off in the other direction.

"Bitch. I didn't like her last time I was here. She seems sneaky to me somehow," her lovely voice snarled as she turned and sneered at the woman. He chuckled. Perception was yet another one of her many appealing assets.

"She is. Why Pascal tolerates her is beyond me," he replied as he cornered the stairs and towed her behind him, all the time listening to her heels clipping along the corridor in her tell-tale gait of long, elegant strides.

"Because she's beautiful, and apparently gives *incredible head*."

Her faux European accent almost made him burst out laughing as he watched her mimicking Pascal's hand twirling. She was rather good at it. Instead, he shook his head and continued downwards, trying to rebuild the tension he needed for the oncoming fight. "I never came down here last time. What's it like?"

He hoped she never *came* at all. Frankly, anything could have happened in those five minutes they'd had alone together before he'd taken her from the bastard. It never took Pascal long to achieve anything, but with any luck, it would tonight.

He turned to the left before reaching the entrance to the club and pulled her towards the office.

"Do you remember the auction, when I told you to control yourself?" Her giggle and waggling eyebrows really didn't help.

"Of course. It's not like I could forget any of it, is it? Why?"

"Because I need that from you now. I want you to stay in control until I touch you, no matter what he does," he replied as he ran his finger along her jaw and gazed into those honest eyes, the eyes he was about to turn as deviant as his own. "Can you do that for me, Elizabeth?"

"Oh, umm... What are you planning? Because I don't know if I can do the hanging from the ceiling thing?" she asked, her soft hands resting on his forearms as if she might bolt at any moment. She might be right to, so he frowned at her as he considered what the fuck he was doing once more.

"Can you control yourself, or can't you?"

He'd walk her straight back out the door if he had to. Well, right after he'd been in and punched the bastard in the face.

"I think so," she said as he watched her steel herself and find her sexy little smile again.

Minx. She'd be fine. He turned for the door and reached for the handle. Her hand on his shoulder stopped him. "Alex, you will stay with me? You won't... you know... go off into your own head or something, will you?" He smiled and brushed his fingers over her lips.

"No, baby, I won't leave you." He watched her whole face soften as she moulded her body against him and nuzzled. Fuck, he loved that

448

nuzzling thing. It really wasn't helping harden him up though so he pushed her upright again and nodded at her. She fixed her dress and nodded back as she plastered on her mystifying smile. It was exactly what he needed, for her to perform.

He opened the door and found Pascal sitting behind his large oak desk with his feet propped up on the table, looking thoroughly bored with a man he was talking to. Actually, he was reprimanding him about something of absolutely no fucking interest at all.

"OUT!" he barked at the adolescent. The boy immediately dropped to his knees in front of Pascal, looking scared to death, and stared at the floor, new fodder obviously. His own angel calmly wandered over to the sofa in the corner and reclined her beautiful backside gracefully. He was instantly in awe of her performance, nonchalant and completely in control, seemingly not in the least bit bothered by his tone, though he'd felt her hand flinch in his before she let go.

"Alexander, dear boy, how-"

He cut him off. He couldn't be bothered with pleasantries. They weren't here for that.

"Send your pet out. Now. We have matters to discuss," he said as he grabbed two chairs and sat them on the Persian rug in the middle of the room, facing each other. Scanning the room for other objects of potential interest, he noticed a new painting hanging of a man alone in the mist. He stood for a second or two and stared. He'd seen it somewhere before and images of New York floated through his brain randomly. Fuck it. It wasn't the time for memories.

"It appears you are not wanted, little thing. Off you go," Pascal drawled as he raised a brow at Alex and tilted his head. He was interested, not entirely happy, but very interested, but then the man always was. He'd also cut his long hair off, which was odd. The jean clad perhaps twenty year-old crawled past him out of the room and closed the door behind him. Elizabeth giggled in the corner. He was going to have to get her to stop doing that. It was bordering on condescending, although he couldn't see her crawling anywhere so maybe he could use it for effect now. He looked over at Pascal and nodded at the chair. It was all that was needed because the man rose after a beat and glided across the room in that effortless way that he always did.

"Take off your jacket and roll up your sleeves," he said as he reached it. The man's smile widened as he threw his jacket on the floor and smoothly removed his cufflinks. He was a damn master at what he did. Every movement was seamless and inexplicably erotic without him even trying. Alex watched and then looked at the chair again. Pascal sat and put his hands quietly on his knees, waiting for instruction, his eyes dancing with devilment as he studied every movement that Alex made, looking for his signs and his cues. This had been going on so long that he hardly had to speak most of the time for Pascal to know exactly what he wanted, what level of game he was going to play.

This time it was going to be very different.

"Elizabeth, crawl to me," he said across his shoulder, hoping to hell that she wouldn't have a tantrum about the command. Pascal looked amused all of a sudden. It didn't bode well, but the shuffling behind him meant that she had at least moved. He was surprised when she landed at his feet, looking thoroughly intoxicating with her knees spread a little looking at the floor. A trained submissive couldn't look better. Hesitating for a second, he looked down on her and pondered the position. He didn't like her down there for whatever reason. Beautiful as it was, it just seemed beneath her somehow now or perhaps unequal. She definitely wasn't unequal to either of them, far superior in some ways.

He moved away and dragged another chair from the corner of the room over towards them, then placing it in front of Pascal's with its back to him, he held out his hand for Elizabeth to take. She instantly placed her fingers in his and stood up so he kissed her hand and sat her in the chair, facing away from Pascal. She seemed almost serene in her demeanour as she held his eyes calmly and smiled softly across at him while he sat himself in the chair, crossed his legs and leaned back to look at her.

"Pull your skirt up and take your panties off."

She didn't blink, didn't change her face at all, just shifted in her seat until she could hook her underwear and then pulled them down her legs provocatively until she reached the floor. Kicking them off over her heels, she held them out to him with a very wicked little smile and ran her tongue over her lips, quietly baring her teeth at him. His cock instantly reminded him what was going on so he scooped them from her and put them in his pocket as he reached forward and pushed her dress up to the top of her thighs. Her eyes lit up with desire as she watched him and he instantly knew she'd be fine. She was absolutely captivating in her gaze as she flushed and opened her mouth a little while he pushed her thighs wide apart.

He looked over her shoulder.

"Make her come," he said as he leaned back again and got comfortable. He still couldn't work out how he felt but his cock was entirely happy about what was going on. Pascal's sex-fuelled gaze was now in full force, licking his lips and tentatively reaching his hands forward to touch her, his whole demeanour becoming charged and ready for command. It was always a sight to behold. The man was damned aggressive in his carnage, thoroughly godlike in his own right and absolutely designed for this. Why he'd chosen Alex as a dominant was still baffling. "Elizabeth, do not come."

Her smile grew as she ran her fingers up her thighs and waited for Pascal's touch. He was being unusually wary for him as his green eyes narrowed a little. Perhaps he was waiting for more instruction. He wouldn't be getting any. He could learn along the fucking way.

He eventually wrapped his arms around her waist and pulled her aggressively backwards so he could reach her thighs and then dragged his fingers into her skin. There was nothing gentle about it, but then there never would be from him, would there?

That first touch was enough to set alight every nerve ending that Alex had. Anger raged quickly as it burned through him, hotly pursued by acute sexual frustration at the vision while his hands unfortunately itched to remove the man's head for his insolence. His eyes flicked to hers and found her still watching him with her mouth parted, now breathing heavily. Pascal's right hand moved upwards towards her neck as his other moved higher up her thigh. Alex instantly stiffened. That throat was his. There was no way he was allowing that.

"No, her throat is mine," he said sharply, sneering at Pascal who smiled quietly and withdrew his hand. He lowered it to her perfect breast as he pulled at her strap so he could get to her shoulder, his favourite spot on any woman. Apparently he liked the feel of bone beneath his teeth.

His eyes followed Pascal's mouth as he licked his way along her shoulder and then groaned as his hand found the apex of her thighs. That light dusting of hair that lined the way to her soft, wet folds was already glistening with desire, highlighting her want. His fists tightened a little but he found himself so mesmerised by watching that he began to relax into Pascal's rhythm, his own personal cadence of movement around a woman's body, her body. It was all so familiar, his damned dexterous precision and her small moans as she tried to keep control of her own body. His eyes shifted to hers as her breathing spiked a little. She was leaning back into Pascal and letting him touch her anywhere he wanted and her eyes were becoming molten pools of yearning for an orgasm she wasn't allowed. Pascal pinched roughly at her now exposed nipples and drew them up into firm pink peaks that begged to be sucked and caressed. He only wished he could, and he wasn't going to allow Pascal to so she'd be waiting for that for a while.

Shifting in his seat slightly as Pascal widened her legs and lowered his fingers, Alex stared at the man and lowered his own zipper, yet another dominant move to keep the smart bastard in his place. He pulled himself free and glared as one long finger swiped her clit and she moaned out loud. She needed something to focus on as she started to lose herself and he was going to give it to her. With long, firm strokes, he moved his hand up and down as she watched and began to regain her composure. The distraction was just what she needed because even as Pascal circled her vigorously, she still remained transfixed on his cock, eyes wide and hungry as she licked her lips and moaned again. Not for the man behind her but for the man in front, the man she loved, the man who wouldn't ever let her go.

"I want you in my mouth," she said huskily. It was sex personified as her body began to tremble a little under Pascal's hand, her milky white thighs tense and quivering as she continued to honour his request by holding herself together for him. Fuck, he wanted nothing more than to throw her on the ground and show her what he wanted to do to her. The room, the atmosphere, the smell was everything he'd expected it would be. Passion and filth echoed in the air as he tried to keep his own sadistic thoughts under control and remain focused on the task, which was to put Pascal in his place. To show him that he wasn't needed until he was called upon, until she was ready, until he made his own fucking decision as to how this was going to happen.

"As you should," he replied as he stared at Pascal and tried to warn him in his own way that he was the one in control here, that he had her attention and her focus, and that it was him that she wanted.

Pascal moved his other hand to her pussy and stretched her wide. Now obviously frustrated with her lack of recognition of his skills, he clearly had every intention of being inside her. It wasn't going to happen. He knew Pascal could make her come. The man could make anything come, for fuck's sake, several at a time in fact. That wasn't what this was about. This was simply about respect and control. Who had it, and who was invited into the fray when he decided it was time.

"No, her pussy's mine, too," Alex stated with another sneer as he held her eyes and watched them darken more. The sweat glistened on her beautiful forehead as she began to writhe under Pascal to avoid him, her breathing rapid just as it should be with two men goading her. She wasn't going to last much longer and damn he was proud of her. Pascal glared at him in disgust so he raised a brow back in challenge. This was the moment he'd waited for, the moment where Pascal would submit and recognise their bond or become aggressive and erupt into another man. Either was fine by him. He'd beat the shit out of him without a second thought if he had to, with far too much enjoyment if he was honest. Fucking confusing Dutch bastard.

They stared at each other for a few moments, Pascal's fingers continuing with their assault as he obviously made up his mind what he was going to do while her enchanting body flexed between them. He continued to stroke his cock, which kept causing moans and pants in front of him. She was probably getting more than frustrated at her obligation to him but that couldn't be helped for the time being. She'd get what was coming soon enough. Frankly, he was surprised she'd lasted this long under the master's hands.

Pascal blinked so he looked back at her and almost came instantly. Her whole body was a raw erotic explosion of fury, her nails embedded in her inner thigh, her chest rising and falling rapidly, and her beautiful lips full and wet as she licked at them and tried to contain herself for as long as she possibly could. He glanced at Pascal's hand and growled at the thought. He wanted her orgasm, wanted it dripping across his own fingers and he was going to have it, regardless of whose hand was presently there.

He switched his eyes back up to Pascal who completely threw him by softening his glare and removing his hands completely as he raised them in the air. He was still pissed but they'd deal with that later. Reaching forward, he grabbed her throat and tilted her backwards. And fuck, did it feel good in his hand. Her neck instantly relaxed as she closed her eyes and let him have her with a sigh of gratitude. His fingers were quick to sink inside her warm, wet pussy as she moaned aloud and clenched hard around him. Her body was coiled so tightly that she damn near exploded on him straight away, so he pushed on her clit once and let her fly while continuing to scowl at Pascal. His point was being extremely well made. Mine. Thankfully, it appeared that the man was completely in agreement.

And fly she did, so much so that as her body arched backward, Pascal had to catch her when the chair fell away beneath her. Surprisingly, he cradled her body softly against him and stroked her hair as she trembled around her orgasm and called Alex's name repeatedly.

The vision was incredible, indescribable even. Never before had he witnessed something so erotically powerful as seeing her fall apart in Pascal's arms while calling his own name, her hair damp with sweat as it stuck to her skin and her legs spread wide as another man's hand gripped her thigh and held her close. Normally this would mean nothing. Pascal would simply be another tool for his amusement but in this moment, in these seconds, all he could feel was emotion, blindingly strong emotion. He let go of her throat and stumbled back a bit as he tried to process what the hell he was in the middle of. He didn't have a damn clue. He couldn't even fathom the look on Pascal's face as he watched her in apparent fascination with some sort of sentiment crossing his face that he'd never known possible of the man. And when Pascal lowered his head and kissed her tenderly as she leaned back into him and began to close her body up again, he couldn't even begin to process what that meant. Did he love her, too? He'd never seen him kiss a woman before.

Were they both in love with the same woman?

He watched her run her hands across her body and link her fingers with Pascal's so that she could raise them to her mouth and kiss them softly. He hadn't got a fucking clue what that meant either so he just gazed at the sight and let it happen. Whatever the hell it was that was unfolding in this room, it was unexpected to say the least and it appeared that suddenly no one was in control at all.

Before he had a chance to think any more about it, she gracefully stood and walked straight at him, eyes still full of hunger as she pushed at his chest aggressively and made him sit. He was so perplexed by the move that he just sat and waited. This wasn't submissive, but then she wasn't, was she? He wouldn't be surprised if she could control them both if she put her mind to it. Maybe that was what was happening?

She dropped to her knees and slowly moved his hand out of the way then sunk those beautiful lips down over his cock. He groaned out loud and tipped his head back. He couldn't focus on Pascal. Christ, he couldn't concentrate on anything but the feel of her glorious mouth around him, so he exhaled a breath and let her take the control from him. Her teeth nipped as she went and dragged back up to the tip of him then she took him straight to the back of her throat, licking at all the places she knew so well and forcing him to release. He was going to come and fucking quickly so he desperately searched his mind for something to stop it, something to prolong the intensity but there was nothing so he opened his eyes to focus on Pascal with a growl. If nothing else, it would further prove the point as to whom she belonged to, or perhaps it was only about who she wanted more. The thought disturbed him for half a second before she cupped his balls and squeezed. He groaned again as his stomach tightened in response and her nails dug in. Three more delicious and mind-altering deep throats later and he felt it build uncontrollably so he let her have him completely. She greedily licked her way up and down his length again and again, pulling every last second of restraint he had away from him until all he could do was hold her head and grunt as he pushed her down on him one last time and then exploded into her throat.

Fuck, everything fused together in that moment, her mouth, his feelings, Pascal's focused eyes, the sounds of lapping and sucking echoing in the room around them. It was magnificent. She was fucking magnificent. He watched Pascal fold his arms and lean against his desk to continue gazing at her in appreciation, or lust, maybe both. Fucked if he knew, but the way the man was watching wasn't about sex. He'd seen his normal reaction to this sort of thing too many times. This wasn't it. This was... something else.

He stroked her jaw until she released him from her mouth and then crawled up onto his lap, one long elegant arm circling his shoulders and the other hand gently teasing his throat. He tilted his head a little to give her better access to it and kissed her lips quietly. Love and lust poured out through their mouths as her tongue found his flirtatiously and she moaned and shifted around on him. She was still very aroused. He wasn't surprised because his spent dick was rapidly beginning to agree again that so was he. His mind flitted with the idea of continuing onward, of having her bend over that desk so that he could fuck her and literally ram the point home to everyone.

His body tensed as other explicit visions began to persuade him otherwise. Pascal's hands weren't helping matters as he gazed at them. The things they would do to her between them were limitless and debauched to say the least. He glanced up at the man and saw the same thoughts crossing his mind as he ran his thumb over his lips in contemplation. Wanker. He wasn't laying another finger on her anytime soon. He growled at his own lack of self-control and frowned. He'd proved what he come here for. Well, he thought he had to some degree but regardless, it was time to leave so he gently moved her until she placed her feet on the ground and steadied herself. Any more thoughts like that and he'd push her too hard. He'd show her too much, and while Pascal would love every damn second, she would be scared to death and probably run for her life.

Standing behind her, he smoothed her dress down and then put himself away so that he could deal with the rest of whatever the fuck this had been. Pascal was still staring at the pair of them, now with his enigmatic smile back in place and a raised brow, clearly he wasn't at all sure what had just transpired either but he appeared pleased with it nonetheless.

The bastard wouldn't be pleased in a minute.

He moved around her and took the four long strides needed to stand in front of the man who had now released his arms and was looking a little defensive. He was right to be because the immediate backhand that Alex gave him across the face was obviously expected. He'd probably been waiting for it and enjoying the prospect.

Masochistic little shit. The man's head slowly turned back to face him with a wry smile and sparkling green eyes as he rubbed at his cheek.

"I probably deserved that." Damn right he did. Bastard.

"I won't have this fucking conversation with you again. She's mine. It will be on my terms," he seethed as he turned and walked to her with every intention of leaving. She stood there looking utterly enticing in her horny come furious stance. Clearly she wasn't entirely sure what had just transpired either but she apparently wasn't very happy with that last move at all. She'd have to get over it. They were fucking leaving, now, so that he could think about yet more confusing shit.

Unfortunately, she surprised the hell out of him by walking straight past him to Pascal with soft eyes and a smile as her hand reached for the dick's face. She grabbed his fingers and placed them on her own cheek, mimicking the same position then leaned in and pressed her lips to his gently. It was only a few seconds but she conveyed so much warmth that Alex inhaled sharply and felt his gut twinge in guilt at the sight. Only she could feel compassion for this sort of moment and Pascal looked almost as shocked at the exchange as he was. A decent woman in this room was unheard of. Christ, a decent woman in this club was unheard of. She beguiled the pair of them with her superiority.

"I think you have made your point effectively, my rose," Pascal said quietly as she released his face and fiddled with the back of his now short hair. She smiled and briefly kissed the man again before turning away and walking back towards Alex with a raised brow. Yes, she had proved her point. The moment had been full of her proving her point and she'd left them both in awe and completely lost as to what would happened next. Maybe it was for her to decide.

"I love you," she said as she linked hands with him and nestled into his side. He kissed her head and looked back at Pascal, still in puzzlement, a strange sense of warmth now spreading across his skin for some unknown fucking reason as the shit raised a brow and nodded at them both.

"Look after her, Alexander. You should know I won't hesitate if you damage her again."

He knew in an instant it was the truth. He'd never seen the man so serious. Whether it was love or amusement was unknown, but he most definitely had a challenger and it seemed it wasn't just for her body. The fact that he felt reasonably comfortable with it was as confusing as the rest of the night.

"We'll be in touch," was his response. It was all that needed to be said. They all knew what it meant so he turned her for the door and chuckled as she looked shyly up at him, batting her eyelashes. Witch. Maybe she knew exactly what she was doing. She stopped abruptly and looked over her shoulder with a giggle.

"I love the hair by the way. Very *Vogue*."

She was right. The man looked better than ever. Infuriatingly so.

"I'm glad you approve, my rose. This way I won't have to tie it back when I taste you for the first time, as and when you agree, that is." She frowned at him. Alex growled. He couldn't help it. The remark was cutting a little close to the bone regardless of what had happened.

"Pascal, really? That's hardly appropriate and quite beneath you," she replied. It was perfect, and so was she and as she let go of his hand and made her way from the room, he watched her arse leave with a tilt of his head. He had a feeling the man behind him was doing exactly the same.

"Do you believe you can be what she needs?" Pascal asked tersely.

He shoved his hands in his pockets and continued to gaze at her long legs gliding up the corridor as her dress sashayed with her until she rounded the corner. He pondered the question for a moment while staring into space. Would he ever be enough for a decent woman? An honest woman? Unlikely. He eventually turned to look at the man and found him pouring two glasses of Scotch.

"Possibly not, but I do want to try." Pascal's snort of laughter as he handed him a glass and sat behind his desk was characteristically sarcastic. Alex frowned at the thought and downed his Scotch. He'd need another to deal with what the hell was going on but the first one felt damn good. He placed the glass back on the desk and wandered towards the door again, suddenly desperate to feel her skin again and hold her close, show her how he felt about her. "I love her, Pascal. Don't get in my way again."

He heard the strides as Pascal came up behind him and stiffened. The man's unpredictability knew no bounds sometimes. It was entirely possible he might explode in fury. He swivelled slowly and levelled his eyes to see what he was dealing with. He was surprised to find him a foot away, gazing at his mouth.

"I had hoped that one day you might caress my lips the same way you did hers," he said in a soft tone as he licked his lips and moved closer. Alex stood his ground and waited. They'd played this game before and it had always ended with Pascal nursing another painful bruise. Oddly enough, it was the last thing he felt like doing to the man at the moment. Having watched him with her, it had created an intimacy they'd never shared before, a true sense of purpose to create pleasure together and not pain. "But it seems it may be time to let you go, dear boy, that maybe it is time for me to take my leave of you."

He stared in shock. He didn't know what the hell to say. The man was his friend, mentor, damn tormentor at times, and now... Well, he hadn't got a clue what he was now but he didn't want him to leave. Ten minutes ago he was fucking furious with the man and now these odd emotional irritations were interfering with his thoughts and morphing them into something inexplicable. If Pascal did have feelings of some sort then he needed to know they weren't reciprocated the way he'd like, but the thought of never seeing him again was strangely terrifying.

"What the fuck does that mean? You've always known I can't give you that, and I don't want-"

"You have no idea what you want or need," Pascal cut in as he spun on his heel and threw his hands in the air in what appeared to be frustration. "And it is becoming boring, quite tiring in fact, trying to decipher these insecurities of yours. Why will you not just free yourself of this?" he continued as he paced around the room and began to mutter to himself in Dutch.

What the hell did he mean by that? Before he got a chance to attempt understanding of the language that was now rapidly getting louder, the man was in his face again, those piercing green eyes firmly directed at his and a mask beginning to form. "No, Alexander, I will not do this with you anymore. Leave now before I lose my temper with you."

Lose his fucking temper? The dick had no right to be losing his temper at the moment. He had been the one in the wrong. He took a step closer to the man in frustration, or confusion. He wasn't sure

459

what was currently coursing through him but he wasn't leaving anytime soon, and certainly not because he had been ordered to. Who the fuck did he think he was talking to?

"I'll leave when I'm damn well ready. What the hell has gotten into you? You know how this is. It's you that showed me the way, for fuck's sake. I don't want you to dismiss-"

"Dismiss? Oh, Alexander, it is you who dismisses this, not I," Pascal cut in again as he raised a brow and sneered. "Why should I still play with you? Tell me and I will, but I'm afraid I am as breakable as others in some respects. So what exactly will I get from your attempt at love with another? Hmm?"

He stared again in complete mystification as Pascal turned from him and wandered across to his desk. Did the man expect him to tell him he had feelings, too? He didn't - well not those sort of feelings anyway. And why the fuck was he doing this now?

"Pascal, this is not about you. I don't care for or need your opinion on my..." He cut himself off this time as the scars on Pascal's chest suddenly appeared in his mind for whatever fucking reason. He tried to shake the thought away but his body stiffened in response, highlighting his want for the sadistic vision. Pascal chuckled in front of him so he looked back across at him with a frown as his fingers began to itch.

"Your confusion is truly remarkable and really quite flattering in certain way. However, unless you embrace yourself, I'm afraid I have no option but to deny you from now on," Pascal said with a wave of his hand, signalling that his soft moment, or whatever the hell it was, was over.

He narrowed his eyes at the man who was now smirking again as if something was amusing him. He couldn't ever remember the man denying him anything so there was nothing funny about his statement whatsoever as far as he was concerned. Pascal sat behind his desk, seemingly absolutely in control of himself again and back in full swing, then picked up his Scotch again and swallowed repeatedly until the liquid was gone.

"But her, well, dear boy, she can have anything from me, as and when she decides that is. Actually, perhaps I should decide for her."

His wink didn't go unnoticed. Christ, the man could goad the angels into hell and it appeared he was currently having a crack at his

460

very own version of one. She wasn't going to be released any time soon.

"Are you challenging me?" The bastard raised an eyebrow and smiled. Apparently he was beginning a game. Clearly the strange emotion he'd witnessed earlier had been pushed aside for now.

"I'm sure we'll find out in time. Your morsel is delicious, Alexander. Unfortunately she has frustrated me and now I am left wanting. It is unfair of her and you know how I feel about that. It is a shame it will have to be this way."

Alex's fist tightened in response as he glared in disgust. Had he not just proved his point effectively enough for the man to back off and give him a chance at happiness?

"I'm warning you, Pascal. If you dare..." The shit laughed out loud as he poured another drink and returned a bored expression as if this were not worth his time. Fucker. What the hell was he trying to achieve by winding him up for Christ's sake? The man had seen his love for her. Couldn't he just say *well done* or *enjoy your life together*? This was becoming too much. Another snide comment and he might just do something he'd regret, like kill the man. Fucking emotions and confusion were beginning to merge everything into some kind of overwhelming need to release each twisted thought his fists were currently encouraging him to.

"Run along now. Your little thing will be fretting." He turned for the door again. He wasn't even going to allow the man his damned annoyance, and that need to kill was firmly embedded now. He needed to fucking leave. "Oh and, Alexander, do send something in on your way out. I am bored. Whatever it is, ensure it looks resilient."

"Get it your damn self, you arrogant son of a bitch," he snarled as he reached the door. Pompous, self-righteous bastard, how dare he try this shit? They wouldn't be coming back here again anytime soon. He shouldn't have tainted her with Pascal's depraved mind in the first place. The fact that he was also craving something a little more resilient himself at the moment wasn't the fucking point.

"Now, now, mother would be rolling in her grave. It's only a game, dear boy."

Anger reared its head with a vengeance. If there was one thing she wasn't it was a game. Alex turned and stalked back to him with a sneer, unable to contain the fury that was rising, the fury that the man had pushed out of him for some incomprehensible reason.

"It's not a fucking game, Pascal. *She* is not a fucking game!"

"She may not be to you," the dick replied with that damned eyebrow and a glint of amusement. He was entering dangerous territory. This may have been fun before but not with her involved and certainly not his feelings for her. What the fuck was the man trying to do?

"I won't let you do this, Pascal. I swear I'll kill you if you defy me on this."

He meant it, every damn word. It was bad enough that he had others threatening her, let alone someone he had considered an ally.

"You'll have no choice in the matter, dear boy. She needs me now."

What the fuck was he talking about now? Did he honestly believe he could be that important to her?

"She does not. She has me," he seethed in reply as he watched him stand abruptly and round the desk smoothly with that devil may care smirk as if they were talking about some other person of no consequence.

They fucking weren't.

"Ah, but you brought her to me, didn't you? You showed her what was possible, as I knew you would because you need me, too, don't you? Hmm? Why will you not admit it? Do you believe she could settle for less now that you've enlightened her? Mmm... Poor Alexander and his feelings of love. You see I told you, didn't I? I warned you what could happen if you fell in love and put yourself in someone else's hands. It complicates everything, dear boy. Did you enjoy watching my fingers on her? Did you want to watch me sink inside and fuck her raw? She was begging for it, wasn't she, panting like a little whore?"

"FUCK YOU!"

Jealousy, fury, pain, excitement, he couldn't put a damn label on what was rising inside him, but the fact was that the fucker was right and it suddenly scared the shit out of him. He stepped closer to threaten the bastard into backing off. The dick licked his lips and moved toward him.

"Oh, darling boy, at last. Shall I bend over here or would you prefer the dungeon? Can she take it as I can? I think probably not. She's not enough for you, is she? Tell me you need me."

He stepped away again, trying to calm down. He wouldn't be forced into this again. Twice had been enough no matter how fulfilling it had been at the time.

"She's everything I need. I love her."

"Oh, don't be spiteful. It is unbecoming and quite dull. Has she seen it all yet, felt the full divine force of you? Have you marked her like you did me? I still relive the moment each time I fuck something else. Nothing has come close."

"I'm not discussing this anymore. It's different now," he replied as he turned and blew out a breath in a bid to stop the rising need to hold the man against the wall and beat the life out of him. He was better now. He didn't need this anymore. She was all he needed.

"It will never be different. You will never contain it and nor should you. You are beautiful just the way you were created. Come, take what you need from me and let me feel you again." Condescending bastard. Unfortunately, his body was desperately agreeing with the thought, too much turmoil and not enough avenues to expel it lately and he *was* ready to blow. Pascal knew him too well and he'd always been able to see it in him. Was that what this had all been, an attempt to make him blow up?

"I'm leaving. I'm not doing this with you again," he said as he hovered on the rug, looking at the chairs, uncertain as to whether his own words were true or not. He brushed his hand over the one she'd been on and balled his fists in frustration at the thought, his fingers still itching with the need to release every indecision buried deep inside. He heard a step behind him and sneered over his shoulder at the man who was pushing his every button with precision. The need for discharge built again and he tried desperately to squash it back down as Pascal neared him.

"You spoil my fun, Alexander. I am bereft without it and your little toy does nothing but diminish you. It's actually quite wretched to watch. Look at yourself. You're fucking pathetic around her as if she might break if you push her too hard. She will ruin you."

He spun so quickly that he saw the glimmer of fear flash in Pascal's eyes before he grabbed the man by the throat and pressed him onto his desk. He lowered his mouth to mere inches from him and squeezed. Unable to hold back every aggressive preference that was now coursing through his veins, he looked into Pascal's eyes and watched them relax into submission.

"I won't stop, Pascal. I will crush the breath from you and feed your fucking innards to your dogs if you continue to goad me. She is everything to me. I won't have you destroy her."

The man's lips began to tremble in anticipation while his pupils dilated. The dick knew exactly what he was doing. Alex shook his head and loosened his grip as he moved upward and away. He shouldn't be doing this. She was waiting. She wouldn't understand this, and she absolutely didn't deserve it, not after what she'd just allowed him, them. Pascal rose in front of him and moved in again.

"Does she enjoy the belt or whip? How many men will she take at once while you watch? Hmm?"

"Pascal, stop this," he mumbled to himself as he walked a few steps backwards again, trying to push the rising rage inwards.

"I do hope she's as pliable as she looks. Has she learnt to hang by her delicate little throat for you yet?" the shit continued, taunting and goading.

"Stop, Pascal. Don't do this. It's different now. I'm not doing-"

"I assume you probably have to cuddle and cajole her pretty little cunt into doing what you want, don't you? Hmm? How will she ever understand you as I do?"

"Stop!" His hands were shaking, his breathing heavy as he tried to look away and focus on anything but the man in front of him.

"I want it, Alexander. Get on with it. Let him go. Let me have him again and-"

"STOP!" he roared as he threw Pascal to the floor and towered over him in fury. Every fibre in his body was primed and ready for demolition, each joint aching for the release the man had pushed him to and was now offering. It was so long since he'd done this, so long since he'd found this kind of expulsion of energy and angst. His brain clouded over in mist as the rage overtook and fuelled his muscles for action.

"Ah, there you are, Sir," the fucker said calmly as he moved his frame and kneeled in waiting, his head hung and arms open wide to the sides as he breathed out a sigh of expectation and licked his fucking lips. Everything slowed, time beginning to evaporate just as it always did and he watched the rise and fall of Pascal's chest as he centered himself, with confusion marring his every thought.

Was this what he needed? Was she enough? What the hell would happen if she wasn't? How could he love her and need this from Pascal at the same time? He thought he was in control of this, thought he could dismiss this need and just hold onto her instead. He shook his head at the sight before him and tried to fathom why the fuck Pascal had pushed this because he had, purposely.

His fists tightened again as he gazed at the scars on the man's ribs and shoulders, the ones he'd asked for, begged for at the time, then flicked his eyes to the sideboard and sneered at the contents.

"Go, Alexander. Get what you need. Get me what I need."

He swung his eyes back to find Pascal watching him like a hawk, trembling slightly in waiting and breathing calmly. Masochist, the man who bowed before him was a fucking conundrum, masculinity personified and yet ready to take a beating and revel in it to perfection. He sneered again at his wandering thoughts and took a step back.

He was a fucking disgrace to her. What would she think if she saw this? She'd be disgusted.

And what the fuck had all the emotion been about earlier? His fists tightened again as he tried to call himself back or push himself forward without care into the very thing he wanted most at the moment.

Right or wrong.

Murderer.

Good or bad.

Useless, worthless little shit.

Decent or indecent.

Sadist.

He cracked his knuckles and took a step forward as he heard Pascal blow out another breath and then close his eyes.

"Alex?" she said from the door. *No.*

He turned his head slowly to look at her, her hand covering her mouth in shock. Repulsion was all over her angelic face as she gazed down at Pascal almost in a state of panic at the sight. *Elizabeth.*

Chapter 25

Elizabeth

Can't breathe, can't breathe.

Running, I'm running. I have no sodding idea where I'm running to, but I'm running. What the hell was that?

What on earth did I just see? I can't breathe I'm running so fast. I have to get away from them as fast as I can and never look back. Yes, just get away and never have to look at either of them again. That's the best thing to do, isn't it?

What sort of fucked up world does he live in? Okay, he told me that there was more that he had to show me but for Christ's sake, what the fuck was he about to do?

His beautiful face was a combination of the calculated rage I saw when he beat that shit up that tried to rape me and those deadened eyes that he had in the Lake District. Unfortunately, horny as hell and primed for something I'd never seen before with eyes full of nothing but cold and distance, he scared me to death. Was he going to somehow mix sex and fighting? And what the hell was Pascal doing on the floor with his arms spread open as if inviting the thought with a smile? The man's clearly a lunatic.

Just keep running, Beth. Preferably away from hell and back towards some sort of ray of light that might give me some clarity. Shit, I enjoyed every second of what happened previous to that, revelled in all the emotion that swirled around the room like silk entwining with lust and longed for more. I would have given them anything if they'd asked. I would have given *him* anything in that moment, my soul, my heart, my body... everything. He owned it all with those eyes and those hands, commanding every single movement from me. But not now, he's a damned monster or something. I guess his *sadistic* term was at least honest but I had no clue as to what it actually meant.

Stupid Beth.

So I'm still running, heels in my hands, as I give every last piece of energy to my legs to get me to safety or at least some sort of normalcy. I bypassed Andrews at speed so that he couldn't trap me into seeing the man I love again and ran like wildfire to find a taxi but I haven't seen one yet. Perhaps if I get to the West End I'll find one. Swinging my way to the left at the junction, I spy one of the many theatres and increase my pace in the hope that I can get there before he finds me, because he's searching for me. In fact, I can feel him almost on me already, like he's seconds behind me and reaching his hands for my throat, refusing to let me go.

God, I love him. Why has he done this? Why wasn't I enough for him? Why wasn't my love enough for him? I put myself in his hands and offered him everything he wanted from me with trust and hope but he's decimated that now. He wants Pascal, doesn't he? Why the hell didn't he admit to it and tell me he was that way inclined? No wonder Pascal's in love with him. They've clearly been together. I'm not competing with that sodding mess. Why would he give me everything, tell me I was his world, his peace and then hide this from me?

There they are, rows and rows of London Black cabs, looking like gifts sent from above to rescue me from insanity and lead me back into the real world. You know the one where my friends and work reside, normal things. Oh shit, the building. Well he can have that damn thing back. Oh my god, he's one messed up individual. Why I thought I could understand him or try to fathom a way through his damned twilight zones and preferences is beyond me. This has been building for far too long. I get one step closer to thinking I've got a handle on him and them, bam, another new version to deal with. Good god, the man wears a business suit every-day and charms the pants of every well-connected landed gentry in the world with that smile but it's not real, is it? Inside he's someone that no one knows about, that no one could ever comprehend or tolerate, well, apart from Pascal that is. He seems to want him all the more for his... perversions. Yes, he had a shitty upbringing, and yes, he's been a bad boy but honestly, does he really think sex and that amount of violence go together appropriately? And was he really thinking about doing that with me?

A bit of rough, even a bit of rougher, is undeniably core clenching but whatever it was that he was about to do to Pascal is not something that should be happening to me anytime soon, regardless of my infuriating intrigue in the matter. I almost stayed. There was one small part of my brain that had her feet firmly planted on the floor, looking on in and panting in adoration at the vision. It was clearly my inner slut because the moment my actual self-preservation kicked in and my feet had taken off, my thighs had screamed in protest treacherously, trying to pretend they couldn't leave. The last thing I registered was an ear-piercing whistle ringing through the corridors as I launched myself from the door.

I raise my hand and try that whistling thing as the next taxi pulls up to the front of the queue. I'm still running. There's people queuing but they better get the hell out of my way because I'm getting in, at speed. In fact, I might even fly into that back door.

"Hey!" a random woman yells as I shove past her and dive into the back of the cab. If she knew what I just witnessed, she'd feel the same way as I do. Panicked.

I ramble off the address, hoping Belle's at home because my bag is in the Bentley. As I slump into the seat, breathing hard, I continue trying desperately to dispel the image from my mind. It's still the same one replaying over and over again. Alex in what must be his full sadistic dominant mode, eyes narrowed to disturbing depths, shirt clinging to every rippling muscle that seemed eerily still as he watched Pascal like a hawk with that slight snarl of disdain. And him, the bloody idiot, kneeling at his apparent master's feet in some sort of trance, waiting for... what?

A horn beeps outside and I swing my head around to see if it's him but nothing happens so I blow out another shaky breath and relax, well attempt to as I smooth my dress down. Just as the cab begins to move, the car door is wrenched open and I flinch instantly as my head shoots to the left.

"Out you come, my rose." *Oh fuck, oh fuck, oh fuck.* "Quite the cheetah, aren't you?"

His dastardly fingers reach in and wrap themselves around my ankles so I kick out furiously in the hope of dislodging them. It doesn't work. Futile isn't enough of a word.

"Oi, mate, get off the girl," my saviour the cabby shouts pathetically from the front. It's a weak effort to say the least. Pascal's eyes narrow as he reaches into his pocket and throws a large bundle of cash through the window. The idiot chuckles back and closes the window as if he's not seen anything. Arsehole.

"Get off me!" I yell out in the hope that someone else might help me. Unfortunately, the two meaty bouncer-like men standing behind Pascal have scared most of them off to God knows where.

"Really, my dear, you'll only excite me. Do I need to gag you?" he says as he yanks my body towards his with a snort of amusement and pulls me from the car with a death grip. I haven't got a hope. Regardless of how much I'm struggling, he has me easily and is, as he says, probably getting excited by my hostility. Perverted shit. Before I can stamp on his foot and make another run for it, he scoops me up and chucks me across his shoulder as if I was some sort of child to reprimand.

"Pascal, let go of me. I don't want this," I yell out loud as I slam my shoes into his back in the random hope of doing some damage. His bark of laughter does nothing to ease my frustration as he ambles along the street.

"You have no idea what you want, my dear. Neither does he. We were just achieving a result when you interrupted." What the hell does that mean? "And your prudish response to that was inadequate, quite unsatisfactory in fact. I had hoped for better than this."

"Oh for fuck's sake, put me down!"

My fear has suddenly turned into seething anger. Not only am I being man-handled but I'm also being humiliated to boot. How dare he? He's not even Alex for God's sake, and why hasn't he come for me anyway? His teeth sink into my arse before I realise what he's doing and I yelp out in pain at the ferociousness of it.

"Never foul your mouth with such language unless my cock's firmly buried inside you," he says as he launches me into the back of his limousine and climbs in after me. I scramble across to the other side in the hope of opening the door. His amused smirk when I ratchet the handle and nothing happens only fuels my anger.

"Let me out of the fucking car!"

He's across the car so quick that I hardly see it happen. His hands are in my hair and pushing me down onto the floor before I can breathe. Awkwardly forcing me forward until my chest lands on the opposite seat, he kneels behind me and starts to push my dress up my thighs to expose my bare arse to him. With one hand grabbing the back of my neck, he roughly holds me in position by pressing his fingers together tightly and barely allowing me to gasp for air. I struggle around in a bid for freedom but I know it's useless and for whatever reason I'm not overly scared, just confused by my core clenching reaction and overwhelmingly lost to what the hell it is that's going on inside my own head.

I resign myself to the fact that this is going to happen and relax onto the seat, hoping that he'll go easy on me, hoping that his deviant hands will remember his kind heart and all those emotions that were flying around in his office earlier. Unfortunately, I'm also hoping that his mouth will be on mine soon so that I can feel his passion and erase some of this knee trembling fear.

His hand wanders over my thighs and up towards my backside, causing me to shake in anticipation of his next move. I have no idea how far he's about to go or what he's thinking about. My body heats in response to my thoughts of how much pressure he'll use, how much he'll push me, how his hands will move differently to Alex's, where he'll enjoy most, how harsh he'll be with his force. Oh god, I'm panting. Why the hell am I panting? I should be fighting him off. I love Alex. What the hell am I doing? I'm being held down, that's what. I'm being forced to submit and do exactly what I'm told. Hang on. No, I'm not. In fact, his fingers are actually being quite soft in their meandering all of a sudden.

"Do you like this, my love?" he says gently as his fingers keep up with their hypnotising rhythm and lull me towards feelings of calm and relaxation. Lips suddenly sweep over my shoulder and soothe my breathing to a more leisurely pace as the car pulls away beneath us. His tongue drags along my collarbone, eliciting all sorts of thoughts while his trousers brush across my skin.

"Mmm..." It's pathetic, but I have no idea what's happening. For all I know, Alex has told him to do this while he takes me back to him, back to God knows what.

"Yes, appealing, isn't it, all this beauty and quietness? The infuriating issue is that this..." he says as he hauls me upright by my wrists and slams me into the side of the car with a grunt, "...is just as fascinating."

My shoulder recovers from the impact as my wrists scream in agony and his belt comes off. He's wrapped it around my arms before I'm aware what's going on and it suddenly occurs to me that I've never felt Alex be as hard on me as this while he yanks me wherever he wants. Pure brute strength radiates across my skin as he delivers the first blow across my backside, causing tears to erupt. I gasp out at the pain and try to move away quickly so he shoves me to the floor and leans over me with a sneer as I look up at him with wide eyes. "Are you afraid, my rose?"

Yes, I suddenly am. Very. I have no clue where the man I know has gone but this isn't him. His intoxicating green eyes are angry, ferociously so, and his sharp cheekbones only intensify his scowl. I nod rapidly in response and try to back away but he drops to the floor and grabs my throat with a vicious grip as he pushes me back towards the window. I gasp out in protest, just as my heart rate accelerates to the same fever pitch as it does when I drift off to my dreamy place. I can't even begin to figure out what that means so I look at the floor and wait. "You are so precious, my rose, but your intolerance is fucking disgraceful and should be punished, severely."

What?

As he's pinning me with one hand, he forces my legs open brutally with his knee until he's inches from my core and then stills as he presses his thumb into my chin, forcing me to turn my head sideways. My fear level shoots up another notch at the way his sneer is turning into a smile. It's not one I like or trust. It can only be described as evil and his hold on me is so precise that I know I've got no room to manoeuvre. This is clearly Pascal in malevolent mode, in complete control of every sound, every breath, every thought. The bastard knows exactly how to manipulate every second of his time with me and he's revelling in it. He moves to my ear and whispers soothingly as if calming a scared little rabbit. He's right. I'm utterly terrified as to what he might do next. Sadly, it seems my inner slut is not threatened at all because she's still panting with lust, even though my feet are itching to kick him away and run to the safety of Alex's arms.

"Are you beginning to understand yet, my rose?" he says as he bites at my neck harshly and rubs his quite blatant arousal into me. My moan of gratitude at his weight and the increased pressure really doesn't help me understand anything at all. "Do you know how much he restrains himself for you, what he withholds because he loves you? I pale in comparison to him when he embraces himself, my dear. He is more than I could ever be."

My eyebrows shoot up at his words as his lips skim over my cheek and find their way to my mouth. Nearly all feelings of fear evaporate as my brain triggers into his words and my body relaxes a little. He's not trying to hurt me, only to teach me a little more about the man I love, to show me something I don't understand, and as his kiss rolls over my lips, I moan out again in appreciation of it. Soft, teasing, warm again, I can't stop my face moving into him as if drawn to potential disaster and relishing it with carefree abandon. It's utterly ridiculous of me but I don't even try to stop it.

"Pascal, I... I don't understand any of this," I reply through our mouths as he moves back to look at me, those damned eyes smouldering with lust and aggression. His fingers squeeze a little harder around my throat so I suck in a quick breath as panic rears its irritating head again. He's clearly just as demented as the man he's just described, no matter what he's said and I know, because I'm feeling him with full force.

"He could break you so easily, my love. You are his perfect dream of pretty flowers and sun-drenched mountains. Imagine betraying that. Imagine his hands wiping away that splendour and replacing it with violence and cruelty. He loves you so desperately, but I'm afraid you can't give him what he needs and it appears he refuses to take it from you anyway," he says quietly as he twists my head around and studies my responses to him, which are problematic to say the least. "A man I used to know once said that love confuses all who lie within it. I think he may have been correct in his analysis, my rose."

Oh.

I rapidly search his eyes for some sort of emotion connected to that random statement and find it pouring out of him. The love I saw before is now firmly back in place as his eyes try to convey whatever feeling he has for me, or for Alex. I'm not sure who he's discussing anymore. And it's all bloody irrelevant anyway because the man I love wanted to do things with him, things I can't begin to contemplate or accept, regardless of his strange explanation. If I can't be what he needs then perhaps he should just take what he wants from Pascal instead, or find someone who can give him what he needs, because while I do love him, I can't bear the thought of anything more forceful than this. It would be too much. Well, I think it would be. I'm not entirely sure my crotch is agreeing with my decision making process, which to be fair is extremely confused given my current positioning under Pascal's hand.

"But I saw him. He wanted you... He looked at you as he has done me in the past. He wants you," I stutter in response as he begins to back away, dragging in a long breath and looking perplexed. I have no idea why but my mouth follows him treacherously.

"He does need me, my rose, but not in the way you might think. He has never wanted that, more is the abominable pity." There's a flash of some kind of hurt in his face before he replaces it with mirth and chuckles a little. "So it seems it is time to do this for him. Come, sit."

His arms wrap around me as he pulls me up onto the seat and undoes the belt around my arms. Warm hands rub at them to bring the circulation back as he gazes down at them with a frown. My kind Pascal has clearly come out to play again and I throw a small smile at him, hoping to ease his bizarre distress. He's only trying to help in his own very odd way. Why he couldn't have just had a conversation is beyond me but then this is Pascal I'm dealing with. Maybe I needed to see this in a different way.

"You didn't hurt me too much," I say as I look up at him and pull my legs up beneath me. He lets go and reaches for the champagne.

"No? Well I restrained myself somewhat. You are too lovely. I see his confusion now." My eyebrow arches in response. I'm not sure what I'm supposed to think about that. Is it that he's scared of Alex? Or is it that his feelings are getting the better of him? And where is Alex? Why is it that Pascal's here anyway?

"Where is he?" I ask quietly as he passes me a glass of bubbles and I drain the lot rapidly. He instantly swaps glasses with me and refills it.

"Never inebriate yourself when my fingers are mere inches away. I only have so much self-discipline and you are thoroughly tempting," is his reply as his very charming and highly dangerous smile engulfs the car again. I relax back into the seat and stare across at him with a soft sigh. Whatever he's been trying to tell me is still an utter mess in my head and I can't imagine how anything else is going to make it better now.

"Why, Pascal?"

It's all I've got. I don't get any of it. I don't understand his need to hurt someone, I don't understand Pascal's want for it, I don't understand how I'm connected to it or how I could possibly fit into it, and more importantly, I don't understand why the hell I'm even contemplating moving forward with any of this. He reaches forward and straightens my dress out so that it covers my thighs again. Given what's just happened, I stare across at him in amazement. Why he's trying to pretend he's a decent man is a complete mystery. "And what the hell are you doing that for?"

"You looked too... ravished. I am attempting for decent," he says with a wave of his hand.

"Decent? You are joking? Nothing about any of this is decent. You're certainly not."

My snort of disgust earns me a reproachful glare so I recall my hostility and try for relaxed again. Gorgeous as he might be, I've just felt what he's capable of and it's quite possible he might launch again at any moment. His jaw twitches with some emotion as a smile graces his mouth again. I've licked my lips before I know it. I'm obviously a very confused little girl.

"Have I not stopped?" Well that's true, I suppose, although I'm still looking at those hands in case they move again. He chuckles at me and stares out the window for a minute in thought as I sip my champagne and try to calm down.

"We all have our demons to play with, Elizabeth. His are born of fear, mine are of remorse or perhaps guilt. However, for now the reason is irrelevant. It is more significant that you realise the amount of release necessary. One cannot simply 'talk it out' as the Americans say," he says as he pulls my feet towards him gently and lifts the champagne from the bucket with a frown. "You should always keep your shoes on, my rose. Do learn to run in them."

And then he does something completely unexpected and takes his shirt off. My mouth goes dry the instant it happens. He's leaner

474

than Alex, more athletic, but still oh so beautiful. Much darker skin covers his undeniably very fit body and as I notice a long scar across his ribs, he moves the champagne to my feet and pours. Ice-cold liquid is quickly replaced by a warm shirt as he softly wipes at my dirty feet and washes away the grime from running on the streets - away from him, away from them. My heart melts a touch for such a gentlemanly act of kindness, and given the reason they're so filthy, I wonder if he feels responsible, if he feels to blame for what I witnessed?

He's probably just got a damn foot fetish.

"Are you scared of him, Elizabeth?"

"No." It's immediately out of my mouth. I'm not scared of him in the slightest. I'm just scared of what I don't understand. He said he'd always stay with me and hear me when I used my safeword, and I trust him with that. I just can't deal with the deceit anymore, the things that I don't know, and the things that he won't tell me. His violence, his past, the reasons he needs this and the reasons he won't let me in far enough to understand this.

"Then why did you humiliate him? Why would you hurt him so?"

Excuse me? I think I was the one who was humiliated, wasn't I? Standing there looking at two men about to go at it in some sort of sexual explosion of... whatever. I rip my feet away from his hands and scoot over to the corner again, suddenly feeling the need to get as far away as possible from his deviant hands and calming words. They're both deranged if they think I'm going to take the fall for this.

"I was the one who had to witness something so... so..." Bizarre, odd, strange... Core clenching. My arms have begun flailing around as I try to get my irritation across.

"Private, emotional, honest," he says with a lift of his brow. "Elizabeth, do you appreciate what an effort it is for him to acknowledge himself and allow it, regardless of the erotic connotation involved, to accept that he needs a man for his release?"

Oh fuck balls, I hadn't thought about it like that.

"Well, I..."

Actually, no. He was happy when I left the room. After being part of some sort of sodding game between them, I had left him smiling. What the hell happened after I left? In those minutes, what occurred to change his thoughts to that of violence?

I narrow my eyes at Pascal and wonder what he did to change the atmosphere. Did he cause this? His sinfully smirking face tells me maybe he did. But clearly I have no fucking clue whatsoever in this world of debauchery and apparent pleasure, so I look at the floor again and try to fathom what happened. I thought he'd gotten what he needed. I thought I'd given him what he wanted from me. The whole office thing was his idea after all.

"He cannot be suppressed, my rose. He may always need this and for your relationship to be whole, you will have to honour his fundamental desire, which is to cause pain. He rids himself of his past in doing so and unfortunately he cannot give you everything until you forgive him this."

Oh my god, what the fuck does that mean? Forgive him? How do I forgive something that has nothing to do with me?

"But he was okay when I left. He was..."

"Aroused, tempted, provoked," he answers for me as he sips his champagne quietly and sits there looking all superior and in control of himself. Handsome bastard. My mind races through the glimmers of restraint he was clawing onto while Pascal touched me, the flashes of hatred in his eyes as he saw my excitement at another man's hands, the way he slapped Pascal as if he was barely holding on to his fury with what he did to me... to himself. To our love. Oh!

"I hadn't thought about it like that." *Idiot, Beth. Stupid, stupid, stupid.*

The car pulls to a stop as I look across at him and wonder what on earth I'm supposed to do now. What am I supposed to say to any of that? God, I'm tired, so bloody tired. If I carry on with Alex, will it always be like this? The constant worry that there's more that I'm going to find out, more that I'm going to have to come to terms with or deal with? I gaze at him uncertainly as he sighs and reaches out a hand for me. For whatever reason, I take it and smile wearily at him.

"My rose, you have some choices to make and I'm afraid you shall have to make them rather swiftly. He is in there, quite possibly eating my dogs to get to you, and while I recognize his dilemma, I would like to save their lives if I'm at all able. He was not all that thrilled about me coming after you."

"Why did you?"

Really, it would have been a lot easier to just let Alex come for me, wouldn't it? While I know Pascal is his friend, he has possibly just pissed the man I love off to the highest degree and he wasn't in his good books in the first place.

"It was time you were made aware of who he is, and because it terrifies him that you might be ashamed of him or that you would leave him for his vices, he would have been manipulative with his reasoning. I believe you deserve better than that, and I also believe that you love him enough to accept him as nature intended him to be."

My eyes become slits because oh, that's good. He knows Alex better than he knows himself. I wish I knew that. Why didn't I know that? I should know that about him, shouldn't I? But he shouldn't have hidden it, should he? Perhaps that's what Pascal means about us being whole. "And I told you I would always be here for you should you need me. That time is upon us now."

"Right." I'm actually a little disgusted with myself for not knowing this stuff. I don't like that it's been concealed from me but I can't deny that I should have been able to see it in him, or maybe feel it somehow.

"Mmm..." Smarmy shit. I have a feeling I could learn a lot from him about the man I'm in love with, the one who's probably demolishing something at the moment. My eyes flick to the window.

"Is he all angry and stuff?" *Stupid Beth, of course he's angry.*

"Quite furious I should imagine." Helpful. I'm now filled with confidence that our reunion will be pleasant and rosy.

"Do you think he'll hit you again?"

"Oh, I do hope so." I roll my eyes at him in reply. The man is seriously psychotic, unfairly attractive yes, but an utter lunatic nonetheless.

"I'm not sure I'm comfortable with all this. I don't know what I'm supposed to think or do. It's not exactly normal, is it?" I blurt out as I stare at the window and wonder what's waiting for me.

"I should hope not. I've been called a lot of things, my rose, but normal has never been one of them. I am very fond of you and we shall have fun while you are worshipped. I believe most women would be delighted with that outcome, don't you?" I skim my eyes over his very compelling torso and concede that yes, the thought is quite

477

tempting, but I can't even contemplate how the hell this sort of thing works, or who dictates when things happen. I would assume it's Alex, but who the hell knows?

Oh my god, could I be any more confused? I narrow my eyes at him and try to formulate some sort of understanding of my situation so he looks back at me with another unfairly enticing chuckle of superiority.

"Do you expect me to share him with you?" Yep, let's get that out there.

"No, my rose. He will need me on occasion and you will be part of that. You must trust me enough to recognise it and bring him to me. He wants you to feel him in that moment and love him for it, even if he doesn't understand it himself yet. This will be in your hands."

Oh right, I'm in control apparently. Great, because I know exactly what the hell I'm doing. Not. That inner slut of mine is throwing the panties she's not wearing out of the window and running for the ominous black door in front of me.

"But no sharing as such?"

"Well, a little. You must let me enjoy him while I can." I roll my eyes again and then frown across at him with the sudden realisation that he might want to... well, do things I'm not entirely comfortable with. I don't even know how I feel about man on man stuff but I'm damn sure I won't have it shoved down my throat. My eyes flick to his groin. I'm a complete slut.

"And you promise there's no man on man stuff? Because I'm not sure I can-"

"Elizabeth, he doesn't want that, although he might do it for you if you pushed him, and I would love that mouth on mine at least once before I die." He's a slut, too, but then I knew that, didn't I? A loveable, strange and undeniably gorgeous rogue. What on earth am I getting myself into?

"Okay." I can't believe I'm agreeing to this. I'm not even sure what it is that I'm agreeing to if I'm honest, but I think I understand to some degree.

"Wonderful," he says, clapping his hands together as if we've just arranged a party or something equally exciting. I suppose we have in a roundabout way. "Now, do you need another drink or are you ready?" he continues as he slips my heels back on and puts my feet to the floor. I gaze across at him and try to consider the fact that he had his hands all over me ten minutes ago as I think about how ready I am for seeing Alex again. There is no clarity forthcoming in the slightest so I nod my head at him and brush my dress down in the hope that I might look as composed and in control as he does. "You look as enchanting as ever, my dear, quite flushed in fact. Now, when you see him, do maintain your dominance over him. He will need it to be honest with you. Do not let him see a hint of fear. He uses it to his own advantage far too well."

Oh, okay. I have no clue what that means but I'll give it a go. I search rapidly for feisty Beth and find her cowering in a corner so kick her swiftly up the backside in preparation for the oncoming battle.

He entwines his fingers with mine and pulls me out of the car with a chuckle then leads us over to the door. Time flies so quickly that before I know it, we're standing in front of his office, surrounded by five Dobermans, all of which are growling and prowling around the bottom of the door as if they're about to tear something to shreds.

"Does this mean he's still in there?" I whisper out as they mill around my feet and then nuzzle their bodies along my bare legs. I freeze a little until one of them whimpers a bit and licks me, so I reach down and scratch him by the ear.

"Well I handcuffed him, my dear, so I would assume so. And given that my beloveds are all still out here, it bodes reasonably well."

My eyebrows shoot upwards. How the hell did he get handcuffs on Alex? A quick flick of his wrist has all the dogs moving out of the way and sitting in a line like soldiers waiting for command, apart for the one who's still nuzzling me. Pascal looks down at it in puzzlement. "I think it's quite telling that the most ferocious and ill-tempered dog I have is trying to bond with you. He's normally quite the cantankerous little thing."

"Ferocious? Hmm... seems like a puppy to me," I reply as I drop down and go nose to nose with him with a small giggle. He rolls onto the floor so I can pet his stomach.

"You weaken even the hardest heart, it seems," he says as he lifts my hand and opens the door. My new friend slips into the room in front of me and growls. Pascal barks out a laugh and nods me forward. "It appears you have a new protector. Do keep him with you. His name is Azaezal."

He turns and walks away from me, leaving me alone and staring at the entrance, wondering what the hell to say next. How about honesty? I think it's high time we did honesty. I pull in a huge breath and try for confident as I stroll into the room as nonchalantly as possible in the hope that I look dominant. I'd love anger, but the thought that I might have humiliated him is not one that fills me with anger, only love. Azaezal is standing in front of the desk, quietly growling at it but I can't see Alex anywhere. I scan the room again and find nothing so wander over to my new protector to find out what he's snarling at and then I notice him sitting on the floor behind the desk.

I inch my way around quietly and look down to see my beautiful man with his hands in his hair and a wooden arm rest broken off the chair hanging from the handcuffs. He was clearly not impressed at the handcuffs. My heart melts at the sight of him all dejected and lost, sitting there on the floor looking like that troubled little boy, his suit crumpled but still managing to look like the thousands it's probably worth. I cautiously walk to the chair and push it away from him so I can sit and look at him while I try and find the right words to say first. Azaezal growls louder, walking over to my feet and sitting between us. Well at least I'm protected.

His eyes focus on my shoes as I cross my legs and gaze down at him. He looks like he might have been crying. His eyes are bloodshot and his hair's a mess, as though he's been constantly running his fingers through it in frustration.

"You run from me but you come back for him?" he rumbles in a very throaty voice as he stares at the dog and sneers at it. He's jealous, great.

"I came back for you," I reply in my most forthright voice. He is absolutely not turning this on me.

"You came back because he made you," he says quietly, still staring at Azaezal as if he questions whether I actually wanted to come back at all. He's right, I didn't, but thankfully after Pascal's strange enlightenment, we have a chance of making this better, of finding a way through this.

"Yes, it was kind of him. He had things to say that I needed to hear, things that you should have told me about a long time ago, Alex. Were you ever going to be honest about this?" He closes his eyes and drops his head back onto the table with a thud.

"So you could run from me quicker?" he replies with a sigh as if he's resigned himself to the fact that I'm leaving him. I watch emotions cross his brow as he sits there, probably chastising himself for frightening me, and also telling himself that I'm too good for him anyway, that he doesn't deserve me. He's so wrong and I wish he could see it. I wish he could see past his father and all the crap that he had to endure so that he could believe in who he is today, the man that I know.

"So I could make an informed decision about what I wanted and whether I could handle it."

He reaches up behind him with another sigh to grab a silver letter knife off the table and begins fiddling with it on the carpet, flipping it over in his hand as if he might throw it at any moment, still with his eyes closed. Azazeal growls again. I assume he's not all that amused by the apparent danger in Alex's hands. I'm not entirely sure I am either.

"It wasn't supposed to happen. The fucking shit pushed me and I wasn't prepared for my feelings." And there they are, his feelings, haunting him and showing him that he's not invincible no matter what he thinks about how irrelevant they are.

"Well you clearly needed it, whatever it is. I mean, I know he's good but I doubt he can control you completely," I reply as I watch him slip the knife into the lock on the handcuffs and magically open them. Why he ripped the arm from the chair is unfathomable given his clear criminal ability. He tosses them onto the floor and stares down at them with a frown.

"Did you fuck him?"

Oh... I have no idea how much to tell him here. Rage could ensue quickly if I give the wrong answer I'm sure, and we didn't actually do anything. I briefly wonder why we didn't. Pascal could have easily kept going because I wasn't exactly saying no at the time, was I? Maybe he meant what he said about *"as and when I agree."*

"Did you want me to?" Good call, turn it back on him and think more about it later.

"No," he replies instantly with a snarl as his eyes meet mine for the first time. They're laced with undiluted fury at the thought. I smile over at him and try to ease his tension on the matter. There's only one man I currently want anywhere near the inside of me and it's not Pascal.

"Good job he was just trying to show me something then. I'm not sure I would have had much choice in the matter had he decided otherwise."

Another sneer lets me know exactly how he feels about that statement. I'm pretty certain the psycho outside will be relishing the aftermath should it actually happen. His dog is just as bad because he's now up and moving steadily closer to Alex with his head dropped. Clearly the man scares dogs, too. I'm really not that surprised.

"Azaezal, go back to daddy. Go," I say with a Pascal type flick of my wrist, hoping it will work because Alex really isn't looking terribly friendly. He turns and licks my leg before barrelling out of the door at speed. I smile after him and picture the reunion with a sigh. Pascal might be an oddity but he has been a very decent man in his own eccentric way, and the fact is I can't stop myself from feeling something close to love for him, regardless of his clear unadulterated perversions.

"What did he show you?" Alex says through gritted teeth as he scowls at me. I can feel my nose twitching as I try to work out what it was that Pascal did enlighten me to - power, force, anger, all-encompassing control maybe.

"You, or at least something close to you, I think." His quiet chuckle and softening face throw me as he gazes down at the floor again and shakes his head.

"You will never be ready for that, and I don't want you to be. You shouldn't have to feel my hatred or anger." He's damn right I shouldn't but that doesn't mean I shouldn't understand it.

"No, that's why he's offering himself to you and that's why I've agreed to it."

His head shoots up as bewildered blue eyes meet mine. Clear confusion flies across his face before he replaces it with another scowl of annoyance. I have no idea if it's with himself or me.

"I don't want you involved. He had no fucking right to draw you into this because it has nothing to do with you."

I reel back into the seat at his tone and stifle the need to run from the room again. How could he try to exclude me from knowing this about him? Why would he even bother with any of it at all if he won't show me all of him? My anger gets the better of me at his dismissal so I plant my feet again and stare down at him. If he loves me, he's going to give me everything or it's a no go as far as I'm concerned. Doesn't he see that I have to show him how much I love him in my own way - at least try to give him something in return for all he's given to me, to give him his peace?

"You don't want me to love you, to cherish every part of you and show you how I feel about you regardless of your needs? You said I gave you peace. Don't you want that anymore?"

"Christ, Elizabeth, you deserve more than witnessing that. You will be disgusted and rightly so. You are worth more than the demons that fuel me," he replies as he pinches his brow. I can see his mind churning over as if he's trying to decipher the code to breaking this stalemate. It could possibly be that he's thinking about letting me go because he knows I won't do this any other way.

"Well, tell me what you want to do then? Do you want to sneak off behind my back as and when you feel inclined and continue to hide this from me? Or do you think you can start being completely honest with me and just be what you are in the hope that I'll love you for it?"

"I don't know," is his quiet response. It's a little unsettling if I'm honest and I suddenly have no idea where his mind is at.

"I won't accept something behind my back, you know that, don't you? I told you I wanted to understand everything about you and I expect you to honour that. I won't love you unless you give me everything," I state firmly. He knows this. He promised me he would try and I expect him to man up and love me like he said he would. He fiddles with the knife again and stares at the floor as he presumably thinks of whatever it is he's currently contemplating and my anxiety level climbs up another notch. He could finish this now. I could be pushing him too hard or something because we all know how fucking disturbed the man is when it comes to real emotions. I had hoped we'd gotten past it but now I gaze down at him, I'm wondering if he really has, if this depth of probing is just too much for him to cope with, let alone try to rectify.

"You left me."

Okay, that pulled me back from my wandering thoughts. His eyes hit mine and I instantly see that little boy again, the worried one, the one who is struggling to understand any of this himself let alone explain it to me with any clarity. The need to lean forward and throw myself into his arms is so intense that I have to grip onto the one remaining chair arm to stop myself. I could so easily make this go away by just dropping down there and letting him guide us back to his version of okay, but it's not enough. I need him to see that. I need him to open up again and fill me with honesty and love regardless of what I'll see when he does.

"I didn't leave you. I ran because you withheld something from me. You made me feel exposed and scared of who you are," I reply, hoping he's getting the message, hoping that he realises how much I need to be inside of his head so I can recognize every feeling he has before he knows them himself, because that's what love is, isn't it? Pure unadulterated honesty with each other, the ability to read minds and sense emotion without thought. His face continues to gaze at the floor until he eventually sucks in a long breath and blows out shakily.

"I've never been more afraid in my life. The thought of you leaving me is... I couldn't breathe without you here. I couldn't bear the thought of you running, and I..." He slowly reaches a hand forward and brushes my leg with his fingertips reverently. His touch is so gentle that I hardly feel it, as if he's scared he'll bruise me, but it's everything I need from him. It's perfect and tears begin to well at the thought of his panic. "You ran and I couldn't fucking breathe."

I'm on top of him before he has a chance to blink, running my fingers through his hair and reassuring myself that he's okay, that we're okay, that we can do this together and find a way to make this work. God knows if we actually can, but the thought that he'll open up enough to let me in with him is overwhelming. His stunned blue eyes gaze back at me as the first small smile lifts the corners of his gorgeous mouth and his hands quietly find their way to my thighs. I draw my hands down his face and let them rest on his jaw, hoping that he's with me, and hoping to Christ that I've got what it takes to endure whatever it is that I'm doing for him.

"I love you, Alex, but I need all of you regardless of how you think I'll react. You have to trust me to love you enough. Not as someone beneath you but as someone who stands by your side and embraces everything you need," I whisper as I place a small kiss on his lips. His arm wraps around my back as he pulls me fiercely towards him and instantly begins the devouring process that I was hoping for, the bond that will bring us back together and help us find our way through this. His sudden halting and pulling back from my mouth has me yearning for more as my body trembles above him, wanting so much to show him, touch him and feel him deep inside me where he belongs.

"I'm not sure how to do this. You'll never understand, and I..." he says in shaky breaths as he stares straight into my soul and burns away any last remaining inch of doubt that we can make this work. Eyes so crystalline blue strip me of every other thought as I lean into him again to lay my lips across his with everything I have. I'll take anything from him as long as he loves me, as long as he trusts me with his emotions and keeps us going forward.

"Just show me, Alex. Let me be part of it with you. Let me feel it all."

I don't get another word in because frantic hands are all over me, gripping on for dear life as he takes every last breath from me with his lips until neither of us have anything left to give with our tongues. Our frenzied attack is quickly becoming a desperate need to find each other again, cement our love and connect all the dots that bring us closer again, away from Pascal and back together, just the two of us, where we belong.

His hands find the back of my head while my fingers work his belt out of the loops so I can feel him as close as possible and satisfy this craving that is all consuming and fraught with need. With fingers fumbling and heaving panting as I try to rip the damn thing off him, he pushes my dress out of the way until I eventually grasp hold of his firm cock and lower myself onto him with a moan of pleasure. Every thought evaporates as he thrusts his hips up to intensify the feeling and pulls me down onto him. I'm almost instantly begging for faster and harder but as his hands hold my hips still, I look up into his eyes and find every emotion I could ever want from him.

"Christ, I love you. Don't ever run from me again. No matter what you see or feel, don't run," he says as he blows out a breath and tighten his fingers against my skin. Clearly trying to contain his movement as much as me, his soft eyes and warm heart sear through me as I rest my hands on his arms and grind down onto him. "I want this slow, baby. Just stay with me and take this slow."

I smile back at him and nod as he moves me away from him then gently pulls me back to make his point very deliberately clear. So that's what we do, right there on the office floor, to remind ourselves what this fucked up situation is really all about.

Love.

Chapter 26

Elizabeth

Trust. Honesty.

Staring down at my Italian bread dough with olives creation, I rip off another chunk to throw onto the baking sheets. I've been at it all morning, creating new stuff to try and take my mind off the fact that I still don't know what was in that sodding envelope. It's infuriating enough that I had absolutely no clue as to what my other half wanted out of his sex life, but now I can't stop thinking about what else he's hiding from me. I've asked him repeatedly about that envelope and he always manages to shrug it off or change directions so masterfully that I've been unable to glean any information. Okay, so I've also been so all over the place about other things that I haven't really tried that hard but it was delivered to me, and I do have a right to know, don't I? I know he's probably just trying to protect me from something but that's not the point, and given my lack of understanding about his preferences, I'm now sure it's got something to do with that. But I've seen it now, haven't I? So he's got no reason to hide it anymore, has he?

I want to know what's in that envelope.

I haven't seen him since Tuesday night and it's now Thursday. He said he had to go to a meeting in Edinburgh of all sodding places yesterday, something to do with gas extraction and economic rejuvenation. What that's got to do with his business I'm not sure but to be honest, I was thankful of the peace at home last night to try get my head around what happened.

After we made love on the office floor, he scooped me up and carried me all the way to the car, promising not to frighten me again, promising that he wouldn't hide things from me again and that he'd give me everything if that's what I really wanted. I wasn't entirely sure at the time if I really did if I'm honest, and Pascal's wink as we unfortunately passed him in the hall didn't really help alleviate my nerves on the matter. Alex stiffened considerably and then gave one of his silent unnoticed nod things, and Pascal looked at the floor. I'm still not sure what any of that means. I should ask him really, given that I'm going to be in a room with the two of them again at some point. Not that it'll be happening again anytime soon according to Alex because apparently I'm not ready. He's possibly right, but it seems my inner slut is not in agreement with him in the slightest because my core is currently clenching even as I throw another dough ball onto the surface.

"Honey, James is here," Belle shouts as Teresa rounds the corner with an empty basket from the front. I freeze mid throw and narrow my eyes at myself. I've called him in to ask him to come on board full time when we move to Defoe Point, which will more than likely be after Christmas but I haven't spoken to Alex about it. He's going to be pissed. I know he is, but James is the best person for the job and I have to think about the business.

"He'll be okay about it eventually," Teresa says softly as she rubs my arm, obviously reading my mind. She loads up some more croissants and heads back out. I smile after her and squash the guilt back down. I still feel like a cow about the Pascal situation.

"Hey, Beth, so what did you want to talk about?" James says as he walks in and jumps up on my very clean work surface. I glare over at him and wonder if he is the right person anymore. Of course he is.

"Hi, off the counters please." He pouts at me and jumps down again. It's cute. It always was but it's ridiculous of a chef to get on surfaces. The fact that Alex and I messed about on the new one is neither here nor there. Besides, it was my work surface.

"Still being a nerd about cleanliness then?" Clearly not with the visions that are now racing through my head. I can't stop my hands moving towards my throat and caressing the very spot that Alex rubbed himself into.

"Yes, and I'll expect you to be if you say yes." His very cute brow rises at me in anticipation.

"Yes to what exactly?"

"A full time position in the company. I need a secondary chef and I thought you'd be perfect if you're interested." His face lights up like a Christmas tree and then flattens again.

"I'm not being funny but how the hell do you expect two chefs to work in here full time?" he says as he scans the kitchen and stretches his arms wide. I giggle in response and reach for the brochure for the new building.

"I don't. We're moving after Christmas and I'm going to need all the help I can get." I throw the paperwork at him and carry on with my dough. "Belle's got a lot of new business and we'll never manage it here so it's time to expand."

"Holy shit, that's one mother of a building," he exclaims as he scans the pictures. He hasn't even seen the new interior yet. He'll be in his own personal heaven when he does. "How the fuck did you manage this?"

"We got lucky." It's all I've got to give. I can't even begin to tell him that Alex gave it to me, given his obvious dislike of the man. I've got to deal with Alex at some point as well so I really don't want any more bad feeling in the mix.

"Really? Well that's great, and yes I'd love to come on board with you. What's the money?" Ah, James, professional as ever. Actually, he'd get on quite well with Alex if they gave each other ten minutes to talk pleasantly.

"Speak to Belle about all that. She's got the contracts drawn up and everything's ready to go so we just need a date when you could start," I reply as I load the last of the baking sheets into the oven and try to think of a way to tell Alex about my decision. I must be frowning because James' hand is suddenly on my shoulder and his face looks concerned.

"Are you okay, Beth? You do want this, right?"

"Yes, of course I do. I wouldn't have asked if I didn't. It's just..."

I haven't got a clue how to put this. How do you say to someone, *"Alex thinks you want to fuck me and isn't at all happy about it and I haven't told him you're going to be working for us so he's probably going to have an explosion of some sort, and while we're at it, he gave me the building so you'd better behave yourself around him and me."* Yeah, it's really not that easy to say at all.

"He doesn't know you're asking me, does he?"

Do I have it written on my forehead or something?

"No," I reply quietly as I stare at the oven and fiddle randomly with some buttons.

"Beth, you need to tell him. What happened between us was a while ago and he clearly doesn't have anything to worry about so he needs to grow the fuck up. I don't know the man but he seems to genuinely care for you so just stand your ground, and I promise I'll only be a dick if he causes it, okay?" His soft chuckle makes me snigger in response. Why I couldn't have fallen for someone as easy as him is beyond me.

Sod it, he's right - my business, my decisions. I've had to put up with enough from him so he'll just have to get over it. Besides, this dominant thing Pascal keeps pushing me toward seems to be working. I even feel like I'm turning into the man sometimes with the thoughts that cross my mind with regard to issues involving Alex, in a random novice type way anyway. Clearly I'll never be as depraved as the man but he certainly knows what he's doing around Alex so I might as well learn something from his rather interesting demeanour. I still can't picture it in its entirety but there's no denying I've changed, or I am changing. Who it's because of I'm no longer sure, but it definitely revolves around dealing with Mr. White and his preferences. I quite like this new version of myself. I feel empowered and enlightened, turned somehow into a more grown up version of my old self, stronger, more adamant in my wants somehow. Alex is just going to have to suck it up and act like a man who loves and trusts his woman.

"Okay," I reply as go over to wash my hands. "Well, as far as I'm concerned, you've got the job then. Belle will sort out the rest."

"Fuck me, that just made my day. Do you fancy lunch to celebrate?"

Should I? Sod it, yes I should. As he said, Alex hasn't got anything to worry about so why shouldn't I go out to lunch with my new chef? I smile across at him and take off my apron.

"Absolutely. Give me ten minutes to sort myself out and I'll meet you in the front."

Lunch is a small cafe up the road from our new building. I couldn't stop myself from taking James along to have a quick look around. He was as much in awe as I was, still am actually. The workmen had just about finished and the last thing we saw as we left were some signs being erected in the car park to do with health and safety, which instantly made me think about new artwork for the building. I'd need to call our design agency to get a larger sign made up of the current signage we use at the shop, which I lovingly created a few years ago. I'd never known I could be arty but the design had flowed out of me at the time as if it had always been in there waiting.

James and I have been busily coming up with all sorts of ideas and new variations on the old menus so that we'll be ready to go when we finally move in. There's no denying we work very well together, his style perfectly accentuating mine. I'm sure it's why we've done so well at some events. And of course every woman that he comes into contact with thinks he's a super cutie, which helps enormously. Unfortunately, it's probably also the reason Alex is so anti James, which is ridiculous because has the man actually looked at himself in the mirror at all lately?

We're just finishing up our coffees when a familiar face strides towards me from the street, looking every bit the Lord in his immaculate business suit and I have no idea how the hell to cope with him at all.

"Well, well, little Beth Scott, what are you doing around here?" *Think quick, Beth.*

"Henry," I squeal in mock delight because I'm sure I should be playing some game of *I'm really not aware that you're trying to destroy my boyfriend and I'm completely thrilled to see you.* The shame of it is that I sort of am. He's like my big brother and good friend all rolled into one so I stand up and give him our usual hug come squeeze in the hope that he won't realise my discomfort.

"And who's this? Have you dumped Mr. White or are you being a naughty little girl?" he asks as he turns towards James.

"Henry, stop it. This is James our new chef if you must know and no, I haven't dumped Alex. We're doing just fine, thank you," I reply, as James stands and shakes hands with him.

"Really? Well that's surprising. I thought you might have seen the light by now and moved on," he says as he stares at me oddly. It's slightly cold and distant, not something I can ever remember seeing from him before. And given that he's being the arsehole in this whole deceitful little game of theirs, he's got no moral high ground over Alex whatsoever.

"What's that supposed to mean?" My hackles are up instantly as my hands land on my hips. James coughs a bit beside me and interjects

491

our little staring contest, reminding me that I, too, am unfortunately a part of their little game simply because I know about it.

"Beth, listen, if it's alright with you I'll be off. I've got some things to organise so I'll pop in to see you next week to sign contracts." I smile over at him as I regain myself and lean in for a cheek kiss.

"Okay, give me a call. Take care." He nods at Henry and wanders off into the crowd. I miss him immediately so I gaze after him before turning back to Henry, who has now sat down. Shit. The last thing I want to be doing is lying my way through a conversation with someone I considered a good friend. Alex might have this crap rolling off his tongue but it's not that easy for me.

"So what is it that the man has that keeps you interested? Apart from his money that is?"

What an arsehole. I can't believe he said that to me. Of all people he should know I'm not interested in that. He's seen me enough surrounded by wealth to know differently.

"What a ridiculous thing to say, Henry. What the hell has gotten into you? I thought you said you were his friend and I assume you're still mine so why are you being such a prat?"

"Calm down, Beth, for God's sake .It was only a joke. You're very touchy about him, aren't you?"

Yes, because you're being a bastard and trying to ruin him. I pull in a breath and try to act nonchalant and ditsy. Perhaps that will make him piss off. Oh god, this is so much harder than I thought. I just want to scream at him and ask him why. Playing games with people I don't know is easy enough, but add real feelings into the mix and it's damn near impossible. I have no idea what the hell to say next so I just look over at him expectantly while he sits there looking all big brotherly and actually quite handsome in his blue suit.

"Look, I'm sorry. I just worry about you with him. I don't know who he's pretending to be for you but I can assure you it's not real. He's not who you think he is and I know because I've been dealing with him for years. He's extremely good at what he does and I would never belittle him for it, but when it comes to relationships... Well, I just wouldn't like to see you get hurt, that's all."

The statement *"he's not who you think he is,"* hits me like a battering ram and I try desperately to keep a straight face. Was it Henry who sent me that text? No, surely not. It must be a coincidence.

It's not possible that he could be involved in this, is it? Why would he anyway? He doesn't know about me knowing his plan so he has no reason to involve me unless he's trying to get me away from Alex for some reason. I know he cares about me but if he's got something to say, shouldn't he just say it so that I'm aware?

"Henry, I appreciate your concern but I'm a big girl now and I am capable of making my own decisions. Alex is wonderful to me and I couldn't be happier, so unless you've got something real to persuade me otherwise, can we just move this conversation away from Alex and I? It's really nothing to do with you."

That should do it. If he's got anything else to add then he'll do it. If not, we'll just get away from this whole discomfort and talk about something else, like him and Sarah.

"All right, Beth, I'll leave it at that. As you say, I'm sure you think you know him better than I do so let's just move on. Why have you hired another chef? Are you expanding?"

Okay, I'm more comfortable with this even though it still has Alex all over it but he doesn't need to know that.

"Yes, business is being really good to us so we've taken on a bigger building to cope with it."

"Well that's good. Where is it?"

"Defoe Point."

"Jesus, how did you get funding for that? I'm surprised Belle didn't come to me for that much money." Shit, good one. How to balls up staying comfortable.

"We have our sources and we're a good bet in this economy, so it wasn't too hard."

His eyes burn mine just like they always did. He can tell I'm lying a mile off and clearly I haven't got any better at being deceitful with him at all. He runs a hand through his blond hair and chuckles as he picks up a sugar cube and pops it in his mouth with a smug grin.

"You're lying, Beth Scott. Where did you get the money?"

"It's none of your business really, is it?"

"Defensive, too... What are you hiding?" he replies as he crosses his legs and leans back with that tell-tale business glint hardening his eyes. It's no wonder he runs a multi-billion pound bank. I snigger at the thought of him and Alex working together. Another formidable team I'm sure. Well, it was. The game they're now playing will more than likely be fatal for one of them. I sigh and look down at my hands as I suddenly remember how big this actually is for both of them. Someone's going to be decimated by the end of it and I doubt it will be Alex.

"Like I said, we're a good bet. Funding was reasonably easy to come by."

I seriously can't do this anymore. The underlying pain of what I know is just too much so I stand up and grab my bag. Henry looks over at me quizzically. "Look, I have to go so why don't we arrange to meet up again soon for dinner or something?"

"Mmm, right," he says as he stares at me without budging from his chair. It's that odd look again. I still don't like it. "I think I'll stay and have a coffee."

"Okay, well, bye then," I say as I manoeuvre my way around the tables awkwardly, elegant as always but just trying to get away from this bloody charade. Damn Alex and his twilight zones of nastiness, and damn Henry for playing in them with him and forcing his hand in the matter. What a pair of idiots.

"Beth?"

"Yes," I reply as I swing my eyes back to him, hoping to hell he's not going to put me on the spot because I know I'll fold if he uses those big kind eyes on me. I always have.

"Just look after yourself, and stay out of things that don't concern you, okay?"

Shit, how the hell did I give that away? I plaster on my brightest smile and pull my bag strap over my head in the hope that I seem completely nonplussed about his comment.

"What are you going on about now?" I reply as I try for clear confusion. His eyes narrow a little but his face does soften slightly.

"Nothing, don't worry about it. Just take care." My hand almost literally slaps me on the back. I think I may have just rescued that little catastrophe, thank god. His sudden frown and cold stare return to tell me that maybe I didn't. Shit... again.

"Oh, okay, bye then... again," I reply as I shake my head at him, still trying to act the ditzy blonde and wave possibly a little too madly. My feet couldn't walk me away faster if I tried.

I have to call Alex. I have to let him know that I may have just fucked up and given the game away. God knows what Henry might do next if he thinks Alex is aware of what's going on. I'm sure he's probably got all his ducks well and truly in a row, ready to launch his attack, but if I've just inadvertently shown that Alex is onto him, he could speed up his little plan to take out White industries. I still can't say I'm comfortable with the thought. Henry still seems the kind soul he always has been to me, but there's no denying that cold look on his face, the one he probably uses every day in business. To be honest, the only reason I really noticed it is because it's the exact same one Alex has when he's pretending to be happy but is actually thinking of something else entirely.

It makes me wonder how many of them in this high-powered world of theirs are ever themselves to everyone. I mean, is it even possible to make that sort of money by just being yourself and enjoying life or is it always double crossing and manipulating all the way? I'm so glad I don't have to deal with that shit every moment of my day. It must be exhausting to constantly worry that someone is hiding something or doing something just to be dastardly and ruin you.

I dig around in my bag for my phone so I can at least give him a heads up on the situation. If nothing else, I don't want him to find out I've been with Henry from someone else. Lord knows what tantrums would emerge if that was the case. He left me last time because of his insecurities and I'm not having that happen again, certainly not after we've just had the rather bizarre Pascal thing to deal with. I flick his name and wait for him to answer. It goes to voicemail. Shit, is he in the air? He did say he was flying up to Scotland so maybe he's on his way back now. I look down at my phone and realise its three-thirty. Wow, where's that day gone? He said he'd be back in London by three today so maybe he's at the office. I swipe around for the ever-efficient Miss Trembell's number that Alex gave me for emergencies and call. She'll know where he is, not that I can tell her about Henry because I don't know if Alex has told anyone, but at least she'll tell me where he is.

"Miss Scott," she replies after one ring, very efficient. Her voice is actually quite scary.

"Oh, hi. Umm, is Alex around?" I don't even know how she knew it was me, but given her efficiency, she may well be psychic or something.

"Yes, Miss Scott, he's on a conference call. Unfortunately, he'll be at least another half an hour. Would you like me to interrupt him or ask him to call you back?" I look down at my watch again and ponder how quick I can get over there.

"No, no, don't take him off his call. I'm sure it's important. I'll come to him instead. I should be able to get there in twenty minutes or so. Could you make sure he knows I'm coming please," I reply as I quicken my pace and head for the taxi rank on the corner.

"Of course, Miss Scott."

"Okay, thanks then. Bye." I have no clue as to whether I should be calling her Louisa or Miss Trembell. It's all far too formal for my liking.

"You're very welcome, Miss Scott. Good bye." My eyes roll back as I switch her off. How many times can the woman say Miss Scott? Well hopefully I'll meet her in twenty minutes so I can ask yet another one of Alex's employees to call me Elizabeth or Beth.

The journey is, thankfully, swift but gives me just enough time to sort my face out and text Belle to let her know I won't be back in today. Luckily enough, I don't need to be and I haven't got to be back in until mid-morning to prepare lunch for a small party so I think I deserve an afternoon off.

So here I am striding across the chequered floor into the White Building, feeling ever so slightly more confident than the last time I was here. It's still intimidating, but given that I'm now actually sleeping with and in love with the man who owns it, I'm trying my best for in control. Sadly, my skinny blue jeans and red t-shirt aren't helping me blend in, but that can't be helped so I pull my leather jacket around me and tuck in my cream scarf, hoping I don't look too out of place. Pascal flits through my mind as if sensing my hesitation and slapping me for it. Then Alex's fierce eyes overpower him as they banish the man from my mind with his order to lift my head. I can't help but smile at the pair of them and their dominant ways. Unfortunately, I do suddenly realise I have no clue as to where I'm going. Alex took me to his apartment in the private lift and I haven't ever been to his office so I'm at a bit of as loss as to what to do next. I approach the main reception desk in the hope that they'll point me in the right direction.

Just as I get there, a tall and very beautiful woman in a dark grey skirt suit approaches me while peering over her glasses. She's probably going to kick out the scruffy girl in jeans, and I can't help fidgeting as I watch her in awe. She stunning. She'd give Belle a run for her money

496

with her business appearance and it really doesn't help that the sway of her hips even makes me think inappropriately.

"Miss Scott, I'm Louisa Trembell. It's very nice to finally meet you," she says, startling me with the most amazing smile I've ever seen. Of course, it would be her, wouldn't it? The woman that Alex spends most of his day with, the one who's perfect at everything she does and the one who apparently is a goddess to look at.

"Oh hi, yes, nice to meet you, too but you didn't have to come and get me," I reply as she extends a hand towards the private elevator we used before and passes me a card. I take it with a frown and look back at her.

"Mr. White has asked that you meet him in the penthouse. That card will get you into the lift, the parking lot below and his private office should you ever need it. It will also get you into the building from the parking lot as long as you enter the correct alarm code. He said you'd know what your code word is," she says with a lift of her perfectly plucked dark brow. She really is far too beautiful for this world but I smile at her as I think of my safeword and assume that's it.

"Okay, thank you. Will he be long?"

"No, I should think about fifteen minutes or so. Can I get you anything at all?"

"No thank you, I'm fine. Please go. I'm sure you're very busy and I can find my way. Well, I hope I can anyway." She giggles a little and leans in with a wink. It's the most seductive vision of a woman I've ever seen and I'm sure I'm practically drooling. Having never been attracted to a woman in my life, I'm surprised to say the least.

"Just swipe everything. He's given you access to every doorway in the building so you'll be fine."

Oh, he has? Wow that's... shit... quite a lot really.

"Wow," is all I've got to reply with. Not only am I utterly drawn to this woman for some unknown reason, I've also been given carte blanche to the entirety of the White Building?

"If you do need me at all, Miss Scott, you can press the hash key on the intercom upstairs. It will come straight through to me at my desk," she says with a soft grin. It almost makes me swoon into her and the sudden thought hits me that Alex has more than likely slept with her. If I can't resist her, no man would ever dare to try. I cough my instant repulsion of the thought away and smile back as graciously as I can, given that I've just met another one of his ex sex partners.

"Okay, thank you," I reply as I turn for the elevator and try not to get wound up about it. He's got a past, and anyone would sleep with him given the chance, wouldn't they? I have absolutely no right to feel irritated about anything but its safe to say that's exactly how I am now feeling.

She doesn't say anything more as I swipe the card over the pad and the door opens so I step in and give her another small smile as the door swings back across in front of me.

"Six," I mumble out as I look around the space and remember the last time I was in here, him making me feel completely inferior as he amused himself with my nerves and intimidation. Well, I'm not that girl anymore and I refuse to feel upset about this. It's ridiculous of me. He's just given me complete access to his offices for God's sake. And I'm about to walk into his penthouse to meet him because I've got very important information to give him regarding things that no one else knows about. He loves me. I really need to get a sodding grip of myself and accept the fact that he's slept with other women, probably a lot of them.

The door slides open, revealing the white foyer and corridor leading to the kitchen area. I smile to myself at the instant reminder of him standing there pulling at his cufflinks and looking like the devil he is as he watched me leave. I was in so much trouble with him in that moment but I'm so glad I gave it a chance. My life would be so much less fulfilling and full of life now if it wasn't for him. I would have missed so much if I'd never gone to his house and let him convince me to try something different. I giggle at the thought as I wander along the marble floor and head for the work surface where I can see the coffee machine calling to me. I flick it on and turn to look around the space. Nothing's changed. It's still devoid of all character and lacks any real sense of him, apart from the painting that's staring at me. I shrug my coat off and throw it on the counter.

Sitting on one of the white breakfast bar stools, I swivel around so that I can look at it while the coffee machine works its magic. It's so sad and lonely that I feel myself being drawn into that little boy's eyes almost instantly. Fiddling with my bracelet, I can't stop my mind wondering why he chooses to keep it here? It's clearly an illustration of how he felt as a child. Does keeping it here help him be the bastard he's known to be? Does it remind him and keep him angry enough to do the same sort of crap that Henry's currently doing to him?

Oh god, it really is depressing, just the way that his poor miserable eyes are pleading with me for help or love in all that grey and dark blue. That shadowy figure in the background looking menacing as he looms over the child with malicious intent must be representative of his bastard of a father. I feel the tears prickling my eyes as the machine starts hissing behind me so I sniff them straight back up and tip off the stool to make our drinks. If he wants to discuss this then I'm sure he will. Until then, my job is to support him and make him understand what true love really is. Pascal's words ring in my ear. *"Maintain your dominance over him. He will need it to be honest with you."* Is that what he needs all the time? Does it make him feel wanted or loved somehow? Or is it just a thing I need to do to keep his respect and let him know I'm not scared of him, even though I am, sometimes anyway?

Is it what he needs to chase his demons away, someone who will accept him body and soul, without the slightest care to his past or what he's been up to? Maybe that's exactly it. Maybe that's what makes me different for him, my ability to see him for what I believe he is now regardless of what he thinks of himself. Maybe he sees that in me and clutches to it like it's a chance at redemption or something.

He asked me never to run, never to leave him, so even if we don't make it as a couple for the rest of our lives, he will know what real emotions feel like. I will make him realise what it means to love and be loved in return, because to be without that makes life meaningless, doesn't it? Regardless of how much money he's got, without love it's pointless.

I potter about with the machine as I make my own drink and set it up for his until the lure of the sofa is just too much. I wander over to the black leather shrouded in the darkened room. Kicking my shoes and socks off, I slouch down so I can gaze out at the twinkling lights of Christmas hanging around London's skyline. It's beautiful and quickly diminishes all thoughts of sleeping with secretaries and crappy childhoods until I find myself simply daydreaming about holidays on yachts and marriage and children and... *Oh for god's sake, stop it, Beth.*

Although he did ask me to move in with him. Would that make him feel more comfortable about revealing himself in his entirety? He said he'd show me anyway, but would he truly appreciate the depth of my love if I said yes? Do I even want to?

Yes, is my brain's immediate response. My inner slut agrees entirely for once but if I'm honest, the thought scares the shit out of me a little. I don't even know what he's going to show me and I'm thinking about giving up my home and moving in with him?

I am, it seems, because I can't bear the thought of not waking up in his arms every day if I've got the chance to do it. What idiot would refuse such temptation? I didn't push him for it. He asked me.

The sudden pressure of his hands on my shoulders alerts me to the fact that he's behind me and I close my eyes and sigh out languidly as his finger runs around the base of my throat.

"You're a very nice surprise," he says as his mouth grazes its way along my neck towards my chin. His hand tangles into my hair as he tips me backwards and climbs over the back of the sofa to land between my legs with clear intent. At some point he's removed his clothes because I'm greeted with his smiling face and a broad, heavy and very naked body pushing down on me. His other hand pulls my wrist above my head as his eyes sparkle to life with mischief. "Now, Elizabeth, what exactly can I do for you?"

"Mmm..." I can't even remember why I came here in the first place all of a sudden as I gaze up and wiggle my hips against him. His very naughty grin reminds me of that small boy and in this moment he just seems like a man in love who's happy with the woman beneath him. None of the money around us is relevant, none of his preferences, none of his inner demons or oncoming battles, just him and me in a quiet moment of love and happiness. His finger runs along my jaw as he stares down at me with soft eyes, and before I know it, I'm agreeing to a request he hasn't even mentioned.

"Yes," I say softly as I reach my lips towards him. He probably hasn't got a clue what I'm talking about, but as his mouth moves across mine purposely, his tongue assaults mine seductively. He teases me with soft strokes and gently nipping teeth until he pulls back slowly and looks back down at me.

"That's a very dangerous word. You do realise that, don't you? It could mean all sorts of useful acceptances," he replies as he moves downwards and begins to undo my jeans. "Yes, string me up, Alex." Oh! His hands yank them down my legs until he tosses them on the floor and moves back towards me. "Yes, bind me tightly and torture me, Alex." My pulse is quickening by the second as his mouth descends onto my stomach and he pushes my legs apart. "Yes, use me as long as you'd like, Alex." His teeth drag along to my core as he pulls the back of my panties across my backside and digs his fingers in harshly. "Yes, fuck my arse and take everything from me, Alex." Oh god, his tongue licks up the length of my core as he throws the panties and clamps down on my very sensitive clit. I almost come instantly as I moan out my pleasure and arch up into him. "Yes, I'll take as much as you can give me, Alex." His fingers push into me slowly and my legs begin trembling with anticipation of what's coming next. "Do I need to go on, Elizabeth? Would you like to revise your statement at all?"

I can't speak. I'm not sure if he expects any answers but he's not getting them. He pushes my t-shirt up until he can roughly pull my bra put of the way and then draws my nipples up into his mouth with his teeth. His fingers begin slowly pushing in and out of me as he grazes his thumb across my clit with soft strokes. My stomach tries its best to hold in the bliss but I haven't got a hope, and frankly, at the moment I don't care. I love the feeling of his weight on me and his expert hands doing exactly what they're made for. My mind briefly flirts with the thought of what on earth else he's got in those hands as Pascal's force hits me and then his calming voice pulls me back to him as his fingers pull out of me.

"Take your top off and turn over for me." Okay, my hands work quickly to remove the offensive item and as I roll onto my front, the leather grates against my already sensitive nipples. "I fucking adore you like this, waiting for me and trembling with need," he says as he hoists me up by my hips so I'm on all fours. "Tell me what you want me to do for you, baby."

I've never been much of a one for demanding with my voice, but thoughts of honesty and trust are running through my head so fast I can't stop them. My mouth opens to speak but his hand clamps over it before I can get the words out.

"Real, baby. You want the real me then I want your exact thoughts, every place you want my hands, my cock, my weight. I need to know how much you can take from me, and I want you to give me every piece of you," he says as he trails his teeth over my shoulders and moves his hand across my backside again. Memories of stinging smacks and probing fingers fly into my mind. He told me he'd take me there, and then I'd be ready for more. Do I want that? He certainly does and I know that because I can feel him asking me for it with that strange sixth sense thing I've got around him. His mouth has moved downward towards the very place we're both thinking about, and the fact that he knows exactly what he's doing to me with his kneading fingers and devilish lips is utterly unfair. Frankly, he might as well say, *"This is what I'm going to do,"* so I can just whimper in agreement as a response.

Then he's there, dragging his talented tongue up the length of my sex and straight across that forbidden place. Oh god, my core contracts viciously as if sensing the potential and relishing the thought. I suddenly realise I'm panting as his fingers join in on the persuasive assault, gently teasing around the area and heightening the feeling of emptiness. My body feels coiled and ready to explode the moment he puts something inside me, somewhere, anywhere frankly.

"Ask me for it, Elizabeth?" Oh Christ, he does know - honesty, trust. I close my eyes to the sensation as his tongue sweeps over me again and his fingers dip inside my wet lips, not enough to give me any satisfaction, just enough to remind me I'm going to have to say what I want. My thighs clamp together in the hope of finishing myself off, but he's on me in seconds, spreading them wide again and not allowing me the pressure I'm craving.

"Please, Alex..." I'm begging. It's dripping out of my mouth like butter. He does this to me, brings me close and then holds me off like I'm some kind of damned ticking time bomb waiting for the command to let rip.

"Please what, Elizabeth?"

"Fuck me," I mumble in reply as coherent thoughts begin to leave me. Small nipping bites travel their way up the inside of my thighs, increasing my need to the point where my core is throbbing with unapologetic desire for the inevitable.

"Where, baby? Tell me where you want my cock buried." Bastard. His fingers continue with their soft wandering until they land on my arse. "Here?" he says as he drags the finger downwards to my wet folds again. "Or here? Tell me."

Oh Christ, my trembling increases to earth quaking as his tongue pushes into that forbidden hole and I moan out around the feeling. It's incredible, unlike anything I've ever felt, and as his fingers move to my clit, I know I'm minutes away from that sweet feeling.

"Are you ready, Elizabeth? Are you ready to give me that last bit of you?" He breathes over my lower back in that low seductive voice of his that will always have me complying with anything he says.

"Oh god, yes," is my instant reply. I'm almost delirious and haven't fully accepted what I've just said yes to until the sudden pressure around my arse is upon me. It's indescribable, pain, pleasure, heaviness. I can't find the words but my body immediately freezes as I realise this is actually happening and I hold my breath in expectation of the oncoming sensation. Fingers probe in and out as he smothers my own juices over the area while firmly holding my hip close to him. My gaze becomes transfixed on the fireplace I'm not actually seeing because my mind is far too engaged in the unusual and quite liberating experience behind me as I remain still and tense with anticipation.

"Easy, baby," he says as he finally pushes his cock against me and I feel him entering me. "Just relax and let me in. You don't know how fucking irresistible you look under me right now, that sexy as sin arse in the air for me, begging and moaning for more. You want all of me then give me all of you."

My body begins to relax as I let myself listen to his words and breathe again. His fingers find my clit again and gently rub across it in small circles as his length starts to stretch me wide. I can't stop the clamping of my muscles everywhere as the familiar build of my orgasm approaches faster than usual and he continues to sink inside me. The small bites of pain seem to dissipate or highlight the effect as he licks the length of my spine in a soothing rhythm and quietly murmurs every thought along the way.

"Fuck," he eventually grunts quietly as he stills and rests his hips against me. "Put your fingers inside your pussy and feel me inside you. Christ, I'm so damn close already." His hand grabs mine and pushes it towards my insides. Linking our fingers, he dips them in and runs my fingers against the hardened wall of his cock buried deep inside me.

I can't even fathom thoughts. I feel so full I can barely breathe, and shit, he hasn't even moved yet but the shuddering that's building only intensifies my heady awareness of him inside me. He leaves my hand there and pulls his back up to my throat as he leans over me and bites at my neck. The slight movement causes my knees to begin their buckling as sensation sweeps over me and I rock backwards into him without any thought. My inner slut is telling my body exactly what I should be doing

"Is this what you want?" he rasps out over my shoulder as he gently pulls out a little and then pushes back in. My body's instant response is to push back against him harder as I feel his cock moving deep inside me with my fingers. "That's it, baby. Show me how to fuck you. Tell me how much you want from me."

"Oh fuck yes, more, Alex, please... I need to-" I'm cut off as he pulls out and drives back in. My body crumbles beneath him as my insides tighten around my fingers to igniting proportions. My own thumb swirls around my clit in vigorous circles, only spurring me further into my bliss as he continues to glide in and out of me with punishing strokes. "Oh god, yes, Alex... Faster."

My teeth sink into the leather of the sofa as he loses himself in his own animalistic state behind me, grunting and groaning as those lights begin fluttering under my eyelids and I drift towards a new kind of paradise. Rough hands lift and turn me until my stomach is against the back of the sofa looking towards that picture. All thoughts of the young tortured boy disappear as I see his scattered clothes in the corridor and feel the grown man behind me, showing me exactly who he is while he takes exactly what he wants with no remorse and relishes in it. As those relentless, passionate thrusts bring me closer to the edge, his hand joins mine to increase the pressure on my clit, pushing me to a new level of enticement and satisfaction as he drives us forward together.

Everything begins to shake as my head tilts back toward him to seek out his mouth in a frenzied attack of tongues and as I close my eyes and let my body go, he bites at my jaw, growling out his own euphoria.

"I'm not him anymore," he pants against me as he wraps his hand around my ponytail and pulls my hair harshly towards him. I grab the back of the sofa and let his hands do all the work as my body spasms against his fingers and a gut wrenching feeling claims every inch of me while I explode in front of him, shaking and quivering like a newly formed siren in ecstasy. Tears spring to the corners of my eyes at his admission as I realise he's been thinking the same thoughts as me. I wind my hand into the back of his hair, searching for more contact to pull us together, and dragging his mouth down to mine again, I kiss him with everything I have.

"No, not him... Someone new," I pant through our lips as the last hard ripple of orgasm swirls through me and he pulls me back down onto him one last time. He wraps his arms around me, and holding me tightly against him, shouts out my name in rapture as he reaches for my throat again gently. My mind whirls with ecstatic feelings of joy and love as he empties himself into a place no one else has ever been, a place just for him to claim purely as his own.

"Someone just for you," he rasps out between heavy breaths as he kisses the side of my face leisurely with that throaty growl of approval. "Only for you. I'll never give him to anybody but you because you made him. You found me."

Tears sting my eyes again as my hand covers his around my throat and I bring it down to my heart. His breathing quietens against my back and that small smattering of hair on his chest brushes occasionally as he continues to twitch inside me, pulsing and reminding me of where he is. What he's just claimed as his, what I offered freely to him for no other reason than to cement a further connection with him and give him every part of me. My mind wanders back to the very reason I said *yes* in the first place - to live with him, to be by his side day and night and promise my life to him if he still wants me to.

"You have it all now, Alex," I say as I squeeze his hand into my chest and lean back onto him. "Every piece of me belongs to you and I want the same from you. Promise me again that you'll give me all of you."

He slowly lifts me away from him until he withdraws himself from me and then gently manoeuvres me until I'm facing him. My legs wrap around him as if they're part of his skin, part of him even, and as his hands find their way to my face to brush away a tear, he gazes across at me with his beautiful eyes shining.

"You've had me all my life, Elizabeth. I didn't know it and I hadn't expected it, but I've always been yours nonetheless. Only you have ever known this part of me and if you want the rest, you can have it. Just promise me you won't run, whatever happens you stand your ground and fight me if you have to, but never run, okay?"

"I've already told you I won't. You couldn't do anything to make me leave." Actually there is one stipulation that my brain rapidly reminds me of. "Well, apart from fuck someone else behind my back that is." His eyebrow raises as a smirk graces his face.

"As opposed to in front of you?" Arsehole. My hand has slapped his chest before I know it. His chuckle of amusement makes me smile at my own stupidity given our rather unusual sex life, but I can't help slapping him again, repeatedly. "Alright, alright, enough. I will never fuck anything behind your back. In fact, I will never fuck anything but you. Is that an acceptable answer for you?"

"Yes, and in that case, my answer is still yes," I reply quietly as I suck in a nervous breath, suddenly worried that I'm overstepping an imaginary line and that he's changed his mind about me moving in with him. His brow furrows in confusion. It doesn't help my state of tension.

"I don't know the question," he says as he grabs a throw off the sofa and drapes it around my shoulders.

"Well that's a first. It's normally me not knowing what the hell's going on," I reply with a small giggle, hoping that I've got this right and that he's not about to embarrass the living shit out of me. He still looks baffled. "You told me that you wanted me with you every morning, that you'd be very happy if I was with you all the time and that if I wanted to I could..." My voice trails off to virtually inaudible as I watch his face change back to one of amusement. He's laughing at me. He knows exactly what I'm talking about and he's fucking drawing it out. I stiffen a little and pull away from him but he yanks me back to him with a chuckle.

"Are you asking if you can move in with me, Miss Scott?" Shithead.

"No, I'm replying to *your* request for *me* to move in with *you.*"

Because he asked me, not the other way around and I won't have this turned on me. His hands are suddenly lifting me and dropping me down onto his already hard again cock. I have no idea when that happened but the feeling is so exquisite that I moan out my gratitude as he impales me and pulls me in tighter.

"Are you my Christmas present? Can I wrap you in an orange bow and tie you to the tree?" he asks with a very gravelly voice as he trails his fingers over my back. My giggle at his statement has him beaming with that glorious panty-dropping smile of his. If I had any on, I would definitely have dropped them by now.

"Orange?" Why orange? "And I don't think people tie their presents to the tree."

"It's a nice colour, like your hair. And I'll tie you anywhere I want," he says as he moves us backwards and stands up. His feet are moving us somewhere as I cling onto him and delight in the feeling of him deep inside, where he belongs.

"Then orange it is, Mr. White. Where are we going now?"

"Bedroom, to celebrate. I've never lived with anyone before so this is definitely a time for you to feel some of my affection," he replies with a lick of his lips and a wink. "And before you remember all the reasons why you absolutely shouldn't move in with me, I need to remind you of why you should."

He opens a door behind me and walks us straight into a bedroom, which has me gasping instantly, not only at the size of the bed but the fact that it's covered with deep orange roses, almost perfectly matching my hair. They're strewn over every surface and filling the room with a sweet, mesmerizing scent. My head swings back to meet his eyes.

"Ever made love on a bed of roses, Elizabeth?" My head shakes a no in utter amazement. When the hell did he do this? And how amazing is it? I have a feeling those pesky fairies have been hard at work again. Either that or someone snuck in while we were on the sofa, which would have been damned impossible to be honest.

"I... I... How did...?" I can't speak. I'm completely blown away. The man is not only a sex god with looks to die for but is now apparently throwing romance into the mix with full effect. I really haven't got a hope and it's completely obvious to me that I'll never love another man like I do him. Not one thing in the world will ever make me question my feelings for him again or my commitment to him. "I... I love you."

"Mmm, good. I haven't had the thorns removed though so don't be too overwhelmed with my romantic gesture. It's self-satisfying to some degree," he replies. His devious smile as he walks us over to the bed and lowers me down onto it has me thinking that we're probably in for a long evening, and that I'm more than likely going to be quite sore by the morning.

And I'm moving in with Alexander White.

Oh god.

Chapter 27

Alexander

Two cups of coffee. He smiled. Would he ever wake up again and only make one? Hopefully not.

He'd left her an hour ago, draped across his bed, surrounded by the roses they'd demolished and sleeping peacefully. It had been quite a task removing himself from her side for the day ahead but she needed rest after the night he'd pushed her through. There's no way she'd be moving a step today without feeling every second of where his body had been last night and rightly so. She was his now, lock, stock and fucking barrel. She'd be feeling a lot more in the future so she might as well get used to the ache and start enjoying it. She was utter perfection and for whatever reason, she was moving in with him. Why she still hadn't run for the hills was a complete mystery but he couldn't remember ever feeling quite so happy. As far as he was concerned, this love she pulled out of him would only get stronger. Even letting his fingers leave her skin this morning had been torturous, as if he might not make it through the day without her touch to soothe his soul. Every breath she made against him relaxed him back towards that serene place he longed for as he continued to battle his own selfish demons regarding his life, his bastard of a father and all the death that shrouded his past ominously. That shit was just waiting to tear them both apart and he could feel it whistling over his skin like the first winds of a hurricane, teasing him with promises of bright horizons while threatening the building tornados like the fucking devil in the background.

Well she clearly knew how to deal with a devil or two. That wasn't the problem. But the violence, the twisted nature of his previous employment and some of his present life, well that she just wasn't going to accept and he knew it with every beat of his heart. She was too good, too kind, too decent, too damn beautiful and regardless of the fact that it was in the past and that he wouldn't be revisiting it any time soon, she would never forgive it, or him for it. So while she wanted everything from him and he'd lied and said she could have all of him, she simply wasn't going to get it all. He couldn't risk it because what was the point of life without her now?

He looked across at the painting and scowled. He knew she'd been staring at it as he'd taken her and she'd given that last barrier between them over to him, the last piece of her body for him to own and claim as his. Christ, he'd been looking at it too and telling himself he'd be everything for her, whatever she needed. Whatever she wanted from him she could have, anything to keep her close to him and safe, to ensure she kept loving him and ridding him of his inner loathing, just not the whole truth. So now, as those eyes stared back at him again from the image reminding him of his guilt and reminding him that he was undeserving of any form of love, he sighed in frustration.

She probably looked at that picture and saw a poor, fragile child that she wanted to protect and cherish like the heaven sent angel she was. All he ever saw was a murderous young man and a father who moulded him to be that way.

"Fuck you," he mumbled under his breath as he snarled at the image and turned away again in disgust. Perhaps he should face the bastard at some point and tell him what he'd done, show him exactly what it felt like to be on the receiving end of a sadist's hand, the hand he'd created with his flawed idea of parenting. Actually, the fucker would probably be proud of his achievement, of the wisdom of his teachings. The thought made his skin crawl as the realization hit him once again that he was no better than the bastard in some ways. Worse really.

His phone beeped in the background, bringing him back to the present. He pressed the button on the coffee machine and swiped across it to find several emails. Opening one, he scanned the document from Jacobs and instantly froze at the information. What the fuck? She'd been with Henry? Why the hell had she been with Henry yesterday? And who the fuck was the other man? Fury was instantly rolling across him in waves as he devoured the rest of the document and tried desperately to quell the rising paranoia. It was damn stupid of him to feel this way given that she'd just agreed to move in with him, but he couldn't stop it from gripping at the blood in his veins and heightening every instinct he had to go and kill the dick, either of them.

He shook his head and threw his phone on the countertop. He had to stop this shit. She loved him, and she meant every word that left her lovely lips because the one thing she wasn't was a liar. There had to be a sensible explanation. He'd just ask her. That's what normal people did in a relationship, wasn't it? Communicated honestly and didn't entertain the idea of games? Fucked if he knew, but at least he was trying to learn.

Another beep alerted him to a text. He swiped it on the table and leant over the phone.

-   **Berlin is hosting this year's event, dear boy. You will both be expected in correct attire. Do not defy me on this, Alexander.**

Defy him?

Fuck.

Well that would be an interesting evening no doubt. He thumbed through his diary, selected the twenty-eighth of December and entered the information. Whether they were actually going to go was questionable. He still couldn't make up his mind if he wanted to kill the arsehole or not, and as he hadn't got a clue who was currently in control of their little soiree, he couldn't quite work out whose decision anything was anymore. Clearly Pascal thought it was his to determine, but watching his hands all over her had been agonising, and having to deal with the whole aftermath of his inability to control himself around the man had been tortuous to say the least. Master fucking manipulator, had he planned the whole thing to end that way or was he really just trying to help with his own deluded sense of appropriateness?

Dominant and submissive, what the hell did that mean to any of them anymore? Who the hell was who in this situation they'd somehow found themselves in? He frowned at how quickly the man had gotten those handcuffs on him. Pascal may have chosen him for his own needs but it certainly didn't mean that the man would bow down to him for any other reason. Was she too much of a temptation for him? Could he be trusted to behave himself? He'd never cared before, just watched on as the man took what he wanted with reckless abandon, but now... She was too important, and the fact that the bastard might have feelings for her too was a concern he wasn't sure how to deal with.

He looked over at the bedroom door and pondered her reaction to the that sort of occasion. She'd taken the auction well enough, Rome too, and with her want for everything from him, perhaps it was exactly what he should show her. What a Christmas line up - an emotional weekend with the family, a debauched ball and then New Year with Henry fucking DeVille. Christ, that holiday was looking better by the second. Mind you, the sudden vision of her in the *correct attire* had him grinning from ear to ear and pressing his cock into the cabinet below him with a groan. He sent a quick email to Louisa to have the jet ready for them on the morning of the twenty-eighth. Either he'd have sorted his head out by then or she'd have made a decision for him.

Scanning through a few more emails, he made some quick responses and then glanced at the time. Six forty-five, should he wake her yet? What were her plans today? In fact, he still didn't know why she'd come over yesterday. Maybe it was to do with Henry; he hadn't given her much of a chance to talk when he'd walked in on her. Frankly, the sight of her in his apartment again had been too much. He'd wanted to fuck the life out of her the first time she was here. He wasn't giving her a chance to leave again before he had a vision to remember. He chuckled and turned toward the machine again. He was waking her up so he could make some more visions to remember.

"Hey," her sleep laden voice said. His eyes turned to see her wandering through the lounge wrapped in the dark blue bed sheet. He raised a brow at her choice of clothing.

"What? My clothes are in here. Don't you like the look?" She pushed one of her very appealing legs through the slit in the material as she collapsed on the chair and gazed over at him with that enticing smile of hers. He wasn't sure whether to take her to bed again or pin her against the window. He walked across to her with the coffee and plucked a few rose petals from her hair. She giggled and took them from him. "So, I was thinking that you might want to tell me why you put those numbers on your back."

"Which ones?" he replied quietly, trying not to narrow his eyes. She really didn't need to know any of them to be honest.

"All of them," she said as her full lips enveloped the side of the glass and he watched her throat swallow. There really was no getting away from this shit, was there? Why the hell did he cover himself in this ink the first fucking place? "When you're ready... I'd just like to know what has been so important to you that you felt the need to ink you skin with the memory."

"Well that's a lot of information you're after, Miss Scott," he replied as he pondered her surname and the connotations of changing it. Would she do that? Marry him? No, why the fuck would she?

"You don't need to hide anything from me, Alex. I love you. You couldn't tell me anything that could make me love you less."

He highly doubted that statement but loved her for it nonetheless. He needed to get off this subject and quickly. She'd just agreed to move in with him; he was damned if he'd give her a reason to change her mind.

"And what have you been hiding from me, Elizabeth? Hmm?" She looked affronted instantly. It didn't surprise him so he chuckled at her and winked.

"Bastard," she replied as she pushed his knee with her foot playfully. "Oh, but on that note, the reason I came here yesterday was to tell you I saw Henry. I think I may have inadvertently ballsed things up a bit." His entire body responded by stiffening and searching her eyes for any sign of dishonesty. She batted them at him and smiled. "Now don't go all ferocious on me, Mr. White. I'm too sore and that's all your own fault so chill out." He snorted out a laugh and walked over to the kitchen to get some breakfast.

"What did he want?" he asked, grabbing croissants, jam and butter.

"Well I don't really know. I was having lunch with James and then suddenly he appeared, sat down and chatted for a bit, then told me he was surprised I hadn't seen the light and left you yet. Next he was informing me that he had no idea who you were pretending to be but he worried about me, and then to top it all off, he told me to keep my nose out of things that didn't concern me. To be honest, I was a bit put out by the whole conversation and given your current, *let's annihilate each other*, predicament, I just wanted to get out of there. So I left, and tried to get hold of you, but you were in a meeting or something. So I came over instead. I just hope I didn't let him know that I knew and therefore you knew, if you know what I mean. Is that confusing? I'm rambling, aren't I?" She glided over to him and sat on the barstool opposite. James the arsehole strikes again.

What the hell was she doing with that jumped up prick? The dick was desperate to get his cock into her. He needed to deal with the bastard and damn quickly. Preferably he could just fuck off and work somewhere else having had his head ripped off and shoved in a very dark hole.

"Why were you with James?" He tried for calm but the sudden aggression in his voice was clearly apparent because the frown he received in return wasn't a happy one.

"I've just told you about Henry and you're worried about James? Jesus, Alex, grow up." She slid off the stool and walked over towards the bedroom again. His eyes narrowed at her back as that fury began to unfurl itself into something more.

"Where the fuck are you going? I asked you a question. Get back here and answer it," he growled, suddenly furious with her for spending any more time with the man than she had to. Henry he could deal with, but James was an unknown commodity. She halted and turned slowly.

"Please don't do this. I work with him," she replied quietly, holding her hands out to him. It wasn't fucking working regardless of her stunning eyes.

"And work includes eating lunch in a damn restaurant?"

"Yes, sometimes it does." Her eyes dropped to the floor. What wasn't she telling him?

"Are you fucking him?" Her face shot back to his in shock. Good, she wasn't fucking the wanker at least.

"What the hell kind of question is that?"

"It's the only reason I can see for you having lunch with another man." Even as he said it, he knew it was ridiculous but he wasn't having her near the man. Pascal's hands were confusing enough. A stranger's were not welcome in the slightest.

"Really? Wow, you only have lunch with women you fuck? Well Christ, that's a lot of lunches you must have had. Was Louisa at one of them?"

What the hell had that got to do with anything?

"Don't change the bloody subject," he seethed as he watched her backside swing away from him casually again.

"What, manipulate it you mean? Damned arrogant, self-centered arsehole. How dare you? If you must know, I had lunch to celebrate with him. I offered him my second chef's job, which he accepted thankfully," she said nonchalantly as she waved her hand about and walked around the corner toward the bedroom. His eyes widened at the thought. It was not fucking happening and certainly not in the building he'd just given to her. Bitch. Christ, he loved her attitude but James? Really? Absolutely not.

"He is not working with you full time," he said tersely as he followed her. The heavy scent of roses assaulted him instantly, reminding him of last night. Visions of her roped wrists and ankles as she gave him ultimate control with her body flowed swiftly through every vein, only increasing his need to do it all again.

"Yes, he is. It's my business and my choice. Suck it up, White," she replied calmly as she brought a rose to her nose and inhaled.

"The fuck it is! Call him and tell him you've changed your mind," he shouted. Either that or he would, with fucking pleasure. She raised a brow and turned for the bathroom.

"Oh, sod off."

"I'm really not joking, Elizabeth. Call him. Now." She looked back and gazed at him with that mysterious smile and a wink. Why wasn't she getting wound up? She almost looked... aroused. Something about it was familiar but he couldn't put his finger on the reaction for the life of him.

"You know you look very appetising when your eyes start turning dark blue? Sometimes they go almost black. Did you know that? It used to be a little scary if I'm honest, not anymore though."

"You will do as you're fucking told," he seethed, taking a step toward her. This was getting old. She would call the idiot and remove him from the equation and show her loyalty to him. She giggled and started picking the petals off the rose reverently. He had no idea what game she was playing but his cock was jumping all over the place in response.

"Alex, I am not, nor have ever been fucking James. I thought the potential threat to your company might be a little more important to you than this stupid feeling you have regarding another man. And given that Pascal had his hands all over me the other day, at your request I might add, I don't think you've got any room to act all jealous about someone who has never been anything other than gentlemanly around me."

"Pascal is irrelevant, James is not. He is a dick and I don't want you to see him again."

That hit a nerve because her face changed instantly from one of arousal to venomous contempt. He was so intrigued by the change that he tried to work out what had caused it. Her eyes were slits and a blush of potential rage shot across her chest.

"You think what you're asking me to do with Pascal is irrelevant? What fucking world do you live in? James is a decent man, one you both could probably learn something from, and he doesn't deserve your wrath. I won't have his name tarnished by your insecurities. He's also the best person for my business. If I tell you I'm jealous of Louisa, will you sack her for me?"

"Why the hell should I sack her?" She threw the rose on the bed and frowned at it, then returned her soul shattering eyes to him.

"You want me to sack James and I've not even had sex with him, so why shouldn't I ask the same of you given that you clearly *have* fucked her?" He took another step, which she backed away from as she held a hand up at him. He had no fucking idea why she did that. Did she expect him to stop?

"I have not fucked her. She's gay." Her eyebrows shot upwards. Clearly she didn't know; well she did now.

"Oh, right... Well that's not the damn point. I'm still not backing down on this, so you can just get over your tantrum and go screw yourself."

He'd had enough of this. He ripped the sheet from her and scowled. She immediately put her hands on her hips and faced him head on. She didn't flinch or falter as she raised a brow in challenge. It was entirely too tempting and he just stifled licking his lips.

"Who does that belong to?" he said, pointing at her flawless body, barely suppressing the groan at the sight before him and willing his damn cock to shut the hell up.

"Me," she hissed at him, glorious.

"Wrong fucking answer," he said as he grabbed her throat and pushed her against the wall. "Who does it belong to, Elizabeth?" She gasped at his ferocity but her eyes refocused quickly. His cock hardened again at her stare. It was the most defiant look he'd ever seen coming from her angelic face and he liked it. Fuck knows why but he did.

"Me, Alex. I give it all to you but it belongs to me." Better, but still wrong.

"I'm going to give you ten seconds to remember what the right answer is before I fuck that opinion right out of your mouth to remind you who you belong to."

It was a promise. He wanted nothing more than to push his cock into her luscious lips and watch her moan around it while he made his point clear.

"Piss off. You don't own me," she said quietly as she pulled in a breath and blew it out into his face. He watched her narrowed eyes glaze a little. She was getting ready for him. Was she really going to centre herself? Did she really think she could outrun him in this? Fuck, maybe she could.

"You're running out of time."

He suddenly felt a little strange, as if something in the air was changing. Gazing into her eyes, he felt the tension crackling around them and felt her pulse pounding steadily beneath his fingers. When had she learnt this much control? Had he taught her this? Had she found a new level of dominance in herself that she was willing to try out? She eventually smiled then floored him by sneering at him in disgust.

"Ten. Do your worst, you piece of shit. Bring a damn whip with you. What are you going to do? Beat me until I relent and give you what you want? It's not going to happen. I've hardened up, Alex. You've made it happen. I'll take anything you can give me and still have my own fucking mind. You want a dictatorship then fuck off and find it somewhere else. I'm sure there's plenty of willing participants out there. I'm not one of them!"

His mind instantly reeled at the thought as he glanced at his hand around her throat and realised she thought he'd hit her over this. His brain fogged with the possibility of what she was suggesting. Would he? No, never. She'd just wound him up. She'd just confused him, and Christ, the thought of her sleeping anywhere near someone else was horrendous. He just wanted her safe and with him. He needed her to understand how important this was, how fucking important she was, to him. His fingers flexed as she put both her hands on his wrist and continued to glare as he shook with anger and frustration.

"Elizabeth..." His body backed away from her slightly. "I would never-"

She cut him off. "You are doing. Are you holding my throat because you need me or because you can't get your own damn way?"

Unfortunately both. He let go immediately and took a step away again. She glowered at him and rolled her neck around as she dragged her beautiful fingers across it. Something close to remorse swept around inside him as that fucking guilt addled his rage again, making him question what the hell was going on. She drew in a long breath and softened her gaze, closing the gap between them again as her hand found his and pulled it back to her throat. "If you want it, Alex, take it. It's yours anyway, but not because you want to bully me into something. Do it because you need me."

He watched her lips moving and realised she was trying to give him an avenue for his fury, a fury she didn't deserve regardless of her decision to employ the dick. Flicking his eyes up to meet hers, he grated his teeth at the image of her over his knee or bound to the chest of drawers behind her so he could ram this crap out of his mind. She rubbed his hand beneath hers and blinked softly in response to his more than likely dark blue eyes. His mind clouded again as Henry, James and daddy fucking dearest swam around behind her like a taunting bunch of reprobates, egging him on to do exactly what his body craved. Fuck, he wanted to beat something, anything, just to relieve the incessant pressure that weighed down on him constantly. But not her.

He let go of her without a backward glance and left the room. He couldn't bring himself to look into those willing eyes a moment longer as utter loathing filled him and tightened his fists in response. He needed something to kill, something that preferably couldn't die because of his actions, so turning along the corridor, he headed for the stairs to go up to the gym. He could use the punching bag or maybe the fucking wall to loose some of this self-created tension. He damn well wasn't using her or her lovely neck.

Slamming the door behind him, he headed straight for the bag in the corner and rallied as many kicks and hits as the damn thing would take from him. Over and over again he threw his pounding fists into the leather until he began to feel his heart rate decrease to a more acceptable level. Sweat beaded across his chest and back as he tried to rip out the venom and land it directly onto his father's face, every punch landing straight on the bastard's body so that he would feel the man he'd created. Ugly, disgusting, powerful, fucking killer... He caught sight of himself in the wall length mirror and doubled his efforts to extinguish the turmoil beneath his skin. More volleys of hits ensued until the bag simply stared back at him, swinging slowly from side to side, tempting more and offering a viable alternative to the woman downstairs. His cock leapt again at the thought so he went at it more forcefully, muscles heaving from the exertion and knuckles sore but breathing controlled and level as he found his way back to normal, whatever the fuck that was. He wouldn't do that to her again. He would never scare her like that again. She wasn't his vengeance. She was his solace and he had no fucking right to make her do anything she didn't want to do. Christ, he damn well told her to fight him, and fight him she had, beautifully, with conviction and grace, and still she'd offered herself up for him. What the hell had he done to deserve her?

He smashed the bag one last time and turned for the mirror again so he could remind himself what he looked like in these moments, what she had to look at and deal with, what she had the backbone to stand up to and face with dignity and warmth. With love.

And there he was, the man of the fucking moment. Dickhead. Dripping with sweat, eyes dark and focused on destruction, hair a fucking mess, knuckles red and filled with tension, muscles on display like the damned back alley fighter he really was underneath the façade. His chest was heaving with undiluted breaths of violence and chaos at the thought of more, at the thought of devastation, and that angry frown was etched into his face as he stared at himself and wondered who the fuck she thought he was. He knew who he was. A disgrace to her, that's what he was, nothing more than a screwed up child in a man's world, playing games to try and stay sane. He turned and without thought, picked up a hand weight and hurled it at the man before him, causing the mirror to shatter into a thousand pieces while he roared out his torment.

Several minutes passed in silence as he continued to stare at the broken glass, now splintering what was left of his image. He half chuckled at the vision. It was probably more like him than the full version had been. Broken and cracked, deep running fissures of hate and revulsion seeping through every pore only highlighting the tortured issues buried within his soul. His disfigured image was suddenly a far more realistic portrayal of Alexander White than the handsome structure his bastard of a father had kindly bestowed upon him. At least his eyes weren't from the arsehole. At least his mother had left him with something good.

His memory shifted to the little wooden box that Mrs Peters had given him and the treasured possessions inside. A pair of broken glasses that bore a striking resemblance to his own and a photo of her with her new-born son, Nicholas Adlin. Alexander White had been born much later, after her husband had destroyed any inch of humanity that she might have forged. Her face was a picture of purity and innocence as she cradled her promise of life closely and smiled up at the camera. God, she was beautiful, soft somehow, not unlike the woman downstairs, and those fragile arms clung to her son like she would never let go. Even in the picture he could see the bruising on the left hand side of her face. He shivered as he remembered his father's right hook and sneered at the thought.

It *was* time to see the bastard. It was definitely time, time to face those fucking demons head on and deal with years of anger and betrayal.

He closed his eyes and let her face sweep over him in the hope of calming the still raging storm. The moment he did, his angel's eyes flooded his thoughts and removed his mother's image. His angel, his air to breathe… What the fuck was he doing in here?

He moved across to the door and heard the elevator open. She was leaving? Shit. He ran the stairs at speed and turned the corner to get to her before she made it out the building. He had things to say, things she needed to hear to help her understand. He needed her. He headed for the lift and noticed it had already left so launched for the staircase. The door slammed behind him, echoing in the concrete fire escape as he took the steps three at a time in order to speed the descent. On crashing through the door into the foyer of the building, he was met by the bewildered stares of varying businessmen and employees as he scanned the area for her.

"Morning, Sir, can I help you?" some random receptionist said as she stared at his body. He quickly realised he still had no shirt on and only a pair of black jeans. He didn't even respond as he headed for the doors and onto the street. Where the hell was she? He looked both ways and ran a hand through his hair as the damn rain poured down on him. Shit, what a fuck up. She offered him everything he'd ever dreamed of and he showed her how much of a complete dick he really was, and then to add insult to injury, he went and stormed away from her like a child rather than talk to her. When was he going to learn how to be a decent man, for God's sake?

A flash of red in the distance caught his eye and he stretched above the crowd of London umbrellas to see if it was her, but the face that turned the corner wasn't her, just some other woman who had red hair, not his angel. He slapped at his pockets for his phone and sighed at the fact that he left it in the apartment. Fuck. He turned and headed back into the building with a frown. She said she wouldn't run. She damn well lied. On reaching the private lift, he realised he hadn't even got his card so stood by the door and banged his head on it repeatedly with a snort of amusement. Jesus, the woman screwed with his head on so many levels; it was ludicrous.

"Well that's an interesting look for the office, dear." He spun his head so quickly it honestly might have fallen off and looked at her face beneath her hooded coat. She smiled and ran her fingers over his tattoo. "Lovely as the visual is, though, I'm not sure the boardroom's ready for it. You in a suit was enough for me to drop the mousse. Imagine what this could cause," she said as she continued her trailing fingers over the hair by his belt and tugged. He winced and let out a small cough as his cock came raging back to life.

"Where did you go?"

"I left a note. I needed a vanilla latte," she replied, shaking her takeaway cup. "And you needed a little space to... whatever it was that you were doing. I have no idea really but given that I didn't feel the immediate need to call Pascal, I thought I'd just let you get on with it."

"Elizabeth, I'm sorry. I..."

"Are you? Good. Don't do it again." She swiped her card over the door and opened the lift. "Should I punish you now? That's how this works, isn't it?" She flicked her head toward the space inside and smirked. "After you, Mr. White."

He looked at her incredulously and wondered where the hell this version of her had appeared from as he stepped inside and turned to her again.

"Are you okay? I mean, I was angry, jealous really and I didn't mean to scare you, but-"

"Six," she said and the doors closed around them. "You didn't. You don't, but we do need to have some ground rules if I'm to understand you better." She circled around him and pressed her nail into something on his back. He peered at her over his shoulder and was rewarded with a very sexy smile as she licked her lips. "Twenty two, six, five, what happened on this date, Alex? Why is the twenty second of June significant to you?"

Of all the fucking dates.

The doors opened and she walked out, throwing the card on the table and moving towards the lounge as if she belonged in the space more than he did. Her long, confident strides swayed along the corridor in front of him and he couldn't help but wonder what the hell Pascal had said to her. She had changed since that night. She was still his angel but had somehow become more confident, more... well, dominant. He suddenly realised it was the same in the bedroom earlier, as if she was the embodiment of the man in a female persona - strong, independent, forthright, with a hint of the primal need to control everything around her, to understand him more and find all the buttons she needed to press to engage the right reaction. The man knew him so well it was unnatural really. Had he shared some sort of secret? He needn't have bothered. She was getting there just fine on her own, but now it was as if she'd jumped six months down a line he never expected himself to entertain.

"What has he done to you?" he asked quietly as he followed her and helped her with her sodden wet coat. She quirked an eyebrow and shrugged out of it with a small giggle of amusement. Christ, he loved that sound.

"Who?" He barked out a laugh and stared at her mouth as she beamed back at him. She knew exactly who they were talking about.

"My tormentor. It seems you've changed a little since your time together. He appears to have rubbed off on you."

"Not yet he hasn't," she replied instantly with a wild smirk and wink. He growled. The thought was fucking disturbing and entirely too appealing for some irritating reason.

"Very, very naughty, Miss Scott. I'm not convinced it's acceptable, though, so I'd stop right there if I were you." She giggled again. "Elizabeth..." He growled it out again, hoping to stop the flow of this particular line of thought, engaging as it was.

"Oh stop it, Alex. And nothing really, he just highlighted some new moves. Whadda ya think?" she replied, twirling her hand around just as the bastard did. He frowned at the similarity and wondered if she understood the implication of what she was doing.

"Don't," he said as he caught her hand and brought it to his lips. Her skin had never tasted sweeter and he licked his lips at the thought of her *hardening up*. "I love you just the way you are, baby. Don't let him change you into someone else. I don't need that from you."

She ran her fingers over his jaw and down to his throat. The instant feeling of peace settled deep inside him and he wrapped his arm around her to pull her closer. Her body pressed into his and her hand ran over those damned numbers again provocatively.

"Twenty-second of June, Alex?" she asked again into his chest. Shit, and so it began. She wasn't going to let it go, was she? Glancing at his watch, he pulled in a long breath, released her and wandered towards the bedroom. Regardless of his need to keep all this from her, he knew this was going to come at some point, that she would dig and dig until he had no choice but to lie incessantly or just tell her the truth, well some of it anyway.

"I can't do this now. I've got meetings in half an hour and then back to backs all day. Then we've got the Tranting charity fundraiser this evening so I'm sorry, I can't answer your questions at the moment." He looked back towards her, hoping to find a peaceful face. He was going to need all her love if they were to get through this and he could only hope she would forgive him his sins.

"What do you mean *we've* got the Tranting charity fundraiser?" she asked with a raise of her brow. He rolled his eyes. He'd definitely told her about this one.

"Check your phone. I sent an email after our last misunderstanding." She narrowed her eyes and delved through her bag. On fiddling with it, she suddenly looked shocked.

"Oh, shit, I'd forgotten about that," she said as she threw it back into her bag and nodded, picking up her coat again. He stiffened and reached his arm for her without thinking.

"Don't-" She cut him off with a hand held high. "I'm not running," she said with a small tilt of her mouth as she wrapped her scarf around her lovely throat and picked up her coffee. "I love you. I'll never run. I just need to get to the shop. I have things to do today and I also need to sort out a dress it seems." His hand dropped away and he released the breath he'd unwittingly been holding.

"Right, I'll pick you up at eight then, from your apartment," he replied as he turned again, now struggling to even look at her with the thought of what that date actually signified.

"Okay, I'll see you later then," she said as he heard her feet walking away from him. He closed his eyes and reached for the door to the bathroom. He needed to shower this morning away and form some sort of coherent plan as to what the hell he was going to do about what he had to tell her. If she was going to understand any of this then she needed to feel what he'd felt when he was younger. She'd need to try and comprehend who he had been at the time and why he'd committed the acts he had.

He turned on the shower and tried not to see the images that were once again flooding his mind. How the hell could he make her see the whys before she comprehended the actual acts themselves? Who the hell was he trying to kid? He was a murderer, of criminals yes, but fundamentally there was no real excuse, was there? No normal person was going to understand the thought process he'd had at the time, and she certainly wouldn't be holding up a damned happy flag of forgiveness, regardless of how much she seemed to feel for him. How did he make a woman so honest understand a tortured soul's deepest flaws? How would she ever realise the dulled sense of morality because of his circumstances? Maybe if she hated him he could make her feel the necessary hatred to kill. That was possible. He chuckled to himself at the thought. He'd have to do some serious damage to make that happen. She couldn't hate anything. She was an angel for God's sake. However, a swirling plan began to take hold, a manipulation of sorts and maybe a way for her to see who he had been.

Stepping out of his jeans and into the shower, he tried to let the water wash away some of the anguish that was presently rolling around his stomach. Before he could do anything to quell the rising panic, he had a long day of meetings, some of which now involved dealing with the potential Henry situation. If she had announced the fact that he knew something, he needed to act accordingly and tighten up his ship. Most of it was already in place for the arsehole's assault but there were a few loose ends, and Tate Westfield was one of them.

Twenty minutes later and he was standing in the lift dressed for the kill, his favourite grey pinstripe wrapping him in a blanket of power as he stared at his reflection and thought about his so-called friend, Mr. Westfield. He still hadn't got a clue whether he was or not. He thumbed through his phone and hit the icon for Conner, the only one he could trust implicitly, and one he still needed to apologise to. He said the word "five" aloud and watched the door close behind him.

"Dude, where the hell have you been?" He chuckled in response to his friend's enthusiastic voice as the lift descended. "Hold on. What the fuck? Oh, I see. Get Miss Peters in here. Right sorry, Alex?"

"Yes," he replied with sudden intrigue as to what his sister was doing.

"Good, you're still there. Umm, I think you might need to see something." He stepped out of the lift, nodded at Louisa and walked into his office with a frown. What did he need to see? And what had Evelyn got to do with it?

"Right, well I was calling to see if you were free for lunch anyway, so why don't I swing by at two? Or I could meet you at Copelli's? Whatever's best for you really?"

"Yeah, okay, just let me..." The silence stretched as he heard nothing but frustrated huffs and puffs coming from the other end of the line.

"Conner, what's going on?"

"I... I'm not really sure. I'll text you later." He heard some rapid keyboard clicking in the background and sat down at his desk. "Do you have investment accounts in Geneva?" What?

"Yes, why?"

"How much?"

"Why the bloody hell is that important to you?"

He flicked his eyes to his own screen and sighed at the ten thousand fucking emails that sprang up in front of him. Scanning through them, he only saw hours of work, including more hours of bollocking people and repairing the damage they'd created or at least limiting it to some degree.

"Are they with Henry?" His ears were suddenly back with Conner at the mention of Mr. DeVille.

"One still is, yes. What the hell are you talking about, Conner?"

"You need to check it out. I'm not sure how but I think you've been hacked and I can't access your accounts to find out what's happening."

"What do you mean you can't access them? You set up the whole bloody system for me, and why the hell are you looking at my financial status anyway?"

"I wasn't. Evelyn was. I've just seen it in her logs, which she's tried to hide from me like the clever little bitch she is. Good job I'm as paranoid as you when it comes to Blutech. I don't know what she's been up to but her handiwork is all over this. Look, give me an hour and I'll call you back, okay?"

"Right."

Before he could add more, Conner ended the call so he stared at the phone, trying to process what the fuck that was all about. Hacked? Who could get through Conner's own security protocol? The man was a genius for God's sake, and what was sister dearest doing anywhere near his accounts? The skin at the back of his neck prickled with tension as he logged into his own banking system and delved into the information on screen. Nothing looked untoward to him but what the hell did he know? Computer genius he was not. Every account still appeared to hold the same amount of wealth as it did a few days ago, or thereabouts. Some a lot more, actually, which made him very happy indeed. At least there was a decent reason he put up with this bullshit every day.

Perhaps he should just give it all up and go live on an island with his angel. She wouldn't need to know any more about his life then, would she? He could just lie in the sun all day and watch her body move around in that languid way that she had about her when she'd been thoroughly used, when she'd been exhausted to the brink of her limits.

"Sir, Magden and Bowdine are waiting for you in the boardroom. Are you ready or would you like me to delay them?" Louisa's voice came ringing through the speaker, breaking him from his little fantasy of peace and unfortunately reminding him of his current obligation. He logged out of the accounts and began sending Conner a quick text to confirm that everything seemed in order at his end.

"No, that's fine, Louisa. I'm on my way."

Picking up the documents that had been laid out for him, he headed to the door. Another hour or two with Tate would hopefully help him gain some sort of idea as to whether he really was friend or foe. Magden and Bodine were trying to sue him for three point two million. It seemed he bought land in California from under their noses just as they'd signed their own paperwork on the deal. Too fucking late. He smirked at the thought of Tate in action. Whatever his feelings for the man, he was extraordinarily good at his chosen profession and he knew he'd be walking away a richer man today.

Wandering to the lift, he glanced back at Louisa who had her head buried in a stack of files.

"Did you say anything to Elizabeth yesterday?" Her head slowly rose as she peered over her glasses at him.

"What do you mean, Sir?"

"She appeared to think we'd... been together in a less than professional setting."

Why he couldn't have just said *fucked* was beyond him. The woman was just as debauched as he was. Gay, yes, but given that they'd originally met in Pascal's London club, the connotation was perfectly acceptable.

"Not at all, Sir. I may have leered a bit if I'm honest but I certainly didn't say anything." He snorted out a bark of laughter and headed into the lift.

"Quite something, isn't she?"

"Oh yes, Sir, quite something indeed," she replied as she lowered her nose into her paperwork again.

He nodded to himself and let the doors close.

"Quite something indeed." She was going to need to be exactly that for what he had to tell her. She was going to need to grip on to every inch of humanity she possessed and try to understand, to feel what he was years before and sense what he could still be if pushed. She'd need to be everything he hoped she could be and more because it was either that or losing her and that shit wasn't happening anytime soon.

He'd die before that.

He simply wasn't letting her go.

Chapter 28

Elizabeth

"Balls to it, I'm not hanging around here a minute longer than necessary. Its three thirty and I need a fucking drink," Belle very nearly screams as she throws her bag on the table and turns the closed sign on the shop window. Teresa and I gape at her and then turn back to each other with the same frown we've used all day. It's the "what the hell" frown.

I have absolutely no clue why she's in such a snit but she is, has been all day in fact. The moment I set foot in the shop this morning she practically ripped my head off about a menu that I apparently hadn't put out for her. I very quickly found it under a pile of her own paperwork and handed it over so she bit my head off about something else. Teresa's had the same dilemma all day while she's tried desperately to avoid the wrath of Belle's temper by ducking into secluded corners every time she's been in the vicinity. Frankly, both of us have been hoping she had appointments so she could get out of here and give us some peace from the tension but no such luck unfortunately. The Belle bitch mode has been forced upon us constantly and to be honest, I need a sodding drink, too.

"Well zippidy doo dah, thank God for that. I can't stand another minute of your crabby arse. You need vodka, lots of it I should say," Teresa says from the side as she chucks a bread roll straight across the room at her. I'm not sure that was the wisest of moves.

"Fuck off." Belle sneers as she brushes the crumbs off her red *Gucci* suit and huffs her way back into the office. My eyebrows raise again at Teresa who looks completely lost.

"Is it time of the month?" she whispers at me. My mind does a quick calculation. It possibly is. We're both around the same time and I'm due anytime now.

"Just about, yes, but I don't think that's it. It never normally affects her like this." It really doesn't. She's a bitch most of the time but she's never overly hostile to us just because of her monthly irritation.

"Well it must be that. There's nothing else, is there? I mean, she just got engaged to a bona fide sex god, for God's sake. Look, let's just get her to a bar and then hopefully we can talk it out of her." I nod my head in reply and watch as Belle storms past us again and heaves the door open.

By the time we've locked up and pulled the shutters down, she's somehow managed to get a cab. Why she's bothered, I'm not sure. The road is filled with bars we could have gone into but it appears she's on a mission of some sort. We both file in behind her and look at her expectantly in the hope that she knows where she wants to go because telling Belle to do anything when she's in this mood is the stupidest thing anyone could ever do.

"Tudors," she snarls at the cabby - yes snarls - as if the poor chap has done something wrong. He simply shrugs and pulls out into the road with no response whatsoever. It's not surprising really. Most Londoners are shitty with cabbies.

"Why are we going there of all places? I'm not exactly dressed for it, honey," I reply as I look down at my black Capri trousers and blue shirt. The fact that I've got my very boring black footwear on isn't helping either.

"Of course you're not. You never are, are you? It's a damn good thing one of us thinks about this shit with some sense," she says as she pulls out a pair of *Jimmy Choos* or something from her *Hermes* bag and forces them on me. "Put those on." She briefly scans Teresa and nods her head in approval. Clearly the fact that she's always been able to do a full day in heels is a bonus this afternoon.

I narrow my eyes at the shoes and then her. She glares back, seemingly daring me for a fight so I capitulate and rip my shoes and socks off. If we're going to row about something I have no idea about then we'll do it in a quieter place than this. Teresa really doesn't need to be involved. Pulling my hair out of its clip, I delve into my bag for lip-gloss and mascara. I don't know much about Tudors but I do know it's full of wealth. It's a direct competitor of INK and Belle often goes there to wine and dine new business, although I can't remember the last time she went. She certainly hasn't been there since she's been with Conner, and I know for a fact he won't go because he hates the place

530

for some unknown reason. Is that why she's chosen there, so she won't run into him? Why wouldn't she want to see him, though? I know they've argued a bit lately, but haven't we all?

Running my fingers through my hair, I glance out of the window and sigh at the thought that I still haven't got anything for Alex for Christmas. People are delving in and out of shops with arms full of bags and gifts, mothers dragging their obviously very bored children along with them as they go, probably trying to desperately get home. The coloured lights along Oxford Street glimmer and glint as the late afternoon gloom begins to descend across London, making me smile at the image of the Christmas tree in the lounge at his house. It's stunning, huge and topped off with an angel, his choice not mine. I wanted a fairy, but he said angels were at the top of his tree as he kissed me. Sweet.

To be honest, the whole decorating of his house makes me suddenly realise that Belle and I haven't even bothered at home this year for whatever reason. We both seem to spend little time there now and given that I've actually just made the rather huge leap of saying I'll move in with Alex, there really doesn't seem much point.

Am I doing the right thing? A sudden bite of nerves has me internally questioning my decision. His morning tantrum about James is still festering around within me. I handled it by simply pretending it didn't bother me - that he didn't bother me, but he did. He always does when he's like that. I dug deep, had an opinion and held firm to it. The idiot will not tell me who I can and can't employ. I just hope that finding my new dominant persona is enough to let him know I won't put up with that type of behaviour, no matter how sexually appealing it might be at the time with those captivating, dark eyes of his and that chest looming down on me. Pascal's eyes floated through my mind, as the man I love's fingers tightened, causing me to question his use of force. *"Remain dominant with him, my dear. He will need it to be honest."*

So I did, and apparently it worked to some degree because he left. I have absolutely no idea what he disappeared to do but I'm pretty sure it had to do with inflicting some sort of pain on something. I'm also pretty sure there wasn't anyone else in the apartment so presumably it was an inanimate object of some sort, thankfully. Having blown out several breaths and pulled myself back together, I opted for giving him a little space by running for coffee. The man I found banging his head on the lift door on my return was quite a sight to behold, standing there in the middle of his own foyer with no more clothes on than I left him in. Clearly every woman in the building was drooling, including me. At first, I wondered what the hell he was doing, and then I realised he was looking for me, that he'd come from his apartment without a thought of how he looked, to find me, because he must have thought I'd run. But I'll never run. I couldn't now, even if I wanted to, because he's too far engrained into me. The thought of not being with him, even with that temper of his, is just too debilitating, too devastating. His temper is his passion for me. It's his way of showing me what I mean to him and I'll take it with a smile because I love him. As long as he realises when he can use it, anyway. He really does need to work on that a bit.

I'm pulled back to the present as the car door opens and Teresa runs toward the very flashy looking building. Expensive is not the word for it. Highly polished chrome wording adorns the front of the cream porch area, inviting you into the venue with a smile. A doorman holds the door open for us as we all barrel through it in the hope of keeping the rain off our reasonably decent hair do's. Well, mine and Teresa's anyway. Belle's looks perfect, as it always does. In fact, short of looking irritated, she looks very flirtatious. She even winks at the doorman. My instincts kick in with a vengeance. Whatever's going on, it seems she's thinking about making it better by the addition of some male company. It's very worrying, almost like she's reverting to bitch mode and forgetting that she's engaged, to a very desirable and wealthy man, who would no doubt kill anybody that touches her, and who is also one of the nicest men I know. Well, nice is a bit of a stretch. I dare say Conner can be very un-nice when pushed, but he does love her and I think the world of him. Has he done something I should be aware of?

Two doors later and we enter what can only be described as a den of iniquity. The low structure of the building screams indulgence with its taupes and creams, and the soft, sumptuous furnishings make me want to curl up and let the venue show me what it has to offer. By the look of the very glamorous bar staff, I would say it probably has quite a lot to offer because the cute, six foot, hazel-eyed model look alike who's currently staring at Belle in hunger is very obviously up for more than serving her a drink. Worryingly, she's giving him her best fuck me eyes right back.

"If you even think about doing that, I'm ripping that damn ring off your finger and having Mr. Avery for myself," Teresa states as she glares at Belle and grabs her arm to lead her away from temptation. I follow rapidly and wave my arm at a boothed area surrounded by candlelight. "What the hell is wrong with you? You're behaving like a complete moron."

She's got a damn good point.

"Come on, honey, spit it out. You've been in a foul mood all day and now you're showing interest in another man? I have no idea what's going on, but you need to get a grip." I inject into the conversation as said cute barman wanders over and inclines his head. I assume he's asking for drinks orders. "Three vodka tonics please," I reply to his unasked question. I'm not giving her a chance to speak and destroy her relationship before she's at least told me what the problem is. He looks at her and licks his lips. She raises an eyebrow then eventually turns her eyes away from him, thankfully dismissing his advances, at least for now anyway. Teresa watches with a tilt of her head as his backside wanders away.

"Teresa, please!" I exclaim as I try to turn the dialogue back to my sister and not the, okay very attractive, barman, who does have a great arse.

"What? That's a fine piece of arse - credit where it's due."

"Clearly, but that's not the point at the moment, is it?" I reply as I glare at her and turn towards Belle again.

"Yes, you're right of course, but Christ, I haven't been seen to in ages. It's actually getting painful down there. Do you think I could just get in a quickie before we...?" Oh for god's sake.

"NO!"

"Okay. Wow... Calm the fuck down. It was just a question," she says as she shuffles about so she can face us again while faffing her dark pixie cut around her face again. Belle snorts in amusement so we both turn to her, thankful for some sort of giggly sound from her.

"So what's going on?" I ask as I look at her and try to see what's behind her eyes. Is it anger, hurt, betrayal? No idea. She always was like a wall of concrete when it came to emotions.

She sighs and opens her mouth. Unfortunately, the return of the barman stops her so we wait until he's disappeared again and look back to her for the continuation of whatever she's about to say. Wall of concrete has suddenly reappeared. It's not helpful.

"Come on, spill it. We can't help if we don't know what's going on," Teresa says as she bumps her elbow into her and smiles. "If he's being a prat then at least let us know what he's done wrong."

Belle picks up her drink and takes a few small sips before sighing again.

"I think he's having an affair."

What? Absolutely not. It's just not him. Well, I don't think it is. Why would he do that? He's just asked her to marry him. It's not possible.

"No, he wouldn't. You didn't see him before he asked you. He was a nervous wreck about asking you. He loves you. You're just being paranoid." She looks back at me in amazement.

"You knew?"

"Well yes, but that's irrelevant at the moment, isn't it? Anyway, why on earth would you think that?"

"All he does is talk about her. It's fucking constant, like she's some sort of genius or something, which she probably is given her brother, but I'm sorry, it's not fucking acceptable and I don't know what to do about it," she seethes as she sips again and crosses her legs.

"Who are you talking about?" Not a clue.

"Evelyn sodding Peters." Oh, that is a little concerning. Alex's sister does seem to have a thing for Conner, but he wouldn't, would he?

"And this would be who?" We both swing our eyes to Teresa. Have we not told her about this?

"Alex's sister - well, half-sister. She works for Conner," I reply as I gaze back at Belle and wonder what it is that I'm supposed to say to her.

"Alex has a sister? When the hell did this happen? We really haven't spent enough time together." No, probably not to be honest.

"Look, honey, she is very senior in his company and unfortunately appears to be very good at what she does so I'm sure he just needs to spend a lot of time with her. It doesn't mean anything's going on between them."

It's all I've got. I can't give her anything else because I'm just not sure. The only person other than the two involved who would possibly be able to answer the question is Alex, and I'm not even sure he would know. Would Conner hide this from him, given the family connection? I can't even believe he'd do it but it is a possibility and Miss Peters is indeed very attractive. Balls, this is not good.

"Well, have you confronted him about it?" Teresa asks as she downs her drink and signals to the peroxide blonde waitress to get us some more. I've hardly touched mine. Belle downs hers as well as if she's on a roll of binge drinking. Unfortunately, I have this thing to go to with Alex so I won't be participating in drunken pursuits today. I can't believe I forgot about it to be honest. I so hate looking like a fool, especially after the morning's activities.

"No," she replies quietly as she looks into the bottom of her glass and I swear I notice her sniff back tears.

"Belle, I really don't think you need to be worrying about this. He loves you. He asked you to marry him in front of a room full of his employees and friends, and her I might add. If he was doing anything with her, do you honestly think he would have done that?"

"I don't know anymore. I just feel like I don't know him at all sometimes, and his constant *Evelyn this* and *Evelyn that* really isn't helping my damn nerves on the matter. I just shouldn't have damn well entertained the idea of doing this with him."

"What?" both Teresa and I shout incredulously at the same time.

"That's fucking ridiculous, Belle. He's wonderful and-"

"Is he? Really? You don't know anything about him, Teresa, and nor do I. He's got secrets and a past that he won't let me in to. He's manipulative, short tempered, actually a damn lunatic with his temper. Yes, he's utterly fantastic in bed but that doesn't mean I've got any fucking clue as to whom Conner Avery is. And yet I stupidly said yes to marrying him, for some unknown reason. Is that the sort of man you'd want to marry?"

We both stare at her with open mouths. Okay, I knew Conner had a temper but I hadn't realised Belle had witnessed it so vehemently. They're supposed to be happy and in love. Mind you, so are Alex and I, and we're regularly doing battle as well. Maybe Conner's as screwed up as he is. I never thought of him as manipulative though, and while I clearly don't know everything about him, I just assumed he was quite a happy chappy really. Maybe his past is entwined with whatever Alex has been up to? No, he said that Conner found him again and pointed him back in the right direction, meaning that they had been apart for a while. But what past could he be hiding from Belle, and why?

"Right," is all that comes out of my mouth because I seriously can't answer that question. Teresa closes her mouth and then picks up her newly delivered drink. I'm not sure when they arrived.

"Quite," she replies with no other comment on the matter.

"Do you want me to ask Alex? He might know."

"He might but do you think he'd tell you the truth if he does? Brothers together and all that. They might not be related but given the code of their little bond, can you honestly say he'd rat out his friend?" Teresa replies as she narrows her eyes at something in the background.

It's a good point but I think he would tell me if I pushed him. He said he wouldn't lie to me and he knows I'd leave him if he did. This dominant thing around him really does seem to work and I've definitely had to put up with enough shit from him so I'm assuming he would tell me something as important as this. Maybe... Actually, I'm not sure. Clearly his manipulation knows no bounds when he needs it. This could be a time when he very much needs it.

"Well, I think he'd tell me - if he knows anything, that is - but I also think he will say that there's nothing going on between them. The only thing he's ever said about Conner and relationships is that he never cheats on anyone. I really can't see that it will be any different now that he's asked you to marry him. Why would it? If you're not a cheater, you're not."

Unfortunately this brings images of Alex and Caroline sodding Anderson flying into my brain. Alex clearly is a cheater - well to his friend anyway. Bastard. Has he apologized for that shit yet? Maybe now would be a good time, because that would be a lovely conversation between them:

"Hey, are you screwing my sister behind my girlfriend's sister's back? And by the way, sorry for fucking your ex behind yours. Glad you forgave me though."

Yes, very pleasant. Actually, that sounds a little incestuous if I'm honest and just a bit weird. There are far too many sisters in that statement for my liking.

"No, he wouldn't, Beth. He might love you but he wouldn't tell the truth about this. He'll more than likely say something like, *'It's none of my business,'* therefore neither denying or confirming that Conner is indeed a cheating bastard."

"Teresa, that really isn't helping," I scathe at her as I take a large gulp of my drink and glance across at Belle, who looks as depressed as I've ever seen her. My heart cringes at the thought. Just as she's lets her emotions go, Conner screws it up? I don't believe it. "This is ridiculous. The guy adores you so I'm going to call him, or go and see him. You're right. It's not fair to put Alex in that position so if you won't confront him then I will." They both stare at me. Belle slowly arches her incredible brow.

"You. Will. Not." If looks could kill I would be dead.

"Well you've got to do something. Sitting around here and stewing about it isn't going to fix anything and it sure as shit isn't going to give you any answers. If there's one thing I've learned in the last few months, it's to ask for what I want," I reply forthrightly. Why Belle is pissing around is completely unknown. The woman's known for her lack of tact, always straight to the point. For God's sake, she's behaving like... well, me, or who I used to be, pre Alexander White.

"Clearly, Miss Kinky," Teresa giggles as she flicks her hand in whip motion. "You go with your new found forcefulness. Take a cat o' nine tails with you."

Belle growls at her, then me. Neither of us can stop the grins that fly to our faces.

"Did she just growl? When did that start happening?" Teresa asks. I giggle in reply and take Belle's hand in mine.

"Come on, honey. Just go and see him and ask him straight out. If he's anything like Alex, he'll be crap under pressure from you. Just look him in the eye and challenge him about it."

"Beth, it's not that simple, and while I appreciate your support, I can't just stomp in there and accuse him of this. I've got no evidence

537

and he'll go crazy, and... well... he scares me a bit if I'm honest," she replies as she hangs her head.

Oh! That's not good. Marcus the dick skips through my head, smiling like the cock he is as images of Belle with bruising all over her erupt. My eyes narrow at her as fury spreads across my skin. If the bastard's hit her I'll kill him.

"Has he hit you? Are you telling me he's capable of...?" Her face flashes to mine.

"No! God no. I don't think he would do that, but... I don't know. He just gets... Oh, I don't know how to explain it." I do. He's clearly just like his friend He might not need the sadistic preferences but he obviously is just as screwed up in a different way.

Jesus, why didn't we just meet normal ones?

"Well fuck him then. Leave," Teresa says from the side. She could have a point. Belle is not up for this type of behaviour, and he certainly shouldn't be putting her through it given that he knows some of what happened to her in the past because I told him.

"I don't want to leave."

"Well, well, Alexander's little innocent... Eliza, isn't it?" What the hell?

We are rudely interrupted by a female voice who is clearly directing her jibe at me. I swing my eyes round to see who the dig is coming from and am greeted by the very unfairly beautiful Cecily Winchester, who definitely knows that is not my name as a smug smile slips across her face. Does she have to look so damned gorgeous in her *Prada* apparel, all long legs and dark, silky hair? I try my best to seem unaffected by her presence but can't help fidgeting with my top in the hope that I look casually elegant. At least my girls are here.

"Cecily, what exactly do you want?" Again, I try for casual given her status with a mob boss or whatever he is, but the sneer that leaves my mouth is definitely not pleasant.

"Don't be so hostile. I only came to say hello. We move in the same circles and I thought I would see how you are." We so do not move in the same circles, bitch. My come-back seriously wants to be FUCK OFF! However, I control the urge and regain some element of nice.

"Fine, thank you, but sweet as that is, I'm in the middle of a private conversation at the moment so I'm afraid we'll have to leave it for another time."

There, that's enough. I've got no more anyway to be honest.

"Well, yes, if we must. Perhaps we could have lunch sometime?" she replies. It's actually quite nice and I narrow my eyes at her because she's absolutely playing some sort of game with me. These sodding twilight people that live in Alex's world seriously don't know how to be normal.

"Yes, perhaps we could." *Not a fucking chance*. She nods at me and quickly scans my girls, who to be fair on them are throwing as many lovely daggers as they can without being overly rude. My eyes notice a man in a black suit approaching in the background and I can't stop the feeling of dread that sweeps through me at his presence. I can't even work out why. I don't know him and have never seen him before, but before I know it, my insides feel like they're churning in fear. It's something about the way he's moving, overbearing or maybe arrogant, long strides moving purposefully as if he's about to kill anything that dares defy him or get in his way. It's all very Alex, but without my ability to see behind his physical presence.

His dark brown hooded eyes and rich brown hair glisten under the dimmed lights as he narrows his gaze on me and stares without any hint of apology. It's highly disconcerting. He's clearly in complete control of himself and the space around him. Unfortunately, as he reaches the table and looks at me, my eyes fly to the floor. He chuckles in amusement at my clear ineptitude, which instantly has me fighting my own neck to look back at him as I rub my bracelet and think of Alex's reaction.

He's not that tall really, not that attractive either, but there's just something about his demeanour. It's extremely cold, very calculating and obviously quite lethal. He scares the living crap out of me for some reason if I'm honest, and I very quickly realise that this is quite possibly Aiden Phillips.

I keep my eyes focused on his and try to maintain some sort of control about myself, but Christ, the man looks like some sort of living evil incarnate. And then he smiles. Oh my god, his face lights up like a fucking Christmas tree. Gone is the potential danger and suddenly there's only a man who would cause women to throw themselves at his feet. It's the quickest transformation I have ever seen. Cecily leans into his side as she suddenly becomes aware that he's looking at me and regardless of my fear, I can't help but feel a little amused by her jealousy. It gives me a much-needed boost of self-worth and I realise that I can deal with this man. I can deal with Alex and Pascal for god's sake and they're frightening enough, and at the same time I might add, together, so to speak. I'm such a slut.

"Who do we have here?" he asks as he eventually breaks eye contact with me and looks across at my girls. I blow out the breath I was holding and stare at Cecily, who's now grinning like the cat that got the damn cream.

"Aiden, this is Eliza, and I'm not sure who these are. Eliza is Alexander's new thing," she very kindly says, nonchalantly waving at my girls. I still hate her.

"It's Elizabeth actually," I mumble in response as I glare back at her.

"Oh, is it? Silly me. Sorry." Bitch.

"Ah yes, Elizabeth Scott. This must be your sister, Annabelle, isn't it?"

Why the hell does he know who we are? My hackles are on instant alert. Okay, I might have met Cecily once and Alex clearly knows the man for some reason, but how does he know my surname and why does he know Belle's name at all? My eyes flick to Belle and Teresa. Teresa's got bitch eyes firmly focused on Cecily but unfortunately, Belle is actually smiling her best *I want you* face. She suddenly stands and offers her hand to him, which he takes, still with that same overly wonderful smile. I have no idea what's going on between the two of them but I'm really not happy about this little conversation.

"Please call me Belle," she says with a hint of sexiness thrown in. Cecily scowls at her and wraps herself in tighter. He abruptly pushes her away like she's completely irrelevant and continues to look at my sister. I'm not sure what game she thinks she's playing but we're not participating in it a moment longer.

"Aiden, it was lovely to meet you but we need to get going I'm afraid," I say as I rise from the booth and nudge Teresa. She instantly stands and grabs her coat. Good girl. Belle scowls back at me so I smile as sweetly as I can manage and hope to hell that she just gives in and comes with us.

"Shame," he says as he continues his assault on Belle leisurely, his brown eyes flashing with open interest as his fingers run across hers. "I was hoping for some entertainment."

Absolutely not. I'm not even sure what to say back to that. Does he think he's going to get an orgy or something? Okay, I'm now into that sort of thing but not with a drugs baron or possible mafia king, regardless of that deceiving smile. His continued stroking of Belle's hand and step toward her indicate that that's exactly what he was thinking, and she's falling for it, or revelling in it. Shit.

"Yes, well, lovely as that might have been, we all have things to do so if you wouldn't mind releasing my friend, we'll be on our way," Teresa says as she grabs Belle's other hand and practically drags her away from the guy. He chuckles again and nods at my feisty little friend as he pulls Cecily back to him.

"Do call me about lunch, Elizabeth," she shouts at me as we hurry Belle and ourselves towards the door. Not a hope.

"Will do," I reply in my most casual voice as I shove Belle out the door, still beaming at Aiden. On reaching fresh air and the safety of the street, I gape at her.

"What the bloody hell was that?"

"What? He's cute," she says as she wanders toward the road, swinging her hips.

"Cute? That's Aiden Phillips. There is nothing cute about a man who hurts, possibly kills, people for a living and deals drugs out to the entirety of the planet."

"Actually, he was quite sexy. Maybe it's the danger thing, or maybe I'm just horny," Teresa chimes in. I roll my eyes at her and push them both forward again.

"Anyway, how do you know that bitch?"

"Same circles apparently," I mumble in reply. I can't even begin to process a conversation about Alex knowing her, or him for that matter.

When we've got quite some distance from Tudors, I feel my heart rate decrease to some sort of normal level and sigh out a breath of frustration. We need to know if Conner's sleeping with Evelyn. I still don't believe he would, but we have to know for sure, and I need to understand why the hell someone like Aiden Phillips would have the slightest knowledge or interest in who we are. While I get that Alex and I have been seen by Cecily, that doesn't explain why he knows what my name is and it also doesn't explain why he would have any interest in me or Belle at all. I'll ask Alex about it later - yet another man I have to discuss with him. I get the feeling he won't be too happy about our meeting today but it's not like I did it on purpose, and I'm definitely not hiding it from him.

Two tube rides later and we're rounding the corner to our apartment building. Belle looks exhausted and Teresa looks like she needs to join a happy party or something. I so need to find her a man, preferably not one like Aiden Phillips or Pascal.

"Are you going to this thing tonight?" Belle asks as we reach the lift.

"Oh, do you mean the Tranting fundraiser? Yes, I didn't know you were though," I reply as we travel upwards.

"Yep, Conner's been badgering me about it. It's important to him for some reason, yet another thing he won't tell me about." Oh, again.

"What's Tranting anyway? Do you know?"

"Nope, no clue."

"Girls really, you need to get your game on. The Tranting Fundraiser happens every two years. It's in aid of Hope Christ's Children's Hospital and there will be some very big players there this evening. I think it's at the Westminster this year." We both stare at Teresa as she wanders into the kitchen and flicks on the kettle. "And given that it's nearly six o'clock, you both better get your backsides in gear. You'll need your finest stuff on 'cause your boys will be in black tie."

And mine is all at Alex's. Great. I rush into Belle's bedroom to see what she's got available. I spy the long, black, incredibly sexy lace creation with a frown. I couldn't pull that off, could I?

"Belle, can I try this?" I shout as I round the corner and present her with it.

"Wear what you like, honey. I'm not going," she replies as she kicks off her shoes and switches on the television.

"What?"

"Not going. He can take the slut instead. In fact call her and see if she wants to borrow something else of mine." This is not good.

"Belle, get your arse in that shower and sort your shit out. This is ridiculous. The man is in love with you and for whatever reason needs you with him tonight. He may need to work on his temper but he is not sleeping with Evelyn Peters."

"Yes, he is."

Oh, I've had enough. Throwing the dress down on the sofa, I find my phone in my bag and text Alex.

-       **Is Conner sleeping with your sister? Love you**

The reply is, thankfully, almost instant.

-       **Definitely not. I'm enjoying this directness by the way. Stimulating.**

I smile at the reply and wander over to Belle, shoving the phone into her hand.

"There. See?"

She looks down at the screen for a few moments then chucks the phone at me and stomps into her bedroom, slamming the door behind her. I'm not sure if she's pissed off with me or herself so I stare at the door and resign myself to the fact that she just needs a little time. Whatever she's doing, I certainly need to start getting ready so I slurp the tea Teresa has plonked down in front of me and mentally run through what else I've got in my wardrobe.

"Do you mind if I stay here tonight?"

"No, of course not. Help yourself, honey," I reply as I check off my list of clothing, underwear and jewellery. I could really use that choker that Alex got for me, although preferably not with the thong thing attached. Actually, maybe that would be nice. I glance at the dress again and notice the lace side panels. Not then, it appears underwear won't be needed at all.

Grabbing my phone, I send Alex a text asking him to bring the choker with him, then realise he might not be going home so send another one to say it doesn't matter. I'll find something to do the job.

"Do you think she'll be okay?" Teresa asks.

"I think so. I'll have a word with Conner later, but she does have to come to this with me. She can't just give up on him for no reason."

"Right, well, she's had ten minutes of moping. You go get yourself ready and I'll get her motivated. Do you think Vodka will help? Or I could do one of my cocktail things." I giggle and point her toward the kitchen.

"I think that would help a lot, honey. Can you get me a glass of wine while you're at it?"

"Yep, go on now. Your hair is a real disaster and Mr. White is going to love this little number so off you go, do your worst."

Standing under the shower, I try to quell the random panic that keeps attacking me regarding Aiden Phillips. He is not the sort of character I want anywhere near my life, or Belle's for that matter. Not that I know an awful lot about the man, but I know enough to be very aware that he is bad news. Why I didn't do a little research when Alex mentioned him is beyond me. I could have been prepared for him today if I had. Clearly my reaction to him was ridiculous. I did not hold myself well at all, and although I did bring my head up in the end, there's no denying that fear seeped through every vein in my body. Now, given that I am currently in a relationship with Alex and have had several dealings with Pascal, I can't quite understand my fear. They are both quite scary enough, so I can only assume he has some very bad things going on his mind that he has the ability to teleport into the heads of others. Or maybe he has no morals at all and I can somehow feel that. I wander out into my room and start the process of gaining some kind of order to my hair, trying to shake off the strange feeling regarding the man. It's almost like he's got a hold over me that I'm not aware of. My eyes narrow at the thought. Does he know something about Alex? He clearly knows him and more than likely has had dealings with him of some sort, but that doesn't mean Alex has been too involved in that world, does it?

The image of him beating up the guy that attacked me comes flying back. It's not pleasant, even if it is a little core clenching for some reason now. What is it about this violence that has become so appealing lately? Are his preferences changing my views on aggression?

An hour later and I wander back out into the lounge to find Teresa slumped on the couch with what looks like a martini in her hand. I didn't even know olives existed in this apartment.

"Where is she?"

"In there, getting very fabulous indeed," she replies. "Seems she's changed her mind about Miss Peters. I think Alex's text did the trick, although I gather she'll be there tonight so I'd keep a watchful eye if I was you."

"Mmm, fair point." Belle in furious mode is not something to be excited about, and is she? Does Alex know? Given their last interaction, I hope so.

"So," she says as she hauls herself upright. "If you've both finished, I'm going to have a bath and chill out for a bit. Do you need a hand into that outrageously sexy thing?"

We both look at the dress as I nod in response. She picks it up and holds it out to me as she begins to unzip the back of it, which keeps going, and going, all the way to the bloody floor until it comes apart in my hands.

"Oh!" I exclaim stupidly as I stare at it.

"Well, yes, it is a bit... risqué, isn't it? No underwear either. Oh, you are going to be naked so quickly once he finds out about this. I'm so jealous," she says with a huge grin on her face. A giggle bursts from my mouth at the thought. He is definitely going to be happy about this dress.

Unwrapping my robe, I push my arms into the armholes and let her zip the back up until it's firmly secured at the back. It skims every contour on me while clinging to each curve a little too tightly if I'm honest. Thankfully, the neckline isn't too low cut. There's still a fair bit of cleavage on show but not overly gratuitous.

"Belle, I'm coming in," I say as I wander in so that I can look in her wardrobe mirror. It's far better than mine. I'm stopped in my tracks by the most breath-taking dress I have ever seen in my life - deep red, slashed almost to the hipbone with ruffles and flowing graciously along the floor behind her. Her hair is up in a seductive do that I've never seen on her before with very hot, cat-like eyes. She looks exquisite and thoroughly edible. If I wasn't her sister, I would be drooling.

"Wow!"

"Is it okay? Not too much?" she asks with a hint of nerves. "It's just I've been such a bitch to him and it seems I shouldn't have been and I just want him to be proud of me and…"

"No, you look… Wow!" Oh my god, she's sniffing back tears. I gallop over to her as best I can in this very tight dress and wrap her up in a sisterly hug.

"Yep, okay, watch the hair for fuck's sake," she says as she pushes me away a little and smiles. She wipes at the underneath of her eyes and gives me a once over. "Right, shoes… Umm… How about these?" She's holding up a pair of equally sexy stilettos, which will probably kill me by the end of the night. "And here, there's a lock for that dress," she continues as she rifles about in her draw and produces a small padlock and key in gold then makes her way behind me and presumably snaps it into place on the zip.

"That makes me feel a little more secure," I respond as I slip my feet into the shoes and take the key from her. It's going in my bag, where it's safe.

"Right, girlies, I think your men might be here," Teresa shouts from the lounge. We both meet her at the window to peer down onto the street. Sure enough there's the *Bentley* and a *Limo* parked out the front. "I am so fucking jealous it's unbelievable. You have to find me one of those," she says as she points to Conner getting out of the *Limo*, looking damn good in a tux, even with blue hair. Alex appears next, looking equally stunning, more so if I'm honest, but then I'm biased. They move toward each other with a smile and a man hug while laughing about something together and I don't stop the sigh that flows freely out of my mouth. It really is very dreamy to watch.

"Okay, let's do this then," Belle says as she plonks my wrap on my shoulders and grabs hers. "Have we got all our shit?"

"Yep," I reply as I pick up my keys and drop them into my bag.

Belle seems to suck in a breath of nerves and then she's back, her face the picture of every magazine cover in the world, that mysterious smile that she achieves with ease firmly plastered across her face as she dares the world to have a clue about what's going on in her head. I don't most of the time so if Conner thinks he'll ever understand her, good luck to him. She downs the rest of her drink and moves to the door, picking up the back of her dress as she goes. Stunning is not enough of a word for her this evening.

"Come on then, snotbag."

Okay, we're back to that. I smile and follow her as Teresa waves her goodbyes and collapses on the sofa again.

Chapter 29

Elizabeth

"I need to show you how much I love you, and I need to apologize for what happened this morning because you deserve so much better than me," he says with those twinkling blue eyes gazing down on me. There's nothing darkened about them, nothing deadly or conflicting, just love shining brightly as he fiddles with a piece of my hair and tips my chin up to him.

I could melt, in all honesty, with the amount of heat that's emanating between my thighs. I've pretty much been doing that since the moment I saw him standing in front of the car, looking all delicious in his tux, and wearing that happy, in love smile that he has when he's relaxed. Why he's so relaxed given our morning encounter is still a little confusing. I'd thought he might be a little fidgety but it seems he's actually in a remarkably good mood. Maybe it's the standing up for myself thing. Who knows? Is he trying to manipulate me into giving up James? He might be. His other tactic hasn't worked, has it? So perhaps he's going with the kill her with love technique. Bastard. That's not going to work either and I hope he damn well knows it.

Unfortunately, regardless of my sudden mental prowess, I'm still utterly devoted to his fingers, which are now heading down the side of my dress and softly teasing my hipbones as his lips meander across my jaw. His aftershave swirls across me in waves while he backs me onto the door in the corridor and presses his body into me, those devious hands hitching up my dress a bit so he can get his thigh in between my legs. It's not going to happen because the dress is just too tight, and I should probably stop him, given our location, but as usual, I'm an utter mess around him, completely open to suggestion and quite frankly, ready for whatever he has in mind. Maybe he's got a teaspoon on him somewhere...

"I missed you today. I need to make us better again. I need to show you," he whispers into my neck as he pulls his fingers back up my thigh towards my backside and that trembling thing starts to build to unearthly proportions again. If I'm honest, I'm still horny as hell from this morning and wish he'd grab hold a bit more. While I still can't get my head around this strange arousal I get from his anger, I am at least accepting that it's here now. It's part of me, or maybe part of us. He creates this in me, this need to give him whatever he wants and let go for him and he knows it. He may not completely understand my head yet, but he knows every inch of this body and what it wants. That inner slut of mine is continually shaking her backside for his hands to play with. He was right this morning when he asked who owned this body. I may have lied and said myself but I don't. He does, and he can have it all, right now. I push back into him in the hope of showing my need but for some reason, he won't allow it as he backs away a bit then continues with his gentle and soft touch as he caresses his way over my skin again.

"Not this time, baby. Let me show you the other man, the one you found," he breathes seductively into my throat as I feel his lips stroke across my collar bone and moan in response. It's beautiful, tender, quiet somehow, and for a moment the sound of the ball downstairs just disappears and the corridor vanishes. All I can hear is his heart and mine beating together, peacefully.

The door behind me suddenly opens and he pushes me calmly back into a room and closes the door behind him. Before I can turn around, he pulls a blue silk scarf from his pocket and lifts it to my eyes with a raised brow, clearly asking for permission. I have no idea why he's bothering because he should know I'll nod my head rapidly like a willing idiot. Given that we've only actually been in the building for an hour and he's already got me into a hotel room, I'm obviously quite up for it. I gaze into his cool blues for a moment, wondering what's going through his mind. Does he feel guilty for his anger, or for the way he was using it on me? Is it always going to be this way between us or will he eventually find a way to control that temper? Because he wasn't like this at first. Is it just his love for me that causes it? His beautiful mouth slips up into smile as he watches me, looking for all the world like he's completely in control of everything around him, and me.

The blanket of darkness comes over my eyes as he ties it off behind me and then his touch disappears, leaving me alone in the dark, waiting for whatever he deems appropriate next.

"A lock?" I hear the amusement in his voice and giggle, wondering whether he'll be able to pick it with an inanimate object that may be lying around the room. "Well that's interesting. Are you trying to keep me out of you, Elizabeth? Are you denying me entrance to my favourite place in the world? Is this my punishment?"

Well I hadn't thought about it like that. I was more worried about other people unzipping the bloody thing, but now that he mentions it, he was a shit this morning. My smile increases to mammoth proportions.

"I've never been a fan of receiving punishment," he says quietly from across the room somewhere. Clearly he's hardly ever had to say sorry let alone be told off about it. Oh! Wait, what about his dad? Shit, not good. *Stupid Beth.*

"Alex, I didn't-" He cuts me off by wrapping a hand around my mouth and pushing his body against my back.

"Don't speak. I want you to listen," he says softly. Oh, okay. I nod into his hand so he backs away again, dragging his fingers across my lips as he does. I hear ice clinking in glasses in the background and slowly turn towards the noise. I don't know what's about to come out of his mouth but the thought of him nonchalantly having a drink while I'm standing here blind is a little disconcerting to say the least, and really not what I was hoping to be receiving at the moment. Instant images of very suggestive positions spring to mind and I can't stifle the snicker of delight that leaves me at the thoughts. What's he doing with ice anyway?

Glass is suddenly being pressed against my lips and I open my mouth willingly. It doesn't occur to me that it might not be pleasant because anything coming from his extraordinary hands is always exceptional. Orange assaults my taste buds, swiftly followed by a heavy kick of liqueur. Ice-cold smooth liquid tumbles down my throat, changing on the way and somehow heating me through to my already overheated core. Delicious. My lips reach forward again as my tongue runs over the rim of the glass for more.

"Do you realise how damn sexy you are? How enthralling you've become?" he asks as I swallow more liquid and reach out to his labels to pull him closer to me. "You're everything to me, Elizabeth. Not a minute goes by when I don't wish I was buried inside you, or simply laying with you in my arms. Before you, I would wake up cold and empty. Now you warm me, you hold me close and tell me you love me as if I'm important to you for no other reason than just being me."

He pulls the glass from me and runs his tongue over my jaw and across to my mouth. My own flicks out to meet him but he pulls away again. "Mmm, sweet. Can you feel that heat travelling down your throat, baby? Did you feel the ice against those perfect lips and then the change as it warmed on the way to your heart? That's what you've somehow done to me, and I don't know why but each new touch from you is sweeter than the last, more intoxicating in some way. I've never felt that before you, that hunger to taste it again, that irrational need to consume something so strongly that it's impossible to be without it. Can you understand that?"

I don't know what my face is doing because I'm just listening. His beautiful emotions are flowing so freely that I'm captivated by the very sound of each word leaving his gorgeous mouth. And if he expects me to give him anything more than a "*yes*" then he's going to be disappointed.

"Yes."

Because it really is all I've got. I can't form coherent thought other than how much I love him, and how much I want to spend every second of my life with him. He gently picks up my hands and pulls them to his neck, caressing his fingers over the back of them as I clasp on to the familiar feel of his skin.

"No you can't, baby. You couldn't possibly because you're too pure and you'll never see what you've given me, or rather what you take away from me. Those moments in my life that are lacking are blindsided by your hands here. They guide me back and fill me with hope and love and dreams of beauty. They threaten me with thoughts of peace and bliss. Just feeling your fingers brushing across my skin is enough to make me believe I have a chance at redemption."

Redemption? My eyes furrow under the scarf. God, that's a big word. I have no idea what that means. What on earth does he think he's done? His hands leave mine and I suddenly feel something cold against the skin on my neck. At first my thoughts are with ice but it's not wet so I frown at the sensation and go to move my own fingers to it.

"No, don't let go of me." Oh. Okay. I feel him reaching around behind my neck and realise that he's clasping something together. I can only assume it's a necklace of some sort and suddenly my hackles rise, because seriously, if he's trying to give me another overly priced gift I'm going to kill him, regardless of his extremely lovely words, which have me almost in tears.

"Do you remember me talking about collaring at the opera?" What? Random. I never did find out what that meant. Is that's what's going on here? Given that I've got a necklace on, I can only presume that collaring has something to do with having something around your throat because that's what you put on a dog. Maybe it is. Actually, I'm not happy with that thought at all.

"Yes, but-" He cuts me off again.

"Don't speak." His mouth brushes against mine oh so softly and I quite literally swoon back into him as I feel his pulse beneath my fingertips. I'm swooning. His tongue, his gentle lips teasing mine open and pulling me towards him, always towards him. Oh god, I'm so in love it's ridiculous. His arms wrap around me until there's no room between us anymore and our kiss heats in desire as my body is crushed in tighter to him. All I can feel is his mouth moving against mine seamlessly in a raw exchange of love and adoration, tasting, not even breathing, just feeling and falling deeper until he slows, quietening each stroke of his tongue as he places small, feather-light kisses across my jaw and eventually back away again. His hands return to mine and he pushes them against his skin, rubbing them backwards and forwards over him while linking his fingers with mine and squeezing them together.

"Collaring is a mutual declaration of commitment and trust between two people. Some would call it a marriage of sorts, the ultimate bond between a dominant and their submissive. It's a theory I've never entertained, never wanted or even thought about."

Okay, where the hell is he going with this? Yes, I love him but I'm not being collared or some such shit. This world of his is bizarre enough without me feeling like a puppy as well. There can't possibly be any sort of equality in that type of thing, can there? Not happening. I'm not entirely happy about the connotation of what I'm wearing on my wrist. Well, actually I'm highly grateful of it in certain situations obviously, but he doesn't own me outside of that.

"Alex, I-" His hand covers my mouth again.

"Elizabeth, do you want me to get some tape?" His voice has suddenly become tense so I rapidly shake my head in response. Absolutely not, although that could be interesting. We haven't done that yet. "Good. I'm trying to say something and I just need you to listen." Okay, listening mode on. My mouth opens at the thought of collaring again and I sense the eyebrow rise so I clamp it closed again. *Shut up, Beth.*

"I watched a collaring ceremony once, and while it was interesting, I had no appreciation of the love that was in their eyes, or understanding of the bond that they wanted with each other. I remember thinking it odd to want that closeness with someone, to want someone so deep within you that they know everything about who you are and what you might need." His fingers brush over mine again as his lips meet mine briefly. I'm mesmerised by his words. All thoughts have vanished as I listen to him speak and feel his breath against my cheek. "To feel so tied to a person that you know you don't even need to speak and they'll give you what you need, help you to fathom the very depths of yourself and accept you for it." Oh god, he's trembling under my fingers. My heart sores to reach him and tell him how much I love him. "I understand that now, baby. You've taught me that," he whispers against my neck. I'm almost crying with joy at hearing the words and suddenly realise that I'm digging my nails into his throat because of the tension in my hands. Quickly sniffing back the tears that are threatening, I loosen my grip on him and wait for more of whatever this utter perfection is. His hands quickly increase the pressure again as if he's lost without it and needs to remind me that it's my throat, that it belongs to me, for my hands only.

"That necklace clasped around you isn't what you think it is. I could never collar someone like you. You should be free to choose for the rest of your life, to make your decisions about me without restraint simply because you will always make the right choice, the morally decent one."

His voice is wavering slightly, full of emotion and barely audible as he heaves in some breaths and becomes silent in front of me. My own throat is catching as I try to think of something to say, but all normality has disappeared. His humility is causing every need in me to rise up to his mouth and show him how much he means to me and what his words are causing inside. All I want to do is lie down and feel his skin against mine so we can undo this morning and move forward into this loveliness that he's creating. My lips reach for him to show him, but as I touch them, he pulls back.

"It's for me, Elizabeth. Those diamonds are symbolic of a collar around me. I'll never leave you, never let you go and I'll love and protect you forever if you want me to, just so that you know how perfect you are, so that you understand my commitment to you and feel safe. You had my throat before this moment, but now you have the assurance that you're in control of it, that you'll dictate what we need and how we need it."

Oh! My head shoots back from where it was and I stare blindly up towards his eyes. What the hell do I say to that? He's collaring himself so that I can be in control? I don't even know if I want to be in control, do I? I doubt it, and I definitely don't want total command over him in any way, although it could clearly be useful in those temper tantrum moments that he has. But what about his own dominance? How's that going to fit in? And is he suggesting he's going to be my submissive? Because that's just ridiculous. Alexander White the submissive? No. This makes no sense at all. I have to find something to say here. Unfortunately, the opening and closing of my mouth seems to have no actual language attached to it. I need to get this bloody blindfold off or something because I'm desperate to see his eyes, those wonderful crystalline blue eyes that sear through me and let me know where his mind is at. Is he doing this for him or for me? And why? Eventually my brain to mouth communication line resumes as I let go of his neck and step away from him.

"Can you take the blindfold off please?" is the first thing that comes out. I'm sure it should possibly be something full of love but I'm so confused by his last words that I can't formulate how I feel.

"No, not yet."

Right, that's completely submissive. Clearly that's not part of the package then and thank God, frankly, because I'm still not entirely happy with this whole Dom/sub thing anyway. In the bedroom is one thing, in the real world? No. Still, I have absolutely no idea what's going on here.

"Umm... why not? You've just told me I'm in control."

"Morally." What on earth does that mean?

"Okay, I'll take it off then." My fingers reach up to my face.

"Do not take that off, Elizabeth," he says quietly in that voice of his that has me trembling instantly. My inner slut leaps at the thought, disabling all coherent thought of confusion, if that's even possible.

I halt the progress of my fingers and relax my hands back down to my sides. "You see the difference between morality and indecency is so slight that sometimes the lines blur. Looking at you in that dress in the middle of the room, with silk wrapped around your beautiful eyes makes me want to string you up and fuck you senseless. It also makes me want to kill anyone who dares look at you. The rage it creates is uncontrollable. Is that morally acceptable or indecent?"

"It sounds bloody fantastic at this moment actually."

Well, the fucking senseless bit anyway because frankly, a good bout of that subspace thing would probably do me the world of good and clarify some of this bewilderment. The rage thing, I have no idea how I'm supposed to feel about that.

"And the fact that I want you to feel pain while I do it, that I might want another man involved?"

My eyebrows furrow behind the silk as I question the ethics behind being bound and dealt pain, and Pascal. Is any of that morally correct or not? It must be if I agree to it, and if he needs it as much as I do then I'm helping him and me, aren't I? But morally good? I'm not even sure what morality means in these circumstances. Really not sure.

"I'm not sure."

"And given your confusion, do you want to be the one who makes those decisions or me? Do you want to tell me what you need or do you want that option taken from you so that I can make those choices for you?" Oh, that's better. That I can deal with.

"You."

"Then you're only morally in control, Elizabeth. In the real world, where decisions are made based on humility and decency, you'll have control. In my world, where decisions are made on unadulterated desire, on pure instinct and immorality, I am. Can you trust me with that?"

My brow scrunches again. It can't be that easy. What about when we don't agree? Given his clear lack of moral integrity in certain situations, he can't possibly believe that this will work.

"But what about those blurred lines?" A small chuckle sounds from across the room.

"Then we'll fight for it." Oh! And then he's suddenly in front of me, lips lingering over mine and breathing ragged as he nips at my lips. "Because I fucking love you fighting me for it. Always fight me, baby. I love that fire in your eyes when you think you're right. You have no fucking clue as to how that makes me feel."

"Alex I..." I have no idea what I want to say other than to tell him how he's made me feel. Confused, yes, but to give up his idea of morality to me is overwhelming. Is this his way of me guiding him back to normal, to accepting a more rational existence? It's certainly his way of opening up to me and showing me how much he needs me, how much he wants me to be there with him every step of the way. My fingers wrap around his neck to pull him closer as his hands draw me into him, those strong arms wrapping around me and making me feel all the things he's promised, to cherish me, to protect me, to love me forever. "I love you."

"Oh, I hope so," he responds quietly as he leans his chin on top of my head and unties the blindfold, slowly revealing his open collared shirt to me. We stand there swaying a little to our own rhythm for a moment as I stare at that throat and try to process thoughts of a collar around it and what that means to him. Hell, I don't even know what it means to me but it sure as shit must mean something big to him. He's Alexander White for God's sake. My hand moves to my own neck to feel the diamonds linked around it and the familiar feeling of my bracelet assaults my fingers. I don't even need to look at it to know that it's the matching piece. It's not as wide as the bracelet, only two rows, but the vintage cut and strict baguette links are all in the same place. I'm not sure if he expects me to wear it every day like the bracelet, but I probably will because the thought of his collar on me, not matter how confusing, is mind blowing. That I own him, that he's given that to me with all the connotations involved, is so overwhelming that I can't help but feel that we've made it, that we've found a way to achieve a togetherness that no one will ever tear apart.

A lone tear hits my cheek as I realise, with acute clarity, that he is it for me. There will never be another who even comes close, and nothing will ever come between us again. We'll learn more and face each other in battle but we'll fall together and find our way back to each other, to this peace we're creating right here and now.

"You're crying, Elizabeth. That's not what's supposed to be happening at the moment," he says as his chest shakes with amusement against me.

"I know but I can't find the words and you're being all lovely and you're giving me something so precious and I don't know what to do with it, and..." I ramble in response into his waistcoat. His fingers lift my chin as he sits in the chair behind him, pulls my stomach towards him and kisses his way across my dress gently. My hands find his hair as he continues up towards my chest.

"You don't have to do anything with it. You do enough by touching me. Your hands quieten everything for me, and that you'll even dare to love me is more than you'll ever comprehend," he says as his handsome, softened face looks up at me with a smile and he brushes his fingers over the backs of my thighs. "That's all you ever need to do. Just keep touching me, because without it, everything else has become pointless."

"Okay."

There is nothing else that comes out of my mouth, literally nothing. What the hell else am I supposed to say to that?

"Okay," he says in reply as we gaze at each other and my smile comes racing back to me at his panty-dropping grin. Moments pass; maybe a sodding eternity passes. I don't know because I'm so preoccupied by his face leaning against me that all sorts of visions are assaulting me. That's where babies grow, in there. Will we have children? A beautiful little boy with bright blue eyes who we'll love together so that I can show him how it should have been. Or a little girl who we can keep protected from all the deviant hands out there and give the world to. His lips graze across the very area again and I sigh in contentment at the thought of family and love and weddings. Is he thinking about these things, too? Perhaps I should ask him about children at some point. We never have talked about it. "I think we need to go and give some money away."

Oh, okay, reality check... I'd forgotten about the charity thing going on to be honest but yes, I suppose we do.

"Right, yes. I just need to sort my face out."

"You absolutely do not. Your face is exquisite just the way it is," he says as he rises up in front of me and cups the side of my face. "What you need to do is put this damned bow tie back on me and then give me the lock to that dress, unless you want me to rip it off you at some point?"

The thought is tempting to be honest and his wicked smirk and suddenly darkened eyes are only furthering my visions. However, given the fact that it's not actually mine, it's perhaps not the best idea.

"Beg me for it." His eyebrows almost shoot off his head and I can't stop the giggle that bursts out of my mouth. "Come on, Alex, I've seen you beg. You're quite good at it, so beg me for it."

"If you want me to beg, I will, but not because of this. So just get your pretty arse over here and do this bow tie before I take matters into my own hands, Miss Scott."

I shake my head at him and swipe my fingers under my ruined eye make-up as I walk up to him and start the process of tying it around his collar. His small groan at my touch only brightens my smile even more as he runs his fingers over my necklace and grabs my backside roughly. I know exactly where that touch is heading, and much as I'm completely up for it, he's right, we should be supporting a charity.

"We don't have time, Mr. White." I giggle at him as I finish the tie and smooth over his broad shoulders.

"Mmm, shame," he says as he holds his hand out and releases me. "Key?"

My brow rises at him and I keep walking to the door, because this is quite a good game and he will definitely be begging me by the end of the evening.

"Negotiation may be required," I say as I turn the handle and glance back at him over my shoulder. Children may be part of it, frankly. His snort of humour as he walks up to me and slaps my arse really quite harshly only heightens what could be a very interesting evening.

"Don't say I didn't ask nicely, Miss Scott."

~

FEELING WHITE

Of course the venue is spectacular, and as I hopefully glide around the tables with Belle, trying my hardest to do this interacting thing that she's so good at, I realise that I'm actually managing it with remarkable success. Something's shifted. It's not a game. There's no manipulation going on or sneakery. I'm just genuinely enjoying being around all these people and their money. Is it because of the diamonds around my neck? Or the implication of them, should I say? It could just be my fourth glass of champagne to be fair.

I reach my fingers up to touch the cool stones and giggle at the thought - collared, Alexander White collared. Who would have thought it? And by Beth Scott, caterer of all people. It's bloody ridiculous to be honest, but as my eyes search the room for him and find him talking to a beautiful woman, I have no feelings of jealousy, only love. So I watch him for a moment and try to figure out the meaning of what he's done this evening as he smiles his fake smile and listens to her rambling on about whatever.

He's so smooth, every movement and inclination laced with exactly what he's hoping to achieve from the situation he's found himself in, or maybe put himself in because it's unlikely he ever does anything unless he wants something from the moment. Was he trying to achieve something other than the very words he said earlier? Why I can't just trust what was coming from his mouth is completely unknown but given his clear ability to manipulate the world, I can't help narrowing my eyes at the thought.

She puts her hand on his arm flirtatiously as she throws her head back in laughter at something he's said. His raised brow and slight stiffening at the move doesn't go unnoticed by me but she clearly thinks she's well in there. Whatever she's got, he needs it, because the very fact that he's putting up with her pathetic attempt at sexiness means there's an ulterior motive going on somewhere. It makes me realise how well I'm beginning to understand him and quietens the nerves about what was going on in that room upstairs. He must have just meant every word. He loves me, he needs me, and he just wants to prove that to me, so why am I still feeling that something else is going on?

"Who's the bitch?" I swing my eyes back to Belle without any care for who the bitch is. Whatever he's doing, he's obviously got a good reason. It's probably to do with yet another twilight zone.

"No idea, and frankly couldn't care less. I do need another drink though," I reply as I waggle my empty champagne flute at her.

"Oh my god, you'll be flat on your arse by eleven. You do know that, don't you?"

"Yep," I giggle in response as a woman in a lemon frilly thing bumps into me and Belle leads us over to the bar.

"What the fuck is that?" Belle whispers as she eyeballs the strange outfit. "And any reason you're getting pissed by the way?"

"Nope, just having a nice time. And no idea at all... Where's Conner anyway?"

"Oh, I think he's talking to some surgeon about something. I left him when they started talking about micro research and sodding computer mumbo jumbo. Honestly, the man's a complete geek sometimes."

On reaching the crowded bar area, we are thankfully presented with two more filled to the brim glasses of lovliness and a couple of high stools to sit on, which is bloody brilliant because my feet are already killing me.

"Did you sort everything out with him?" I ask as I search around for blue hair and hope he's not in ear shot.

"I'm just going to forget about it. It's clearly me making up shit in my own head and you're right, why would he propose if he was having an affair? I still hate the woman but I need to get over it. She's not worth me worrying about, is she? Actually, is she? You've met her. What do you think?"

"I think she's nicer than she appears but you know what I'm like. I always look for the good in people. She may be the bitch from hell for all I know. Only time will tell, I suppose. But I really don't think you need to worry about Conner. He loves you, desperately."

"Mmm... Oh, and while we're at it, why didn't you tell me about my proposal? A little warning would have been bloody nice?" she says as a man brushes her back with his coat. She turns and glares at him.

"Oh, I'm sorry. Actually, I'm not. Would you two ladies like a drink?" he says as he leers at Belles chest. To be fair, my sister has a very good set of boobs and she has rather got them on display this evening.

"No, engaged, fuck off," she replies as she flicks her ring finger at him. He's clearly either not attractive enough or she's completely in love again so I snort out a laugh and return my stare to the room because the look on his face is killer. "Now, warning?"

"It wasn't my place to warn you, and anyway, I didn't want you having too much time to think about it. We both know you would have said no if that was the case."

"Alright, Snotbag, when did you grow up and become the seer of all things?"

My eyes swing back to Alex to find him in what appears to be a heated discussion with a large older man. Again, I'm not sure that the room can see his reactions but I can. Every tensing muscle is priming for something. That slight jaw twitch and his fingers tightly gripping his brandy glass show me every emotion, or rather lack thereof, now coursing through him. Those blue eyes of his narrow slightly as he plots something and smiles charmingly with that ever-rising brow. He's clearly getting frustrated as he holds that enigmatic smile and appears to the rest of the room like he's in absolute control of whatever he's discussing. I giggle to myself as I realise that I've become the seer of all things where Mr. White came into my life and asked me to read him. Well, not asked, but it was the only way I was ever going to get some sort of handle on him, wasn't it? See him for who he really is and love him for it. My ability to understand him suddenly astonishes me because I'm absolutely sure that not one other person in this room sees who he is as much as I do. They certainly don't feel him in the same manner. While a part of me wishes they did, there's a small part of me that's completely delighted that he only gives it to me, just for me, just like that throat of his.

My groin twitches inappropriately at me mid-thought and of course he somehow knows this and turns towards me, that wicked lip curl of his sending all sorts of carnal messages straight across the space between us as if he were mere inches away.

"Snotbag, honestly, if you're going to drool all over him all night, why don't you just go get a room or something?"

"Already did," I dreamily reply as he continues his assault of the eyes, licks his lips and then turns back to towards the man again.

"What a slut." Oh my god.

"Sod off. I am not. Okay, maybe I am a little bit. But he does look very hot in that tux, and those butchering hands are quite..."

"Yes, very hot." What the hell? I swivel around to see her gazing in the other direction at a very smart looking Conner ambling towards us. Oh, thank God for that.

"Hey, ladies, what are you getting up to over here all on your lonesome?"

"Hardly alone, dear," Belle replies as she scans the bar area and then nudges Mr Up-Himself purposely. I have no idea what the hell she's doing so look on in amazement.

"Changed your mind have you, darling?" he says as he swings back round to her and looks straight down her cleavage, again.

"No she fucking hasn't, Jack. That's my fiancée you're looking at." Oh!

Her smirk at the situation has me giggling instantly so I roll my eyes at Conner's irritated glare and drop down from the stool to go in search of my man, who appears to have disappeared.

"Conner, she's winding you up. She was only just saying how hot you look. I need the loo. I'll see you both in a bit," I say to them as I wave them both off and begin to weave my way through the array of tables to look around for Alex.

It really is very extravagant in here and I can't help but wonder about all the money involved in creating such an affair. I mean, okay, they're all doing it for a very reputable charity but honestly, if all the contractors involved had just given a certain amount of money over and then the guests had put their hands in their pockets, wouldn't it have accumulated the same in the end? It just seems an awful lot of fuss to go too to give money to a charity. Having said that, I don't suppose people are as happy to hand that cash over until they're inebriated so maybe this is the best course of action. What the hell would I know?

An elderly couple are standing in the way as I finally get to the corridor that leads to the bathroom, so I smile sweetly at them and squeeze past, trying not to intrude on their clearly private moment. I can't help letting my mind envisage a future with Alex. Will we still be together when we reach that age? Married? Children? Grandchildren? Oh god, the thought has me instantly wobbling on my too tall heels and trying to make it to the bathroom in time. I've yet to move in with the man and I can't get these damn visions out of my head. Mind you, he has just told me he'll give me forever, hasn't he? That he'll love and cherish and protect me for the rest of my life if I want him to, that he'll never leave. I wish I didn't have this underlying feeling that there's something he's not telling me. I could honestly roll my eyes at myself because what the hell else do I want from the man? He's doing everything every woman on the planet could ever dream of and yet I still want more - like those bloody numbers on his back. Pascal really doesn't help with his *maintain your dominance over him* speech, as if I'm supposed to keep pushing him forever until he gives me every last shred of thought or memory. Maybe I am.

Pushing the bathroom door open, I'm instantly bombarded by all sorts of scents and smells coming from the fifteen women who are applying varying creams and potions to their skin. I have absolutely no idea what any of them are and can only assume this is the world of the obscenely rich. I have one moisturiser and obviously a small arsenal of make-up brands, but what the hell are these women doing to themselves? Frankly most of them look utterly beautiful anyway. Why they need to keep putting stuff all over themselves is beyond me but as I close the door, I realise they're possibly all just as nervous of their appearance as I am.

Having done the necessary deed, I walk over to the cabinets full of varying creams to indulge myself in a little of the same beautifying experience and find myself staring into the mirror as I wash my hands. The woman looking back at me seems so far removed from what she used to look like. Everything about me is glowing, make-up done to precision, hair perfectly coiffed, highlighting the diamonds twinkling around my neck. I look down at my bracelet and smile at the thought. He's done this to me, given me this ability to shine and be comfortable with who I am. I don't even need to re-touch my face or hair because it all looks wonderful, exactly the way he would want it, exactly the way I now want it to be. Shaking my head at my reflection, I turn from the mirror to leave.

"You're right, darling. You don't need to do a thing. It's no wonder you've captured his heart," a woman's voice says from behind me so I turn to see where it came from. The smile that greets me seems genuine, but given her potential bitchery, I'm not falling for it completely. She did try the oneupmanship the last time I saw her and I will not let her destroy anything for me, or Alex, or Conner and Belle for that matter.

563

"Evelyn," is my short reply. I'm not sure if I'm mad, irritated or just a little confused about her but I'm apparently not having any of her little games again this time.

"That sounds a little hostile, Beth. Have I done something to offend you?" she replies as she swishes her frankly astounding red dress and re-applies her lipstick. Could she have chosen another colour? Given Belle's choice this evening, I have a feeling this is not going to end well at all.

I narrow my eyes a bit and turn back for the door because she knows exactly what she did the last time we were together and I'll be damned if I'm going to pretend everything is fucking rosy in our garden. I'm also just a little bit wary of her interest in Conner, which clearly leads me to that suspicious feeling that I really don't like in the slightest. It's probably best to just avoid her and carry on with my Alex hunting instead of dealing with anything untoward. Unfortunately, her effortlessly glorious frame follows behind me and grabs at my hand to stop me so I shake it off and swing back to her in the corridor.

"Beth, please?" I huff out a puff of air and straighten my dress as I realise that I'm going to have to get this off my chest and face it head on.

"It's not hostile, Evelyn. It's distrustful. I'm always on his side. Do you understand that? Always. So be warned I won't put up with any shit from you. Do not try to manipulate me to suit your own advantage again. He's an absolute master at it and I can see it coming a sodding mile off." Not that I did last time but that's not the point.

"Well, that told me I guess," she replies with an award winning smile as she walks over and links arms with me. I stiffen instantly. "Oh stop it, Beth. Believe me, we're on the same team here. I just couldn't help having a crack of the whip last time we met, so to speak. I was the one meeting the great Alexander White for God's sake."

I'm gaping I'm sure. Is she insinuating that she knows about Alex's preferences? And is she also suggesting that she was on the back foot because I'm pretty sure it was him, for once, which caused all sorts of problems for me at the time. Actually if it hadn't happened, we wouldn't have had the breakdown and utterly amazing sex, but at the moment that's not the point.

"I don't even know what that means."

"Oh, I think you do. Really, Beth, I would never have thought it of someone like you. And is he always so intimidating? He's actually not too bad when he gets rid of that glare of his, is he?" she says nonchalantly as she saunters us back toward the ballroom and the oncoming traffic seems to part the room for her. Jesus, how does this family seem to manage that?

"Umm... No, he's quite lovely when you get past the pissed off frown," is my response, because while I still don't trust her completely, she seems to be saying all the right words.

"Actually, I haven't seen him yet. I was talking to Conner earlier and he-"

"Elizabeth Scott." Holy shit.

And there's that voice that has me instantly trembling, and not in a good way. My eyes turn to the side to see a very distinguished, if not scary, looking Aiden Phillips standing five feet away. What the hell is he doing here? Regardless of that very well cut tux, the man is not to be trusted in any way, shape or form. He may be completely gorgeous in a disturbingly effective way, but that aura is still oozing its way all over me like the damn plague. My eyes quickly dart around for Alex because I could really do with him right now. Unfortunately, my saviour seems to appear in the form of Evelyn who takes half a step in front of me and casually tilts her head towards him. His amused chuckle at her soft yet unyielding stare is completely erotic and unfairly attractive, given his mob boss status.

"And you are?" he asks her as he approaches. Try as I might, I can't make my mouth function as his body gets closer and zaps that underlying current of evil at me. She looks back at me and narrows her eyes a little at my inability to speak. Eventually my brain engages enough to remember some degree of pleasantries.

"Hello, Aiden. How are you? This is Evelyn Peters. Evelyn, this is Aiden Phillips."

I have absolutely no clue whether she's ever heard of Aiden Philips or not, but true to form, she hasn't flinched in her demeanour. Not one hair out of place, not one shaking bone in her body as she extends a long manicured hand and does that absolutely in control of herself thing. Yet another family trait, it seems.

"Aiden," she says with a raised brow as he walks closer to me and wraps an arm around my back while shaking her hand. My whole body is instantly in shock. I have absolutely no fucking clue what I'm supposed to do with his arm around me. Why the hell has he done it? One casual encounter in a bar does not mean it's acceptable in the slightest. I should run, or maybe push him off me, but that would probably offend him and I'm certain that's not the correct thing to do. Where the fuck is Cecily sodding Whinchester when I need her? My eyes rapidly scan for Alex again as I try my best for relaxed and smile back at Evelyn who is now looking a little confused to say the least.

He's still nowhere to be seen and even though I have no desire to engage in this any further, I quickly make the decision that it's probably best to just keep this short and sweet and get the hell away from the guy.

"No Cecily tonight, Aiden?" I ask in the hope that maybe we can just do chit-chat and move on.

"No, not tonight. Amira is here with me," he replies, as if it's completely fine to be discussing mistresses and wives in the same sentence. He's still looking Evelyn over with equal interest as his fingers graze my waist. This is so not okay. If Alex sees this, he's going to explode.

"Aiden Phillips," Evelyn says as she flicks her eyes to my waist and then back up to his. "I assume you do know who you're holding there? I'm not entirely sure your attention will be very welcome."

She's got a damn good point. Unfortunately, he laughs and tightens his hand on me as he once again looks her over.

"I'm entirely sure that anything I do will be more than acceptable, Evelyn."

I'm agreeing with Evelyn to be fair, but his utter complacency at the fact that Alex may walk around the corner at any minute is so confusing that I just stare at him and try to back away a little. Nobody would say that sort of thing about Alex. I mean, I know he's some sort of master criminal, drug dealing lord or something, but I've never met anyone who would stand up to Alex. Well, maybe Pascal. The thought occurs to me that Evelyn would be very good for Pascal. Where the hell that came from is anyone's guess. He looks down at me with that unfairly radiant smile of his and snorts at my wide eyes.

"Do you want me to let you go, Elizabeth?" Oh god, yes.

"Umm... Yes, please. I think Evelyn is probably right and I'd hate to cause a scene."

His eyes narrow at me as I try once again to disentangle his arm from me while he holds me firmly against him. Shit. I hope this isn't pissing him off. I'm sure he might flip out or something any minute now. Honestly, there's just something about the man that makes me think he might just pull out a gun and start shooting anything that moves, myself included.

"Aiden," his voice says from somewhere behind me. I blow out a breath at the authority in it and look straight at the floor. This could go very wrong, very quickly. I was only dancing with Henry and he left me. James looks at me and we argue so the fact that Aiden has got his hands all over me is definitely not going to go down well.

Without so much as a glance, Aiden chuckles and keeps looking at Evelyn who is still not unbalanced by the man at all. Apparently he's not even the slightest bit concerned that Alex has arrived because he's actually increasing his hold on me again, fingering my hipbone almost casually.

"Alex," he replies confidently. Alex? Why the hell is he calling him that? Nobody calls him that but close friends.

Alex's fingers brush my arm as he wanders around me, growling very quietly and stands next to Evelyn, seemingly at ease with what's happening in front of him. My head shoots up again to find her smiling at him and I can't help the little puff of tranquillity that settles as I watch them close together. It's still damn freaky given their similarities but lovely nonetheless. But why the hell isn't he exploding? I try once again to pull myself from Aiden, but without making a scene, I can't. He simply won't let me go. Alex's brow rises at my move but nothing else as he turns to Evelyn and kisses her on the cheek. Why the hell isn't he helping me? Is this some sodding twilight game I'm not aware of? He's giving me nothing to work with at all, and apart from that enigmatic smile, I can't see a bloody thing that's crossing his mind. Oh god, I thought I'd just about figured him out.

Apparently not. I have no idea what the fuck I'm supposed to do now so I stop my fidgeting and wait. Eventually I'll find a way out of this without pissing off a Mafia boss, or my boyfriend. Well, I hope I will, but as I feel Aiden lean down and kiss my shoulder softly, I'm instantly pretty damn sure none of us will come out of this unscathed.

Chapter 30

Alexander

It was taking everything he had, every muscle primed, every sense honed on demolition. This wasn't the same as before. This was pure, undiluted rage direct from his heart and it was all because of his feelings for her. Kill, destroy, rip out the bastard's guts and roll around in the blood until the fucking idiot was buried six feet under without an inch of skin left on his mutilated body. He could hardly bear to watch the man's fingers as they stroked across her dress firmly and claimed some sort of ownership of the woman he loved. What the fuck sort of game he was playing was completely unknown because he more than likely knew exactly who Elizabeth Scott was, given their meeting with Cecily last week.

He watched as her breathing began to shallow out at the man hands and hoped that she would just keep it together and breathe her way through it. She was clearly uncomfortable, flustered even, because the blush across her chest and fiddling with her bracelet indicated her stress levels were high. She was trying to move away at first. He'd seen it and thanked her for it but at the moment, she just needed to stand still and hold herself together. If Aiden thought for one minute she was special in any way, the dick would do as much damage as possible, and probably expose the past to the highest fucking degree just to have some fun.

She blinked across at him with narrowing eyes as he held his smile and looked past her towards the main threat in the situation. The fact that his new-found sister was also here was equally perturbing. He'd just found some family, and he was damned if both of them would be seeing his past tumbling from another man's mouth before he had the chance to explain it.

"Pretty little thing you've got here, Alex." Dick.

"Yes, quite beautiful," he replied as he glanced over at her and caught the slight tilt of her mouth and her eyes smiling back at him. "Useful, too, but dull most of the time."

That didn't go down as well at all because the sudden angry frown that flew across her stunning face was deadly to say the least. She opened her mouth to speak so he glared at her and hoped to God that she got the message. This was the only way he could keep her safe at the moment and the only way to keep control over the situation they'd found themselves in.

Why the hell was Aiden here anyway? More than likely another step forward in his attempt to become a real businessman. And how did he even recognise Elizabeth? They'd never met. Cecily must be here somewhere, but he'd seen Amira earlier. Surely Aiden wasn't taking his mistress and wife out together now?

"She doesn't appear that dull to me. Besides, they really don't need to speak that much, do they?" That may have been true before her, but not now.

Evelyn stiffened and snorted in derision at the same time as Elizabeth tried to move away again. He wasn't sure if Aiden knew anything about him having a sister, but he was pretty sure she'd handle herself if need be so he levelled his eyes back on the woman he loved.

"Stop fidgeting, Elizabeth. You're making a fucking scene. Stand still."

Her eyebrows shot up as she stilled instantly and looked back at him in surprise. His whole body tensed at the thought of giving her to the dick. It wasn't going to happen anytime soon but if he could just get the man to believe she was yet another whore, perhaps he could make all of this finish before it started.

"Aiden, I'm a touch thirsty. Would you like to go and get a drink?" his frankly fantastic sister asked as she moved a step towards him and stretched out a hand. Clearly Evelyn had picked up on something happening underneath the surface and was trying her best to diffuse the atmosphere. The man looked back at her and smiled. It was his ownership smile, the one that said he'd do whatever the fuck he wanted and nobody would tell him any different.

"Yes, why not. I think we'll all go, shall we? I've got a suite upstairs."

Fuck that. Not in a million years was that shit happening.

"I don't think so." Elizabeth's beautiful lips snarled as she yanked her body away from him and glared back in contempt. His fists tightened as Aiden reached out and grabbed hold of her wrist harshly before she got a chance to move away any further.

"Now, now, pretty, got a temper, have you?"

"Fuck off," she spat back at him quietly as she tugged her arm to try and loosen his hold. It was absolutely glorious and utterly enticing, just not what was needed at the moment. Or maybe it was.

He watched for a moment as the wrestling continued and pondered the best response. Eveyln shifted beside him, probably to interrupt, so he held up a hand and stopped her before she got a step closer. She glared at him as well so he rolled his eyes and resumed his watch of Elizabeth who was doing really very well. The crowd around them hustled and chatted about their business without even noticing the little tug of war that was currently occurring until she accidently bumped into a women behind her.

"Oh god, I'm so sorry," she said, still trying to wriggle her arm free of Aiden's hold.

"No problem," the orange dress replied as she glanced at Aiden. He rewarded her with an award-winning smile and licked his lips. The dick was far too attractive for his own good. The woman batted her fucking eyelashes in response and looked back at Elizabeth. "You're a lucky girl, honey."

"Doubtful at the moment," she mumbled in response as the women walked off and she continued her struggle.

"What exactly are you playing at?" Evelyn whispered to him as she sipped her champagne and continued to watch the show. "Why aren't you stopping this?"

"I have my reasons. Just stay out of this," he replied, never removing his eyes from the woman he loved as she snarled ferociously and tried to keep her composure.

"I think you're out of your bloody mind."

"You're possibly right."

Christ, she was beautiful, bitch-like eyes drilling straight into the face of Aiden Phillips as if he was the lowest form of scum on the planet. Not one small part of her seemed fearful as she stood up to him and refused to cower in a corner like every other woman did, or offer herself up to him on a platter and roll around in the money he'd give her afterwards. No, this woman couldn't be bought at any price. She wouldn't accept anything she wasn't one hundred percent committed to or one hundred percent morally comfortable with. He gazed at her long legs standing firm as she eventually snapped her hand away from the man and sighed at the thought. How the hell was she ever going to understand? Christ, even he didn't understand anymore, although the current need to kill was very definitely in full force at the moment.

"You're lucky we're in a room full of people, bitch," Aiden said as he stared her down. She glared in response and smoothed over the front of her dress in an attempt to contain herself. It clearly wasn't working because her fury was bubbling. He could see it and loved her all the more for it. She abruptly swivelled her head to look back at him with confusion marring her brow and opened her mouth.

"I don't know what the hell sort of game you think you're playing, but I'm not part of it. If you think I'm doing this for you, Alex, you're wrong," she hissed quietly.

No, and she shouldn't. He would never ask that of her but unfortunately, that's not what Aiden needed to hear in this moment. He raised a brow and stared at her for a few seconds as thoughts took hold. He supposed he could punch the man. It probably wouldn't help in the long run but he could at least get her out of here and away from the danger. He was going to tell her it all anyway so what did it matter? He glanced across at the Endigo brothers who were watching Aiden like a hawk, always there to back the dickhead up when needed. No, that plan wasn't going to work at all.

"You'll do anything you're fucking told. Get over here," he said as he held out a hand and watched her eyes widen. She didn't move in the slightest, just stared back at him in shock with her bottom lip trembling a little and sudden glistening eyes.

Evelyn shifted again. Christ, he hadn't got a bloody clue how she might react, and the potential irritated response she might deliver could really screw this up so he did the only thing he could think of.

"And you can keep your damned mouth shut, too, Evelyn. In fact, just fuck off. I don't want you here. Elizabeth is more than enough entertainment," he said as he caught Aiden narrowing his eyes at the scene. Elizabeth was still glaring beautifully, her hand now hovering in

571

mid-air as if she might slap something. They both deserved it at the moment, and he was damn near walking himself straight into those manicured fingers, but Aiden's amused chuckle as he reached his hands towards her again brought him back to the moment with acute clarity.

"I'm surprised you're letting this go on as long as you are, Alex. It's not like you to let them get away with this crap." Shit.

He grabbed at Elizabeth and yanked her toward him so quickly she didn't have a chance to move away. If that bastard's hands touched her one more time, he might well do something supremely stupid. She squealed a little in response and struggled to get away so he clamped the back of her neck firmly and held her at his side.

"Stand still. You're becoming a pain in the fucking arse," he sneered as he tightened his grip on her neck and felt her stiffen against him.

"Alex, please, you're hurting me," she whimpered under him. His heart damn near broke at the thought but such was his life, and at the moment, she was caught right in the centre of it.

"Good. Perhaps you'll stop with this little temper tantrum then."

"I've had enough of this shit, whatever it is," Evelyn snarled as she swished her dress around and leant into him. "You really are the bastard they say you are, aren't you?"

He sucked in a breath - yes, or he had been before the woman in his fingers changed everything. Thankfully his sister turned her body and sashayed away from them to safety. At least she was out of it now and he could concentrate on the woman in his hands.

Aiden was now sipping at his drink and standing eerily still in that thoughtful guise of his so he levelled his eyes back at the man and loosened his hold of Elizabeth a little.

"I smell deceit, Alex," the man said. Fuck.

"No, what you smell is fear, Aiden. I'm afraid she hasn't quite got the message yet," he replied. She immediately twisted in his hand and looked up at him. Christ, if there was one time when he needed her to look at the fucking floor this was it, because her soul-tearing eyes reached in and softened every hard edge again.

"Fear? Hmm... I don't think its fear. From what Cecily said, there's not a chance of it. What don't you want me to know, Alex?"

FEELING WHITE

Oh for Christ's sake, the shit wasn't going to let it go, was he? Maybe if he got them all in a room he could turn the conversation to business and get off the fucking subject. Or maybe if he could just wind her up to the point of exploding, she'd give him a reason to drag her from the room and away from Aiden.

"Nothing at all, Aiden. Now, you were mentioning your room. Shall we go and get on with it?"

Her whole body tensed and before he realised what had happened, she'd spun from his hand and slapped him so hard the sound echoed in the room. Several guests turned to see the commotion as she stumbled backwards into a man who caught her and steadied her fall. He lifted his hand to rub his cheek and watched as she stared at him in disgust. If only she knew how much he was disgusting himself at the moment. She could have it all. He was going to give it all, just not in this room, and certainly not coming from Aiden Phillips' mouth.

"Not very scared at all," Aiden said as he sipped his drink again and looked across at her. "I think you might be in love with her, Alex. Is that what you don't want me to know?"

"Don't be so fucking stupid, Aiden."

"She doesn't know, does she? Are you worried I might blurt it out and tell the world what you are? Or is it just her you're bothered about?" the dick said as he moved over towards her again. She instantly recoiled a step and glared at him.

"She doesn't know what? Alex, what the hell is he talking about? And why are you being such an arsehole?"

"Aiden," he growled as he moved a step towards her. She backed off again.

"Oh, it is just her, isn't it? Ha, Alexander White's finally been caught. It's funny really. You should just be honest, Alex, then she'd definitely know fear."

He watched her face as she stared back at him with her hands out to the side as if begging for some sort of answer. It was only her he could see. The clinking of the glasses, the other people milling around and conversation had all disappeared. Shit. This wasn't how it was supposed to happen. He was so focused on the potential amusement that was about to drop out of Aiden's mouth that he could think of nothing else to say. Gone were scheming games, gone was the ability to think rationally and manipulate his way out of this. He just needed to get her away from the man. There was only one choice, and she was just going to have to do this his way.

"Get to the damn car, Elizabeth. You've embarrassed yourself enough for the evening."

"Umm... Fuck off. How about that for a reply?" she said. He very nearly rolled his eyes because it was utterly beautiful, and he had told her to fight him, hadn't he? What a fucking disaster. Aiden laughed. Dick.

"I'm not going to say it again. Do as you're fucking told."

She glared for a few moments then slowly reached up behind her neck, undid the clasp on her necklace and dropped it on the floor in front of him.

"I don't know what on earth is going on here but I'm not doing it anymore. I'm so tired of all this crap," she said as she turned her body and began to walk away so he reached out and grabbed hold of her arm.

"Elizabeth. Pick. That. Up."

"No."

"If you want me to make you do it, I will. Don't fucking test my patience."

"You can't make me do anything." He raised a brow, and Aiden chuckled again.

"I can assure you he can, pretty. He's killed for less." Fuck.

He spun so quickly on the dick that Aiden actually took a step back. Good, the fucker should beware. He didn't want to do this in here, but he was getting damn close regardless of the two goons in the background who were moving closer.

"Aiden, shut the fuck up. Look around you for God's sake."

"I don't understand." His eyes turned back to her before she could get another word out.

"Pick. It. Up."

"If I were you, I'd just do what he says, pretty. Really, Alex, you're losing your touch." Wanker.

"Stay out of this, Aiden," he said as he glared at her and tugged at his collar. Fucking bow ties.

"Why? I'm enjoying it. I've never seen you nervous before."

"Aiden, I swear if you-"

"You swear what? Don't fucking threaten me, you imbecile," he cut in as he offered a hand towards her. "You could always leave with me instead, pretty. I'm not nearly as bad as he is."

She frowned at his outstretched fingers and then back at Alex as her mind presumably whirled at what the man was suggesting.

"Alex, what is he-"

"Shut up and get moving."

He scooped the necklace off the ground and started to walk them off through the throngs of people in the hope of leaving the dick behind, or at least taking this somewhere quieter. She struggled in his grasp as she tried to make him let go, but he wasn't letting go. He'd told her that. He'd never fucking let go of her and as he rubbed the diamonds in his hand and thought of the hotel room earlier, he hoped to hell that she'd understand this.

"Alex, let go of me. I don't understand what's going on, and I..."

He dragged her faster as she struggled to keep up. He just needed to get her away from Aiden. If she was going to hear this, it was going to come from him, and only him, in his way. It was the only chance he'd have at making her understand.

"Please, Alex, stop. I have no idea-"

"Where are you going? You can't take this amusement from me, Alex."

He stopped abruptly and turned to face the dick.

"Aiden, back off. Just remember I've got as much on you. Don't push me into using it."

"Now, now, talk about temper tantrums. Unless you're going to be useful to me in some way, I would suggest you check yourself and rein it back in, Alex. She's only another whore, for fuck's sake."

Venom gripped his spine as he stared into the eyes of his former employer and furiously searched for something to calm the impending storm. How fucking dare he?

Elizabeth struggled again in his hold, which quickly brought him back to the problem at hand: her. He swivelled again without any further thought on the arsehole behind him and stormed onwards towards the exit. Andrews - he needed Andrews. Where the hell was he?

His eyes scanned the entrance foyer as they arrived to find Andrews reading a paper calmly.

575

"Car," he very nearly shouted across the space. Andrews immediately dropped the paper and made for the door with a confused expression.

"Alex, stop."

His step faltered as he heard the familiar voice of Conner behind him somewhere. He huffed out a breath and kept moving. Conner wasn't what he needed to deal with at the moment on top of everything else.

"Oh look, the fucking boy scout's arrived," Aiden drawled.

Jesus, could this get any worse? He kept moving to the kerb and waited for the car to drive up. Perhaps if Andrews could get his arse into gear, he'd get through this unscathed. Unfortunately, Conner was right behind him.

"What the hell are you doing?"

"Conner, please, tell him to... Ow, you're hurting me again. Please..."

"I've told you to shut up, Elizabeth," he cut across her as he turned to face Conner. Where the fuck was the car? She stilled again and looked at the floor so he shook his head and frowned at Conner.

"Man, what the hell's going on?"

"Nothing, we're leaving that's all. Elizabeth's tired," he replied as he scowled at Aiden who was damn well laughing. Conner's brows rose slowly, only highlighting the deceit. He never could lie to the man. What the fuck was that about?

"She's not going anywhere with you in this frame of mind. I can see it a fucking mile off. Have you forgotten what happened in New York?"

Absolutely not. He sneered at the thought as visions of that dungeon crawled into his head and reminded him of himself, so he loosened his hold on her a little as she sniffed back tears and fidgeted.

The car pulled up at exactly the right moment so he opened the door and shoved her glorious backside into it before Conner got a chance to do anything about it. Slamming the door, he turned to find the furious looking blue hair staring back at him.

"She's tired, Conner. And there's nothing wrong with my frame of mind."

loyalty to Alex or concern for Elizabeth was questionable, but thankfully he seemed to be agreeing with the plan.

"For fuck's sake, Alex, take me home, will you?"

He sighed and shook his head as he turned away from her and looked out at the London skyline flashing beside them, magnificent in its glory as it continued onward as far as the eye could see. Tall skyscrapers lined the sky with their lights glinting and showing the world that it never stopped, never closed down, never forgot that its job was to keep trading and be what it was designed to be. A money making empire with a cutthroat attitude towards business and all that got in its way - his home, the place that had helped to create the young man he'd been and the grown one he'd now become. The juxtaposition was fucking hilarious really. In reality, the only difference was he didn't use a knife anymore, or at least didn't unless he had to.

He pinched his brow and continued to gaze out the window, wondering how this was all going to end. Would she allow him this and forgive him his sins, or was this whole thing going to destroy everything he'd found in her.

"I love you, Elizabeth, and I'm sorry, but I'm not taking you home."

"Well, this is a fine way of showing me how much you love me. I'm not sure you know the meaning of the damn words anymore, Alex. Look at me and tell me what's going on or I swear to God I'm leaving. You told me you'd be honest with me so what the hell is it that you think you're doing?"

What needed to be done.

He didn't reply, just kept looking away from her and hoped she'd remember what he'd just said because it would be the last time she'd be hearing a loving word from his mouth for a while. The only words she'd be receiving would from the version of himself she didn't know, the one he didn't really want her to know anything about, but unfortunately, it was the one she needed to see to get them through this.

A car horn blared beside them as Andrews turned the corner into the airport and smoothly travelled along the tarmac towards the plane. Briefly stopping at the checkpoint, he glanced across at her and noticed her face in the moonlight, that angelic halo drifting around her red hair again as it reflected in the window beside her. Christ, what was he doing? The thought of subjecting such beauty to his hands was very nearly enough to make him change his mind and tell Andrews to take them home again. She turned to look at him as the car pulled off again, her eyes watering slightly as she continued her stare and drove herself deeper inside him with every breath.

"I won't play your games anymore, Alex. Whatever this is, don't make me hate you for it. I love you. Please don't break us apart when we were getting so close. I don't care what Aiden was talking about. Just explain it and then we can move on. It really doesn't matter. Let's just go home and talk about it," she said as she reached a hand across towards him.

He watched those fingers descend until they landed softly against his own, allowing him to revel in the feeling of her warmth for a moment. Probably the last time she would show any affection towards him, given what she was about to experience. Hate... Was she even capable of it?

Her tender touch disabled any thoughts of pain or torture for a few seconds as he gazed at her bracelet in hope and ran his finger across hers gently. Much as he might like to stop this, it wasn't possible anymore. She needed to know the truth and then make her judgement on him, her morally decent one. He pulled his hand away with a sigh as the car pulled to a stop outside the plane.

"We're not going home, Elizabeth," he said as he opened the door and felt the wind hit him with force. He looked up into the sky and shoved his hands into his pockets as Andrews opened her door and helped her out.

"But I don't want to go, Alex. Please... I've got commitments here and I can't just... well you can't just take me. It's kidnapping if I say no, isn't it? Michael, tell him. He can't just-"

"Your commitment is to me and nothing else, Elizabeth. You'll do as you're told."

She looked instantly shocked again and opened her mouth in retaliation so he walked straight past her towards the steps and nodded at Phillip as he reached them.

"Bring her in, Andrews," he called over his shoulder.

"Michael, no, stop it. What are you doing? Let go of me for fuck's sake," was all he could hear behind him as he climbed up the steps and tilted his head at Tara. She might be useful to some degree.

"Mr. White, Sir," she said with a smile. The woman was clearly a glutton for punishment. He was pretty sure he'd been rude to her the last time she was here, but then she was a whore, wasn't she? He shook his head and continued on to the main cabin, still listening to the scuffling that was being created by the love of his life as Andrews hauled her through towards the seat.

"Fuck off, Michael. Don't ever touch me again. How fucking dare you?" her lovely lips snapped as Andrews let her go and retreated a step. He chuckled a little at her hostility and turned to Andrews.

"You can go now. I'll call you when we land."

Andrews stood there for a moment, looking thoughtful. This was worrying. He raised a brow at the man in expectation. He really didn't want an argument but he'd damn well have one if it had to be done. The woman currently glaring at the pair of them was his only concern, and that need to kill something was still bubbling along under his skin quite effectively so a few minutes of kicking the shit out of something would work out quite nicely for him.

"Fine," Andrews eventually said as he glanced over at Elizabeth and then back at him. "Have a good trip."

"A GOOD FUCKING TRIP? ARE YOU BOTH FUCKING INSANE? Alex, I don't want to be here. What the hell is going on?" she screamed as she bolted for the door.

Without a second thought, he lunged across the space and caught hold of her. She could go into the damn bedroom if this was the way it was going to be. She immediately struggled in his hands and began kicking out at him, those heels of hers spiking into his shins with precision as she slapped her hands around his face. It seemed her viciousness lesson had been very effective indeed.

"Get the hell off me, you psychopath," she snarled again as her nails scratched across his cheek on the way through the corridor. He very nearly laughed at the statement. She might not be that far from the truth to be honest.

She abruptly stopped trying to attack him and put both her hands on those walls to try and stop the forward momentum, fuck knew why because he was twice as big as her and intent on showing her exactly how brutal he could be.

"Keep trying, Elizabeth. We both know how much I like it."

583

"Fuck you," she spat as she began her kicking again and grabbed onto various hand holds in the hope of stopping them.

He rounded the corner, threw her down the bed and brought his fingers up to his face as she rapidly crawled backwards towards the headboard. She was magnificent in her animalistic sneer as she hovered on all fours and panted from fighting him, her fingers still grabbing onto the sheets as if she might rip it to shreds any minute. It was taking everything he had not to climb on that bed and fuck the living hell out of her. Everything ached with need as her eyes drilled into him again and beckoned the desire that he was trying to dampen.

His phone suddenly beeped in his pocket and her eyes shot to his pocket, which was close to his cock. More visions swam of those lips doing exactly what they were designed to do so he licked his lips and raised a brow at her.

"Not a fucking hope, White. You've got no right to-" He was across the room so quick she didn't have a chance to move. It was just what he needed to start the process.

Grabbing her by the ankles, he flipped her over onto her stomach and placed his knee into her lower back so he could hold her still. Then reaching for the drawer, he grasped the tape and grabbed at her arms, which were scrabbling around for some sort of purchase. She hadn't got a chance. He was too quick at this, too fast, too many years doing exactly this because this was what he needed, the fear.

"I've got every right, Elizabeth. I'll do as I please."

"Alex, get the fuck off me," she screamed into the sheets as he pulled her elbows together behind her back. Three wraps of black tape around them and she was still struggling beautifully, then she abruptly stopped and stilled under him. He chuckled at her response. As good as she was at reading him, behaving wasn't going to get her a damn thing this time round. This was completely different.

He hauled her up and yanked her to the end of the bed then reached for the intercom.

"Phillip, take off as soon as you like."

"Sir, you're not buckled in and-"

"Get this fucking plane off the ground."

The pitch of the engines changed around them as he watched her reaction to what was happening in the room. She looked nervous again. Her anger had dissipated to some degree and her lips were slightly parted in expectation. There was no arousal that he could see, only a slightly anxious twisting of her body as she tried her hardest not to look at him and flicked her eyes to the door again. He took off his jacket and shirt and casually tossed them onto the bed as he sat into the leather chair and looked across at her. His phone beeped again, reminding him of the incoming message, so he reached for it and pulled up the text.

- **Of course, dear boy. I assume you're ready to be honest.**

Well, it seemed the man did know what he needed. How did he know that shit? He glanced over at her again and noticed her inching away from him to the other side of the bed. Where the hell she thought she was going was completely unknown.

He chuckled at her. She looked damn good nervous, always had. Not nearly as intoxicating as when she was happy and in love, but fear still suited her well. It heightened every carnal plea inside his body to give in to itself and show her exactly what his hands were capable of.

"Look at me," he said. She shifted sideways and tried to contain her balance as the plane increased its speed and the front wheels lifted off the tarmac.

"I... I don't want to. I don't know who you are right now."

"No, you don't. But you wanted to know, didn't you? So that's why we're here."

Her head turned back towards him slowly as she presumably got the drift of what he was trying to say, those lovely lips of hers gently parting as she gazed at him with interest.

"And this is your random fucking way of telling me something?"

"No, of showing you someone, of teaching you."

She narrowed her eyes at him and moved her arms around again. They were probably hurting by now. He'd bound them too tight, purposefully. She would definitely understand pain by the end of this flight and hopefully be a step closer to grasping his idea of normal, of the years of abuse. Not the beauty of pain in submission, which she revelled in, but the never ending hurt of being assaulted.

"Alex, please, we don't have to do this. Just take this off and we can talk about-" He cut her off by standing and retrieving a knife from the drawer. She wasn't getting it. Talking about this wasn't going to help. "What is... What's that? Why have you got a knife?" she asked as her eyes shot to his again.

He shoved her harshly until she landed on her back on the bed and then grabbed the bottom of her dress as he looked up into surprised eyes.

"Ask me again," he said quietly as he cut the dress at the hem and watched the blade slice through the black silk. She squirmed away a little. "And I suggest you keep still."

"What?" she replied, as the material creaked under the strain of the tear and he slid it up a few more inches past her knee. "Alex, please. I don't know... Stop, please."

"You asked me a question earlier today. I want you to ask me that question again."

Her eyes refocused on the blade as she tried yet again to back away as it got closer and closer to her thigh. His cock hardened instantly at the thoughts now racing around his mind at her wide eyes and heavy breathing, and that delicious gasp of panic at the cold steel brushing against her skin only intensified every need consuming him

"I have no idea... Alex? Oh my god, what are you...?" She gasped again and became completely still as the blade sliced its way across the silk by her naked clit. Try as he might, he couldn't stop the need to push the flat of the blade against her, to let her feel it on her skin. The cold metal touching something so hot, probably needy regardless of her situation, must have been confusing as hell.

"Think, Elizabeth," he whispered as he rubbed it again and then tried to shake himself free of the current mind fog she was placing him in. Christ, what he wouldn't give to just forget this whole thing and move on to fucking her, slowly. Her small moan at the pressure really wasn't helping him maintain any control so he quickly sliced the rest of the dress straight past her breasts and up to her throat.

She recoiled from the blade at her neck and stared at him in shock as that nervous fear flew across her face again, eyes now wide and glistening again as her lips trembled. He damn near exploded in his pants like a fucking teenager.

"Do you... Do you mean the date thing?" she asked hesitantly as she tipped her chin away from the blade. "Alex, please, I don't like what you're doing here."

"Yes," he replied as his mouth unconsciously found its way to her jaw and licked its way upwards towards her ear. Fuck, she smelled good, and that trembling was beginning to radiate across her body as she flicked her eyes away from him and squirmed again. He growled at himself and pushed his cock into her thigh as desire reigned and began to strip away the last shred of decency he was clawing onto.

"Alex, I-"

"Just fucking ask me," he sneered as that calm descended and began to tear every preference from him, every thought, every need boiling to uncontainable. Shit, he needed to back away from this. She wasn't ready. What the fuck was he doing? He loved her, and was now scaring her, on purpose. Presumably that wasn't fucking normal but it couldn't be helped. This was the only way to make her see. Her eyes narrowed slightly. Maybe she was ready.

"Okay, if that's what you want. What happened on the 22nd of June, 2005?"

He stilled as the words fell from her lips and closed his eyes. There was no getting away from it now. She'd asked and he was going to answer, truthfully. Every feeling connected with the acts was going to be heard, whether she wanted to hear it or not. With a sigh, he slowly removed his hand until the blade moved safely from her throat and kissed the very spot it had been lying against. His lips lingered as he tried to convey for the last time the depth of passion he had for her, the need.

He slowly peeled himself from the bed and watched her eyes following him away as he backed up towards the chair and sat down again. She wriggled her body upwards until she was leaning against the headboard and staring back at him, still with narrowed eyes. He almost chuckled at the fact that all fear had apparently disappeared at the thought of information. Only she could dismiss the situation she was in to find out more about the man she loved.

He gazed at her for one last moment as he memorised the look on her lovely face, the face he'd probably never see again in the same light once she knew. Beauty, innocence and love radiated across it, that halo still firmly imprinted around her as she looked at him with adoration still pouring off her regardless of her circumstances.

"It's okay, Alex. Tell me. I told you I wouldn't run," she said quietly as she tilted her head and smiled softly. Unlikely this time

587

round, not that she was going to have a choice in the matter. He noticed her twitching her shoulders and frowned at the thought of the tape. She shouldn't be bound for this, should she? Why did he think she should? She should be free to attack him if she chose to. He deserved her viciousness if she wanted to give it. That's what he wanted from her, wasn't it? Absolution, some sort of acceptance. He abruptly stood and moved his way behind her so that he could slice the tape off again and peel it from her skin. She looked instantly confused again but rubbed at her arms as he dropped the knife down on the bed in front of her and wandered back to the chair. Her eyes glanced at the knife by her knee and then back at him as she shuffled her way out of the remains of her dress. Utter perfection sat before him, her knees tucked up as she rested on one hand and kicked off her heels. That creamy skin called to him. Oh Christ, how it called to him, her love, her acceptance, her need for him.

"Pick it up," he said. She shook her head and scowled at it.

"Why would I do that?"

"Just pick it up, feel the weight of it, get used to it in your hand."

She gingerly moved her hand to the steel and clasped onto the black rubber handle. It wasn't a big knife, just another switchblade, not much bigger than a large penknife really, but it was still good enough to kill with. His fingers itched as he watched her turn it over in her hands with a small shrug of her shoulders and caught her lips reflected back at him from the blade.

"I don't understand what you're trying to tell me. I don't even know why you've got a knife, let alone why you-"

"I killed two men on that day - one with a knife, the other with my hands."

Her eyes shot back up to his in complete shock so he held them firm. This was real. She needed to know this now. Her mouth opened and then closed again as she still stared. There was no gasp, no scream, no disgust, no running, just shock. Was it the actual words he'd said or the meaning behind them? He couldn't read a goddamn thing that was flashing across her face because other than shock, it was completely blank. "So, we are going to spend a few days learning about who you've fallen in love with. I will be completely honest about who I am, or rather have been, and you will keep that with you at all times," he said as he nodded at the blade. "If you feel the need to use it at any point, feel free to do so. I won't stop you. Neither will anyone else. I told you you had my throat, and I meant it. It's yours to do with as you wish."

Her mouth opened again as her eyes returned to her hand. Those elegant fingers that gripped the hilt tightened and then let go altogether and he watched it tumble onto the sheets again.

"Hands made for butchery," she mumbled as she stared down at the blade. A small smile crossed his lips. He couldn't have put it better himself.

"You wanted the truth. Now you have it," he said as he crossed his legs and let his eyes caress her body, every inch of it perfection, flawless, unadulterated exquisiteness.

"I just wanted you," she replied softly, still looking at the blade. "To understand why and try to..." She stopped talking as her eyes welled in tears and her body seemed to curl up into small ball.

"Then you shall have me, in my entirety. If you still want me by the end of this, that is. But you're not going to like any of it so you may as well be prepared for who you're about to see."

She scowled at the knife again and edged away until she was far enough away from it to tentatively kick it onto the floor beside the bed. Clearly she wasn't that enamoured by the object, not something he understood in the slightest.

"I'd like to be alone for a while," she said as she crawled her way under the sheets and pulled them up to her shoulders, her attempt, no doubt, at trying to end the conversation so she could process the information he'd just delivered, more than likely trying to find an excuse for his behaviour and give herself time to dismiss it.

That wasn't how this was going to work. She needed to hear it all, to feel it deep down in her soul and understand, to feel him for what he really was. This wasn't a case of naughty boy syndrome, or even screwed up adolescence. No, he was a murderer and a sadist, and while he'd done it all for varying reasons pertaining to an abused childhood, they weren't enough to absolve it.

He'd never asked for nor needed absolution before now, but at the moment, he was desperate for it. If she chose not to forgive him, his world would mean nothing without her in it. She could use that damn blade and cut the heart right out of him for all he cared, but she'd do it after he'd given it his all, after she'd seen it all and understood the very depths of his tortured fucking soul.

"Try, Nicholas. Reach for me and try to win the game, boy. One day you'll have learnt a lesson from this and remember who taught you how to live, who showed you how you'd need to be to achieve anything of worth."

Daddy fucking dearest.

He stood up with a sneer at the memory and moved over to the bed to look at her face. Still angelic as she lay there with her eyes closed, seemingly at peace with that red hair tumbling around her cheeks and her legs tucked up into her stomach. He reached for the cover and slowly pulled it down her body to reveal her skin again and sighed at what was about to come.

Love... He mouthed the word to himself, a word to absorb all the revulsion and banish it to the furthest corners of his mind again. Could the feeling break through the hate he was about to create for her?

Christ, he hoped so, because there was no point living without her now.

THE END... FOR NOW

Acknowledgements

There is one person I have to thank for putting up with my constant keyboard tapping every evening and it's my wonderful partner. I love you, more than words can say.

Without your support through the last year or so, I couldn't have achieved any of this and you'll never understand how much that means to me. But hopefully, if you look inside the characters, you'll find a bit more of me that you've allowed to open up and free itself from its box.

Me x

To all the book blogs that have supported, helped, guided and forged a path for me, I love you all, without reservation. However, special mentions go out to: Orchard Book Club, Rachel Brightey. Bound by Books Book Reviews, Rachel Hill.

My editor – Heather's Ren Pen Editing x

My PA – Leanne Cook – Love you, honey x

And of course, you guys. Anyone who has read the second part of this story and enjoyed it is warmly thanked and acknowledged as super wonderful. I hope you've enjoyed the further journey of my characters and if they've resonated with you in some way, be it small or large then I've achieved my goal, which was to provoke thought and entertain you.

CEH x

****

THE WHITE TRILOGY CONCLUDES

With

Absorbing White
Final book in the trilogy
By
Charlotte E Hart

****

Printed in Great Britain
by Amazon

17480713R00336